PUNJAB

Also by Rajmohan Gandhi

A Tale of Two Revolts: India 1857 and the American Civil War (2009)
Mohandas: A True Story of a Man, his People and an Empire (2006)
Ghaffar Khan: Nonviolent Badshah of the Pakhtuns (2004)
Revenge & Reconciliation: Understanding South Asian History (1999)
Rajaji: A Life (1997)
The Good Boatman: A Portrait of Gandhi (1995)
India Wins Errors: A Scrutiny of Maulana Azad's India Wins Freedom (1990)
Patel: A Life (1989)
Understanding the Muslim Mind (1987)

PUNJAB

A History from Aurangzeb to Mountbatten

Rajmohan Gandhi

ALEPH BOOK COMPANY
An independent publishing firm
promoted by *Rupa Publications India*

Aleph Book Company
7/16 Ansari Road, Daryaganj
New Delhi 110 002

First published in India in 2013 by
Aleph Book Company

Published in paperback in 2015

Copyright © Rajmohan Gandhi 2013

All rights reserved.

No part of this publication may be reproduced,
transmitted, or stored in a retrieval system, in any
form or by any means, without permission in
writing from Aleph Book Company.

ISBN: 978-93-83064-08-3

1 3 5 7 9 10 8 6 4 2

Printed and bound in India by Thomson Press India Ltd., Faridabad

This book is sold subject to the condition that
it shall not, by way of trade or otherwise, be
lent, resold, hired out, or otherwise circulated
without the publisher's prior consent in any form
of binding or cover other than that in which
it is published.

For loved friends and torch-bearers of insaniyat,
*Khushwant Singh (who started in Sargodha and Lahore and lived in New Delhi)
and Mubashir Hasan (who began in Panipat and lives now in Lahore);
and in memory of Pyarelal Nayar (1899-1982), who loved Punjab, Bengal and
India before and after the three were divided*

CONTENTS

Preface 9
Introduction: Why a Punjab History 15

1. Punjab Until Aurangzeb's Death 23
2. 1707-1757: Collapse of Authority 62
3. 1757-1799: Adina Beg Khan, Afghans and the Sikhs 99
4. 1799-1849: Ranjit Singh and His Successors 130
5. 1849-1859: British Punjab and the 1857 Rebellion 187
6. 1859-1919: Imperial High Noon 235
7. 1919-1922: Together for Freedom 279
8. 1922-1942: Collaboration and the Separation Call 298
9. 1942-1947: Independence and Trauma 323
10. 1947: *Insaniyat* Amidst Insanity 367
11. Postscript: Divided Punjab and the Future of *Punjabiyat* 376

Notes 389
Bibliography 416
Index 421

PREFACE

Apart from the considerations cited in the Introduction that follows, personal reasons drove me to understand and tell this story. The poisonous winds of 1947 had buffeted millions, and also me, then a boy going from eleven to twelve and living in Delhi, a city which received (and enacted) its own share of convulsion that year.

Two years before that, in November 1945, I had faintly absorbed the drama of three Punjabis, a Hindu, a Sikh and a Muslim, officers all in Subhas Bose's Indian National Army, being tried together at the Red Fort for treason against the British Empire. The sound 'Dhillon, Sehgal, Shah Nawaz' had entered Delhi's air.

Half a century later, on my first visit to Lahore, I was struck (like many others) by the strong similarities between Delhi and Lahore, including an identical mix of Mughal and British monuments. Interest turned into a bond, and I made several subsequent visits to Lahore, none more enriching perhaps than the one made in 2005, when my wife Usha and I interviewed two dozen or so persons with memories of how Hindus and Sikhs had saved Muslims, and vice versa, in the Punjab of 1947. From those carriers of history we learnt of the *insaniyat* which in numerous priceless instances defeated the insanity of that year.

In Lahore I also learnt that many in the city continued to miss, more than half a century after 1947, its Hindus and Sikhs.

Surely this former Punjab, a single entity so different from today's two Punjabs, required to be understood. The need for this understanding was further heightened in the 1980s, when I lived close to the conflicts associated with Sikh militancy in Indian Punjab (which took the lives of some people I knew) and could not escape the impact of the Indian army's assault on the Golden Temple, the assassination of Indira Gandhi, the carnage that followed, and the indignities that Sikh friends in Delhi suffered.

Much earlier, in 1948, my assassinated grandfather, the Mahatma, had joined the numberless victims of Punjab's and the subcontinent's angers. Punjab had become a part of my life, a question-provoking yet precious part, and I needed to understand it as well as I could.

I should confess that I grew up in Delhi with a mild anti-Punjabi prejudice. The Delhi where I was born in 1935 was not the more-or-less Punjabi city it would become after 1947. In those early days, Delhi's was a non-Punjabi world, despite the fact that from 1858 until 1911 the British had administered the city as part of their Punjab province. (Punjab had been the Empire's base for crushing the Great Rebellion in Delhi, an exercise in which Sikhs and Punjabi Muslims mainly, but also Dogras and Gurkhas, had enlisted on the Empire's behalf.)

Yet this earlier Punjab connection was scarcely noticeable in Delhi in the years preceding 1947. I, and people like me, can remember a time when Banias, Bengalis, Jains, Mathurs and Muslims—to name them in alphabetical order—seemed to be, at least from some perspectives, Delhi's dominant communities.

As British India's capital from 1911, and hungry therefore for bureaucrats, journalists, accountants, clerks and typists, Delhi also attracted many south Indians. Since my mother was Tamil, our family had contacts with several south Indian families living there. (My Gujarati father did not bring to us— my siblings and myself—quite as many Gujarati contacts, possibly because Delhi seemed to contain fewer Gujaratis than Tamils, though our Gujarati neighbours at the time, the Pandyas, were like family.)

With 1947, Delhi changed demographically, linguistically, and food-wise. Muslim boys in my school—we didn't have a great number—vanished from one day to the next. One of them, a classmate, was called Javed Akhtar. (Javed's father, Chaudhri Muhammad Ali, then one of Delhi's top civil servants, would serve as Pakistan's Prime Minister in the 1950s. Later I would learn that Javed and his father were not merely Muslim, they were 'Arain' as well, as was General Zia-ul-Huq, the Jalandhar-linked ex-student of St. Stephen's College, and that Arains constituted one of Punjab's significant groups.)

Even as Muslim boys disappeared from my school, a number of Punjabi boys, Sikh and Hindu, materialized. Several Punjabi teachers also suddenly appeared.

Hitherto run jointly by a Bengali principal (a lady of Brahmo extraction, I would much later learn), a wheelchair-confined Jain 'chief', and a Sikh founder or co-founder who always remained in the background, the school obtained a new Punjabi principal. With a mix of pride and sadness, Kapur-saab at times spoke in his gentle, deep voice of his 'Gov'ment College, Lahore'.

From Kapur-saab and the other newcomers in my school, I learnt that Punjabis were a wonderfully gifted and friendly lot who loved the places they came from. (In due course I learnt also to gauge their respect for Tamils and other south Indians by, among other things, their love of dosas.) My silly bias was blown away.

As Punjab was traumatized in 1947, Delhi started becoming Punjabi-ized. Even if they belonged to non-Punjabi-ized tracts, at least two generations of Indians and Pakistanis were affected by Punjab's suffering. That long-lasting trauma, or rather the need among Indians and Pakistanis to get out of it, is probably the strongest impulse, even if mostly in the subconscious, behind this inquiry. I was venturing into it under a half-recognized pull to assist, never mind how poorly, in healing the wound.

While most accept that there can be no reconciliation without truth, establishing historical truths clinically is an impossible exercise, for you cannot cross-examine long-dead witnesses: the writers of diaries, memoirs, police reports, newspaper stories, personal letters, and authorized and unauthorized biographies, which form the staple of history's raw material.

Yet it may be possible and also desirable to strive for a balance in historical perspectives by studying, in Punjab's case, a variety of conflicting accounts as, for example, those provided by different Sikh, Muslim, Hindu and British sources. Even if ultimately futile in recalling the past's exact reality, such an attempt may yet, God willing, serve the causes of truth-telling, understanding and reconciliation.

This study does not claim to offer hitherto unknown facts or documents. However, though the cellar did not yield hidden bottles, the searcher has distilled available wines, including overlooked ones. Apart from posing a few questions thus far unasked, this study seeks to interrogate, contextualize, balance and distil known material.

As I researched and wrote this story, long-gone Punjabi friends re-entered my mind and moved me: Principal Mahendra Nath Kapur; early family friends Dr and Mrs Krishna; that witty and dedicated Gandhi companion and scholar, Pyarelal Nayyar; his redoubtable sister, Dr Sushila, who helped so many refugees and non-refugees in her long public life; their brother Mohan Lal and mother Tara-ji; the fearless Amtus Salaam of Rajpura, whose loving warmth for person after person totally concealed her loss of numerous relatives in 1947; Rajkumari Amrit Kaur, who for freedom's sake farewelled palace comfort and whose forebears I would meet in my research; Gulzari Lal Nanda, twice (each time very briefly) India's prime minister; and several others.

Had they been living, these friends would have been of help and guidance for this study. So would have the gifted historian, biographer and generous friend, Balram Nanda, who lived until 2010 but, sadly for me, did not delay his passing by a year or two. Some Punjabi schoolmates of mine have also gone, including the determined Mohanjit Singh and the brilliant and blunt Vijay Chaudhri.

Even so, these persons, and other friends still living, 'connected' me somehow to the Punjabis of the eighteenth and nineteenth centuries whom I encountered in the course of my research.

Others helped with insights, information, questions, memories of 1947, or access to knowledge about earlier periods. I should specially thank those connected with the archives of Pakistan preserved in a place in Lahore believed also to contain Anarkali's tomb, where I had the opportunity to look at papers from the times of the later Mughals, Maharaja Ranjit Singh and the British; and also Syed Babar Ali and his remarkable team at the Lahore University of Management Sciences (LUMS) for the time I spent there in 2011 for my research. The Lahore Museum proved helpful too. In its archives I was fortunate enough to find a Kangra School portrait of an eighteenth-century viceroy of Punjab, Adina Beg, whose career had caught my interest. The museum kindly furnished me with a photograph of the painting, which appears in this book. I don't believe it has been published elsewhere.

Most of my study was done amidst the rich South Asia collection of the University of Illinois at Urbana-Champaign, where I have spent twenty-four semesters during the fifteen-year period between 1997 and the end of 2012. While the authors of the works I researched provided much of the information presented in this study, I owe a good deal also to colleagues at the university, and appreciate the university's funding of the research in Lahore in 2011. The campus's Varun Goel, graduate student in geography, valuably assisted with the maps.

I was fortunate, too, that Ishtiaq Ahmed, the reputed Lahore-born political scientist who has lived for years in Sweden, read the manuscript and suggested improvements. His comprehensive study, published in 2011, of Punjab's 1947 trauma was of invaluable help. I am greatly indebted to him. Helpful thoughts were also given by Professor Amita Sinha of the University of Illinois. Only I am responsible, I should add, for this study's opinions and shortcomings.

David Davidar's enthusiasm about publishing my Punjab story has meant much to me. I thank him and his gifted Aleph team, including Ritu Vajpeyi-Mohan, a meticulous editor, and Aienla Ozukum, for their hard work on the text and for suggestions that have enhanced its clarity, as also Bena Sareen for evoking undivided Punjab on the striking cover.

I thank my wife Usha, daughter Supriya, son-in-law Travis and son Debu for supporting this work with love and criticism.

Now that, despite difficult odds, this book has 'happened', I have a few prayers regarding it: that it might prod some to pursue their own research into Punjab's history and ask new questions; that a few reading this work may conclude that there was more to the Punjab story than they had thought, more complexity and richness perhaps, or maybe more humanity in the Other side than previously realized, and that our inherited, unexamined beliefs regarding what occurred in Punjab's history may need revising.

R.G.
Urbana, Illinois
26 November 2012

INTRODUCTION:
WHY A PUNJAB HISTORY

When employed today, the noun 'Punjab', which has come down from the Persian word for 'five rivers', usually means either Pakistan's largest province (with a population in excess of ninety million in 2013) or its immediate eastern neighbour, the Indian state of Punjab (containing twenty-eight million people), while the adjective 'Punjabi' characterizes the people, ways or things connected to either of the two Punjabs, or both.

In this study, however, 'Punjab' signifies the subcontinent's Punjabi-speaking region as a whole, or what old-timers remember as undivided or 'British' Punjab. (In consonance with current popular practice in both India and Pakistan, this study will speak of Punjab rather than 'the Punjab' of traditional usage.)

A hundred years or so ago, around 1914, British Punjab, stretching all the way from Attock in the northwest to the borders of Delhi, seemed ideally placed to lead the subcontinent towards economic progress and inter-communal understanding. The Raj had provided stability to the area for six decades. While diverse in religion, sect, caste and class, the vast majority of Punjabis spoke the same language or a closely-related variant. Water gushing in its great rivers and canals, Punjab's agriculture was vigorous.

Although even in 1914 prominent Punjabis were apt to quarrel in the press and from public platforms over the situation of Muslims, Hindus or Sikhs, the population seemed to live in peace. Nine decades earlier, and prior to British rule, Ranjit Singh's indigenous kingdom had presented a marked contrast to the instability which enabled the British to conquer the rest of India.

Why did this promising Punjab witness division and carnage in 1947? For clues we *have* to go not merely to what happened between World War I and 1947 but also to earlier history.

There are global reasons too for recalling Punjab's past. In August 2012, after a white gunman in America killed six innocent Sikhs in a gurdwara in Oak Creek, Wisconsin, Harpreet, an eighteen-year-old Sikh woman about to enter the University of Texas in Tyler, urged fellow-Americans via a large poster, 'I am a Sikh, please don't hate me.' Circulating her plea on Facebook and Twitter, Harpreet also told CNN: '[Y]es, my skin is brown and my hair is dark but that does not make me and my family Muslims or terrorists'.[1]

Several Sikhs in America quickly dissociated themselves from any suggestion that it was acceptable to think of Muslims as terrorists. We must assume that Harpreet herself did not intend to convey such a suggestion. That she was neither a Muslim nor a terrorist is what she was declaring. Yet Harpreet's remark was a reminder that the Sikh-Muslim relationship, for centuries a major question in Punjab, is now a factor in our world as a whole.

Pakistan's Punjab province, almost wholly Muslim, holds today a population larger than that of Egypt, Iran or Turkey, a fact which makes Pakistani Punjab by itself *one of the most important Muslim regions in the world*. More than half of all Pakistanis—the people who belong to supposedly the world's most dangerous country—live in Punjab. Moreover, Punjab's relationship with Pakistan's other provinces, Sindh, Balochistan and Khyber-Pakhtunkhwa, is critical to that country's future.

In India, Punjab has produced two prime ministers (Inder Kumar Gujral and Manmohan Singh), twice the same acting prime minister (Gulzari Lal Nanda), and one president (Zail Singh), as well as the assassins of Prime Minister Indira Gandhi. While posing tough problems for the Indian state, Punjab has also performed as one of India's growth engines: the Punjabis' energy has powered India's agriculture and military, even as the other Punjab has powered the military and agriculture of Pakistan.

In the twentieth century, Sikhs from undivided Punjab helped in the process that transformed western Canada and California. In earlier centuries, Punjab was the gateway for a series of invasions into India. In the middle of the twentieth century, the subcontinent's partition bisected and traumatized Punjab and Bengal while the rest of the region remained intact.

Though several angles reveal Punjab's significance, its histories are scant. Latif's *History of the Panjab* was published in Lahore in 1889, nearly 125 years ago, that is. Thereafter British civil servants wrote their district gazetteers, scholars of Sikh history produced major works, Ranjit Singh's rule (1799-1839) was recorded by contemporaries and analyzed by later scholars, British Punjab was portrayed by its architects, and studies and novels sought to capture the shock and shame of the 1947 killings and migrations.

Historians have delved into other aspects of Punjab's story, too.

- the influence of the still-popular eighteenth century poets Bulleh Shah and Waris Shah

- the 1857 Revolt and Punjab
- Punjab as the Empire's garrison state
- the Bhagat Singh phenomenon during 1929-31
- the Muslim League's 'Pakistan' resolution of March 1940, and more

Yet, after Latif's oft-quoted, controversial and now dated work of 1889, there has been no new history of Punjab as such, no attempt to tell Punjab's story from, say, the end of the Mughal empire to the finis of the British one—except for Ikram Ali Malik's study of the 1799-1947 period, which however excludes the eighteenth century. Though Punjab's *Sikh* story has often been presented, as well as stories of partition, the history of Punjab itself, *assuming that Punjab had a personality of its own,* has been captured rarely or not at all.

If undivided Punjab had a personality and history of its own, then it follows that we cannot fully understand its descendants, the modern Indian states of Punjab, Haryana and Himachal and Pakistan's Punjab province, or indeed modern India and Pakistan, without confronting that personality and history.

While constituting invaluable intellectual wealth, the Sikh histories available today—all deriving from the Sikh faith's deep involvement, right from its founding, with Punjab's language and soil—easily outweigh any studies available of aspects of Punjab as a whole, or of Punjabi Muslims (even though Punjabi-speaking Muslims have always outnumbered Punjabi-speaking Sikhs), or of Punjabi Hindus.

Moreover, an important question has not been addressed in existing scholarship: *Why was Punjab's Muslim majority unable to fill the power vacuum when, post Aurangzeb, the Mughal Empire retreated from the province?* In fact, eighteenth-century Punjab as a whole, post-Aurangzeb and pre-Ranjit Singh, has received meagre attention in India and Pakistan, and the same is true of the contribution of Punjabi Muslims to nineteenth-century Punjab.

There were gaps, and I yielded to the urge to try and fill them while capturing, if possible, the heart of the entire story, starting with Aurangzeb, of pre-1947 Punjab.

With the death of Aurangzeb, the last major Mughal, central authority over Punjab started to erode. The ensuing contest for regional power involved a couple of outside forces, Afghans and Marathas. The contest also involved Punjab-based Mughal governors who looked either for independence or for an Afghan umbrella. And it involved a local minority, the Sikhs.

The local majority, Punjab's Muslims, stayed aloof from the contest, which ended in favour of the Sikhs. Available accounts imply that until the British conquered Punjab, the more numerous Punjabi Muslims lived almost invisibly in the shadow of the Sikh minority. What were they doing? What were their hopes, fears, struggles? The questions called for answers.

Varying a good deal among themselves—in tribe, dialect and local customs—Punjab's Muslims thought of themselves as both Punjabi and Muslim, and were so seen by others. Today they dominate a powerful Pakistani institution, the army. They also dominate Pakistan's business, industry and agriculture. By virtue of numbers, they greatly influence Pakistani politics as well. Smaller ethnic groups in Pakistan (Sindhis, Pashtuns, Balochis and the so-called Muhajirs, Urdu-speaking descendants of refugees from northern and central India) frequently criticize Punjabi hegemony.

Yet the story of Punjabi Muslims has been neglected by historians, including by those in Pakistan. In part, the neglect is linked to the status in Pakistan of the Punjabi language. Not Punjabi but Urdu, the language spoken before partition by Muslims and numerous Hindus in northern India and yet seen by many as 'Islamic' (a language, moreover, which Punjabi had helped evolve), has been Pakistan's national language ever since that country's inception.

Indeed it was Punjab's Muslim leadership which steered the successful campaign to declare Urdu as Pakistan's national language. It was a way of showing Muslim Punjab's love for Islam.

But this readiness to yield first place to a language different from theirs was not necessarily an 'Islamic' preference. Nor did it necessarily mean a magnanimous refusal by Pakistan's Punjabis to impose their language on the country's linguistic minorities: Sindhis, Pashtuns and Balochis.

A widespread belief among a section of Punjabi-speaking Muslims that theirs was a folk idiom rather than a literary language and one, moreover, that enjoyed a special relationship with the Punjabi Muslims' supposed historic foes (the Sikhs), helped remove Punjabi as Urdu's competitor. In fact, these Punjabi Muslims frequently claimed that Urdu rather than Punjabi was the language they spoke, even as (in Indian Punjab) many Punjabi Hindus claimed that Hindi not Punjabi was their language.

Thus Punjabi became the 'Sikh' language, Urdu the 'Muslim' language, and Hindi the 'Hindu' language. Language was uprooted from ground-level and tied to religion rather than to the varied people who spoke it, or the tract where it was spoken.

Yet the people of Punjab, in Pakistan and in India, whether Muslim,

Hindu or Sikh, continued and continue to speak (and sing) in Punjabi. In culture and politics alike, *Punjabiyat* or Punjabi-ness appears to be alive in both Pakistan and India, even though defining or analyzing *Punjabiyat* is not easy, and even though undivided Punjab has been gone for more than six decades.

Defining *Punjabiyat* may be hard, yet we know that it is symbolized by poets like Amrita Pritam and Faiz Ahmed Faiz, and by storytellers like Saadat Hasan Manto and Khushwant Singh. We know too that immortal singers like the Jammu-born Kundan Lal Saigal (who died in 1947), Kasur's Noor Jehan (*d.* 2000), Amritsar district's Muhammad Rafi (*d.* 1980), and Nusrat Fateh Ali Khan (*d.* 1997), who was born in Lyallpur (now Faisalabad), enriched *Punjabiyat* with their Punjabi or Hindi-Urdu songs.

Artists like them and Punjabi-origin movie stars from Bollywood like Nargis (*d.* 1981), Dev Anand (born in 1923 in Gurdaspur district's Shakargarh tehsil, now in Pakistan, *d.* 2011), Raj Kapoor (born in Peshawar in 1924, *d.* 1988), Sunil Dutt (born in Jhelum in 1929, *d.* 2005), and the Amritsar-born Rajesh Khanna (*d.* 2012) kept *Punjabiyat* alive for future generations.

However, most Pakistanis today do not know that Lahore, Rawalpindi, Faisalabad, Multan and other towns in Pakistani Punjab held significant Hindu and Sikh populations before 1947. An even larger number of Muslims lived in Amritsar, Jalandhar, Ludhiana, Ferozepur and other towns in what today is Indian Punjab, a fact of which most Indians are unaware. Rural Punjab, too, in both its halves, used to contain the 'Other'.

Not to recognize the Punjab that was, or to imagine that Punjabi history started only in 1947, is to erect—in India and Pakistan both—a granite wall between our lives and those of our grandparents and thus ensure a failure to understand ourselves.

■

Large in area, undivided Punjab was varied in soil, temperature, dryness or dampness, population density, religion, caste and sect. What was common to the area and to almost all its inhabitants was the Punjabi language, which seems to have existed for a thousand years or more, though spoken in several variants and written in more than one script. *Their language seemed to reveal the Punjabis as a distinct people*; not homogeneous by any means, yet distinct.

Punjab's boundaries were marked in the west and northwest by the Indus and tracts belonging to the Baloch (or Baluch or Biluch) and Pashtun (or Pakhtun or Pathan) tribes, in the north by the Himalayas and Kashmir, in the east by the Jamuna, and in the south and southwest by the Aravalli Hills and the Thar Desert. Though substantial portions of western and southern Punjab were desert-like, other areas were fertile, including the Himalayan foothills and tracts close to the rivers.

Presenters of Punjab's stories often divided the region into its doabs, a doab (or doaba) being the space between two rivers, and pointed out that each doab possessed special physical and linguistic features, often a different agriculture and, at times, a different politics.

We too will use the doab device, first employed, it seems, by Emperor Akbar, who evidently gave each doab its name.[2] So there was (and is) the Chej (or Chaj or Jech) doab between the rivers Chenab and Jhelum, the Rachna doab between the Ravi and the Chenab, the Bari doab between the Beas and the Ravi, and the Bist (or Bet) doab between the Beas and the Sutlej. The space between the Jhelum and the Sindhu (Indus), the great continental river which formed the western boundary of Punjab and of which the five Punjabi rivers were tributaries, was (and is) the Sindh Sagar doab.

While Punjab's western-most doab was called the Sindh Sagar doab, its eastern-most region, south and east of the Sutlej was, in Akbar's time, known as Birun Panchnad, i.e. outside the five rivers, birun being the Persian word for 'outside' and panchnad a Sanskrit expression for 'five rivers'.

But the phrase 'panchnad' (or panjnad) was also used more narrowly for a short southbound stretch of water, starting well to the south of Multan, where the five rivers flowed as one. The eastern frontier of the Birun Panchnad land was the river Jamuna. Since the Jamuna flowed past Delhi, 'Delhi doab' was another name for the large Birun Panchnad area. In later times, the Sikhs would use the term 'Malwa' for much of this area, while the British would think of this space south of the Sutlej as 'cis-Sutlej' territory.

While it is often meaningful to locate a Punjabi place or person in a particular doab, equally convenient is the British-era breakdown of Punjab into five geographically contiguous divisions, which, ignoring the rivers, were named after cities.

Thus there was the Rawalpindi division in the region's northwest, which included the districts (and towns) of Gujrat, Shahpur, Jhelum, Rawalpindi, Attock and Mianwali. In the middle of British-run Punjab was the Lahore division, to which the districts of Lahore, Amritsar, Gurdaspur, Sialkot, Gujranwala and Sheikhupura belonged.

Punjab's southwest constituted the Multan division. This contained the districts of Montgomery (now Sahiwal), Lyallpur (now Faisalabad), Jhang, Multan, Muzaffargarh and Dera Ghazi Khan. The eastern division, named after Jullundur (now Jalandhar), included the districts of Kangra, Hoshiarpur, Jullundur, Ludhiana and Ferozepore. The fifth division, named at times after Delhi (which the British administered for fifty-three years as a part of Punjab) but more often after Ambala, occupied the southeast and contained the districts of Hissar, Rohtak, Gurgaon, Karnal, Ambala and Simla (now Shimla).

Of the five divisions, those of Lahore and Jullundur appeared to be the most fertile. While Muslims formed a majority in the Rawalpindi, Lahore and Multan divisions, they were a minority in Jullundur and Ambala. A sixth Punjab-linked space—not contiguous and not called a 'division' by the British—comprised numerous princely states where the British did not directly rule.

Many of these princely states lay in the Himalayan hills to the north or east of the Rawalpindi, Lahore or Jullundur divisions, but some occupied Punjab's broad plains, such as Bahawalpur, which stretched extensively to the east and south of Multan, and Patiala, Nabha and Jind, which formed enclaves within the Ambala division. While Bahawalpur was predominantly Muslim, as was Kashmir, the large princely territory to Punjab's north, non-Muslims formed a clear majority in almost all the rest of these princely states.

Independent India's states of Punjab, Haryana and Himachal and Pakistan's Punjab province constitute modern re-arrangements of the five British-era divisions of Punjab and the sixth 'princely' space.

■

After an opening chapter on Punjab's historical background, this study proceeds with the 1707 demise of Aurangzeb, which, as has been mentioned earlier, left a vacuum in Punjab and triggered a scramble for power. For the rest of that century, Punjab remained unstable.

Three forces—invading Afghan rulers, Mughal governors and sons-of-the-soil Sikh chieftains—clashed for control. Punjab's unchanging eighteenth-century picture of continual clashes between these three forces was only disturbed twice: in 1739, when the Iranian Nadir Shah raided Punjab and Delhi, and in 1758, when for a transitory spell a Punjabi Muslim called Adina Beg governed Punjab in the name of the Maratha Confederacy.

In the last three decades of the eighteenth century, Sikh chiefs dominated the city of Lahore. Inaugurated in 1799 and controlled from Lahore, the considerable kingdom of Ranjit Singh and his heirs lasted for half a century. After defeating the Sikhs first in 1846 and again in 1849, the British ruled Punjab for a century until 1947, when under Mountbatten's viceroyalty Punjab was partitioned, tearing up that Punjab which is the subject of our enquiry.

This, therefore, is Punjab's story from the time of Aurangzeb to the time of Mountbatten, preceded by a backdrop recalling Punjab's Mughal and pre-Mughal past. That the span focused upon has to be book-ended with non-Punjabi names is only one of the ironies of the Punjabi story. Perhaps the irony contains a clue to Punjab's personality.

Punjab's society and economy, as these evolved, form part of the inquiry, but this is essentially a political history, told chronologically and by confronting a procession of interesting characters involved with Punjab—Muslim, Sikh, Hindu and British characters, rulers and poets, gurus, Sufis, avengers, reconcilers, district officers from afar, political leaders, journalists and others.

In the process, several historical questions are examined. These include the secret of Sikh success from the 1760s to the 1840s; the inability of Punjab's Muslim majority to fill the eighteenth-century power vacuum—their unwillingness to enter the contest for power which the Sikhs, Afghans and Marathas had energetically joined; the pluses and minuses of British rule; Punjab's history of revenge and counter-revenge; but also a less known, and contrasting, history of cooperation.

The study also touches upon the condition of Punjab's women; the evolving politics of the region's Hindus and Sikhs; the relationship between Punjabi Muslims and the British; and the oft-ignored role of Punjab's far-flung and long-settled Pashtun families.

Also examined is the question of why the Gandhian or nationalist Congress movement, which swept much of India from 1919 to 1947, failed to make sufficient headway in Punjab, despite a promising start there in 1919. The salience of Punjab's Unionist Party from the 1920s and the initial slowness with which Muslim Punjabis embraced the call for Pakistan are also looked at.

Towards the end, the study addresses two interconnected yet separate questions which Punjabis and non-Punjabis continue to ask. Why did partition occur? And why did upheaval and tragedy accompany it? A short subsequent chapter provides a few true stories of *insaniyat's* victories over the tragedy-cum-insanity of 1947. Trends after 1947 in divided Punjab, and prospects for the future, are lightly touched upon in the concluding chapter, which should be seen as a postscript.

Onward, then, to Punjab's story.

Chapter One

PUNJAB UNTIL AURANGZEB'S DEATH

Before moving to the period that is the focus of the book, a quick scan of the history that preceded it would provide a useful perspective. This earlier, and oft-turbulent, story may be told in three parts, one relating to pre-Mughal Punjab, the second to Mughal Punjab, and the third to the Punjab of the Sikh Gurus.

Punjab was the seat of the ancient Harappan Civilization. Persians ruled it (with the Beas as their eastern boundary) in the sixth century BCE, and Alexander's historic foray followed two centuries later. The Macedonian's march was succeeded in Punjab by the feats of Chandragupta Maurya (claimed by some as a Punjabi) and his minister, Kautilya, and by the rise of Buddhism linked to Asoka and his empire. Located between the Jhelum and the Indus, the town of Taxila grew as a centre of learning and trade.

Menander the Greek (Milinda) ruled the western doabs before the start of the Common Era. Panini, Sanskrit's first grammarian, was born in what is now Attock, east of the Indus, possibly in the fourth century BCE.

During the first three CE centuries, Kanishka and his Kushan successors, most of them professing Buddhism, controlled parts of Punjab. Then the Gupta kings enjoyed sway. Chinese scholars curious about the country of the Buddha tramped across Punjab's soil. Harsha ruled over, and for a time from, Punjab in the seventh century. Early in the eighth century, entering mostly by sea, the Arabs conquered Sindh and moved from there into Multan but could not establish a lasting empire.

Twenty-five miles west of the town of Jhelum, at a height of 3,200 feet, stood Tilla Gorakhnath, an ancient Jogi monastery. Gorakhnath, the reputed founder, may have lived close to the tenth century.

The stormy attacks launched early in the eleventh century from Ghazni in east-central Afghanistan by Mahmud, who was of Turkic origin, changed India and Punjab forever. In vain was Mahmud resisted by brave Hindu princes of the Pal clan of the 'Hindushahis,' as they were called, identified by some scholars with the Janjuas, one of the dominant groups in Punjab's northwestern region, between the Indus and the Jhelum.[1]

Other Punjabi tribes—Gakhars, Khokhars, Syals and Bhattis—are also said to have 'fought valiantly' but to no avail against Mahmud.[2] Even an unprecedented joint force, apparently assembled in 1008-09 by several Rajput princes of northern India, failed to stop Mahmud as he swept across today's Khyber-Pakhtunkhwa and parts of Punjab. A fierce final resistance offered by a Pal scion in Nandana Fort on the Jhelum ended in 1015, and Lahore fell in 1021.

Though a principal city of the Pals, Lahore was at this point seen as secondary to the great trading city of Multan, which was also closer to Mahmud's attackers, who usually crossed from Ghazni into India via the Gomal Pass, about 200 miles south of the Khyber, and used Multan as their resting place and base.

Multan's great merit was its location. Three rivers merged before passing Multan on their way towards the Indus. Sailing downstream from Multan to the Indus, and along the great river to Thatta on the Arabian Sea, was an inexpensive exercise for cargo boats. Even the Sutlej was not very far from Multan, and in the eleventh century the same may have been true of the river Ghaggar, long-extinct from our perspective.

Accessible by land as well, Multan was ideal for commerce, including international trade with Persia, Central Asia and the Arab world. Nevertheless, Mahmud made Lahore, on the banks of the Ravi, his second capital and 'appointed Sukhpal, also called Nawaz Shah, in charge of the conquered region'.[3]

Quite a few Central Asians sought opportunities in Lahore. One of them was Syed Ali Hujweri, better known as Data Ganj Baksh, who died in the 1070s after writing *Kashful Mahjub* (Unveiling the Veiled), his well-known study (in Persian) of Sufi thinking. Though he wrote disapprovingly in the book of his new city ('In the country of India I myself had become a captive among uncongenial folk in the town of *Lohanor*, which is a dependency of Multan'[4]), Hujweri was loved and honoured there. The Lahore shrine where he is entombed is today one of Pakistan's famed sites.

Hujweri was more orthodox in his Islam than four famous Sufis who appear in a chain about two centuries after him: Moinuddin Chishti, Qutbuddin Kaki, Baba Farid and Nizamuddin Auliya. Two of these four—Baba Farid and Nizamuddin Auliya—were born on the subcontinent, the former in Multan and the latter in Badayun, a town near the Ganga in today's Uttar Pradesh. All four served during the rule of the so-called Delhi Sultanate, which was created following the triumph of Mahmud's successor in invading the region, Muhammad or Muizuddin or Shahabuddin—as he is variously known—of Ghor. Called Ghori after the Afghan region he came from, which lay to the west of Ghazni, Shahabuddin, like Mahmud, was of Turkic origin.

After first losing (in a battle fought in Tarain in eastern Punjab) to Prithviraj Chauhan or Rai Pithora of Ajmer in 1191, Ghori returned the following year and defeated the Rai on the same battlefield. This was a significant victory, for Prithviraj had been master of, among other places, Delhi, India's capital in legend and history. Taken prisoner along with his master, Prithviraj's court poet, Chand Bardai, who may have been raised in Lahore, wrote a ballad, *Prithvi Raj Raso*, said to contain flavours of the Punjabi language.[5]

The battlefield successes of Mahmud of Ghazni and Shahabuddin of Ghor owed much to the Turks' skills as horsemen, to the quality of their horses, and to clarity in command-and-control. The Rajput forces resisting them did not lack 'in numbers' or 'the martial spirit', but evidently they were 'inferior in terms of organization and leadership...and did not have a unified command'. While each Rajput prince was inclined to be his own commander, Turkish officers were 'dependent on the will of the sultan' and 'totally loyal' and obedient.[6]

On his path to Tarain, which lay south of the Sutlej and north of Delhi, Ghori had defeated the successors of Ghazni's appointees in Multan and Lahore. He did not however stay to rule India from Delhi or anywhere else. Handing over the territories he had gained to his slave Aibek, Ghori left for home. Soon Aibek installed himself in Delhi as king; he and his successor Iltutmish lived in Rai Pithora's fort.

These two were the first monarchs of what historians have called the Delhi Sultanate, a rubric for the three-century rule over much of India by four dynasties—Slave, Khilji, Tughlaq and Lodhi (or Lodi)—the first three predominantly Turkic and the last one Afghan, though some claim an Afghan origin for the Khiljis too. However, influenced as they were by Persian culture, India's Turkic rulers employed Persian as the Sultanate's court language.

The Sultanate's control over the Punjab region was tenuous, largely because of raids throughout the thirteenth and fourteenth centuries by Central Asia's Mongols. Unprecedented in the speed of their terrifying spread across Asia and Europe, remarkable in their military prowess and hugely destructive in their raids, the Mongols repeatedly pillaged not only Iran and the Arab world but also India, especially Punjab. Though the Mongols stopped (or were stopped) before reaching Delhi, they destroyed much of Punjab.

In the upper Sindh Sagar doab, not far from the Khyber, the Gakhars were, at times, able to block the Mongols, who therefore often invaded via Multan. 'For three centuries this unhappy district (Multan) bore the brunt of the great racial disturbances caused by the Central Asian upheavals.'[7] But many other parts of Punjab were also laid waste. For long periods, the Beas was the frontier of the Sultans' Indian kingdom, with the Mongols enjoying sway in the large Punjabi areas west of the river.

Recalling, in a Persian text, this period of Punjab's history, a Hindu Punjabi called Sujan Rai Bhandari would say in 1696: 'So long as the Mongols of Balkh and Kabul raided the Punjab every year, this country remained in a ruinous state, and one only saw devastation all around.'[8] With only sporadic help coming from Delhi-based kings and no rulers from their own region, the people of Punjab coped as they could with the attackers, largely by getting out of the way. Many left Punjab. The population shrank.

In addition to being harried by marauders like the Mongols, the people of Punjab (and other places) paid heavily in taxes for the Sultanate's pomp and extravagance, a glimpse of which has been left by Ibn Battuta, the fourteenth century Moroccan traveller. Executing, as demanded, a bond to live in India, Battuta and 'a party of distinguished men from Khorasan, Bokhara and Samarkand', all expecting to fill high positions in the Tughlaq Sultanate, journeyed from Multan to Delhi in the year 1333, escorted by a deputation sent by the Sultan, Muhammad bin Tughlaq. Ajodhan, where Baba Farid was buried, was one of the places they passed through.

Battuta was impressed by the Sultan's postal system. Operated by relays of horses and fast runners, this network had taken Battuta's message from Multan to Delhi and brought back the Sultan's answer.

At state banquets served on the march, the Sultan's chamberlain 'stood up and bowed in the direction in which the Sultan then was. All the guests followed suit. After this homage to the sovereign, they sat down to their meal'. Water and sweetened drinks were served in cups of gold, silver or glass, followed by large pieces of roast meat (a fourth or a sixth of a sheep for each guest), pastry, halwa, other varieties of meat cooked in butter, onions and ginger, chicken-and-rice, samosas, sweets and small cakes, pomegranate juice, betel leaves and areca nuts.

'At the conclusion of the feast, the ceremonies of grace after meal and homage to the sovereign were performed in the same manner as before its commencement.' After arrival in Delhi, Battuta wrote a poem in praise of

Muhammad bin Tughlaq. It fetched him a reward of 55,000 dinars.[9]

The Sultan's lifestyle was imitated by officers and chiefs in the provinces, adding to the burden on the peasantry. Except for brief periods when a ruler happened to be considerate, farmers were heavily taxed. On the other hand, the adoption and increasing use of the Persian wheel may have helped agriculture, including Punjab's, during the Sultanate, which in some periods also saw a growth in trade and the creation of new towns.

Numerous conversions to Islam took place in Punjab during the Sultanate, whether from Hinduism, Buddhism, a localized faith, or agnosticism. There seems to be little solid information on how these conversions occurred and whether or not force was used. Some scholars seem certain that the Sufis—the ones we have named and a great many others, including, for instance, Bu Ali Qalandar of Panipat (1209-1324)—were primarily responsible, and that the majority of conversions were real and voluntary.[10]

After speaking of Baba Farid and three other Sufi pioneers who evidently were Farid's contemporaries and close friends—Bahauddin Zakaria of Multan, Jalaluddin Bukhari of Uch-Bahawalpur (about hundred miles due south of Multan), and Lalshahbaz Qalandar of Sindh province—a Pakistani writer asserts:

> These saints and their associates/disciples converted most of the Rajput/Jat tribes [of Punjab]...to Islam. This process of conversion, begun in the early 13th century, continued till the close of the 19th century.[11]

As writers like the one just quoted see it, the Sufis attracted a large following by demonstrating a distance from wealth and power, connecting with the people and the land, stressing God's love and mercy rather than his wrath, ignoring ethnic or religious labels, speaking and composing poetry in the Punjabi language, and singing their poems with the aid of a one-stringed instrument.

Thus Baba Farid seems to have said to his disciples, 'Give me not a knife but a needle. I want to sew together, not cut asunder.'[12] We know, too, that Farid's thirteenth-century Punjabi verses refer to Punjab's flowers and fruits, trees and thorns, birds in flight and in ponds, the tiger, the swan, the falcon, the crow and the dog.[13]

There is historical evidence of widespread Sufi activity in Punjab in the thirteenth and fourteenth centuries. Moreover, many a Muslim clan today names the Sufi who, the clan believes, converted its ancient ancestors. However, it was not Sufi influence alone that propelled conversion. Prisoners of war taken by the Sultans may well have accepted Islam to escape death, while others may have done so to escape the jizya, the poll-tax levied by the Sultans on non-Muslims for, as was claimed, the latter's protection.[14]

Yet conversions out of necessity probably accounted only for a small percentage, and evidence that large-scale conversions were obtained under duress has not been unearthed. We should note, too, that the vars or ballads contained in the holy book of the Sikhs include a few that honour Punjabi Muslims of Rajput origin who evidently accepted Islam voluntarily in the period when Ghazni's successors ruled from Lahore.[15]

Two other explanations for conversions have been offered. One is that groups of nomadic tribes, including perhaps some Jat and Gujjar clans, ran into Islam before the Hindu caste system absorbed them.[16] The other is that the 'untouchables' of Punjab's Hindu society were attracted by the Islamic value of equality. While plausible, these theories remain conjectural and lack little prospect of being backed by accounts, giving time and place, of actual conversions.

Who were the people of Sultanate-era Punjab that we are speaking of? We know at least one thing about them: except for recent migrants from Central Asia, the great majority spoke Punjabi (in more than one dialect), though the Pashtuns, Baloch and Kashmiris living in the region probably used their own tongues. The population farmed, or worked with the loom, leather or wood; as oil-pressers, smiths, barbers or scavengers; as merchants or traders, priests or religious teachers.

Projecting backwards from British estimates made between the 1880s and the 1910s, and using British-period terminologies, Punjab's Sultanate-era population may have included

- farming castes like (in alphabetical order) Arain, Awan, Jatt (or Jat), Kamboh, Rajput and Saini;
- pastoral castes like Gujjar and Ranghar;
- trading or vending castes like Arora, Bania and Khatri;
- so-called 'menial' and 'untouchable' castes like Chamar, Chuhra and Julaha;
- Brahmins;
- Islam-teaching Shaikhs;
- Sayyads claiming descent from the Prophet;
- immigrants of Afghan, Arab, Iranian or Turkic origin; and
- Baloch, Pashtuns and Kashmiris.

During the Sultanate, and also later, the first four of the categories listed probably made up the bulk of the population, with the likelihood that the 'menials' and 'untouchables', taken together, comprised more people than any other category.

The listing or classification offered is neither complete nor tidy. Nor will everyone accept it. The number of Punjab's castes—zaats or jaatis or biradaris—was, and is, in the hundreds, and calling one of them Rajput or Jat, farming or pastoral, trading or soldiering, indigenous or foreign, can set off a sharp dispute. While it is true that Punjab's story is better understood with the help of a population breakdown, no matter how imperfect, we should retain a question mark whenever the origin or occupation of a jaati or biradari is described.

Early British scholars (who were also, usually, administrators) ran into assertions by the almost wholly Muslim Arain and Awan biradaris that their forebears were Arabs or other West Asians. Also, it was possible for a particular biradari to be viewed as Jat or Jatt (both spellings have been used) in one part of Punjab and Rajput in another. Clans seen as Rajput included Bhattis, Dogras, Gakhars, Janjuas, Tiwanas and Wattoos (to give, in alphabetical order, a sampling of names), though some of these zaats claimed an alien rather than a Rajput origin.

Bhinders, Chahals, Chathas, Cheemas, Dhillons, Gills, Maans, Sandhus, Sidhus, Siyals and Waraiches were only some of the hundreds of Punjab's Jatt clans. While many farming castes were soldiering castes too, some from the trading Khatri and Arora castes worked as clerks or accountants.[17]

Though we have unavoidably spoken of 'Hindus', 'Muslims' and 'Sikhs' in pre-British Punjab, we should remember that classifying and counting people as Hindus, Muslims or Sikhs was a British idea to begin with. Before British officials started to record a Punjabi's religion, the latter did not necessarily or primarily think of himself as a Muslim, Hindu or Sikh. If asked who or what he was, he might have mentioned his zaat or village before speaking of his religion.

Rulers and their courts often stressed their religion, sometimes armies fought under a religious flag, and at times clans changed their religion, but the people did not necessarily see themselves as being 'Hindus' or 'Muslims' above everything else. Looking chiefly to their survival, they also looked to their zaat, for caste loyalties were strong and, usually, strongly enforced.

To sum up in respect of conversion to Islam in Punjab, roles may have been played by conquest, prolonged rule, Sufis, the practice of untouchability, and policies such as the jizya. In addition, we may surmise, repeated ferocious attacks by anti-Muslim Mongols helped the conversion to Islam of several clans and tribes, starting with their chiefs.

We may speculate that the chief of a Punjabi tribe, caste or clan—whether or not he thought himself a 'Hindu'—was willing to embrace Islam after he found no Hindu raja around him able to organize resistance against the Mongols, whereas Delhi's Sultan and his Muslim functionaries in Multan, Dipalpur and Lahore often attempted to do so. That the new religion was recommended to the chief by a Punjabi-speaking Sufi who practiced renunciation and appeared to treat all human beings alike may have contributed to the conversion.

Of Sultanate-era defence in Punjab against the Mongols, the historian Muhammad Mujeeb has written:

> The bases of the defending armies were Lahore, Multan and Depalpur from where they could operate freely and manoeuvre as required... The defence bases were in charge of the most outstanding generals, two of whom, Jalauddin Khilji and Ghyasuddin Tughlak, were raised to the (Delhi) throne.[18]

The scholar who quotes Mujeeb in his book argues that as the political structure in Punjab crumbled during the Mongol attacks, and towns and the countryside were repeatedly devastated, the Sufis provided order and meaning to society. The Sufi silsila (chain or sequence), he suggests, gave a sense of belonging to those within the order and won the admiration of those outside, while the Sufi khanqah (meeting-place and hospice) gave the public, including Hindus, opportunities to hear the Sufi teaching of brotherhood. 'Khanqas not only brought Hindus and Muslims together, but they also narrowed the gulf that divided the Muslims of foreign origin and local converts.'[19]

The grassroot co-existence celebrated by the Sufis was backed philosophically by the doctrine of wahdat-ul-wajud (unity of being). Espoused by several though not all Sufis, the doctrine seemed akin to the Hindu concept of advaita (non-duality). Seeking common ground with Hindus, some Muslims suggested that non-duality also signified monotheism.

But the growing world of Indian Islam was also a varied world, and there was unease about wahdat-ul-wajud among orthodox sections of the ulema, the scholars of Islam. They preferred 'There is no god but God (or Allah)' to 'God is everywhere and with everyone'.

Hindus did not like it if a Muslim cleric dismissed their beliefs as polytheistic or idolatrous, and Muslims were puzzled and also offended when, observing caste rules, Hindus avoided their touch. Yet, the fact remains that many from Punjab's varied tribes and castes—Jatts, Rajputs, Gujjars, Gakhars and others—accepted Islam during the Sultanate era, so that the Punjab that Babur, the first Mughal, entered in the 1520s had a substantial Muslim presence, probably constituting a majority west of the Ravi, with roots in most cases in Indian soil. Not surprisingly, given the shortage of solid evidence, there is disagreement on the percentage of the 'foreign' element among the region's Muslims.[20]

A large majority of Punjab's Muslims were Sunnis. Shia groups included followers of the Ismaili sect, which had first entered the subcontinent not long after the Arab attack on Sindh in the seventh century, but Ismailis were a small minority among Punjab's Shias.

Punjab's Hindus included a variety of 'high', peasant, 'menial' and 'untouchable' castes and despite Islam's successes made up a substantial part of the population. By acknowledging Sultanate suzerainty, more than a dozen Hindu Rajput rajas and zamindars managed to retain large tracts in the hills to the north and east of Punjab. Many other Hindus—usually Brahmins, Khatris or Aroras—filled mid-level administrative positions across Punjab. Quite a few Hindus learned Persian, the Sultanate's official language, and often taught it to Muslims in Punjab. The accountant of a Muslim-majority village or group of villages was frequently a Hindu.

Evidently Punjab was largely peaceful during the final half-century of the Lodhi Sultanate. In that half century, some Hindus rose to become diwans (ministers) and provincial governors.

■

Before leaving the Sultanate and moving to the Mughals, we may note the marks left on Punjab's history by two Sultanate-era individuals, Amir Khusro (1253-1325) and Amir Timur (1336-1405). A poet and musician of exceptional talent, Khusro, a Turk born on the subcontinent, was a disciple of Nizamuddin Auliya, the Sufi mystic. While delighting in the Sultanate's expansion and Islam's spread, Khusro called 'Hind' or India his 'motherland' and, even with its Hindu majority, 'a paradise on earth'. He thought that Muslims might find much to admire if they penetrated the heart of the seeming idol-worshipper.[21]

Though Khusro spent several years in both Lahore and Multan, and wrote about the former city, he did not compose Punjabi verses or songs.

His languages were Persian and Hindawi, a half-way house towards Urdu, a language born on the subcontinent from the interaction of Turkic ruling elites with Punjabi-speakers in the regions of Multan and Lahore, and with Hindi-speakers living in and around Delhi.

Timur's legacy on the subcontinent is of a different sort. Possessing both Turkic and Mongol blood and professing Islam, Timur created a Central Asian empire and is today a hero in his native Uzbekistan. However, during his 1398-99 attack on India he not only spelt death and devastation for the Indian Sultanate and the Hindu population of Delhi, he also destroyed much of whatever the Mongols had left of Punjab.

Reaching Delhi by 'a more southerly route', the tall, strong but lame invader sacked, stripped and knifed the capital as none before or since, and returned to the Northwest's passes via Lahore and northern Punjab, keeping 'close to the foothills during his return'[22] and plundering, destroying and killing all along his new route. Though surviving for another 125 years, the Sultanate would never fully recover from this catastrophe, while a Punjab unable to forget the Mongol attacks reeled afresh.

One Punjabi who bravely stood up to Timur was Jasrat Gakhar, sometimes called Jasrat Khan Gakhar (or Khokhar). (Almost four centuries earlier, Gakhars had similarly tried to stop Shahabuddin Ghori.) Whether Jasrat was a Hindu or a Muslim is not known for certain; whether or not Punjab's Gakhars and Khokhars are the same is another evidently unresolved question. What seems clear is that like other Gakhars occupying the land that lay on the route of invaders, Jasrat and his father Shaikha frequently changed sides in order to survive. After Shaikha was executed as a traitor by Timur, Jasrat fought Timur. Though captured, he escaped and struggled for control, often with success, in different parts of Punjab and in Kashmir. He died in 1442.[23]

Occupying the same northern high ground in the Sindh Sagar doab (in the Rawalpindi division of the future), the Gakhars and the Janjuas (from whom, as we noted, the Hindushahi Pals may have sprung) have been seen as traditional foes.[24]

■

Mercifully, raids into Punjab ceased after Timur's invasion, and 'a revival began'.[25] Many who had left, or their descendants, returned to the region. Trade increased. However, in the 1520s—125 years after the invasion—Timur's descendant Babur, a warrior-poet-scholar who wrote in Turkish and Persian, marched into India (also via the Khyber), not to capture treasure and return, but to stay and rule.

Overcoming those in the way (including the Gakhars and the Bhattis), Babur demanded that the Lodhis of Afghan origin then heading the Sultanate should hand over the Delhi throne to Timur's rightful heir, namely himself. Rejecting the demand, Ibrahim Lodhi fought Babur's forces in a gory battle in Panipat in eastern Punjab in April 1526. Thanks largely to Babur's cannons, Lodhi was defeated and killed, and India's Mughal Empire began.

Babur, who had earlier captured Kabul, would write in his journal of 'the big market in Kabul where 10,000 to 20,000 men [from India]' would annually bring 'slaves, cloth, sugar, aromatic roots, etc.' and where every year Indians bought 7,000 to 10,000 Central Asian horses.[26] Reached via the Khyber and Rawalpindi, Lahore was Kabul's chief trading partner, just as Multan was Qandahar's, and thus also, in the 1520s, a big mart.

But henceforth, both Lahore and Multan would tender unqualified obedience to the Delhi throne. Except for a fifteen-year period (1540 to 1555) when the Afghan Surs held that throne, the Mughals would occupy it for more than 300 years.

The Mughals' connection to Timur, and through him to the Mongols, posed a problem for many Punjabis. Thus it has been said that Akbar—the third Mughal emperor, and the son of Babur's son Humayun—could not, at the start of his reign, quickly 'erase from the minds of the people the bitter memories of the invasions of Changiz and Timur. No genuine love and sympathy was felt for the Mughal Dynasty and the masses if not actually hostile were quite indifferent to its fate'.[27] The coldness was also connected to the blood spilled in Punjab during Babur's invasion and again during Akbar's actions against rivals.

The stability provided by Akbar proved a springboard for prosperity. Punjab's soil, aided by hard-working farmers freed from the fear of marauders and aided also by the Persian wheel, pushed up high-quality rice, cotton, wheat, sugarcane, jowar and opium. It also bred horses, mules, camels, buffaloes and cattle, and gave forth grape, melon, watermelon, mango, peach, fig and mulberry.

Rocks in the northern Sindh Sagar doab contained salt. A few large spaces, reserved as imperial hunting grounds, accommodated tigers, cheetahs, antelopes, foxes and hyenas. In addition, there were jungles and forests, including Lakhi Jangal in southern Punjab, extending from both banks of the Sutlej.

While nobles lived in homes of stone, all other homes were built out of earth and wood. Floors were of pounded earth often covered, especially in a Hindu home, with cow dung. While the rich showed off silk or gold at festive occasions, the common people were scantily clothed, with males, and girls below ten, wearing a cloth around the head and a smaller cloth to cover the private region.

Except in periods of famine, most Punjabis had enough to eat. Crops were sown either in May or June and harvested in November or December, or in January or February, to be harvested in April or May.

An illiterate heir who fought while in his early teens to reclaim the Mughal throne, which the Afghan Surs had briefly seized, and who went on to reign for half a century, Akbar enjoyed a special relationship with Punjab even though the battles he waged there had hurt the region. On his way to the throne in Delhi that his grandfather Babur had taken, young Akbar had to subdue enemies in Punjab and rout a challenger, Sikandar Sur. A wise guardian, Bairam Khan, had aided Akbar.

Akbar was India's emperor from 1556. By 1595, i.e. ten years before his death, Punjab's cities—including Lahore, Gujrat and Sialkot in the north, Multan in the southwest, and the eastern towns of Firozepur, Panipat, Thanesar, Sirhind and Sultanpur—were manufacturing cotton fabric of different kinds (calico, chintz and muslin), satin from silk, carpets of wool and cotton, shawls, brocades and embroidered cloth, swords, bows and daggers, plates and dishes, paper and leather, felt and quilts, candied sugar, and oils and perfumes. Boats were built in the northern town of Wazirabad on the Chenab, Arabian horses were sold in Multan, and there was a timber mart in Khizrabad in eastern Punjab's foothills.[28]

Punjabi cities of strategic significance included Rohtas in the northwest (on the route from Kabul via the Khyber Pass to Lahore), where Sher Shah Sur had built a fort, and—in eastern Punjab, watching the paths to Delhi— Jullundur in the Bist doab (sometimes also called the Jullundur doab or, simply, the Doab) and Ludhiana, south of the Sutlej. Cities like Jullundur, Sialkot (in the Rachna doab), Rohtas (Sindh Sagar doab), Multan suba's Dipalpur, half-way between Multan and Lahore, and Delhi suba's Sirhind headed the sarkar around them.

Manufacturing and urbanization were facilitated by the order provided by the Mughals and earlier Delhi-based Sultans. Akbar's Punjab comprised three portions:

- the province or suba of Lahore, a large region governed from the city after which it was named, which grew on the Ravi's banks at Punjab's centre;

- the equally spacious suba of Multan, which included much of present-day Sindh and was managed from Multan city, situated about 230 miles southwest of Lahore city and just east of a joint Jhelum-Chenab-Ravi stream (these three rivers merged north of Multan);
- and large eastern tracts (part in fact of the suba of Delhi) governed either from Delhi or from the town of Sirhind.

▪

Ruling first from Delhi and then from Agra, Akbar treated Lahore as a third capital of his large empire and built a fort there. Journeying across Punjab and staying there was usually a necessity for him, to conquer Kabul or Kashmir for example, or to chase away Hakim, the half-brother who eyed the Mughal throne from hideouts in modern Afghanistan and had established himself in Punjab, or to expel the former guardian when Bairam Khan turned rebellious, or to move to the charms of annexed Kashmir. The emperor was aided in his campaigns by a road that Sher Shah Sur had earlier built from Bihar via Agra to Punjab, a highway that Akbar would extend westward to Peshawar and eastward to Bengal.

Later in his reign, from 1585 to 1598, Akbar reigned almost continuously from Lahore. During this thirteen-year period, and at some other times, the people of Punjab, kept no doubt at a safe distance by the imperial police, saw the strongly-built but somewhat short Akbar in a variety of settings: riding in a cavalcade of elephants, horses and camels; crossing a turbulent river (losing companions on occasion); leading troops to battle; organizing famine relief; visiting the tomb of a saint; hunting animals; and so forth.

Though his 'court was the most splendid ever held in India',[29] Akbar was evidently not addicted to pursuing pleasure. Questions such as the tax levied on the peasant, the coin the populace used, the grain-seller's weights, the cloth-seller's measuring-rod, the price of gold and silver, or the degree of permissible cruelty in punishing crime, commanded his attention.

So did the structure of his administration, which he raised on the edifice left by preceding rulers of India: Sher Shah Sur the Afghan, Akbar's father, Humayun, Humayun's father, Babur, Afghan and Turkic kings who had ruled from Delhi before Babur, and earlier Hindu chiefs.

An elite class of mansabdars—all named by Akbar, all serving at his pleasure, each occupying an assigned rung on a hierarchical ladder, and all expected to be battle-ready—governed India as his servants/officers, some at the royal court in the capital, the rest in the provinces. Recompensed with money and other riches and with lands on which they collected tax, the mansabdars possessed considerable prestige and wealth.

However, on death a mansabdar's property went not to his family but to the emperor, a practice that did not promote thrift. Required to provide soldiers to the empire, a mansabdar was liable, moreover, to be moved from post to post and place to place, e.g. from looking after the treasury in the capital to leading troops at a battlefront near Kabul. On the other hand, a Hindu trader or moneylender selling or lending to a mansabdar could, unlike the noble, accumulate wealth and bequeath it.

When given military control over a suba, the mansabdar was called a nazim or governor. If given financial control as well, he was something like a viceroy and called the subahdar. Each suba contained a dozen or so sarkars, each of them led by a faujdar, usually a military officer. Each sarkar contained a number of parganas or mahals, and there were several villages in every mahal or pargana. Most sarkars contained at least one town, where a kotwal was in charge of security.

Controlling his mansabdars and, as needed, moving them around were time-consuming exercises that contributed to Akbar's chief goal: expanding and consolidating his empire. With expeditions launched from his Punjab base, Akbar quelled rebellions by Pashtun tribes and by chiefs in present-day Afghanistan. He also scattered Central Asia's Uzbeks who had challenged the Mughal throne.

Mansabdar Man Singh, the Rajput prince, and Mansabdar Todar Mal, Akbar's 'finance minister', led some of these expeditions. Also sent to the Pashtun front, Raja Birbal, one of the emperor's closest friends, was killed there in 1586. Upon receiving the news of Birbal's death Akbar did not eat for two days, it seems.[30]

Most of Akbar's mansabdars were descendants of nobles who had migrated from Central Asia to India, or new migrants. A few, as we have seen, were indigenous Hindus. It does not appear that Punjabi Muslims—whether converts or descendants of converts—were among them. Even Akbar's army did not contain many Punjabis. It seems that 'the newly converted Muslims of the Punjab... were never recruited in the Mughal armies'.[31]

Nonetheless, having pushed the northwestern frontier of his empire to beyond Kabul and Qandahar, which now served as 'the twin gates of Hindustan',[32] Akbar gave Punjab a degree of peace not experienced in the region for centuries. Individuals rebelled here and there, none more celebrated in modern times than Dulla Bhatti, a Muslim Rajput chief from Pindi

Bhattian, about seventy miles northwest of Lahore, who was executed in Lahore for his revolt. Punjab's population and economy grew under Akbar. Visiting Lahore during Akbar's reign, a Portuguese Jesuit, Father Antonio Monserrate, thought the city was 'second to none either in Asia or in Europe with regard either to size, population, or wealth'. He found it 'crowded with merchants, who foregather there from all over Asia' and was surprised that Lahore Fort had 'a circumference of three miles'.[33] Published sixty years after Akbar's death, John Milton's *Paradise Lost* included Lahore among the East's fabled cities.

Broadly speaking, Akbar's time saw peaceful co-existence between Punjab's diverse groups—Muslims and Hindus, Sunnis and Shias, foreign elites (Turkic, Afghan, Iranian, Uzbek), who found openings in the Mughal empire, and locals (Muslim and Hindu Punjabis plus descendants of earlier migrants from Central Asia). To promote inter-faith dialogue, Akbar created in Lahore a building called Khairpura where, in his presence, Muslims, Christians and Jews held forth, and another called Dharampura where pandits discoursed on Hinduism. But we should mark that such meetings or conversations had to be 'guarded by soldiers clad in armour and steel'.[34]

Akbar's tolerance did not necessarily mean that all his officers were humane, or that the weak in Punjab were safe. On one occasion, Mirza Lahori, son of a governor of Lahore in Akbar's time, Mirza Quli Khan, 'buried alive in the ground a servant of his for no offence… but simply to enlighten himself on…what becomes of the dead after burial', while at another time Mirza Lahori carried off, 'in the streets of Lahore, the bride from a Hindu wedding party'. When the family laid their grievance before the governor, they were told 'they ought to be glad that they were now related to the Subedar of Lahore'.[35]

European Jesuits conversed with the king in Lahore and elsewhere, and Akbar approved the publication of *Dastan-i-Masih*, a life of Jesus, written jointly by a Father Jerome and a Muslim scholar.[36] But the Jesuits failed to win him to Christianity. Akbar's unwillingness to keep only one wife was the Jesuits' explanation for their failure, but the Emperor's chief concern was his empire's stability, which his conversion would have put at risk.

Akbar's tolerance for different faiths has been linked to his disappointment at Sunni-Shia discord and also to an incident which occurred in northwestern Punjab in May 1578. It seems that shortly after crossing the Jhelum into the town of Bhera and 'about to begin hunting', he 'all of a sudden' had an intense mystical experience. While skeptics would call it a fit, the Emperor's chroniclers state that after the occurrence Akbar 'got his hair cut short and standing under a fruit tree distributed gold and silver among the poor'. 'The hunting programme was cancelled.'[37]

But one of the Lahore conversations on religion led to the assassination of a learned Shia, whereupon, it seems, Akbar had the assassin put to death 'by being bound alive to the leg of an elephant'.[38]

After Akbar's death (in Agra), the brilliant and influential Islamic scholar, Shaikh Ahmad of Sirhind (1563-1624), questioned the genuineness of the Emperor's Islam, even though Akbar was buried as a Muslim under Islamic rites. Offended by the freedom that Akbar's regime gave to Hindus, Christians, Zoroastrians and other non-Muslims, as well as to Shias and Sufis, the Shaikh called for a return to what he saw as pure Islam. Others criticizing Akbar along similar lines included Abdul Qadir Badauni, a scholar in the Emperor's office.

Such critics also disliked Akbar's alliances (including marital) with Hindu princely families from Rajasthan, and the elevation of Hindus like Raja Todar Mal Tandon, the minister who managed the empire's finances until his death in Lahore in 1589, and Raja Man Singh (hailing from today's Jaipur), who led Akbar's armies in battle or governed Kabul or another imperial province.

Detractors like Badauni and the Shaikh of Sirhind had supporters in the Mughal court in Delhi and Agra and among the clerics, but Akbar's approach was approved by the public, including in Lahore and elsewhere in Punjab. We may consider the comment of a Jesuit Father when Akbar died:

> He was a prince beloved of all, firm with the great, kind to those of low estate, and just to all men, high and low, neighbour or stranger, Christian, Saracen (Muslim), or Gentile (Hindu); so that every man believed that the King was on his side.[39]

Five years before Akbar's death, a monarch in a far country, England's Elizabeth I, granted a royal charter to nobles and businessmen forming a trading association called the East India Company.

■

In hindsight, the emperor's most interesting intervention across Punjab's religious boundaries occurred in 1574, when he gifted the land on which would rise the Golden Temple of the Sikhs, as the disciples of Guru Nanak, who had died three years before Akbar was born, were slowly becoming known. Their lines starting and, in effect, ending together, India's Mughal emperors and the Gurus of the Sikhs would often come into conflict in the seventeenth century.

In the Punjab of the 1570s, however, Guru Nanak, who had died in 1539, was remembered lovingly and reverentially by Muslims and Hindus alike, and referred to as Baba or Father Nanak. People recalled his compassion and directness, and his message that humility in one's heart was more important than any Hindu or Muslim rite. God, he taught, was eternal and formless but was the Truth, and focusing on the Name could attract His grace.

Whether Muslim or Hindu, Punjabis had responded positively to Baba Nanak, but a small new community of 'Sikhs' (pupils) saw itself as a distinct group and spoke of Guru Nanak as its first Guru. In 1574, when the third Guru's daughter was getting married to one who would become the fourth Guru, the Mughal emperor gave, as a wedding gift, an area of land in a place in the Bari doab not yet called Amritsar.

We have already briefly encountered another Baba from a much earlier period of whom Punjabis of the sixteenth century also spoke warmly: Baba Farid (1173-1266?), scion of an aristocratic Muslim family, a descendant, it was said, of Omar, the Prophet's Companion, and apparently a son-in-law of Sultan Balban of Delhi. Despite such connections, Farid, a second-generation immigrant who spent many years in Multan, was a renunciate prescribing union with God as the ultimate human goal, and also a sensitive poet conscious of the hardships of ordinary Punjabis around him.

He composed poems in a form of Punjabi, as, much later, Guru Nanak too would do, though in Farid's time his language was probably called 'Multani', even as 'Lahori' was apparently the name for the Punjabi variant spoken in and around Lahore.[40] Like Guru Nanak after him, Baba Farid suggested that at a basic level a Muslim and a Hindu were the same, sharing the joy and pain of being human.

It is conventional today to speak together of Guru Nanak and the nine Gurus who succeeded him, and similarly common to speak in one breath of the four great Sufi teachers: Baba Farid, who died in or close to 1266 in Ajodhan, latter-day Pakpattan on the western bank of the Sutlej, a hundred miles east of Multan, his celebrated master Qutbuddin Kaki (who died in Delhi in 1236), Farid's famous disciple Nizamuddin Auliya (who died in Delhi in 1335) and Qutbuddin's master, Moinuddin Chishti (who died in Ajmer in 1233).

Yet the connection between Baba Farid and Baba Nanak (who was a poet too) is not to be dismissed. It is likely that Akbar recognized it in his time. Not only was it known that the founder of Sikhism had visited Farid's

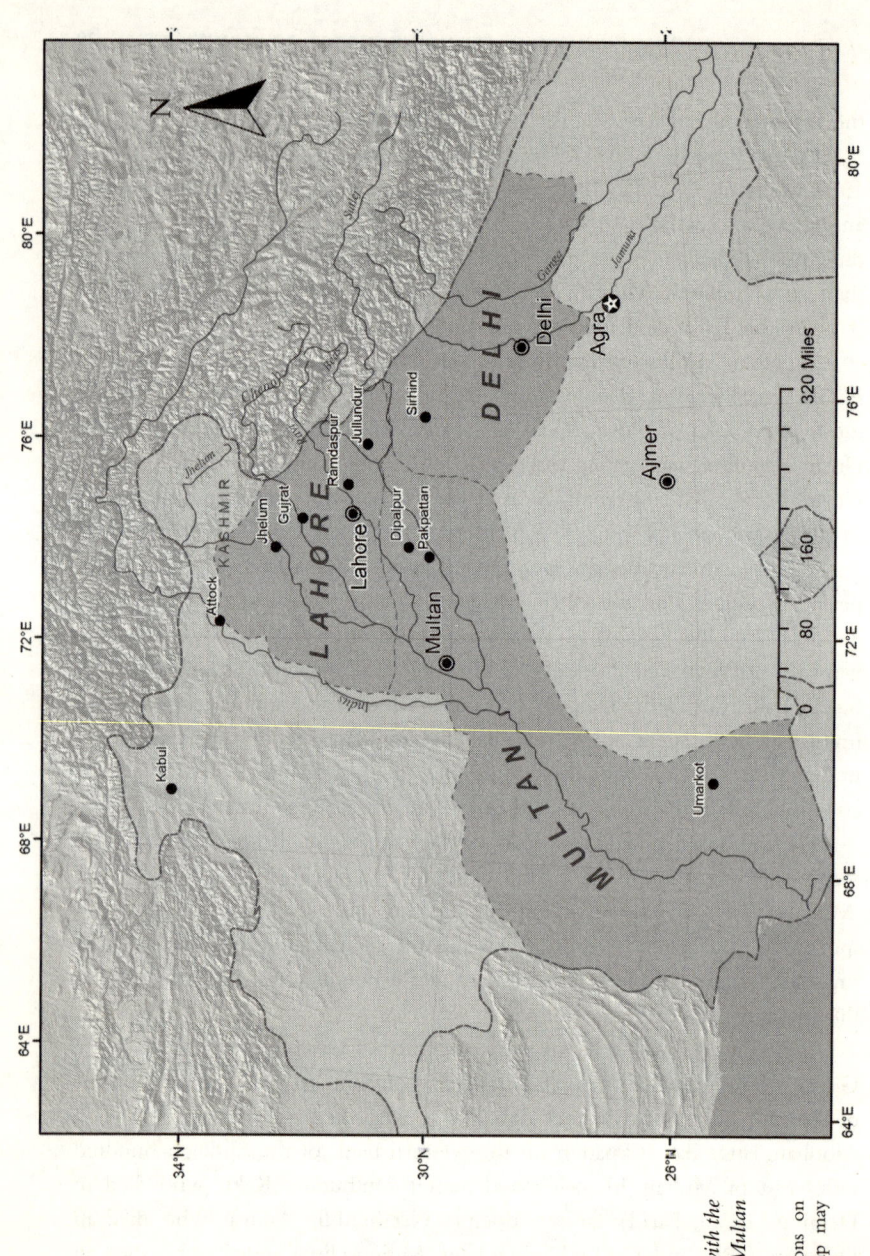

Akbar's Punjab with the subas of Lahore, Multan and Delhi

(Lines and locations on this indicative map may not be exact.)

shrine in Ajodhan, even as Akbar himself had done more than once; several of Farid's poems and hymns were loved by the early Sikh community and would soon enter its holy book, the Granth Sahib.

In 1604, a year before Akbar died, the Granth Sahib, compiled by the fifth Guru, Arjan Dev, was installed in Amritsar at the site the emperor had provided. Earlier, in 1588, a renowned Lahore-based Sufi, Mian Mir (1550-1635) had evidently journeyed to the site—at the invitation of Guru Arjan Dev—to lay the foundation for a Sikh temple, the Harimandir, close to a tank, already sacred to the Sikhs, that Guru Ram Das had built.

Its administration left in the Guru's hands, Amritsar functioned as an autonomous town within suba Lahore. Yet in 1606, only a year after Akbar's death, Arjan Dev was executed (and also, Sikhs believe, tortured) in the very fort in Lahore that Akbar had constructed.

Jahangir, Akbar's son and successor, had ordered the execution. We know from Jahangir's own writing that he was jealous of Guru Arjan Dev's popularity and that a gesture from the Guru towards Khusrau, a son rebelling against Jahangir, had outraged him.

> [Clothed] in the garments of sainthood and sanctity, [Arjan Dev] had captured many of the simple-hearted of the Hindus, and even of the ignorant and foolish followers of Islam... They called him Guru, and from all sides stupid people crowded to worship... him... At last, when Khusrau passed along this road, this insignificant fellow... came out and did homage to him... When this came to my ears,.. I commanded that he should be put to death.[41]

Honouring or blessing a rebelling son was a capital offence, doubly so when a potentially assertive community was growing around the offender. We may mark, too, that seven hundred supporters of Khusrau, presumably all of them Muslims, were impaled in Lahore under Jahangir's orders.[42]

■

Shah Jahan, who followed Jahangir to the Mughal throne, was born in 1592 to one of his father's Rajput wives in Lahore, where the sister-and-brother duo of Nur Jahan (another of Jahangir's wives) and Asaf Khan wielded great influence, for Jahangir had made Asaf the governor of suba Lahore. The parents of Asaf and Nur Jahan were Iranians from Qandahar who had fled that city and found refuge in Akbar's Indian empire. In 1612, Shah Jahan married Asaf's beautiful daughter, Mumtaz.

When Jahangir died in 1628 (in Kashmir), Shah Jahan was not his obvious successor. Though his older brother, the rebel Khusrau, had died in imperial custody, Nur Jahan, who bore no children to Jahangir, was determined that Prince Shahir Yar, her son-in-law from a previous marriage, should succeed her husband. But the stratagems and resources of her brother, who was similarly resolved in favour of *his* son-in-law, Shah Jahan, were more successful, even though Jahangir had signed a will nominating Shahir Yar.

Defeated and captured in battle by Asaf's army, Shahir Yar was then strangled in Lahore along with Khusrau's son Dawar Baksh, whom Asaf had earlier installed as a mock king to foil Shahir Yar. Other grandsons of Jahangir were also executed, and Nur Jahan was imprisoned.

Deception, war, fratricide, and the murder or blinding of closely-related rivals would mark virtually every succession in Mughal times, as it had done during the Sultanate.

An earlier project of Nur Jahan's had been more successful. While reigning as India's powerful queen, she built in Agra an elegant mausoleum for her father, Ghiyas Beg, also known as Itmad-ud-daulah. But it is in grounds very close to Lahore, across the Ravi, that Jahangir, Nur Jahan and Asaf Khan lie buried. Cherishing his links with Punjab, the emperor had left instructions to be interred there. Largely the creation of Jahangir's successor Shah Jahan, the graceful imperial tomb is one of Lahore's prize possessions.

Though Shah Jahan, in his turn, would lie in Agra—next to Mumtaz, underneath the wonder he created as an eternal resting place for the wife who predeceased him by thirty-five years—his links were stronger with Delhi, where he built the Red Fort and the Jama Masjid and, abutting these two grand edifices, a whole town called Shahjahanabad, which replaced Agra as the Mughal capital.

In Punjab, meanwhile, Lahore had overtaken Multan in numbers and economic activity. While the river Ghaggar disappeared, silt damaged navigation along the Indus, undermining Multan's advantages, but also affecting, towards the end of the seventeenth century, Lahore's trade.[43]

For the sake of Lahore city, and in particular perhaps for the gardens he had created there for imperial pleasure, Shah Jahan had a canal built in the upper Bari doab that brought waters from the mountains of Kashmir. Aided first by the policies of Akbar and later by those of Shah Jahan, suba Lahore evidently contained 28,000 villages during the seventeenth century, compared with around 10,000 villages in suba Multan.[44]

Shah Jahan's association with Lahore, the city of his birth and of his marriage to Mumtaz, was also strong. In that city (and also in Kashmir) the builder-king laid out the Shalimar Gardens. Palaces were built inside the Lahore Fort, which grandfather Akbar had first constructed. Shah Jahan's chief engineer for such projects was a Kurdish general, Ali Mardan Khan,* who as governor of Qandahar (which Jahangir had lost) crossed over to Shah Jahan's standard and restored his province to the Mughals.

The emperor's chief engineer may have been an 'import' but Lahore's artisans and architects, too, were responsible, generation after generation, for the city's classical buildings and gardens. We may note, too, an impression that a team of architects from Lahore may have contributed to the design of the Taj Mahal.[45]

Aided by the Persians, Qandahar again shook off Mughal control, as did Kabul. A series of expensive forays by troops that included thousands of Hindu Rajputs failed to restore Delhi's supremacy in the Pashtun country, even when the Mughal army was led to the periphery by the emperor himself, or by his third son Aurangzeb, or by eldest son Dara Shikoh, the father's favourite, who lived in Lahore as viceroy for the Mughal territory between that city and Kabul.

Shah Jahan had spent lavishly out of a large revenue extracted from the populace. The Belgian traveller, Francois Tavernier, 'who witnessed [both] the commencement and the completion' of the Taj Mahal, would claim that the undertaking required the labour of '20,000 daily for twenty-two years'.[46]

Shah Jahan's other construction projects were also expensive, as were his military campaigns beyond the Khyber and expeditions to Kashmir, Tibet, and the south. His 200,000-strong standing army and magnificent court were additional large burdens. Despite these expenses, the Mughal territory was left with an abundance of rupees, gold, silver and pearls at the end of Shah Jahan's thirty-year reign.

The reigns of Akbar, Jahangir and Shah Jahan and the viceroyalty of Prince Dara did much to bind Lahore and its people, and Punjabis as a whole, to the Mughal empire. Though alien rather than Punjabi, the Mughals impressed Punjab with their grandeur, and while the populace paid for the opulence, it gained from the empire's stability.

By the end of Shah Jahan's kingship, Punjabis appeared to view the Mughal umbrella as reassuring rather than foreign. Though the Mughals employed Persian rather than Punjabi as their administrative language, many

---

*Also buried in Lahore.

Punjabis were now relating themselves to the Mughals and perhaps even beginning to 'own' the Mughals.

•

The new relationship was reflected in the role of Hakim Alimuddin, a native of Chiniot, the wood-carvers' city on the Chenab's southern bank, about 110 miles west of Lahore. Having attended, in Lahore, to the medical needs of Shah Jahan before the prince ascended the imperial throne, Alimuddin rose from office to high office until Emperor Shah Jahan made him the subahdar of Lahore.

Earlier, Alimuddin had identified himself wholly with his native Chiniot, where he dug many wells and built a hospital, an inn, a mosque and a madrassah. It is legitimate to see Alimuddin—'simple in his mode of living and dress'[47]—as Lahore suba's first Punjabi viceroy, even if, as is possible, he had alien forebears.

Called 'Wazir Khan' by now, in 1634 Alimuddin built what a future historian would call 'the chief ornament of the city of Lahore...an architectural monument of surpassing beauty and elegance',[48] the Wazir Khan Mosque. Endowing resources for its upkeep, Alimuddin also ensured space beside the unique mosque for future book-binders, painters and writers.

•

To return to Shah Jahan, his emperorship ended in 1657, eight years before his death, when a sudden illness that seemed incurable triggered an abdication. Dara took over as regent, but brothers Murad (the youngest), Shuja (the second) and Aurangzeb (the third) were not slow to claim the throne, except that Aurangzeb pretended, in a letter to Murad, that he would stand down in the youngest brother's favour. Aurangzeb added that a kingship in 'this deceitful and unstable world' was the last thing he wanted.[49]

All four brothers were Mumtaz's children, as were sisters Roshanara and Jahanara. Having died twenty-six years earlier, Mumtaz did not witness the fratricide among her sons that followed the emperor's illness. But Shah Jahan, who recovered—though not in time to regain control—would learn in the prison into which Aurangzeb confined him that Dara had been killed, that a fleeing Shuja had disappeared into eastern regions beyond Bengal, never to be heard of again, and that Murad had been trapped and executed by Aurangzeb.

Before being imprisoned, Shah Jahan had realized that much of the Mughal army was backing Aurangzeb against Dara and Shuja, and indeed against himself. For as long as he was able, the father tried to support Dara, sending 'camels laden with silver and gold coins' with which the favourite son might enlist an army. But commanders in Agra and Delhi declared for Aurangzeb, and Dara escaped from these two cities to Lahore. He had lived there, earlier, in the mansion where his mother Mumtaz was born. Previously belonging to her mansabdar father, Asaf, the property had become imperial on Asaf's death.

We are informed that as viceroy Dara was 'very popular among the people of Lahore',[50] where he had written a biography of the old Sufi venerated in Lahore, Mian Mir, who died near Lahore in 1635. After Mian Mir's disciple Mulla Shah, who became Dara's teacher or Pir, had also died, the prince erected a spacious mausoleum over his Pir's remains and planned for 'a more superb shrine over the remains of Mian Mir'.[51]

Desirous, like his great-grandfather Akbar, of winning the goodwill of India's Hindus, prince Dara was also—unlike Akbar—a serious scholar who wrote or commissioned works of lasting interest on mysticism and on similarities among religions, including *Sirr-i-Akbar* (The Great Secret) and *Majma-al-Bahrain* (Mingling of the Oceans). Dara's dialogue with Baba Lal, a Hindu thinker, 'regarding bridging the gulf between race and race, creed and creed, Hinduism and Islam', was held in Lahore in the home of a rich Hindu, Chander Bhan, who wrote down the conversation.[52] Apparently the prince was a also friend of a French Jesuit priest, Father Buzee.[53]

Dara's feeling for Punjab and its chief city was expressed in verse:

> May God keep the Punjab all flourishing!
> May He preserve the country of the saints!
> Oh, may Lahore be always full of bliss!
> May plague and death be always far from it![54]

As for the city's reciprocal sentiment, one scholar has spoken of 'Dara Shikoh's affectionate remembrance in many a Lahori heart'.[55]

For a while it seemed as if Lahore might give Dara not only sanctuary but also a militia, but Aurangzeb pursued his brother with an immense army and chased him out of the city, towards Multan and Sindh. While Dara sought allies in Sindh and in Gujarat, Aurangzeb turned his attention to Shuja, who was advancing from Bengal. Shuja's men were stopped west of Allahabad and beaten back towards Bengal. Meanwhile, in Jun, a small territory in eastern Sindh, Dara lost his wife to illness. After asking trusty servants to carry her remains to Lahore for burial, Dara was aiming for Qandahar when the ruler of Jun, spotting an opportunity for reward, betrayed Dara and Dara's son into the hands of Aurangzeb loyalists.

Brought in chains with his son to Delhi, Dara, the philosopher-prince greatly liked by the people, was made to ride 'on a sorry elephant' through the streets and subjected to a mock trial, where he was accused of apostasy. Had he not suggested that Hindus too were monotheists, that much was similar between Islam and Hinduism? A verdict of guilty was quickly obtained. When soldiers arrived to pick him up for execution, Dara fought back with a small knife until he was overpowered and killed.

> His body was exhibited on an elephant to the populace, while his head was brought to Aurangzeb, who had it wiped and washed in his presence, and being satisfied of its identity, shed tears.[56]

Deposed by Aurangzeb in 1658, Shah Jahan lived on for another eight years. To dilute Dara's continuing appeal, Aurangzeb sought the hand, for his son Akbar, of the late prince's daughter, who lived among the detained in Agra. Shah Jahan successfully resisted the pressure, as did the girl, who declared that she would rather kill herself than become Aurangzeb's daughter-in-law.

From their windows in Agra, the trio—father, daughter and granddaughter—could see the celestial tomb of Mumtaz, the wife, mother and grandmother who had died at the age of thirty-eight. To that tomb was taken, in 1666, the body of seventy-four-year-old Shah Jahan. Ordering a grand procession, Aurangzeb walked behind the funeral car 'in solemn sadness and with tears in his eyes'. Apparently, the 'suspicion was never removed that the aged king had been removed by poison', and it was said that with the death behind him Aurangzeb was 'ready to march for Kashmir with a contented mind'.[57]

•

The lives of India's Mughal emperors and of the Sikhs' Gurus were intertwined, and we have already touched on aspects of the Gurus' history. But more of it should be seen.

Guru Nanak was born in 1469 into the Bedi clan of the Khatri caste of Hindus in a Punjab which had seen Timur's brutal invasion only seventy years earlier. The Punjabis with whom Guru Nanak shared his vision in the last decade of his life (the 1530s) had seen Babur march across their land and were aware of the gruesome battle of Panipat. Addressing Babur directly, Guru Nanak wrote:

Deliver just judgments, reverence holy men, forswear wine and gambling.../ Be merciful to the vanquished, and worship God in spirit and in truth.

He added:

The Primal Being is now called Allah, the turn of the shaikhs hath come...
Babur ruled over Khorasan and hath terrified Hindustan.
The Creator taketh no blame to Himself;
It was Death disguised as a Mughal who made war on us.
When there was such slaughter and lamentation,
didst not Thou, O God, feel pain?
Creator, Thou belongest to us all.[58]

Thus, for Guru Nanak the Creator belonged to Muslims and non-Muslims alike. (The 'shaikhs' were Sufi or other Muslim teachers.) As for Babur, in Nanak's eyes he was neither a barbaric foreigner nor the great enemy, only a great sinner who had caused great pain. A story that Guru Nanak was once imprisoned by Babur is joined by another suggesting that the Guru bestowed good wishes and recognition on Babur.[59]

Apparently the Guru's first utterance after a mystical experience was, 'There is no Hindu, there is no Mussulman.'[60] This rejection of a Hindu-Muslim divide was a reminder of the thought of oneness sown in Punjab by Baba Farid and nourished thereafter by several others.

Before dying (in Kartarpur, on the Ravi), Guru Nanak named as his successor a disciple, Lehna, a Khatri of the Trehan clan, who became known as Guru Angad. In choosing Lehna, Guru Nanak rejected the claims of his sons. In 1552, Guru Angad named Guru Amar Das, also a Khatri but of the Bhalla clan, as the third Guru.

While Guru Amar Das, who died in 1574, also rejected his sons' claims, he named his son-in-law, Guru Ram Das, a Khatri of the Sodhi clan, to follow him. Before his death (1581), the new Guru selected his youngest son, Arjan Dev, to succeed him. All the Gurus who followed were Guru Arjan Dev's direct descendants, which made them direct descendants also of Guru Ram Das and, through his daughter, of Guru Amar Das, the third Guru, as well.

Thus the Gurus were all from the 'high' Khatri caste of traders and administrators but within that caste from middle-level clans or sub-castes. More importantly, the growing community of their followers, increasingly known as Sikhs (from sishya, Sanskrit for pupil), came from a variety of castes, including peasant Jats, priestly Brahmins, trading Khatris and Aroras, and 'low' or 'menial' castes. Apart from a few Muslims, most were, or had been, Hindus.

At the langar, the community kitchen attached to a gurdwara, all Sikhs sat down together to eat. Caste taboos had been broken, and a measure of equality introduced. But they had also become a distinct community, which for writing used a new script called Gurmukhi ('from the Guru's mouth'), first popularized by Guru Angad. Twice a year, during spring on Baisakhi day and at Diwali before winter's onset, the community congregated at Amritsar. Its offerings for the langar and other expenses were collected by masands, the Guru's agents.

The future would see sharp disputes, continuing to our times, concerning the relationship between Hinduism and Sikhism, and between Islam and Sikhism. The Sikh faith is popularly seen as being closer to Hinduism than to Islam, yet it is not as if Islam made no contribution to it. According to a modern scholar of Punjabi history,

> The idea of a single god, of a single book containing the revelation or the doctrine of salvation, the concept of brotherhood among the believers whatever their origin, social background or caste, are some of the major contributions that almost eight centuries of Islamic rule brought to Punjab's culture and mentality.[61]

Violence did not mark the transition from one guru to another. But there were disappointments and rival claims. Asserting that he was the new guru, Guru Nanak's son Sri Chand refused to recognize the installation of Guru Angad who, as a result, moved from Kartarpur to Khadur, also in the Bari doab and, we may add, in the 'Lahore division'.

The Gurus and their families had to deal with the empire's functionaries. When Guru Ram Das named his youngest son, Arjan Dev, as his successor, Prithi Chand, his oldest brother, tried, it appears, to get local Mughal administrators to support a claim to his father's position. However, Prithi Chand 'had to be content with a share in the income' from the Amritsar land, where Guru Arjan Dev established, in accordance with his father's wish, a centre for teaching the principles of the Gurus, and compiled what ere long would be known as the Sikh scripture, the *Adi Granth* or the Granth Sahib.[62]

In 1598, Emperor Akbar and Guru Arjan Dev met in Goindwal. One result was that the rate of revenue in suba Lahore was lowered, increasing the Guru's popularity among the growing ranks of his farmer followers, and not merely among Sikhs.[63]

According to some versions, the death sentence ordered for Guru Arjan Dev by Akbar's son Jahangir was commuted to a heavy fine which the Guru could not or would not pay. Cruelly afflicted, he died. Other accounts say that the tortured Guru disappeared. Whatever be the truth in allegations (apparently current in the late eighteenth century) that a Hindu diwan in Lahore had played a role in the Guru's torture, it is indisputable that Jahangir disliked him and had ordered his death.[64] One person who welcomed the death was Akbar's sharp critic, the Shaikh of Sirhind.

Nominated at the age of eleven as the sixth Guru, Guru Hargobind, his father's only son, is said to have 'girded two swords, one symbolizing his spiritual authority'—his piri—and 'the other his temporal power'—his miri. At some point, not surprisingly, he 'encouraged his followers in martial activity'.[65] Building in Amritsar a fort called Lohgarh and also (facing the Sikhs' temple) a platform from where he pronounced on earthly matters, the Guru, who preferred horses or arms as offerings rather than money or grain, wore royal regalia and raised a dedicated army. Many of the horses in his stable were bought in Kabul.

Some Sikhs criticized Guru Hargobind's interest in arms, and the Guru's throne was claimed by Guru Hargobind's uncle, Prithi Chand, and later, after Prithi Chand's death, by his son Miharban. Yet many in the community agreed that physical force was needed for its protection.

Jahangir had the Guru arrested and kept in detention in a fort in Gwalior, seventy-five miles south of Agra, but the incarceration was followed by cordial relations between the emperor and the young Guru, apparently helped by the fact that both were avid hunters. In any case, while the Guru was aware that the emperor held powerful cards, Jahangir knew of the Guru's influence in Punjab. Sikh tradition holds that during this spell of rapprochement the Lahore-based diwan who had tortured Guru Arjan Dev was handed over to the Sikhs, who avenged their Guru's suffering by torturing the diwan before killing him.

After Jahangir's death, however, Mughal administrators in suba Lahore obtained Shah Jahan's assent to an attack on the Guru's fort in Amritsar. This was successfully repulsed, but the Guru abandoned Amritsar and went to the place where Guru Nanak had died, Kartarpur on the Ravi. There too he was attacked, but two Mughal commanders were killed and the Guru's unafraid force was again victorious.

Realizing, however, that in suba Lahore he would not be left alone (despite the goodwill apparently entertained for him by the viceroy in Lahore, Dara Shikoh[66]), the Guru moved to Nalagarh, a territory of a Hindu Rajput vassal of the Mughal ruler in east Punjab's hills. There, in a town called Kiratpur, the Guru lived unmolested for eight or nine years, along with his 'stables, horsemen and matchlock-men'.[67] He died in Kiratpur in 1644, fourteen years before Aurangzeb would depose Shah Jahan.

By this time Guru Hargobind had attracted numerous followers in central and eastern India, including Khatri traders from Punjab settled in those distant regions. On the other hand, Jats seemed predominant in his Kiratpur-based army and also among the Sikh masands (agents) who travelled across the empire.

In the Punjab plains, however, the Guru's opponents had found a clear field. The Amritsar centre was taken over by the Guru's cousin Miharban, who claimed he was Guru Nanak's successor, a claim also made, after Miharban's death, by his son Harji. In the early 1640s—before Guru Hargobind's passing— his own grandson, Dhir Mal, whose father Gurditta had predeceased the Guru, left Kiratpur and returned to Kartarpur, taking with him the original *Adi Granth* that Guru Arjan Dev (Dhir Mal's great-grandfather) had prepared.

Apparently willing to mend fences with the Mughals, Dhir Mal accepted from Shah Jahan revenue-free land in Kartarpur. Thus Dhir Mal in Kartarpur and Miharban/Harji in Amritsar presented themselves as alternative rallying points for the Sikhs. Refusing to yield, however, Guru Hargobind nominated Dhir Mal's younger brother, fourteen-year-old Har Rai, as his successor.

Though a conflict between Mughal commanders and the Rajput chief of Nalagarh forced young Guru Har Rai to move for a while from Kiratpur to Nahan, the hilly land of another Hindu vassal of the Mughals, he was evidently back in Kiratpur, twenty-eight years of age, when Aurangzeb captured the Mughal throne.

Told that the Guru had tried to help Dara, the new emperor summoned him to Delhi. In response, Guru Har Rai sent his elder son, Ram Rai. Detaining Ram Rai, Aurangzeb also tried to cultivate him. Three years after Aurangzeb's ascension, Guru Har Rai died, but not before nominating Har Krishan, his younger son, who was only five, as the next Guru. The emperor's reply was to summon Guru Har Krishan, too, to Delhi, where, at the age of eight, the boy-Guru died of smallpox.

The Mughals at this point saw three actual or potential claimants to the throne of the Sikh Guru: Ram Rai, their hostage in Delhi, Dhir Mal in Kartarpur and Harji in Amritsar. But they were to be surprised for, before dying, Guru Har Krishan had evidently indicated (historian Grewal informs us) that his baba or 'grandfather'—more precisely his grandfather's brother—Tegh Bahadur, the fourth of Guru Hargobind's five sons and an uncle to brothers Dhir Mal and Guru Har Rai, would be the next Guru.[68]

Grewal's account goes on to state that when, in 1664, this forty-three-year-old son of Guru Hargobind heard that he had become the ninth Guru of the Sikhs, he was in Bakala village in the upper Bari doab—in Punjab's Lahore division—expecting to spend the rest of his life there in peace and quiet, just as he had spent the previous twenty years. Bakala was the village of his maternal grandfather and Tegh Bahadur had gone there at the age of twenty-three from Kiratpur, presumably with his mother, following the death of his father Guru Hargobind and the ascension of his nephew Guru Har Rai.

As a seat for the new Guru, however, Bakala was vulnerable: it was too close to the centres in Amritsar and Kartarpur from where, respectively, nephews Harji and Dhir Mal, supported by masands and followers, were competing for the loyalty of the Sikhs. Repairing to Kiratpur in the hill country, Guru Tegh Bahadur ran into opposition there from his brother Suraj Mal, the youngest of Guru Hargobind's sons. However, he was welcomed in the neighbouring hill territory of Bilaspur, also run by a Hindu vassal of the Mughals. There the Guru established his seat in a place called Makhowal.

Angry with Dhir Mal, a follower of the Guru plundered the Kartarpur property, but the Guru seems to have returned all the looted possessions to Dhir Mal, in keeping with a tenet of his that forgiveness was 'the most meritorious austerity', unparalleled by any other virtue.[69]

In 1665, a year after his ascension, the Guru began six years of travel in Mughal subas in the Gangetic plains, visiting Sikh sangats or congregations in Agra, Allahabad, Banaras and Patna, where, shortly after he left the city, his wife gave birth to his only son, Gobind Das, the future Guru Gobind Singh. He journeyed, too, to Dhaka and Assam. In all places, the sangats, a majority of them composed of Khatri settlers, honoured Guru Tegh Bahadur, celebrated his son's arrival, and gave offerings.

The Guru travelled across the empire with the knowledge and consent of Mughal officials—there was contact between the worlds of the Guru and the emperor. Part of the Guru's eastern journey was in fact made in the company of one of Aurangzeb's Rajput generals.[70]

But the imperial establishment was perturbed at reports of Sikh temples being constructed in several of the empire's towns and of the Guru's masands carrying collections from the temples to the Guru. A displeased Aurangzeb ordered that the masands should be driven out of the temples. Then, in 1669, he ordered that the temples should be demolished.

By 1671, when the Guru returned to Makhowal, the empire's Sikhs were facing a grave situation. Preparing himself for dark eventualities, the Guru also tried to strengthen his flock. The conquest of fear was now a central message from him. 'Do not fear,' he urged. Significantly, he also advised, 'Do not frighten.'

He wore the sword bequeathed to him by his father, Guru Hargobind, and it seems his following called him 'Sacha Badshah' or the True King, which is also how, decades earlier, Guru Arjan Dev had at times been addressed.[71]

Two years later, Guru Tegh Bahadur left the comparative safety of Makhowal and went from village to village in the sarkar of Sirhind and other northern and western portions of suba Delhi, preaching his message to sangats comprising farmers and zamindars. Given Aurangzeb's attitude, this was a bold exercise.

Guru Tegh Bahadur was back in Makhowal when, in May 1675, a deputation of Brahmins from the valley of Kashmir called on him and reported on religious persecution by the Mughal governor of suba Kashmir. Anguished by the news, the Guru took a decision. For the right to believe, he would take the ultimate risk: he would go to the heart of the empire and there proclaim his faith.

Nominating young Gobind Das as his successor, he left Makhowal for Delhi. Arrested when he crossed from vassal territory into the Mughal pargana of Ropar, he was kept in custody for four months in the sarkar of Sirhind.

Brought to Delhi in November, he was asked to perform a miracle to prove his nearness to God. On refusing to do so, he was told to embrace Islam if he wished to remain alive. To show that business was meant, three of his companions were put to death in his presence. When Guru Tegh Bahadur said he would not accept Islam, he was beheaded. The event occurred on 11 November 1675 at the eastern end of Chandni Chowk, right across from the grand entrance of the Red Fort. Loyal Sikhs (from the 'untouchable' Chuhra jati) bravely carried the Guru's severed head to his nine-year-old son and successor in Makhowal.

■

As we near the end of this chapter, we may interrupt the narrative of the Sikh Gurus to obtain more of a picture of the Mughal empire in the latter part of the seventeenth century. The sixth Mughal Emperor, Aurangzeb, who ruled from 1658 to 1707, sought to impose an austere lifestyle on his subjects and tried to banish music, singing and dancing. Championing frugality, he sewed caps to show how to earn one's bread. Word also spread that the emperor spent time copying the Qur'an in his own hand. A text of the Qur'an in his writing went as a gift to Mecca.

In his regime, Muslims were forbidden to touch liquor. Non-Muslims were asked—in 1679, four years after Guru Tegh Bahadur's death—to pay the jizya, a practice Akbar had abolished more than a century earlier. Tax was resumed on lands given to non-Muslims for religious purposes. Some Hindu temples were destroyed even when there was no rebellion to crush.

Diligent in religious observance, Aurangzeb was a tenacious fighter as well. The empire under Aurangzeb's long rule increased in area. New territories annexed included 'Little Tibet' beyond Kashmir in the north, Chittagong beyond Dhaka in the east, and, in the south, the Muslim kingdoms of Golconda and Bijapur. But the empire invited rebellions.

South of Delhi, thousands of Jats showed defiance, as did Satnamis in Narnaul pargana in the Delhi doab. In the northwest, the poet Khushal Khan Khattak stirred the Pashtun country into revolt, and Aurangzeb had to take a force there himself. In India's middle, Rajasthani clans who had been loyal to the Mughal throne for a century became restive. In the Maratha country in the south, Shivaji created a Hindu kingdom and ruled it until his death in 1680. Though Shivaji's son Sambhaji was captured and killed in 1689, the Marathas refused to be subdued.

Dates reveal the pressure on Aurangzeb. His expedition to Kabul took place in 1673, Shivaji's coronation in 1674, Guru Tegh Bahadur's execution in 1675. Spying was tightened by him, and Shias harassed along with non-Muslims. While some Hindu temples received grants during his reign, and the percentage of Hindus appointed to senior positions may even have gone up, two great temples, one in Mathura and the other in Banaras, were among the Hindu shrines demolished; some link the Mathura demolition to the Jat rebellion.

Built in Lahore between 1671 and 1673, the Badshahi Mosque, so unadorned that it contains only two inscriptions, is Aurangzeb's greatest architectural contribution. It rose under the eyes of Fidai Khan Koka, the emperor's foster-brother, who was made Lahore's governor to build the mosque. For over 300 years it would be the world's largest mosque. Stones forming this imposing structure included many previously gathered by Dara for Mian

Mir's mausoleum.[72]

But Punjab did not hold Aurangzeb's attention for long. His youngest son, Akbar, made an alliance first with rebel Rajputs and later with Sambhaji, Shivaji's son, forcing Aurangzeb to a military campaign in the south—the Deccan.

Combining with Maratha and Rajput elements and also with Shiite-leaning Muslim chieftains in the Deccan who had ties with the ruler of Persia, young Akbar seemed capable of offering himself as a rival emperor. The Deccan campaign against his son and the son's allies kept Aurangzeb in the south for years.

∎

The tenth Guru, Guru Gobind Singh, whose leadership of the Sikhs commenced during Aurangzeb's rule, received literary, religious and military training in the hills around Makhowal in the principality of Bilaspur. Within a few years, he learnt Persian and Sanskrit and also turned into a skilled horseman and shot. If a vassal land like Bilaspur, free from direct Mughal rule, provided a degree of safety to the young Guru and the band around him, the prevalence in that hilly tract of the cult of the goddess of retribution (Devi, Durga or Chandi, as she was variously known) probably contributed to their embrace of militant struggle.

The Hindu rajas of these hill states, frequently in conflict with one another, maintained a tricky relationship with their Mughal overlord. While harbouring the young Guru and his growing force was risky, for it could annoy Aurangzeb, it nonetheless provided strength against an unfriendly raja next door. So when in 1685 Bilaspur thought it prudent to ease out the nineteen-year-old Guru, neighbouring Sirmur (also called Nahan) was willing to give him space. There, in a place by the Jamuna called Paunta, Guru Gobind Singh built a fort and raised a force.

Three years later, the Guru's force was victorious in a hard battle in a village called Bhangani against an army from neighbouring hill states that intended to subdue Sirmur. Unwilling, however, to be embroiled in future feuds on behalf of Sirmur, the Guru—his position strengthened by the Bhangani triumph—returned to the territory of Bilaspur, where, on the bank of the Sutlej, he built a new base, Anandpur, in the vicinity of Makhowal. It soon attracted men and resources.

By 1688, Aurangzeb's empire was under great strain. A sequence of rebellions had shaken the confidence of its officers. Military campaigns had crippled its finances. No longer sure that lands awarded would remain with them, leading nobles in Punjab and elsewhere milked the peasants tilling their lands. Unrest grew.

As for the emperor himself, from 1680 he was mired in the Deccan, attempting to quell Maratha and other rebellions, and moving from place to place with hundreds of thousands of soldiers and camp-followers. A huge city of tents, complete with bazaars, elephants and camels, moved with the emperor.

On these southern marches he kept himself informed of events in the hills east of Punjab. Learning that Anandpur had become a magnet for the Sikhs and others dissatisfied with Mughal rule, Aurangzeb ordered his officers in 1693 to ensure that crowds did not assemble there. Yet by now some of the hill rajas too were willing to stand up to the Mughals, although others remained loyal. Resisted by rebelling rajas and by Guru Gobind Singh, three successive Mughal forces sent to enforce submission returned in failure.

The Guru seemed safe in Anandpur, but as the seventeenth century drew to a close, his was not the only Sikh voice being heard in Punjab. In the doabs, the successors of Prithi Chand seemed dominant. In fact, the Guru's message went out more to sangats located outside Punjab or in the cis-Sutlej tracts.[73] 'In terms of followers, the doabs of the Punjab [seemed] virtually lost to the successors of Guru Hargobind.'[74]

Recognizing that an empire in crisis could hit out at one like him, and facing dissension in the Sikh community at the same time, Guru Gobind Singh produced a radical response in April 1699. Articulated on Baisakhi day in front of a large gathering in Anandpur, this reply included a new and militant rite for becoming a Sikh (sipping sweetened water after the Guru had stirred it with a double-edged sword), the right of any five 'new' Sikhs to similarly baptize others, the elimination of intermediaries (masands) between the Guru and the Sikh, and the obligation of a new Sikh to keep his hair uncut, carry a sword, and call himself a Singh.

The word for a lion, 'Singh' was also, as we have seen, the name used by the Mughal empire's Rajput mansabdars. Now, thanks to the Anandpur decree, a Sikh from a 'low' caste could in minutes become a Singh. The Guru also decreed that anyone baptized by five of the baptized would belong to the elect Khalsa, an honour hitherto restricted to those directly initiated by the Guru.

In a dramatic gesture, Guru Gobind asked to be baptized himself by five of the new Singhs. He declared, moreover, that while any five of the initiated, no matter how humble, could make one a Singh, neither masands nor the followers of Ram Rai, Dhir Mal or Prithi Chand were entitled to do so.

Thus bestowing to his following—at a single event—pride, militancy, equality, a new look, and the status of the chosen, the thirty-three-year-old Guru had also deepened the bond between the follower and himself.

Before long, however, Anandpur's armed Singhs frightened the hill rajas, who asked Mughal officers in adjacent imperial territory to intervene. The coming together of Mughal faujdars and hill rajas, plus a proposal of honourable peace, induced the Guru to leave Anandpur for a friendly territory across the Sutlej. The faujdars also withdrew.

Bhim Chand, one of the rajas, then attacked the Guru's force, only to be routed, and a triumphant Guru rode back to Anandpur. When, following this success, Sikh ranks grew, the hill rajas presented themselves to the Mughal court as vassals entitled to protection and formally sought support for expelling the Guru from Anandpur.

After enduring a long blockade mounted by a combination of imperial and vassal forces, and receiving an assurance, sworn on the Qur'an, of safe passage, the Guru agreed, in December 1704, to leave Anandpur. But the promise was false, and a large body of Mughal troops attacked the Guru and his party while they were crossing a thick stream near Ropar.

Although the Guru, two of his older sons and some others eluded the attackers, his wife, mother and two minor sons were separated from him. In the one-sided fighting that ensued in a place called Chamkaur between Mughal troops and the Guru's remaining band, the two older boys and all his followers were slain. Apparently, 'the Guru had insisted ... that if not the first, his sons must not be the last to die'.[75]

But the Guru survived. Evidently two Pashtun horse-dealers, Nabi Khan and Ghani Khan, saved the Guru's life by describing him as a Muslim pir to a Mughal patrol looking for him. As Pashtuns, the two may have had their own reservations regarding Mughal rule, but they may have responded also to the Guru's personality and plight. Preserved carefully and fondly in Sikh tradition, the story of the risky service performed by Nabi Khan and Ghani Khan suggests that multiple if unrecorded life-saving acts of this kind probably occurred in Punjab at this and other times.

To return to the Guru, shock followed escape, for he learned that his minor sons, Zorawar and Fateh, had been put to death by Wazir Khan, the Mughal faujdar of the sarkar of Sirhind, into whose hands the boys, their mother and their grandmother were betrayed. One version states that the boys, defiant in bearing, were bricked alive in Sirhind town, and that the grandmother died of shock. Another account has the boys executed.[76]

While the Muslim ruler of Malerkotla, not far from Sirhind, is said to have protested the killing of the boys, it appears that a devoted Sikh follower managed to escort the Guru's wife, Mata Sundri, to Delhi. On learning of what had happened to his youngest sons, the Guru himself, Sikhs believe,

> composed as ever, bent upon his knees and lifting his hands to God in prayer uttered: 'These two, Thy trust, I have rendered unto thee'; and digging up a shrub with his knife, he made this prophecy: 'Just as I have torn this shrub from its roots, so shall this tyrannous empire be destroyed, root and branch.'[77]

Faithful Khalsa surrounded the Guru as he moved southwest and formed a force in tracts east of the Sutlej, including the forested Lakhi Jangal, near modern-day Faridkot and Bathinda. Month by month, the force grew in numbers.

Nursing a powerful drive, a daring leader who believed in God and his own destiny now bonded—through shared danger, a common language, and the breaking of caste barriers—with a Singh following where a majority, scholars tell us, were Jat clans who equated honour with revenge.[78]

Some of these Jat clans had acquired wealth and acreage. Over successive decades, the migration of Jats into good soil in central and eastern Punjab and their consequent economic advancement had coincided with their embrace of Sikhism. The outcome of Guru Gobind Singh's relationship with these rising Jat Sikhs was a community which was also a potent force.

The much larger population of Punjab's Muslims had not thrown up a comparable association. No Punjabi-speaking chief, landlord or Sufi had attempted—or felt the need—to create such a community or force from among the region's Muslims, who, as we have marked, belonged to a variety of tribes, castes and clans, including Rajput and Jat.

Whether or not they were Muslim, survival had for centuries been the chief concern of most Punjabis. A low profile was the standard Punjabi response as, stripping the countryside and razing towns, invaders or 'rightful heirs' rode across Punjab. Occasionally, as we have seen, communities like the Gakhars, Janjuas or Bhattis fought an invader, yet such battles were the exception.

'Let the Turanis, Rajputs, Iranis and Afghans do the ruling and fighting; we will stay alive.' This appears to have been the Punjabi motto. The Punjabi who collected taxes for the empire from a set of villages—usually the landlord for those villages—was an essential intermediary between the Mughal administration and the population. Often he was a Muslim. Frequently he became rich and influential. At times he headed a clan of fellow-kinsmen. But raising a local army, or establishing control over a sizeable neighbourhood, or supporting one side in a battle for the Mughal throne, was a dangerous exercise that a Punjabi landlord or zamindar generally steered clear of.

Aspiring to a senior post in Punjab's Mughal administration, or even a place in the Mughal army, was also deemed risky. The long history of alien armies riding over Punjab, and of outsiders governing the region, had convinced most Punjabis that it was not their destiny or duty to rule, a belief corroborated by the fact that for much of the time the Mughals had ruled well. The latter, on their part, did not try to weld Punjabi Muslims, or any section thereof, into a force. The thought did not enter the Mughal mind.

As a modern writer puts it, 'The Punjabi Muslims... had a negligible role in the elite power groups which controlled Punjab. The Mughals who were ruling Punjab from 1526 to 1748 kept their own hand-picked governors, mostly of Turkish, Persian or Pathan descent. Merely being Muslim did not qualify the Punjabi for a respectable place in the Mughal hierarchy.'[79]

The large tracts across which the endangered Guru had moved from Anandpur in the hills to the jungles near Bhatinda contained Muslims in fair numbers. There appears to be no evidence that these local or Punjabi Muslims actively supported Mughal forces against the Guru's band. Their acceptance of the Mughal umbrella notwithstanding, there was no compelling reason for Punjabi Muslims to join the hunt for the Guru.

In stark contrast to the Muslim Punjabis was the fighting army of the Guru. As the seventeenth century ended and the eighteenth began, the Guru's army was in fact the only Punjabi force in existence. The sole opposition the Sikhs faced, besides the Mughal emperor's armies, was Wazir Khan, the Sirhind faujdar. If Sikh sources suggesting that Wazir Khan was a distant relative of the ruler of Malerkotla are correct,[80] then it is likely, from what we know of the origins of the Malerkotla chiefs, that the Sirhind faujdar had an Afghan background. He mounted an attack on the Guru but was repulsed near Muktsar.

Learning of these events, and not wishing to face another rebellion in yet another part of his weakening empire, Aurangzeb tried to conciliate the Guru, sending an emissary with a letter and the offer of an estate. Guru

Gobind Singh's response was the well-known *Zafarnama* (Epistle of Victory), in which the Guru justified his stand and charged the emperor with betrayal. But he did not rule out a meeting.

Composed in 1705 in Persian verse, the letter accused the Mughals of violating a sacred oath, credited the Guru's survival to God's grace ('My Lord, vanquisher of enemies, brought me to safety'), reminded the old emperor that while the world was a temporary abode, God was a strict judge, and demanded punishment of those who had betrayed and mercilessly killed his band, including his sons. Anxious to soften the Guru, Aurangzeb, in response, asked Munim Khan, the governor of suba Lahore, to render assistance to the Guru and persuade him to meet the emperor in the Deccan.

While declining the help offered by the Lahore governor, the Guru agreed to meet Aurangzeb and proceeded southwards. On the way, when he was in Rajasthan, he learnt (in March 1707) that the emperor had died.

■

When, in February 1707, death overtook him, the sixth Mughal emperor was in a camp near Aurangabād in today's Maharashtra, far from Delhi and Punjab. He had crossed his eighty-eighth birthday.

'Of small stature, with a long nose, a round beard, and an olive skin', Aurangzeb 'usually wore plain white muslin' and 'applied himself assiduously to business'. At times he was seen with 'a cheerful, smiling countenance... Under him the Moghal empire reached its greatest limits'.[81]

But it had been fatally overstretched. Sikhs, Jats, Marathas and Pashtuns— and others—persisted with their rebellious mood, and the emperor's personal frugality was of little help to a treasury emptied by military campaigns and by the king's mobile city. Likewise, Aurangzeb's personal faith in Sunni Islam, no matter how sincere, offered poor comfort to Muslims who feared that the emperor's intolerant zeal might one day invite the hostility of India's non-Muslim majority.

Dark clouds were glimpsed by the old king himself, and guilt and fear invaded his mind. As we have seen, one of his sons, Akbar, in the past a favourite, had joined Sambhaji against the emperor and then gone into exile in Iran. Another son, sent to prison by the father, had died there. The eldest daughter, a poet, had been imprisoned for corresponding with her brother Akbar. Of the three sons who were around as Aurangzeb neared his death, the oldest, Muazzam—also jailed by the father at one point—was viceroy at Kabul, Azam was camped near Aurangzeb, and Kam Baksh, the youngest, was also in the south, in the kingdom of Bijapur.

Kam Baksh, the current favourite, had been born to Udepuri, an 'exceedingly handsome' woman from Georgia in the Caucasus—described by one historian as 'a Christian lady'—who was sold as a child into Dara's harem and later, following Dara's killing, absorbed into that of Aurangzeb.[82] To this son, who had spoken of his afflictions, the emperor wrote:

> Son of my soul... Now I am going alone. I grieve for your helplessness. But what is the use? I have greatly sinned, and I know not what torment awaits me... Let not Muslims be slain and reproach fall on my useless head. I commit you and your sons to God's care. I am sore troubled.[83]

We do not know whether the Guru's *Zafarnama* had contributed to the king's contrition. As for Punjab, to which Aurangzeb could give little time, its agriculture and trade had declined during the final phase of his reign, with the copper paisa and the silver rupee losing in value.

■

Yet Punjab had experienced a protracted spell of peace. In the words of the modern historian Jagtar Singh Grewal:

> The province had come to enjoy an appreciable measure of peace under the Lodis during the latter half of the fifteenth century... This peace was only temporarily broken during the two hundred and fifty years following: first, by Babur's invasions in the 1520s and then, at the beginning and the end of the Sur interregnum from 1540 to 1555. From Akbar to Aurangzeb the province remained almost entirely peaceful.[84]

This assessment of a long span of peace enjoyed by Punjabis is significant, for we have seen that momentous events that could have caused great conflict had taken place during this period, including the 1606 execution, in Lahore, of Guru Arjan Dev and the 1675 execution, in Delhi, of Guru Tegh Bahadur. If, however, peace did largely prevail, it would suggest that people in seventeenth-century Punjab—Muslims, Hindus and Sikhs—saw the executions not as evidence of unalterable Muslim-Sikh or Muslim-Hindu hostility but as ugly consequences of fear gripping a ruler, Jahangir in the first case and Aurangzeb in the second.

That enmity was not the norm even at the height of Aurangzeb's rule is also perhaps indicated by the tone and content of *Khulasat ut-Tawarikh*, written in Persian in 1695, twelve years before the emperor's death, by

Sujan Rai Bhandari, a Hindu from the Bari doab town of Batala, which in British times would belong to the Lahore division. In this work, which among other subjects deals with the rulers, rivers, landscapes and heroes of Punjab, Bhandari refers to the saints honoured by the region's Muslims, the Gurus of the Sikhs and the shrines of the Hindus, and offers no depiction of hostility between communities.[85]

The absence of hostility in Bhandari's account does not by itself prove the prevalence of peace on Punjab's broad surface. Yet we may surmise that, privileging survival and used to co-existence, people in places like Lahore, Amritsar and Batala did not believe in innate Muslim-Sikh enmity. Their instincts were probably confirmed by the story that a renowned Sufi had journeyed from Lahore to lay the foundation for the Sikh temple at Amritsar, and had done so at the invitation of Guru Arjan Dev. They had heard, too, that their popular viceroy for many years, the Mughal prince Dara Shikoh—Jahangir's grandson, and the one they had hoped would succeed Shah Jahan—was this Sufi's disciple.

And they knew that, like Guru Tegh Bahadur, this prince too had been executed under Emperor Aurangzeb's orders. Aware that many Muslims in Lahore and elsewhere in Punjab had been shocked by the Gurus' executions, aware also that many a Muslim prince had been slain by his Mughal brother, at least some seventeenth-century Hindus and Sikhs also knew that Aurangzeb's great-grandfather Akbar had abolished the jizya and gifted land for the Amritsar temple.

We may accept another surmise. When the seventeenth century ended and, a few years thereafter, when Aurangzeb died, some Muslim, Sikh and Hindu Punjabis may have managed to remember the older story of a connection between Guru Nanak and the Sufis.

However, even if they remembered all this, recognized the advantages of peaceful co-existence, and hoped for days of tolerance to return, an apprehension preyed on their minds. They wondered whether Punjab's seeming calm would survive an event even more traumatic than the execution of two earlier Gurus: the cold-blooded murder of the present Guru's minor boys.

Chapter Two

1707-1757: COLLAPSE OF AUTHORITY

Hearing in Kabul, where he was viceroy, that his father had fallen critically ill in the Deccan, Muazzam, Aurangzeb's sixty-three-year-old son, raced across the Pashtun country and Punjab towards Delhi. When he learnt en route that his father had died, he proclaimed himself emperor. In April 1707, in Lahore, he was met by the suba's governor, Munim Khan, and by Munim's son, Mozuddin, who was the governor of Multan. The father-and-son duo, descended from a Turkic noble, offered their services, troops and artillery to Muazzam, known also as Shah Alam or Bahadur Shah I.

Possessing a liberal temperament missing in his father, Bahadur Shah was unsuccessfully challenged by the brothers Azam and Kam Baksh. The former was defeated and killed in a battle south of Agra in June 1707, and the latter two years later, in the Deccan. For the first battle, Bahadur Shah received symbolic support from Guru Gobind Singh.

When the Guru learnt of Aurangzeb's death, he was aware that both Azam and Kam Baksh were encamped in the south, where he was headed. Betting on Bahadur Shah, the Guru turned around and journeyed north towards Agra, where, in July, he met the new emperor.

According to Latif's *History of the Panjab* (1889), Bahadur Shah gave 'tents, elephants and horses' and the title of a commander of 5,000 to the Guru.[1] Evidently Bahadur Shah encouraged the Guru to hope, first, that Sirhind's Wazir Khan would be brought to justice and, second, that the Anandpur site would be restored to the Guru.[2]

For several months the Guru stayed in Agra near the new emperor, whose priority however was to subdue the Deccan-based Kam Baksh, his late father's final favourite. In November 1707, when Bahadur Shah and his army set forth to crush the challenger, the Guru and a band of followers journeyed alongside. 'For nearly a year, Guru Gobind Singh remained close to the imperial camp',[3] hoping to hear the assurances he had asked for.

However, Bahadur Shah was reluctant to act against the hill rajas of the north. His focus was on Kam Baksh. To win allies in the Deccan, the emperor released the late Shivaji's twenty-five-year-old grandson, Shahu, a Mughal hostage for eighteen years, and recognized Shahu's claim to an autonomous Maratha throne. He thus met the Marathas half-way but refrained from supporting the Guru.

In September 1708, when the imperial camp halted near Nanded on the banks of the Godavari, the Guru concluded that enough was enough. The justice he wanted would have to be secured without Bahadur Shah's aid. Detaching himself from the emperor's camp, he stayed on in Nanded, where he was offered respectful greetings by a thirty-eight-year-old Hindu Rajput from Kashmir who seemed to possess 'an iron will and unswerving determination under his saintly clothes'.[4]

After living the life of a hunter and warrior in the hills of Kashmir, this Rajput had turned into a renunciate (bairagi) called Madho Das without, however, forgetting the tales of Rajput humiliation at Mughal hands. Wandering through the south's Maratha country, he had lapped up the lore of Shivaji, the chieftain (then dead for less than thirty years) who had defied the Mughals and established a Hindu kingdom.

The spark ignited by the Shivaji story became a fire when Madho Das encountered Guru Gobind Singh, and heard, perhaps from the Guru himself, his harrowing story. Revenge replaced renunciation as Madho Das's goal. Through revenge he would exact for the Guru the justice that Bahadur Shah would not or could not provide.

Baptized by the Guru, Madho Das became Gurbaksh Singh, 'the Singh saved by the Guru', though history would call him, among other names, Banda (the Guru's 'man' or 'slave'), or Banda Singh Bahadur (Banda the brave lion), or Bairagi Banda.

From the Guru he received a sword, five arrows, trusty companions, an edict, and, most crucially, an instruction. This, according to Grewal, was 'to lead the Singhs in the Punjab against their oppressors'.[5] The edict, addressed to Punjab's Sikhs, required them to support Banda Bahadur. According to another scholar, the Guru also directed Gurbaksh Singh to see himself as his associates' equal, 'never their superior', and 'not found a sect of his own'.

> Thereupon the Guru gave [Banda Bahadur] detailed instructions to proceed to Punjab along with three other Sikhs,... wait for reinforcements (which the Guru would arrange)... and, later... march on Sirhind, lay siege to the city and seize and personally execute Wazir Khan... [and thereafter] settle accounts with the chiefs of the hill states... The Guru himself would join them at a later stage.[6]

The degree of the Guru's confidence in Banda Bahadur (joined by the admonition against personal ambition) prompts the question whether his decision to quit the emperor's march, stay on in Nanded, and take into his own hands the issue of justice in Punjab was made before or after he saw Madho Das. Sikh tradition is perfectly clear that it was made before.

After a few days' stay in Nanded, the Guru was stabbed by an Afghan named Jamshid Khan who was evidently 'connected with either Wazir Khan or an imperial officer'.[7] Word of the assault reached the marching emperor, who, according to some sources, sent surgeons ('one of them an Englishman'[8]) to treat the forty-two-year-old Guru, who however died on 7 October 1708.

During the several days between the assault and his demise, Guru Gobind Singh could have nominated, like his predecessors, an individual as the next guru. He did not. Instead he declared explicitly that their scripture—the Granth Sahib—would henceforth be the Sikhs' permanent Guru, and also that they would be led by the Khalsa as a whole, i.e. by elect Singhs acting together.

One clear implication of this instruction was that, whatever his merits or mission, Banda Bahadur was not the next guru. Early in 1709, Banda started for Punjab, resolved to accomplish the tasks given to him by the now martyred Guru.

Banda's departure from Nanded for the north coincided with a battle waged near Hyderabad in the Deccan between Bahadur Shah and Kam Baksh. It ended in the former's victory. A mortally injured Kam Baksh was brought to the victor's camp and treated by surgeons (again including Europeans) in the emperor's service. 'I never desired to see you like this,' said the older brother, whereupon the dying brother, looking at the crown-wearing Bahadur Shah, offered these honest last words: 'I never desired to see *you* like this.'[9]

In the second half of 1709, Bahadur Shah was still attending to matters in the south when with silent feet and fierce face Banda Bahadur suddenly showed up in Punjab, well to the east of the Sutlej. With the sarkar of Sirhind in Delhi doab as his target, he began to enlist Sikh peasants. Needing money for his growing force, he plundered Mughal treasuries in Sonepat and Kaithal.

A historian from this period, Khafi Khan, would write that 'in two or three months' time nearly five thousand horse and eight thousand foot joined [Banda Bahadur]. The number... was increasing daily and great booty was falling into his hands. Soon after, about nineteen thousand men, armed and equipped, took to plunder and persecution'.[10]

Banda Bahadur has rightly been credited for his force's swiftness and ability to surprise, but circumstances also favoured him. Oppressed by insecure landlords, Sirhind's peasants, many of them Sikh and Hindu Jats, were in extreme distress and looking for a radical leader. Remembering, moreover, what had happened to Guru Gobind Singh's sons, they enlisted under Banda. Landowning Jat Sikhs provided Banda with money and horses.

As for Punjab's Muslim zamindars, they were no longer in awe of the Mughal establishment or sure of its future. Helping Mughal officers to suppress Banda was not necessarily a good investment. Another factor aided Banda: for a few years mansabdars had not paid their soldiers, who therefore went from chief to chief in search of a job, producing a significant 'floating armed population' that Banda was able to tap into.[11]

Just as crucially, Banda took full advantage of escalating weaknesses in the empire's capital. Though the new emperor was seen by his officers in Delhi as kindly and liberal, and his rejection of Aurangzeb's restrictive policies was widely welcomed, he was not only far from Delhi and Punjab at this time but officers thought him weak too. They felt no pressure to protect the empire's positions in the sarkar of Sirhind, with, for instance, the prime minister, Munim Khan—the former subahdar of Lahore—'postpon[ing] radical measures to a later day instead of nipping the evil in the bud'.[12]

To servants and foes alike, the imposing empire that Babur had founded one-hundred-and-eighty years earlier suddenly looked extremely vulnerable. Within the empire's establishment, the pendulum had swung, following Aurangzeb's death, from puritanical zeal to hedonism, from fear of the ruler to contempt for him.

In November 1709, while mansabdars in Delhi and Agra sought their pleasure from dancing-girls and intoxicants, Banda Bahadur's force suddenly descended on Samana, an undefended town in Sirhind sarkar. Samana's alleged offence was that two wanted men lived there: the professional executioner who thirty-four years earlier had severed Guru Tegh Bahadur's head, as well as this man's son, who, some thought, had carried out the order to execute Guru Gobind Singh's minor sons. 'Nearly 10,000 Muslims are said to have been massacred in this town and immense booty was acquired.'[13]

More towns and villages were laid waste. Since Usman Khan, the Muslim chief of Sadhaura, northeast of Samana, was believed to have persecuted a Muslim pir friendly to Guru Gobind Singh, a massacre was carried out in Sadhaura. The avenger's ranks swelled. 'Thirty to forty thousand infidels served under [Banda Bahadur's] banner', Khafi Khan would write, adding that Banda 'issued orders to imperial officers to submit and retire from their posts'.[14]

We do not know how many officers retired in response to the demand.

What we do know is that Delhi sent no reinforcements to Sirhind. However, Faujdar Wazir Khan was there. Expecting an attack, he assembled a coalition of forces from the area, including from nearby Malerkotla, which was run by a Pashtun nawab.

'Located on the main highway between Delhi and Lahore', Sirhind was 'where some of the Mughal nobility had constructed large buildings and gardens. It was famous for the manufacture of chintz and red muslin and... as a marketplace for the products of neighbouring urban centres from where foreign traders could obtain merchandise conveniently'.[15]

The battle for Sirhind took place some miles outside the town in May 1710 and resulted in Banda Bahadur's victory. Wazir Khan was killed, though not by Banda Bahadur's hand. Many others were also slain. The town of Sirhind was razed to the ground and apparently all its Muslim inhabitants put to death. Retribution had yielded to revenge, which had turned to bloodlust.

A horrifying picture of the atrocities visited upon Sirhind's residents, and on Wazir Khan's corpse, has been painted by a British writer, John Malcolm: 'Every atrocity that the most wanton barbarity could commit, every cruelty that an unappeased appetite for revenge could suggest, was inflicted upon the miserable inhabitants.'[16]

All Muslim officers in the sarkar of Sirhind were ousted, their places taken by Banda Bahadur's men, several of whom came from 'low' castes. 'A low scavenger or leather dresser... had only to leave home and join [Banda] when in a short space of time he would return to his birthplace as its ruler, with [an] order of appointment ... [T]he well-born and wealthy went out to greet him and escort him home [and]... stood before him with joined palms, awaiting his orders.'[17]

Much of the land between the Sutlej and the Jamuna now lay at Banda's feet, but he had no wish to rest. Hearing that Hindus were being harassed east of the Jamuna, he crossed that river in July 1710 and plundered the town of Saharanpur, among other places.

Soon he forayed north of Sirhind, too, into the Bist (Jullundur) doab and, crossing the Beas, into the Bari doab, in both instances to suppress local Muslims who had hoped to replace waning Mughal authority. Bolstered by Banda's raids, local Sikhs captured important towns including Rahon in the Jullundur doab and Batala and Pathankot in the upper Bari doab. The Sikhs of the doabs had been as deeply affected by the deaths of Guru Gobind Singh's sons as had the cis-Sutlej Sikhs, and were equally alive to the openings presented by the empire's inaction.

Especially in and around Sirhind—in the area the Sikhs called 'Malwa'— and, north from there, in the Jullundur doab, Banda 'changed the class structure of land holdings' by 'liquidating many of the big Muslim zamindar families'. 'Large estates were... broken up into smaller holdings in the hands of Sikh or Hindu peasants.'[18]

Among the victims of Banda Bahadur's campaign in eastern Punjab were Muslim Arain farmers who grew fruit and vegetables. According to an Arain narrative, 'their land was taken away and given to the Jatts who then on a large scale converted from Hindu to Sikh'.[19]

Not checked by any force, Banda Bahadur reached the gates of Lahore itself but these could not be breached. Mughal authority had survived in Lahore. Yet Banda himself was more than free. From a captured imperial fort in Mukhlispur, not very far from Anandpur, he now commanded a belt of mostly hilly territory that extended westward from the Jamuna to the Ravi, crossing the Sutlej and the Beas along the way.

Renaming his command centre Lohgarh, or the iron fort, he issued from there a new coin and introduced his official seal and year, commencing from the date of his victory at Sirhind.[20] Both the coin and the seal were issued in the name of Guru Nanak and Guru Gobind Singh.[21] He also took a wife, from the hills. The hill rajas who had joined the Mughals to expel Guru Gobind Singh were not attacked, but that was largely because, sensing the empire's decline, some of them were now helping Banda, who belonged to their Rajput caste.

Questions arise. Had the former bairagi become a prince, forgetting the Guru's admonition? The Punjab where Banda now found himself was not only dangerous. It was heady. The downtrodden worshipped him. Big men feared him. Mughal chiefs were not to be seen. In such a climate, Banda Bahadur could easily have thought that his destiny was grander than he had imagined.

Or was something happening that was less personal and more 'Sikh'? Had Banda glimpsed a future Sikh state in Punjab? Or at least the end of Mughal rule there? We do not know. In any case, an attempt by him to enlist princes from Rajasthan in a dharam yudh (holy war) to protect 'Hindu' interests against 'Muslim tyranny' was unsuccessful.[22]

In December 1710, Banda was given battle by the sixty-six-year-old emperor himself. Returning at last from the Deccan to Delhi, Bahadur Shah did not pause in the capital but marched with his army directly to Lohgarh, where Banda's besieged force, 'beggarly dressed', as Khafi Khan put it, offered 'wild attacks' to the imperial army, producing 'terror and panic' in the latter.[23] But numbers and resources won out, and Banda was forced to flee in disguise to the Bari doab.

Bahadur Shah followed in pursuit but failed to capture the avenger who was also a challenger. With Banda in mind, the emperor announced that Lahore would now be his capital. From Lahore he sent commanders to find Banda, who had concealed himself, along with his wife and a band of followers, in hills in the upper Bari doab.

When one general returned empty-handed, a frustrated Bahadur Shah ordered his confinement within the fort. Sikhs were forbidden from entering Lahore but, determined to disturb its peace, Banda's tireless men 'came to the suburbs at night by swimming the Ravi and retired before daybreak'.[24]

Though the emperor alienated Lahore's Sunni clerics by allowing the expression of Shiite views from the imperial platform, the people, who preferred to call him Shah Alam, seemed to like him. Hindus were glad that under his rule jizya was no longer being collected. 'He was most popular in the Panjab', says Latif,[25] in part because Shah Alam's mother, one of Aurangzeb's wives, was the Punjabi-speaking Bai Begum, daughter of the Muslim ruler of Rajauri, a Jarral Rajput. In February 1712, however, while still in Lahore, the emperor died.*

Another gory war of succession took a fresh toll of Mughal princes, officers and generals. Part of this war was fought in Lahore, throwing that city and other parts of Punjab into 'great confusion'.[26] A fierce sandstorm on the banks of the Ravi made the scene murkier. Banda was forgotten. Free to roam again, he retook Lohgarh, defeated Bayazid Khan, the faujdar of Jammu, and killed Shams Khan, the faujdar of Sultanpur in the Jullundur doab.

The victor in the succession war, Jahandar Shah (one of Bahadur Shah's sons), was soon accused of being shameless enough to 'seize wives and daughters' while 'passing through the bazars' of Delhi, and charged also with being afraid of the naked sword.[27] After eleven months as emperor, Jahandar was dethroned in January 1713 when a nephew, Farrukh Siyar, defeated him after another bitter battle.

Helped to the throne by nobles including the intriguing Sayyid brothers (whom we will shortly discuss), Farrukh Siyar ordered Abdul Samad Khan, the Turkic[28] subahdar of Kashmir, to Lahore, ordering him to subdue the Sikhs.

An energetic general with influential relatives in the Delhi court, Abdul Samad Khan forced Banda out of the sarkar of Sirhind before the end of

---

*One of Lahore's gateways was named after him and is still called the Shah Alami Gate.

1713, but the daring rebel soon surfaced in the upper Bari doab, where thousands of Sikhs rallied to his support. Arms and horses were provided to him by rajas and zamindars, many of them Hindus, in the hilly areas to the doab's north, around Jammu.[29]

In March 1715, after Samad Khan's forces and those of Banda had skirmished with one another for over a year, an exasperated Farrukh Siyar sharply rebuked the governor but still sent him reinforcements. Led by their chiefs or landlords, a few Muslim clans of the Bari doab also supported Samad Khan—Punjabi clans like the Bhatti Rajputs, Kharals and Wattus, as well as Afghans long settled in Kasur. While the region's Arains, too, would have opposed Banda, some Muslim Jats may have assisted him.[30]

Though pushed into isolation in a small fort in the village of Gurdas Nangal, four miles from today's Gurdaspur town, Banda Bahadur and his band defied the imperial army. Surviving on flesh, grass, leaves and bark, 'the infernal Sikh chief and his men', Kamwar Khan would write, 'withstood all the military force that the great *Saltanat-i-Mughalia* could muster against them for eight months'.[31] Eventually, however, in December 1715, Abdul Samad Khan was able to starve them into dissension and submission.

After their surrender, many in Banda's force were killed in Gurdas Nangal. Others were beheaded on the banks of the Ravi, en route to Lahore. According to Latif, the returning governor made a 'triumphant entry' into the city 'with a long train of Sikh officers and men, headed by Banda'. The prisoners, all in chains, were made to sit on emaciated donkeys or camels; a 'jeering and cursing mob' followed them.[32]

The next day, Samad Khan and his son Zakariya Khan led the prisoners on their long march to Delhi. A Briton who was in Delhi in February 1716 wrote of witnessing a procession into the city of 'some 800 live Sikh prisoners' along with about '2,000 bleeding heads of the rebels borne aloft on poles', adding that 'the Sikhs vied with one another in precedence of death'.[33] Most of the bleeding heads belonged to Sikhs captured and killed on the road from Lahore to Delhi, for Farrukh Siyar had issued an edict that 'every Sicque falling into the hands of his officers should, on a refusal of embracing the Mahometan faith, be put to the sword'.[34]

In June 1716, after another parade of humiliation, Banda Bahadur and all Sikh prisoners were executed; many, including Banda, were tortured before being killed. Khafi Khan would record that no Sikh prisoner accepted Islam to save his life. The execution of Banda and his close companions took place near the tomb, just south of Delhi, of the Sufi saint, Shaikh Qutbuddin.

Banda's four-year-old son, too, was killed.

Backed by the royal edict, Samad Khan sought 'to extirpate the race' from Punjab.[35] Counter-revenge seemed to know no limits and brooked no ambiguity. Hindus and Muslims were required to keep their hair short, with Hindus asked to remain beardless as well. While Punjab's Hindus wondered about their future, its Muslims too may have questioned a policy which for the excesses of some targeted a whole people, a people linked, moreover, to Guru Nanak and the Sufis. As for the Sikhs, says Latif,

> These extreme measures... spread terror and consternation throughout the Sikh nation. Those who remained of them fled to the mountains to the north-east of the Panjab or concealed themselves in remote jungles. Many who could not abandon their homes changed their external appearance, had their beards and moustaches clipped, and gave up their outward forms of worship.[36]

In their new 'homes' in the hills and forests, and in the desert in southern Sirhind (or Malwa, as they preferred to call it), the Sikhs lived on wild vegetables and the animals they could hunt. They cheered themselves by giving 'very flattering names to even the meanest articles of diet'.[37] While Banda's excesses had divided Punjab's Sikhs, Samad Khan's policies reunited them.

Many poor Muslims in the region, too, may have sympathized with the Sikh struggle against the upper class of ruling officers and landlords, and the Sikhs, most of them Jats, may have received quiet support from Muslim Jats.

With nothing to lose except their hunger, the Sikhs fought back within two or three years, raiding villages 'at the foot of the hills, and on the outskirts of the Lakhi Jungle and the Malwa desert'.[38] Motivation they plainly had, but circumstances also came to their aid. A succession of revolts across Punjab, all triggered by the empire's weakness, paralyzed the Lahore government.

In 1716, a zamindar named Qatil in Gujrat pargana in the Chej doab mobilized fellow zamindars, built a fortress, and revolted, preventing the realization of revenue by imperial officers. Further to the west, Awan zamindars in the Sindh Sagar doab refused to pay revenue, which was also withheld in Sialkot pargana in the Rachna doab. Other zamindars in the Bari doab used the absence of authority to rob villages; and the road from Lahore to Multan became vulnerable to rebelling landlords.[39]

Rivalries in the Delhi court, where, as we have marked, Samad Khan's relatives were influential, added to Punjab's problems. Delhi-based enemies of Samad Khan and his Turani relatives abetted revolts in Punjab to weaken the governor.[40] One revolt, on behalf of long-settled Pashtuns in Kasur, thirty-five miles south of Lahore, was led by Hussain Khan Kheshgi, another by Isa Khan Munj, a landlord in the Jullundur doab. Both rebellions contained a local-versus-outsider element.

■

According to Khafi Khan, the Kheshgi revolt of 1720 was instigated from Delhi by the brothers Abdullah Khan Sayyid and Hussain Ali Sayyid. For twelve years or so following Bahadur Shah's ascension, these brothers were possibly the Mughal court's most influential members. Hailing from the Jamuna-Ganga doab, sons of a subahdar and for a time viceroys themselves (of Bihar and Allahabad, respectively), they had played a role in Bahadur Shah's ascension to the throne and a larger one, five years later, in that of Farrukh Siyar.

Their success flowed from the 'national' or Hindustani card they played. Nobles linked to the Indian soil should band together, the brothers whispered, to reduce the influence of the court's Turani and Irani elements. Moreover, the brothers seemed willing to share power with the empire's native rebels, and willing also to see the Pashtuns as native or Hindustani.

Until the Sayyid brothers' rise, rivalries in the Mughal court usually carried a Turani-versus-Irani (and therefore also a Sunni-versus-Shia) stamp, with an assumption that while the Turkic element produced better warriors, the Iranis were abler administrators. The less influential but more Indianized Afghans were a third factor, but now the Hindustanis had also begun to assert themselves.

As the empire rapidly weakened in the years following Aurangzeb's death, this 'nationalist' argument was the basis for the brothers' alliance with the growing power to the south of Delhi, the Marathas. Though Shivaji had died in 1680, and his son Sambhaji was killed in 1689, bands of Marathas—led first by Sambhaji's brother Rajaram and after his death (1700) by Rajaram's widow Tarabai—had continued to harass the Mughals. Following Aurangzeb's death, uncontested Maratha raids in southern, western and central India became more and more frequent, even as Sambhaji's son Shahu, released by Bahadur Shah, claimed the Maratha throne.

But real Maratha power was in the hands of the adroit Chitpavan Brahmin, Balaji Vishwanath. An early backer of Shahu's claim (as against that of Tarabai and her son), Vishwanath was named the Marathas' Peshwa, or premier, in 1713. In a crucial deal, Vishwanath and the Sayyid brothers agreed that Shahu would exercise sovereignty in the Maratha homeland. Not only that. In imperial territories where Maratha forces enjoyed influence, revenue would be shared, the Sayyid brothers conceded, between them and the Mughals.

Farrukh Siyar repudiated the deal. In 1718-19, however, backed by thousands of Maratha soldiers who had advanced all the way to Delhi, the Sayyid brothers succeeded in blinding, deposing, imprisoning and killing Farrukh Siyar. Within a year, three kings succeeded Farrukh Siyar. All three were his cousins (and Bahadur Shah's grandsons), and all owed their ascension to the Sayyid brothers, whose deal with the Marathas was reinstated through an imperial firman.

■

Encouraging local revolts in Punjab against the Mughal governor, Samad Khan, was in keeping with the brothers' 'nationalist' line. However, the brothers' good fortune ended shortly after they had installed eighteen-year-old Muhammad Shah as emperor (1719). While Shah remained on the throne for nearly thirty years, Hussain Ali Sayyid was killed in 1720, and Abdullah Sayyid died in prison in 1723. Meanwhile, Sikh rebels had taken full advantage of the fallout in Punjab of happenings in Delhi.

> When the Delhi government was in the throes of revolutions (1717-19) and the *Subahdar* of Lahore was busy in dealing with the serious revolts of Isa Khan Munj and Husain Khan Kheshgi of Kasur, the Sikhs found an easy opportunity of entering upon a career of pillage and plunder.[41]

The landlord Isa Khan Munj, born into a Muslim clan of pastoral Rajputs, controlled highways across the Jullundur doab where he repeatedly robbed travellers and traders. Even the Lahore governor, Samad Khan, 'could not proceed [from Delhi] to Lahore without taking elaborate precautions'. Acknowledging Isa Khan's power, Bahadur Khan had made him a mansabdar. From Jahandar Shah, Isa Khan extorted the faujdari of Lakhi Jangal.[42]

But no one gave Samad Khan as much trouble as Nawab Hussain Khan Kheshgi from Kasur in the Bari doab. In 1720, the forces of Kheshgi, who by distant origin was a Pashtun, fought the governor's much larger army in the fields of Harchoki outside the town of Chunian, twenty miles west of Kasur. The nawab was killed in what one writer terms an epic battle 'entrenched in the cultural psyche of the people of Punjab'.[43]

Here we may interrupt our narrative to acknowledge a Hindu image of Kasur as Lahore's rival, a picture buttressed by a Ramayana-linked legend that while Lahore was connected to Rama's son, Lav, Kasur was the city of Lav's twin, Kush.

We saw earlier that in 1715, five years prior to the battle of Harchoki or Chunian, Kasur-based Pashtuns had supported Abdul Samad Khan against Banda. Now, in 1720, Samad Khan was viewed as a declining empire's harsh proconsul, against whom all in Punjab were asked to unite. Only four years after Banda Bahadur's execution and the decree against the Sikhs, at least parts of Punjab were stirred not by what Sikhs and Muslims had done to one another but by the roughness, felt by all, of an empire nearing its end.

But the Kheshgi revolt was also a bid for control, and not merely an expression of popular feeling. In fact, both the Kasur revolt and its suppression 'brought great hardship on the people who were repeatedly required to cough up taxes to finance the [rival] armies'.[44] The impact of Sikh raids elsewhere in Punjab was similar. Money plundered from local treasuries was replaced through fresh levies on cultivators and traders, who were often a raid's direct victims as well. The cost of capturing the raiders was a third charge on them.

■

Some Sikhs, meanwhile, dissociated themselves from Banda's methods. A bid by Banda's followers to take control of the temple at Amritsar was foiled by other Sikhs. Bhai Mani Singh, a lifelong companion of Guru Gobind Singh, was appointed to look after the temple's affairs. But rebellion continued to attract a section.

> While the Sikhs in general, and even a large number of the Singhs, lived as peaceful citizens of the Mughal empire, the professed rebels, or the *tat-khalsa*, lived as outlaws in the less-accessible tracts of the province plundering or killing the government officials and their supporters.[45]

As attacks on Punjab's roads increased, and 'highways traffic came almost to a close',[46] the Delhi court eventually bestirred itself. In 1726, emperor Muhammad Shah moved Samad Khan, now much older than before, to Multan, and Samad Khan's son Zakariya Khan was made the Lahore subahdar. That Zakariya had married the sister of Qamruddin Khan, prime minister in the Delhi court, facilitated the promotion.

For a while, mobile columns of light cavalry raised by the youthful new governor drove away rebelling Sikhs from 'all the centres of population' to 'their old retreats', and peace and quiet seemed restored, but in two years' time small groups of Sikhs were again sallying forth and exacting tribute from 'defenceless villages and often waylaying travellers'.[47]

Zakariya Khan's first response was wise. Suppression having failed, he tried conciliation. The emperor was persuaded by him to give the Sikhs the jagir of a few villages close to Amritsar (worth a lakh of rupees a year), and their leader the title of nawab. The offer was accepted by the tired rebels, who took to peaceful pursuits, with many of them settling in Amritsar.

From 1734, their leader, Nawab Kapur Singh, and his colleagues gave the recent rebels an organized life in Amritsar under the watchful eye of Bhai Mani Singh. But inactivity was soon found unsatisfying, and the Sikhs dispersed either to their homes or to Malwa.

Zakariya Khan now blundered. Complaining that many had left the Amritsar settlement, he withdrew the jagir. To earn their keep, the ex-rebels, he said, should either join the imperial army or settle down as farmers. 'The Sikhs resented this action and took to their old course of plunder.'[48] The subahdar blamed Bhai Mani Singh, who was in his late sixties if not older. When, in 1737, Bhai Mani Singh was unable to pay the fee demanded for a Diwali congregation in Amritsar, he was, by the governor's order, put brutally to death in Lahore.

The result was a hardened Sikh resolve to paralyze Zakariya Khan's administration, which in the 1720s and 1730s also faced rebellions by Muslim zamindars in 'almost the entire upper northern tract in the Chej, Rachna and Bari doabs'. These zamindars included Panah, a powerful leader of the Bhatti Rajputs, whose influence in this upper belt extended all the way west from the Ravi to beyond the Jhelum, another landlord named Mian Khan, and a third landlord, Mir Mar, who apparently organized loot and plunder 'in the region between Lahore and the Sutlej'.[49]

■

Across India, meanwhile, the empire continued to decline in prestige and prosperity. To keep potential rebels in line, new nobles and jagirs had been created, which reduced the income from crownlands; the governors who collected this income therefore sent smaller sums to Delhi.

Enjoying a reign that would last for thirty years, the emperor, Muhammad Shah, we learn, was 'extremely handsome, of a strong and splendid build, and possessed natural intelligence and foresight'.[50] But he lacked judgment. 'A certain girl named Koki, the daughter of a *faqir*... fascinated him so much that... her signatures were put on state papers and she issued orders in her own name.'[51] A 'dancing girl of charm and beauty' named Udham Bai also acquired influence in the palace, with the emperor raising her 'to the dignity of a queen'.[52]

More serious was Shah's unwillingness to confront the challenges to his empire, a weakness shared by his prime minister for twenty-four years (1724-48), Zakariya Khan's brother-in-law, Qamruddin Khan. In the words of a contemporary historian,

> Whenever the officers of the Deccan or Gujarat or Malwa* reported any Maratha incursions to the Emperor, His Majesty, in order to soothe his heart afflicted with such sad news, either visited the gardens... or rode out to hunt; while the grand *wazir* Qamaruddin Khan [sought] to assuage his feelings by gazing at the lotuses... or hunting fish in the rivers.[53]

Even as the king and his ministers looked away, and the court's Turani, Irani and other factions slashed at one another, the empire was losing territory or authority or both. By the mid-thirties, the Marathas had occupied large portions of Gujarat and central India and, without any resistance from the court, plundered areas close to Delhi. In 1737, the Maratha leader, Baji Rao, appeared at the very gates of Delhi, without however attempting to occupy the capital.

Some provinces declared virtual independence, including Hyderabad in the south, where Asaf Jah, Qamruddin's predecessor as grand wazir, established himself as viceroy in 1725, starting a Sunni dynasty of the Nizams. In the east, Saadat Khan, the leader of the court's Irani faction, inaugurated a Shia dynasty in Awadh, after being named viceroy there in 1722.

South of Delhi, and close to the imperial capital, Suraj Mal consolidated the influence of the Jats, turning Bharatpur and its environs into an independent region in the 1730s. East of Delhi, but west of Awadh, Rohillas of Pashtun origin began to assert autonomy in what before long would be called Rohilkhand.

A few pushes, and the empire would crumble. The first of these came in 1739, from the northwest. As so often before, Punjab was stepped on and squeezed.

Two years prior to this invasion by the Iranian ruler, Nadir Shah, Zakariya Khan, the Lahore subahdar, had been made governor also of Multan, following the death of its subahdar (Zakariya's father, Samad Khan). 'The weakness of

---

*In central India, not to be confused with the 'Malwa' in Sikh discourse

the court at Delhi' having 'raised him to the rank of satrap',[54] Zakariya Khan exercised absolute authority in all of Punjab.

He built spacious palaces for his residence and also a new mosque in Begumpura, near Lahore. His chief minister was Lakhpat Rai, a Khatri who had also served Zakariya Khan's father. Lakhpat Rai's brother, Jaspat Rai, acted as Zakariya Khan's secretary and counsellor.

The satrap was successful in some ways. In the doabs, peasants were given advances for cultivation. Lahore's Hindu traders liked Zakariya Khan, whose soldiers guarded the highways. Some abandoned villages were repopulated. But sternness with the Sikhs continued. Captured Sikh plunderers 'were daily brought in chains and executed in the streets of Lahore',[55] and their captors rewarded.

But Zakariya Khan's soldiers could not be present everywhere in Punjab. Avoiding a direct engagement with them, Sikh and other outlaws persisted in pillaging.

∎

Nadir Shah, from 1736 the ruler of Iran, had been born in 1688 into a poor Turkic family in Khorasan, a region where Iranian generals and Afghan chiefs were in conflict. Victories over Afghans, and his prowess as soldier and commander, had made the tall, powerfully-framed, black-bearded and sun-tanned Nadir Shah an Iranian hero and eventually, despite his being a Sunni, the king of Persia.

Pique was mixed into Nadir Shah's desire for India's riches: the Mughal emperor had failed to greet his accession to the Persian throne; Nadir Shah's enemies had found shelter in the Mughal province of Kabul; and so forth. In the summer of 1738, leading a large army of Turkomen, Iranians, Pashtuns and others, he advanced without resistance into Ghazni and then, after a fight, took Kabul, where he emptied the Mughal strong-rooms that Shah Jahan had filled with riches a hundred years earlier.

Long forgotten by Delhi's effete and distant Mughal court, Kabul's governor, Nasir Khan, was at this time encamped in Peshawar, which belonged to his province. Collecting 20,000 men at the Khyber Pass, he tried with their aid to resist Nadir Shah's column of cannons and his large and well-trained army of 125,000, many of them on horseback. Failing miserably, Nasir Khan saved his own life by surrendering. Those of his men who could not flee were killed.

In November 1738, Nadir Shah, inspirer of awe and dread, entered

Peshawar, from where he sent a letter to Muhammad Shah in Delhi, claiming that he had entered India 'purely out of zeal for Islam and friendship for you' and expressing outrage that infidels in the Deccan had dared to exact tribute from the emperor's dominions.

But after crossing the Indus and entering Punjab, he apparently commanded his army 'to ravage the country and to freely use both fire and sword in all places'. The region 'was seized with terror', and Nadir Shah's 'victories and brutalities became the topic of all circles'.[56] After the Indus, the Jhelum was crossed and then the Chenab. The Persian was aiming for Lahore.

Towns and villages on the way were pillaged and inhabitants massacred. To arrest Nadir Shah's march, Zakariya Khan at first assembled his army twenty miles outside Lahore. Quickly, however, he fell back to positions near the city's entrance, just east of the Ravi. After a river-bank battle in which many of Zakariya Khan's soldiers were slaughtered, the subahdar sued for peace and saved Lahore's inhabitants.

The price exacted included a great many elephants and twenty lakh rupees. The Lahore treasury lacking the sum demanded, the city's wealthiest inhabitants, most of them Hindus, produced the money. The Persian installed himself in the Shalimar Gardens that Shah Jahan had built, had a gold coin struck in the name of 'Nadir the Sultan', announced that Zakariya Khan would remain governor in Lahore, and proceeded towards Delhi, taking as hostages a son of the governor and also a son of Diwan Lakhpat Rai, the chief minister.

Reaching the bank of the Beas, Nadir Shah ordered the execution of 1,007 men taken prisoner by his army after entering India. Carnage continued in the Jullundur doab. Crossing the Sutlej, Nadir Shah reached Sirhind on 5 February 1739, Rajpura on the 6th and Ambala on the 7th.

Led by its ruler, Muhammad Shah, the Mughal empire offered battle in the fields of Karnal, not far from Tarain or Panipat, sites of earlier battles for the throne of Delhi. Though possessing more men and elephants, the Mughal army, short on practice, was easily routed. According to one estimate, 30,000 were slain on the Indian side, including many princes and nobles.

Submitting even as the Lahore governor had done, emperor Muhammad Shah offered his crown to Nadir Shah, but the Persian said he would be satisfied with supplies of money, jewels, gold, silver, horses, elephants, camels, slaves, and craftsmen. The levy was crushing but lives and the throne were spared.

The Persian was honoured in the chastened capital's Red Fort and people thought the worst was over until a false rumour in Delhi's bazaars that Nadir Shah had died touched off the killing of several of the Persian's soldiers. Nadir Shah's revenge was to order a massacre of Delhi's citizenry and the ravaging of its wealth. Within nine hours, 20,000 were killed, large sections of the city flattened, and riches removed from homes.

Muhammad Shah and his nobles begged again. Eventually sheathing his sword, Nadir Shah ordered an end to the killing and plunder. Then, before an assembly of nobles, Nadir Shah personally replaced the imperial diadem on Muhammad Shah's head.

But the ransom demanded was increased, and the Mughals were required to cede to the Persian monarch all territory west of the Indus as well as, east of the river, four parganas in suba Lahore, including Sialkot and Gujrat. The Mughals' collapse before Nadir Shah enraged Punjabis like the poet Ali Haider (1690-1758), who wrote: 'They should die by eating poison, these Hindustanis have no sense of shame. The Turanis are so devoid of honour...'[57]

Nadir Shah took back with him, in an enormous procession of soldiers, elephants, camels, horses and mules, the entire Mughal treasury, including the Peacock Throne that Shah Jahan had commissioned and the fabled Kohinoor diamond, as well as crores of rupees, plus a Mughal princess seized as a wife for one of his sons. For this return journey, Nadir Shah chose a more northern route, via Sialkot, and stripped new places in Punjab of their wealth and possessions. Seizing their opportunity, Sikh bands plundered the rear of Nadir Shah's returning army.

Ordered to produce a fresh large sum from Lahore's citizens, Zakariya Khan showed up with the money before Nadir Shah crossed the Chenab. Commanding Zakariya Khan to accompany him for the crossing, Nadir Shah asked the governor, referring to the Sikhs, 'Who are these people?'

'Faqirs who visit the tank at Amritsar every six months,' replied Zakariya Khan. 'Where do they live?' asked Nadir Shah. 'Their saddles are their homes,' replied Zakariya Khan.[58] From those saddles the Sikhs would penetrate place after place in the years ahead.

After the crossing, Zakariya Khan was allowed to return to Lahore, with an instruction to pay into the Persian treasury twenty lakh rupees every year as revenue from Nadir Shah's Punjab parganas. The recent Mughal satrap was now Nadir Shah's servant in a desolated Punjab but still, in the early 1740s, its most powerful individual. In the mind of the future, however, a humbler contemporary would rival and perhaps overshadow the image of Zakariya Khan.

In twenty-first century Punjab, no poet seems to be quoted more readily or more often than Bulleh Shah. Born around 1680 either in a village called Uch Gilaniyan in suba Multan, or in the village of Pandoke near the town of Kasur in suba Lahore—the ambiguity proving his modest background— Abdullah Shah soon had his first name shortened into Bullah or Bulleh.

Though hardly famous, his ancestors were Bukhara-origin Sayyids long connected to the Multan area. One of them was a disciple of the thirteenth-century Sufi saint buried in Multan city, Bahauddin Zakaria. Bulleh's father, Shah Muhammad, however, lived much closer to Lahore, in the neighbourhood of Kasur. A teacher affiliated to the village mosque in Pandoke, fifty miles from Kasur town, Shah Muhammad was well-versed in Arabic, Persian, and the Qur'an.

Also learning Arabic and Persian and familiarizing himself with the Qur'an, the son, who spent much of his life in and around Kasur, and some of it perhaps in Lahore, displayed a deep spiritual hunger and an equally deep understanding of the world around him. The first attribute may have contributed to his never marrying (his sisters too remained single) and to his finding a mentor, Shaikh Inayat Qadiri.

Born into the Arain biradari where small farmers predominated, this mentor belonged to a Sufi school led by one we have previously come across: Guru Arjan Dev's friend and Prince Dara's mentor, Mian Mir. Shaikh Inayat eventually became a successor at Mian Mir's seat in Lahore.[59]

A Sayyid glorying in an Arain guide is an element in Bulleh's appeal and lore. Taunted by relatives that he was being initiated by an Arain, Bulleh Shah is said to have replied,

> He who calls me a Sayyid will be punished in hell; He who calls me Arain will ride swings in heaven.[60]

Anguish caused by a protracted withdrawal of Shaikh Inayat's approval was responsible for some of Bulleh's most powerful love poetry, which merges three longings: for the beloved, for the guide, and for God. When after the long separation Shaikh Inayat reconnected with his disciple, recognizing him by voice though not by appearance, he enquired, 'Can this be Bullah?' 'Not Bullah but *bhullah* (lost),' replied the poet-disciple. The relationship was restored.

Bulleh's unorthodox utterances so displeased the clerics of Kasur that on his death (around 1758) he was denied a spot in the town's cemetery. In 1982, however, Taufiq Rafat, one of Bulleh Shah's modern translators, would write:

> Today the cemetery where orthodoxy had refused him burial ground is mostly in ruins, encroached upon by a fast-growing town whose hard-pressed denizens defecate on its collapsed graves. The tomb of Bulleh Shah... and the area around it is... the only place free of collective refuse and the privileged of the city pay handsomely to be buried in the proximity of the man they had once rejected.[61]

Expressed in the Punjabi idiom of the central doabs (Rachna, Bari and Bist)—the idiom of towns like Gujrat, Sialkot, Lahore, Kasur, Amritsar and Jullundur—Bulleh's poetry employed a deceptively simple free verse. Sounding like spontaneous speech, it is a poetry as easily understood in today's Punjab as it was during his lifetime.

Revealing knowledge of the Qur'an, of Rumi, and of Hindu and Sikh traditions, Bulleh's poems attack hypocrisy in biting language, with images of rogues inhabiting mosques, temples and gurdwaras.

> 'Hats off to those who a lost coin reimburse/ But have no such scruple about a fat purse.'[62]

Other images he offers include cotton and the spinning wheel, the sweeper-woman, kind females trying to save Bulleh from himself, and the Punjabi countryside's birds and crops. Losing the big 'I' in love for God is part of the message of one who wrote also of 'the truth that cannot be spoken—or withheld'. Again and again Bulleh Shah rejects the insistence, 'I am this, not the other.' He writes (Taufiq Rafat's translation):

> Neither Hindu nor Muslim/I sit with all on a whim.
> Having no caste, sect or creed/I am different indeed.
> Neither thirsty nor quite slaked/I am not dressed nor naked.
> I do not laugh, do not cry/And neither stay nor go by.
> I am neither sinner or saint/ Knowing not sin nor restraint
> Bulleh tries hard to shirk/ The embrace of Hindu and Turk.[63]

(All across India, 'Turk' was a popular if inaccurate synonym for 'Muslim'.)

Bulleh Shah was face-to-face with the upheavals in and around Lahore glimpsed by us: Banda Bahadur's raids; the Sunni-Shia controversy when Shah Alam reigned from Lahore; the near-chaos following Shah Alam's death; raids by Sikh outlaws; the Hussain Khan Kheshgi revolt in Kasur; the suppression of Sikh risings by Abdul Samad Khan and Zakariya Khan; the destructive march of Nadir Shah's army (which stripped Kasur too on its way to Delhi); and more.

His guide's apparent enmity with Hussain Khan Kheshgi contributed to Bulleh Shah's coolness towards the Kasur revolt,[64] but a stronger reason was the suffering the revolt brought to the people of the area.

Linked to the Sikh gurus via his guide's mentor Mian Mir, Bulleh Shah seems to have been more than sympathetic to them and evidently wrote of Guru Tegh Bahadur as a ghazi or martyr for his faith.[65] His opposition to 'us versus them' was certainly reminiscent of what Baba Farid and Guru Nanak had taught.

But the carnage associated with Banda hurt Bulleh Shah's heart, which, despite the poet's dislike of hierarchy and privilege, was saddened also by the ebbing away of Mughal-era security, inadequate as that was. Bulleh's poetic spirit was political as well: seeing where Punjab was heading, he was troubled.

Rafat has suggested that 'the full bitterness' of Bulleh Shah's 'Punjab has gone to the dogs' statement can only be understood against the backdrop of the Mughal empire breaking up and of a 'Punjab being persistently rent by petty chiefs and marauders'.[66] While Bulleh's comments on contemporary political scenes were 'random and oblique,'[67] the poet wrote these lines (tr. Rafat):

> The Mughals quaff the cup of poison/Those with coarse blankets are up
> The genteel watch it all in quiet/They have a humble pie to sup
> The tide of the times is in spate/Punjab is in a fearsome state.[68]

By 'those with coarse blankets', Bulleh Shah evidently meant the Sikhs.[69] Remembering, however, his philosophical kinship with Guru Nanak's message, modern Sikhs appear to join Punjab's Muslims in celebrating Bulleh Shah's life and verse, as do Hindu Punjabis.

■

Another Arain slowly rising in influence was Adina, son of Chunnu, born around 1710 in Sharaqpur, eighteen miles south of Lahore. The future would know him as Adina Beg Khan, but the last two names, with their Turkic or aristocratic associations, were later acquisitions.

Extreme poverty took the unlettered Adina as a domestic servant, a gardener perhaps, to homes of Mughal officers in the fecund Jullundur doab. Proximity to the officers engendered a desire to join their military force, which he did, becoming an adept soldier. But how high could an Arain rise in the Mughal army? Since soldiers worked at times with revenue collectors—cultivators had to be coerced to cough up—Adina succeeded in becoming a revenue collector in the village of Kang in the sarkar of Sultanpur in the Jullundur doab, the 'unvarying fertility' of which had been marked by a succession of travellers, starting with Hiuen Tsiang in the seventh century.[70]

Lala Shri Niwas, a rich Sultanpur banker, noticed Adina's drive and ability and obtained for him the revenue contract for five or six villages. The next year Adina started collecting revenue from a whole pargana. Impressed by his reliability, the Sultanpur faujdar, with whom Adina deposited his collections, entrusted Adina at times with carrying all the revenues from his sarkar to Lahore, where Adina came to know the suba's treasury officer.

When, towards the end the 1730s, the Sultanpur faujdar died, Adina, armed with an introduction from the treasury officer in Lahore, swiftly called on the satrap, Zakariya Khan, and sought the position that had fallen vacant. Zakariya Khan demanded security; Lala Shri Niwas provided it.

Appointed faujdar by the satrap, and becoming 'Adina Beg Khan', he made Shri Niwas his immediate assistant and the banker's brother, the Persian-knowing Bhwani Das, his office superintendent. Adina's great break was however followed by the plague of the Nadir Shah invasion, of which the Jullundur doab and its Sultanpur sarkar, the latter situated on the main road between Lahore and Delhi, were major victims.

Adina Beg Khan's work during and after the invasion was impressive. He restored order, provided relief, and secured, by ransom, the release of some prisoners. Learning of Adina's performance, and anxious to curb growing Sikh influence in the Jullundur doab, Zakariya Khan named him the nazim or governor for the doab as a whole, ordering him at the same time to punish the Sikhs.

Nazim Adina Beg Khan affirmed that he would indeed punish the Sikhs but, as Punjab moved into the eighteenth century's fourth decade, he did not quite do so, for he saw clearly that times had changed. Mughal decline was irreversible, and the future was wide open.

The empire that had controlled Punjab for two centuries was not only on its way out; it had been squeezed dry by Nadir Shah. Another invasion from the northwest was not impossible. Meanwhile, the Marathas' reach was extending by the day. As for the Sikhs, they were not only defiant; unlike the Mughals or the Marathas, they belonged to the land, which they knew intimately. Moreover, they had scores to settle.

Aware also of the strength of the Jullundur Sikhs, Adina Beg saw that he could no longer align himself exclusively or irrevocably to the declining Mughals. Earlier we had marked a common Punjabi guideline: 'Let others do the ruling and fighting; we will stay alive.'

Adina Beg did not share it. This unusual Punjabi wanted to do the ruling and was ready, if necessary, for fighting. But like all other Punjabis, he too needed to survive. To do so in the Punjab of the 1740s, loyalty to one power was less important than balancing all powers. Adina would profess total loyalty but practice balance.

When he noticed inaction against Jullundur's Sikh rebels, Zakariya Khan sent a tough order, and Adina had no choice but to ask the rebels to leave the doab. The Sikhs sent a vakil, Jassa Singh Thoka, also known as Jassa Singh Ramgarhia, to negotiate, but the wily Adina hired him for a position in his office. The equally astute Jassa Singh took the position. Obliged to leave the doab, the Sikhs crossed the Sutlej and entered the Sirhind sarkar, where they created problems for the imperial government.

■

Nadir Shah having denuded the Lahore treasury, Zakariya Khan had no money to pay his soldiers. His way of raising it was to imprison the diwan, Lakhpat Rai, whose brother, Jaspat Rai, then proceeded to demand arrears from all nazims and faujdars. Lakhpat Rai was released but Adina found himself behind bars for being in arrears.

Zakariya's second son Shah Nawaz replaced Adina as the Jullundur nazim. After a year, however, Adina was freed—largely, it seems, because of the loyalty to him, in the teeth of persecution and torture, of the Hindu brothers, Shri Niwas and Bhwani Das[71]—and named deputy governor under Shah Nawaz.

Here we may pause to absorb the hazards of medieval life, which in India continued into and beyond the eighteenth century. Prison, torture and the possibility of unnatural death were predictable milepots in the career of every ambitious individual, and treachery an indispensable tool for advancement. Yet, ambition would not be stilled, preferring to remember instances, which also occurred, of a prisoner escaping, or the probable killer being himself killed.

Along with this general truth we may mark a particular one, namely Adina Beg Khan's ability to work very closely, on a round-the-clock and daily basis, with Hindus and Sikhs. Perhaps this was more common in eighteenth-century Punjab than we may think; it is more than likely that there were other Adinas, whose names we do not know, who at different levels and in different sites in Punjab—crop-fields, ferry-points, bazaars, karkhanas, offices of the empire's functionaries, and elsewhere—worked closely with persons from a variety of religious traditions.

■

Zakariya Khan died in 1745. The Sikhs did not mourn the departure of a viceroy they had defied and who had shown them little mercy. Yet, Zakariya Khan 'was an able administrator [who] did much to relieve the suffering caused by the Persian invasion'.[72] In Lahore, grief at his death was such that 'for three nights in succession no lamp was lighted in any house', and 'thousands upon thousands of lamenting residents followed his coffin'. So recorded Anand Ram Mukhlis, a contemporary Hindu historian.[73]

The spot in Lahore where, along with his wife, father, mother and other relatives, Zakariya Khan is buried is today a neglected and forgotten ruin. Not far from it stands a tower in which—so it was said—the viceroy's unmarried sister, Sharaf al-Nisa, keeping a double-edged sword at her side, daily recited the Qur'an for an hour.

Her death-bed request to be buried in that tower without dome or lamp but alongside the Qur'an and her bejewelled sword would later be immortalized by Iqbal.[74] After Lahore came under Sikh control, a group of Sikhs apparently broke open the tower, believing that it contained treasure, and removed the Qur'an and the sword.[75] Sharaf al-Nisa had died, like her brother, in 1745.

Did Zakariya Khan miss a trick, in the years before his death, by not declaring Punjab's independence from both Nadir Shah (who would be assassinated in 1747) and the dying Mughal empire? In the south of India, Asaf Jah had established his independent chiefdom, and Saadat Khan had done likewise in Awadh, but Zakariya Khan did not emulate them.

It has been suggested that the Sikhs' rise to power, which we will shortly witness, might have been pre-empted in the early 1740s if a satrap like Zakariya Khan had declared Punjab's independence.[76] We do not, however, know whether the thought entered his mind, or whether an independent set-up led by him would in fact have attracted enough support in Punjab to thwart Sikh opposition.

Zakariya Khan's death touched off a bitter rivalry for the viceroy's position, especially between his sons Yahya Khan and Shah Nawaz. Neither was favoured by the emperor, Muhammad Shah, who wished to clip the wings of his court's Turani faction, which was led by the prime minister, Qamruddin Khan. As we saw earlier, Qamruddin's sister was Zakariya's wife, i.e. the mother of the two rivals, one of whom, older brother Yahya, had in addition married Qamruddin's daughter.

The 'solution', reluctantly accepted by the emperor, was to name Qamruddin himself as Punjab's formal viceroy, make Yahya the deputy viceroy, and retain Shah Nawaz as the Jullundur nazim. The younger brother was in addition given a quantity of money and jewels.

■

Having to serve two temperamental brothers, one hovering close-by in Jullundur, the other, more distant, in Lahore, with each boss openly hostile to the other, was a risky undertaking, but the tactful Adina Beg survived it. When, in the summer of 1746, Yahya Khan and his diwan Lakhpat Rai demanded another round of tough action against the Sikhs, Adina Beg persecuted the Sikhs and proved his loyalty to Yahya.

But when a physical clash between the brothers became unavoidable, and 'balance' had to yield quickly to choice, Adina fought on the younger brother's side. Supported by Adina, Shah Nawaz won the first round and, imprisoning Yahya Khan, seized power in Lahore, only, however, to lose a second and more important one in September 1747, when Yahya escaped and joined his uncle, the grand wazir, in Delhi.

When Shah Nawaz, still in control in Lahore but fearful of the price his revolt would exact, asked Adina for advice, his deputy's mind reached out to the northwestern lands beyond India, where an Afghan general, Ahmad Shah Abdali, had just succeeded to portions of the kingdom of Nadir Shah. Said Adina to Shah Nawaz:

> You are no more than a nephew to *Wazir* Qamruddin Khan, but your elder brother Yahiya Khan is his son-in-law besides... Rest assured that neither the Emperor nor the *Wazir* would leave you undisturbed... You have only one recourse—of joining Ahmad Shah Abdali's party. He is a powerful and successful man and openly aspires to the Crown. He will look upon your joining him as the most unexpected favour [from] heaven.[77]

Having served with Nadir Shah's invading army in 1738-39, the Afghan was familiar with India. An excited Shah Nawaz sent him an envoy carrying a simple message: 'Crown to Ahmad Shah and wazirship to Shah Nawaz.' In order to win the Persian segments of Ahmad Shah's soldiery, Shah Nawaz even claimed in this message that he had become a Shia.

But 'balance' also required playing the informer. To secure the confidence of the Delhi court, Adina Beg now informed Qamruddin that Shah Nawaz was turning against the emperor and seeking Abdali's aid. In a warning to which an inducement was joined, the wazir told his nephew that 'their family, at all times attached to the Emperors of India, had never been defiled by the crime of ingratitude and treason', but added that loyalty, plus the uncle's exertions, could earn for Shah Nawaz 'the five provinces of Kabul, Kashmir, Thatta (Sindh), Multan and Lahore'.[78]

Both messages produced the effect desired. While Abdali agreed to invade India, his inviter, Shah Nawaz, chose to defend the empire against Abdali. By January 1748, Abdali and his army had arrived outside Lahore, where, supported by Adina Beg Khan, Shah Nawaz put up a brief resistance before decamping in the dead of the night for Delhi.

■

This was the first of Ahmad Shah Abdali's ten Indian invasions. Only twenty-six in 1748, he belonged to the Abdali or Durrani tribe of the Pashtuns. His person was 'tall and robust', his face 'remarkably broad, his beard very black, and his complexion moderately fair'. Though he mixed freely with his soldiers, his appearance was 'expressive of an uncommon dignity' and toughness.[79] When Nadir Shah was killed, his Durrani (Abdali) contingents had unanimously 'elected' Ahmad Shah as the Persian king's successor in the Pashtun country.

His resources augmented by the artillery, rockets, elephants, camels and horses that Shah Nawaz had left behind, Abdali struck coins in Lahore and compelled chiefs in Punjab and the hills to pay him allegiance and tribute. After mercy was begged and money put up, Lahore's citizens were spared. Following a forty-day stay in the city, Abdali advanced towards Delhi.

Nine years after Nadir Shah's humiliating sweep, what remained of the empire in Delhi presented, in March 1748, a surprisingly robust fight in Manupur, nine miles from Sirhind. Joining the defence, which was led by Prince Ahmad, the emperor's son, and Qamruddin, the old wazir, were soldiers provided by Rajput princes and Rohillas from east of the Jamuna. The flight of Shah Nawaz, who was detained after arrival in Delhi, had alerted the court, and Abdali's pause in Lahore had given the empire time to prepare.

Though Qamruddin died of a cannon shot that hit him in the knee, his body was propped up on the back of an elephant, and the death was kept concealed. Luck played a part, with the rockets that Abdali had acquired in

Lahore going off and panicking the Afghans more than their Indian foes. Prince Ahmad fought more valorously than expected, and Adina Beg Khan, who had joined the fray, was wounded twice, but the hero on the victorious (and much larger) Indian side was Muin-ul-Mulk, also known as Mir Mannu, the son of Wazir Qamruddin and thus the cousin of Shah Nawaz and Yahya Khan.

Along with the remnants of his army, Abdali returned rapidly to his regions across the Khyber. Ominously if not surprisingly, 'the watchful Sikhs harassed the king's rear'.[80] Yet Abdali's defeat and retreat had brought Punjab back to the Mughal empire. In a just reward, Mir Mannu was named its viceroy.

Only a month after Manupur, however, the emperor died, ending a reign of more than thirty years. He was succeeded by Prince Ahmad, who for a change did not have to kill or blind anyone to reach the throne. But that throne had lost most of its prestige, wealth and power.

■

Profiting from the Mughal-Abdali confrontation, the Sikhs were more active than ever, and across a wider area. Energetic Sikh leaders surfaced not only in the cis-Sutlej Sirhind or Malwa area (Haro Singh and Karora Singh) and in the Jullundur doab (Jassa Singh Ahluwalia), but also in the Bari doab (Lajja Singh and Hari Singh) and in the Rachna doab (Charhat Singh).

Establishing himself in Lahore in June 1748, Muin sent punitive expeditions in pursuit of the Sikhs. The battle of Manupur had created an aura around him, and for a while Sikh forces retreated. But they also forged an unspoken understanding with Adina, who had been retained as the Jullundur faujdar. Though instructed by Muin to curb Sikh power, Adina was willing to let that power survive even as he made a show of moving against it.

He had no alternative, for the Sikhs were not only the most active force around him, they were also local. The Mughals, by contrast, a pale shadow of their former selves, were neither of the soil nor (Muin apart) focused. Another factor favouring the Sikhs was the attachment for Guru Nanak's teaching nursed by Muin's Hindu diwan, Kauramal.

Given Muin's firm orders, Adina could not remain entirely inert against the Sikhs. In the late summer of 1748, he and the Sikhs fought a hard battle that took 600 Sikh lives but obliged Adina to retreat. Later in the year, after the rainy season, the Sikhs became bolder and hundreds of them reoccupied Amritsar, building there a small fortress called Ram Rauni.

Along his troops Muin marched from Lahore to Amritsar and ordered

Adina to bring a force from Jullundur, which Adina did. Ram Rauni's besieged Sikh group took many casualties but persuaded Adina's Sikh assistant, Jassa Singh Thoka, who was in the contingent from Jullundur, to cross over to their side. Diwan Kauramal, to whom Thoka appealed for aid, in turn persuaded Muin that winning over the Sikhs was wiser than trying to crush them.

Muin's offer of a quarter of the revenue in Patti pargana was accepted by the Sikhs. While ready himself to negotiate with the Sikhs, Adina had opposed Kauramal's proposal that Muin should do so, for Kauramal was his chief rival.

Though it looked as if the Sikhs were pacified, a significant move in the opposite direction had been made in Amritsar. In March 1748, different Sikh jathas or groups agreed to form a Dal Khalsa, an army of the Singhs, under the leadership of another Jassa Singh—Jassa Singh Ahluwalia[81]—who advanced the idea that the Khalsa should one day govern Punjab.[82]

A year later, in December 1749, Abdali again invaded Punjab and demanded the revenue from Nadir Shah's four parganas. Believing that Punjab had passed to him, Mir Mannu opposed the claim and assembled his forces just south of the Chenab to resist Abdali. But Delhi's Mughal court conceded Abdali's demands over Muin's head, whereupon the Afghan returned to his country.

Two years later, in December 1751, Ahmad Shah Abdali again entered Punjab and besieged Lahore for four months. 'Neither Abdali for want of artillery nor Muin for lack of reinforcements from Delhi could make short work of this long affair.'[83] All the land within a fifty-mile radius from Lahore was laid waste by the Afghans. Inside the city, flour could not be had, lamps could not be lit, and horses chewed rotten sacks and the straw of old huts.

Arguing that the enemy was formidable and Muin's own forces raw and unaided, the Diwan proposed negotiations, adding that, with the countryside too barren to feed his soldiers and horses and the hot summer about to set in, Abdali would accept suitable terms and return to his country.

Sharply opposing the suggestion of the Diwan (who, to Adina's dismay, had been given the governorship of Multan by Muin), the Arain argued for attacking the enemy, in order, according to some historians, to have Kauramal eliminated.[84] But perhaps Adina was also anxious to weaken, if possible, the Afghan threat to Punjab.

Mir Mannu agreed with the Jullundur faujdar but the assault failed, and Kauramal was indeed killed. Apparently Adina 'treacherously withdrew' after Kauramal was slain, and Muin was forced to surrender.[85]

It would take Adina a little time and effort to regain respect, but Mir Mannu, the victor of Manupur, secured it right away when, accompanied only by three aides, he walked up to Abdali's triumphant camp and had this conversation (doubtless in Persian) with the Afghan:

Abdali: Why didn't you submit earlier?
Muin: I had another master to serve.
A: Why didn't that master come to your help?
M: He thought his servant could take care of himself.
A: What would you have done had you captured me?
M: I would have cut off your head and sent it to my master at Delhi.
A: Now that you are at my mercy, what should I do to you?
M: If you are a shopkeeper, sell me (for a ransom). If you are a butcher, kill me, but if you are a king, grant me your grace and pardon.[86]

When the conversation ended, Abdali, it seems, embraced the surrendering Mughal viceroy, conferred a new title on him, gave him the very turban that he, Abdali, was wearing, and proclaimed him the subahdar of Punjab. Except that this now was an Afghan Punjab, snipped off from the Mughal empire.

When a Durrani envoy called in Delhi on the emperor, the latter 'put his seal' on the shrinkage, and the Afghan returned to Qandahar, but not before ensuring that another Mughal province, Kashmir, had been conquered by his troops.[87] Sukhjiwan Mal was named the Afghan's governor in Kashmir. On his part, Adina was able, in 1752, to give his name to a town he had established on the bank of a canal in the Bari doab. Adinanagar stood in fertile, foot-of-the-hills country eight miles north of modern Gurdaspur.

■

Emboldened afresh by the depletion of Muin's resources, the Sikhs increased their raids, and Adina was again asked to punish them in the Jullundur doab. This he energetically did, for he had 'to wash away the suspicions attached to his treachery at Lahore'.[88] Many Sikhs were killed in Makhowal, but Adina, the 'able but artful chief', once more 'entered into a secret understanding with them' by which the Sikhs agreed to limit their raids and Adina agreed not to go after them.[89]

Calling Adina 'a man of marked ability', a future British officer studying the history of Jullundur district would record that 'in this battle [at Makhowal]' Adina 'was supported by the bulk of the Ramgarhia Confederacy (the followers of Jassa Singh Thoka)' and add that Adina 'gave the Sikhs favourable terms and indeed took many of them into his pay'.[90]

Muin, who maintained a ruthless policy towards the Sikhs, was 'kept in humour' by Adina, who from time to time sent to Lahore forty to fifty Sikh captives from his doab.[91] The viceroy had them executed. In November 1753, however, Muin suddenly died, probably from poison, and six months later his two-year-old boy, proclaimed viceroy by Muin's widow, also died, again, apparently, of poison.

The subahdari was now claimed by the widow, Surayya Begum, also known as Murad Begum or the Mughlani Begum, 'a lady of remarkable address and unbounded ambition'.[92] She sent agents to Qandahar and also to Delhi to obtain ratification for her claim but was opposed by Bhikari Khan, a Turkic general who had served in Lahore as Muin's closest advisor.

With de facto control in her hands, the Begum had Bhikari Khan imprisoned in her palace. While Abdali saw no need to disturb her, the court in Delhi was too feeble and divided to intervene. Turani nobles were fighting the Iranis, who were led by Safdar Jung, the wazir at this time.

Safdar Jung, on his part, was exasperated by the king's tolerance of an overbearing eunuch, Javed Khan, a favourite of the king's mother, Udham Bai. The wazir went so far as to stab Javed Khan to death, whereupon the emperor and his mother had the wazir removed. When Safdar Jung mounted a rebellion, his opponents called in the Marathas for aid. Safdar Jung was put down but the Turani nobles who with Maratha support had won out now made the emperor their target.

In June 1754, the emperor, Ahmad Shah, was deposed by the new Turani wazir, Ghaziuddin, also known as Imad-ul-Mulk, a grandson of an earlier wazir, Asaf Jah, the founder of Hyderabad's dynasty. In Ahmad Shah's place, Imad-ul-Mulk installed a son of Jahandar Shah. The successor called himself, after one of Aurangzeb's titles, Alamgir II.

Delhi's climate of scandal-cum-chaos was matched by that of Lahore, where the Begum, it seems, 'abandoned modesty'. Encouraged by 'the shameless examples of the highest dignitaries in the Delhi court', she carried on an affair with an officer that was 'on the lips of everybody big and small in Lahore' and later tried also, it appears, to seduce a youth barely out of his teens called Tahmas Beg Khan Miskin, whom 'she really loved'.[93] Moreover, senior officials were being ordered about by eunuchs in the Begum's employ.[94]

Offended by such reports from Lahore, the Turanis of Delhi asked a Lahore-based officer of Uzbek origin, Khwaja Mirza Khan, who was one of the late Muin's trusted colleagues, to exercise control in Lahore, but Abdali sent soldiers from Qandahar who restored the Begum to power.

Bhikari Khan, her foe, was murdered, with the Begum herself participating in the killing. However, her mother's brother, Abdullah Khan, who had been the Begum's agent to Abdali, saw no reason why he should not rule instead of an unruly niece. He imprisoned the Begum.

Much of Punjab was now beyond Lahore's reach. Multan had its own governor who worked under Abdali's orders. The four parganas ('Char Mahals') of Punjab that Abdali had inherited from Nadir Shah, including Gujrat and Sialkot, were run by a Durrani appointee. The Sikhs controlled large portions of the upper Bari doab, including Amritsar, Batala and Pathankot.

In his soil-rich Jullundur doab, Adina Beg Khan too profited from the squabbles that preoccupied Delhi and Lahore. Independent of any master, he had augmented his resources and won prestige by maintaining peace and order in his doab, a state of affairs not obtaining in Lahore or Delhi or much of Punjab. Meticulous in administration, he had also shrewdly handled landlords, cultivators and traders.

In April 1755, Adina won fresh laurels after Rohillas from east of the Jamuna, who too felt themselves independent of all masters, including the Delhi emperor, attempted to take over the territory of Sirhind as well as portions of the Jullundur doab. Adina quickly put together a force of 'about 50,000 horses and the same number of foot'[95] to fight them. The force included his own soldiers, others raised by his doab's Muslim zamindars, and—significantly but not surprisingly—an army of Sikhs. The Adina-led alliance defeated the Rohillas.

A grateful Alamgir II gave the Arain a grand new title but more meaningful was the fact that Adina now controlled both the Jullundur doab and the large sarkar of Sirhind. The hill rajas, too, offered Adina allegiance.

Lahore was the ambitious Adina's next target, and he moved his force against it. The capital fell easily because Abdullah Khan, the Begum's uncle, had lost the loyalty of most of his soldiers. In the autumn of 1755, the Arain became the master of much of Punjab, in part at least because of his alliance with the Sikhs.

But Adina was too intelligent to make Lahore his base. Wanting to be as far as possible from Qandahar, he remained in Jullundur, handing responsibilities in Lahore to a deputy, Sadiq Khan, who had been Sirhind's faujdar when the Rohillas attacked that territory.

Adina's control over Lahore was short-lived. Even as he had turned to the Sikhs, the Begum, freed by Adina's attack, turned to the Afghans for aid.

Responding promptly, Abdali sent to Lahore two contingents led by a general, Jahan Khan. In December, the Begum was restored as Abdali's subahdar, but with her uncle as the deputy, and Sadiq Khan fled to Sirhind. Among those taken captive to Qandahar was Khwaja Mirza.

Even in Adina's own doab, the Sikhs, his allies from time to time, measured their strength against his. In November 1755, Jassa Singh Ahluwalia compelled Adina to acknowledge Sikh control over Fatehabad on the Beas. By now the Sikhs were organizing themselves not 'principally... as bands of plunderers but to wage a joint... resistance against the state'.[96]

■

Resenting her uncle's interference, Mughlani Begum, Abdali's governor in Lahore, now played a crucial card she possessed: the betrothal, a while earlier, of her daughter Umda Begum to the new wazir in Delhi, Imad-ul-Mulk, a Turani kin. Through an agent she appealed to the wazir to come to Lahore, marry the daughter, and remove her deputy, the uncle.

He would indeed come, the wazir replied. But his reasons were his own. Married by now to Ganna Begum, the daughter of a Delhi noble and an 'unrivalled beauty',[97] the wazir was more interested in the Mughlani's wealth than in her daughter. He entertained two other hopes. The first was of bringing the Mughlani back to Delhi, if necessary forcibly. The second hope was of restoring Lahore to the empire he was serving, to which the Mughlani had brought shame.

Not wishing to alert the Afghans, he set out on what was described as a hunting expedition in the cis-Sutlej territory but aiming in fact for Lahore. Also, he coordinated his moves with one who was a reliable foe of the Afghans and capable, if opportunity arrived, of governing Lahore for the empire—Adina. 'Stop at Sirhind,' Adina advised, 'Don't go farther.'

The wazir stopped in the sarkar of Sirhind in the town of Macchiwara, 120 miles east of Lahore. But Adina's soldiers as well as the wazir's, several thousand in all, showed up in Lahore to, as they said, offer presents to the governor and her uncle and accompany the bride-to-be on her journey to the distinguished and 'eager' groom.

The ploy worked to perfection. Seeing the troops arriving to 'honour' him, the shrewd uncle, Abdullah Khan, realized what was happening and quietly escaped to the hills near Jammu. The Begum, her hands freed, launched wedding preparations, showered gifts, and sent her daughter to the wazir's camp. Three weeks later, on 28 March 1756, she was seized before dawn in her palace and moved all the way to the wazir's camp. Upon facing him the Begum swore revenge, but Imad-ul-Mulk took her, as well as her daughter, to Delhi.[98]

Adina was again appointed the empire's viceroy at Lahore. Once more he chose to remain in Jullundur; he knew that Abdali would react. Sayyid Jamiluddin served as Adina's Lahore-based deputy and restored some order but in October 1756 Afghan troops were back in Lahore.

The Begum's uncle, Abdullah Khan, had not taken things lying down. Proceeding from Jammu to Qandahar, he returned to Lahore with contingents of Abdali's troops and became, formally, the Afghan's Lahore viceroy, supported by a deputy, Khwaja Mirza, the Uzbek who had worked for Zakariya and who returned from Qandahar after a year's captivity.

Enraged by what they viewed as a coup against their king by the wazir and Adina, the Afghan troops 'thoroughly plundered' the city of Lahore. Many inhabitants, including Jamiluddin, had however fled the city 'with or without porters'. Yet Abdullah Khan and Mirza could not freely govern what was left of Lahore as 'they were constantly harassed by the Sikhs'.[99]

■

As 1756 drew to its close, Alamgir II looked at the empire that his namesake and forebear had ruled for half a century, felt wretched, wondered who could save it, and thought of Abdali. No doubt the Afghan's troops had behaved badly in Lahore, but there, the king reasoned, his wazir had supplied clear provocation. No doubt the Afghans had for centuries fought the Turanis over India's crown, but if the only hand that could keep the empire in one piece was an Afghan's, so be it.

Najib-ud-Daulah, Rohilla rebel and sometime Mughal governor, was born and raised in the Pashtun country before he moved to a spot northeast of Delhi. He too thought of Abdali, who for the first time in ages had provided a stable government to the Afghans.

Both king and rebel invited Abdali to invade India, as did a third person. A captive of Wazir Imad-ul-Mulk but also the mother of his betrothed, and his relative in other ways, Mughlani Begum had thought of Abdali from the moment she was seized from her Lahore palace. Being the resourceful woman she was, she managed, from Delhi, to send a private letter to the Afghan. 'I am ruined by...treachery,' she wrote, adding what she thought would interest Abdali:

> Goods and cash worth crores of rupees lie buried to my knowledge in the palace of my late father-in-law (Qamruddin) besides heaps of gold and silver stored inside the ceiling. Complete disagreement exists among the emperor, his wazirs and nobles. If you invade India this time, the Indian Empire with all its riches of crores will fall into your hands.[100]

In understanding Ahmad Shah Abdali, the Begum was closer to the mark than the king or Najib. Abdali was more interested in money for consolidating the Afghan kingdom he had created than in saving India's tottering Mughal empire. His troops needed money, and the Afghan people, who included enemies of his, needed to know that only Abdali brought them glory.

On 15 November 1756, heading a large army, he crossed the Indus at Attock. On 20 December, crossing the Jhelum and the Chenab along the way, he reached Lahore via Gujrat, both *his* cities. His general, Jahan Khan, went after Adina Beg Khan, who with his force lay some twenty-five miles southeast of Amritsar. Adina quickly fled, at first southward to Hansi in the cis-Sutlej drylands, and then, north and east from there, to a niche, hard of access, in the Kangra Hills.

On 10 January, Ahmad Shah Abdali crossed the Sutlej. That no one stopped his advance—that India's soldiers did not fight—disgusted Abdali, or so he claimed. It was part of his excuse for the plunder and devastation of Delhi by his army that began on 28 January.

But the real provocation, apart from the trick played in *his* Lahore, was that the king and nobles in Delhi had not met his demands, conveyed through an envoy on 14 January, for two crore rupees plus the hand of the emperor's daughter, plus Sirhind and all territory west of it.

The wazir had sent Mughlani Begum to meet Abdali in Karnal and pacify him. Najib joined Abdali on 16 January, and on the 20th Imad-ul-Mulk presented himself. The wazir was reprimanded, taunted that 'the first officer of the empire of Hindustan could make an abject submission without striking even one blow',[101] and ordered to join Abdali's retinue.

When the empire's nobles said in Delhi that they did not know where treasures were concealed, Abdali raised the heat. Ordered to reveal a hiding-place, an ex-wazir, Intizam-ud-Daulah (a son of Qamruddin), said: 'This moment, beyond this one ring I have on my finger, I have not control over even one rupee.'[102] Threatened with torture if he did not produce one crore that very day, Intizam pointed to his father's widow, saying she would know where any treasure was buried.

Shulahpuri Begum, 'the daughter-in-law of one grand wazir, the widow of another, and the mother of a third',[103] was then told that unless she showed the spot, iron pins would be driven under her fingernails. She pointed. After six hours of digging, coins worth sixteen lakhs and gold and silver vessels were recovered. Larger treasures belonging to Intizam and other nobles were excavated.

His hunger not appeased, Abdali demanded a levy from every house in the Mughal capital, which was divided into wards for exaction, with Afghan troops posted at every corner. In many cases torture led to death, there were many suicides, and many rapes.

Her resources not exhausted, Mughlani Begum gave Abdali information on the worth of each noble and on virgins in the imperial harem. On 20 February 1757, she also made a personal offering of jewel-laden trays, at which point Abdali exclaimed that now he would think of her as more than a daughter: she was now his son.

Having won the Afghan's warmth, the Begum arranged a sweet revenge on Imad-ul-Mulk. When told by Abdali to produce all his gold and jewels, the miserable wazir had pleaded poverty, whereupon he was openly disgraced, and his servants were beaten. Now he was required to properly marry, in a grand ceremony, the Begum's daughter, Umda.

Abdali attended the event (20-21 February), gave presents, magnanimously restored Imad as 'wazir', and commanded that Ganna Begum, Imad's wife of 'unrivalled beauty', be handed over to Mughlani Begum for service as a bondmaid. The wazir was in addition forced to divorce the other women in his harem.

The Afghan's generals were ordered to attack the Jat kingdom that Suraj Mal had established south of Delhi and to raid the Mughals' earlier capital, Agra, where, for a change, the Mughal governor, Fazil Khan, offered tough resistance. Najib, the Rohilla chief, joined this campaign, which witnessed horrific brutalities, exactions and killings in Brindaban, Mathura and Agra, provoked by Fazil Khan's resistance and also, in Latif's words, by the Hindu inhabitants' 'enormous crime of defending their faith and honour'.[104]

Abdali himself captured the fort at Ballabgarh. He had taken Mughlani Begum on this southward expedition, during which he promised her, as a fief, the territories of Jullundur doab, Jammu, and Kashmir.

What stopped the expedition and the bloodshed was a cholera outbreak. Reddened by wanton killing, the river Jamuna turned on the Afghan army, which daily lost one hundred and fifty men to water-borne cholera. There

Contest for Punjab, 1750s

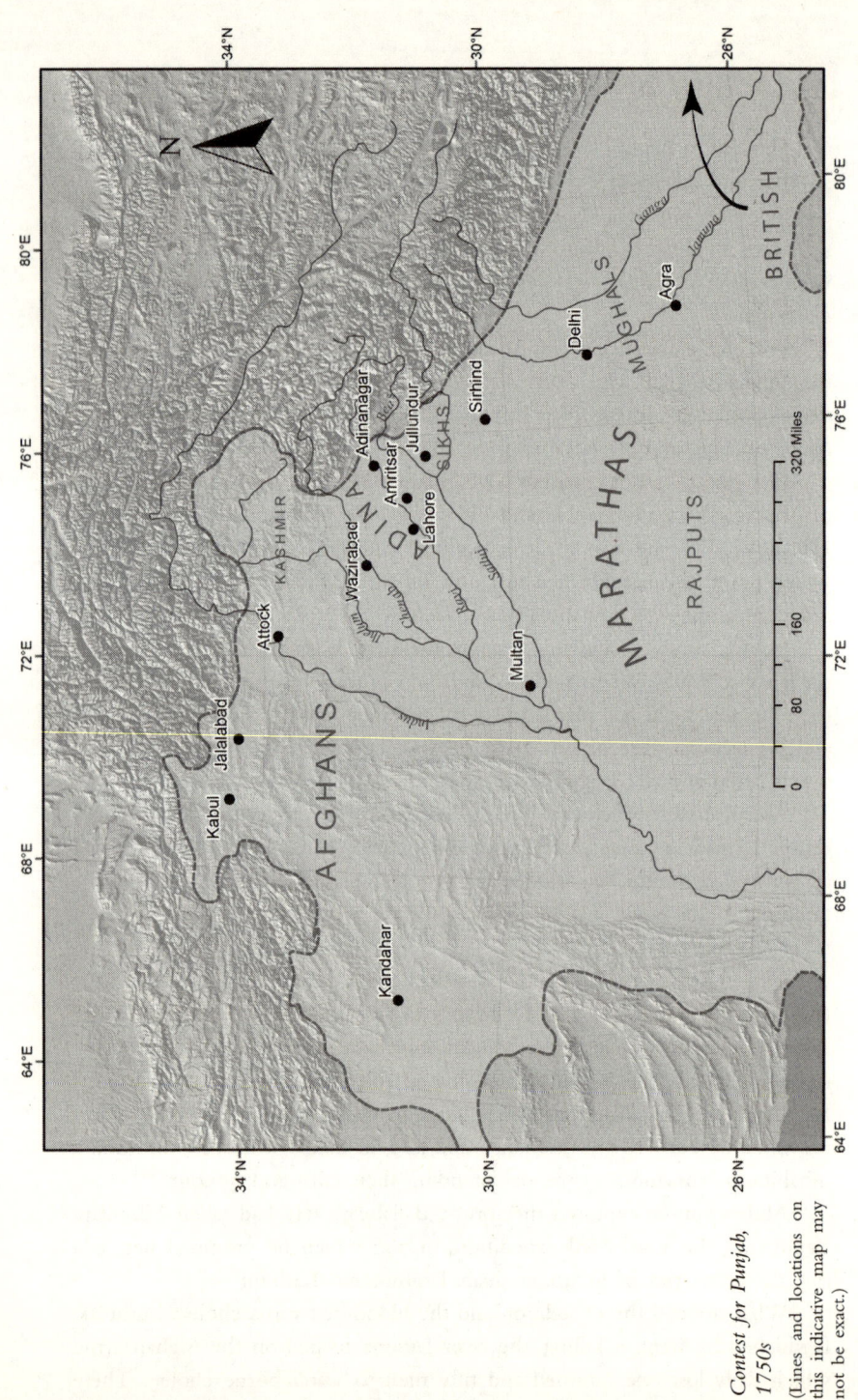

(Lines and locations on this indicative map may not be exact.)

was word, moreover, of a rebellion closer to his Afghan home. At the end of March, Abdali felt he had to turn around and return.

For carrying the immense booty he and his troops had seized, every elephant, camel, horse and donkey in Delhi and the territories they raided was commandeered. Loading goods on their horses, Abdali's cavalry marched back on foot. Abdali's own booty was apparently loaded on 28,000 camels, elephants, mules, bullocks and carts. The late Muhammad Shah's widows were also taken by him, as well as Hazrat Begum, a sixteen-year-old daughter of that emperor, whom Abdali took 'forcibly into wedlock', but 400 maidservants who were being dragged away managed to escape.[105]

Before the departure, Zohra Begum, daughter of Alamgir II, was married to Timur Shah, Abdali's son. Alamgir II, who too had been forced to contribute treasure, was reinstated as 'emperor'. Abdali named the humiliated Intizam as India's new 'grand wazir', and Najib, the Rohilla chief, as the head of the Mughal army.

On his way back, however, 'the Sikhs plundered [Abdali's] baggage, and cut off the stragglers of the Afghan party'. Evidently the Afghan king was 'much incensed'.[106]

■

Not only all of Punjab and Sindh, but the sarkar of Sirhind too was ceded to the Afghan. In the summer of 1757, a throne remained but the Mughal empire's authority had gone. In Punjab, the empire ceased to exist even in name.

Willing to exercise control in Punjab was the local chief, Adina Beg Khan, who had avoided a confrontation with Abdali. In his hideout in Khali Balwan in the Kangra Hills, Adina waited for the after-effects of the Abdali storm to subside. Would the Afghans remain in Punjab to rule it? If not, thought Adina, Mughal power having exited, he could capture the land. But he knew that the Sikhs too wished to control Punjab.

In Delhi, more than one force was willing to replace the Mughals, above all the Marathas, who by now dominated not only much of western and central India but had extended their reach into eastern India, where, in 1751, the Mughal province of Bengal was forced to cede Orissa to them.

Though wary, Abdali was another candidate for replacing the Mughals. 'He... is the most likely person... to restore the ancient power of the empire, should he assume the title of king of Delhi.'[107] A Briton, Alexander Dow, would write this in 1768, but, as we have seen, this opinion was widely held eleven years earlier, on the eve of the Abdali raid of 1756–57. If he occupied Delhi, Abdali would clearly rule over Punjab as well.

And then there were Dow's compatriots. More than a century earlier, England's East India Company had set up 'trading' settlements on the west coast (Surat in 1612, Bombay Castle in 1638) and in coastal south India (Fort St. George, Madras, in 1639). Later, in 1690, the Company established itself at Fort William in Calcutta. These outposts accrued from permissions humbly obtained from India's Mughal rulers and their provincial administrators, and also from the Company's judicious interventions in coastal power struggles.

For footholds in India, the English company had faced European rivals from Portugal, Denmark, Holland, and France. In the seventeenth century, the main white rivalry in India was between the British and the French. By mid-eighteenth century, England's prospects seemed brighter.

That Mughal authority was expiring was by this time known everywhere, from the northwest's Khyber to each coastal town. Like the Marathas across much of India, and the Sikhs and Adina in Punjab, the East India Company in its coastal outposts was willing to flex muscles and seize opportunities. Only three months after Abdali's arrival in Delhi, a Company force led by thirty-two-year-old Robert Clive defeated twenty-year-old Siraj-ud-Daulah, Bengal's Mughal viceroy but in reality the territory's young ruler, in the Battle of Plassey (or Palashi), near the satrap's capital of Murshidabad.

Thus, by the autumn of 1757 the British had obtained Bengal even as the Afghans had annexed Punjab, Sindh, and the northwest. In reality, however, Punjab had no ruler.

Chapter Three

1757-1799: ADINA BEG KHAN, AFGHANS AND THE SIKHS

Believing that Abdali had conferred on her the Jullundur doab and the territories of Jammu and Kashmir, Mughlani Begum sent a messenger—her young staffer Miskin—to Adina's hideout with a khillat or robe of honour. The Begum desired that Adina should govern the Jullundur doab, or the Doab as it was called, on her behalf.

But she had been tricked. Authority over all of Punjab, Sirhind, Jammu, and Kashmir had in fact been given to Abdali's eleven-year-old son Timur Shah, who was left behind in Lahore, which meant that Jahan Khan, Timur's guardian and Abdali's trusted general, was the real ruler of these territories. 'Now that your brother Timur Shah is the viceroy there,' Abdali told the Begum, 'what will you do with the provinces?'[1]

Towards the end of the autumn of 1757, a firman from Timur and a letter from Jahan Khan reached Adina, ordering the Arain to 'present [himself] at our service'. If he did not comply, Adina was told, 'the whole country of the Doab will be laid waste and you will be pursued in the hills'.[2] Wary of offering himself to the Afghans in Lahore, Adina sent no reply. Jahan Khan made good on his threat and pillaged several Doab towns, whereupon Adina sent word that he would serve as Timur's agent and raise revenue for the Afghans. But, pleaded Adina, he should be excused from the court in Lahore, for if he left the Doab, even briefly, the Sikhs would take over the territory.

Jahan Khan did not trust the ambitious Arain but needed the revenues that only Adina could raise. When Adina agreed to send thirty-six lakh rupees annually, he was given an Afghan khillat and named Timur's governor for the Doab; however, to ensure loyalty and punctual payment, Adina's Hindu agent Dilaram was required to attend the Lahore court.

Impatient for an early instalment of revenue, Jahan Khan imprisoned Dilaram but the ever-resourceful Mughlani Begum contrived Dilaram's escape. At this an infuriated Jahan Khan personally caned the Begum, extorted jewels from her private collection and placed her in harsh confinement.

Though instructed to come to Lahore—to plan, he was told, the suppression of the Sikhs—Adina refused to show up. Instead he sent agents with presents for Prince Timur and a request for pardon. At least two Hindus, Dharamdas Taranjia and Chaudhri Jodha Nagri, and the Muslim chief of Kapurthala, Rai Ibrahim Bhatti, were among the emissaries Adina sent to Lahore.[3]

He would be pardoned, Adina was informed, but attend court he must. When he did not, troops were sent to seize him, but Adina retired to the foothills—and struck an alliance with the Sikhs, taking many of them into his pay and granting them the right to plunder.

Commanded by Murad Khan, Afghan troops crossed the Beas into the Doab but ran into Sikh soldiers who fought with 'indescribable fury'. Led by Sodhi Barbhag Singh and Jassa Singh Ahluwalia, and 'intoxicated with opium and bhang', the Sikhs routed the Afghans and looted their possessions.[4] Murad fled to Lahore. Shocked by Murad's defeat, Jahan Khan stormed out of Lahore to meet the retreating soldiers. At Batala, he confronted Murad Khan and 'out of extremity of rage' ordered that the commander be caned.[5]

Saved by the Sikhs, Adina gave them leave, early in December 1757, to pillage the entire Doab, including the city of Jullundur. Fired by prospects of loot and also by anger against Nassir Ali, a city resident accused of anti-Sikh excesses, the Sikh soldiers were merciless. 'Children were put to the sword, women were dragged out and forcibly converted to Sikhism' and carried off as wives. The town was burnt down. Mosques were defiled by pigs' blood, and flesh was thrust into the mouth of Nassir Ali's dead body, dug out of the grave.[6]

Another contingent sent to the Doab by Jahan Khan was not resisted either by the Sikhs, who were busy pillaging, or by Adina, who had retired to his hideout in the hills to weigh his options. Should he continue his alliance with the Sikhs? Attempt a rapprochement with the Afghans? Or send a feeler to a third force, the ascendant Marathas, who in September 1757 had been invited to Delhi by Imad-ul-Mulk (Mughlani Begum's father-in-law)?

Imad's approach to the Marathas had been made over the heads of the king, Alamgir II, and the grand wazir, Intizam. Arriving in Delhi in large numbers, and led by Raghunath Rao, brother of the Peshwa in Poona, the Marathas not only drove Najib, the Abdali plenipotentiary, out of the capital, they also seized Saharanpur, Najib's town north of Delhi, and threatened Abdali's easternmost Indian territory, Sirhind, which lay west of Saharanpur, with only the Jamuna in between.

Harassed continually by the Sikhs but not attacked in battle, the troops sent by Jahan Khan to the Doab and also to Kashmir returned to Lahore without achieving any solid result. At this point neither the Afghans nor the Sikhs nor Adina ruled the Doab. Chaos prevailed. This was true also of Sirhind and in fact of much of Punjab. Even the environs of Lahore were not safe from Sikh forays. Every night, thousands of Sikhs burst into the suburbs for plunder but no force was sent out to repel them. This anarchic state lasted from November 1757 to February 1758.

But Adina had made up his mind: he would urge the Marathas to extend their sway up to the banks of the Indus and, in the process, drive the Afghans from Punjab. In repeated secret messages to Raghunath Rao, Adina pointed to the 'rich harvest of spoil within their reach' in Punjab and promised on his own part to pay them one lakh rupees for every day of marching and ₹50,000 for each day of halting.

This, despite the fact that Jahan Khan's deputy, Khwaja Mirza Khan (an Uzbek officer), had succeeded in confronting Adina in his hilly redoubt. Asked to prove his loyalty to Abdali, Adina not only provided explanations, he purchased Mirza Khan by offering the Uzbek his daughter in marriage.

■

Joined to the dream of planting their flag on the Indus's shore, the lure of Punjab's riches was irresistible for the Marathas, who, crossing the Jamuna westward, made their first attack on the territory of Sirhind at the end of December. Abdali's governor there, Abdul Samad Khan, a Pashtun general, quickly patched up a conflict he was having with a Sikh chief, Ala Singh of Patiala, and entrenched his forces in Sirhind town.

In January 1758, Malhar Rao, the Marathas' general, returned to the Jamuna's eastern bank after securing a tribute of five lakh rupees from Samad Khan but, at the end of February, the Marathas resumed their invasion of Sirhind and Punjab, this time with an immense army headed by Raghunath Rao.

When, on 5 March, the Marathas reached Ambala, Adina wrote to Prince Timur and his general-cum-wazir, Jahan Khan, that the Marathas from the Deccan had materialized like 'a bolt from the blue' and that he, the Afghans' agent, was joining them only 'out of policy'. They should not 'delay even for an hour' but advance at once against the Marathas.[7]

Unsurprisingly, the Maratha army, numbering around 200,000, received support from the Sikhs. Sirhind town, where Samad Khan had shut himself, was besieged, and though the Afghan governor managed to escape, he was quickly captured. 'As the Marathas and the Sikhs thought of nothing but plunder, they so thoroughly looted the inhabitants of Sirhind, high and low, that none, either male or female, had a cloth on his or her person left.'[8] Houses were pulled down, timber carried off, and floors dug up for hidden treasure.

For the moment at least, all the Indians—Sikhs, Marathas, Mughals like Imad and Muslim Punjabis led by Adina—had united against the Afghans, who sensed their sudden isolation. At first, Jahan Khan thought to confront the coalition. Taking an army, he moved from Batala in the Bari doab to the western bank of the Beas and camped there for eight days, hoping to cross into the Jullundur doab. But an advance guard sent by him returned with reports of Samad Khan's capture and of the Marathas' remorseless advance into and across the Doab towards the Beas.

Left with no alternative, Jahan Khan not only ordered a retreat of his forces to Lahore; he advised Timur Shah to retire to Afghanistan. Carrying everyone and everything back to their country was a challenge. The prince, his mother, all the other Afghan ladies, the chiefs, the troops, and their baggage had to be swiftly moved across four rivers—the Ravi, Chenab, Jhelum and Indus. The task seemed even more daunting when word arrived that the Maratha-led alliance had crossed the Beas and that an advance force headed by Adina and a Maratha general lay encamped just fifteen miles from Lahore.

Hurriedly, the entire Afghan establishment evacuated Lahore and moved in the direction of Kabul. The women rode in litters on camels and horses, guarded by eunuchs. Hundreds of carts loaded with property made repeated trips by day and by night to the next town or river, and soldiers set fire to goods they could not carry.

Lahore was abandoned to the 'Indian alliance' led by the Marathas. Among the many who accepted the new rulers was Khwaja Mirza Khan, Adina's son-in-law, who had served the Mughals before aligning with the Afghans. Now, like Adina, he was with the Marathas, as were a number of former Mughal officers and soldiers.

The Afghans crossed the Ravi without major mishap but the Chenab near Wazirabad was another story. Although Timur, Jahan Khan and their women made it across the cold, deep, and swift-flowing Chenab, many soldiers were caught east of the river when thousands of Maratha and Sikh soldiers, and Adina and his troops pounced on the fleeing Afghan army. To the attackers' delight, the treasure Timur had accumulated in Lahore still lay on the river's eastern bank.

Many of the trapped soldiers (Afghan, Uzbek, Qizlbashi and others) were slain and the rest dragooned into the victors' armies. Transporting the seized booty to Lahore took several convoys. Afghans allowed to live were driven back in bonds by Sikh soldiers and brought to Amritsar where with blows and whips they were made to remove the rubbish that Jahan Khan's troops had dumped into the Sikhs' holy tank.

Though the claim that their standard was raised on the walls of Attock on the Indus's eastern shore has been disputed,[9] the Marathas, led by Raghunath Rao and aided by the Sikhs and by Adina, had pushed the Afghans out of India. However, Raghunath Rao did not pursue the Afghans beyond the Chenab. He returned to Lahore, as did Adina.

Asked by the Marathas to produce the sum of money he had promised, Adina asked for time. The enraged Marathas looted his camp. Quietly submitting, Adina arranged, on 12 April 1758, a grand celebration of Maratha triumph, spending a lakh of rupees on a magnificent platform in the Shalimar Gardens for Raghunath Rao to sit on. All of Lahore was illuminated, and rose-water flowed in the Shalimar's fountains.

A placated Raghunath Rao conferred the title of nawab on Adina, leased the province to him for seventy-five lakh rupees a year, and left. The Marathas were not inclined to remain in Punjab or rule it directly. The province was too close to potential attackers from the northwest and too far from their Poona capital. Moreover, the Sikhs had already started harassing them.

Governing Punjab and Sirhind, raising revenue and coping with the Sikhs was left to Adina. Aware that Abdali would want to avenge the treachery, Adina chose not to function from Lahore, Kabul's classical target. Appointing his son-in-law Mirza in charge there, with Mirza's brother Said as deputy, Adina fixed Batala as his own headquarters, while giving responsibility for Sirhind to an old associate, Sadiq Beg Khan. With Mirza declaring that he did not want the Mughlani Begum's sticky presence in Lahore, she was asked to accompany Adina to Batala in the Bari doab, close to Adinanagar.

■

After years spent in 'toil, danger and anxiety',[10] the Arain who knew when to be bold and when to submit had realized his dream. 'The Sikhs he [had] amused, the Delhi Court he despised, the Afghans he bewildered, and the Marathas he effectually influenced in his favour to break the power of both the Sikhs and the Afghans and to obtain his own independence.'[11]

All of Punjab, from the Indus to the Jamuna, was now his to govern without serious hindrance, for Delhi was hopelessly weak, the Afghans had gone, and his Maratha suzerains lived too far away to give trouble. As for the Punjabis, whether Muslim, Hindu or Sikh, they had known of Adina for about twenty years. His 'vigour, discipline and good government' had made him popular with a peasantry milked by invasions, clashes and depredations.[12]

The viceroy's ability to collect the seventy-five lakhs for the Marathas depended on the well-being of peasants and merchants who had not felt safe for years. Security would return to Punjab if the Sikhs ceased their attacks. Adina tried to win the cooperation of the Sikhs, among whom he had influential friends.[13] In the end, he 'advised the Sikhs to cease their lawless activities. But they defied him, so he decided to subdue them'.[14]

Allies turning on one another has been a staple of our story. It happened again in the summer of 1758 as Adina sought to suppress defiant Sikh groups who had fought at his side only a few weeks earlier. Initially possessing an army of 10,000 horse and foot, Adina mobilized fresh support from chiefs and zamindars in every doab and territory. His backers included Gakhar, Janjua and Gheba chiefs from the Sindh Sagar doab; Chaudhry Rahmat Khan Waraich from the Chej doab; Raja Ranjit Dev of Jammu; several zamindars from the Rachna doab; many chiefs from the Bari doab, including a Sikh zamindar, Nihan Singh Randhawa; and chiefs and merchants from Adina's own Jullundur doab.

This fighting force quickly assembled by Adina was unprecedented in at least two ways. It was, for one thing, a native or Punjabi force, very different from the outsider armies—Afghan, Mughal, Maratha or whatever—whose weight Punjab had borne for decades. Second, it was a force drawn from a variety of castes, tribes, regions and religions. No one before Adina had put together such a composite army.

Adina's enemy, which too sought control over Punjab, was also native to the region. In fact, as we have marked earlier, the Sikhs inspired by Guru Gobind Singh comprised the first substantial Punjabi force seen in centuries. Half a century after the Guru's death, new generations of recruits were providing numbers and skills to a dozen or so autonomous Sikh 'armies' dominating different parts of Punjab, each with its own chief.

While Adina's force had behind it the authority of the state, the Sikh rebels felt bolstered by two inner convictions, one religio-political and the other psychological. Believing that the Khalsa was destined to rule, the Sikhs also felt they had deep scores to settle. In the Punjab of the late 1750s, order or authority thus stood on one side and passion on the other. However, the Maratha empire, which had given Adina authority, wholly lacked, among

Punjabis, the prestige the Mughals had enjoyed half a century earlier. If anything, the viceroy's personal prestige was larger than that of the new empire. Despite the broad support he had mobilized, Adina lost the first round. A 'strong body of Sikhs' surprised him by showing up close to Adinanagar. The viceroy sent his diwan, a Hindu named Hira Mal, and another influential Hindu, Guru Aqil Das of Jandiala, to deal with them. However, in a fierce battle fought near the town of Qadian, Hira Mal was slain, his troops fled, and his baggage was seized by the Sikhs. The defeat occurred even though a few prominent Sikhs had fought alongside Hira Mal.[15]

The records state that Adina was 'chagrined' at the defeat and death of his diwan. His subsequent acts show that he became vengeful as well. Ordering village and clan chiefs to join his forces, the viceroy also 'made them take an oath that they would attack the Sikhs and drive them away' and that any Sikh found would be captured or killed.[16] Going by what a contemporary Batala-based historian named Ahmad Shah wrote, Adina made headway:

> All Punjab zamindars submitted to [Adina] and started devising plans for rooting out the Sikhs. Of all the zamindars of Punjab, the Randhawas showed the greatest readiness in destroying [the rebels]... The Sikhs were very much perturbed and relaxed their activities. Some fled away and hid themselves.[17]

Since rebels were hiding in the jungles, one of Adina's trusted nobles, Mirza Aziz Baksh, was tasked with cutting down trees and given 'one thousand carpenters with steel hatchets and axes' for the purpose.[18] Ahmad Shah, the Batala historian, adds however that 'a body of Sikhs, bolder than the rest, showed the greatest gallantry', proceeded to Amritsar to protect Sikh sites there, and took shelter in the Ram Rauni mud fort, where ten years earlier another Sikh band had displayed bitter resistance.

In the end, Mirza Aziz was able to take the fort, but not before many in his force fell to the matchlocks and arrows of the intrepid Sikhs, a few of whom stormed out on foot or horseback to attack Adina's multitudes. Some of the Ram Rauni Sikhs escaped but most were captured or killed.

Other Sikh rebels fled towards the Malwa region, as they called it, which overlapped with the sarkar of Sirhind. There Sadiq Beg Khan was ready for them with his guns, and though the Sikhs again surprised government troops with daring counter-attacks, they eventually had to run and hide when they did not fall.

Adina kept Muslim, Hindu and Sikh chiefs contented. Men like Ranjit Dev of Jammu, Ghamand Chand, chief of the Kangra hill state, Barbhag Singh of Kartarpur, and Rai Ibrahim of Kapurthala became his 'great allies'.[19] He cut his army's costs by rotating his soldiers every six months. Ingenious as well as zealous in collecting revenue, he fined a Jullundur qazi who had been caught with a heap of ground poppy thirty thousand rupees for 'violating the Qur'anic injunction' against intoxicants.[20]

In the middle of the summer of 1758, Adina seemed poised to give Punjab what it had long lacked, a native-led administration which understood the needs of peasants and traders. However, two 'acts of God' intervened. First, rains due in July and August failed completely and a severe famine hit Punjab. The price of wheat rose sharply.

Adina's impulsive response was a blunder. Wishing to starve out the Sikhs of the Manjha (the central Punjab area around Lahore, Amritsar and Batala), he prevented the import of wheat from Malwa, a ban that hurt Manjha's Muslims, Hindus and Sikhs alike, apart from hardening Sikh opposition. The poor were 'hit... extremely hard and they left their homes migrating in all directions'. Recording this history in the early 1860s, Aliuddin, a writer in British employ in Lahore, would add the comment, 'With the will of God the Sikhs grew stronger daily.'[21]

Then, secondly, Adina himself suddenly fell ill. 'Colic' is how the illness was described. Within days, on 15 September, he died in Batala. It is unlikely that he was more than fifty years old. In accordance with his will, Adina was buried in Khanpur, near Hoshiarpur, in the part of Punjab he was attached to and where he had lived the longest, the Jullundur doab.

An autonomous government of Punjab, led by a native Muslim but interested, it would seem, in the well-being of all its residents, had ended after less than five months. Perhaps it would have ended even if Adina had lived on, for an outraged Shah Abdali was pacing across the Indus and the Khyber, waiting for a ripe moment to avenge the humiliation Adina had helped inflict on his son.

Another humiliation, nursed elsewhere, was avenged soon after Adina's death. 'The Sikhs, out of revenge for the Khan's recent harshness to them, dug out his grave and burnt his dead body.'[22] However, the Marathas named Adina's widow as the Doab's governor.

As for Mughlani Begum, after Adina's death she found shelter in Jammu city, the capital of Raja Ranjit Dev's principality. Two years later, when Abdali again invaded India, he bestowed on her the revenues of the sarkar of Sialkot, but a year thereafter, in 1761, she invited ignominy by marrying Shahbaz, one of her eunuch servants.

This bold and scandal-scarred peeress of the Mughal empire would die in poverty in Jammu in 1779. The powerless Mughal nobles who scorned her did not in her case 'separate private life from public life, though regarding themselves they sedulously maintained this distinction'. Evidently a woman did not merit the exoneration the men readily gave to themselves.[23]

■

When Adina died in Punjab, a king—an emperor to be exact—still sat on the Delhi throne. But the empire of Alamgir II was shrunken, decrepit and toothless. True, Najib, the Rohilla chief—to Abdali a fellow-Pashtun—was his important ally, and Intizam, the grand wazir, was loyal to him, but Imad-ul-Mulk, the wazir humiliated by Abdali, was not. More influential at this juncture than the emperor, Imad was in cahoots with the new power, the Marathas, and had invited them to run Delhi.

In the spring of 1759, a year after the Marathas, Sikhs and Adina had pushed Timur and Jahan Khan out of Punjab, Alamgir II wrote to Abdali:

> Imad-ul-Mulk is thinking of killing me. If Your Majesty comes to this side, I may be saved from this tyrant, otherwise there is no possibility of safety either of me or of my sons.[24]

Throwing his weight behind the invitation, the Rohilla chief, Najib (who had been expelled from Delhi by the Marathas), secured written endorsements from several Muslim religious leaders and nobles and forwarded them to Abdali, who replied that he would 'come to India in [the] winter and do what was due [for] Islam'.[25] True to his word, and accompanied by 'enormous hordes', Abdali arrived in Lahore in October 1759. On their approach, such Marathas as had stayed on 'fled from Punjab without striking a blow',[26] while the man holding charge in Lahore, Khwaja Mirza Khan (Adina's son-in-law), submitted to the Afghan king.

In Delhi, however, Imad acted. Murdering both the emperor and the grand wazir, he placed another prince on the throne, titling him Shah Jahan III, and urged the Marathas to resist and repulse the Afghans. The stage was set for 'India', represented by Imad (Shah Jahan III was a puppet in his hands) and above all the Marathas, to fight the Afghan ruler, Abdali.

The people and chiefs of Punjab, whether Muslim, Sikh or Hindu, largely sat out the year-long contest between the Marathas and the Afghans that followed, which was carried out in forts and fields to the north of Delhi and thus very far from either side's 'home'—Kabul for the Afghans and Poona for the Marathas. Efforts to prevent river-crossings, cut off escape routes and deny water, fodder and supplies to the enemy culminated in a huge and gory battle fought in Panipat in Sirhind sarkar on 14 January 1761. It was won by Abdali's forces.

Apart from superior numbers, the Marathas possessed modern artillery supplied by the French who continued to compete in the subcontinent against the British. But Maratha generals did not know the north Indian terrain as well as Abdali and his ally Najib did. Moreover, Maratha mobility was impeded by the presence in their camp of innumerable family members of both sexes and also of pilgrims wishing to see north India's holy places in the protective company of soldiers.

To everyone's surprise, Abdali won over the support of Shuja, the Shiite noble who controlled Awadh. In contrast, the Marathas failed to enlist the support either of Rajasthan's chiefs or of the Hindu Jats around Delhi, although for a few days one Sikh leader, Ala Singh, like most Sikh chiefs a Jat, procured food and fodder for the Marathas. But that was an exception. Abdali's logistical stranglehold was such that, in the climactic battle of 14 January, Maratha soldiers and horses struggled on empty stomachs.

Along with many thousands of soldiers, Vishwas Rao, the son of the Marathas' Peshwa, and the thirty-year-old Maratha general, Sadashiv Rao, were slain that day. Evidently the Peshwa had hoped that a victorious Vishwas Rao would sit on the Mughal throne. Instead Abdali saw to it that Shah Alam II (son of Alamgir II), whose sister had been married four years earlier to Abdali's son Timur, replaced Imad's puppet Shah Jahan II as the Mughal emperor. Imad fled,* as did several Maratha chiefs.

The day after his great victory, Abdali visited the tomb in Panipat of the thirteenth-century Sufi saint, Bu Ali Qalandar, and offered thanks to God. His troops were allowed two months' free time in Delhi, where, yet again, the nobles were plundered and the people squeezed. On their journey back to Kabul, which commenced on 22 March 1761, Abdali's troops, loaded with plunder and booty, were once more molested by groups of Sikhs who followed Abdali 'all the way'.[27] During the Panipat battle, the Sikhs had been

---

*Later Abdali pardoned him.

perfectly content 'to watch the Afghans and Marathas destroy one another's hopes of dominance'.[28] But Abdali's prestige had soared.

■

Two days after Panipat, the British—rulers of Bengal from 1757—defeated the French in a crucial encounter at India's southern end. Three years later, in another critical battle at Buxar in eastern India, Bengal-based British forces defeated a combination of Mughal nobles backed by Shah Alam II. One consequence of this 1764 event was that the East India Company successfully claimed the revenues of Bihar and Orissa as well. Another consequence was that the autonomous territory, west of Bihar, of Awadh, in earlier times a Mughal province, consented to British 'protection'.

The Company was moving westward. Delhi too was now in its sights though not in its hands. The Company 'recognized' Shah Alam II as India's 'emperor' but he was only a title-holder without resources. The Marathas, still the leading Indian power despite their Panipat defeat, also recognized Shah Alam II and hoped to use him. Since Abdali seemed unwilling to occupy Delhi, it appeared that before long either the British or the Marathas would control that capital.

■

Punjab was another matter. It seemed distant to both the British and the Marathas. To Punjab's Muslim landlords and chiefs, it was a home where they hoped to survive. To the Sikhs, it was a home they wished to rule. To Abdali, it was a place where his son and officers had been humiliated but also a territory that he, and before him Nadir Shah, had annexed.

Abdali left behind officers to rule in Punjab: Khwaja Mirza Khan to run the Char Mahal area west and north of Lahore; Khwaja Abed Khan in charge of Lahore; Saadat Khan and Sadiq Khan in the Jullundur doab; and Zain Khan in Sirhind.

Once Abdali returned to Kabul, these deputies were swiftly dealt with by the Sikhs. A large Sikh force confronted and killed Khwaja Mirza Khan on the eastern bank of the Chenab. We do not know what happened to his wife, Adina's daughter. The Jullundur doab too was overrun by the Sikhs, and in Sirhind both Zain Khan and the Pashtun ruler of Malerkotla were pinned down.

Nuruddin, a Jammu-based Afghan general ordered by Abdali to subdue the Sikhs, was driven back at Sialkot by Sikh soldiers led by Charhat Singh

Sukerchakia. In reply, Khwaja Abed Khan, Abdali's governor in Lahore, tried to besiege Sukerchakia's base in Gujranwala—south of Sialkot and north of Lahore—but the bid misfired. Other Sikh forces—soon to be called misls or missals (from the Persian for 'alike'), each under an independent chief and usually comprising the chief's kinsmen—rallied to Sukerchakia's support, including by attacking Afghan officers wherever found.

A fleeing Abed Khan was pursued by Sikh contingents led by the Ahluwalia misl into Lahore, where he was killed. Lieutenants of Jassa Singh Ahluwalia, chief of the Ahluwalia misl, announced their leader as Punjab's new king. Seizing the royal mint, they then struck, so the report goes, 'the first Sikh rupee' in the name of Jassa Singh. Minted in November 1761, the coin, which honoured a misl chief rather than a Guru, was however quickly withdrawn.[29]

Word of Afghan reverses and of the coin the Sikhs had struck elicited a silent, swift and sudden Abdali invasion. Bringing a large yet lightly equipped army, he quickly crossed four of Punjab's rivers in the winter of 1761-62 and arrived as far as Jandiala, east of Amritsar, where, he had been told, a large body of Sikh soldiers had surrounded his Hindu ally, Aqil Das.

Learning at Jandiala that this Sikh army had retired, south of the Sutlej, into the Sirhind area, Abdali marched in pursuit at unprecedented speed, covering 120 miles inclusive of two river-crossings in less than forty-eight hours. Accompanied by family members and loads of baggage, the Sikh army lay encamped at village Kup, seven miles north of Malerkotla, when, as dawn broke on 5 February 1762, Abdali showed up, taking the Sikhs by surprise. The height of winter was not the customary time for an Afghan invasion.

Facing an unexpected attack on their forces and also on families and supplies, misl chiefs Jassa Singh Ahluwalia and Charhat Singh Sukerchakia, both present at Kup, instructed their soldiers to form circles around the families and retreat but also fight, even as Abdali ordered his army to cut off the Sikh soldiers from their families and baggage. It was a hopeless task for the Sikhs, yet many in Abdali's army were slain. A much greater number of Sikhs were killed in what has entered Sikh history as the *Wadda Ghallughara* (Great Carnage). Figures vary from 8,000 to 30,000 Sikh dead.

When, at the end of a gruelling day of killing-and-running, the rival armies reached a river, both sides dropped weapons and quenched their thirst. Thereafter the Sikhs galloped off, first to Barnala, twenty-five miles southwest of Malerkotla, and then into a desert, where Abdali called off the chase.

Ala Singh was the Sikh chief of Patiala, the territory where Abdali had ended up. A year earlier, at Panipat, Ala Singh, who belonged to the Phulkian misl, had procured food and fodder for the Maratha army. Ordered now to submit to Abdali, the Sikh chief procrastinated, whereupon he was seized and imprisoned. An angry Abdali wanted Ala Singh to 'rid himself of the most visible symbol of Sikhism by getting himself clean-shaved', but the Afghan king's first minister, Wali Khan, successfully intervened and a large tribute was deemed sufficient punishment for Ala Singh's vacillation.[30]

On the way back to Lahore, Abdali instructed the destruction and desecration of the Sikh shrine in Amritsar. Wali Khan 'pleaded against the move' but Najib, Abdali's Rohilla ally, supported it.[31] In acts the Sikhs would not forget, the temple was blown up with gunpowder and the sacred tank desecrated with the flesh and blood of cows. Cart-loads of Sikh heads were brought from Kup to be displayed on the gates of Lahore, which was back under Afghan control.

Abdali stayed on for nine months in Punjab, attempting to subdue the Sikhs. To this end, officers and soldiers were 'despatched in every direction' but they 'came back defeated'. While emboldened Sikhs committed 'depredations [in] the very suburbs of Lahore', Afghan forays in pursuit of Sikh rebels destroyed villages in several parts of Punjab, alienating Muslim peasants as well.[32] Journeying at this time from Sirhind to Sialkot, Miskin (now a staffer for Zain Khan, the Afghan in charge of Sirhind) saw that 'dearness of flour prevailed everywhere'.[33]

Raja Ranjit Dev of Jammu was one of the Hindu allies enlisted by Abdali at this time. With Dev's prodding and help, Abdali ousted Sukhjiwan Mal, the capable Kashmir governor he himself had installed a decade earlier. Apart from failing to cough up the revenues desired by Abdali, Sukhjiwan Mal had also moved closer than Abdali liked to the Delhi emperor, Shah Alam II. His resistance overcome, Sukhjiwan Mal was captured, blinded, and 'trampled down by horses to death'.[34] Nuruddin, one of Abdali's generals, replaced Sukhjiwan Mal as the Kashmir governor.

Before leaving for Kabul in December 1762, Abdali made another Hindu, Kabuli Mal, his Lahore governor, a gesture aimed at placating the Sikhs. But Sikh fighters on horseback harassed Abdali right until the moment when, with his army, he crossed the Ravi to return to his country.

As the bulk of the Afghan army crossed over to the opposite bank, the Sikhs emptied their matchlocks in the direction of Abdali, who, seated on his horse, was still on the Lahore side of the Ravi. For some minutes a motionless Abdali acknowledged the Sikhs' boldness. Then he suddenly counter-attacked with his swordsmen and scattered the Sikhs before crossing the Ravi with seeming casualness.[35] If carnage and brutality marked the Abdali/Sikh confrontation, so did guts, on both sides.

■

Abdali's departure was the signal for bids by Sikh misls to possess as much as possible of Punjab, including Lahore, and to rebuild Amritsar and its temple. In Sirhind, Zain Khan was attacked and killed. (Ala Singh, however, managed to buy the ruins of Sirhind for ₹25,000.) Malerkotla, next to Sirhind, was sacked and its chief, Hingan Khan, slain. East of Sirhind and across the Jamuna, Najib's Rohilla tracts were raided.

In Lahore, Kabuli Mal, the governor, was told to hand over all the city's butchers to Sikh soldiers who were ready to execute the 'cow-killers'. Though Kabuli Mal evaded the demand, he had to cut off the noses and ears of some of the butchers.

Advancing north from his Gujranwala base, Charhat Singh Sukerchakia, who led the Sukerchakia misl, 'devastated the country as far as Jhelum, and took possession of the fort of Rohtas'.[36] Even Multan, thus far a safe Afghan province, was plundered by a Sikh raid in 1764.[37]

By the late 1760s, a dozen or so different Sikh misls had between them taken over much of Punjab. The leader of a misl controlling a large or small territory was in effect the territory's ruler. In addition to the three misls already named—the Ahluwalia, Phulkian and Sukerchakia—there were four others of some prominence, the Bhangi, Kanhiya, Ramgarhia and Nakkai.

For several years the most influential misl was that of the Bhangis, who acquired their name from the intoxicant bhang many in the misl consumed. Both Lahore and Amritsar came under Bhangi control, as also portions of western Punjab. While the Nakkais held territory south of Lahore, the eventual conquerors, the Sukerchakias, started off with only the town of Gujranwala, north of Lahore, in their possession. The Ahluwalias dominated spaces between the Ravi and the Beas. East of the Beas, and up to the Himalayan foothills, the Kanhiyas and the Ramgarhias were strong; the Phulkians controlled Malwa (Sirhind).

In each territory, the dominant misl levied a rakhi (protection tax) on Sikh and non-Sikh peasants. On occasion two misls combined to rule an area; at times several misls together formed a dal khalsa to launch an attack on an Afghan post.

■

Provoked by Sikh blows to the prestige won by him at Panipat, Abdali invaded Punjab four more times—in 1764-65, 1766-67, 1767-68, and 1769-70—before he died in Afghanistan's Suleiman mountains in April 1772. While the Sikh misls survived these attacks, Abdali managed to preserve his hold (mostly through vassals) in Kashmir and some other pockets in the Himalayan hills, and also in Multan and Sirhind.

Thanks to an accompanying writer's eyewitness account (offered in Persian), we have details of the 1764-65 invasion, in which Abdali was joined by Nasir Khan, the Baluch chief. Nur Muhammad, the writer, is an admirer of both Abdali and Nasir Khan, and a critic of what he and his chiefs saw as the Sikhs' unwillingness to 'fight a regular battle' or 'face men in the field', to use Nasir Khan's words quoted by Nur Muhammad. 'They come like thieves to fight', Nasir Khan seems to have added.

Annoyance at the Sikhs' refusal to directly confront an organized army is accompanied however by pictures Nur Muhammad paints of daring from both sides in unexpected encounters, and of Sikh tactics. He describes a battle in the Jullundur doab:

> The Sikhs fought as they had done the previous day... They came roaring like a lion and went away slyly like a fox. They came, discharged their guns from a distance and held back. They did not flee but delayed fighting. When the Shah marched, [the Sikhs] constantly followed the Afghan troops, and when the Durrani halted they fought with him.[38]

Calling the Sikhs 'cunning' and 'crafty', Nur Muhammad also speaks of at least one occasion when the Sikh soldiers organized themselves 'into a regular battle array', with one Sikh general 'fearlessly standing like a mountain' and another 'who looked like a lion in stature'.[39]

After reaching Sirhind and Karnal, the Afghan and Baluch armies turned back. In Sirhind, which Abdali found in ruins, his ally Ala Singh of the Phulkian misl claimed that he had tried to prevent Sikhs from destroying the city. The Patiala chief brought gifts for Abdali and promised to repopulate Sirhind.

Giving Ala Singh the title of raja—thus making him the first Sikh to be called a prince or king—Abdali, who hoped to divide the Sikhs, also announced Ala Singh as his Sirhind governor. In 1765, 'Ala Singh was probably the most powerful of the Sikh chiefs not only of the cis-Sutlej region...also of the Punjab proper'.[40]

As soon as Abdali's back was turned, Sikh forces re-entered Lahore and ousted his governor, Kabuli Mal. Two Bhangi chiefs and a Kanhiya divided up the city and its revenues between them, Lehna Singh controlling the fort and the walled city, Sobha Singh (of the Kanhiyas) ruling areas south of the walled city, and Gujjar Singh taking over the lands between the Fort and the Ravi.

To mark the Sikh occupation of Lahore in the summer of 1765, a coin in the name of the Gurus was struck. Prominent Hindus pleaded with the Sikh trio not to tyrannize Lahore's Muslims. The appeal worked, and the city's Muslims felt thankful for 'a kind senior person' called Nathoo Shah.[41] Apparently 'most of the upper-caste Hindus stood by the Muslims' at this time.[42]

When, eighteen months later, Abdali again invaded Punjab, he invited the Sikh chiefs of Lahore to become his subordinates. The offer was spurned. Avoiding a direct battle, the Sikhs once more inflicted damage through surprise attacks. But Lahore's Sikh rulers moved out of the city, which Abdali entered in December 1766.

Urged by Lahore's leading citizens, Muslim and non-Muslim, to reinstate the 'just and liberal' Lehna Singh as his viceroy, Abdali offered the post to the Sikh chief, but Lehna Singh declined. Stating that to serve the Afghan king would lower him in the estimation of the Sikhs, he also returned a basket of Kabul's dry fruit that Abdali had sent him. Making a present of his own to the king, a sack of inferior grain, Lehna Singh explained that while dry fruit was the food of kings, the grain he was sending was what 'a poor zamindar' like him lived on.[43]

On this expedition, Abdali again visited Sirhind, where, Ala Singh having died, the Afghan named Amar Singh, the late chief's grandson, to succeed his grandfather. As the new governor, Amar Singh issued coins in Abdali's name. But it was obvious to Abdali that Punjab as a whole had slipped from his control, and that the Sikhs would run most of it, including Lahore, the moment he left.

Except for brief Afghan interludes, the Sikhs indeed controlled Lahore for the rest of the century and beyond, but Lahore's economy had taken a beating and its rich suburbs were depopulated. Many if not most well-off Muslims and Hindus moved out, the former to diverse locations, the latter mainly to Jammu.[44] Evidently the Sikh chiefs stored arms and ammunition in the Badshahi Mosque. It would also be alleged that they used the Mosque as a stable.[45]

■

Why was the Punjab vacuum filled by Sikh misls and not by Punjabi Muslims, who comprised the majority? For one thing, the misls were aided by the suffering from Afghan attacks of the Punjab peasantry, whether Muslim, Sikh or Hindu. Of the steep slide in living conditions from the 1730s to the 1770s, a future district officer would write:

> There was no authority to maintain peace or order. It was devastated again and again by the invading armies of Nadir Shah and Ahmed Shah Abdali and the prosperity which had been slowly built up in the previous two centuries gave place... to desolation and misery... Tribe fought against tribe, village against village; all but the strongest positions were abandoned, homesteads were deserted, and the face of the country became a wilderness. Every village was sacked, burned or deserted, the continuity of village life was broken. Old owners fled for safety to the jungles or to fortified towns, in some cases disappearing forever.[46]

Here the Gujranwala tract, north of Lahore and south of the Chenab, was being spoken of, but other parts of Punjab offered similar scenes. Squeezed dry by Abdali's raids across Punjab and his battles with the Sikhs—realizing, as a popular saying went, that 'only what was held in the mouth and hands was theirs, everything else belonged to Abdali'[47]—Punjabi villagers welcomed the Afghans' foes.

When, in the opening chapter, we looked at the devastating Mongol attacks during the Sultanate, it was suggested that Punjab's non-Muslims may have formed a positive view of Muslims and Islam because some Sultans had resisted the invaders. Muslim peasants and menials in eighteenth century Punjab were similarly appreciative of the Sikhs' resistance to Nadir Shah and Abdali.

Secondly, Punjab's Muslim chiefs offered the Sikh misls no competition or challenge. Contrasting histories marked these two sets of chiefs. While a majority of the Sikh misls were led by warriors from the countryside—men like Jassa Singh Ahluwalia, Gujjar Singh Bhangi and Charhat Singh Sukerchakia who enlarged their territories through successful attacks on Afghan positions— many of Punjab's Muslim chiefs had secured their estates not via the battlefield but by taking opportunities offered within the Mughal framework.

That structure was now dying or dead but Punjab's leading Muslims, more interested in survival than in control, showed no urge to salvage it or to create an alternative. Earlier, while many Muslim Punjabis relied on the Mughals, the gory Aurangzeb–Dara battle that Lahore witnessed had disillusioned them, and they found Aurangzeb's victory troubling. The puritanical and intolerant features of his rule, and his neglect of Lahore, undermined their loyalty to the Mughals.

His successor, Shah Alam, was liked in Lahore where he died, but the violent struggle for succession on his death did nothing to reassure Muslim Punjabis, who felt they had been left without an anchor or umbrella. When the empire collapsed, Muslim Punjabis had no time to mourn or welcome its end; they had to deal with the Afghans and the Sikhs.

The Punjab of this period was not witnessing a contest between Muslims and non-Muslims. Only a few years earlier, Adina had put together a composite force. Even in the 1760s and 1770s, almost all the Sikh misls contained a few significant Muslim leaders. Some misls encouraged the building of mosques in their territories while prohibiting the public call for prayer and in some instances putting to death butchers who killed cows.

But the misls possessed a drive not noticeable among Punjab's Muslim notables, whose ranks included guardians of estates containing the tombs of early Sufi teachers—sajjada nashins, as they were called. Many of these guardians were descendants of famed Sufis. A Mughal or Sultanate umbrella had sheltered their estates in the past, lending the custodians wealth and prestige, which survived in most cases. But none of them seemed interested in political power.

Sufi descendants apart, several hardy Muslim clans inhabited Punjab at this time. The Gakhars, Janjuas and Ghebas of the hills around Rawalpindi and Jhelum, and the Awans, Bhattis, Kharrals, Chathas, Cheemas and Waraiches of the plains, were some of these Punjabi clans, each with one or more chiefs. Long-settled Pashtun or Baluch chiefs controlled other pockets of Punjab.

While we do not know a great deal individually about Punjab's Muslim chiefs of this period, evidence that any of them wished to shape Punjab's future is hard to find. Some of Punjab's Muslim groups and the Pashtuns of Kasur and Multan fought defensive battles for local control, but never to take over large chunks of Punjab. Tenacious, tough and independent-minded as they often were, they did not covet the seat of power in Lahore.

By contrast, the Sikhs aimed for Lahore right from Banda's time. Like their historical foes—the Mughals—these Sikhs believed that they were meant to rule over a large territory. Reflected in the seals and coins of Banda Bahadur (issued in 1711) and Jassa Singh Ahluwalia (1761), such a belief could, in hindsight, also be read in the flag (*Nishan Sahib*), which was raised at every gurdwara from the 1620s, when Guru Hargobind led the community. The flag featured a double-edged sword surrounded by a pair of single-edged swords (kirpans). In this image some could see the hint of a future state, even though Guru Gobind Singh said that 'Sword' was a synonym for God. Other regal symbols present in the courts of some of the Gurus, e.g. the fly-whisk and the canopy, also encouraged a belief in the Sikhs' destiny to rule. Having faith in their destiny, fighting prowess, and right to rule, and possessing also the traits of dash and opportunism, the Sikhs in eighteenth-century Punjab foreshadowed in some respects the British imperialists of the eighteenth and nineteenth centuries.

While a steadily-nursed religio-political conviction about Khalsa Raj, and a psychological yearning for revenge, motivated the Sikhs, Punjab's Muslim chiefs, who had accepted the Mughals, possessed no comparable impetus.

> Racially the 'Punjabi Muslim' and the 'Punjabi Sikh' were the same people, the Sikhs belonging to one of the farming castes, the Jats, to which many 'Punjabi Muslims' belonged. But… the 'Punjabi Muslim' suffered from no religious oppression. Thus the Sikhs who were as plainly Punjabi as the Punjabi Muslims became remarkably militant while the Punjabi Muslim remained placidly submerged in his… routine life.[48]

In 1739, Mukarrab Khan, the Gakhar chief, sided with Nadir Shah in the Persian's victorious battle with the Mughals in Karnal, just to the north of Delhi, thereby winning the title of nawab from Nadir Shah. Mukarrab Khan then defeated Pashtun rivals of Yusufzai and Khattak stock to the west of the Gakhar country and Punjabi rivals (Chibs) to his east, captured the city of Gujrat, and became master of the northern tracts between the Chenab and the Indus, with the Jhelum in between.[49]

Despite a record like this, and despite the fact that Afghans and Sikhs were fighting one another, Mukarrab Khan did not try to carve out a Gakhar-controlled kingdom in Punjab. On the other hand, Gujjar Singh of the Bhangi misl, which had its base in Amritsar, not only entered Lahore in 1765, and, along with Lehna Singh and Sobha Singh, ruled that capital; later that year he forayed from Lahore into Gujrat and ousted Mukarrab Khan from his own Gakhar base.

While a Gakhar chief who in 1739 had journeyed a long distance to fight seemed content, in the 1760s, to remain in his corner (perhaps he felt old), Gujjar Singh had the audacity to unseat Mukarrab Khan in unfamiliar tracts remote from his home. Gujjar Singh went on to seize also the territory in the Chej doab of Rahmat Khan Waraich, an ally, earlier, of Adina's.

The Sikhs' drive for power was sharpened by religion. Muslim groups too were capable of invoking religious zeal, but there was a significant difference. While his religion reached the Sikh peasant in his own language, inviting an unreserved embrace, this was not necessarily the case with the Muslim peasant, who was also Punjabi-speaking but who usually received his Islam in Arabic.

The Punjabi psyche had always privileged survival. This psyche was practical, yet also skeptical. Punjabis smiled at misfortune but did not expect great dreams to be fulfilled. In the eighteenth century, the Sikh Punjabi broke free of this psychological trait while his Muslim fellow-Punjabi did not.

Then there was the skills' advantage—in riding horses, for one thing—and also, more importantly, the alliance advantage. Gujjar Singh's success in the Gakhar territory was aided by a strong input from the Sukerchakia misl of Charhat Singh, which had its headquarters in Gujranwala. Acting in concert, the Sikhs captured the crucial Rohtas fort. Their alliance was then cemented by the marriage of Charhat Singh's daughter with Gujjar Singh's son.

Though in the future they would fight one another, for the time being Sikhs across Punjab had found a common purpose. They felt they were a single people. On the other hand, Muslims across Punjab saw themselves as belonging to a clan, tribe, locality or landlord, not to one another.

We have no evidence of attempts for an alliance between, say, Mukarrab Khan and Rahmat Khan Waraich (a Jat), or between Mukarrab Khan and Rai Ibrahim, the Bhatti Rajput ruler of Kapurthala in the Jullundur doab, a powerful chief who in the 1750s had cooperated fruitfully with Adina Beg Khan, as had Rahmat Khan Waraich. It was not until the mid-1770s that Ibrahim Khan was ousted from Kapurthala by Jassa Singh Ahluwalia of the Ahluwalia misl. We cannot tell whether a Gakhar-Waraich, Gakhar-Bhatti or Waraich-Bhatti alliance was feasible in the 1760s. All we know is that no league of Muslim chiefs emerged at this time.

Even within a smaller area, e.g. the Jhelum region, 'local [Muslim] tribes such as Gakhars, Janjuas, Gujjars, Jats and Khokhars', some containing horsemen every bit as skilled as the Sikhs, 'never united to prevent the Sikhs' uprising'.[50]

Let us cast a look at four other Muslim-run principalities of this period: Multan and Bahawalpur in lower Punjab; Kasur, which lay to Lahore's south in the Bari doab; and Jhang in the Rachna doab.

In Multan, there had been no warfare for two hundred years, from 1548 to 1748. Peace helping commerce, Multan city again served as an emporium for trade between Hindustan and Persia, recalling much earlier times. After 1752, following Abdali's invasion, Multan was absorbed into Afghanistan's sphere of influence and lost some of its stability. Functioning either as a province of Kabul or ruled by Pashtuns who acknowledged Kabul's suzerainty, it also yielded to the Bhangi misl for short spells. From 1779, Multan was ruled by Nawab Muzaffar Khan, a Pashtun from the Sadozai clan to which Abdali also belonged.

The large tract of Bahawalpur, south of Multan and extending east of the Sutlej towards Rajasthan, was in the hands of autonomous chiefs descending, it appears, from Arabs who had travelled centuries earlier to Sindh and thence to Punjab. These Bahawalpur chiefs—the Daudpotras as they were called—submitted to the Afghans only when the latter showed up in force. At other times in the eighteenth century they functioned as independent rulers. Although the Daudpotras intruded into Multani territory from time to time, thoughts of annexing Multan or expanding northwards did not burden their minds.

Led by Pashtuns settled in the area from the time of Emperor Akbar, Kasur, situated close to Lahore, was strongly fortified. In 1763, it defied for days a combined attack launched by four leading misls before yielding. Taken over by the Bhangi misl, it was however recovered by Nizamuddin Khan in 1794. Though there were (and would be) moments when Kasur challenged Lahore, it lacked allies.

Jhang, lying in the Rachna doab and controlled for decades, if not longer, by Muslim Siyals, was seized in 1772 by Jhanda Singh of the Bhangi misl, but Ahmed Khan Siyal won it back.

Tied to Punjab by origin or their forebears' long domicile, these Muslim chiefs (we have glanced at only a few amongst them) were thus capable of independence, defiance and resilience. What they lacked was what some Sikh chiefs possessed, a strategy for Punjab as a whole.

Also, 'Sikh rural society was far more egalitarian than the Muslim'.[51] Sikh leaders, most of them Jats, profited from the spirit of equality accepted in many of the misls. Such a spirit was generally absent in the more steeply hierarchical military force of a Muslim chief or landlord in Punjab, who was often a Rajput when he was not a Sayyid (claiming kinship to the Prophet), or a Shaikh (suggesting a link to a Sufi teacher), or a Mughal, and only in some cases a Jat, even though Jats were perhaps the largest single community among Punjab's Muslims at this time.

Moreover, Muslim Jats were rarely bunched together the way Sikh Jats were, and the latter were luckier in the quality of their lands, which provided them with sizeable surpluses for fighting.

It was Jat culture, and not Sikhism alone, that had helped produce the Sikh misls' camaraderie, which proved valuable in battle. The Afghans and long-settled Pashtun chiefs like the ones in Kasur also possessed an internal camaraderie, which was drawn from Pashtun culture, but—except when Abdali crossed into Punjab with his host—Afghan numbers were small compared with those of the Sikhs. Moreover, Afghans did not belong to Punjab.

The Sikhs' egalitarian outlook and fight against Abdali's armies appealed also to Punjab's Muslim peasant, even though incidents like the slicing off of butchers' noses and ears did not go down well with him. Like the Sikh, the Punjabi Muslim usually saw an Afghan officer as an outsider and an Afghan raid as a calamity.

Obliged to quit Delhi eastward for Awadh after Abdali sacked the Mughal capital, poets such as Mirza Sauda and Mir Taqi Mir, writing in Persian or Urdu, had sharply criticized the invader.[52] Similar opinions resided in the minds of Punjab's Muslims and were probably expressed in robust Punjabi.

Despite a common adherence to Islam, Punjabi Muslims did not join the Afghans in their battles against the Sikhs. Often they stood non-aligned, even as, during the Panipat battle of 1761, the Sikhs had remained neutral between the Afghans and the Marathas. On occasion, Punjabi Muslims tilted in favour of the Sikhs.

To identify an additional factor, Sufi influence, especially noticeable in the western doabs, and the Sufi teaching that labels were unimportant, may also have contributed to the willingness of Punjab's ordinary Muslims to accept a Sikh misl's rule.[53]

We may conclude in hindsight that, spurred by psychological and religious impulses, the Sikhs successfully captured a current of pro-peasant Punjabi nationalism which they had also helped create. If, perceiving the current, a few Muslim chiefs had together provided an alternative rallying stage for Punjabi nationalism, could they have attracted Sikh and Hindu allies and gone on to fill the vacuum that the Sikh misls eventually filled? We do not know, and the question is purely rhetorical. There is no evidence that after Adina any Muslim chief envisioned a rallying platform, or grasped the potential in an all-Punjab, pro-peasant strategy.

In the end, Sikh success was aided by the unity that seemed to exist among the dozen or so misls of Punjab, at least when confronting the common Afghan foe. Considering that the misl chiefs were all ambitious men who had risen to leadership via raids of plunder—men who saw one another as rivals—their apparent unity was surprising. But with Mughal decline, Punjab's large spaces could accommodate a number of ruling groups. At least for the time being, cooperation among the misls made sense. On the ground, unity was enforced through decisions taken in a general assembly. Such an assembly was held at Amritsar or, when necessary, even on a battlefield, but always in the presence of the Granth Sahib. Its decision was characterized as a gurmatta (literally the Guru's decision) and carrying it out became a Sikh's religious obligation.

Also helpful to the misls was their willingness, for the sake of pragmatism and smoother governance, to end the exclusions marking earlier Sikh history. Descendants or followers of notable dissidents from the Sikh past like Sri Chand and Dhir Mal, as well as the Bedis, Sodhis, Trehans and Bhallas coming down from Guru Nanak, Guru Ram Das, Guru Angad and Guru Amar Das, obtained recognition from misl chiefs.

At the end of the 1760s, therefore, it seemed that, between them, the different misls had begun to give Punjab something like a semblance of government. The thought entered the Punjabi mind that the Mughals' old enemies were close to becoming their successors. The vacuum left by Mughal decay (in Punjab it was Mughal demise) would be filled not by Punjab's Muslim majority but by its Sikh minority.

Far to the south of Punjab, interestingly enough, a father-and-son duo, Haider Ali and Tipu Sultan, minority Muslims in a territory which was overwhelmingly Hindu, would lead Mysore's defiance of impending British rule in the very period, the 1760s to the 1790s, which saw the Sikh rise to power in Punjab.[54]

■

No text gives a better picture of life in Punjab of this period (and preceding periods) than Waris Shah's celebrated *Heer*, composed in 1766. Its story was not Waris's original creation. Punjabis had been reciting it from Akbar's time: they believed that the events unfolding in *Heer* had actually occurred in areas around Jhang during the fifteenth century. Several writers before Waris had presented their versions of the Heer story, including Damodar Das Arora of Jhang. Earlier, Lahore's famed poet, Shah Hussain, had turned to the story for some of his verses.

Like his predecessors, Waris paints northwestern Punjab as the backdrop for the old love story of Heer and Ranjha. He gives us the Chenab, its boats and its boatmen; peasants who farm and men who herd cattle; green grazing grounds and women spinning cotton into yarn; the feudal system, including a clan chief and a daughter ready to outwit or defy the father; mullahs, jogis and sufis; 'vituperative arguments' and 'soliloquies';[55] and more.

It is as a Muslim that Waris portrays the Muslim world to which Heer and her beloved belong. Before starting the story, he offers a 'contemplation' of God Almighty—'Who made love the first principle of creation'—veneration for the Prophet, honour for the Four Companions, and an ode to Baba Farid.[56]

Waris's *Heer* superseded earlier versions because the blunt and earthy Punjabi of his verses was what the peasants spoke; because his 'bait' metre offered the rhythm they loved; and because the love he narrated—the longing for each other in Heer and Ranjha, which Waris likened to the longing for God in each soul—was what, in reality or imagination, they too possessed. The Punjabi peasant or goat-herd might not have known comfort or dignity, but he or she was capable of love, or of imagining it.

In Waris's story, Wahiduddin Ranjha (or Dheedo, as the village called him) was an unmarried, wayward but attractive Jat youth in Takht Hazara, east of the Jhelum, in upper Chej doab. He loved buffaloes and his flute but, despised by his brothers and taunted by their wives—the latter resentful that Dheedo was not falling for them—he left his village and journeyed south. Before long, after crossing the Chenab and entering Jhang, he ran into Heer, the beautiful but arrogant daughter of the chief of the Siyals, who were Jats too but ranked 'higher' than the Ranjha clan to which Dheedo belonged. (Siyals of a later time would claim Rajput descent.)

Smitten by Dheedo, Heer found him a job as a herdsman in her father's fields. When her 'shameful' love for an inferior like Dheedo was discovered, the family quickly arranged a more suitable match for Heer, but unexpected events intervened in her favour, frustrating the opposition of her parents and the views of a qazi, who was brilliantly debated by Heer. Finally, the local king and her parents appeared to permit Heer's marriage with Dheedo.

Happiness was at hand but the fates blasted it. 'The ship sank even as it touched the shore.' Heer was poisoned, whereupon Dheedo too ended his life. Some earlier versions of this story had concluded by sending the young pair to Mecca to live there happily for the rest of their lives, but Waris chose a more realistic if tragic ending.

While the date of Waris's composition is provided in the text, we do not know the year of the author's birth. It seems that he was born around 1720 in Jandiala Sher Khan, near Sheikhupura, northwest of Lahore. The village was inhabited by Muslim peasants and a few Sayyid families. Waris's father was probably a Sayyid.

Like Bulleh Shah, born four decades before him, Waris appears to have studied in Kasur. From Kasur he went to Pakpattan, Baba Farid's resting place, where Waris is said to have practiced austerities. After teaching in an old mosque in another village, he moved northwest of Pakpattan to Malika Hans, where his *Heer* was written.

Exile is part of its theme. In answer to a message from the brothers and sisters-in-law asking him to return to Takht Hazara, Dheedo says: 'Moments that sail past do not return; fortunes lost will not come back; a word uttered cannot be recalled; the released arrow does not revert to the bow; the escaped soul does not re-enter a dead body.' But the secret of Waris's influence is not his memorable imagery. It is his understanding of the human heart.

The text refers to 'the stormy years' when *Heer* was composed, a time when 'peasants turned into rulers', 'thieves became barons' and 'governments were formed from house to house'. It speaks also of the author himself being 'looted by roving bands'.[57] All this is stated tersely at the end, but it is the older love story, not Punjab's clashes of his time, that Waris recounts.

How 'a bleeding Punjab, turbulent and chaotic without a moment of peace and stability,' produced powerful poetry has been explained by suggesting that despite constant clashes 'there still were large areas left', away from the routes of armies, 'where peace prevailed' and poetry could be composed and recited.[58]

This was certainly true. Parts of Punjab were indeed spared clashes. Earlier in the century, Banda's fierce attacks were essentially confined to Sirhind and the Jullundur doab. The later invasions of Nadir Shah and Abdali damaged more of Punjab, yet life went on in many places, marked no doubt by danger and watchfulness.

Heer was turned to, and clung to, as knowledge of the violence, as distinct from the violence itself, spread to every corner of Punjab. Indeed, Waris himself appears 'to have recited it to huge spell-bound audiences'.[59] We can believe that the common people of Punjab identified with Heer and Ranjha, whose background was similar to theirs. Through the dice of war or fate, ordinary Punjabis were losing lives or loved ones. Through *Heer*, where love was stolen by fate, they felt closer also to those from whom love was stolen by war.

While Heer's 'long lament',[60] to which Waris had given eloquent tongue, found an echo in the hearts of many eighteenth century Punjabis, domination and consequent exile—two of the threads that run through *Heer*—were part of the daily experience of many Punjabis, whether Muslim, Hindu or Sikh. They responded to 'a passionate, sensitive and resourceful Punjabi girl' like Heer who stood up to patriarchs and bigots.[61]

In this period, there were Muslim poets besides Waris who wrote kissas or stories in the genre of *Heer*. Even if these other kissas did not attain equal fame, they were (and are) widely recited. The fact that none of them contained 'an iota of communal bias or antagonism' suggests, in the view of at least one writer, that—despite the clashes we have been recording—amity 'among Hindus, Muslims and Sikhs... subsisted in the eighteenth century' in Punjab.[62]

If, therefore, we wish to imagine Punjab as it was during the last four decades of the eighteenth century, we can, among other things, picture to ourselves a large rural audience listening to Waris Shah—a laughing and crying audience of Muslims, Sikhs and Hindus, even perhaps including, to one side, a knot of women. Galloping horses and falling bodies should not be allowed to fill our entire mental screen. If there was war in Punjab, there was also peace.

■

By the time of the last two of his invasions (1768-69 and 1769-70), Abdali had been weakened within his kingdom, and he was ill. Dissensions in his camp and his soldiers' reluctance to fight distant battles ended these invasions almost as soon as they were launched. Two years after his final attempt into India, the king died.

His Indian invasions were only one facet of the life of Ahmad Shah Abdali (or Durrani). For the people of Afghanistan, where he lies in a tomb in Qandahar, his Indian campaigns are marginal to his greatest achievements: the creation of an independent Afghanistan and the establishment of standards for it. Inside Afghanistan, he won over the people before he won the tribal chiefs, treated defeated rivals and chiefs with respect and as equals, genuinely consulted a council of advisors, stopped cruel forms of punishment like cutting off noses and ears, and made it unlawful for a master to kill a servant.

In 1870, an anonymous writer in the *Calcutta Review*, almost certainly a Briton, would describe Abdali thus: 'Courtly, farseeing, singularly patient... a poet, a divine, and a man who took a profound delight in the society of the learned... he was above the influence of the harem, a foe to drunkenness, and renowned for his generosity and charity.'[63]

Indians did not notice all these qualities on the numerous occasions when this dominant eighteenth-century figure raced across Punjab. But they acknowledged the speed and skills of Abdali's army, the king's personal bravery, his brilliance as a general, and his efforts at diplomacy. However, they could not forget the greed and cruelties associated with his invasions, the massacres at the hands of his soldiers, or the destruction and defilement at Amritsar and elsewhere.

A British writer would say that Abdali was 'fitted for conquest but incapable of empire'.[64] Certainly, the expectation that Abdali would occupy the virtually vacant Delhi throne was belied by him. Even in respect of Punjab, there is no evidence of attempts by him to provide a stable or people-friendly administration.

But perhaps it was less for empire and more for money that he raided India. Not, chiefly, money for himself; we should note the verdict of J.P. Ferrier, writing in 1858, that 'the revenues of Afghanistan… never found their way into [Abdali's] private coffers'.[65] When the Sikhs harassed him or blocked his path, he (and the Sikh chiefs as well) invoked religious duty for motivation, but it was not primarily for Islam that Abdali so often marched into India.

■

Abdali's son and successor, Timur Shah, was conscious of the Indian territories his kingdom had lost and also eager to strengthen his bond with his wife's brother, Shah Alam II, who in name at least was still the emperor of Hindustan. Supported by the Marathas, Shah Alam II returned to Delhi in 1772, after he had spent a few years in Allahabad under the protection of the Marathas' rival, the East India Company.

The British were nervous about a possible Afghan-Maratha-Mughal alliance, but the Sikhs occupying most of Punjab made sure that Timur and Shah Alam II would not be able to join forces. Timur managed, however, to recover Multan from the Sikhs who had seized it. Early in 1780, Timur and his force wrested the city and left a new Afghan governor there. En route, Timur's force had defeated the Sikhs in a tough battle at Rohtas.

The following year, Timur again entered Punjab's southern regions and restored his writ in Bahawalpur, where the chief, Bahawal Khan, had stopped paying the tribute that Timur's father had always exacted. In 1785, Timur once more sent his forces into India, this time to nail down his control over Kashmir. There was fierce resistance but Timur's generals prevailed.

At the end of 1788, angered by word from Delhi that Shah Alam II had been deposed and blinded by his Rohilla wazir, Ghulam Qadir, Timur again crossed the Indus in an attempt to join up with the emperor. But the Sikhs once more blocked his path, and all that Timur could do for his brother-in-law was to send a letter to the British Governor-General in Calcutta, Lord Cornwallis, urging him to protect the emperor.

∎

The quest for power sharpened Sikh rivalries. In a 1774 battle waged in Jammu, Charhat Singh of the Sukerchakia misl and Jhanda Singh of the powerful Bhangi misl, fighting on opposite sides, were both killed. Before his death, Charhat Singh had become master of large and contiguous territories in the three doabs between the Indus and the Ravi. In 1776, Jassa Singh Ahluwalia entered into a league with the Bhangi, Sukerchakia and Kanhiya misls to expel Jassa Singh Ramgarhia from Punjab. The bid was successful, and the Ahluwalias took over Ramgarhia lands in the Jullundur doab.

Power, however, was shifting in favour of the Sukerchakia misl, which after Charhat Singh's death was headed by Maha Singh. Defeating, among others, the chief of the Muslim Chathas of Gujranwala, Maha Singh added to the lands that Charhat Singh had not only captured but also capably administered.

In the Gujranwala area in the 1770s, the Jat Chathas of Wazirabad and Rajput Bhattis of Hafizabad (Muslims in both cases) offered 'fierce resistance' to the Sukerchakias, whose attack was aided by Sahib Singh of the Bhangi misl. Describing the conflict, the (British) writer of the *Gujranwala Gazetteer* wrote that, besieged for weeks in his fortress in Manchar, Ghulam Muhammad Chatha eventually surrendered after Maha Singh assured him safe passage to Mecca, but the promise was 'basely broken'.

Ghulam Muhammad was shot and his fortress razed to the ground. Rasoolnagar in Chatha country was renamed Ramnagar. The *Gazetteer* noted that the treacherous killing of Chatha and his resistance was remembered 'in many a local ballad' in Gujranwala.[66]

The Bhattis of Hafizabad tehsil, who were Muslim Rajputs, did not cease their resistance to the Sukerchakias until 1801, when their leaders were killed and their possessions captured. Some Bhattis fled to Jhang.[67]

In 1785, the Sukerchakias, led by Maha Singh, combined with the Ahluwalias to defeat the Kanhiyas in a fierce battle fought near Batala, the Kanhiya base. Though Gurbaksh Singh, son of the Kanhiya chief, Jai Singh, was killed in this battle, his far-sighted widow, Sada Kaur, persuaded her father-in-law that her daughter should be betrothed to the victor's five-year-old son.

Helped by several factors, including this alliance with the Kanhiyas and the support he received from Sada Kaur, five-year-old Ranjit would soon become the future ruler of Punjab, thus fulfilling a wish expressed two years earlier by William Forster, an English traveller into Punjab. Forster had hoped for the emergence of 'some ambitious Sikh chief' who would defeat all rival misls, 'absorb their power', and 'display... the standard of monarchy'.[68] Punjabis worn out by unending instability nursed similar desires.

At eighteen, Ranjit Singh succeeded his father Maha Singh as the chief of the Sukerchakia misl and the inheritor of its rich territories. In 1799, when he was only nineteen, he led an army that took over Lahore from discredited Sikh governors. In 1801, when he was twenty-one, he was crowned king, the investiture performed by a direct descendant of Guru Nanak, Sahib Singh Bedi.

There were significant Afghan interludes. Timur's successor, Zaman Shah, invaded India in 1797. He had been urged by Indian admirers (chiefly the Rohillas but also Tipu in Mysore) to occupy the Delhi throne before non-Muslims (i.e. the British or the Marathas) seized it. The Afghans' Sikh vassal in Patiala and Nizamuddin Khan, the Pashtun chief of Kasur, backed the idea of a fresh Afghan bid.

The Gakhars were sympathetic to Zaman as he entered the country, and the Afghan king reached Lahore without much trouble. Along the way, in Gujrat, Sahib Singh, the Bhangi chief, offered a weak resistance before escaping. Seventeen at the time, Ranjit Singh also moved from Gujranwala to Amritsar, where his mother-in-law, Sada Kaur, the leader of the Kanhiya misl, urged him to fight.

Lahore, however, was illuminated for three nights in Zaman's honour. While its Sikh governors moved out, a few prominent Sikhs of Lahore submitted to Zaman. But unrest in his kingdom summoned the Afghan king back home, and Lehna Singh and Sobha Singh returned to Lahore. Both soon died, however, and were succeeded by their sons, Chet Singh and Mohar Singh, neither of whom was liked in Lahore.

Heeding Sada Kaur's plea, Ranjit Singh managed to inflict a humiliating defeat on Zaman's commander, Shahanchi Khan, in Ramnagar/Rasoolnagar on the banks of the Chenab. In November 1798, a stung Zaman Shah was once more in Lahore, his entry assisted by Kasur's Pashtun chief. On the way to Lahore, Zaman's army plundered Gujrat and Gujranwala where, Sikh soldiers

Competing Sikh misls, 1780s

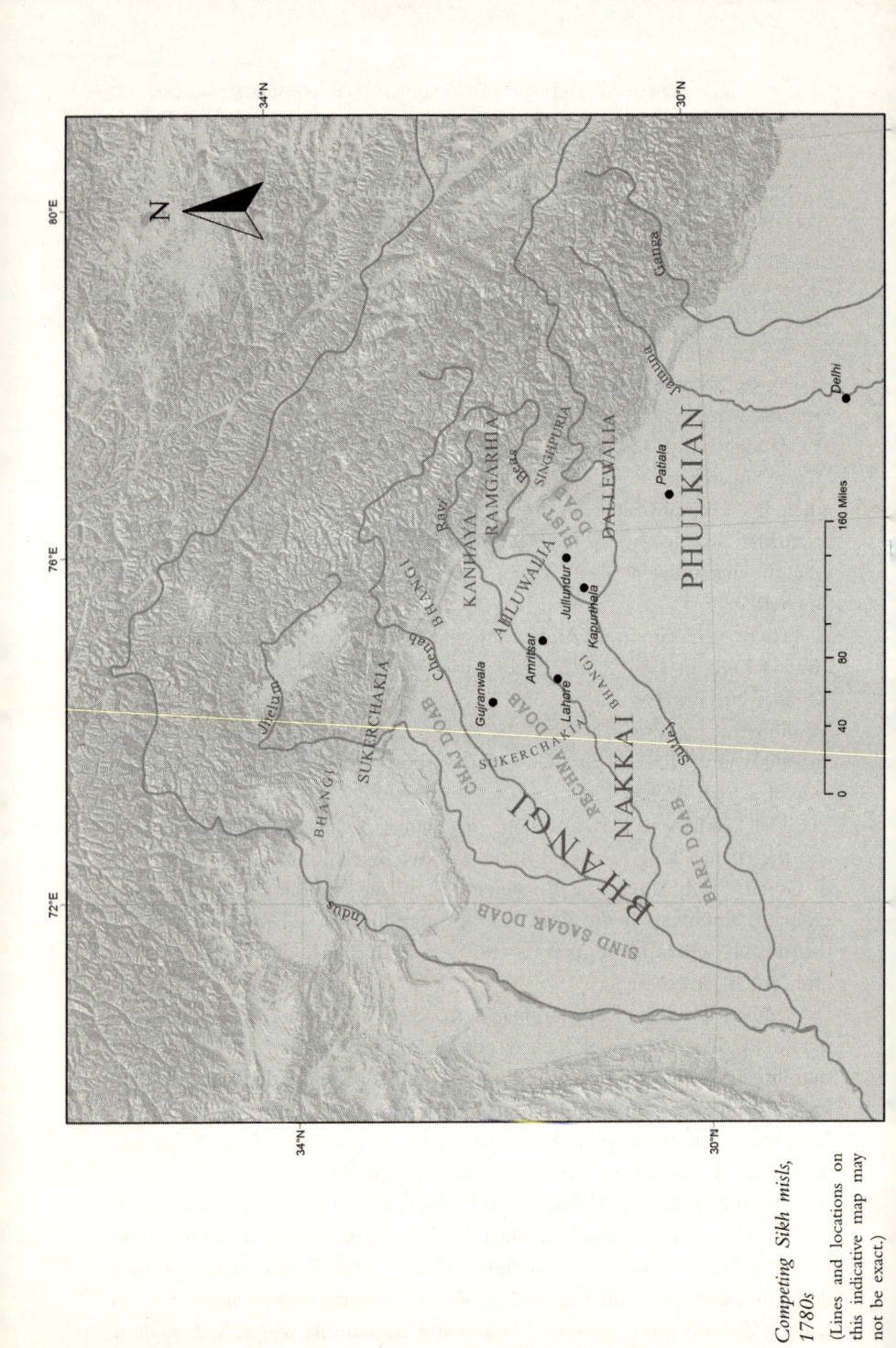

(Lines and locations on this indicative map may not be exact.)

having retreated, the towns' Muslims became the Afghan army's main victims. In Lahore, many Sikhs offered presents, it seems, to Zaman. Kasur's Nizamuddin Khan hoped to be named Zaman's subahdar in Lahore; Ranjit Singh 'also sent his representative to Zaman to negotiate' for that position.[69] While Latif states that eighteen-year-old Ranjit Singh paid Zaman 'homage in person' at this time,[70] it seems that Ranjit Singh's diplomatic move was joined to a readiness to do battle: the story is told of a daring Ranjit riding up to a tower in the fort in Lahore and shouting, 'O grandson of Abdali, come down and measure swords with the grandson of Charhat Singh.'[71]

All in all, Zaman seemed to command awe over many people across Punjab, including the Sikh raja of Patiala and the Hindu chief of Kangra in the hills. However, by January 1799 Zaman was obliged to leave Lahore for Kabul, where his brother was again creating trouble. In fact, Zaman's rule in his own country was on its last legs. This time he had quit Punjab for good, 'never to disturb it again',[72] for he was soon deposed, blinded and imprisoned in Kabul. 'Had Shah Zaman remained content with his Afghan possessions,' it would be said, 'and not coveted India, he would not have lost the kingdom of his ancestors.'[73]

In July 1799, displacing Chet Singh and Mohar Singh, Ranjit Singh occupied Lahore, 'as much with the willing cooperation of its leading Hindu and Muslim residents'[74] as with the assistance of his Sikh forces and of Sada Kaur.

Leaders of the Bhangi and Ramgarhia misls and Nizamuddin Khan, the Kasur chief, joined hands in the following year in an attempt to oust Ranjit Singh, but the young ruler prevailed over the combination in a clash in Bhasin village, situated between Lahore and Amritsar. After 1802, when, supported by the Ahluwalias, Ranjit Singh, now twenty-two, captured Amritsar, where the Bhangi misl had been dominant, he was free to replace Punjab's patchwork quilt of tracts under misls with a unified kingdom.

Chapter Four

1799-1849: RANJIT SINGH AND HIS SUCCESSORS

Historians disagree on whether Ranjit Singh was born in Gujranwala, the Sukerchakia seat, or close to the town of Jind at the southern end of Punjab's Malwa region—his mother's father was Jind's Sikh chief. At an early age, the dark-skinned Ranjit was hit by small-pox, which blinded his left eye and left permanent pits on his face. Short in stature—his head dominated the body—Ranjit loved horses. Apparently his ugly appearance was transformed the moment he mounted a horse. Well before entering his teens he became an expert horseman and shot, but he never learnt to read or write.

Though among the smaller misls to start with, the Sukerchakias had acquired substantial tracts in and around Gujranwala, which Ranjit inherited. Three years after marrying Mehtab Kaur—daughter of Sada Kaur, the widow who owned the Kanhiya misl's lands—Ranjit Singh took a second wife, Raj Kaur, a sister of the chief of the Nakkai misl. Both marriages were aimed at augmenting Sukerchakia power, for Ranjit had also inherited the fierce ambition that had driven his father Maha Singh and grandfather Charhat Singh.

Ranjit seemed to covet power more than affection, of which he did not receive much from Mehtab or her mother. The child Mehtab's betrothal to Ranjit was above all the political response of a cornered woman whose husband had been killed by the boy's father. Like her son-in-law, Sada Kaur separated feelings from interests. If the Sukerchakias expected gains from an alliance with the Kanhiyas, the latter hoped to profit from the Sukerchakias' rapid ascent.

Young Ranjit Singh's willingness to become a king revealed boldness, for it went against his Jat background and against Sikh tradition as well. It was also bound to invite hostility within his misl and from chiefs of rival misls. Ranjit Singh reckoned, however, that the populace, longing for a return of Mughal-era stability, would welcome a monarchy. Moreover, he and his advisors remembered that Punjab's numerous chiefs offered allegiance and money to a king or viceroy in Lahore.

Some of these chiefs, especially in the hills, were called rajas, and Abdali had designated the Patiala chief a raja too. In these circumstances, why shouldn't Lahore's ruler be a maharaja? Also influencing Ranjit Singh's step was the birth of Kharak Singh, a son from his Nakkai wife, Raj Kaur. That the child could be turned into an heir-apparent was evidently an 'irresistible' pull for the father.[1]

Wishing, however, to be a people's monarch, Ranjit Singh sat in a chair or on a carpet while granting an audience, rather than on a throne. The new coins he ordered carried Guru Nanak's name, not his. While the Khalsa Sarkar, as his government was called, and the new Khalsa Durbar (the court), bore a clear Sikh-Hindu imprint (few at the time stressed differences between Hindu and Sikh beliefs), Ranjit Singh desired Muslim loyalty as well. As far as he was concerned, he would be a king for all Punjabis.

Even during his first takeover of Lahore, which occurred two years before his investiture as Maharaja, Ranjit Singh's earliest public acts had been to pay homage at two mosques: the city's greatest, the Badshahi Mosque built by Aurangzeb, and the most-frequented one, the Wazir Khan Masjid that Shahjahan's Chiniot-born governor had created. Also, he made a Muslim, Imam Baksh, the city's kotwal.

Disregarding objections to monarchy from Muslim clerics, Mughal kings had claimed that they were upholding Islam from the throne. Ranjit Singh similarly ignored Guru Gobind Singh's warning to Banda Bahadur against princely dreams. But he treated Sikh religious leaders with respect.

In the years to come, these religious leaders would at times censure Ranjit Singh. 'In personal terms, he was not a model of uprightness or chastity,' observes Amrik Singh, adding, 'he had a number of concubines.' His 'countless acts of dalliance' were objected to. Once 'it was even decided to flog him publicly' for a transgression.[2] Not wanting a confrontation, Ranjit Singh submitted to the punishment, which however was not carried out.

Following Ranjit Singh's coronation, many were drawn to his court and to Lahore: sons of chiefs, doctors and scholars, artisans and craftsmen, and others.

■

By the year 1800, much of India had fallen into the East India Company's hands. Ruling eastern India from the 1750s, the Company became the south's master as well in 1799, when Tipoo Sultan was defeated and killed. In 1803, the Company's soldiers took Delhi, overcoming the Marathas propping up the Mughal throne, and turned Shah Alam II—Babur's descendant and successor—into its pensioner.

But moving west of the Jamuna called for caution. Autonomous Sikh chiefs were in power in Patiala, Nabha, Jind, and elsewhere in the region between the Jamuna and the Sutlej. Intriguing with local landlords, a rogue British adventurer called George Thomas had indeed established himself, in 1797, as the ruler of Hansi, a town well to the south of Patiala. Yet, when Thomas sought support for a march across Punjab to plant the Union Jack on the Indus's shore, his request was turned down by the Calcutta-based Governor-General.

Not only was Punjab devoid of order, and an unknown quantity; beyond it lay Afghanistan, the source of recent and ancient invasions into India. The Company did not thirst for an encounter with the Afghans.

Ranjit Singh's installation in Lahore brought a new element into the picture. On behalf of superiors in Calcutta, Collins, the British Resident in Delhi, had in fact been watching Ranjit even before he became Maharaja. Was he the one capable of controlling Punjab? If so, a stabilized Punjab could become a buffer against Afghanistan.

The English were 'willing, even eager to fight the Afghans to the last Sikh'.[3] It suited them that a Sikh-led Punjab should cope—and, if it came to that, fight—with Muslim Afghanistan. 'The most far-sighted of all the external forces' present in India, with agents in many parts of Punjab, the British had discerned Ranjit Singh's potential. 'Through their agents they urged the Sardars to unite under Ranjit Singh.'[4]

Another reason for keeping a British eye on Ranjit was to catch signs of Sikh-Maratha or Sikh-French negotiations. The French, on their part, had relied on the Marathas, whose soldiers seemed 'better disciplined than the Sikhs'. Three French generals had helped direct Maratha forays in northern and central India. The ouster of the Marathas from Delhi was a blow to their hopes, yet the French looked for future Maratha victories across India, which, given the quarrels among Maratha chiefs, might yet pave the way for French dominion.[5]

■

Defeating, in the year 1800, the Kasur-Bhangi-Ramgarhia combination (which was also a Muslim-Sikh combination) in the Battle of Bhasin, Ranjit Singh had also cultivated the prestigious Ahluwalia misl and its leader, Fateh Singh. Given the hold on the Sikh imagination of the late Jassa Singh Ahluwalia, and the abilities of his successor, Fateh Singh, this made sense.

Also, Ranjit Singh had enlisted a talented young Muslim aide with a Sufi background, Fakir Azizuddin Bokhari. Azizuddin, son of a hakim called in to check Ranjit Singh's eyes, was learning Unani medicine in Lahore, but his gifts lay in diplomacy and flowery, persuasive speech. Recruited as the new ruler's mouthpiece, Azizuddin soon became Ranjit Singh's chief confidant and minister for foreign affairs. Two brothers of his, Nuruddin and Imamuddin, also entered Ranjit Singh's service.

Ranjit Singh's first encounter with the East India Company took place in Amritsar in the year 1800, when he was not yet Maharaja. This was a meeting with Mir Yusuf Ali, the Company's emissary sent to probe the Sikh leadership and detect the chances of any Sikh-Afghan alliance.

At this juncture, the Company saw the Jamuna as its western border. The Sutlej was Ranjit Singh's frontier from the opposite end. Between the Jamuna and the Sutlej lay, as we have seen, a number of independent chiefdoms— Patiala, Nabha, Jind (ruled by Ranjit Singh's uncle) and the like—most of them Sikh-run.

After talking with Sikh chiefs in Patiala and elsewhere in cis-Sutlej Punjab, Yusuf Ali arrived in Amritsar for a meeting with Ranjit's mother-in-law, Sada Kaur. Requested by the Kanhiya chief to join the discussion, her son-in-law talked with the emissary in Amritsar and then invited him to Lahore for further talks.

Yusuf Ali reported to the Company that in these conversations Ranjit Singh admitted nothing more than friendly relations with Zaman Shah. Writing himself to Collins (the Company's Resident in Delhi), Ranjit Singh recounted his face-offs with the Afghans during the previous year (1799), including the challenge he had hurled up the Fort tower in Lahore to Zaman. Also provided was an account of how, thereafter, Ranjit Singh salvaged the cannons the Afghan had lost while crossing the Jhelum on his way back to Kabul and then, for friendship's sake, returned them to Zaman Shah.[6]

That Ranjit Singh volunteered such an explanation to the Company revealed his awareness of British power. He was also talking to the French, and said as much to Collins. Officers from France in the employ of Scindia, a key Maratha chief, had in fact met him in 1799. Three years later (after a French general suppressed George Thomas of Hansi), a French mission called on the Maharaja in Lahore.[7]

While ready, when needed, to be humble and folksy, the unlettered, one-eyed Ranjit Singh possessed both an imperial goal and key ingredients for reaching it, including diplomatic skill and curiosity. To become master of a large area, he would need to get at the secret behind imperial armies, and to let one imperial power know of his links to the other.

Meanwhile, he would subdue local armies and add to his territory and revenues. After a bitter fight, Nizamuddin Khan, the Kasur chief, was defeated but his territory was not seized. An indemnity plus Kasur's acknowledgment of Lahore's suzerainty were deemed sufficient.

However, parts of the territory of Sansar Chand, the ambitious Rajput chief of Kangra, were annexed and given over to Sada Kaur and her Kanhiyas. The alliance with the Ahluwalias was solemnized beside a Sikh holy tank in Tarn Taran in 1802 before 'hundreds of thousands of peasants and Sardars', with Ranjit Singh and Fateh Singh exchanging turbans and thus becoming dharam bhai or brothers in the faith.[8]

Together, the two proceeded westward into the Rachna and Chej doabs, accompanied by their armies. The Muslim landowners of Pindi Bhattian were 'persuaded' to associate themselves with the new Punjab. Consisting of 400 choice horses, their tribute pleased Ranjit Singh. In Chiniot on the Chenab, Jassa Singh Doloo, a Sikh chief, offered stubborn resistance. After being defeated, he was taken into the Maharaja's service. The Jhelum too was crossed, and Fateh Singh took over tracts seized from Muslim chiefs to its west.

Because Kasur's Nizamuddin Khan had flexed his muscles while Ranjit Singh and Fateh Singh were in the north, Kasur's walls were pounded with guns brought from Lahore. Resisting and defeated again, Nizamuddin was once more allowed to run Kasur as a fief. A keen practical sense told Ranjit Singh that vassalage was less expensive than governing new pieces of territory with his own limited forces, and less productive of lasting hostility.

In 1802, the great province of Multan, Kabul-controlled for decades, was invaded by a large Punjab army with the Maharaja at its head. To save his city, Muzaffar Khan, the nawab of Multan, paid an indemnity and agreed to share future revenues with Lahore rather than with Kabul, whereupon Ranjit Singh and his troops withdrew.

Even more important for the Maharaja was his triumph (also in 1802) in Amritsar, where Bhangi influence had remained strong despite the misl chief's defeat and death two years earlier. Apart from being Sikhism's chief city, Amritsar was now a bustling centre for trade and manufacture. Coinciding with the decline in Lahore, years of stability under Sikh rule had brought prosperity to the city. Much of the trade of Kashmir and Central Asia with Hindustan took place in its bazaars, and numerous Kashmiri traders and artisans had settled there.

Taking Amritsar was essential for anyone wanting to be Punjab's master, and doubly so for a Sikh. While Mai Sukhan, the late Bhangi chief's widow controlled one part of the city, including Govindgarh fort, and was said to have the support of the Ramgarhia misl, the rest of Amritsar was divided among nearly a dozen Sikh families. There were disputes galore over rents and taxes.

Encircled by the combined forces of Ranjit Singh, Fateh Singh and Sada Kaur, the fragmented city offered little resistance. Ramgarhia support failed to materialize, and Amritsar was taken piece by piece. Persuaded to surrender, Mai Sukhan accepted a pension from Lahore for herself and her son.

From Govindgarh fort, which he took over, Ranjit Singh obtained Ahmed Shah Abdali's powerful Damdama gun. Used to good effect in the 1761 Panipat battle, the gun had since passed through a series of Afghan, Sikh and Punjabi Muslim hands. It had last been seized by the Bhangis from the Chathas of Gujranwala district. Ranjit Singh proudly took the Damdama to Lahore.

In Amritsar, he also acquired the backing of the Nihangs, the body of militant ascetics who for generations had served as 'the suicide squads of the Khalsa armies'.[9]

The year 1802 saw the betrothal in Lahore of three-year-old Kharak to a Kanhiya girl. At the festivities, Ranjit Singh's eye fell on an attractive Muslim courtesan called Mohran. He asked her to move to his harem and apparently married her.[10] Later a coin was minted in Mohran's honour.

■

Drawn by word of Ranjit Singh's swift triumphs, soldiers from outside Punjab sought employment under him. These included deserters from the armies of the East India Company, 'mainly Hindustani Muslims and a few Eurasians'.[11] When a platoon of deserters paraded before him, Ranjit Singh saw—for the first time—soldiers marching in step and making battle formations in instant obedience to crisp commands.

Though his Sikh troopers cracked jokes about the deserters' strange 'dancing', and declared that Hindustani foot-soldiers could teach nothing to Sikh horsemen, Ranjit Singh employed the deserters right away, ordering them to drill his soldiers and create an infantry. He also directed some of his soldiers to cross the border, join the Company's army, and learn its techniques.

Results were quickly seen. When, in 1803, Ranjit Singh led his troops to obtain the submission of Jhang, the cavalry of Ahmed Khan Siyal—'Punjab's best breeder of horses'[12]—clashed with Ranjit Singh's new infantry (and older cavalry and elephants) and was worsted. Though Ahmed Khan slipped away to Multan, Jhang acknowledged Ranjit Singh's suzerainty. Once more Ranjit Singh rejected the thought of governing a defeated territory, and Ahmed Khan returned to Jhang as Lahore's autonomous vassal.

The Jhang success encouraged Ranjit Singh to reconstitute the Sikh military into three wings. The first wing, which he commanded himself, included the best of his generals. Much of it trained in the European style, this wing possessed cavalry, infantry and artillery branches, the last led by a Muslim, Ghausa Khan. A second wing consisted of soldiers supplied as needed by a clutch of the once-powerful Bhangi sardars who had received their lands back by undertaking to provide soldiers for the Maharaja. The third wing comprised soldiers from misls allied to Ranjit Singh, including the Kanhiya and Nakkai. Altogether, the Maharaja's army probably had 24,000 soldiers by 1809 and 50,000 by 1821.[13]

■

Events favoured Ranjit Singh and the British rather than the Marathas and the French. After falling out with the cis-Sutlej Sikh chiefs, who earlier had thanked them for ousting George Thomas, the French left the Malwa region because Scindia, their Maratha paymaster, needed them in Delhi, where the British, led by Lord Lake, were determined to expel him. But French support made little difference, and Scindia was forced to leave Delhi.

However, another Maratha chief, Jaswant Rai Holkar, remained active near Delhi. Supported by the Rohillas, Holkar tried also to induce the Afghans to move yet again into India. In 1805, Lake pursued Holkar steadily westward upto and beyond the Sutlej. The Maratha chief and his large army (accompanied by the Rohillas led by Amir Khan) crossed the Beas, reached deep inside the well-recognized territory of Lahore's ruler, and asked for the Maharaja's support. The British stopped at the Beas.

His boundaries violated by both the Marathas and the British, Ranjit Singh faced a difficult choice. Arriving in Amritsar, Holkar demanded a 'Hindu' alliance against 'Christian' Britain. Ranjit Singh did not fall for this 'religious' line, in part because his agents had informed him of Holkar's messages to Kabul. Aware, however, that the Maratha chief's French-trained soldiers were better disciplined than his, he did not wish to take them on.

Meanwhile he gauged the strength of Lake's army. Confident that the British would do him no immediate harm, he had quietly entered their camp on the Beas and met Lake.[14] What he saw in the camp was enough for him to withhold a positive response to Holkar.

The Maratha accused Ranjit Singh of lacking in 'courage and valour'.[15] The Maharaja's private comment about Holkar was earthier, yet, not wishing to be crushed between the British and the Marathas, he played for time. Fortune was in store for him, for the East India Company changed its Governor-General in Calcutta and revised its policy. The new appointee, Lord Cornwallis (who had earlier fought a war in America on the losing British side), was instructed by London to conserve funds, not make fresh annexations, and allow Holkar to retreat unmolested.

The Marathas and the Rohillas returned across the Sutlej and left Punjab for good. All that now remained between Punjab and the British power to its southeast were the cis-Sutlej chiefs. While everyone assumed the Jamuna to be the Company's western border, Ranjit Singh needlessly volunteered to Lord Lake that he saw the Sutlej as his eastern/southern frontier.

On 1 January 1806, three parties signed a treaty in Lahore: the Company, Ranjit Singh, and Fateh Singh Ahluwalia. The two Sikh chiefs agreed to cut themselves off completely from Holkar and his soldiers, while the British undertook not to send their armies into Punjab or seize the two chiefs' possessions.

■

Quarrelling among themselves, the cis-Sutlej or Malwa Sikhs urged Ranjit Singh to visit Patiala and sort out their disputes. Though Sahib Singh, the new Patiala ruler, saw himself as the first among the Malwa chiefs and disliked conceding Ranjit Singh's superior status, Nabha's rivalry with Patiala had left him with no choice.

The invitation to Patiala, and stops en route and on the way back, enhanced Ranjit Singh's influence in Malwa and in the Jullundur doab. The people seemed to love him, chiefs offered large presents, and his arbitration was accepted by the disputants, who included the raja of Jind, Ranjit Singh's uncle.

On his way back to Lahore, in Jullundur, Ranjit Singh was asked by the brother of Sansar Chand, the Rajput ruler of Kangra, to relieve Kangra's fort, which Gurkhas led by Amar Singh Thapa had besieged. (The Gurkhas had for some time been pressing westward into eastern Punjab's hilly borderlands.) Though Thapa urged Ranjit Singh to stay neutral, the Maharaja camped at Jwalamukhi (an ancient pilgrimage site inside Kangra) and ordered Lahore's troops to relieve the fort. 'Swearing vengeance on Ranjit Singh', the Gurkhas retired to Mandi and Suket.[16] Sansar Chand thanked Ranjit Singh at Jwalamukhi and left a tribute.

The Maharaja was still in the hills when, in 1807, word reached him that Mehtab Kaur, his first wife—the daughter of Sada Kaur—had given birth to twin boys, Sher Singh and Tara Singh. Stories that the boys were either illegitimate or born to another woman would soon be passed around, including by Kharak Singh, the Maharaja's first-born, and by Kharak's Nakkai mother, Raj Kaur; but Ranjit Singh believed the boys to be his and became strongly attached to Sher Singh in particular.[17]

Returning to Lahore, Ranjit Singh learnt that Kasur was again defiant. Though Nizamuddin Khan was dead, his brother Qutbuddin Khan, supported by a large band of Ghazis and also by Muzaffar Khan of Multan, had repudiated Ranjit Singh's suzerainty.

The Maharaja's first response was to send Fakir Azizuddin to Kasur. When Azizuddin's honeyed words failed to change Qutbuddin's mind, Ranjit Singh led an army to silence the defiant city. The force included pieces of artillery and also the Nihangs he had acquired in Amritsar. He would pit the Nihangs against the Ghazis.

Kasur's strong walls withstood a month's volleying from Ranjit Singh's guns but were breached when a heavy charge of gunpowder, placed in a tunnel that Sikh miners had dug, was fired early one morning in March 1807, creating a large gap. 'Phula Singh's Nihangs charged through the breach', the fort was seized, and a captured Qutbuddin was brought before Ranjit Singh.[18]

The Maharaja forgave the rebel. Though ousted from Kasur, Qutbuddin was allowed to retain tracts he held in Mamdot, across the Sutlej. 'The acquisition of the mythological rival of Lahore from its [Muslim] owners' was seen as advancing Ranjit Singh's 'prestige and popularity amongst the *Khalsa*'.[19] After extinguishing the Kasur defiance, Ranjit Singh marched to Multan to punish Muzaffar Khan for having assisted Qutbuddin's revolt. Once more Muzaffar Khan avoided a battle by offering submission and paying money.

Another quarrel concerning Patiala—this time a dispute between Sahib Singh, the ruler, and his wife, Aas Kaur—obliged Ranjit Singh to repeat the journey to Malwa. Taking a large army with him, Ranjit Singh again arbitrated with success, and received substantial presents not only from Sahib Singh and the Rani but also from rulers of the other places where he stopped.

Two developments marked the return journey from Patiala. One, despite waging a hard battle in the hills, Ranjit Singh failed to subdue the raja of the hilly state of Sirmur, who had refused to acknowledge the Maharaja. Second, large chunks of the Jullundur doab were integrated into Ranjit

Singh's kingdom. Tara Singh Gheb, the doab's most prominent chief, having died, his wife was awarded a pension by the Maharaja, but Gheb's forces were absorbed into the Lahore army, and his large Dallewalia estates merged with those of the kingdom.

Among those joining Ranjit Singh's establishment at this time was Mohkam Chand, earlier an advisor to the Bhangis and a commander of their forces. Ranjit Singh made Mohkam Chand, who was a Khatri, a diwan, asked him to look after the newly-acquired Dallewalia territory and sent him on a successful campaign to reduce the Rajput chiefs of Pathankot, Jasrota and Chamba.

Acting on Mohkam Chand's shrewd advice, Ranjit Singh also called an assembly of all the chiefs of Punjab. By accepting the invitation to attend, a chief would admit the Maharaja's suzerainty. Abstaining, he would qualify for punishment. While the many attendees were given presents and khillats, those who didn't show up—including the chiefs of Sialkot, Akhnur, Gujrat and Sheikhupura, and even the Kanhiyas—were pursued by the forces of Ranjit Singh and Fateh Singh Ahluwalia and coerced into submission.

Another recruit, 'a handsome Brahmin youth from Meerut' called Khushhal Chand,[20] was a less happy choice. At first a soldier in Ranjit Singh's army, Khushhal Chand—who became a Sikh, changing his name to Khushhal Singh—soon headed the palace bodyguard and later became the royal chamberlain. All entering the palace had to be cleared by him. A nephew he brought into the Court, the future general Tej Singh, would earn a disreputable name in Sikh history.

■

Soon enough the diverse cis-Sutlej chiefs, thirty or so in all, had to decide whether to yield either to Ranjit Singh, who controlled Lahore, Amritsar and Jullundur, or to the British, who occupied Delhi and Meerut. Since most of these chiefs were Sikh, the Maharaja expected them to submit formally to his Khalsa Durbar. But the British had other ideas.

Napoleon's meteoric rise in Europe, and in particular the 1807 Treaty of Tilsit signed between him and the Russian Tsar, allowed talk of France expanding eastward, backed by Russia. To protect newly-won Delhi from their European rivals, the British would erect barriers in Persia, Afghanistan, Sindh and Punjab—through diplomacy.

To each of the four territories, the Company assigned a different skilled diplomat: Malcolm to Persia, Elphinstone to Kabul, Pottinger to Sindh, and

Charles Metcalfe to Punjab.

Also, the Company physically 'defended' Delhi, presumably from the French and the Russians, by stationing a detachment of troops ninety miles north of it, in Karnal. The Company was feeling confident. In 1808, its coffers were fuller than they had been three years earlier, when Cornwallis, the Governor-General at the time, instructed an end to operations in Punjab against the Marathas. His successor, Lord Minto, felt no difficulty in sending troops to Karnal, thereby also declaring an interest in Malwa.

Some steps taken by the Lahore kingdom had served the Company's interests. The 1807 takeover of the Dallewalia lands in the Doab, and a thoughtless incursion by Mohkam Chand across the Sutlej (near Ferozepur), created panic among the Malwa Sikhs who feared expropriation by Ranjit Singh. Early in 1808, an ouster by Ranjit Singh's forces of the Muslim ruler of Malerkotla had a similar impact.

However, the Company's officers could not deny the British depiction of the Jamuna as their boundary. When it was reported that Ranjit Singh wished to make a pilgrimage to Haridwar, which lay within the Company's India, Charles Metcalfe—the man who had been named envoy to the Lahore kingdom—was asked by his superiors not only to receive the Maharaja with due courtesy but also, once the pilgrimage was over, to accompany him 'to the border' at the Jamuna.

And when the Malwa chiefs called on Seton, the new Resident in Delhi, and directly sought British protection, the Company's response was, if anything, negative.

During the months it would take for British policy to firm up, twenty-four-year-old Charles Metcalfe met the twenty-eight-year-old Maharaja and his officers on numerous occasions and in different places across Punjab: Kasur, Malerkotla, Gungrana (Ludhiana district), Amritsar and Lahore. (Because Ranjit Singh cancelled the pilgrimage, no meeting had occurred in Haridwar.) Having to wait on Ranjit Singh during the latter's travels was presented by Metcalfe as a trial. Whether he actually felt it or not, the envoy feigned umbrage at supposed slights from his Asian hosts.

One admires nonetheless the detailed reporting of the envoy, which is the source (hardly an unbiased one) of most of our knowledge of the protracted negotiations, conducted during several months in 1808 and in January 1809, between the Company and the kingdom of Lahore. One admires equally the files surviving in the archives of Lahore's Punjab Secretariat, where may be seen—in the exquisite handwriting of the copying clerk of a bygone age—

the assessments of a bright young envoy who often faced six or more men on the opposite side, several of them also endowed with impressive talent. Before his first meeting with the Maharaja (in Kasur), Metcalfe was presented with an elephant, a horse, pearls and shawls. Describing this meeting to Edmunsone, the chief secretary in Calcutta, Metcalfe reported that the Maharaja wanted either the Governor-General or Metcalfe to declare that 'the British Government would never interfere in any of the concerns of the Sikh chiefs'.

Evidently Metcalfe replied that as an envoy he could not make or announce policy, whereupon Ranjit Singh asked whether Metcalfe would not at least 'promote' his views to the Governor-General. 'I will assure you that I will promote friendship between the two states,' Metcalfe answered. The Maharaja then asked if one of his representatives could accompany Metcalfe to Calcutta to meet Minto. Metcalfe made a joke to stall the request.[21]

Like other Europeans meeting Ranjit Singh, who only spoke Punjabi, Metcalfe had taken interpreters with him, who, in the opinion of one scholar, may have been Punjabi-knowing Muslims.[22]

In his letter to Edmunsone, Metcalfe quoted Ranjit Singh as saying that all Sikhs were 'the peoples of my nation, my brethren'. In the envoy's opinion, the Maharaja wanted the 'right to subjugate and oppress according to his pleasure all the independent Sikh chiefs on our Frontier'.

Claiming that he had been subjected to 'a grave attack' designed to elicit the commitment sought by the Maharaja, Metcalfe urged the Governor-General and his colleagues to 'conceive an assemblage of nine persons in which eight are endeavouring by all manner of means to obtain a particular point from one'.

After another meeting (in Gungrana), Metcalfe passed on to Edmonsone 'all the information I possess concerning Runjeet Singh's powers'. This included the size and weaponry of the Maharaja's armies. With due immodesty, Metcalfe claimed that his facts had been gathered not from inquiries, which would have been indiscreet, but from 'silent observation and unsought communications'.

Metcalfe then penned sentences that revealed the empire's readiness to discern and exploit native differences:

> I have occasionally mentioned the disaffection prevailing among the Chiefs of this country. This is almost universal, and if at any future period the ambition and encroachment of Runjeet Singh should compel

the British Government to go to war against him, it might perhaps be taken advantage of to destroy effectually his power. Sardar Futeh Singh [Ahluwalia] has been supposed to be particularly attached to the Raja but he is in reality particularly discontented with him.

The quiet character of Futeh Singh who was the equal if not the superior in rank and power of Runjeet Singh has yielded to the bold commanding spirit of the other, and he has been the ladder by which Runjeet Singh has mounted to greatness.

Now, however, added Metcalfe, Fateh Singh was not 'the companion and friend of an equal as formerly, but the nominal favourite of a master'. There was an outward show of intimacy but no confidence. Metcalfe added that he was mentioning 'the circumstances of this chief' as this was a 'case [which] may be entitled to [future] attention'.[23] Though being asked to talk first with Fateh Singh and Mohkam Chand before meeting the Maharaja was interpreted by Metcalfe as an insult, it had given the envoy a chance to cultivate Fateh Singh.

Interestingly enough, Metcalfe told Ranjit Singh in Kasur that if Afghanistan were to feature in the Maharaja's territorial designs, 'the British Government would not interfere'.[24] The Maharaja was not impressed, for he knew that another British diplomat, Mountstuart Elphinstone, had been assigned to enlist Kabul, even as Metcalfe was trying to bring him round. What Ranjit Singh did not know was that in 1809 in Peshawar—at the time the winter capital of Afghanistan—Elphinstone would sign a treaty with Shuja, the Abdali descendant then occupying a fiercely contested Kabul throne.

Earlier, Ranjit Singh had sent Azizuddin's brother Imamuddin to Patiala, Metcalfe's first stop on his mission, to welcome the envoy, a conscious attempt to suggest that Patiala was his vassal. For similar reasons, the rulers of Jind and Kaithal (in relative terms the most pro-Ranjit chiefs of Malwa), were summoned to Lahore for consultations. Metcalfe's counter-move, much resented by Ranjit Singh, was to ask some of the Malwa chiefs to meet him in Kasur.

The talks were marked by gamesmanship of this sort and also by presents, hugs, flattery, accusations, threats, proposals and counter-proposals. When, on one occasion, Mohkam Chand said to Metcalfe, 'You haven't seen the Sikh soldiers in battle,' the envoy offered a predictable retort: 'You haven't seen the British.'[25]

Apart from Ranjit Singh, Lahore's negotiating party included, among others, Fateh Singh, Fakir Azizuddin, Mohkam Chand, another Diwan named

Bhawani Das (who had previously served Zaman Shah), and an aide of Fateh Singh called Prabh Dial, who was said to know the English mind. When, in Kasur, Metcalfe launched into an oration about French designs and France's callousness towards allies, the Lahore team first applauded the envoy and then asked pointed questions.

Were the French targeting the Lahore kingdom or the British? *Where* (asked Azizuddin) did the Company draw its 'immutable' western boundary? *When* (the Maharaja asked) was the French invasion expected? Might not Shuja (the Afghan ruler) ally with the French? And so forth.

In his report for the Governor-General, Metcalfe conceded that the one-eyed Ranjit Singh 'acted the principal part' in the discussions, at times overruling his ministers. The envoy added that the Maharaja showed 'pertinacity' and 'anxiety' but was 'correct and polite'.[26]

The question about the real French target annoyed Metcalfe. To Azizuddin's query about the boundary, the envoy's answer, supplied after a long pause, was, 'Karnal', the place where British troops had latterly been sent. When, replying to the Maharaja, Metcalfe said that the supposed invasion's time could not be ascertained, Ranjit Singh observed, 'In that case, there is time for us to think things over.'[27]

In Malerkotla (a Malwa territory where, as we know, he had ousted a Muslim chief), Ranjit Singh told Metcalfe of suspicions in Lahore that Punjab was a British target, to which Metcalfe's counter was to refer to stories about the Maharaja wanting Delhi. Though not eyeing the former Mughal capital, Ranjit Singh did harbour hopes in another direction. He coveted Sindh, a desire the British would thwart.

In any case, the Maharaja did not believe in a French threat to Punjab or Delhi.

For ten years or more, the British had watched and liked Ranjit Singh. As late as in June 1808—a month before Metcalfe's mission commenced—a Captain Matthews had called on the Maharaja in Lahore and judged him to be 'a man of excellent understanding, possessed of a most liberal, generous, friendly mind, untinctured with prejudices of any kind'. Matthews also reported that Ranjit Singh, 'a most capital horseman', wanted 'Europeans into his service'.[28]

But Metcalfe's encounters convinced him and his superiors of the Maharaja's independence. He was not going to be a subordinate partner. However, Metcalfe also saw that attaching Malwa to the British would please the cis-Sutlej Sikhs without inviting a confrontation with the Maharaja.

To their delight, the British discovered that the Malwa chiefs desiring British protection were backed by Sada Kaur. Not only that. Her daughter, Mehtab Kaur—the Maharaja's wife—had personally called on Captain Matthews in Lahore to say, on her mother's behalf, that 'if the British decided to invade the Punjab, they could count on [Sada Kaur's] support', i.e. the support of the Kanhiya misl.[29]

Ranjit Singh was stunned when, in December 1808 in Amritsar, Metcalfe presented him with an accusatory letter from the Governor-General. Claiming that he was 'surprised' and 'concerned' to learn that the Maharaja aimed at 'the subjection of chiefs who have long been considered under the protection of the power ruling in the north of Hindustan', i.e. the British, Lord Minto proceeded to remind Ranjit Singh of his remark three years earlier to Lord Lake that the Sutlej was his kingdom's boundary.

The Governor-General followed up this letter with 'an 'irrevocable demand' that all territories beyond the Sutlej taken by the kingdom 'be restored forthwith'.

The enraged Maharaja's first response was to find a horse and gallop for a run. When his anger subsided, he left Amritsar for Lahore and summoned advisors. Mohkam Chand led the hawks in proposing defiance. Following his urging, Punjabis were asked to be ready for battle. Within days, tens of thousands rallied. Forts were strengthened and stocked with provisions for a long war.

But even Mohkam Chand could not assure success against the better-trained and possibly larger army the British could mount. Others in the court recommended appeasement and the avoidance of hostilities. Azizuddin was one of them. He was 'strongly backed behind the scenes by Sada Kaur'.

Swallowing his pride, Ranjit Singh yielded. For a while, he pressed for one small face-saver. He should be allowed, the Maharaja urged, to retain Faridkot across the Sutlej, which he had lately taken. (Faridkot's chief had defied his supposed master, the Patiala ruler, an act the Maharaja claimed he was obliged, as Punjab's paramount chief, to undo.) 'Only Faridkot,' the Maharaja requested, 'nothing else.'

Even that was not conceded. The pressure on Ranjit Singh was not withdrawn even when it became utterly clear, after Napoleon attacked to his west and took on Spain, that a French invasion of India in the near future was impossible. As British historians would admit in the future, the 'danger from France' to the Company in India had only been a pretext much of the time.[30]

If the Malwa territories had in fact been living under the British umbrella, why, Metcalfe was asked in a meeting in Lahore, did the British cold-shoulder the chiefs who had called on Seton in Delhi? Again, when the raja of Patiala encountered a major difference with his rani, why did the two turn to Ranjit Singh, not to their British 'protectors'? Metcalfe felt no need to provide answers.

Earlier, before Lord Minto's tough messages were communicated to the Maharaja, Metcalfe had reported to Calcutta that Ranjit Singh, tired from travels across Punjab, had been 'resting in [the] arms' of 'his favourite mistress, Mohran'. What Calcutta and London would not learn for years to come was that Metcalfe himself soon found an Indian mistress, apparently a Sikh woman, who bore him children.[31]

■

On 2 January 1809, in pursuance of the new British policy, Major David Ochterlony* advanced north from Delhi with three infantry battalions, a cavalry regiment and some artillery. On 9 February, he issued a proclamation declaring that all Malwa chiefs were under British protection and calling on the Lahore kingdom to move all its forces to the north or west of the Sutlej.

As Ochterlony moved up towards the Sutlej, chiefs welcomed him in several places, including Patiala, Nabha and Jind. Apparently Raja Sahib Singh of Patiala received the British commander with 'childish joy'.[32] Sada Kaur, too, praised the British advance. In Malerkotla, the nawab was reinstated. The important city of Ludhiana became British. And the Union Jack was planted on the Sutlej.

For a while it looked as if the British would move beyond the Sutlej and attack Ranjit Singh's core territory. Metcalfe had suggested something like that, and an Amritsar street-fight between Nihangs and Shias seemed to provide a pretext. Ranjit Singh moved quickly to quell that stir, but on his side too there were calls for war. Mohkam Chand thought that Holkar and the Rohillas should be tapped for an alliance against the British.

But the suggestions of Metcalfe and Mohkam Chand were rejected and peace factions prevailed on both sides. Faridkot was evacuated on 3 April and, on 15 April 1809, a Treaty of Friendship was signed in Amritsar between

---

*Born in America and joining the East India Company in 1777, David Ochterlony would engage in battles or negotiations with Sikhs, Gurkhas and Rajputs and take several Muslim concubines or wives in Delhi, where he served as Resident. He died in Meerut in 1825.

Calcutta and Lahore, whereby the two sides promised perpetual friendship to each other, with the British side acknowledging the Lahore kingdom's sovereignty north and west of the Sutlej.

Clearly, the Treaty had a victor and a loser: the British had leapt up to the Sutlej. Moreover, though this was not spelt out, the losing party's rights north and west of the Sutlej were also circumscribed. Having killed Ranjit Singh's bid for a unified Punjab, the British were not about to concede any rights to him in relation to Afghanistan or Sindh.

■

Ranjit Singh's response to the loss of face across the Sutlej was to tighten his grip within the kingdom. In December 1809, Kangra was coerced into submission. Sansar Chand yielded after his son, a 'guest' in Lahore of the Maharaja, was placed behind bars. Chamba, Kulu, Mandi and Suket were among the hill states that joined Kangra in accepting vassalage. The Gurkhas were starved into retreating altogether from the hills around eastern Punjab, but Ranjit Singh noted their grit.

Jammu, too, was subjugated. In the Jullundur doab, Sikh chiefs resisting the Durbar's authority were ousted from their lands, and Jullundur town was absorbed. Khushab, northwest of Lahore, was tamed. Salt mines in what the British would later call the Rawalpindi division were brought under the Durbar's control.

Led either by Ranjit Singh himself or by a trusted commander, these 'whirlwind operations' put an end to the independence of most Sikh misls. Despite their roles in providing wives for Ranjit Singh, the Nakkais and the Kanhiyas were, respectively, 'wiped out' and diminished.[33]

But the Maharaja still lacked what, for prestige and revenue, he most desired: the large territories of Multan and Kashmir. Technically, these two territories were under the Afghan umbrella. In practice, fully autonomous Pashtun chiefs ruled both. In 1811, a fresh attempt by Ranjit Singh to take Multan failed, the fort of Multan successfully defying the Durbar's army and artillery.

The Maharaja found some compensation for the Multan disappointment in grand celebrations in Lahore and Amritsar for the wedding in 1812 of his first son, Prince Kharak Singh. Representing the Governor-General of India, Ochterlony came for the event, as did the rajas of Kangra, Patiala, Nabha and Jind. The nawabs of Bahawalpur and Multan sent family members. By this time, even Charles Metcalfe had nice things to say about the Maharaja.

From his new position as the Company's Resident in Delhi, Metcalfe told the Governor-General in Calcutta that Ranjit Singh, 'irresistibly supreme' in Punjab, was 'manag[ing] his government with ability'.[34]

■

The Lahore-Kabul equation remained crucial. With Kabul's support, Ranjit Singh could subdue both Multan and Kashmir. Equally, with Ranjit Singh's support, a claimant to Kabul's throne could overcome rivals.

Even more crucial was the role of the British, capable by now of tilting the scales in any clash in India. When Ranjit Singh attacked Multan in 1811, its ruler, Muzaffar Khan, had appealed for help to the Company and even offered to hand over the city and its fort. The Company demurred. Aiding Multan would have violated the Amritsar treaty.

Interestingly enough, Ranjit Singh too had asked for British support for his bid against Multan. On 12 August 1810, Colonel Ochterlony's 'assistant munshi' in the Maharaja's Court in Lahore forwarded Ranjit Singh's 'application for assistance' to his master in Ludhiana.[35] Ochterlony consulted the Governor-General, who authorized the Colonel to reject Ranjit Singh's request 'for cooperation in his meditated attack on Multan'.[36]

As for the Afghans, they were furiously fighting one another. Installed on the throne with the backing of Fateh Khan, the influential wazir, Prince Mahmud had blinded the deposed Zaman Shah. Battling it out with Mahmud was Shuja, who held the throne from 1803 to 1809 but was removed in 1810. Escaping from the conflicts in Kabul, the blinded Zaman and his harem, as also the harem of Shuja, sought asylum in Lahore, a city that Zaman had previously entered as a conqueror. A 'remarkable instance of the mutability of fortune', said Elphinstone, who ran into Zaman on the route from Afghanistan into Punjab.[37]

As for Shuja, he had somehow landed up in Kashmir as a prisoner of the Afghan governor there, who, however, was Fateh Khan's foe. It was a bizarre picture.

Anyhow, when Fateh Khan proposed to Ranjit Singh a joint invasion of Kashmir and a division of its revenues, the Maharaja agreed. In 1813, large armies of Fateh Khan and Ranjit Singh, the latter led by Mohkam Chand, raced to be the first to reach Kashmir's capital, Srinagar. Although Kabul's army won the race, Mohkam Chand succeeded in rescuing Shuja and bringing him to Lahore.

Kashmir was now in the hands of Fateh Khan, who was hardly eager

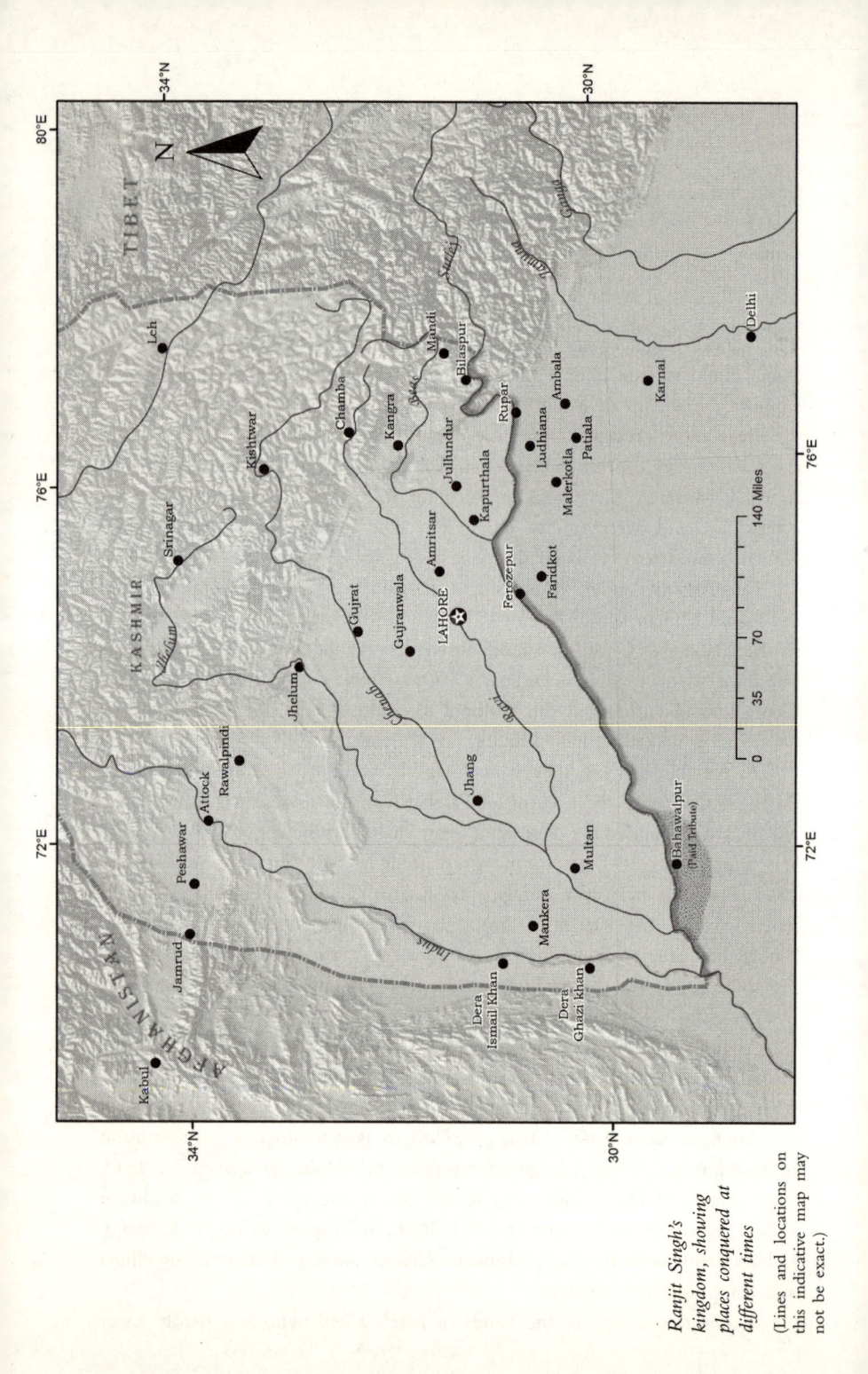

Ranjit Singh's kingdom, showing places conquered at different times

(Lines and locations on this indicative map may not be exact.)

to share its revenues with the Maharaja. However, something that seemed of almost comparable value was held by Shuja and his blinded brother Zaman, Ranjit Singh's hostages in Lahore: the Kohinoor diamond which their grandfather, Ahmed Shah Abdali, had captured from the Mughals in Delhi. In fact Shuja's chief wife, Wafa Begum, had offered to the Maharaja an 'invaluable diamond', presumably the Kohinoor, if he rescued her husband from his chains in Kashmir.[38]

Wafa Begum's subsequent word that the jewel had been pawned in Kandahar was disbelieved by the Maharaja. In June 1813, taking with him a detachment of soldiers to Lahore's Mubarak Haveli, where the refugee and his family were housed, Ranjit Singh asked Shuja for the Kohinoor. Reluctantly, the Afghan prince instructed a servant to fetch it from his harem. A small roll of cloth was brought; when it was spread open, a large diamond was revealed.

Bhawani Das, once Zaman Shah's advisor and now one of Ranjit Singh's dewans, had accompanied the Maharaja to Shuja's refugee quarters. He confirmed that it was the Kohinoor. 'Rewrapp[ing] it in the same cloth', and without saying another word of thanks, goodbye or anything else, the Maharaja quickly stepped out with what he had extracted.[39] In his version of the Kohinoor transfer, Latif writes that Shuja and his family were deprived of food for some days before they agreed to part with the diamond.[40]

Shortly afterwards, more jewels from the harems of the Afghan princes were removed. Ranjit Singh having drastically reduced the refugees' rations, no resistance could be offered. A deeply offended Shuja tried clandestinely to encourage an invasion of Lahore by Fateh Khan—hitherto his principal enemy—and also by the British. Letters from Shuja's camp proposing an attack were intercepted by Ranjit Singh's men. Confronted with the letters, Shuja denied any knowledge or connection, but Ranjit Singh totally disbelieved him.

Even so, laxity in the Durbar's cordon and daring in the Afghan refugees enabled first the chief wife and then Shuja himself to escape from Mubarak Haveli. Wafa Begum got out in November 1814, Shuja in April 1815. Crawling out of a secretly-dug tunnel, Shuja, two sons of his, and a band of supporters journeyed via Sialkot, Kashmir, the Kulu hills and Simla to reach Ludhiana, where Wafa Begum had already arrived.[41]

Ludhiana, the Afghan party's new place of refuge, was of course Britain's forward headquarters, near the southern bank of the Sutlej, from where Colonel Ochterlony operated.

No matter how dazzling or priceless, the Kohinoor did not slake Ranjit Singh's thirst. He wanted Kashmir and attacked it with all the forces at his command in the summer of 1814. Though Mohkam Chand was old and ill by now, another gifted commander, Hari Singh Nalwa (a Khatri Sikh from Gujranwala), was among the attackers, as were Mohkam Chand's grandson, Ram Dyal, Mian Ghausa, the artillery chief, and the Maharaja himself. Also joining the invaders was a Muslim Punjabi, Agar Khan, the Rajput raja of a chiefdom adjacent to Kashmir, Rajouri, annexed by Ranjit Singh two years earlier.

The large and expensive expedition failed. From his listening post in Ludhiana, Ochterlony reported to the Governor-General in Calcutta that the Afghans holding Kashmir had defeated Ranjit Singh in a battle north of the Pir Panjal range. The retreat of the Maharaja's forces was 'so disorderly' that it 'became a disgraceful flight', added Ochterlony.[42]

This was in August 1814. In October, Mohkam Chand died, adding to Ranjit Singh's gloom. But soon there were compensations. Some lands in the Sindh Sagar doab were subjugated in 1815-16. Even though most of it lay east of the Sutlej, the large principality of Bahawalpur was compelled to pay tribute in 1816.

Then, in 1818, Multan was brought to its knees. For centuries a major constituent of the trading world, Multan was also famed for its mosques, shrines and tombs. In earlier periods, before its destruction, possibly at the hands of Mahmud of Ghazni, the city's Sun Temple used to attract quantities of pilgrims and wealth. Four attempts by Ranjit Singh's forces to take the Multan Fort had failed, but information received early in 1818 that the Afghans were busy in a war with Iran, and, indeed, that Fateh Khan had been wounded in that conflict, convinced the Maharaja that the hour for a grand assault had arrived.

A 20,000-strong army, led by a new commander, Diwan Chand, was commissioned for the task. Its artillery was under Ilahi Baksh. All boats on the Ravi and the Sutlej were commandeered, grain and war material stored along the invasion route, the Zamzama gun wheeled towards Multan, and a relay of messengers set up between Lahore and the battlefront.

Muzaffar Khan's Ghazis tried to stop the Lahore army outside the city but their swords and spears were helpless against the invaders' muskets and artillery. A steady Multani gunfire kept the attackers from entering the city but two weeks of bombardment blew down an intervening wall, and the Durbar's immense army moved in.

'Rising like a mountain' in the middle of the city, the fort of Multan was protected by a wide and deep moat. This moat was dry—it was the month of March—yet its size kept the fort's brick-and-mud ramparts safe from the Durbar's guns. Weeks of pounding failed to destroy the ramparts, and Ranjit Singh, who had chosen this time to stay in Lahore, became anxious. Eventually, however, the Zamzama's power, plus mines laid by daring Nihangs who braved enemy gunfire, created gaps large enough for the Durbar's troops to go through.

The resistance which was then offered by Muzaffar Khan, who had ruled Multan for thirty-nine years, among other things founding the city of Muzaffargarh, his sons, and other clansmen, all coming out in martyrs' green with swords drawn and beards perfumed,[43] would be immortalized in poetry and historical records, including in an 1818 text by Fakir Muhammad Issa Qadri and a later British gazetteer, which acknowledged 'the heroic defence' put up by the nawab and his sons.[44]

Muzaffar Khan, several of his sons, and a nephew were among the defenders killed. Giddy with their triumph, the victors set houses on fire and committed outrages on women, writes Latif.[45] In Lahore, a Ranjit Singh delirious at the word of victory—his biggest triumph thus far—gave the messenger a pair of gold bracelets and rode out on an elephant, showering pieces of gold and silver on the cheering crowds outside his palace.

But when two young sons of Muzaffar Khan, captured alive, were brought to him, Ranjit Singh embraced them in acknowledgment of the family's bravery. Also, when, three weeks after the Multan triumph, the festival of Id-ul-Fitr arrived, the Maharaja paid homage in a Lahore mausoleum to the memory of Mian Ghausa—the deceased founder of Ranjit Singh's artillery—thereby indicating to his Muslim subjects that he was not an enemy of their faith.

Yet, Multan's defeat chastened other Muslim chiefs in its large neighborhood—in Bahawalpur, Dera Ghazi Khan, Dera Ismail Khan and elsewhere—and brought to Ranjit Singh an additional annual revenue of ₹7 lakhs.[46]

Ranjit Singh gave Multan's governorship to Sawan Mal, apparently an Arora from Gujranwala. Administering the city and province of Multan for over twenty years, Sawan Mal replaced—according to a future British assessment—the 'disorganized' and 'happy-go-lucky' rule of Pashtun 'aristocrats' with 'a government conducted on the strictest of business principles'. Viewing 'inherited wealth as contraband', Sawan Mal, it was said, would 'lend money to a Jat to buy a plough or dig a well' but 'keep a Multani Pathan out of his estate and think he did God a service'. The British appraisal goes on to assert that Sawan Mal made the district 'the most contented in India and yet at the same time made it yield every rupee of income that [could] be squeezed from it'.[47]

The year also saw the start of the ascendancy in the Lahore court of the Dogra brothers from Jammu: Gulab Singh, Dhian Singh and Suchet Singh. Distantly related to the raja of Jammu, these brothers, who were Hindu Rajputs, had joined Ranjit Singh as simple soldiers after Jammu was subjugated by him. Their abilities and good looks won promotions, with Dhian Singh replacing Khushhal Singh as the Maharaja's chamberlain in 1818.

■

Multan's defeat was followed by a civil war in Afghanistan that enabled Ranjit Singh to extend his kingdom beyond the Indus in the northwest and also to conquer Kashmir.

In the summer of 1818, Fateh Khan was murdered by Prince Kamran, son of the very man, Mahmud, whom he had installed as king. Occupying key positions in Afghanistan and Kashmir, brothers of the killed wazir swore vengeance. The conflict that ensued had a tribal dimension too, for Fateh Khan and his brothers were Barakzai Pashtuns as opposed to the Sadozai clan to which Abdali's descendants, including Shuja, Mahmud and Zaman, belonged.

Racing to capture Kabul, 'the rival factions had left their south-eastern frontier with the Punjab practically undefended'.[48] Grasping his opportunity, Ranjit Singh launched (in October 1818) a large invasion of the Pashtun city of Peshawar, which was about sixty miles west of the Indus, ten miles east of the Khyber Pass, and 150 miles east of Kabul.

Attock city, which lay on the Indus's eastern bank, already belonged to the Maharaja, having been handed over in 1813, along with its Akbar-era fort, by its Afghan chief, Jahandad Khan. Following his usual policy, Ranjit Singh had retained Jahandad as his Attock chief.

The invading army's leaders included Hari Singh Nalwa and the Nihang chief, Phula Singh. Except for an initial ambush in which Pashtun tribesmen killed an entire reconnaissance party, the Durbar army met with little resistance. On 19 November, the Maharaja and his army entered Peshawar. The next day he rode on an elephant through its bazaars—'the first time in 700 years that the city saw an Indian conqueror ride through its streets'.[49]

Appointing Jahandad Khan as his Peshawar governor, Ranjit Singh left the city to return to Lahore, but his man was quickly deposed by one of the late Fateh Khan's brothers, Dost Muhammad, who, however, offered the Maharaja an annual revenue of ₹1 lakh and an acknowledgment of Lahore's suzerainty over Peshawar. Dost Muhammad's offer was accepted by Ranjit Singh.

Kashmir too lay undefended. Though certain that Ranjit Singh would again invade Kashmir, Kashmir's Afghan governor Azim Khan (another of Fateh Khan's brothers) had gone to Kabul to avenge his brother's killing. Before leaving, Azim Khan sent agents to Ludhiana to urge Ochterlony to take Kashmir under British protection. The Amritsar Treaty had tied the Company's hands, the colonel replied.

Left in charge of Kashmir, Azim Khan's younger brother Jabbar Khan blundered by persecuting Hindu Kashmiris. Many of them left the Valley, including Jabbar Khan's revenue minister, Pandit Birbal Dhar. Showing up in Lahore, Dhar advised Ranjit Singh that an opportune moment for seizing Kashmir had arrived.

Crown Prince Kharak Singh (formally named as Ranjit Singh's successor in 1816) and Diwan Chand led the invading army, which the Maharaja accompanied. Included in the attacking party was a man familiar with Kashmir's terrain, Raja Sultan Khan, who was released after seven years in prison. Until Ranjit Singh annexed it in 1812, Sultan Khan had ruled the principality of Bhimbar, which lay to the south of Kashmir's hills. Also taken for the Kashmir assault were the Nihangs.

As Dhar had predicted, there was little by way of defence. Sighting the Maharaja's forces, Jabbar Khan and his outnumbered Afghans troops escaped into the hills. In July 1819, Kharak Singh and Diwan Chand entered Srinagar as conquerors but forbade looting or molestation.

Ranjit Singh was still in the plains, bringing up the rear, when he heard that 'paradise-like Kashmir had come within [his] possession'.[50] Returning to Lahore, he appointed Mohkam Chand's son Moti Ram as the governor in Kashmir.

While troops were sent to different parts of Kashmir to eliminate pockets of Afghan defiance, Fakir Azizuddin was asked to prepare a report on the people, climate and produce of Kashmir, which apparently brought ₹70 lakhs in annual revenue to Lahore, apart from extending the kingdom's borders to Tibet and China.

His victories in Multan, Peshawar and Kashmir were still fresh when three new sons were born to Ranjit Singh. The mothers, Rattan Kaur and Daya Kaur, had been the wives of Sahib Singh Bhangi, who died in 1811. In conformity with Jat custom at the time, Ranjit Singh had taken both widows under his wing. Remembering his recent triumphs, the Maharaja named the boys Multana Singh, Peshaura Singh and Kashmira Singh.[51]

But even as he celebrated his good fortune he had to deal with a problem—the Pashtun tribes in the Hazara region between Peshawar and Kashmir were rebelling. The party sent from Lahore to quell them included Fateh Singh Ahluwalia, Prince Sher Singh (Ranjit Singh's second son), the prince's grandmother Sada Kaur, Ilahi Baksh, the chief gunner, and young Ram Dyal, who was the late Mohkam Chand's grandson and the son of Kashmir's new governor.

However, tribesmen captured and killed Ram Dyal, whereupon the shattered father, Moti Ram, renounced his governorship and retired to Benares. He was replaced as Kashmir's governor by Hari Singh Nalwa, while Fateh Singh Ahluwalia was asked to administer Hazara and fortify police posts there.

As for Sada Kaur, her daughter Mehtab (Ranjit Singh's first wife) had died by now and her relations with the king had soured. After refusing to attend Kharak Singh's wedding, she objected to his investiture as Crown Prince, and complained repeatedly that Mehtab's sons, i.e. her grandsons, Sher Singh and Tara Singh, were being ignored.

The Maharaja, who remembered Sada Kaur's support for Ochterlony's push in Malwa, found her ceaseless criticism hard to bear. He knew, moreover, that his mother-in-law, now in her seventies, was in a position to call in British support, for some of her lands were located south of the Sutlej.

Around February 1822 (when Nau Nihal, Prince Kharak Singh's son, was born), Ranjit Singh decided to act against Sada Kaur. She was journeying east from Lahore when a body of horsemen sent by the Maharaja caught up with her. Sada Kaur was brought back to Lahore and placed in detention.

In related steps, all Kanhiya forts were occupied and their militia absorbed into the Durbar's army. Batala, the ancestral seat of the Kanhiyas, was given as a jagir to Sada Kaur's grandson, Prince Sher Singh, who did not—perhaps could not—do anything to protect his grandmother or her interests. Other Kanhiya lands were joined to Kangra.

Ranjit Singh did not see Sada Kaur again. She died in confinement in 1832, 'full of angry recriminations against the Maharaja'.[52] Whatever remained of her personal possessions was attached to the kingdom after her death. It was a sad end for one of the most remarkable women in Punjabi history.

The Maharaja's relationship with Fateh Singh Ahluwalia, the prince of Kapurthala (Jullundur doab), also worsened during the 1820s. While Fateh Singh's role in the Maharaja's court steadily declined, that of Dhian Singh, the royal chamberlain, grew rapidly. Given the title of raja, Dhian Singh would soon be named chief of the council of ministers.

When Ranjit Singh objected to a fort that Fateh Singh was building, the annoyed prince, who owned lands in British Punjab as well, crossed the Sutlej and asked for British protection, whereupon the Maharaja seized Kapurthala and other estates belonging to Fateh Singh. Finding to his disappointment that the British would not go to war to recover his possessions, and assured by Ranjit Singh of forgiveness if he returned, Fateh Singh re-crossed the Sutlej in 1826 and knelt down at the Maharaja's feet in Lahore. A tearful embrace followed, and Fateh Singh got his lands back, but the independent prince, for long a partner, had become a vassal.[53] He would die in 1837.

■

As for Ranjit Singh's expanding kingdom, the biggest gains after the triumphs in Multan, Peshawar and Kashmir had occurred in 1821 in the large Sindh Sagar spaces west of the Jhelum, to which Kabul thought it had claim. Advancing at the head of a large army, the Maharaja found a regional ally in Ahmed Yar, a leader of the Tiwana clan of the Muslim Rajputs of Khushab, a place he had subdued ten years earlier.

In this demanding expedition, during which Ranjit Singh's men dug wells as they moved forward, the towns of Bhakkar, Dera Ismail Khan (west of the Indus), Mankera and Leiah (or Layyah) were all captured without any challenge from Kabul. After enduring a fortnight's siege, the region's most influential chief, the nawab of Mankera, surrendered his fort and accepted the Maharaja's offer of a jagir in Dera Ismail Khan.

Here we may mark as an aside that most Muslim rulers of these overwhelmingly Muslim chiefdoms, as also the Kabul kingdom, employed Hindu ministers or accountants.[54]

The Sindh Sagar conquest conferred on the Maharaja an image of invincibility.[55] At his kingdom's opposite end, in the hills abutting east Punjab, Ranjit Singh 'subverted more principalities' than the Mughals had.[56] But he annexed few of them. Mandi, Suket, Bilaspur, Chamba and Kulu, vassals earlier to the Mughals, now conceded Ranjit Singh's suzerainty and sent contingents to the Lahore Durbar.

The hill rajas enjoyed internal autonomy but the Maharaja regulated succession when they died and also their dealings with one another. In 1824, when Kangra's ruler Sansar Chand died, the Maharaja acknowledged his son Anirodh Chand's succession only after obtaining a lakh of rupees from him. Also dying in 1824, Ramanand, a 'great banker of Amritsar' (as Latif describes him), left eight lakhs of rupees. Evidently this wealth was seized, and Lahore's city wall was rebuilt with it.[57]

After Gulab Singh, the oldest of the Dogra brothers, quelled disturbances raised by Muslim petty chiefs, he was given Jammu as a jagir.[58] Before long, all three brothers were called rajas, and Dhian Singh named the wazir. The wazir never sat while in attendance on the Maharaja, even if others took seats, but Ranjit Singh asked that Dhian Singh's boy Hira, still to enter his teens, should always be seated. Hira was unusually attractive, even more so than his father and uncles, whose looks were admired by many, Europeans included.

'Dotingly fond' (writes Latif) of Hira, the Maharaja soon conferred on him the title of raja and asked Anirodh Chand to give one of his 'two beautiful sisters' in marriage to the boy. Believing their ancestry to be superior to that of the Dogras, Anirodh and his mother evaded the proposal.

To escape an offended Maharaja's reach, Anirodh crossed the Sutlej into British Punjab, but not very long thereafter mother and son both died. Cousins of Anirodh obtained much of the Kangra estate with the aid of the Maharaja, who married two of Anirodh's half-sisters himself and, in 1829 arranged—'with great pomp' in Lahore—Hira Singh's marriage to 'a maiden of equal degree'.[59] We are not told what happened to Anirodh's full sisters.

∎

Visiting Punjab in 1831, the East India Company's officer and diplomat, Alexander Burnes, estimated that Ranjit Singh's kingdom contained only around 100,000 Sikhs.[60] 'The paucity of Seikhs in a country ruled and governed by them is remarkable', he would write.[61] Burnes thought, however, that in the areas where the Sikhs were most concentrated, they amounted to a third of the population. The historian Grewal suggests that Sikhs in Ranjit Singh's dominions numbered around 1.5 million, making up 12.5 per cent in a population of about 12 million.[62] Another scholar gives a 14–15 million figure for the total population.[63]

According to Grewal, who cites Burnes's impression that Sikh numbers were rising year by year, more than half of the kingdom's population, and 90 per cent of its Sikhs, lived in a 'core region' formed by three contiguous spaces: the upper Bari and upper Rachna doabs (which included the future

British-era districts of Amritsar and Lahore) and the Jullundur doab.[64]

Differences in these estimates notwithstanding, Muslims were a clear majority in the kingdom, and Hindus a large majority among the rest. Since Sikh-Hindu differences were not underlined at the time, it can be said that Sikh and Hindu elites jointly formed the kingdom's ruling class, of which, according to Grewal, over 50 per cent were Sikhs. Moreover, Jats from the 'core region' formed the bulk of the Sikh ruling class.

For the first time in centuries, Punjab's Muslims were thus being governed by a non-Muslim establishment led by Jat Sikhs. While the Maharaja was a believing Sikh, he was not setting up a theocracy, and his establishment included Muslims. We have noted Ranjit Singh's reliance on Fakir Azizuddin and his brothers and on Muslim artillery commanders; his occasional alliances with different Muslim chiefs; and his willingness to let several Muslim chiefs run their territories as autonomous vassals.

Persian was the Durbar's official language, many Muslims served in his army, and Muslim jurists presided over the courts where his Muslim subjects sought justice under Islamic law. Unani medicine was dispensed without cost in numerous dispensaries overseen by Fakir Nuruddin. Schools where the Qur'an and the Arabic language were taught continued to exist, with widows teaching young boys and girls.[65] If Ranjit Singh's visits to Muslim mosques and shrines are also taken into account, as also the fact that the Muslim women he took into his harem or married were not asked to change their faith, then it becomes hard to conclude that his was an anti-Muslim kingdom.

A French scholar of Punjab, Jean-Marie Lafont, offers the opinion that the kingdom's administrative and military structure 'reflected the multiethnic and multicultural diversity of the 14-15 million inhabitants of the Punjab'. Lafont goes so far as to add that the people experienced a 'feeling of belonging' and 'a Punjabi ethos and culture' was created, 'at least between Indus and Sutlej, from the Himalayan foothills to the frontiers of Sindh'.[66]

Yet Muslims did not have much say in the kingdom's management. The Maharaja's favourite officers were Dogras, Sikhs and Brahmins. Among the latter were Pandit Ganga Ram, who was 'placed at the head of the military office',[67] and, following his death, his successor, Pandit (later Raja) Dina Nath, both from Kashmir.

The three Fakir brothers were close to the Maharaja, but they were wholly deferential if also at times influential. Muslims in his army were recognized and rewarded but not, it would seem, tapped for advice. Allowed to remain a Muslim, Mohran was for spells his favourite consort but never a counsellor. He held free and frank talks with Europeans and a few Sikhs and Hindus in his court but not, it would seem, with Muslims in his employ or outside. This was the result not of animus but of circumstances, of where and amongst whom he had been raised, and of his path to power.

With some Muslim chiefs, notably those of Multan and Kasur, he fought repeated and bitter battles, but these ended, as we have seen, with Ranjit Singh acknowledging his foes' valour and granting them a place in his kingdom. A few Muslim clans in the Lahore and Rawalpindi divisions, including Chathas and Bhattis, continued to resist his rule, but their defiance was neither victorious nor essentially religious. They fought him not as Muslims against a Sikh but to remain masters of their tracts. Elsewhere, and especially in Multan and Kasur, the Pashtun clans he had overthrown continued to resent his rule.

According to one view, 'the Multani Pathans or the Chahttas or the Bhattis who had resisted the Sikhs were persona non grata' in the Maharaja's kingdom.[68] A more serious charge, widely believed in today's Pakistan, is that 'many Muslim mosques were turned into powder magazines and stables'.[69] There is little doubt that some were, especially in Lahore, where guns and ammunition were stored in the Badshahi Mosque, but perhaps more to show who was boss than to hurt Islam.

Lafont has written of Lahore's Sunehri Mosque, built in 1753 by the Mughal officer Nawab Bhikari Khan, who, as we saw in chapter 2, was killed in 1754 by, among others, Mughlani Begum. Noting that the mosque was turned into a gurdwara 'when the Sikhs took over' (presumably before Ranjit Singh began his rule), Lafont also informs us that in the late 1820s a group of the Durbar's Muslim officers persuaded the Maharaja to restore it as a mosque. They were supported by the Fakir brothers and also by Jean Francois Allard, an important French officer in the Maharaja's service, who provided personal funds for redoing the mosque's golden domes.[70]

Later, in 1834, when Allard sought Ranjit Singh's permission to return to France so that his Lahore-born children could receive a Christian education, the Maharaja said, 'Every person should be free to follow the religion he chooses... You can go.' Apparently the remark was published in the French press.[71]

According to Lafont, after Ranjit Singh took over in Lahore, the city's Muslim community 'continued to enjoy the possession of most of its mosques and sacred monuments', though, adds the Frenchman, the tomb and mosque of Shah Sharaz (d. 1692) were destroyed to make a ditch designed to protect important buildings.[72] Other Mughal-era monuments that were damaged, or raided for marble, included the graceful tomb of Jahangir.

On the other hand, Amritsar's Harmandir and the ancient Hindu shrine at Jwalamukhi in Kangra were provided with funds and with gold and marble. In Lahore, Ranjit Singh built a gurdwara named after Guru Ram Das and a mausoleum for Guru Arjan Dev.[73] The use of Gurmukhi was encouraged. Textbooks in that script were produced, a few of them even reaching, it seems, some Muslim girls.[74] For the Hindus' spiritual benefit, 'simple copies of the Bhagavat Puran and the Shiv Puran were copied repetitively at Lahore'.[75]

While Ranjit Singh respected the faiths of others, his kingdom displayed unmistakable symbols of his own faith. At times an elephant with a bejewelled copy of the Granth Sahib placed in a golden howdah would precede the elephant carrying Ranjit Singh, also seated in a golden enclosure.[76]

The kingdom was not free of religious tension. Bans on the slaughter of cows and restrictions on public calls for the Islamic prayer were imposed in many places. However, such bans could not be enforced in overwhelmingly Muslim localities.

It has been argued that 'the Punjabi and the Pathan Muslim for the first time suffered religious oppression during the Sikh time, from roughly 1780 to 1849'.[77] This assessment may need to be qualified in the light of some eyewitness accounts. Thus Alexander Burnes would relate that Sikhs looking after Ranjit Singh's thoroughbreds had 'repaired and beautified' a mosque frequented by a Muslim physician, turning it into 'a conspicuous white building that glitters in the sun', because the physician had cured the horses from disease.[78]

Joseph Wolff, a travelling Jewish doctor turned Christian evangelist who met Ranjit Singh, was also said to have been 'impressed with Ranjit's liberal views on religion and the futility of making forcible conversions'.[79] Wolff thought, too, that by defeating several Muslim chiefs in battle, the Maharaja had conveyed to the Muslims that 'the edge of the sword [was] not always evidence of the truth of religion'.[80]

We may conclude this short reflection on Muslims in Ranjit Singh's kingdom by noting that the forebears of several prominent Muslims of twentieth-century Punjab, including Fazl-i-Husain and Khizr Hayat Tiwana, were the Maharaja's officers or allies.

■

While nothing like a major Muslim revolt was mounted in Ranjit Singh's Punjab, religious rebellions took place in the Pashtun region west of the

Indus. In 1824, Phula Singh, the Nihang chief, and Balbhadra, who led Gurkha soldiers enlisting under the Maharaja, were both killed in a fierce battle with Pashtun tribes who had seized Peshawar. Yet the Pashtuns lost about 4,000 men and Peshawar was retaken by the kingdom's army, which was headed by Diwan Chand (who would die in 1825), Hari Singh Nalwa and two French commanders, Allard and Jean Baptiste Ventura.

Two years after this battle, the region's most resolute rebel surfaced. He was neither a Pashtun nor a Punjabi but a Hindustani named Sayyid Ahmed, born in Rae Bareilly near Lucknow. A follower of Delhi's famed Islamic ideologue, Shah Waliullah (1703-62), Sayyid Ahmed found the demise of Muslim rule in Delhi and Lahore unbearable.

Though opposed both to the British and the Sikhs, he focused more on the latter. Interestingly enough, India's new British rulers did not impede his journey via Sindh to Peshawar, nor that of the numerous fighters he enlisted in Uttar Pradesh and Bihar.

One of Sayyid Ahmed's recruiting pamphlets, issued in north India in the mid-1820s, alleged: 'The Sikh nation has long held sway in Lahore and other places. Their oppressions have exceeded all bounds. Thousands of Mohammedans have they unjustly killed... No longer do they allow the call to prayer from the mosques, and the killing of cows they have entirely prohibited.'[81]

Recruits, arms and donations were raised in several Indian cities, and towards the end of 1826 a jihad commenced in the tribal areas around Peshawar. For a while, Yusufzai, Khattak and other Pashtun tribesmen responded fervently to Sayyid Ahmed's call, and Peshawar was vacated by the Maharaja's Pashtun governor. An army, again led by the Maharaja's French commanders, Allard and Ventura, played a part in the recovery of Peshawar.

Ranjit Singh used money and clan rivalries to divide the tribes and, from time to time, the kingdom's organized force to subdue them. In the summer of 1830, troops led by Prince Sher Singh, the Maharaja's son by Mehtab Kaur, Hari Singh Nalwa and Allard won a major battle against the rebels. Claude Wade, who had taken over in Ludhiana as the East India Company's chief Punjab-watcher, conveyed to the Resident in Delhi a 'detailed account sent by agents in Lahore of action between Sikh troops under Sardar Hari Singh and the insurgents under the fanatic Sayad Ahmed in which the latter were defeated'.[82]

However, in a reversal from earlier clashes between Afghan soldiers and Sikh bands, the Maharaja's organized regiments were now being ambushed by determined Pashtun bands, and some battles were daringly won by the jihadists.

What eventually put an end to Sayyid Ahmed's bid was Pashtun resentment of Hindustani jihadists. 'When Ahmed was accused, as many say unjustly, of assigning maidens one by one to his needy Hindustani followers, the people were greatly incensed.' This was the finding of Olaf Caroe, student of Pashtun history and a future British governor of the North West Frontier Province.[83]

Desertions and even murders occurred, and Sayyid Ahmed was trapped between the kingdom's forces and hostile tribesmen. In May 1831, a Sikh party led by Prince Sher Singh surprised and killed an isolated Sayyid Ahmed at Balakot.* Defiance of Sikh rule would, however, continue in the Pashtun country, at times supported by Kabul.

Interestingly enough, it has been claimed that 'not a single Muslim chief of any standing' in Punjab supported the jihad, which 'did not disturb the even tenor of life' in the kingdom.[84]

∎

Napoleon's defeat in 1815 had ended any French hopes of displacing the British from India, but it also freed some French and Italian officers for service outside Europe, including in Punjab. In 1822, two French commanders, Jean Francois Allard and Jean Baptiste Ventura, whom I have referred to earlier, were among the first Europeans to join the Maharaja's army. Within a few years, more than fifty whites or Eurasians were on Ranjit Singh's payroll, of whom the best known, besides Allard and Ventura, were Claude August Court and Paolo Avitabile from France and Italy respectively.

From 1829, the Maharaja also employed the Austro-Hungarian homeopath, Martin Honigberger, as his personal physician, and two years later he facilitated a journey to the Himalayas by the French geologist and botanist, Victor Jacquemont.

Always conscious of the British next door, Ranjit Singh was glad to have officers who had fought the British and could train his army along European lines. Though most of his ministers and commanders advised against the employment of foreigners on handsome emoluments, they were overruled.

However, conditions were imposed. The Europeans were required to abstain from smoking, shaving or eating beef. They were required, too, to marry local women and had to obtain the Maharaja's permission before leaving

---

*Destroyed in the 2005 earthquake and then rebuilt

Punjab. Not given prominence in his court, they were also discouraged from confabulating with one another.

Thanks to the French and Italians, the Maharaja's military officers wore uniforms inspired by Napoleon's army. Allard and Ventura led a mobile, Lahore-based special force, the Fauj-i-Khas. Court (who found a Kashmiri wife, Fezli Azamjoo) and Paolo Avitabile were in charge of two separate brigades, also Lahore-based. In 1830, Avitabile's brigade was moved to Peshawar.

Units of the Fauj-i-Khas stood on the Sutlej's right bank—the kingdom's border. Across the river, a Fauj detachment provided security to Lahore's agent in Ludhiana in British Punjab—there had been one right from 1809. The French were thus represented in northern India, close to the British, via the Fauj's Khalsa colours.

According to Lafont, the employment of European officers led to an increase in the proportion of regular troops in the kingdom's army. Apart from Punjabis, Purbiahs (easterners) and Gurkhas had also enlisted. Some of the Purbiahs were deserters from the Company's armies. As for the Gurkhas, Ranjit Singh had appreciated their grit ever since 1809-10, when he fought them in the hills.

No matter how impactful, the Europeans in Ranjit Singh's military did not upstage the Punjabis. Ilahi Baksh remained in charge of artillery, Hari Singh Nalwa was now the Maharaja's chief general, and Prince Sher Singh, twenty-three in 1830, seemed an inspiring young commander.

■

The army's supreme commander—the kingdom's central figure and driving force—was the Maharaja himself. By 1830, the fifty-year-old king, given to hypochondria, was beginning to feel old and unwell. Four years earlier, thinking his end to be near, he had sent Fakir Imamuddin to Ludhiana to plead for the services of a British physician. The Governor-General sent a Dr Murray, whose ministrations worked.

Another Scot saw Ranjit Singh several times during 1831 and 1832: the explorer, diplomat, linguist and spy, Alexander Burnes. Connected to the poet Robert Burns, Alexander Burnes would be assassinated in Kabul in 1841. After conversing with the Maharaja in diverse settings—in a garden, in the royal court, on a hunt, during a drinking party, and so forth—Burnes wrote:

> Nature has indeed been sparing in her gifts to this personage and there must be a mighty contest between his mind and body... he has but one

eye, is pitted with small-pox, and his stature does not certainly exceed 5 ft. 3 in. He is entirely free from pomp and show, yet the studied respect of his court is remarkable; not an individual spoke without a sign, though the throng was more like a bazaar than the court of the first native prince of India...

I never quitted the presence of a native in Asia with such impressions as I left this man; without education, and without a guide, he conducts all the affairs of his kingdom with surpassing energy and vigour, and yet he wields his power with a consideration quite unprecedented in an Eastern prince.[85]

Ranjit Singh's love of horses being no secret, in July 1831 Burnes brought to the Maharaja, as a gift from the King of England, 'a team of five massive dray horses'[86] and, as a present from William Bentinck, the Governor-General of India, a grand coach which, given the condition of roads, could only be transported, it was explained, by water. The presents would legitimize a trip from the Arabian Sea up the Indus River to Ranjit Singh's border and on to Lahore, enabling Burnes to pick up closer knowledge of the topographies of Sindh and Punjab.

Interested himself in Sindh, Ranjit Singh was disappointed that the amirs of that land had permitted the British diplomat to sail up the Indus, and he harboured no illusions regarding Burnes' purpose. But a gift from the English king could not be declined without incurring imperial wrath, and the dray horses had tempted him anyway. The 'exploring' gift-bearer was not only allowed into the kingdom and into Lahore, he was feted, and in Burnes' presence guns repeatedly boomed in salutes to the British monarch.

Four miles outside Lahore, twenty-six-year-old Burnes was welcomed by Fakir Azizuddin and Raja Gulab Singh from Jammu, whose brother, Raja Dhian Singh, was the royal chamberlain. Several days of gift-giving (the Maharaja reciprocated handsomely) and talks followed.

When Burnes and the Maharaja talked about how his kingdom might obtain Sindh, Ranjit Singh spoke warmly and also openly of the 'bravery of his nation, who were very free from prejudice, would carry eight days' provisions on their backs, dig a well if water were scarce, build a fort if circumstances required it'.[87]

The Scot's first night in Lahore had been spent in the home of the Frenchman, Allard. The city's Frenchmen told Burnes that Ranjit Singh had 'no equal from Constantinople to India', adding,

> The most creditable trait in Ranjit's character is his humanity; he has never been known to punish a criminal with death since his accession to power... Cunning and conciliation have been the two great weapons of his diplomacy.[88]

But British cunning proved superior. Burnes was able to report to Bentinck not only that the Maharaja was excited by the British horses, *and* that he desired Sindh, but also that—like the cis-Sutlej Sikhs—Sindh's amirs wanted British protection, for they were fearful of Ranjit Singh and his army. The British response to this intelligence was to redouble their 'conciliation' of the Maharaja with events of pomp and ceremony.

These included a grand affair in Ropar, in British Punjab, on 26 October 1831, where Governor-General Bentinck lined up British troops on both sides of a road on which Ranjit Singh, seated on an elephant, and his 1,000 horsemen in coats of mail, would ride. The Maharaja was housed in a magnificent tent atop a hill. Next to the tent was erected a silver pavilion resembling a Hindu temple; and close by was a wheat-field where clever ploughing had produced the outlines of birds and horses.

The next day, on his side of the Sutlej, the Maharaja outdid the British. Wine, dancing-girls, diamonds, silks, gilded thrones, Azizuddin's eloquent flattery—everything was employed. But Bentinck plainly told Ranjit Singh that the British would not let him cross his southern boundary into Sindh.

A year later, in December 1832, Captain Wade journeyed from Ludhiana to Lahore and obtained the Maharaja's seal on a treaty signed by the British and by Sindh's amirs of Hyderabad, Khairpur and Mirpur. With that seal, Ranjit Singh formally renounced his ambitions regarding Sindh. Some staunch Sikhs deplored the apparent caving in and the carousals preceding it. There was a bid to kill the Maharaja but the assailant was stopped and seized.

∎

When recording their impressions, those who met the Maharaja would always mention his curiosity. Burnes, for one, jotted down a string of Ranjit Singh's enquiries. During Ropar's grand festivities, when the Maharaja met British military officers, he apparently 'asked a hundred searching questions' about weapons.[89] Jacquemont, the French botanist whose research Ranjit Singh supported, would write:

> He is the first inquisitive Indian I have seen; and his curiosity balances the apathy of the whole of his nation. He has asked me a hundred

thousand questions about India, the British, Europe, Bonaparte, this world in general and the next, hell, paradise, the soul, God, the devil and a myriad others of the same kind.[90]

A fierce drive and skill at arms (and with a horse) had taken the young scion of the Gujranwala-based Sukerchakia clan of Jats to a seat of power that he turned into a throne. More than an abundance of soldiers, it was an image established over the years of irresistible strength that constituted his military secret.

But drive and military skills alone cannot account for the fact that in a place and period of considerable instability, this short, unprepossessing king invited no challenger, faced no revolt, and kept his throne for nearly forty years; or for the fact that, despite his appearance, informality and background, Punjabis, whatever their religion, and Europeans, whatever their nationality, saw him naturally as the Maharaja.

Curious among the incurious, pragmatic where others were ego-driven, usually content with autonomous vassals rather than desiring direct rule, and employing talented individuals, he possessed another quality rare in his times: he did not kill defeated or captured foes. Armed with these virtues, the short man stood tall in his age.

If an officer, civil or military, failed in his mission, or offended the Maharaja in any way, Ranjit Singh would levy a fine on him, often a stiff one. Or, before the whole court, he would strike the presumed culprit with a sheathed sword. After a while, however, the officer's standing and incomes were usually restored.

There were weaknesses. Apparently he liked, at times, to show off his jewels, including, on special occasions, the Kohinoor. He threw gold and silver at nautch girls. He was also accused of being a hoarder, and of continually raising his demands for tribute. At times he drank to excess. He was not content with a few wives. In his biography, Khushwant Singh names twenty-two women who had a relationship with the Maharaja and quotes a statement by a son of his, Prince Dalip Singh, to a French journal in 1889: 'I am the son of one of my father's forty-six wives.'[91]

Dalip Singh's mother, Rani Jindan, said to be beautiful, was perhaps the Maharaja's last and youngest wife. He married her in 1835. Two years earlier, he had married Gul Bahar, described by Latif as 'one of the *demi-monde* of Amritsar', with 'great pomp and ceremony'.[92]

The weaknesses were common but the virtues exceptional. His subjects saw Ranjit Singh as 'one of the best princes that has ever reigned in India'.[93]

His European officers (and other European visitors) were apparently struck by the 'free and direct approach of the Sikhs' in Ranjit Singh's court. The absence of 'sumptuous decorum' or 'endless processions' contrasted with images of the earlier Mughal durbars of Agra or Delhi. Though it had a king, the Lahore court seemed 'republican' and displayed 'straight-forward habits'. It was 'patriarchal' and 'warrior-like' but observed little by way of etiquette or ceremony.[94] As far back as in 1783, years before Ranjit Singh's takeover, the English traveller, Forster, too had found 'a large vein of popular power' and 'an equality of rank' in the Lahore ruled by the Sikh trio we looked at in the preceding chapter.[95]

The Maharaja retained much of the Mughal governance structure. Thus a province or region was headed by a nazim or governor. Under the nazim was a kardar who collected revenue and enforced order in each of the region's parganas or ta'alluqas. In each pargana, a qanungo maintained revenue records. A village had its muqaddam or headman and its patwari or accountant, and a group of villages its chaudhari or chief.

Most nazims and kardars in Ranjit Singh's time were Sikhs. Kotwals looked after the security of towns—for some years at least a Muslim was the Lahore kotwal. Personally appointing all nazims, kardars and kotwals, the king was also the ultimate judge who installed several adalatis (judges) at different levels. The army, likewise, was headed—brilliantly and inspiringly—by the Maharaja. For years there was no prime minister or wazir though, eventually, Raja Dhian Singh, the Dogra chamberlain, rose to become a wazir.

The kingdom's servants were paid partly in cash but mostly through a jagir, an assignment of land and its revenue. Around 40 per cent of the kingdom's revenue went in jagir to officers, servants, soldiers, religious institutions (Sikh, Hindu and Muslim) and defeated chiefs.[96]

After decades of clashes and uncertainty, Punjab's cultivation, trade and manufacturing (including textiles, metal work, pottery and silverware) all evidently grew during Ranjit Singh's rule, helped by safer passage for trading caravans and by banking facilities. Amritsar grew more than Lahore and Multan, but the latter also saw trade and prosperity, as did towns like Batala, Jullundur, Hoshiarpur, Sialkot, Gujrat and Wazirabad. The production of Kashmiri shawls rose, and Kashmiri weavers moved into Amritsar, Lahore and other cities.[97]

Calcutta's Marwaris, who traded across Hindustan, and Sindh's Shikarpuris, who traded with Iran and Central Asia, did commerce in Amritsar and Lahore. To help one Marwari trader, Ranjit Singh seems to have built in Lahore a stable for cargo-bearing camels and donkeys and fifteen shops.[98] Recalling such initiatives, Lafont sees Ranjit Singh as a 'great Indian ruler who modernized his state in an effort to create a place for it in the concert of nations'.[99]

Other parts of India did not throw up anything like his remarkable kingdom. However, though lasting for about five decades, it was entirely dependent on one man. The Maharaja's subjects had no idea of what would happen after Ranjit Singh, for he failed to create a council of civilian and military officers to assist the successor he had named, his eldest son, the feeble-minded Kharak Singh.

The Maharaja well knew, and his subjects suspected, that his court was shot through with intrigue. Yet for all his extraordinary inquisitiveness, which every interlocutor noticed, he did not seem curious about the future of his kingdom. Eager to learn all he could about European armies and British guns, he did not ask the more difficult question: how could ambitious claimants be restrained from going for one another's throats once he was no more?

His successors would need more than the weapons of war with which he had won his kingdom. His army, consisting of around 50,000 soldiers in 1821, had more than 80,000 men in the late 1830s. Punjab had in fact been turned into a militarized state. The army's size and the large emoluments of its European and Punjabi commanders were draining the kingdom's treasury, but the price being paid was more than economic. The gun had been established—or reinforced—as Punjab's arbiter.

During the 1780s, when Ranjit Singh's father and other misl chiefs captured portions of Punjab, thereby laying the beginnings of the Maharaja's kingdom, two countries that experienced revolutions, America and France, had given themselves constitutions. One of the Maharaja's Frenchmen may indeed have spoken on the subject to him, or to Fakir Azizuddin.

There was no call for Ranjit Singh or his compatriots to dream of a republican constitution. However, something like a council to aid governance was not beyond imagination or accomplishment. Had he created one in his lifetime, and demanded loyalty for it from the army, it might have reinforced his successors.

■

Lahore's appearance, scarred in the second half of the eighteenth century, did not greatly improve during his reign. Visiting Lahore in 1809, an unnamed English officer would write that

> the ruins of Lahore... afforded a melancholy picture of fallen splendor. Here the lofty buildings and Masjids which fifty years ago raised their tops to the skies and were the pride of a busy and active population are now crumbling into dust... On going over these ruins I saw not a human being, all was silence, solitude and gloom.[100]

Viewing Lahore more than twenty years later, Alexander Burnes wrote in June 1831:

> We moved among its ruins... The mosques and tombs, which have been more stably built than the houses, remain in the midst of fields and cultivation as *caravan serais* for the travellers. The houses are very lofty, and the streets, which are narrow, offensively filthy from a gutter that passes through the centre. The bazars of Lahore do not exhibit much appearance of wealth, but the commercial influence of the Panjab is to be found at Amritsar, the modern capital.[101]

Even in 1838, the English traveller, Charles Masson, would say:

> [The earlier] extravagant praises bestowed upon [Lahore] must however be understood as applicable to a former city, of which now only the ruins are seen... The present city is nevertheless very extensive and comprises many elegant and important buildings.... Without the walls are scattered on all sides the ruins of the ancient city which are still wonderful...[102]

However, innovations in painting and literature were seen. While poets like Ahmad Yar (1768-1842), Sawan Yar and Jafar Beg wrote in Persian or Punjabi about the Maharaja, Qadir Yar (1802-1892) produced new and popular verses recounting old Punjabi tales like *Sohni Mahiwal, Puran Bhagat* and *Raja Rasalu*. Thanks to the Maharaja's Frenchmen, some paintings of the prolific Imam Bakhsh Lahori, who ran a workshop in Lahore from 1827 to the 1850s, went to Paris, where they were liked.

Euclid was translated from Arabic into Punjabi in this period, and the Maharaja had a Muslim cleric called Ali Ahmed, well-versed in mathematics and astronomy, brought from the North West Frontier to Lahore to teach elite young men, including Lehna Singh Majithia, who would acquire a name as an engineer-mathematician, and Ranjit Singh's grandson, Nau Nihal Singh.[103]

■

Having subjugated chief after chief in his neighbourhood, but blocked by the British from advancing into Sindh, Ranjit Singh often let his mind travel to Kabul. If in the past Lahore had acknowledged Kabul or Kandahar, it seemed to him fair that Kabul should now pay tribute to Lahore. That, however, is not what Shuja, the British guest in Ludhiana, or Shuja's Kabul-based rival, Dost Muhammad, or the British thought.

Shuja's presence in Ludhiana had given the British influence over him, but Ranjit Singh too managed to send him an offer: if Shuja would assure him Peshawar, give up his claim to the Sindh Sagar doab, agree to ban the slaughter of cattle in Afghanistan, and send horses and fruit as tribute, Ranjit Singh would help him regain the Kabul throne. Ignoring the offer, Shuja tried (with British consent) to obtain the throne through his own effort, believing that Pashtun tribes would rally to his standard.

Ranjit Singh allowed passage across Punjab to Shuja and his party, but in a battle in Kandahar in the summer of 1834, Dost Muhammad easily repulsed Shuja, who returned to Ludhiana. On his part, the Maharaja directed Hari Singh Nalwa to govern Peshawar and get closer to Kabul.

The year 1834 saw unrestrained fighting between Nalwa's force and Pashtun tribals. The latter's ambushes and sniping were countered by the destruction, under Nalwa's command, of whole villages and the construction of a series of forts. 'The name of Nalwa became a terror in the tribal territory', and Pashtun mothers would for years frighten children into good behaviour by speaking of 'Haria', after Nalwa's first name.[104]

Soft power too was used by the Maharaja. Fakir Azizuddin and Josiah Harlan, an American in the Maharaja's service who had earlier worked for Dost Muhammad, were sent as emissaries to the Afghans. Later, Harlan would claim success in setting Dost's brothers against him, 'exciting their jealousy of his growing power'.[105]

Nalwa serving as its governor, Peshawar was annexed to the kingdom in 1834. For a time, Dost remained quiet in the hills. Three years later, however, when Nalwa was ill and confined to his bed in Peshawar, and the Maharaja was busy in Lahore with the nuptials of his grandson, Nau Nihal Singh, Dost Muhammad launched a large assault.

Nalwa rose from his sickbed and led a counter-attack. In gory battles fought along the Khyber Pass, about 6,000 Punjabis and 11,000 Afghans were killed, but Nalwa and a son of Dost were among the dead. A British witness would report that Hari Singh Nalwa received four wounds: two from sabres, one from an arrow (which Nalwa pulled out himself), and the fourth from a gunshot. Before dying, he instructed his men not to give out word of his condition.[106]

The Afghans retired to their hideouts and the Khyber continued to mark the Sikh kingdom's northwestern frontier. Shaken by Nalwa's death (yet attaching the bulk of his wealth to the kingdom), Ranjit Singh named Allard, the Frenchman, as Peshawar's military governor. After three years at home, Allard had returned to Lahore in 1837 as France's Agent.

Dost's next move was to involve the Russians, who sent a diplomat and funds to Kabul. The Tsar accepted Dost's stand that Peshawar belonged to Kabul. Though perturbed by the Russian move, the British realized that while Dost might settle with them too if they recognized his right to Peshawar, Ranjit Singh would be infuriated. Instead, they chose to try a coalition with Shuja and Ranjit Singh.

Eventually accepted by the Maharaja, the British plan was to create an Army of the Indus, to be formed by British, Sikh and Afghan contingents. Supplied by a Shuja living as an exile in Ludhiana, the last contingent would understandably be the smallest. The Army of the Indus would aim to restore Shuja to the Kabul throne and make Afghanistan friendlier to the British and also the Sikhs.

Though the British explained that they would move towards Kabul via Sindh, not by marching across Punjab, the Maharaja was not excited. He would have preferred to take Kabul by himself, or along with Shuja, but without the British. Yet, he was old and unwell, and his army was not in a position to go alone into Afghanistan or resist the British who were pushing him.

Earlier, when the British had asked him not to move into Sindh, he had firmly rejected pressure from his hawks to enter Sindh anyway, saying to them, 'What happened to the 200,000-strong Maratha army that fought the British?'[107] The Maratha empire had disappeared in 1817 after they lost their last battle, fought in Poona, against the British.

The Maharaja fully expected the Company to chip away at Punjab and eventually absorb it. As British historians would later frankly acknowledge, the Company 'had long cast covetous eyes on [Punjab]'[108]. Ranjit Singh did not miss this reality. Years earlier, when shown a map of India where British-conquered South India, Bombay, Bengal and UP were painted in red, he had exclaimed, 'Sab lal ho jaega (It'll all become red).'[109] In his view, it was good to stand up to the British but unwise to provoke a clash with them.

The Afghans, on the other hand, feuding among themselves, seemed to offer scope for the Sikh kingdom's expansion.

■

Something like the plan for the Army of the Indus probably existed in their minds when, in 1837—the year when a seventeen-year-old woman named Victoria became the Queen of England—British dignitaries led by General Sir Henry Fane, commander-in-chief of the Company's armies, attended the magnificent wedding in Lahore of Prince Nau Nihal Singh, the Maharaja's grandson and Prince Kharak Singh's son. At receptions, young Hira—Dhian Singh's son—came across as

> the most superbly dressed of the Omerahs and the reigning favourite of the day. He was literally one mass of jewels; his neck, arms and legs were covered so thickly with necklaces, armlets and bangles, formed of pearls, diamonds and rubies that it was difficult to discover anything between them.[110]

In the following year, 1838, the idea of the Army of the Indus was put explicitly to the Maharaja by an official British delegation sent by the Governor-General in Calcutta, Lord Auckland. Ranjit Singh chose to receive the party in Adinanagar,* the town near the Kangra hills that Adina Beg had founded eight decades earlier. The Maharaja had raised buildings and trees in Adinanagar, which he frequently visited. For the benefit of the British visitors, great tents were erected and troops paraded.

Sir William MacNaghten, the leader of the British delegation (which included Alexander Burnes, recently back from Afghanistan), read out a letter from the Governor-General proposing an Anglo-Sikh treaty to restore Shuja. The kingdom's first minister, as he was now being called, Dhian Singh, indicated visible disapproval, an opinion in which he was ardently joined, once the British had left the room, by most ministers. Only two, Fakir Azizuddin and Bhaia Ram Singh, argued for accepting the proposal.

In the end, the Maharaja agreed with these two, thinking it better that a restored Shuja should be beholden to the Sikh kingdom too, not just to the British. Earlier, Burnes had thrown in an alleged remark by Dost Muhammad regarding the Maharaja: 'I can't do that brute any harm, but I will torment him a good deal yet before I have done with him.' Ranjit

---

*Now called Dinanagar, the town is part of Indian Punjab.

Singh was duly stung.[111] His acceptance of alliance was conveyed to the relieved British by Azizuddin.

To obtain the Maharaja's signature, however, the Governor-General himself had to travel, at the end of 1838, to Ferozepur, a British-held army town on the Sutlej. Here, about forty miles south of Lahore, the two armies—the Company's and that of the kingdom—met each other as allies, together forming the Army of the Indus. Curiosity, concealed suspicion and anticipation filled the Ferozepur air. There were drinking parties. Words of flattery also flowed. Dancing girls, carpets and jewels were on show.

For many, the star was the Maharaja himself. Lord Auckland's sister, the writer Emily Eden, who with numerous Britons had accompanied the Governor-General to Ferozepur, would say of Ranjit Singh:

> He said he understood that there were books which contained objections to drunkenness, and he thought it better that there should be no books at all than that they should contain such foolish notions... He has made himself a great king; he has conquered a great many powerful enemies; he is remarkably just in his government; he has disciplined a large army; [and] he hardly ever takes away life, which is wonderful in a despot...[112]

Emily Eden and the others found the Maharaja to be lovable, popular in the 'British' town of Ferozepur—and ill.

His seal to a treaty was obtained but the infirm Ranjit Singh returned a 'No' to a proposal for stationing a British Resident in Lahore, and hoped the British would not insist. In Ludhiana, to no one's surprise, Shuja too signed the treaty. It was agreed that, accompanied by Prince Taimur (Shuja's son) and Captain Wade, the kingdom's soldiers in the Army of the Indus would enter Kabul through the Khyber Pass. Along with Shuja, the British would aim to meet them in Kabul by way of Sindh, Quetta and Kandahar.

In the end, the 9,500-strong British contingent, too, embarked from Lahore. Kandahar was reached at the end of April, and there, on 8 May 1839, Shuja was once more enthroned as the king of Afghanistan. Separately, a Muslim contingent of Ranjit Singh's army, led by Shaikh Basawan, escorted Prince Taimur through the Khyber Pass and into Kabul. When, some days later, Shuja, the British, and the kingdom of Lahore jointly organized a victory parade, Ranjit Singh's Muslim troops carried his colours on Kabul's streets.

The Maharaja heard that Shuja had reached Kandahar, but by this time he was seriously ill. On 27 June, four weeks before Basawan's entry into Kabul, he died. To save him, medicines of every variety—homeopathic, allopathic, hydropathic and more—had been tried, as also a powder of pearls and precious stones administered personally by Fakir Azizuddin. Nothing helped.

From his death-bed, Ranjit Singh managed to press saffron on Prince Kharak Singh's forehead, affirming the eldest son's succession, and also to enjoin Dhian Singh to stand by the heir. Yet, there were those who thought that Kharak Singh's half-brother, Sher Singh, had deliberately and for long been 'carefully kept at some distance on the frontier while the influence of the Dogra family reigned supreme in the Court'.[113]

The funeral fire that turned the Maharaja's body into ash also burnt alive, evidently with their consent, 'four of the Ranis', including Raj Devi, daughter of Sansar Chand of Kangra, and 'seven of his slave-girls'. Ten years after British India had declared sati to be unlawful, all eleven solemnly mounted the platform of cremation in the kingdom. It seems that Dhian Singh too offered to sacrifice himself but was prevented from doing so.[114]

■

Triggered by clashes over succession, killings and revenge-killings occurred. Some wanted young Nau Nihal, who was on his way to Kabul when the Maharaja died, to succeed to the throne, not Nau Nihal's father, the opium-eating Kharak. They were foiled by Dhian Singh, who took advantage of Nau Nihal's absence and arranged a crowning ceremony for Kharak on 1 September 1839. Resenting, however, the growing influence over Kharak of Chet Singh (a relative by marriage of the new Maharaja), Dhian Singh switched over to Nau Nihal's camp, conspired with the prince, and murdered Chet Singh.

For a year, Nau Nihal, supported by Dhian Singh, the wazir, seemed to manage well as the de facto ruler; people claimed, apparently with truth, that his grandfather had spoken of the prince's 'Alexander-like' qualities.[115] But Nau Nihal died in an accident on the very day, 5 November 1840, on which his father, Maharaja Kharak Singh, died of disease (or was poisoned): a palace gate collapsed on the prince while he was returning from his father's funeral.

Six princes now remained as real or potential contenders: the twins Sher Singh and Tara Singh (Sada Kaur's grandsons), who were in their mid-thirties; Peshaura Singh, Kashmira Singh and Multana Singh, who were in their early twenties; and Dalip Singh, the two-year-old son of Rani Jindan, the youngest of Ranjit Singh's wives.

On 9 November 1840, Sher Singh (Kharak's half-brother) was proclaimed the Maharaja, but Kharak's widow, Chand Kaur (who did not recognize

Sher Singh as her late husband's half-brother), asserted the future right to the throne of the baby that Nau Nihal's widow was carrying, and her own right, in the meantime, to act as Regent.

To start with, Dhian Singh, the wazir, backed Maharani Chand Kaur, but finding that she was listening more to a Sikh noble, Attar Singh Sandhanwalia, than to him, he switched again. Dhian Singh's brother, Gulab Singh, however, remained with Chand Kaur.

The splits divided the army. Objecting to their commanders' loyalties, soldiers killed several of them, including two whites, Foulkes and Ford. To win over the soldiery, Prince Sher Singh and Raja Dhian Chand offered pay increases, gratuities and promotions, which only augmented the power of the panches (soldiers representing their fellows). Also, many more soldiers were recruited.

Privately, everyone sought British support for his or her goal. Publicly, rivals were accused of intriguing with the British. Those involved in such exercises included, it seems, Chand Kaur, her rival Sher Singh, the Sandhanwalias (who were Chand Kaur backers), the now divided Dogra brothers, even the European generals, Avitabile and Ventura.

Chand Kaur seems to have offered the British 'a large slice' of Punjab if they supported her against Sher Singh, who too was willing to cede a portion of the kingdom to the British if they backed him against Chand Kaur.[116]

Worse was to follow. Thanks, it would be alleged, to 'Dhian Singh's manipulative skills', Nau Nihal's child was aborted in his widow's womb, and Chand Kaur's murder was arranged.[117] The Sandhanwalias switched over to the Sher Singh camp—and then, on 15 September 1843, killed him.

> Ajit Singh [Sandhanwalia, nephew of Attar Singh] came up to the platform on which Sher Singh was sitting and on pretence of presenting him with a new double-barrelled gun, suddenly pointed the weapon at him and shot him dead. He then cut off his head and stuck it at the end of his spear.[118]

At the same time, Sher Singh's son, the boy prince Partap Singh, was killed by Ajit's uncle Lehna Singh. Dhian Singh was inveigled into the fort and shot in the back. The wazir's corpse was cut into pieces. All in his bodyguard were also killed. Dhian Singh, observes Grewal, 'had served himself well but also served the state faithfully for nearly a quarter of a century'.[119]

With the aid of the soldiers' panchayats, the murders were quickly avenged. Dhian Singh's widows declared they would not allow the cremation of his body 'until the heads of the Sandhanwalias were placed at its feet'.[120] The next day, along with several hundred of their troops, Lehna Singh and Ajit Singh were slain by the soldiers and their severed heads placed at the feet of Dhian Singh's dismembered body. The widows then went into the flames, as did Dhian Singh's body parts, and, presumably, the heads of Lehna Singh and Ajit Singh.

Hira Singh—Dhian Singh's son, the Maharaja's favourite, in earlier scenes the boy hidden by the jewels on his person—emerged as the leader of what used to be the late Sher Singh's faction. Now six years old, Dalip Singh, son of 'the comely' Rani Jindan,[121] was named the new Maharaja, and his mother the Regent, but Hira became the wazir.

Those who thought that this arrangement might at last please the tortured souls of Ranjit Singh and Dhian Singh were soon to think again. First, Hira Singh tried, with the help of his uncle Gulab Singh, to eliminate Princes Peshaura Singh and Kashmira Singh. Then, after Hira's other uncle, Suchet Singh, claimed the wazir's seat, Hira killed this uncle.

Hira's luck ran out when his mentor, Pandit Jalla, a Brahmin from Jammu, made provocative remarks about the character of Rani Jindan. The Rani's brother, Jawahar Singh, successfully exhorted the army panches to act against 'the insolent Brahmin' and his supposed protector, Hira Singh. The wazir and the Pandit ran for their lives, aiming for sanctuary in Jammu with Gulab Singh, the sole survivor of the Dogra trio.

But infuriated Sikh soldiers caught up with the two and their 1,000-strong Dogra army. On 21 December 1844, the escapees and their army were all killed. Impaled on spears, the heads of Hira Singh and Pandit Jalla were brought to Lahore and paraded.

In the summer of 1845, the panches were running the military, now enlarged to 120,000 soldiers and costing 50 per cent more than in 1839, but civilian matters were in the hands of Rani Jindan and a small group that included her brother Jawahar Singh and two leftovers from Ranjit Singh's time, Fakir Nuruddin (whose more famous brother, Azizuddin, had died by now) and Diwan Dina Nath.

Prince Peshaura Singh rose in revolt against them in August but was killed on Jawahar Singh's instructions. The panches demanding revenge, Jawahar Singh was killed on 21 September. Mounting his funeral pyre the next day, Jawahar Singh's four wives prophesied the Khalsa's overthrow and widowhood for the soldiers' wives.

The curse would work. Two wars between the kingdom and the Company, one fought in 1845-46 and the other in 1848-49, would extinguish the kingdom and the lives of tens of thousands of its soldiers, most of them Sikhs.

•

Before turning to these wars, we may, first, acknowledge in a few words the similarities between this era and earlier Mughal and Sultanate times, and, secondly, look briefly at what happened in Afghanistan after Shuja recovered his throne in the summer of 1839.

That during his reign Ranjit Singh took no life outside of battle constituted a striking exception, yet a few practices, some of them quite sobering, continued not only from one generation to the next, but also from one century to the next, ignoring any Sultan/Mughal or Mughal/Maharaja divide. These included

- plots for access to the throne by the contenders' wives, widows, and in-laws;
- the state's officers playing both civil and military roles;
- seizure of officers' assets after their death, even when they had served loyally and effectively;
- treachery;
- and the killing, for throne's sake, of brothers, half-brothers, cousins, and uncles.

Killings for revenge or a throne were common not only across generations but also on both sides of the Khyber. In November 1840, after he had scored some victories, Dost Muhammad was captured by William MacNaghten, Britain's envoy to Afghanistan—the one who had brought to Ranjit Singh the proposal for restoring Shuja—and exiled to India.

For a few deceptive months, the British thought that Afghanistan was like a conquered Indian province. Garden parties were held in Kabul. Cricket and Shakespeare were played. The command of British forces in Afghanistan, which included thousands of Hindustanis, was given to an old and infirm general, William Elphinstone. The Company's bribes to tribal chiefs were discontinued.

But soon enough the chiefs rose in revolt, with Dost's son Akbar emerging as their leader, and a series of jolts occurred. First, in the summer of 1841—two years after his restoration and the victory parade in which the British and the Durbar had joined—Shuja was deposed. (He would be killed in February 1842.) Next, in November 1841, Burnes was killed in Kabul. In the following month, MacNaghten was murdered and his body dragged along the streets of Kabul.

This was only the prelude. In January 1842, over four thousand of the Company's Bengal army troops, and thrice as many camp-followers, perished 'amid the blood-stained snows of grim Afghan passes' while attempting to retreat from Kabul to Jalalabad.[122] More than 3,000 of the troops were Hindustanis; the wives of many of them were among the camp-followers. Elphinstone himself was talked into becoming an Afghan hostage and would die a captive some years after the massacre of his army.

Thus the British in Afghanistan too had been afflicted by a curse. In the autumn of 1842, different Company regiments managed simultaneously to assault Kabul. In revenge for the killings of Burnes and MacNaghten, the city was razed and its great bazaar reduced to ashes. However, Britain's Afghan adventure, presided over by Lord Auckland, was now over. The regiments returned to India, and a freed Dost Muhammad was allowed to re-enter Afghanistan and occupy its throne.

In what sounded like a new policy for an autonomous buffer zone to the west of British India, the new Governor-General, Lord Ellenborough, claimed that Punjab and Afghanistan together—'the rivers of the Punjab and the Indus, and the mountainous passes and the barbarous tribes of Afghanistan'—'would be placed between the British army and [any] enemy from the West'.[123]

The Company's defeat in Afghanistan was followed six months later by a compensating, if hardly heroic, conquest of Sindh. (Four decades later, a British writer would call the annexation 'one of the deepest blots on our national escutcheon'.[124]) In February and March of 1843, Sindh's amirs were humbled by the Company's army led by a sixty-one-year-old general, Charles Napier, and Sindh became a British province.

■

The Afghanistan debacle made Punjab, and the Khyber Pass, even more important for the British. If Ranjit Singh's successors would not control Punjab and secure the Pass, the British would have to do it themselves, no matter what Ellenborough had declared. Moreover, Punjab not only had rich soil and capable farmers; it also threw up, as the Company's agents and travelling dignitaries had noticed, hardy fighters.

In 1831, Colonel James Skinner,* who had raised cavalry regiments for the Company's Bengal army from 1803, was greatly impressed by the deportment of the 1,000 horsemen that Ranjit Singh had brought to the grand Company-kingdom party at Ropar, and by the 'accurate firing' of the Punjabi gunners on show.[125] Before and after Skinner's comment, other Britons had reacted similarly. Punjabis could make a priceless addition to the imperial army.

In global terms, this was a significant consideration for England, for although Napoleon's defeat had checked France, Russia was flexing its muscles. More disturbingly for British pride, America was rising. After overthrowing the British in the 1770s-80s, it had expanded in size, numbers and power.

The man keenest to make up for the loss of America by expanding in India was an energetic British lord and politician, James Broun-Ramsay, the tenth Earl of Dalhousie, who would become the Governor-General of India in January 1848, before the start of a second war between Britain and the Sikh kingdom, but after the Company had won the first war. Some of Dalhousie's thinking was also shared by his immediate predecessor as Governor-General, Henry Hardinge, a veteran of wars in Europe.

The British had four distinct armies in India. The smallest consisted of the purely British 'Queen's Regiments'. The other three were the racially mixed 'presidency' armies of the East India Company: the Bengal, Bombay and Madras armies that, along with British rule, had grown from the 1750s onwards in each of the three 'presidencies'. In the 1840s, these three armies contained around 40,000 whites and 250,000 Indians. No white served under an Indian, and the highest paid Indian earned less than the lowest paid Briton.

It was the Bengal army that supplied the units that officers like Lake, Ochterlony, Wade and Fane commanded in areas close to Punjab, as also the units that in 1839 went with Shuja to Afghanistan and paid a heavy price. From 1840 to 1842, the Bengal army also sent units to fight British battles in China.

More than half of the Bengal army's Indians (the Hindustanis, as they were called) were high-caste Hindus from Awadh, the Shia-ruled autonomous principality under the Company's umbrella, with Lucknow as its capital. About a third of the Bengal army's Hindustanis were Muslims, also mainly from modern UP and Bihar.

If Britain's Indian possessions stretched westward to include Punjab, a

---

*Founder of Skinner's Horse, still a unit of the Indian Army.

great new recruiting ground would open up.

■

Despite Ellenborough's words of 1842, the British were willing, in 1845, to extend beyond the Sutlej towards the Indus and the Khyber. *Punjab's leaders, on their part, were keen that the British should.* The panches had horrified the kingdom's aristocratic chiefs and nobles by their insolence. Supported by several chiefs, Maharani Jindan evidently approached the British with the suggestion that 'they may destroy the [kingdom's] army' and take the boy-king under their protection.[126] Gulab Singh offered the British his 'cooperation' provided Jammu and some other tracts were left with him.[127]

Simultaneously, the people were 'warned' by the Durbar that the British were preparing for war. Diwan Dina Nath 'solemnly confirmed' such a report, which was not false, for the Company had indeed collected men and war materials on the borders. But it was hardly the entire truth.[128] A pledge to save the state was duly taken on Ranjit Singh's samadh, and the panches were asked to suspend their authority for the sake of the kingdom.

But the two men invited to lead the defence, Lal Singh, who was named wazir, and Tej Singh, who was made the army commander, had decided (or been told) to scuttle the defence. Like Tej Singh (a nephew of Khushhal Singh), Lal Singh was a Brahmin converted to Sikhism. It was said, too, that Lal Singh was Rani Jindan's paramour.

Though the war was not real, its casualties were. It was agreed between 'the junta at Lahore' and British agents that the kingdom's army should cross the Sutlej and show itself as the aggressor. On 11 December 1845, the river was crossed not far from Ferozepur, which contained an isolated British force of 7,000. Two days later, Hardinge not only declared war on the kingdom; he said he would serve in battle under Hugh Gough, the Bengal army's commander-in-chief.

Hindustanis made up more than half of the units assembled under Gough. In the first engagement, fought near Mudki, the British side lost more than 900 men but the kingdom's army was repulsed with an even heavier loss. We are told in *The British Conquest and Dominion of India* by Sir Penderel Moon, a historian who served in Punjab in the 1940s, that Tej Singh had scrupulously 'refrained from attacking [Ferozepur] and secretly informed the British of his goodwill'.[129] However, Lahore's soldiers fought with great bravery, proving their prowess.

In the next round, after Gough attacked Pheru Shah, where the main Sikh force had gathered, the kingdom's soldiers showed even greater strength. It seems, however, that they also 'barbarously mutilated' wounded enemy soldiers.[130] Fearing, during a tense moment, that the British would lose, Hardinge instructed the destruction of confidential papers. But 'the irresolute or traitorous Tej Singh'—to use Moon's description—ordered abrupt withdrawals of his army and aided the British. Gough in any case was in no mood to lose, and in Pheru Shah the attacking Bengal army won.

However, its Hindustani sepoys came across as reluctant fighters. The ill-fated Afghan campaign had demoralized them. Moreover, some of them harboured sympathy for the only independent native government left on the subcontinent. According to Moon, 'The Sikhs were deeply impressed by the toughness of the British soldiers and never forgot it. The Hindustani sepoys they despised.'[131]

Whether or not the Pheru Shah defeat displeased Rani Jindan, it forced her to substitute Gulab Singh for Lal Singh as wazir. The change was of no help during the next battle, the biggest of this war, which was waged in Sabraon (not far from Ferozepur) on 10 February 1846. Penderel Moon tells us that Henry Lawrence, the Company's new Political Agent in Ludhiana, had obtained 'from the treacherous Lal Singh sufficient information to prepare a rough sketch of [the Sikh entrenchments in Sabraon]'.[132]

This time the Hindustanis fought better, but the chief architects of the kingdom's defeat were its own Lal Singh and Tej Singh, both of whom played their chosen roles. After bringing thousands of soldiers across the Sutlej to Sabraon, Tej Singh not only took himself back to the river's western bank, he also destroyed a portion of the bridge of boats on which the soldiers had advanced.[133]

Forced to retreat under British fire, the kingdom's soldiers were massed on the broken bridge over the Sutlej when the Company's army gunned them down. British artillery completed the annihilation. Many of the wounded Sikhs were 'mercilessly slaughtered' by the Company's army in revenge for the cruelty in Pheru Shah and its alleged repetition by Sikh soldiers at the start of the Sabraon battle.[134]

Among the heroes of the lost battle of Sabraon was a white-bearded veteran of Ranjit Singh's armies, Sham Singh Atariwala. Clad in white and riding a white mare, Sham Singh was killed with fifty others in a gallant last stand.

Almost 10,000 Sikhs were killed in Sabraon, and all the guns they had moved across the river were captured. Around 2,400 died on the British side but its victory was complete. Two days later, the British crossed the Sutlej, occupied Kasur, and pondered the terms they should impose on Lahore.

At first they intended to reduce, bind, and drain Punjab, not run it. The latter option would cost money and also, perhaps, more blood. The Durbar was required to cede to the Company all of the fertile Jullundur doab; to forgo every cis-Sutlej claim; to drastically reduce its army and cavalry; to host in Lahore a British Resident and a contingent of British troops; and to pay an indemnity equivalent to a million and a half sterling.

All terms were accepted by the shattered party, but its treasury was empty. How would the Durbar pay the indemnity? One man had an answer. Like all the others at the helm in Lahore, Gulab Singh had kept in close touch with the British. Unlike many of the others, the Dogra chief had also ensured that his personal coffers were full. The deal he proposed was accepted by all parties. Let the Durbar surrender all the hilly lands between the Beas and the Indus to the Company; for a million and a half pounds, he would buy the lands from it.

Thus was the Raja of Jammu transformed into the Maharaja of Jammu and Kashmir. Had he wanted to, he could have become the Maharaja of Hazara as well, but Gulab Singh did not wish to be saddled with that turbulent area.

Henry Lawrence was named the Company's first Resident in Lahore. In a letter to him, Governor-General Hardinge referred to Maharaja Dalip Singh, who was now eight, and said: '[T]he native prince is in fetters and under our protection and must do our bidding.'[135] Punjab would be run the way its Resident, Henry Lawrence, desired.

■

Shah Mohammed's *Jangnamah,* a Punjabi lament on the kingdom's defeat, was evidently written soon after the defeat of the Sikhs by the British and their quislings. Said to be a high-born Muslim, and a son or nephew to Sultan Mahmud, one of the kingdom's artillery officers (who is named in the ballad), the poet, Shah Mohammed, is scathing about Rani Jindan, Tej Singh, and the British.

Intriguingly, he sees Punjab and 'Hind' as the warring parties, rather than Punjab and the Company (or the British). In his poem, the British and Hindustani soldiers are both fighting for 'Hind'—or, one could say, for Delhi. It is a Lahore vs. Delhi fight, reminiscent of earlier tensions between Punjabis and Mughals. Shah Mohammed is not a Mughal fan.

In speaking of the Sikh soldiers, he hails their bravery but reminds us also of their overbearing conduct. However, his ballad's primary significance lies in its assumption of a common loyalty for the Sikh kingdom of its Muslims and Hindus, the latter term embracing, in the poet's mind, Sikhs as well. The poet asks, 'How in the midst of Musalmans and Hindus, living happily together/Had a scourge of sorts [i.e. the British] descended from nowhere?'[136]

His poem claims that Punjabi Muslims did not see their Sikh rulers as anti-Muslim. According to Shah Mohammed, all Punjabis, Muslims and non-Muslims alike, were pained and angered by the defeat, even though the Rani and a few others (the writer mentions 'Pathans') 'greeted the Feringhee with presents'.[137] If his poem is true to its time, we can say that the kingdom's chief tensions at this time were not religious.

Expressing a sense that by its doings the kingdom had incurred divine wrath, the poem nonetheless preserves hope for the future while also breathing an apprehension that the British triumph would endanger a precious asset, trust between Muslims and non-Muslims. Shah Mohammed hints that this trust was fragile.

> God willing, good things shall happen again/What if the soldiers have lost the lustre of their mien?
> Great commonality does exist between the Hindus and the Musalmans/
> None should ever dare break this common silken bond.[138]

A wholly different point emerges from another comment on the 1845-46 war, this one by a modern historian.

> The ultimate blame for what happened to the Sikh State rests neither with the Dogras, nor with the Brahmins, who subverted it from within, nor with the British who triumphed with the help of traitors. In the end the Sikhs themselves are responsible for failing to protect the magnificent legacy of an exceptional man.[139]

What is interesting about this frank verdict is its failure to speak of Punjab's Muslims, who constituted the majority in the kingdom's population. As key groups influencing 'what happened to the Sikh State', the Dogras, the Brahmins, the Sikhs and the British are all appraised, but not the Muslims, who evidently 'took' what happened without causing it to happen. It is a reading that confirms the concern of Punjab's Muslims with survival, preferring that to control.

■

The British soon found that they could not control Punjab without running it. At the end of December 1846, Henry Lawrence, the Resident in Lahore, was empowered to 'direct and control the duties of every department'. Rani Jindan was removed as Regent and later banished from the kingdom and thus separated from her son. Lal Singh, too, was removed as wazir and sent to Dehra Dun for allegedly colluding with Imamuddin, the Durbar's nazim in Kashmir, to prevent its transfer to Gulab Singh.

In some provinces, including sensitive ones close to Afghanistan, British political agents were posted to 'advise' the kingdom's nazims, who, except for the odd Hindu or Muslim, were Sikhs. More rulers than advisors, these political agents were quick to exploit anti-Durbar sentiments among Pashtuns or other Muslims. But in two provinces, Multan in the south and Hazara in the north, independent-minded governors resisted British officers and British demands, provoking what some would call the second Anglo-Sikh war.

To begin with, the Multan dispute was between the British-led Lahore Durbar and the province's nazim, Mulraj, whose father, Sawan Mal, had significantly augmented Multan's agriculture and revenue before being killed, in 1840, by a disgruntled former employee. Mulraj succeeded to his father's office but was told that his confirmation as governor was contingent on his sending sufficient funds to Lahore.

Dissatisfied with what Mulraj was willing to cough up, Lahore sent a new governor, Kahan Singh, to Multan, along with two young British officers, Patrick Vans Agnew and W. A. Anderson, and 500 Durbar troops. This was in April 1848, by when Dalhousie had succeeded Hardinge as Governor-General in Calcutta and Frederick Currie had replaced a sick Lawrence as Lahore's Resident or de facto ruler.

Multan's soldiers, more numerous than the Durbar contingent, killed the two Britons sent by Currie, refused to accept Kahan Singh as governor, and induced the Durbar's soldiers to stand with them against the firanghis. Whether or not Mulraj had incited his soldiers, he was no longer in a position to defy them.

Three parties—Mulraj, his soldiers, and the Durbar's contingent—now stood as one in an anti-foreigner alliance. Elsewhere in Punjab, too, the news from Multan caused many Sikh soldiers to desert regiments loyal to the British-led Durbar and join those prepared to rebel.

Meanwhile, Herbert Edwardes, a British officer posted across the Indus in Bannu, received a plea for help that Agnew had written shortly before dying. Currie in Lahore received a similar letter, but it was the junior officer on the periphery rather than the Resident in the capital who mobilized a riposte. Playing on their resentment of Sikh rule, Edwardes collected levies of Pashtuns and Balochis against the governor of Multan and also enlisted support from the nawab of Bahawalpur.

A mixed Edwardes-led force assaulted Multan and hoped that the city's Muslims would join in overthrowing Mulraj. As we know, Multan's walls and fort were not easy to breach. For seven months, from June 1848 to January 1849, Mulraj and his force, which contained Sikhs, Hindus and Muslims, endured a siege, which however became harder to defy once Currie and Dalhousie sent heavy guns and more troops under a General William Whish.

In Hazara, the standard of revolt was raised by its governor, Raja Chattar Singh Atariwala. As clan chiefs, the Atariwalas had long enjoyed esteem west of the Jhelum. The prestige was enhanced when Chattar Singh's daughter was betrothed to Dalip Singh, the boy-Maharaja.

Posted in the region, two young British officers, James Abbott and John Nicholson, had distrusted Chattar Singh, but Currie in Lahore not only dismissed their suspicions, he sent Chattar Singh's son, Sher Singh, to Multan to reinforce the siege against Mulraj. A large contingent of the Durbar's Sikh soldiers accompanied Sher Singh.

In Multan, to Currie's shock, Sher Singh almost joined hands with Mulraj. Thanks perhaps to Edwardes, the hands did not fully join. According to Grewal, 'A forged letter arranged by Edwardes to fall into the hands of Mul Raj made him suspicious of Sher Singh.'[140]

Yet Sher Singh had become a rebel. In October 1848, he left Multan with a sizeable Sikh army to join his father in Hazara. Before leaving, he issued a proclamation asking all Punjabis to rise against the foreigners. The prospective brother-in-law of the Maharaja spoke of the 'oppression, tyranny and violence' with which 'the *firanghis* have treated the widow of the great Maharaja Ranjit Singh' and 'the people of the country'.[141]

Hitherto, Dalhousie had been eager to declare war but wary. For one thing, he did not know how the Afghans, over whom the resilient Dost Muhammad was again exercising sway, would react. Most of all, however, Dalhousie wanted an unassailable pretext, which Sher Singh's proclamation had supplied. Privately expressing delight that matters had reached 'the crisis I have for months been looking for', he laced his public announcement with rage at Sher Singh's statement.

Unwarned by precedents, uninfluenced by example, the Sikh nation has called for war, and on my word they shall have it and with a vengeance.[142]

Though Dalhousie was suggesting that all Sikhs were behind Sher Singh's rebellion, this was not the case. Many remained on the side of the British-controlled Durbar. A factor influencing them was the sympathetic personality of Henry Lawrence, who had listened with understanding to the dying kingdom's Sikh officers and was expected to return to the helm at Lahore.

Following Dalhousie's decision, Gough advanced the Bengal army against Sher Singh's soldiers, who lined themselves on the western bank of the Chenab. On 22 November, at Ramnagar, they repulsed a British attack. But they were forced to proceed westward across the Chenab, which Gough and his men also crossed. The British were helped, in this phase of the fighting, by the Rachna doab's Chathas and Bhattis, who had never reconciled themselves to Sikh rule.

A lull lasting weeks followed. The British were waiting for reinforcements from Multan, which was close to falling, and especially for the big guns deployed there. On his part, Chattar Singh was negotiating with Dost Muhammad, who controlled the Pashtun areas the Sikhs wanted to pass through.

But Abbott and Nicholson, too, were parleying with the Afghan. However, when Chattar Singh agreed that Peshawar and the Khyber would be ceded to him, Dost enabled Chattar Singh's soldiers to cross Pashtun territory and advance towards the army of his son Sher Singh.

Anxious to prevent a union of the two Sikh armies, Gough engaged Sher Singh's force in Chillianwala, on the Jhelum's eastern bank, on 14 January 1849. The result was the Company's worst defeat in its long history in India. After losing nearly 3,000 officers and men, the Bengal army withdrew. The Sikh forces of father and son were able to come together, move east, and cross the Chenab.

Within days, however, guns sent by Whish from Multan arrived, along with many soldiers. Its defences breached at last, Multan was stormed on 2 January, and its citadel taken on the 18th. Mulraj surrendered on 22 January. On 13 February, not far from the town of Gujrat, Gough attacked the combined forces of father and son with one hundred big guns and an increased number of troops. 'After a short fierce fight, [the Sikhs] gave way.'[143] On 13 March, the 16,000-strong Sikh army laid down its arms and its horses.

British eyewitnesses captured the sad sight of the Sikh soldier 'flinging down *tulwar*, matchlock and shield upon the growing heap of [surrendered] arms' and the 'more touching sight still' of the 'parting for the last time from the animal which he regarded as part of himself'. The soldier 'caressed and patted his faithful companion on every part of [its] body, and then turned resolutely away. But his resolution failed him. He turned back again and again to give one caress more [until] he tore himself away for the very last time, brush[ing] a teardrop from his eye.'[144]

On 29 March 1849, at a ceremony in Lahore Fort, ten-year-old Dalip Singh was told to sign a document. Writing his name in Roman letters, the boy-king renounced, on his behalf and on behalf of all heirs and successors, every 'right, title or claim' to Punjab. All of the kingdom's property, including the Kohinoor and other jewels, now belonged to the British. The Sikh kingdom gone, all of Punjab was annexed to British India. The proclamation of annexation, read out that day by Dalhousie's Secretary, Sir Henry Elliot, 'was received by those present with silence'.[145]

Though cleared of the charge of planning to kill Agnew and Anderson, Mulraj was sentenced to death for rebellion, a punishment commuted to exile for life. Kept in prison in Allahabad, Chattar Singh and Sher Singh were released five years later. On the victorious side, Lord Dalhousie was made a Marquess. Desiring friendship with the victors, Dost Muhammad agreed to cede Peshawar and adjoining lands up to the Khyber to British-owned Punjab.

We may end this chapter with a judgment, not a kind one, on Punjab's nobility during the 1840s.

> A number of chieftains opted for either resistance or collaboration as much out of a desire to humiliate and destroy personal enemies as out of a desire to either expel or retain the influence of the *firangis*... For instance, the descendants of Sham Singh Atariwala (the hero of Sabraon) actively participated in the war against Chatar Singh Atariwala and his sons... in order to avenge an old family dispute... [T]he leaders of the rebellion eventually identified their rivals at the darbar—rather than the British—as their real enemies.[146]

Chapter Five

1849-1859: BRITISH PUNJAB AND THE 1857 REBELLION

Depending upon whether we take as its starting point Henry Lawrence's appointment in 1846 as Punjab's *de facto* ruler or the 1849 annexation, British rule in Punjab would last for 101 or 98 years, or twice as long as the preceding Sikh kingdom. Earlier, from Akbar's 1556 conquest of Lahore to the 1712 death in that city of Shah Alam, the Mughals had ruled Punjab for 156 years.

During the nine turbulent decades between Shah Alam and Ranjit Singh—i.e. for almost the whole of the eighteenth century—domination over Punjab was primarily, as we saw, a contest between Afghans and Sikhs, except for rare spells when a Mughal officer such as Zakariya Khan or Mir Mannu, or a Punjabi Arain like Adina Beg, ruled over the region.

As the Sikh kingdom lay on its death-bed, at least three Britons were nursing precise ideas on how 'their' Punjab ought to be run. The first was Henry Lawrence, born in 1806 into a large northern Irish family with Scottish links. Though Henry's father, Alexander, acquired fame for gallantry in 1799 in the East India Company's war in southern India against Tipoo Sultan, the family remained poor.

The East India Company was a firm of British merchants who not only 'throve and trafficked and ruled in Leadenhall Street' in London but who 'could at their pleasure command the services and unsheathe the swords' of redoubtable generals.[1] Luckily for the Lawrences, a family friend, John Huddlestone, had returned from Madras to become a director of the Company and an MP as well.

Huddlestone found Company appointments in India for young Henry and four of his brothers. Before leaving one after the other for India—a voyage of more than five months past Africa's southern tip—Henry and three of his brothers trained at Addiscombe for service with the Company's armies; only John, the fourth son, went to Haileybury, where appointees to the Indian Civil Service were educated.

Joining the Bengal Artillery in his teens, Henry fought a war in Burma, where he nearly died of illness, before discharging civil and military roles across India: in eastern UP, where he is said to have surveyed every village in four districts around Gorakhpur; in Ludhiana; in Ferozepore; and in the Khyber region. During his Gorakhpur phase (1829-30), he married a cousin, Honoria Marshall. At the Khyber, in the summer of 1842, a daring stand by him enabled the Company's regiments to force the Pass and reach Kabul, where the loss of thousands of British and Indian lives during the previous winter was brutally avenged.

Posted next as the Company's Resident in Nepal, Lawrence concluded that the children, most of them half-native, of India-based British soldiers deserved residential schools and started giving most of his savings to create such 'asylums'. This was the origin of the still-existing Lawrence Schools* in Sanawar in the Simla hills, Lovedale in the Nilgiris and Murree in Pakistan.

After the 1845-46 battles in Punjab to which Hardinge had summoned Lawrence, the Governor-General appointed him as the Lahore Resident, with authority to regulate every department of a vanquished Durbar over which, in theory, a boy-king reigned.

This powerful Resident held the view, rare among India's British rulers, that they had to win the confidence of those they ruled, especially of those who had joined the Company's armies. In 1843, fourteen years before the 1857 Revolt, Lawrence had expressed this view in writing.[2] As Resident he opposed the idea of annexing Punjab: he thought he would reconstruct the Durbar by coaxing or coercing its squabbling chiefs. Soon, however, he found himself governing Punjab through the young British 'advisors' he had placed alongside the Durbar's nazims or governors.

Energetic, intrepid, and frequently arrogant, these young officers—they would be called 'Lawrence's men'—were fervently loyal to the Resident, who acquired the image of a paternalist and friendly ruler.[3] One of the 'men', Harry Lumsden, helped Lawrence raise new regiments, including the Corps of Guides, in the Frontier region.

These regiments were combined into the 'Punjab Irregular Force', so described because it fell outside the Company's 'regular' armies of Bengal, Bombay or Madras. This Punjab Irregular Force (PIF) was directed not by the Company's Calcutta-based commander-in-chief but by Punjab's Resident. Mainly consisting, to begin with, of Sikh soldiers, PIF soon enlisted many Muslims, Punjabis as well as Pashtuns.

---

*Long since opened to children of all backgrounds.

Another of Henry Lawrence's 'men' was James Abbott, stationed between 1846 and 1849 in Hazara, which Ranjit Singh and his successors had found hard to subdue. Yet 'advisor' Abbott seemed to win the confidence of Hazara's inhabitants, who in 1849 stood by his side in the fort of Srikote throughout a siege of six months enforced by Nazim Chattar Singh's large army, before that army was defeated by the British.

Abbott would thereafter rule over Hazara for five more years. With—so it would be claimed—'fatherly kindness', he helped turn 'a wild and desolate region into one of the happiest and most peaceful districts of the Punjab'.[4] Hence, to this day, the name Abbottabad for Hazara's chief town.

Quickly winning the confidence of many Punjabis, Henry Lawrence was especially liked by the Sikhs, who welcomed the openings that PIF offered as also Lawrence's empathy for their chiefs. Though eventually unsuccessful, his resistance to the annexation of Punjab was also appreciated by the Sikhs, who forgave the early and unpopular decision by Lawrence to exile Rani Jindan.

With the support of devoted aides and, as he hoped, of cooperating Sikh chiefs, he planned to 'stem the tide of annexation which was soon to swallow up many of the independent principalities of India'.[5] As long as Hardinge, who had become a close friend, remained Governor-General, Lawrence's hope had a basis. It vanished when, early in 1848, Dalhousie replaced Hardinge.

Not only was Lord Dalhousie ardent about annexation, he resented talk in Punjab in 1849—after Lawrence returned there, from a sick-leave spell in Britain, as *Sir* Henry Lawrence—that the Resident's iqbal (prestige) could ensure a peaceful settlement without further war or annexation. Antagonistic towards the Resident, Dalhousie decided—in the words of an admiring British writer—to 'put his foot down and show his subordinate that, *iqbal* or no *iqbal*, it was Lord Dalhousie and not Henry Lawrence who would have the last word on each question as it came up'.[6]

■

Five years younger than Henry Lawrence, and differing sharply on how Punjab should be governed, was his brother John, who also found himself in Punjab in 1846. Tall and strongly-built, John was the only 'civilian' in the Lawrence brotherhood. He too had wanted to join the Company's imperial army, but Alexander, the father maimed in Seringapatam, desired lower risks for at least one of his sons.

John was therefore steered towards the ICS. As we have seen, he attended Haileybury College, where he picked up Bengali. Before that he had studied at a day school in Bristol where, he would afterwards recall, 'I was flogged every day of my life at school except one, and then I was flogged twice.'[7]

A course in Calcutta, where John learnt Persian and Hindustani, was followed by spells as a district officer in Delhi, Panipat (in today's Haryana) and Etawah (today's UP). These were successful stints even though—like many civilians and soldiers from Britain—John was susceptible in the summer's heat to 'a pining for home and an absolute detestation for India'.[8]

He did not like Delhi, where he spent the early 1830s, and thought of its Red Fort, where the Mughal king and his numerous relatives lived on the Company's pensions, as the 'sink of the city'. As John Lawrence saw it, while 'slavery, polygamy and concubinage' prevailed within the Fort, Delhi's population outside the Fort enjoyed freedom under the Company's British laws.[9]

John's boss at this time, the Resident and Commissioner of Delhi, was Thomas Metcalfe, a brother of the Charles Metcalfe whom we saw negotiating with Ranjit Singh in 1808-09. John Lawrence's biographer, Bosworth Smith, creatively imagines his subject, twenty-one or so at the time, sheltering a young woman escaping from the palace 'with stripes on her back', or 'punish[ing] a scoundrel born in the purple' when the latter crossed the Fort's perimeter and entered the 'British' city.[10]

Contrasting John Lawrence's outlook with that of his older brother, a contemporary officer called Lionel Trotter would write: 'Henry's sympathies, roughly speaking, were all on the side of the old aristocracy while John was equally zealous on behalf of the masses who lived by the labour of their own hands and brains.'[11] In the late nineteenth century, when biographers often connected character traits to racial ancestry, it was said that, between the brothers, Henry possessed more 'Irish warmth' and John greater 'Scottish sternness'.[12]

John came into his own during his duties (1834-37) in Panipat in cis-Sutlej Punjab, which was British-run from 1809. Equipped with gun, dog and horse and supported by a small British and Indian staff, Lawrence helped provide a secure climate to the Panipat countryside.

It would be said that peasants entering its fields no longer carried arms, whereas earlier they seldom 'went out to plough or to herd their buffaloes without sword, shield, and often a long matchlock over their shoulders'.[13] This farming-under-arms, as one may call it, was probably a reality in several pockets of Punjab even during Ranjit Singh's rule and certainly during earlier periods when armed bands routinely snatched local power from one another.

Lawrence's secret, which went beyond 'Scottish sternness', was later explained by one of his colleagues in Panipat, Charles Raikes:

First, he was at all times and in all places, even in his bedroom, accessible to the people of his district. He loved his joke with the sturdy farmers, his chat with the city bankers, his argument with the native gentry. When out with his dogs and gun he had no end of questions to ask every man he met. After a gallop across country, he would rest on a charpoy and hold an informal levee of all the village folk, from headman to barber. *Jan Larens sub jaanta,*' the people said. ('John Lawrence knows everything.')

Second, added Raikes, Lawrence was 'never above his work'. He himself did what needed to be done, whether it was arresting someone or settling a dispute over land; he would do the latter by going to the spot instead of waiting in his court for the disputants. Third, said Raikes, Lawrence shook off all flatterers.[14] Finally, Raikes speculated, the young white officer's height and strength won him a 'potent' image 'among the natives of India'.[15]

At the end of 1845, John Lawrence, thirty-four at the time, had completed his Panipat and Etawah duties and a furlough in Britain (where he found a wife) and was back in Delhi, serving as its magistrate and collector, when—sensing the likelihood of war against the Sikh kingdom—Governor-General Hardinge arrived from Calcutta. In the old Mughal capital, so we are told,

Hardinge's discerning and soldierly eye [took] the measure of the young Magistrate, the vehement swift-riding man, with the honest and eager face, careless of dress and appearance who never seemed to count any work too hard or to think any duty too little [for] his own hands [and] knew every man in the place... [16]

This Delhi meeting between Hardinge and John Lawrence was followed by what we have seen: the military engagements in Punjab of Pheru Shah and Mudki in which the Governor-General served as a soldier under Gough. Finding British soldiers 'exhausted', Hardinge, who already had Henry Lawrence at his side, evidently 'wrote in his own handwriting and in hot haste a pressing note to John Lawrence asking him to find transport for [a] siege train with... heavy guns, stores and munitions from Delhi'.

Apparently John Lawrence 'speedily' organized in Delhi 'a train of four thousand carts, each driven by its own owner', 'pushed forward' to the Punjab front 'the supplies and munitions' required, and vindicated Hardinge's confidence in him.[17]

When, some weeks later, the defeated Lahore kingdom was divested of the Jullundur doab, the Governor-General named John Lawrence the Doab's commissioner even as older brother Henry was made Resident in Lahore. In the years that followed, the younger brother registered notable successes in the Doab, starting with a proclamation of religious liberty.

As a future biographer of John Lawrence would put it, 'Once more the call to public prayer, which the Sikhs had silenced, awoke the dawn from the minarets of the mosque.'[18] All were free, the commissioner declared—Muslims, Hindus, Sikhs and Christians—to observe their own religious and social customs, but none would be permitted to meddle with those of their neighbours.

Second, John Lawrence insisted on a low land tax. 'Mind,' he told a junior officer, 'you assess low. If you don't, I shall be your enemy for life.' But a light assessment was accompanied by a penalty if a well was not dug, or a tank not repaired, or trees not planted. A farmer who improved his land paid less tax.[19]

John Lawrence's innovations in the Doab included the removal of transit and customs duties that the Sikh kingdom had been levying on produce and manufactures, and a change in how zamindars in the doab's hill tracts, including Kangra, paid their revenue. Instead of having to pay in rice, they could now give cash, which meant that crops other than rice could also be sown.

Also, chiefs in the hill tracts were allowed to supply money to the Company rather than levies of soldiers, hitherto the standard method of appeasing the superior power ruling the plains. Though the change risked setting armed men loose, it brought money to the government. The commissioner was ready, moreover, to take discharged soldiers into the Company's army.

In addition, Lawrence dented a practice among some in the Bedi clan of killing baby girls. The justification for the practice was this. The clan that produced Guru Nanak would lose prestige if its girls married into inferior clans; if they married within the clan, it would be like incest. The only solution was to kill the girl-child.

Some of the Jullundur-based Bedi clans petitioned John Lawrence to be allowed, under the principle of non-interference with religious and social customs, to bury their daughters at birth, a 'custom' they claimed to have followed for 'the last four centuries'. Confronting the Bedi elders, John Lawrence first obtained an admission that their scripture did not justify the practice. Then, 'before some hundreds of people', he told the Bedi elders 'that Government would not only never consent to such a villainous crime being perpetrated but that we should certainly hang every man who was convicted of such a murder'.[20]

In proclamations and letters to all chiefs, John Lawrence also announced 'the severest penalties' for sati and another tragic practice: the destruction of 'leprous persons by burying them alive or throwing them into water'.[21]

■

A third man with strong views on Punjab was Lord Dalhousie (1812-60), India's Governor-General from 1848. Born James Broun-Ramsay, Dalhousie was a year younger than John Lawrence and six years younger than Henry. As Governor-General, he wielded greater authority than either Lawrence brother, but his Calcutta base lay more than a thousand miles east of Lahore.

In Dalhousie's case, too, his India interest had come down from his father, the 9th Earl of Dalhousie, a blue-blooded Scot who served in the 1820s as commander-in-chief of one of the Company's Indian armies. Prior to that, the older Dalhousie served as Canada's Governor-General for six years. His childhood years in North America contributed to the younger Dalhousie's belief in an expanded Indian empire, owned and remade by the British, that might make up for the loss of America.

A vigorous politician, the young peer had been president of the board of trade, an influential cabinet post, before he was offered the top Indian appointment, which he accepted on condition that his hands would be left free. Arriving in Calcutta in January 1848, Dalhousie proved staunch in his imperialist and modernizing convictions and resolute in his conclusion, quickly formed, of Indian inferiority.[22]

India's native chiefs repelled him from the start. Dalhousie thought that as Governor-General he would hasten the demise of India's 'decadent' customs and 'worthless' institutions, provide efficient (and also profitable) white rule, set up universities and a network of rail and telegraph lines, and extend the empire's boundaries.

We cannot be surprised, then, to learn—from John Lawrence's biographer—that between Henry and John Lawrence, Dalhousie's 'own views and sympathies were in close agreement with those of the younger and... more practical brother'.[23] In Dalhousie's eyes, one of Henry's faults was his closeness to the previous Governor-General; in Henry Lawrence's eyes, one of Dalhousie's faults was that he was not the courteous Lord Hardinge.

When Dalhousie took over in Calcutta, in name at least the Sikh kingdom still existed, with Henry Lawrence as the Resident in Lahore and John Lawrence ruling over an annexed Jullundur doab. However, an ill Henry Lawrence had to leave for England, whereupon the younger brother acted as Resident in Lahore, and the Governor-General and John Lawrence developed a strong relationship.

When, a year later, the battles of Multan, Chillianwala and Gujrat were fought, Dalhousie showed impatience not only with Henry Lawrence, who had returned, but also with the British army's commander for the Punjab operations, General Hugh Gough. In a strongly-worded letter to Henry Lawrence in February 1849, Dalhousie asserted his supreme authority over civil and military leaders, expressed dissatisfaction with Gough's performance, and said that as far as the Governor-General was concerned, the army '*will* cross the Jhelum this season and please God, the Indus also'.[24] In the end, as we know, the Sikh army was defeated and its kingdom annexed, but the Indus was not crossed by the British.

While Henry Lawrence had failed to prevent annexation, everyone including the man himself assumed that he would run annexed Punjab: his iqbal was high in the province and 'Henry's men' ruled almost all its sections. But though Dalhousie could not prevent Henry Lawrence from governing Punjab, he conspicuously clipped his wings.

The Governor-General decreed that a Board rather than a single man would administer Punjab. While presided over by Henry Lawrence, the Board would include his brother John and a third member, Charles Mansel, a civilian from the 'North-Western province' of the time (i.e. much of today's UP minus Awadh, where an autonomous nawab ruled).

Dalhousie gave Henry Lawrence the tasks of raising new regiments, disarming the people, and restoring peace between the Company and still-influential members of the defunct Durbar. Henry's brother was assigned revenue and finance, while police and justice were placed under Mansel, who before long was succeeded by Robert Montgomery, Scots-Irish by birth like the Lawrences and like Mansel an NWP civilian.

∎

Two factors blessed the start of British Punjab. One, the province's Muslim majority felt glad at the end of Sikh rule. Ranjit Singh was not anti-Muslim, yet his Khalsa sarkar had restricted Muslim practices. Indeed, according to Ian Talbot, 'most of the leading Muslim families of West Punjab [had] supported the British during the Sikh Wars'.[25]

Second, Punjab's Sikh chiefs saw in Henry Lawrence a ruler willing to blot out the humiliation of their defeat and assuage their bitterness. Though less swayed than his brother by Sikh sentiments, John Lawrence, too, recognized Sikh valour. Punjab's Sikh chiefs sensed his respect even if they did not directly hear what John Lawrence would later say:

> We began the [military] campaign [against the Sikhs]... by despising our foes; but we had hardly begun it before we learned to respect them, and to find that they were the bravest, the most determined, and the most formidable whom we had ever met in India.[26]

Including portions the British were already ruling, the Punjab after annexation was split into six administrative divisions: Lahore, Multan, Jhelum, Leiah,* the Jullundur doab and Ambala (i.e. the cis-Sutlej space). A commissioner headed each division, a deputy commissioner (DC) governed each district within a division, and one or more assistant commissioners supported each DC. All officers were British, about half of them from the military.

On annexation, President Henry Lawrence and his Board built forts along the Afghan frontier and raised ten 'irregular' Punjabi regiments, five cavalry and five infantry, commanded by the Board. Remembering their bitter defeat, the Sikhs stayed aloof to begin with, but soon they too entered the new regiments. The Frontier Guide Corps, conceived by Henry Lawrence, was strengthened. Dalhousie decided, however, that the Peshawar valley would be defended not by PIF but by 10,000 'regular' troops of the Bengal Army, of whom 3,000 were Europeans.

The raising of new regiments was matched by the disarming of the general population. Six months after annexation, a proclamation asking for weapons was 'everywhere placarded', though Hazara and the trans-Indus tracts were exempted. The chief aim was to recover the Sikhs' arms. In response, apparently 120,000 weapons 'of every size and species... from the cannon or the rifle of the nineteenth century down to the bows and arrows of the time of Porus and Alexander' were surrendered.[27]

According to Bosworth Smith, the Punjab which the British took over contained very few prisons.[28] Not wishing to look after prisoners, the Sikh Durbar had punished criminals by mutilation. One of its European generals, Avitabile, given charge of the Peshawar region in the kingdom's final phase,

---

*The Jhelum and Leiah divisions were later combined into the Rawalpindi division.

seems to have had men blown from guns.[29] Henry Lawrence and his colleagues ended mutilation and built twenty-five jails.

Also absent in the Punjab they had annexed—so the British would claim—were balance-sheets, roads, bridges, public conveyances, proper schools and hospitals.[30] Aiming to supply what was missing, the Board sought above all to win the peasants' goodwill. John Lawrence ensured that the land tax was halved or, in some places, cut to a fourth. But it had to be paid in money.

The tax reduction did not hurt the Board. For one thing, Multan's substantial revenues were now flowing into the Lahore treasury for the first time. This was true also for revenues from other outlying parts. In addition, large sums came in from estates confiscated from stubborn foes of the British.

The treasury was again not hurt, and the people felt relief, when, on 1 January 1850, the Board abolished all transit and town duties. During the kingdom's final years, according to Bosworth Smith, 'a piece of merchandise crossing the country had to pay duty some twelve times over',[31] though little of what was paid ever reached Lahore.

Fortunately for the Board, there were three good seasons after annexation. With thousands of Punjabi soldiers returning to farming, grains were abundant. But the farmers were unlucky, for prices fell sharply. The province's intake of revenue would nonetheless go up from 134 lakh rupees in 1849 to 205 lakh in 1857.[32]

When Henry Lawrence was Resident rather than President, a civil engineer, Colonel Robert Napier, had worked with him. Now Napier was charged with building canals and roads across Punjab. The roads—'military roads, roads for external and internal commerce, [and] cross and branch roads'—came first. The great road of Sher Shah of Sur that Akbar had extended would soon become, thanks in part to Napier's planning, the Grand Trunk Road connecting Peshawar, Lahore and Delhi to Calcutta.

In the first three years after annexation, '1,349 miles of road were cleared and constructed' in Punjab, 853 miles were under construction, 2,487 miles were 'traced', and 5,272 miles surveyed.[33] For rural Punjabis, the emergence of roads snaking past them was a phenomenon both impressive and unsettling.

Even though the chief purpose of Shah Jahan's seventeenth-century canal, brought down from the Himalayas, had been to water Lahore's Shalimar Gardens, pre-British Punjab, especially the Multan region, was not ignorant of canal irrigation. To demonstrate its interest in Punjab's farmers, the Board dug a 247-mile canal for irrigating not an imperial garden in Lahore but farming lands outside Adinanagar, Amritsar and Patiala. To emphasize the contrast, the British canal also originated from the Ravi river starting-point of Shah Jahan's canal.

■

The cornerstone of British Punjab, soon to be romanticized, was the district officer—the deputy commissioner (DC) or his assistant. The lore was that a district officer could do or be anything: he was 'publican, auctioneer, sheriff, road-maker, timber-dealer, recruiting-sergeant, slayer of wild beasts, bookseller, cattle-breeder, postmaster, vaccinator, discounter of bills, and registrar'.[34]

The DC worked not in an office or courtroom but from the back of a horse or in a tent, which was his 'locomotive home during some five months in the year'. He rode about 'redressing human wrongs' or sat 'under an immemorial tree or beside the village well' to settle a dispute, and was unafraid of floods, riots and assassins. British writers would claim that most district officers were energetic, sagacious, punctual, devoted to justice and 'loving' students of 'the native character', and therefore successful.[35]

This starry-eyed portrait was not altogether false. Through its district officers the Board did transform Punjab. However, to get closer to the complex reality we should look at a specific district officer rather than the generic or anonymous one.

Like the Lawrence brothers, John Nicholson came from Scots-Irish stock. Like them he had a patron in the East India Company. In his case the patron, James Hogg, was an uncle, his mother Clara's brother. Having made a deal of money as a lawyer in Calcutta, James Hogg returned to Britain in 1834 as 'a leading proprietor of East India Stock'[36] and went on to become the Company's director and (twice) its chairman. He also entered Parliament and received a baronetcy.*

John Nicholson's father was a doctor whose brother, Richardson Nicholson, went to India as a mate on an East India Company ship and found a position in the Company's Opium Department at Mirzapur in eastern UP. John was only eight when, in 1830, his father died. Growing up as the oldest of seven fatherless siblings and mixing with numerous maternal and paternal cousins, John learnt early how to find his own private world within a crowd, a useful preparation for India.

In 1839, when he was a tall but still growing sixteen-year-old, John

---

*Quintin Hogg or Lord Hailsham (1907-2001), member of British cabinets from the 1950s to the 1980s, was a great-grandson of Baron James Hogg.

sailed for India to join the Bengal Infantry as a direct cadet, without having to go through the Addiscombe training school.[37] Uncle James had arranged the exemption. Growing to a strong six-foot-two, John, we are told, kept his head high, always looking ahead, or at the sky above, but never at the ground.

He possessed a fiery temper. Soon after arriving in India, he challenged another British cadet, some months senior to him, to a duel with guns 'for presuming to teach him his duty'. Others intervened and the duel was averted.[38] At the end of 1840, after what to him was a hot and boring spell in Ferozepore, the Company's army town on the Sikh kingdom's border, Nicholson was sent with his 27th Native Infantry to Jalalabad.

In Peshawar en route, Avitabile, the Sikh kingdom's European governor, 'hospitably welcomed' Nicholson and his regiment. At the Khyber, 'thanks to the suasive influence of British gold', the Afridis guarding the Pass let the soldiers through.[39] In the summer of 1841, when Afghan hostility to Shah Shuja and the British suddenly escalated after a year of calm, John Nicholson, now eighteen, was asked to escort 600 ladies from Shuja's harem trying to reach Kabul.

What happened to the harem is not known, but Nicholson and his British and Indian companions were pushed into a fort in Ghazni by anti-Shuja, pro-Dost Afghans and besieged. Months later, in March 1842, i.e. only weeks after the death in the Afghan snows of thousands of Indians and Britons, Nicholson and his companions surrendered.

Extreme cruelty to the captives was followed by kinder treatment, including a dinner in Kabul given by Dost's son Akbar, and then by release, but the road back to Jalalabad and Peshawar was barred to them. Britons taken captive elsewhere in Afghanistan were also released, including George Lawrence, another of the Lawrence brethren.

By this time the British had managed to send in units from India to avenge the humiliating deaths of the previous winter. Having reached the Bamiyan area, Nicholson and party joined hands with incoming British regiments and took part in the vengeance enacted in Kabul in September 1842.

Afterwards, as he and the other British left Kabul in their Afghan clothes, Nicholson regretted the 'lightness' of the retribution. In a letter to his mother, he said he was 'sorry to leave Kabul while one stone of it remained on another'. Earlier, following Akbar's dinner, he had written to his mother that the Afghans were 'the most bloodthirsty and treacherous race in existence' but also among 'the handsomest' he had ever seen, possessing great 'natural innate politeness'.[40]

Before leaving Kabul, George Lawrence introduced John Nicholson to his brother Henry, who had played a crucial role in forcing the Khyber Pass for the regiments of retribution. On his trudge back to Peshawar, Nicholson ran into the dead body of *his* brother, Alexander, who had just arrived in India, no doubt courtesy of Uncle James, only to run into an unexplained death in Pashtun territory.

After another spell in Ferozepore and a new one in Moradabad (western UP), Nicholson met Henry Lawrence again in 1845 on the battlefront at Sabraon. Henry Lawrence liked young Nicholson's self-confidence, capacity to endure, and ability to lead. In early 1847, after a term in Jammu and Kashmir, where Nicholson trained Gulab Singh's soldiers along European lines, Nicholson became 'an assistant to the Resident in Lahore', or one of Henry Lawrence's white Punjabis.

After performing duties on the Resident's behalf in Lahore, Rawalpindi, Peshawar, and elsewhere, Nicholson provided intelligence and logistics for the 1849 war against the Sikh army, riding furiously past battlefields, bringing information and organizing supplies. His exertions were supported by Raja Muhammad Khan, the head of Rawalpindi's Gakhars.

On annexation, Nicholson was made the deputy commissioner (DC) of Rawalpindi. Writing in the 1890s, his biographer, Lionel Trotter, would claim that Nicholson's 'subjects (in Rawalpindi) received him with open arms... [and observed] the contrast between a grinding Sikh tyranny and the strong yet upright, even-handed sway of an English sahib'.[41]

Already, then, this twenty-seven-year-old DC, who had not administered any territory thus far, possessed 'subjects'—he was Rawalpindi's king. Adds Trotter: 'The name of this particular sahib was in every mouth and local rumour had already magnified him into the foremost hero of the late campaign; the great warrior whose arms had routed the hosts of Sher Singh and delivered the Punjab from its Sikh oppressors.'[42] In other words, a king with a mythical aura.

In Rawalpindi, Nicholson took interest in a fifteen-year-old youth from a once-privileged Jat family, Muhammad Hayat Khan of Wah, and paid for his studies. Hayat Khan would become his 'orderly', a servant-aide. White Punjabis like Nicholson often took a close and continuing interest in a servant or subordinate, but other 'subjects' were usually ignored and no 'subject' was seen as an equal.

During a furlough that followed, Nicholson travelled to Europe, tried to intervene in a conflict between Hungarians and Austrians, enviously examined, in Berlin, a new German weapon (a needle-musket), and resisted urgings from another of Henry Lawrence's white Punjabis, Herbert Edwardes, to find a wife.

'Return not alone,' Edwardes had written from India. 'How good it is to be helped by a noble wife who loves you better than all men and women but God better than you.'[43] But, as Trotter would put it, Nicholson 'perhaps loved his profession better than any woman he had seen; or perhaps his heart, for all its tenderness, was less inflammable than his temper.'[44]

India, Nicholson would say, was 'like a rat-trap, easier to get into than out of'.[45] There is no evidence that he loved Lahore, Pindi, Kashmir, Moradabad or Ferozepore or indeed any part of India. All the testimony suggests the opposite. If he liked the profession of a soldier-ruler, evidence indicates that he especially liked the ruling part.

Returning to Punjab in 1852, Nicholson was made the DC of Bannu, which at this time included Dera Ismail Khan. His friend Herbert Edwardes had been the Bannu DC until 1851 and proven 'his mastery in the art of governing a fierce and lawless people'. 'Bad specimens of Afghans', Edwardes would call them, adding, 'Could worse be said of any human race?'[46]

Nicholson liked the Bannu posting because of its nearness to Peshawar, where, in 1853, Edwardes took charge as commissioner of the entire Peshawar division, which included Bannu. Nicholson was glad to be in the company, from time to time, of Edwardes and his wife. There was a new road now between Bannu and Peshawar, and riding the sixty miles was no hardship for Nicholson.

Apparently the man who had followed Edwardes in Bannu—Nicholson's immediate predecessor—did not 'tame' its unruly tribes and raiders. Nicholson rose quickly to the task. Taking 1,500 mounted police, he chased raiders into their hills. When the raiders evaded the chasers, Nicholson mounted a blockade. 'Serious pressure' was inflicted on the raiders, whose 'headmen came into Bannu, submitted, and asked for terms'.

'Pay a rupee a head and behave well in future,' replied the DC. Apparently the raiders 'had learnt their lesson'[47] or, perhaps, Nicholson did not want a continuing war in the hills. Not much later, when a clan chief, allegedly a cattle-lifter by night, was killed in a scuffle with Nicholson's soldiers, the DC had his body cut up and displayed in the market.[48]

On the other hand, Nicholson retained corrupt native officials in their posts until better replacements were available. Preferring to go by his impulses, Nicholson was found one day, in Bannu, kicking 'a bundle of regulations' across the floor and saying to a visitor, 'This is the way I treat these things.'[49] Nicholson's image in Bannu was of a 'hard-hearted, self-willed tyrant' to begin with. Later, claims Thorburn, who served in Bannu some years after him, 'as [Nicholson's] self-abnegation, his wonderful feats of daring, the swift and stern justice that he meted out to all alike, became known, this impression gave way to a feeling of awe and admiration and the people became so cowed that during Nicholson's last year in office raids, robberies and murders were almost entirely unknown'.[50]

Nicholson liked to flog. Thorburn would record a conversation between two Bannu disputants who had come to him for a verdict. One said to the other. 'Turn your back to the sahib, he will see it waled from the whipping which Nicholson gave you.' The other replied, 'You need not talk, for your back is well scored also.'[51]

Soon after Nicholson's arrival in Bannu, a tribal chief meeting him is said to have 'hawked and spat out between himself and Nicholson, a dire insult and meant as such'. 'Orderly!' the DC shouted, 'Make that man lick up his spittle and kick him out of camp.' The order was carried out. On another occasion, a mullah failing to salute the DC was compelled to remove his beard. Recording the incidents with approbation, Nicholson's nineteenth-century biographer adds: 'Nicholson never brooked the faintest show of insolence towards an officer of the ruling race.'[52]

Evidently Henry Lawrence and his wife Honoria tried from afar to interest Nicholson in religion. We do not know if they succeeded. At times Nicholson assisted Pashtun children. Thus in 1854 he wrote to Edwardes of 'a wretched Waziri child who had been put up to poison food'. Asked by Nicholson (who spoke Punjabi, Hindustani and Pashto) whether it wasn't wrong to kill people, the boy seems to have said, 'Yes, it is wrong to kill with a knife or sword.'

'Why?' Nicholson asked. 'Because the blood left marks,' the boy replied. Nicholson found a tribal elder, known to the boy, to take him in as a foster-son. He wrote to Edwardes: 'I have seldom seen anything more touching than... the child clasping the man's beard, and the man with his hands on the child's head.'[53]

Nicholson gets humanized also in the story of his complex relationship with Neville Chamberlain, an army officer who obtained a position coveted by Nicholson. In a letter to Chamberlain, Nicholson acknowledged the former's superior claims, but when no answer came back he was incensed. Learning, much later, that his letter had never reached the addressee, Nicholson, who had fanned the flame of imagined insult, could only hang in shame 'the head he usually held so high'.[54]

Not every district officer was as vain, harsh, vindictive, successful or awe-inspiring: Nicholson does not personify British Punjab. Yet the ruling class to which he belonged shared at least a few of Nicholson's virtues and weaknesses.

•

> Within three years after the great surrender (1849), Ranjit's crude kingdom had been transformed, as if by magic, into one of the most thriving, best-ordered provinces of British India. Three years of just, wise, unflaggingly provident rule aided by a series of favouring seasons had raised the youngest of our possessions to a level with Bombay or Bengal. Thanks to the tireless zeal of Dalhousie himself and all who worked under him from the Lawrence brothers to the youngest member of the Punjab Commission, the Lahore Board could already declare that 'in no part of India had there been more perfect quiet than in the territories lately annexed'.[55]

This is Lionel Trotter, Nicholson's biographer, speaking near the end of the nineteenth century, but other writers, official and non-official, British and Indian, said similar things at the time. Thus Syad Muhammad Latif, a Punjab-based judicial officer of Hindustani origin, would write in the 1890s of Britain's 'victories of peace and civilization' in the province and of how its Muslim, Sikh and Hindu religious leaders 'blessed their English rulers'. Added Latif: 'From the hardy yeoman and the sturdy peasant to the thrifty trader and the enterprising capitalist, all rose in robust prosperity.'[56]

These evaluations should be discounted by a good percentage. It was natural for an empire to boast and its Indian officers to flatter. Yet what remains after hefty discounting is impressive all right.

Meanwhile, to return to the Punjab Board, that august body nearly lost one of its greatest prizes, the Kohinoor diamond, which had become the property, following annexation, of Queen Victoria. Receiving firm instructions from Dalhousie for its protection, the Board had decided that the jewel would be safest in the custody of Member John Lawrence. John put the thing in his waistcoat pocket.

When, after some days, Dalhousie sent word that the Queen wanted it brought to her, the Board relayed the requisition to John Lawrence, who felt his pocket, did not find the thing, and said nothing. Later that day, asked about it by his master, John Lawrence's servant said that he had indeed found a glass object in master's waistcoat and placed it in a tin box. Fortunately for the Queen, and even more so for John Lawrence and the entire Board, the glassy thing was still in that box.[57]

But the Lawrence brothers were not hitting it off. After having struggled in vain to prevent annexation, Henry Lawrence tried 'to ease the fall of the privileged class'. He thought that 'the more that could be left to the Sirdars of their dignity, their power, their property, their immunities, the better'. Disagreeing, John Lawrence said in a letter to his older brother that 'our very existence depends on our gradually reducing the power and consequence of the chiefs'.[58]

This and other differences were aired before Lord Dalhousie. 'The friction, the tension, the heartburning, were intense.'[59] In the end, the brothers and the Governor-General concluded that Punjab could not be ruled by a divided Board, and both brothers conveyed to Dalhousie their willingness to resign.

> The Governor-General, whose own views and sympathies were in close agreement with those of the younger and more practical brother, caught at so fair an opportunity of completing his own handiwork.[60]

To Henry Lawrence's chagrin, his offer to resign was accepted and he was asked to proceed to Ajmer as Resident for Rajputana. Trying to soften the blow, Dalhousie explained that even as Punjab needed a single head, it also needed a civilian, which unfortunately Henry was not, whereas John was. Did not his twenty-year experience qualify him, Henry asked, for *any* role in India? Dalhousie was unmoved. Retaining his low opinion of India's princes, Dalhousie would say in sarcasm that Henry thought of himself as the king of Punjab.

Henry Lawrence's mortification was matched by disappointment among officials, chiefs and the public in Punjab, for the retired President had seen 'with his own eyes every portion of his province, and converse[d] freely with every class among his subjects, and with each and all of his subordinates, as far as possible in their own homes'.[61] Also, he had unsettled the prejudices of many a white Punjabi. 'No one ever dined at Sir Henry's table,' one of them would say, 'without learning from him to think more kindly of the natives.'[62]

In February 1853, John Lawrence was named the chief commissioner of Punjab, with Robert Montgomery assisting him as judicial commissioner and Donald Macleod as the Commissioner for Revenue. 'A few days later, Sir

Henry's haggard face and gaunt figure passed away for ever from Lahore.'[63]

As for the newly-appointed chief commissioner, his devoted biographer would say that whatever John Lawrence did and wherever he was—at summer's peak he repaired with his wife and children to a three-roomed house in Murree—'his finger was always on the pulse of his province'.[64]

With native princes and at durbars, he spoke Persian and Urdu-Hindustani comfortably, though not, it would seem, Punjabi. From the Board's time, Urdu was the official language of Punjab's Ambala and Jullundur divisions, and Persian that of the western divisions.

■

By now Dalhousie had eased out several Indian princes under his doctrine of 'lapse', which enabled the paramount power, i.e. the Company, to absorb any state which, in the Governor-General's judgment, lacked a suitable male heir. Applying this doctrine, the states of Satara, Jaitpur and Sambalpur had been absorbed in 1849. Jhansi would 'lapse' to the British in 1853.

The Mughal heir, Bahadur Shah Zafar, seventy-eight years old in 1853, continued to live on a Company pension in Delhi's Red Fort. For form's sake, the Resident, Thomas Metcalfe, continued to salaam Zafar, but Dalhousie wanted the king out of the Fort.

The Governor-General was modernizing India. In 1853, the telegraph was brought to several places including army cantonments, and rail lines began to be laid, starting with western India. Edwin Blood, a nineteen-year-old American from Massachusetts who had found a job in Calcutta, would write in his journal that India had 'become a field of glory' for Dalhousie, a 'genius' in Blood's eyes.[65]

John Lawrence, the chief commissioner, would on occasion differ with the Governor-General, as when Dalhousie wanted James Outram, a general who had supervised in Sindh, to become the Peshawar commissioner, whereas Lawrence wanted Herbert Edwardes in that position. Lawrence's argument, which won the day, was that Peshawar required a civilian rather than a military chief:

> That assiduous attention to the routine of administrative details, that prompt response to all references, however apparently trivial, and that exact attention to instructions, can only be secured in officers regularly trained to their duties. We are strangers in language, colour and religion to the people who beyond the Indus are peculiarly intractable, fanatical

and warlike. To reconcile them to our rule requires the most careful and able management.[66]

The two agreed in respect of an audacious soldier, William Hodson, to whom Dalhousie had given command of the Frontier Guides. His manner had made Hodson unpopular 'with both natives and whites'; his honesty with money, including some of Henry Lawrence's funds entrusted to him, had come into question; and he was charged also with 'cruel treatment of a rich native chief named Kader Khan'. In 1855, with Lawrence's full backing, Dalhousie deprived Hodson of his command.[67]

For preventing an advance towards India by Russia and its ally Persia, Dalhousie wished to bolster Dost Muhammad in Afghanistan. If Lawrence was cool to the idea, the Bannu DC, John Nicholson was positively opposed. To Herbert Edwardes, the commissioner in Peshawar, Nicholson, wrote (May 1854):

> I hope you will never forget that [the Afghans'] *name is faithlessness,*[*] even among themselves.... In Afghanistan son betrays father, and brother brother, without remorse... Even the most experienced and astute of our political officers in Afghanistan were deceived by that winning and imposing frankness of manner, which it has pleased Providence to give to the Afghans, as it did to the first serpent...[68]

But Edwardes, who had forged links across the Khyber, strongly backed Dalhousie's line, and Nicholson's opposition and Lawrence's misgivings were overridden. On 20 March 1855, at the mouth of the Khyber, chief commissioner John Lawrence was obliged to sign a treaty with a son of Dost Muhammad whereby the Company and Afghanistan agreed to befriend each other's friends and oppose the other's enemies.

No matter how steady the Lawrence hand at Punjab's helm, Dalhousie saw himself as the province's creator. As a modernizer, he 'wanted to make Punjab not only a model province but a paying investment'.[69] With such a Governor-General, Lawrence needed both frankness and tact.

In the summer of 1855, Dalhousie made up his mind to annex the territory of Awadh, even though it supplied the bulk of the Bengal Army's Indian soldiers, and even though, in a treaty signed in 1837, the Company had promised not to annex it. Exactly when Lawrence learnt of this decision,

---

*Italics in the original.

which was implemented early in 1856, is not clear, but his biographer, who had the benefit, after his subject's retirement, of several interviews with him, is certain that Lawrence strongly supported Awadh's annexation.

The chief commissioner and the Governor-General met for the last time in Calcutta in February 1856. To make the long and hardly easy journey from Lahore, John Lawrence took his first 'holiday' in fourteen years. 'Of all from whom I part in India,' Dalhousie had written to him, 'there is not one from whom I shall sever myself with more sincere regret than from yourself, my dear John.'[70] In March 1856, within days of Dalhousie's departure from India, the chief commissioner was made Sir John Lawrence.

■

Dalhousie's successor in Calcutta was Charles John Canning, whose father had died as Britain's prime minister. Like Dalhousie, Charles Canning too had served in the cabinet before coming out to Calcutta, where, right away, he was confronted with troubling events to India's west. Persia having claimed Herat and received Russia's backing, Dost Muhammad asked for British aid. In July 1856, London announced that a Persian attack on Herat would be taken as an attack on Britain.

While not willing to send troops into Afghanistan, the British decided to mount a naval demonstration in the Persian Gulf and land a British force on Persia's shores. When Canning sought John Lawrence's opinion on a commander for the force, the chief commissioner suggested his brother, Henry Lawrence. In the end, however, James Outram was chosen, a decision made by Her Majesty's Government in London, not by Canning in Calcutta.

But Canning asked John Lawrence to sign a new treaty with Dost Muhammad, reaffirming British support. Edwardes in Peshawar was again more enthusiastic than Lawrence in Lahore about a treaty with Kabul, but Canning agreed with Lawrence that a large British presence in Afghanistan should be avoided. It would, Lawrence argued, 'eat up resources and incite the people'.[71]

Before Lawrence cautiously rode out with a small party towards Dost's camp at the Khyber, British troops were told to be ready for treachery and to attack if gunfire was heard. Measured booms did ring out, but Lawrence was being saluted, not gunned. On 7 January 1857, an agreement was signed.

Conspicuously absenting himself from the ceremony was John Nicholson, by now posted in Peshawar as its DC, under Commissioner Edwardes, and expected therefore to be part of the chief commissioner's durbar. But

Nicholson's 'intense feeling of hatred for the Afghan nation' had made him 'go off' to 'the furthest end of his district'.[72]

Begun in November 1856, the Anglo-Persian war, in which many Indians of the Bengal Army also took part, ended in April 1857 with British victory. Persia withdrew its claims to Herat, which was returned to Afghanistan.

■

John Lawrence dismissed serious anxiety when, in the spring of 1857, he first learnt of discontent among the Bengal Army's Hindustani sepoys over greased cartridges for a new rifle, the Enfield. Though some Punjab-based sepoys, too, were refusing to touch, taste or handle the cartridges, believing them to be greased with cow-fat or pig-fat, Lawrence thought that the sepoys' thrill at the new rifle's 1,000-yard range would overcome other reactions.

It was odd, certainly, to learn that two native regiments in the Calcutta region had to be disarmed and disbanded in March, and that in April a sepoy of the 34th Infantry, Mangal Pandey, had been executed there: Pandey had disobeyed British officers and also tried to kill two of them. Even odder was a report that for no obvious reason peasants around Agra and Meerut were passing chapatis from village to village.

Reminding himself that India was a strange land, Calcutta very far, and his own Punjab safe, Lawrence set off early in May—his wife and child with him—for Rawalpindi, en route to Murree in the hills, for already Lahore was very hot.

On the morning of 12 May, a terse telegram, tapped out in Delhi on 11 May and relayed from Ambala, reached Lawrence in Rawalpindi. Sowars from Meerut, the telegram said, were burning houses and killing Britons in the Mughal capital. Ambala had also sent off that word to Lahore, where Robert Montgomery had been left in charge, and to Peshawar, where Edwardes was the commissioner. Another telegram quickly followed: originating in Meerut, this one spoke of Europeans killed in that city by Hindustani sepoys on 10 May.

The word from Meerut, where British soldiers outnumbered Hindustani sepoys, was even more shocking than the telegram from Delhi, where only a few British soldiers were stationed at the time. Thanks, however, to the telegraph, the British in Punjab heard of the Delhi killings and Meerut mutiny before the news reached Punjab-based sepoys.

The Punjab of May 1857 contained 36,000 sepoys belonging to different 'native' or 'Hindustani' regiments of the Bengal Army. Twelve 'European' regiments stationed in Punjab contained about 11,000 British soldiers, mostly massed around two cities at the province's opposite ends, Peshawar and Ambala. PIF—the Punjabi Irregular Force, including the Guides—comprised 14,000 men, Pashtuns and also Punjabis, almost all stationed in the trans-Indus frontier region. In addition, there were 15,000 native military police in Punjab. The military police's Lahore division was headed by Richard Lawrence, another of the Lawrence brethren.

While Indian soldiers outnumbered white ones in most places in Punjab, this was especially true of Lahore, Rawalpindi, Ferozepore, Jullundur and Hoshiarpur, and even more so of Amritsar, Gurdaspur, Sialkot, Jhelum and Multan.

Since the telegraph line between Lahore and Rawalpindi was down, preventing consultation with the chief commissioner, Montgomery and his colleagues in Lahore acted on their own. So, at first, did Edwardes and Nicholson in Peshawar. While these men, and district officers elsewhere in Punjab, sought to prevent mutinies by Hindustani regiments stationed near them, a jolted Lawrence also thought of how Delhi might be recovered. Lawrence's 'spirit', his biographer argues, 'was imperial, not provincial'.[73]

Jumping out of his bed in Rawalpindi after receiving the first message, Lawrence sent a telegram to the Bengal Army's commander-in-chief, General George Anson, who was in Simla at the time, urging him to descend on Delhi with a force, and another to Governor-General Canning in Calcutta, requesting him to get China-bound British troops diverted to India.

Not forgetting the ultimate boss in London, on 15 May Lawrence wrote also to Ross Mangles, the East India Company chairman, calling the revolt 'the greatest crisis which has as yet occurred in India' and urging 'most strongly... that a large body of European infantry be despatched to India as soon as may be possible'.[74]

In Punjab, through bold manoeuvres that required silent planning and sudden execution, Hindustani regiments were disarmed in one station after another, an outcome aided by Indian informers and by the fact that everywhere in the province heavy guns were in British hands.

On 12 May in Lahore, within hours of the receipt of the telegram about Delhi, a 'trusty Brahmin clerk' (as Bosworth Smith would describe him) spoke to Richard Lawrence, who commanded Lahore's military police, about the four native regiments (three infantry and one cavalry) stationed in the Mian Mir suburb. Laying 'his finger on his throat', the agent said, 'Sahib, they are up to this.'[75]

Passed on at once to Montgomery, the remark was enough for Lahore's acting boss. Asked by him to organize their regiments' immediate disarming, British officers in Mian Mir at first resisted the request, but they were quickly persuaded. To ensure surprise, a previously arranged ball was meticulously gone through on the 12th night. In the morning, the blow fell on Mian Mir's Hindustani sepoys.

Though greatly outnumbering the station's British soldiers, all of whom belonged to five companies of the 'European' regiment—the 81st—the Hindustanis were stunned on hearing the shouted order, 'Pile arms!' Yet pile arms they did, for at the same instant they saw 'a long line of Artillery' facing them and heard 'the rattle of ramrods' in British hands.[76]

Montgomery oversaw this intrepid manoeuvre at Mian Mir, which would be repeated across Punjab in the days to follow. Usually it was the local commissioner or DC, acting on his own or under orders from Lawrence or Montgomery, who demanded a native regiment's disarming and with effort persuaded its British major or colonel to accomplish it. In some places, senior British officers demonstrated solidarity with *their* sepoys, as they thought of them, by adding their personal swords to the arms piled up by the Hindustanis.

Before the day of the 13th ended, one company of the 81st was on its way, in hastily-collected carts, from Lahore to Amritsar. In the morning, the Bengal Army's stations in Amritsar and in neighbouring Govindgarh fort, places critical to Sikh sentiment, were made secure. Earlier, on the 12th, Montgomery had sent messengers from Lahore to Ferozepore, which held a large arsenal; to Multan, where a British artillery company was stationed next to a Hindustani regiment; and to Kangra, which influenced opinion in adjoining hill districts.

Through messengers and where possible through the telegraph, Lawrence (who stayed on in Rawalpindi, sending his wife and child to Murree) and Montgomery instructed officers elsewhere in Punjab in the following terms: 'Send all treasure to the nearest military station. Let Punjabi police escort it. Distrust Hindustani guards. Stop and read all sepoys' letters. Act firmly but show no alarm.'[77]

There were failures. Though Ferozepore had been alerted, the 45th Native Infantry stationed there broke out and joined the rebels in Delhi. In June, three native regiments successfully revolted in Jullundur and reached Delhi. This was a blow to Lawrence, who had not forgotten his years in the Jullundur doab. There was, too, defiance by regiments based in Sialkot, Jhelum and Rawalpindi.

On the other hand, in Multan, which, with Delhi in rebel hands, was the sole link between Punjab and the outside world, sixty British artillery men, led by Major Crawford Chamberlain, skilfully disarmed around 3,500 Hindustani soldiers. Upon learning of the Jullundur debacle, Lawrence had instructed the major in Multan to take the risk and disarm the Hindustanis. Prior to this action, Chamberlain and his colleagues had hesitated for four weeks, while the sepoys, on their part, had hesitated to revolt. Nor had the sepoys forged links with the Multanis who only eight years earlier had given the firanghis a difficult time.

In Peshawar, Herbert Edwardes apparently received the telegram about Delhi, relayed by Ambala, on 11 May, a day before Lawrence in Rawalpindi or Montgomery in Lahore got it. On the 12th morning, after Edwardes had learnt also about Meerut, he wrote to his wife that he expected the mutiny to spread to 'every station'. If, however, it came to the Peshawar area, he was confident that 'we shall, please God, make short work of the mutineers', for 'we have three European regiments in the valley, and all the artillery is European'.[78]

Contributing to Edwardes' confidence was the Anglo-Afghan treaty for which he had pressed. Persia, one of the treaty's targets, had since been defeated. Edwardes expected Dost Muhammad to continue his policy of friendship with the British.

Also present in Peshawar in May was its DC, John Nicholson. On the 13th, Edwardes, Nicholson, an old major-general (Thomas Reed) and two brigadiers (Sydney Cotton and Neville Chamberlain) held a five-man 'council of war' in Peshawar. While Reed, Cotton and Chamberlain were accountable to the commander-in-chief of the Bengal Army, Edwardes and Nicholson served Punjab's administration, under Lawrence. But they too had been trained in the army.

This 'war council' took a few decisions. One was that Chamberlain should lead a Delhi-bound Movable Column that would suppress rebellions in Punjab along the way. (More than a century earlier, in the late 1720s, 'moving columns' of light cavalry raised by a youthful new governor, Zakariya Khan, had scattered Punjab's rebelling Sikhs.) Another decision was that, after obtaining Lawrence's approval, new PIF units should be raised in and around Peshawar.

A young record-taker at this 'war council', Frederick Roberts (a future general), would afterwards refer to the 'sense of power' that John Nicholson, whom he was meeting for the first time, exuded during the discussions.[79]

After a building in Peshawar had been identified where British families could, if need arose, take refuge, Reed, Chamberlain and Edwardes rode out to Rawalpindi to confer with John Lawrence. At this meeting, held on or around 16 May, it was agreed that retaking Delhi, where Zafar, the old king, had evidently blessed the rebellion, was essential. The white Punjabis confabulating in Rawalpindi understood that Delhi's 'name and prestige and that of the restored Mogul sovereignty' would exercise influence 'in every Sepoy cantonment and in every native bazaar from Peshawar to Calcutta'.[80]

Lawrence backed the idea of fresh PIF units and the proposed Movable Column, but he rejected Reed's suggestion, which Edwardes had supported, that Nicholson should accompany the Column as its 'civil and political officer'. Nicholson was needed, Lawrence said, in Peshawar, but the chief commissioner was conscious also of the unpredictable impact of Nicholson's masterful personality on the Column and on Punjabis it would encounter on the path to Delhi.

Nicholson himself felt that the Movable Column was what life had prepared him for. In less than a month, he obtained his heart's wish. The Column's chief, Brigadier Neville Chamberlain—the man against whom Nicholson had nursed a flame for a time—was summoned to the front in Delhi, as was old General Reed; and Reed and Lawrence agreed between them that Nicholson was the only man available to replace Chamberlain. Not only would John Nicholson accompany the Column; made brigadier now, he would command it.

Before Nicholson left Peshawar for his new charge, he and Edwardes did harsh, toilsome, gory and bold things in the frontier region. They read sepoy mail, executed suspected spies, tried to raise new PIF units, and, on 22 May, disarmed three native regiments in Peshawar. 'The doomed regiments, taken completely by surprise and unable to act in concert, obeyed, each in turn, the order to pile arms.'[81] Lawrence called the Peshawar disarming 'a masterstroke'.[82]

Before the disarming, not many chiefs in the Peshawar valley had helped with recruiting. An 'old Afghan chief', friendly for some time to the Edwardes couple, told Nicholson that 'this was a crisis in which the sahibs must rely upon themselves'. After the disarming (Edwardes would later write), 'Khans and Urbabs who stood aloof the day before appeared as thick as flies and were profuse in offers of service'.[83] Hundreds lined up to join the PIF.

The next day, Nicholson, riding his 'great grey charger', chased a group of rebelling sepoys of a Mardan-based Hindustani regiment who were marching off towards the hills of Swat 'with drums beating and colours flying'. 'Mile after mile and hour after hour the chase continued' until the hunter found his prey. According to his lionizing biographer, 'Nicholson's great sword fell[ed] a Sepoy at every stroke'.[84]

We are told that those not slain by Nicholson and his men fell into the rough hands of pro-British tribesmen. Only fifteen years earlier, a brutal fight had found Pashtun tribesmen ranged against a joint British-Hindustani force. Now, in the summer of 1857, the Pashtuns seemed willing, in another brutal clash, to side with the British against the Hindustanis.

Cheered by the Pashtun reaction yet perturbed that Hindustanis from Jullundur had joined the rebels in Delhi, Lawrence proposed moving all British troops from the Peshawar region to the Delhi front. To turn necessity into virtue, he suggested that Peshawar 'be given' to Dost Muhammad, along with a request 'to take charge as our friend'.[85]

Spelt out in a letter that reached Edwardes in Peshawar on 11 June, the proposal was also advanced by Lawrence to Canning, his chief in Calcutta. For two months, the latter did not respond. Perhaps it took time for Lawrence's message to reach the Governor-General—the telegraph line to Calcutta was frequently cut by rebels. Edwardes, on his part, firmly opposed Lawrence's suggestion.

Also opposed to the idea were Nicholson, who was still in Peshawar when Lawrence's letter arrived, and Brigadier Sydney Cotton, who commanded Peshawar's British troops. Writing to Lawrence on behalf of all three, Edwardes 'insisted strongly on the absolute need of holding on to Peshawar', which was 'the anchor holding the Punjab'. If the anchor was removed, 'the whole ship will drift to sea'.[86]

Suggesting that Lawrence's proposal arose from panic, Trotter, Nicholson's biographer, would speculate that while Nicholson, with a mother in Ireland, had no wife, and Edwardes' wife was in Britain at the time, Lawrence—older than those two, and in poor health—was affected by the nearness, at the moment of crisis, of his wife. 'Edwardes and Nicholson', observed Trotter, 'were young, hopeful, audacious, and their womenkind were all safe in their far-off island homes'.

As for Canning, when, in August, he finally responded to Lawrence, his message was clear: 'Hold on to Peshawar to the last.'[87] But John Lawrence did not withdraw his proposal. To him the Indus, not the Khyber, was India's natural frontier; he wanted as few points of contact as possible with the Afghans; and if a choice had to be made, he thought Delhi more important than Peshawar.

On the night of 11 May, after rebel soldiers from Meerut had coerced

Zafar in Delhi's Red Fort into blessing them, the old king proclaimed himself Hindustan's sovereign. Many Europeans and Indian Christians were murdered in the city that day. Not long afterwards, British women and children who had taken refuge in the Fort were also killed, though not with Zafar's consent.

In the days that followed, several Hindustani regiments of the Bengal Army flocked into Delhi from stations east of it in the doab between the Ganga and the Jamuna. They had emulated the sepoys of Meerut, which however remained under British control, as did Agra, the NWP capital.

In the last week of May, a British force from Meerut led by Brigadier Archdale Wilson was stopped by the rebels at Hindan, twelve miles east of Delhi. The bigger force for which Lawrence had been pressing General Anson in Simla eventually left Ambala on the night of 24 May, but desertions, shortage of transporting animals and illnesses delayed its advance towards Delhi.

Several succumbed to cholera, including Anson himself, but, led now by General Henry Barnard, the Delhi Field Force (DFF), as it was called, reached the Ridge overlooking Delhi on 8 June, after having been augmented the previous day by Wilson's force from Hindan. A furious fight took place on 8 June but the Ridge was captured by the British.

Earlier, in Karnal, the DFF had been joined by Delhi's magistrate, Theo Metcalfe, one of several Metcalfes who had served the Company. Having escaped from the Delhi killings of 11 May, Metcalfe was returning in vengeful mood to assist its recapture.

But by this time the British had suffered major reverses in Awadh's large and prosperous capital, Lucknow, and also in Kanpur, fifty-five miles southwest of Lucknow and the army-cum-transport town on Awadh's edge. Awadh's chief commissioner at this juncture, counterpart to Punjab's John Lawrence, was none other than Henry Lawrence. In March 1857, Canning had moved the older brother from Rajputana to head freshly-annexed Awadh.

On 30 May, rebel sepoys and loyalists of Awadh's deposed nawab forced the new chief commissioner, all the Europeans of Lucknow, and about 700 Indians loyal to the British inside a few buildings within the so-called Residency area, and besieged them. Lucknow's population seemed to support the rebels.

Anticipating trouble, Henry Lawrence had prepared the Residency for defence and put in stores for its inmates' survival. Three days before the siege began, he wrote to Lord Canning:

> Hitherto [Awadh] has been kept quiet, and we have played the Irregulars against the line regiments; but being constituted of exactly the same

material, the taint is fast pervading them, and in a few weeks, if not days—unless Delhi be in the interim captured—there will be but one feeling throughout the army, a feeling that our prestige is gone, and that feeling will be more dangerous than any other.

Religion, fear, hatred, one and all have their influence; but there is still a reverence for the Company's *ikbal*—when it is gone we shall have few friends indeed. The tone and talk of many have greatly altered during the last few days, and we are now asked, almost in terms of insolence, whether Delhi is captured, or when it will be.[88]

On 5 June, a week after the start of the Lucknow siege, Kanpur fell to its four native regiments' rebelling sepoys, who began a sustained attack on hundreds of Europeans, some of them unwell or old, huddled together in barracks in a compound called the Entrenchment, and led by an old general, Sir Hugh Wheeler. A four-foot-high mud wall surrounded the compound.

Travelling to Delhi and to the DFF massed on the Ridge, the news from Lucknow and Kanpur cheered the rebels and depressed the British. Week after week, the British shelled Delhi's walls from the Ridge, but the counter-shelling from the city seemed bigger. On 2 July, the men on the Ridge heard British-trained bands heralding the entry into Delhi of five more rebelling regiments, along with heavy guns they had seized.

Disappointment on the Ridge was matched by disorder inside Delhi, where Zafar did not have the money to pay salaries to the mounting ranks of sepoys, who tried forcibly to take what they needed from the city's merchants, whose supplies had shrunk because armed robbers had taken over the countryside around Delhi. Both the city and the Ridge faced shortages, sickness and death.

The British on the Ridge sent spies into Delhi, defended their rear against rebel forays and their front against assaults, and waited. They knew that John Lawrence was organizing reinforcements, European and native, and aiming to send heavy batteries for breaching Delhi's walls.

Elsewhere, too, the British were reacting. Summoned by Canning, forty-seven-year-old Colonel James Neill and his 1st Madras Fusiliers reached Allahabad via Calcutta on 9 June. Another senior officer drafted by Canning, sixty-two-year-old Henry Havelock, who had commanded a division in the Anglo-Persian war that had only ended in April, brought a column to Allahabad at the end of June. Also at the end of June, 700 men of the 5th Fusiliers, who thought they had left England for China, arrived in Calcutta. Thanks to interventions by Lawrence in Rawalpindi and Canning in Calcutta, they had been redirected upon reaching Singapore.

Along with their columns, Havelock and Neill marched westward in scorching heat towards Kanpur and Lucknow and, if need be, Delhi. In some villages near Allahabad, British soldiers killed aged men, women and children for alleged association with the rebels. Many were simply 'burnt to death'.[89]

The British columns were still far from Kanpur when, on 25 June, after three weeks of bombardment, illnesses and deaths at the Entrenchment, General Wheeler sued for peace. The man to whom he submitted was Nana Sahib, a descendant of the Peshwas, who lived near Kanpur and whom the sepoys had accepted as their ruler. From the besieged Lucknow Residency, Henry Lawrence had smuggled out a letter asking Wheeler not to trust Nana Sahib, but Wheeler yielded before the letter arrived.

The Entrenchment's surrendering men, women and children were assured safe passage to Allahabad by Nana Sahib. Two days later, at Kanpur's Satichaura Ghat, Wheeler and many other Britons were killed while boarding boats in the Ganga for the promised journey to safety. The rest from the Entrenchment were either shot or detained. In the middle of July, under the aegis of Nana Sahib, the imprisoned were all slaughtered, including women and children, in the well-known Bibighar massacre.

Before this, on 4 July, Henry Lawrence had been killed inside the Lucknow Residency by a rebel-fired shell exploding near him. As the fifty-one-year-old officer lay dying, he uttered words for his tombstone: 'Here lies Henry Lawrence, who tried to do his duty.' The shelling continued while a short prayer was said over a hurriedly-dug grave, and 'a few spadefuls of earth speedily covered' Lawrence's remains.[90]

■

In Rawalpindi, an immediate question for John Lawrence, when he first heard of the outbreak, was about the Sikhs. Only eight years had passed since Sikh soldiers were defeated after giving the British their toughest Indian battle. The Khalsa sarkar had yielded place to a Punjab where Muslims were the Sikhs' equal. Now that there was an anti-British rising, would the Sikhs not join it? Having only recently moved from battlefields to their farms, would they not respond to a call to arms to settle scores with their victors?

Aware as Lawrence was of the Sikh soldiery's disdain for the Hindustanis, or the Purbiahs as Punjabis often called them, he knew that Sikhs and Hindus had been close during Sikh rule, and that knowledge made him cautious. On 18 May he wrote to Robert Montgomery in Lahore:

> I will not therefore consent to raise levies of the old Sikhs. There is a strong feeling of sympathy between Sikhs and Hindus, and though I am willing to raise Sikhs gradually and carefully, I wish to see them mixed with Mohammedans and Hindus.[91]

Accordingly, a new regiment raised in Mian Mir on 8 June, the 25th Punjabis, was a mixed one, comprising Punjabi Muslims, Sikhs and Hindu Dogras. But if Punjab called for caution, it also offered the British hope. Writing twenty-five years later, Bosworth Smith would frankly acknowledge elements in the Punjab of 1857 which encouraged the British:

> There was the hatred of the Sikh for the Mohammedan who had persecuted him, and whom he had persecuted in turn. There was the contempt of the hardy Punjabi, whatever his caste or creed, for the less manly races of Oude or Bengal. Finally, there was the hope of plundering the revolted city, the home of the Mogul, under the *Ikbal* of the Company.[92]

Battle-itch, hate, contempt and greed. The ingredients were waiting to be utilized, and a strategy presented itself to John Lawrence. Recall, with due care, the Sikh love of war. Stir and use the dislikes: Sikh resentment of Muslim rule, Muslim resentment of Sikh domination, Punjabi disdain of the Purbiah. Spread word of the chance to plunder Delhi under British protection.

As Bosworth Smith would candidly put it, Lawrence 'could afford in the crisis of our fate to put arms freely into the hands of one of these sections (Sikh and Muslim), in full confidence that they would use them, not against their common masters but against their own (Indian) brothers'.[93]

Lawrence's wariness about levies of former Sikh soldiers did not last, and turning Sikhs against a Mughal king did not prove hard. Yet Lawrence's keenness on a 'mix' in new army units persisted. To Brigadier Sydney Cotton he wrote on 10 June:

> My proposition for a regiment of ten companies is four of Sikhs, two of Hill Rajputs, two of Punjabi Mohammedans, two of Pathans. In Peshawar, if you like, you might have a third of Pathans.[94]

In this letter, Lawrence called the Pathans 'braver' than the Sikhs but lacking the latter's 'sustained courage', less willing than the Sikhs to be disciplined, less loyal, and more likely to quit the service after collecting 'a little money'. The Punjabi Muslim was to him 'a brave soldier, with perhaps less dash than the Pathan, but more steady and less fanatical'.[95]

By the end of the Revolt, the army and military police of British Punjab, which also included much of today's Khyber-Pakhtunkhwa, would present a total of 58,000 men, of whom 11,000 were Europeans, 24,000 Muslims, 13,000 Sikhs, 2,000 Dogras, and 8,000 other Hindus. With 'watchful care', Bosworth Smith informs us, Lawrence had ensured that the large force contained 'men differing from each other in religion, birthplace, habits and dialect'. 'The somewhat sinister maxim, *divide et impera* [had] been acted upon', adds Bosworth Smith, with 'triumphant results'.[96]

Lawrence's policy towards the Sikhs was influenced, it seems, by Nihal Singh Chachi, a Sikh soldier who after surviving in Jalalabad in 1842 had served British officers in Lahore before annexation and thereafter. Among Lawrence's numerous acquaintances named in Bosworth Smith's two-volume, 1,051-page biography, Nihal Singh Chachi is the *sole* Indian. Serving Lawrence too as an aide-de-camp, Nihal Singh told his master, in respect of the old Sikh chiefs, 'You had better employ them, or they may go against you.'

Taking what he judged to be the lesser risk, Lawrence sought Nihal Singh's assistance in drawing up a list of 'all the Sikh chiefs who had suffered for the rebellion of 1848' and 'wrote at once to each of them', inviting the chiefs to retrieve their situations by enlisting, along with their retainers, on the Government's side.[97] The effort was amply rewarded. As for the Sikh rajas of Patiala, Nabha, Jind and Kaithal—allies of the British even during the Anglo-Sikh wars—they required little persuasion. Money and soldiers outpoured from them. Lawrence came up with thumb-rules for himself and his far-flung officers:

> Trust Irregulars and native Punjabis but 'utterly distrust' the Bengal Army's native or 'regular' contingents. Bring the Irregulars from the frontier to the interior. Send the Bengal Army Regulars to the frontier—far from Delhi and amidst the Pashtuns who have no love for them. Where possible disarm the Regulars; if mutiny occurs, destroy them on the spot; if they take to flight, 'raise the native populations against them and hunt them down'.
> Find out the Sikh chiefs living in your district and enlist onto your side their martial instincts and their natural hatred of the Hindustanis. Collect camels and beasts of burden at suitable points, so that the troops

moving to the front may face the enemy in the best possible condition. Concentrate bodies of mounted police. Arrest every wandering Fakir, guard every ferry, examine every Sepoy's letter. Remain calm.[98]

Despite the stress and his ailments, Lawrence stayed calm himself during the rebellion, and once even made a twenty-four-hour visit from Pindi to Murree to see his family. A visitor in Pindi saw Lawrence 'pulling up his shirt-sleeves and feeling his muscles', evidently 'a very favourite attitude of his'.[99]

■

Lawrence had found General Anson, the Bengal Army's Simla-based C-in-C, indecisive, slow, and reluctant to speak out. Canning, the Governor-General, was far away and often hard to reach. Communication was difficult even with Agra, where John Colvin was governor. In the circumstances, John Lawrence functioned—in his own mind, in the eyes of most Britons west and north of Delhi, and even in some rebel eyes—as de facto Governor-General and de facto C-in-C.

When Anson proved unwilling, despite repeated requests from Lawrence, to send a firm message to Punjab-based sepoys, the chief commissioner issued, on 1 June, his own manifesto, presumably in Urdu and Hindi, and had it 'posted and circulated at all the stations of his province'.

> Sepoys! You will have heard that many Sepoys and Sowars of the Bengal Army have proved faithless to their salt... An army is assembled and is now close to Delhi, prepared to punish the mutineers... I warn you to prove faithful to your salt; faithful to the Government who have given you and your forefathers service for the last hundred years.
> The British Government will never want for native soldiers. In a month it might raise 50,000 in the Punjab alone... All will unite to crush you... Already from every quarter English soldiers are pouring into India.

Aware that sepoy ranks contained virtually no Sikhs, Lawrence added:

> The Hindu temple and the Mohammedan mosque have both been respected by the English Government. It was but the other day that the Jumma mosque at Lahore, which the Sikhs had converted into a magazine, was restored to the Mohammedans. Seize all those among yourselves who endeavour to mislead you.[100]

'The prime instigator' himself of the advance towards Delhi of which he was warning the rebels, Lawrence backed that advance with officers, soldiers, provisions, and animals of transport. To retake Delhi he was prepared to strip Punjab. In and from Rawalpindi, in the sweeping yet not necessarily false words of his biographer, Lawrence was 'hearing everything, weighing everything, deciding everything, directing everything'.[101]

With the aid of intelligence agents, the situation on the Ridge opposite Delhi, too, was being monitored by him. From his years as Delhi's magistrate, Lawrence had a precise idea of the walls and bastions the British needed to breach. Aware of the role Lawrence was playing, rebels within Delhi's walls sought at times to restore flagging spirits by parading a fair-skinned, well-built and chained Kashmiri as a captured John Lawrence. Or so the story went.[102]

While prescribing stern punishment in the war against rebels, Lawrence restricted cruelty in a few instances. He also tried, without success, to limit the roles of turbulent men like John Nicholson and William Hodson. In fact, if Bosworth Smith is to be believed, Hodson might not have obtained his opportunity for the role he would play but for an intervention by Lawrence's Indian 'advisor', Nihal Singh Chachi.

'Hodson would do good work to Delhi', Nihal Singh is said to have told Edward Thornton, the Rawalpindi-based commissioner for the Jhelum division, who met Lawrence daily. 'The Chief commissioner ought to employ him.' 'But,' replied Thornton, 'Hodson is one of three Englishmen in India who cannot be trusted.' To Nihal Singh that was of no account in the war against mutineers.[103] His advice was acted upon, and Hodson, as we shall see, played his controversial part.

Bragging by Frederic Cooper, the Amritsar DC, about what he did on 1 August shocked Lawrence. After chasing and capturing 303 out of 400 or so disarmed Hindustani sepoys who had escaped the previous day from their Lahore internment, Cooper had them shot, in batches of ten, in Ajnala, near Amritsar. After 237 bodies were dumped into a deep well, Cooper ordered his Sikh and Muslim police to produce the remaining sixty-six prisoners.

Only twenty-one could be brought out—the rest had suffocated to death in the small room into which they had been packed. Cooper sent a gratified report of the proceedings to Lawrence, who called the dispatch 'nauseous'.[104] Cooper himself would remain proud that as 'a single Anglo-Saxon supported by a section of Asiatics' he had 'coldly presid[ed] over so memorable an execution'.[105]

On 1 June, two months before the Ajnala cruelties, Commissioner Edwardes in Peshawar had written to Lawrence about 120 deserters of the 55th Native Regiment captured with arms in their hands. Earlier they had joined in imprisoning their regiment's British officers, who however were not killed.

Edwardes told Lawrence that he, Nicholson, the DC, and Cotton, the army head, had decided to 'make an awful and lasting example by blowing them away from guns before the whole garrison. Five can be placed before each gun, and two troops of artillery will throw sixty of them into the air at once. A second round will finish the matter.'

Lawrence had no formal right to intervene. It was an army matter, and in Peshawar, Cotton spoke for the army. However, he wrote to Edwardes questioning the decision.

> [O]n full reflection, I would not put them all to death. I do not think that we shall be justified in the eyes of the Almighty in doing so. Our object is to make an example to terrify others. I think this object would be effectually gained by destroying from one-fourth to one-third of their number.

He wrote also directly to Cotton:

> I trust that you will not destroy all the men of the 55th who have been seized... Such a wholesale slaughter will, I think, be cruel and have a bad effect... Men in similar circumstances will have no inducement to yield but rather to fight to the last... [These sepoys] saved the lives of their officers when in their power. These circumstances entitle them to consideration, which I beg they will receive at your hands.

Following this counsel, 40 of the 120 were blown by guns in Peshawar on 10 June. Eighty were spared.[106]

■

Except for a few events in September, when Muslim peasants of the Dhoond tribe attacked Murree in the name of Delhi's Mughal king, and Ahmad Khan Kharal (or Kharral) led a more serious revolt in a region lying between Lahore and Multan (in today's Sahiwal district), Punjabis, whether Muslim, Hindu or Sikh, initiated no rebellion against the British. This was in marked contrast to what happened in 1857 in places like Delhi, Awadh, the Rohilla division of today's UP, and Jhansi.

To the average Punjabi, the swift disarming of Hindustani regiments was a sign that the British would defeat the rebels, a likelihood strengthened by British control over the ferries, which ruled out rebel incursions from outside Punjab. Moreover, while the province's Sikhs had no desire for a Mughal future, Punjabi Muslims were negative about the Khalsa past. The British present was an acceptable alternative to most Punjabis.

This large-scale unresponsiveness to the revolt by Punjabis was punctuated from time to time by isolated instances of sympathy for the rebels in parts of Punjab. When on 9 June Jullundur's Delhi-bound rebel sepoys released prisoners and plundered houses of government in Ludhiana, many of Ludhiana's Muslims joined in the actions.[107] Evidently entertaining sympathy for the Mughal throne, these Ludhiana Muslims were also impressed by the sepoys' ability to shake off British control. Prominent in backing the rebels was Abdul Qadir Ludhianvi, one of the city's leading Arains.[108]

Earlier, in May, in a region south of Rawalpindi, unidentified 'clan heads in the Bar tracts of Shahpur district' appeared to have 'met secretly to pledge themselves to a common... action, should the locally cantoned sepoys rise in mutiny',[109] but the area's Hindustani sepoys were prevented from rebelling and no action ensued.

The 'winning-side' image was an element in Sialkot on 9 July, when two troops stationed there, the 9th Bengal Cavalry, consisting of Hindustani Muslims, and the 46th Native Infantry, comprising Hindu and Muslim Hindustanis, revolted and marched off on the road to Gurdaspur, in the direction of Delhi. Encountering no resistance in Sialkot, whose European soldiers had left earlier to support the bid to retake Delhi, the sepoys were joined by hundreds from adjacent villages, some of whom carried arms.

On 12 July, when the rebels from Sialkot neared Gurdaspur, they found John Nicholson and his Movable Column facing them. Sialkot had telegraphed Rawalpindi about the rebels, and Lawrence had instructed Nicholson, who was in Amritsar, to confront them with his Column, an encounter we will soon look at.

The jail in Sialkot had been unlocked on 9 July by the rebels and a few Europeans were murdered, but the majority were spared. In addition to women, children and the elderly, military officers too were spared. In fact, 'Colonel Farquharson and Captain Caulfield were repeatedly offered Rs 2,000 and Rs 1,000 a month, respectively, with six months' leave every hot weather, if they would only consent to throw in their lot with the mutineers',[110] a gesture that impressed Lawrence.

After the native regiments left Sialkot, faithful servants ingeniously protected the lives of the city's Europeans from attacks by the Revolt's sympathizers, but 'the Europeans' houses and the Parsees' shops were completely gutted'.[111]

According to the *Sialkot Gazetteer,* 'the Sadr Bazaar was partially plundered, but the shops of Muhammadan traders were scrupulously respected'.[112] These traders were seen as well-wishers of the Mughal throne.

That throne's surviving iqbal was occasionally a factor elsewhere in Punjab as well. However, even in Sialkot the upper hand quickly went to the British. On the morning of 10 July, Sikh levies helped MacMahon, a young Briton who took charge, in clearing Sialkot's cantonment of plunderers and supposed plunderers. In the process, twenty-four men were shot dead. Jail officers and other Indian employees thought to have connived in the disorder in Sialkot were hanged after a quick trial, and 'villages whose inhabitants had taken part in the plunder' were fined.[113]

We may glance at rebellions in four other Bengal Army stations in Punjab. The defiance in Jhelum (7-8 July) was a response to the sepoys' glimpse of European troops arriving to disarm them. An ensuing battle took forty British and many times more Hindustani lives, but the local population did not support the rebels. In Rawalpindi, too, where, in John Lawrence's presence, a native regiment was disarmed on 7 July, the sepoys found no local backing.

'Why take away our arms? We committed no fault,' the disarmed sepoys asked Lawrence, who replied: 'True, you had not; but your relations and friends and countrymen had. We only do it to protect ourselves. The arms are not yours, they belong to Government, to give or to take away.'[114] Forty sepoys who ran off in Rawalpindi were shot or captured in pursuit.

Also attracted to the Mughal throne, Ferozepore's disarmed 10th Native Cavalry, consisting mostly of Hindustani Muslims, broke free on 10 August and made it all the way, via Hansi, to Delhi, along with many horses.

The Peshawar-based 51st Native Infantry, also previously disarmed, was less fortunate. A rumour that the regiment's men had obtained arms and hidden them triggered a search. While 'the young Afghan and Sikh levies' directed to search the 51st's lines were performing (25 August) 'the congenial task of looting the huts of their hereditary foes'—this is Bosworth Smith writing—the regiment of 870 men 'rose as one man'. Facing guns, they ran towards Jamrud, near the Khyber. All 870 were killed in pursuit or, after capture, by a firing squad. 'The whole regiment... had ceased to exist.'[115]

Bosworth Smith is uneasy recording this vapourization, on the heels of a rumour, of 870 human beings, yet even twenty-five years after the event he offers no regret, whether his own or Lawrence's. While drawing attention to the Sikh and Pashtun levies' looting, he implies, in respect of the British, that they only performed a stern duty. His stance conveys the long life of

1857's partisan spirit.

To return to 1857 Punjab: On 1 September, about 300 villagers of the Dhoond tribe, which disliked British rule even as it had disdained Sikh rule, attacked Murree, but an advance warning from Hakim Khan, a Dhoondi who had served Mrs. Lawrence as a personal attendant, enabled Murree's British to push back the attackers, who returned to their hills. Pro-British pirs and a Hindu called Uman Chand then led forces to punish the Dhoondis. The villages of Dhar and Jawa were burnt down, and cattle and other property seized from these and other villages.[116]

■

Staged south of Lahore and north of Multan in a region that included Harappa and also Pakpattan (where Baba Farid is buried), the Gogera Rebellion (named after one of the region's tehsils) is the best-known Punjabi face of the 1857 Revolt. Gogera's Ahmed Khan Kharal, a leader of the pastoral Kharal (or Kharral) tribe, was the one who, according to a British gazetteer published in 1883-84, 'roused all the important tribes' on the Ravi side of a district now known as Sahiwal.[117] John Lawrence was forced to give weeks of his time to the rising that ensued, in which Wattoos, Joyas, Fatianas, Sials and others joined the Kharals.[118]

It seems that emissaries from Delhi, crossing the Sutlej at the end of May 'from the direction of Sirsa and Hisar', had inspired Ahmed Khan, described by the gazetteer of the 1880s as 'a man above the average—bold and crafty'.[119] We must assume that the idea of restoring Mughal rule appealed to him. Calling the area's tribes 'turbulent', the gazetteer adds:

> On the night of September 16th, Sarfraz Khan (a Kharal and Ahmed Khan's rival) informed the Deputy Commissioner that Ahmed and other chiefs had gone home to commence the rebellion.... Jhamra was burnt... Kamalia was plundered and the *tahsil* at Harappa captured... Mr Berkley, Extra Assistant Commissioner, was killed near Kaure Shah, and Major Chamberlain, who had come up with troops from Multan, was besieged at Chichawatni. For some time the situation at the civil station was extremely critical... In the nick of time, however, reinforcements led by Colonel Paton arrived from Lahore.[120]

Three heavy guns, a company of European infantry, and a detachment of Sikh cavalry accompanied the colonel. So did Nihal Singh Chachi, Lawrence's 'most trusted orderly'.[121] The rebels attacked the incoming British force but were repulsed by artillery. Paton reached Chichawatni and relieved Chamberlain, who joined a counter-offensive against the rebels. Fresh reinforcements brought all the way from Multan, Jhang and Gurdaspur also took part in the action. Ahmed Khan was killed early on, along with a son of his, but others at once took his place; Murad Fatiana, Shujaa Bhadroo and Mokha Wehniwal have been named as being among them.[122]

'Several actions were fought,' the gazetteer informs us, and though most rebels were 'armed only with clubs and stones and pitchforks',[123] the insurrection ended only in November. Its 'leaders were executed or transported and, still worse [for the insurgents]', continues the gazetteer, 'thousands of cattle belonging to [them] were seized and sold'.[124]

A notable Punjabi living in exile in London, nineteen-year-old Prince Duleep Singh, was unwilling to condemn the Revolt. When the British foreign secretary, Lord Clarendon, complained of Duleep (or Dalip) Singh's attitude, Queen Victoria answered that a young Indian prince barred from his ancestral throne and compelled to live in Britain should not be expected to denounce Indians.[125]

After spending over two months in Rawalpindi, John Lawrence boarded, on 15 July, an ordinary mail cart and left for Lahore, which was four days away, accompanied only by a European aide. Journeying like this right after the revolts in Sialkot, Jhelum and Rawalpindi was reckless but it showed the chief commissioner's confidence. On the 19th he reached Lahore.

Command at the Ridge outside Delhi was now in the hands of Archdale Wilson, who pressed Lawrence for reinforcements. While the armies of Havelock and Neill seemed stuck around Lucknow and Kanpur, troops that had sailed from Britain would take months to arrive. Punjab was thus the sole source for additions on the Ridge.

Lawrence's response was to ask Nicholson, on 22 July, to hasten towards Delhi with the Movable Column even while he, Lawrence, provided that Column with more men from 'his almost exhausted province'. Eventually the Column became 4,000-strong.

Needing no persuading, Nicholson commandeered batteries and gunners for his Column without consulting any civilian or military officer in Punjab. An annoyed Lawrence could do nothing except offer broad advice. 'You would get on equally well,' he wrote to Nicholson early in August, 'and much more smoothly, if you worked *with* men rather than by ignoring them.'[126]

Emperor Aurangzeb, the sixth Mughal

Guru Gobind Singh and his Khalsa army

Nadir Shah on the Peacock Throne in 1739, after defeating Emperor Muhammad Shah

Ahmad Shah Abdali marched into India ten times after Nadir Shah's invasion

Waris Shah (1722–1798), author of Heer Ranjha

Maharaja Ranjit Singh

Contemporary portrait of Adina Beg Khan, Viceroy of Punjab, 1758

Henry Lawrence (1806-1857), 'father' of British Punjab

John Lawrence (1811-1879), Henry's brother and chief of British Punjab

John Nicholson (1822-1857), the Empire's soldier

Muhammad Iqbal (1877-1938),
poet and philosopher

Fazl-i-Husain (1877-1936),
founder of the Unionist Party

Sikander Hayat Khan,
Premier of Punjab, 1937-42

Khizr Hayat Tiwana (right), Premier of Punjab, 1942-47, with Master Tara Singh (centre) and Muhammad Ali Jinnah in 1945

Evan Jenkins, Governor of Punjab, 1946-47

Lord Louis Mountbatten (1900-1979), last Viceroy of India

We have jumped forward. It was on 22 June that Nicholson took the Column's command from Chamberlain in Jullundur, where three regiments had mutinied. A few days later, at a party in the home of Edward Lake, commissioner for the Jullundur division, Nicholson displayed his arrogance. Prominent among Lake's Indian guests was the strongly pro-British Mehtab Singh, a former Sikh general who was also a close relative of the Raja of Kapurthala. Noticing that, like all the British present, Mehtab Singh had kept his shoes on during the reception, Nicholson decided to show off his power.

After most Indian guests including members of Mehtab Singh's entourage had stepped out of the front door, and the Sikh dignitary's turn to leave arrived, Nicholson rasped out an order to him in Hindustani: 'Take your shoes off and hold them in your hands as you leave.' Adding, 'I want your followers to see your humiliation,' Nicholson declared: 'If I am the last Englishman left in Jullundur, you are not to come into my room with your shoes on.'

Mehtab Singh had come to Lake's house, not Nicholson's room. All the same, Nicholson's biographer informs us, 'Mehtab Singh, completely cowed, meekly did as he was told.' All 'swaggering about' in the Jullundur area apparently ended after this demonstration by Nicholson of British dominance over Indians, and his own dominance over everyone around him.[127]

Using deception—and formidable batteries—Nicholson's Column disarmed, in Amritsar and elsewhere, several Punjab-based Hindustani regiments. On one occasion, after 1,500 had thus been disarmed and detained, an old Sikh colonel who had fought against the British at Gujrat is said to have remarked, 'You (the British) have drawn the fangs of 1,500 snakes. Truly your fortune is great.'[128] In the Punjab of 1857, flattery was realism's sibling.

■

Nicholson was in Amritsar on the morning of 10 July when two messages about the previous day's Sialkot rebellion reached him. One was sent from Lahore by Montgomery. The other message, apparently brought by 'a young bandsman of the 46th Native Infantry, who had galloped his ponies all the way from Sialkot', consisted of a few words hurriedly scrawled by MacMahon: 'Troops here in open mutiny... Bring the movable column at once if possible.'[129]

Realizing instinctively that his task was not to protect Sialkot's Europeans but to prevent Sialkot's Hindustani regiments from reaching Delhi, Nicholson also surmised, correctly, that the mutineers would aim first to reach Gurdaspur. He would surprise them there.

Throughout the 10th of July, ponies, bullocks and carts assembled by Montgomery trudged on the road from Lahore to Amritsar, for Nicholson wanted his men not to have to march on foot all the forty-four miles to Gurdaspur. Armed with big guns, rum, bread and milk, and sitting on or walking alongside the transport sent from Lahore, Nicholson's force, largely European but with a contingent also of Sikh and Muslim Punjabis, moved out of Amritsar that night. In the morning, after a march of twenty-six miles, it halted for two hours in Batala.

At 10 a.m., the eighteen-mile trek to Gurdaspur began. Outnumbering the ponies, the men took turns on foot. A few dropped dead in the heat but many sang as they marched. By 6 p.m. the last of the force had reached Gurdaspur, near the Ravi's eastern bank. Unaware that the Movable Column was approaching, the Sialkot regiments also made it close to Gurdaspur that day, arriving on the Ravi's western bank.

Let us pause to recognize an asymmetry. Thanks to British chroniclers, we know something about the march of Nicholson's column. Of dramas in the Hindustanis' march from Sialkot, or other rebel treks—their thrills and fears, songs and laughter, fortunes and mishaps, or even names or faces—we know nothing.

The next morning (12 July), Nicholson was delighted when his spies reported that the Hindustanis were crossing the river by a ford at Trimmu Ghat, only nine miles west of Gurdaspur. Had they travelled further south before crossing the Ravi, the Sialkot regiments would have eluded Nicholson's force.

Now the river would be at their back and Nicholson's battery in front. As Nicholson's battery, men and guns were moved with stealth and speed to Trimmu Ghat, the Ravi's waters rose by the hour. Trapped without an escape route, the outnumbered Hindustanis put up a fierce defiance. Most were killed. Nicholson's individual role in the battle he commanded was to 'cleave a man literally in two' with his sword and say to his aide-de-camp, 'Not a bad sliver that!'[130]

His reputation soared. He possessed, it was said, a successful commander's secret: he knew what to do and how to do it. In Lahore, on 22 July, he was welcomed as a hero by a Lawrence finally back from Rawalpindi. Two days later, rejoining his men after talks with Lawrence, Nicholson announced that they were proceeding to Delhi.

Serving Nicholson while his Movable Column forayed across Punjab, his orderly, Muhammad Hayat Khan of Wah, would accompany him also to Delhi. Jullundur, Ludhiana, Ambala, Karnal, Delhi—that was the route.

Through forced marches the Column reached Ambala on 6 August. While the Column would continue on foot, Nicholson himself boarded a mail-cart and arrived on the Ridge outside Delhi on 7 August.

Sick of General Wilson's irresolution, officers and soldiers on the Ridge were galvanized, we are told, by the arrival of 'a man cast in a giant mould, with massive chest and powerful limbs', a 'long black beard', a 'deep sonorous voice', a 'commanding' appearance, 'features of stern beauty', an air of 'immense strength, talent and resolution', and an advance reputation of being a 'military genius'.[131]

This is not only the language of a long-gone, hero-worshipping age, it is language written soon after Nicholson's death, which, as we will see, coincided with the recapture of Delhi. It gives an idea of Nicholson's image among Britons in 1857 and for at least half a century thereafter. Trotter's 1897 biography, from which these descriptions are taken, would go through ten editions by 1905.

Rejoining his Column before it neared Delhi, Nicholson led its entry onto the Ridge on 14 August. His Column had 4,200 men, of whom 1,300 were Europeans. Sikhs comprised a majority of the rest, but Punjabi Muslims, Pashtuns and Dogras were also among them.

Nicholson realized that the British were fortunate to be perched on the Ridge. In a letter to Herbert Edwardes—perhaps his closest friend—Nicholson called the Ridge's position 'a perfectly providential one'. Formed of solid rock, the Ridge, Nicholson pointed out, had 'strong buildings on it in front', while a river and a canal not only protected its flank and rear, they provided water.[132]

On the Ridge he met up with a young brother of his, Charles Nicholson, and with a few old friends including a recently-injured Neville Chamberlain. Some on the Ridge thought Nicholson haughty and aloof, but neither Nicholson nor his admirers doubted for a second that he should direct the storming of Delhi. But replacing General Wilson with a very fresh brigadier would have caused irreparable division and confusion. For one thing, even if *hors de combat* for the moment, the highly-regarded Chamberlain was senior to Nicholson.

Replacement was not attempted. Instead Nicholson assumed charge of difficult operations while he and everyone else awaited the arrival from Punjab of what Lawrence had painstakingly assembled—a 'long train of heavy guns drawn by elephants and of bullock wagons loaded with shot, shells, and ammunition of all kinds'[133].

This siege-train had left Ferozepore on 10 August with, it was said, 'a weak escort'.[134] On the 24th, Wilson was informed by spies that a large body of rebels, equipped with sixteen guns, had marched out of Delhi in the direction of Najafgarh, with three aims: cutting off supplies to the Ridge, harassing it from the rear, and intercepting the siege-train.

Nicholson was asked to block the rebels. Taking with him sixteen guns, 2,500 soldiers and also Theo Metcalfe, 'who knew the whole district well', he launched out on the 25th morning 'in a drenching rain'. Apparently riding well in advance of his column and reconnoitring enemy positions, Nicholson once more secured a decisive win.

The march to the battle in Najafgarh took the whole day, the battle itself only an hour. Most rebels, several thousand in number, tried to escape British firepower by abandoning their heavy guns and rapidly retreating. While massed on a bridge during their flight, scores of rebels were shot. After 'passing a night without food or shelter on the ground they had won', Nicholson's army returned to the Ridge with the rebels' guns and a loss, through death or injury, of four of its officers and ninety-one of its men.[135]

The biggest victory thus far for the British, Najafgarh was a huge jolt for the rebels, who did not thereafter send out any attacking force from Delhi. When agents from Zafar showed up at the Ridge to discuss a truce, they were rebuffed. From Lahore, an admiring Lawrence wrote to Nicholson of his desire to 'knight you on the spot'.[136] The thirty-four-year-old maverick was not knighted but Lawrence named him the future commissioner for Punjab's westernmost division, Leiah.

Edwardes, meanwhile, had written to Nicholson of their shared loss in the death of Henry Lawrence, a father-figure to both. In his reply of 1 September, Nicholson penned remarks unusual to him:

> If it please Providence that I live through this business, you must get me alongside of me again, and be my guide and help in endeavouring to follow [Sir Henry's] example; for I am so weak and unstable, that I shall never do any good of myself.[137]

On 4 September, elephants of the siege-train lumbered up the Ridge, dragging guns that would breach Delhi's walls. Men diverted from building roads and canals in Punjab started to erect batteries near Delhi's bastions, amidst shelling and firing by the rebels. By 7 September, the batteries were up.

In Lahore, Lawrence remained anxious. He had emptied Punjab of all but 1,000 European soldiers, many of whom were sick. 'In the Punjab we are by no means strong', he said in a message to a still-undecided Wilson, urging him to launch an immediate assault on Delhi. 'Every day's delay is fraught with danger', he added.[138]

A ferocious cannonade felled parts of Delhi's walls on 11 September but Wilson seemed averse to ordering an assault. If the general hesitated one more day, Nicholson told a friend on 13 September, he would propose Wilson's supersession. That day, Wilson reluctantly gave the green-light for storming Delhi. In a war council, the general announced that Nicholson would lead one of the attacking columns.

Nicholson, we learn, had 'gained his heart's desire'.[139] On the morning of 14 September, four separate columns launched into Delhi through breaches in the city's northern and western walls, between Kashmiri Gate and Lahori Gate. Occupying every height and foothold on the walls or near them, the rebels fought back with death-forgetting resolve. Shells, bullets and chunks of masonry were poured on soldiers blasting or clambering their way inside, and stone and sand pushed into the breaches.

Noticing his men slowing down behind him, Nicholson, who was leading the entry at Lahori Gate, turned around to urge them to press forward. At that precise moment, a rebel bullet hit Nicholson in the back. Men in Nicholson's column would afterwards claim that the shooter was a rebel sepoy called Kaleh Khan, and claim also that Nicholson's twenty-four-year-old orderly, Hayat Khan, caught his master as he fell.[140]

Though reluctant to concede significant roles to *any* Indian on the British side, Trotter too writes that someone, 'probably an orderly... immediately caught [Nicholson] and laid him on the ground' inside a protected recess 'and tended him'. The 'faithful' Hayat Khan, to use Trotter's adjective for the helper he does not himself name, remained at his master's side as he was carried first to a makeshift clinic and later to the field hospital atop the Ridge.[141] Evidently the doolie-bearers lingered along the way, joining in the plunder of nearby houses and shops, and it was only late in the afternoon that Nicholson was brought into the field hospital.

Other Britons too had been wounded or killed, and it appears that Wilson thought of ordering the assault's recall. When, on the 15th evening, Chamberlain informed him of Wilson's thinking, the wounded Nicholson—as Chamberlain would later write—remarked, 'Thank God I have strength to shoot him, if necessary.'[142]

Another injured man was brought to Nicholson's side—his brother Charles. Casualties mounted but Wilson did not order a withdrawal. Between the end of May and 20 September, more than 4,000 would be killed on the British side, many of them Indians, but Delhi was back in British hands. Among those guiding the columns inside the city was its magistrate before the rebellion, Theo Metcalfe.

On the first day, 8 officers and 265 men among the attackers were killed, including 103 Indians, while 52 officers and 822 men were wounded, including 310 Indians. Rebel casualties were many times these numbers. Delhi's civilians killed in the revenge that followed amounted to a larger figure still; civilians displaced and plundered formed a multiple of that number.

Major General Archdale Wilson established himself (20 September) as Delhi's military ruler in the Red Fort's principal state room, the Diwan-i-Khas. Zafar and his sons had fled their palace. The king was discovered in Humayun's Tomb by William Hodson, the officer recommended to a wary Lawrence by his Sikh aide, Nihal Singh.

Heading espionage first from the Ridge and now from Delhi, Hodson brought Zafar, his wife Zeenat and their son Jawan Bakht back to their Fort, to be imprisoned there, on 21 September. Hodson had promised them their lives, and the three surrendered.

The following day, three other Mughal princes also hiding in Humayun's Tomb, Mirza Mughal, Mirza Khizr Sultan, and Mirza Abu Bakr, surrendered to Hodson, who had taken one hundred cavalry with him to the Tomb. En route to the city, Hodson shot the three princes dead with his own hand.

To his family he wrote that he was 'very tired but very much satisfied with my day's work'.[143] From MacDowell, Hodson's associate that day, we learn that Sikhs in the raiding party 'shouted with delight' when Hodson murdered the princes.[144] Some Britons, however, and John Lawrence was among them, would object to Hodson's playing 'the part of policeman and magistrate, judge, jury and executioner all in one'.[145] Within a few days of Hodson's deed, twenty-one other Mughal scions were hanged, and the Mughal dynasty was wiped out.

His brother Charles would recover but John Nicholson died of his wound on 23 September. 'Then,' the Revolt's chief British historian, John Kaye, would write, 'from city to city, from cantonment to cantonment, went the chequered tidings; Delhi had fallen, the king was a captive—but John Nicholson was dead.'[146]

■

Before dying, Nicholson evidently uttered a few wishes. One was that his mother in Ireland should not give way to grief. Another was that Hayat Khan should be promoted, a request acted upon by John Lawrence. After being appointed assistant to deputy commissioners in Bannu and Kohat, Hayat Khan would serve as political assistant to General Frederick Roberts in the Anglo-Afghan War of 1878-80 before becoming a judge.[147]

Bloodlust found free play in recaptured Delhi. Wilson ordered that anyone found with a weapon should be killed, not taken prisoner. In the event, the empty-handed too were slain. Sikh and Muslim Punjabis, Pashtuns and Gurkhas joined the British in the slaughter. The Punjabi/Hindustani 'divide' was shrieked up. 'Poorbeah dogs' and 'quaking' Hindustanis, as they were dubbed, received no mercy.[148] Delhi's residents were not spared. Without remorse, a British official wrote at the time:

> All the city people found within the walls when our troops entered were bayoneted on the spot; and the number was considerable, as you may suppose when I tell you that in some houses forty or fifty persons were hiding. These were not mutineers but residents of the city, who trusted to our well-known mild rule for pardon. I am glad to say they were disappointed.[149]

An order from Wilson to let go of women and children was flouted, and civilian officers joined the killers. Clifford, Gurgaon's assistant commissioner, whose sister had been killed in Delhi in May, claimed that 'he had put to death all he had come across, not excepting women and children'.[150]

'In one episode outside the walls of the fort,' Queen Victoria's biographer would write, '400 mutineers were hanged simultaneously, while British officers seated beneath sipped whiskies and sodas and regimental bands played.'[151] Rev John Rotton, who had been ministering on the Ridge, defended vengeance.[152] Referring to Wilson's instruction to 'make no prisoners but put all armed rebels to death', George Dodd would observe in 1858:

> This was attended to; but something more was done, something darker... The sense of hatred towards the mutinous sepoys was so intense, the recollection of the atrocities at Cawnpore was so vivid, that vengeance took [the] place of every other feeling. The troops did that which they would have scorned to do against the Russians in the Crimean war—they bayoneted men no longer capable of resistance.... [M]any a dark-skinned inhabitant of Delhi fell under the bayonet.[153]

Though Calcutta's Britons had called him 'Clemency' Canning because of his disapproval of earlier cruelties near Allahabad, the Governor-General seemed to welcome Delhi's vengeance:

> In the name of outraged humanity, in memory of innocent blood ruthlessly shed, and in acknowledgment of the first signal vengeance inflicted upon the foulest treason, the Governor-General-in-council records his gratitude to Major General Wilson and the brave army of Delhi.[154]

However, to his credit Canning successfully resisted pressure to raze Delhi's Jama Masjid, Shahjahan's seventeenth-century creation, as did John Lawrence, even though Lord Palmerston, the British Prime Minister, had backed the demand.

In March 1858, a military court found the eighty-three-year-old Zafar guilty of playing a prominent role in 'an international Islamic conspiracy' to seize power in Delhi and kill its Christians, and sentenced him to exile and life-long imprisonment. Some months later, Zafar, Zeenat and Jawan Bakht were taken to Rangoon, where Zafar died in 1862.

Ignoring the reality that Hindus constituted the bulk of the Bengal Army's rebels, the prosecution had claimed that 'Hinduism [was] nowhere either reflected or represented' in the Revolt.[155] The line revealed the core of a firm new policy: separate Hindus from Muslims, and never again permit the two to join hands.

■

General Wilson said the Delhi result was 'unhesitatingly attributable' to John Lawrence. 'Through him Delhi fell, and the Punjab, no longer a weakness, became a source of strength,' said Canning.[156]

Before the Revolt, the British had administered Delhi from Agra, the NWP capital, but rebel control over much of NWP snapped the Delhi-Agra link, so that it was Lawrence, the Punjab chief commissioner, rather than John Colvin, the NWP lieutenant-governor, who guided the British on the Ridge. Colvin died a few days before Delhi's recapture, and Lawrence continued to oversee its functioning under military rule. Early in 1858, he spent a month there.

After Delhi was regained, Lawrence's Punjab reinforced the British effort to capture rebels in what in our times we know as UP, including Awadh and the Rohilla country. In their thousands, Sikh and Muslim Punjabis joined the armies of Havelock and Colin Campbell, a new general sent from England, which in November relieved the besieged in Lucknow's Residency and later, in March 1858, recaptured Lucknow.

An earlier foray into Lucknow (September 1857) had taken the life of Colonel Neill, author of the grim revenge, forever linked to his name, enacted at Bibighar in July, when captured rebels were whipped into licking the blood-covered floor before being hanged. Two months later, after leading another attack into Lucknow, General Havelock died of dysentery, but the Residency's inmates had been safely removed to Kanpur.

In March 1858, when Campbell's army finally forced Lucknow's rebels out of the city, his Sikh soldiers—sent from Punjab—took part in the plunder and atrocities that William Howard Russell of the London *Times* would report. Also in Lucknow and joining the scramble for booty, William Hodson, sabre in hand, 'dashed into a room' in the Begum Kothi that held promise.[157] Shot through the liver, he staggered back. A Sikh carried Hodson in his arms to a doctor but the Briton died within hours.

Even though he had helped recruit them, the rising number of Punjabis in the army troubled Lawrence. Only a month after the fall of Delhi, he said in a letter to the newly-arrived Colin Campbell (15 October 1857):

> There is some danger that our officers, in their horror of John Pandy, may go into the other extreme and make too much of John Sing.[158]

Linked to Mangal Pandey, 'Pandy' was now the favoured British term for a sepoy. A few months later, writing to another English general, Mansfield, Lawrence repeated his worry:

> In round numbers the Punjabi troops of various kinds cannot fall short of fifty thousand men!... If we allow the Punjabis to feel their strength, we may one day have as much trouble with them as with the Hindustanis.

Their use against surviving rebels, added Lawrence, called for astuteness.

> I would leave... a greater proportion of Sikh cavalry in Rohilkund, where the people to guard against are Mohammedans, and take more Mohammedan cavalry into Oude, where the Hindu element among the mutineers abounds.[159]

Thanks in part to Punjabi soldiers, Rohilkhand and Awadh were back in British hands by the summer of 1858. In June, the brave young Rani of Jhansi was killed in Gwalior. Though neither Nana Sahib nor Begum Hazrat Mahal of Awadh, who defied the British in Lucknow, were caught, the two had been forced to leave India for Nepal's marshes.

In London, Parliament marked the British triumph by abolishing Company rule and asking Queen Victoria to assume the governance of India. In her name, Parliament and ministers would control India, where the Governor-General would henceforth be called Viceroy as well.

John Lawrence played a role in the framing of new policies. No longer opposing an increased regard for India's princes and chiefs—the Revolt had settled that question in favour of his late brother's stand—Lawrence argued against severity in punishing supporters of rebels, and also against aligning British rule with Christianizing efforts in India, a course advocated by a group that included Herbert Edwardes.

Others, notably Canning, thought like Lawrence. Read out in November 1858 by Viceroy Canning in Allahabad, a Proclamation by the Queen assured native princes that their rights and dignity would be protected. While all Indians were promised 'due regard' for their 'ancient usages and customs', British officers were warned that 'interference with the religious belief or worship of any of our subjects' would incur the monarch's 'highest displeasure'.

As for surviving rebels, the Proclamation added that except for those 'who have been, or shall be, convicted of having directly taken part in the murder of British subjects', they would be guaranteed their lives; some would receive punishment and the rest pardon. Though some Indians and Britons regretted the abandonment of social reform, the new policies were widely welcomed.

In February 1859, after military rule ended in Delhi, the city was formally ceded to Punjab, becoming one of its districts. Punjab's head would henceforth be called lieutenant-governor rather than chief commissioner. But it was Robert Montgomery who became Punjab's first lieutenant-governor, with jurisdiction over Delhi as well, for forty-seven-year-old John Lawrence had decided that it was time for him to return to England. He left India in February.

'War is at an end,' Canning declared in July 1859, adding, 'Rebellion has been put down... Order is re-established; and peaceful pursuits have everywhere been resumed.'[160]

Chapter Six

1859-1919: IMPERIAL HIGH NOON

In Punjab and across India, the Revolt's suppression was followed by decades of imperialist success. After describing, in a 1904 gazetteer, the War's impact in Jhelum district, a British officer wrote: 'The subsequent history of the district is more social than political; the quiet routine of ordinary administration has never been interrupted.'[1] The verdict could have applied to the whole of Punjab.

While the Empire had absorbed the Revolt's lessons, Punjabis and other Indians, generally speaking, had not. One major lesson was that Muslim-Hindu partnership had given the conflict its strength. Another was that an elite-people divide had ensured its failure; in particular, the Revolt's principal leaders had built no solid link with the Indian peasantry.

An astute Empire carried forward its strategy of keeping Punjab's Muslims, Hindus and Sikhs focused on their religious identity and divided from one another. In addition, India's British rulers decided, post-1857, to

- Separate Christianity from British rule;
- Recognize the sensitivities of India's chiefs and aristocrats, but
- Rule Punjab and the rest of India as a superior race, dismissing any notion of equality between rulers and subjects, and yet
- Offer Punjabis and other Indians a better quality of life through a network of roads, railway lines, post and telegraph offices, canals, schools, hospitals, colleges, universities and law courts;
- Cultivate, in particular, the farmer;
- Recruit new soldiers for the Empire's armies from rural Punjab but underscore every recruit's distinct religion and caste, ensure that Indian hands stayed far from big weapons, and, finally,
- Aim to make the soldier the Empire's agent in his village.

Part of this imperial strategy was spelt out, we saw, in Victoria's 1858 Proclamation. The rest emerged over a period of time as the Empire's civil and military officers in Punjab, Calcutta and London asked themselves and one another how Punjab, which had not only escaped the Revolt but played a crucial role in ending it, could continue to influence India in the Empire's favour.[2]

The strategy of providing quality while refusing equality was vulnerable. Even so it worked for about sixty years. Any hitches that arose were overcome.

Peace was maintained. Canals built between 1860 and 1920 brought about ten million acres of new land under the plough. Ownership of land passed more widely from a village community or a tribe to the individual farmer. His title to the land was recorded and preserved. The rate of land revenue was lowered even if collection was now more stringent.

As Punjab's agricultural production increased, so did the government's revenue. British banks, ships and agencies handled India's exports and imports, including Punjab's exports of cotton, wheat and oilseeds. By controlling the rupee-sterling ratio and defraying home charges from revenues in India, the Empire made certain that it was 'a major co-sharer' in Punjab's growing wealth.[3]

Trade expanded in Punjab. Land was monetized and agriculture commercialized, but some farmers did worse than others. Money-lending prospered and Indian banks were born, yet rural debt also grew as farmers borrowed from urban and rural moneylenders, mortgaging their land. Often land was alienated.

Cities grew. Tree-lined avenues emerged in the 'civil lines' of Lahore, Amritsar, Rawalpindi, Multan and Ludhiana, where British rulers and their immediate Indian juniors lived, while 'cantonments' lodged soldiers and their officers. Around 5,000 British soldiers were quartered in Rawalpindi, about which a British gazetteer would say in 1895:

> The lands around the town are very fertile... There are no city walls, and no relics of antiquity to catch the eye. The town is essentially modern, and owes its growth and prosperity to the existence of the large cantonment beside it... There are many good substantial brick buildings to be seen in every direction... As a rule the streets are wide and regular... The town is probably the cleanest in Northern India. [Possessing] a fine new railway station [and] a picturesque little church,... it offers nice views including of the Pir Panjal hills of Kashmir, pleasant gardens in the European areas, and lots of birds and animals in the (European-area) woods of the town.[4]

Started by the government and by Christian missionaries, new schools expanded literacy. Higher education opened up. Lahore's Government College started in 1864 and the University of the Punjab on 1 January 1882, also in Lahore. A medical college had opened in 1860 in the city, Forman Christian College (a Presbyterian institution) in 1866, and a law college in 1870.

Although an education administrator in the province called G.W.Leitner attempted to revive Arabic, Persian and Sanskrit, English elbowed out the classical languages. Leitner's wish to use the vernacular for transmitting western sciences in schools was also not fulfilled, with Urdu rather than Punjabi becoming the medium of instruction up to the matriculation level.

Slowly yet steadily, a new if small Indian middle-class emerged, educated in English and entering government service or professions like teaching, medicine and the law. In the bureaucracy (which remained white at senior levels) and also in the professions, sections of Punjab's Hindus—chiefly Khatris, Aroras, Brahmins and Banias—advanced far more rapidly than the province's more numerous Muslims.

■

Until the 1880s, when a Russian threat via Afghanistan was again imagined, Indians in the army were wanted only for internal security, and preventing another rebellion was the Raj's sole military concern, for which divide and rule was accepted policy.

In 1858, when the Empire's Peel Commission—named after Jonathan Peel, HMG's Secretary of State for War—looked at military policy in India, a three-man Punjab team comprising John Lawrence, Herbert Edwardes and Neville Chamberlain urged that Indian soldiers be confined to their provinces. Stationing them outside would facilitate a pan-Indian network and again stimulate a 'community of feeling throughout the native army'.[5]

The Punjab trio's second recommendation was that a native regiment should contain potentially adversarial companies. Thus, a Punjab-based regiment might have a ratio of say two companies of Sikh Jats to two of Punjabi Muslims, one of Hindu Jats (or Dogras) and two of Pashtuns. This thinking also meant that at the all India-level the three armies of Bengal, Bombay and Madras should remain segregated and have little to do with one another.

We can look also at what Charles Wood, Secretary of State for India in London, wrote to the Viceroy, Lord Canning, in 1861: 'If one regiment mutinies, the next regiment [should be] so alien that it would be ready to fire into it.'[6]

The ideas were implemented. Until 1895, the three Indian armies stayed separate. Stationed as before across northern India, including in Punjab, the Bengal army was now more and more Punjabi, less and less Hindustani, and also more and more Gurkha. Its regiments were confined to their province of origin, and within a regiment companies were placed so as to be able, if need arose, to check one another. As a senior official put it, it was desirable for different groups to be 'mixed promiscuously through each regiment'.[7]

By 1870, Punjab was supplying 35 per cent of the Bengal army's soldiers. The percentage was impressive, yet the army's non-Punjabis, including the Gurkhas, ensured that neither the Sikhs nor the Punjabi Muslims dominated the Bengal army, while the two main Punjabi groups also 'balanced' each other.

The policy changed in significant ways in 1890, five years after General Frederick Roberts, who had commanded the Madras army from 1880 to 1885, took charge of the Bengal army. We had come across Roberts in Peshawar in May 1857, when as a junior officer he took notes at the 'war council' that Edwardes, Chamberlain and Nicholson held after receiving the telegrams from Delhi and Meerut.

Convinced in the 1880s that the Russians were a real threat in the northwest, Roberts—the leader of a news-making march from Kabul to Kandahar in 1880—was even more certain that what the Raj needed was not 'balance' in its Indian armies but efficiency, which, he had concluded, could only be bred by native 'martial races'.

In the 1880s, Roberts was not the only British officer who believed that specific 'races' in the region—Sikh Jats from central Punjab, Muslim Gakhars, Janjuas, Awans, Tiwanas and Khattar Jats from northwestern Punjab, Hindu Jats from districts like Rohtak and Hissar, Hindu Dogras from Kangra and Jammu, the Frontier's Pashtun tribes, and the Gurkhas of Nepal—were martial in a sense in which most other groups were not. Whether blood alone provided this supposed quality was not a question discussed by advocates of the martial-race theory. They, in particular General Roberts, simply pushed the theory and the Empire acted upon it.

There were several consequences. First, the Bengal army's 'martial' regiments of Gurkhas, Jat Sikhs and Punjabi Muslims increasingly took over tasks that lay in the domain of the Madras and Bombay armies, including in Burma, until the time came in 1895 when the three armies were combined into a single Indian army divided into four regional commands: Punjab, Bengal, Madras and Bombay.

A second consequence was the steady abandonment of mixed regiments and support for 'mono' regiments, which were seen as simpler to organize and likely to be more efficient. Though divide-and-rule remained imperial policy, it was no longer a regimental tactic.

Not only was there no effort for closer relations between, say, the Sikhs and Pashtuns in the army, or between Sikhs and Punjabi Muslims, but the Raj required Sikh units in its army to be properly Khalsa—strictly turbaned and bearded—even as it simultaneously acknowledged the traditional standing, in their respective strongholds, of the 'martial' Muslim tribes providing recruits: Tiwana, Gakhar, Janjua and Khattar Jat.[8] It made strategic sense to uphold two rival forces, Sikh fundamentalism and Muslim conservatism, both pro-Empire in this period.

In a third outcome, recruitment was now increasingly confined to a few locations and a few castes or tribes. In the town of Rawalpindi, officers recruited Punjabi Muslims of the Salt Range—Gakhars, Janjuas, Awans, Khattars and Tiwanas. Amritsar was where Jat Sikhs were taken into the army. For Hindu Jats from Rohtak, Hissar, Gurgaon and western UP, Delhi was the recruitment centre. For Dogras, the centre was Jullundur town. Pathans were taken in Peshawar. Communities that lost out included Ahirs, Gujjars and the Awadh groups who earlier had entered the Bengal army in sizable numbers.

As a result of this recruitment process, a rural community's social structure was often reproduced in a company or regiment, where the subedar major was likely also to be an elder in his village.[9]

A fourth consequence was that the Punjabi percentage in the Indian army steadily rose. 'By the year 1900, Punjab was supplying more than half the combatants of the entire Indian Army.'[10]

Finally, recognizing that the loyalty of the expanding numbers of Punjabi soldiers would be 'won or lost in [their] homes and villages, not in the regiments',[11] the Raj sought to unify its military and rural policies:

> It was no coincidence that the 'martial classes' coincided with the dominant landholding elements of rural Punjab. The grafting of the army's regiments onto the social base of Punjab's rural order demonstrated a masterful appreciation by the military and the state in rural Punjab that the essence of a reliable and stable military lay in a contented peasantry.[12]

■

After providing estimates in 1855 and 1868, India's British rulers conducted a comprehensive census in 1881 and every ten years thereafter. If essential for governance, the census also fitted perfectly into imperial strategy since, among other things, it recorded an Indian's caste, sub-caste and religion, and the numbers from each category, thereby supplying competing Indians with ammunition for mutual political warfare.

Taking British Punjab and the region's princely tracts together, the population of Punjab rose from an estimated 17.6 million in 1855 to 20.8 million in 1881 and to 25.1 million in 1921. The highest population concentrations were found in and around Lahore, Amritsar, Gurdaspur and Sialkot and in the Jullundur doab. Density dropped sharply in the arid zones to the west of this fertile base, in the inhospitable northern hill tracts of Chamba and Kangra, in the water-starved expanse of the Bahawalpur principality and, a little less sharply, in Hissar in the southeast.

The number of towns in Punjab went up from 168 in 1881 to 185 in 1921, with an average population of around 18,000 in a town. In 1921, Lahore, which in 1881 had a population of 149,000 (slightly less than Amritsar's 152,000), was twice that size, holding 281,781 people, having greatly overtaken Amritsar, which had a population of 169,218 in 1921. Rawalpindi now contained 101,142 individuals, while five other cities had a population of over 50,000: Multan, Ambala, Sialkot, Jullundur and Ludhiana. As for the countryside, census figures confirmed that fertile lands close to rivers contained more Jats and Rajputs (whether Sikh, Muslim or Hindu) than members of other rural communities.

In terms of religion, the Muslim percentage in Punjab went up from 47.6 in 1881 to 51.1 in 1921. While the corresponding Hindu number went down from 43.8 to 35.1, the Sikh percentage rose from 8.2 to 12.4, and the Christian from 0.1 to 1.3.

Part of the decline in the Hindu percentage and the rise in the Sikh was explained by a change in self-description. Many previously calling themselves Hindus now reported as Sikhs. While in 1881 less than 54 per cent among the Jats of Punjab described themselves as Sikhs, in 1921 the percentage went up to 80. The percentage of Hindu Jats went down from about 40 in 1881 to less than 10 in 1921.[13]

■

The Britons studying Punjab's 'tribes and castes' found no sizeable portion of the province peopled exclusively by a single 'caste' or 'tribe' or even by two 'castes' or 'tribes'. Every district came across as a mixture.

Gujars or Gujjars (who were Muslim and Hindu), Jats or Jatts and Rajputs (both divided into numerous sub-groups and also into Muslims, Hindus and Sikhs), Awans and Arains (almost all of them Muslim), and Khatris and Aroras (almost all Hindu or Sikh) were found virtually everywhere in Punjab but in significant numbers in some districts. Clans like Gakhars, Janjuas and Ghebas—almost wholly Muslim—were concentrated in the British-era's Rawalpindi division. 'Menial' or 'low' castes were noticed right across the province and in large numbers.

As one moved from west to east, cultural and demographic changes appeared 'with some suddenness about the meridian of Lahore, where the great rivers enter the fertile zone and the arid grazing grounds of the West give place to the arable plains of the East'.[14]

Western Punjab contained a higher Muslim percentage, a larger Pashtun and Baloch percentage, and a higher proportion of pastorals and nomads than central or eastern Punjab. It also seemed to have, in comparison with central or eastern portions, a more egalitarian culture, a lower population density, and fewer towns. The Sikhs were numerically strongest in the middle of the province but not in an absolute majority in any entire district.

The British noticed that many Muslims had retained pre-Muslim or clan names, even though they could have adopted Arab or Persian names, or names implying descent from the Prophet, his Companions or his tribe, or from a Sufi—names such as Sayyad (or Sayyid or Syed), Qureshi, Alvi, Siddiqi, Farooqi or Shaikh. A great many Punjabi Muslims chose not to claim such a genealogy, even if others did. As a recent study puts it,

> Why does not a Noon, Tiwana, Minhas, Wattoo or Bhatti claim to be descendants of the Prophet or the Companions? Because they are not. They do not feel ashamed to say that they are Rajputs, Jats etc. They are even proud of it. And why should they not [be]?[15]

■

From the late 1880s, the province saw significant internal migration as land was granted to farmers who moved into new 'canal colonies' coming up in arid lands in western Punjab. As a result, population density went up dramatically in the districts of Montgomery (afterwards Sahiwal), Multan, Lyallpur (later called Faisalabad), Jhang and Muzaffargarh, all in the province's Multan division, and in the district of Shahpur in Rawalpindi division.

Vetted and chosen by Punjab's district officers, migrants into the canal colonies came mainly from seven heavily-populated districts: Amritsar, Gurdaspur and Sialkot (Lahore division); Jullundur, Hoshiarpur and Ludhiana

(Jullundur division); and Ambala. In these districts population density went down.

Two-thirds of the canal colony migrants were Muslim, Sikh and Hindu Jats. The rest included Arains, Sainis, Kambohs and Rajputs. Another percentage consisted of Muslim farmers from adjacent dry tracts in Dera Ghazi Khan, Mianwali and Jhelum districts.

The case for new canal colonies was obvious: rivers had surplus water, barren lands were waiting to be farmed, fertile districts were overpopulated. But the colonies were also of huge political value. Turning the Raj into the giver of land and water, and making Punjabis more beholden to it, the canal colonies became a tool with which the Empire rewarded loyalty or bought it. As we will see, these colonies also enabled the Empire to tighten its military link with Punjab.

Etched by new canals and new rail lines and marked by green new rectangular fields, new market towns and new railway stations, the colonies raised wheat, cotton, mules, mares, studs and camels for the Empire's markets and armies. Entrepreneurs, mostly Hindus and Sikhs, started processing and semi-manufacturing plants, including cotton ginning and pressing factories, on colony plots earmarked for just such a purpose. And the Empire extracted revenue from everything the colonies raised and produced.

For untold generations, the colonies' lands had been used by 'Janglis': goat- and camel-herders cut off from 'civilization'. The Raj tried to settle these 'Janglis' in reserved segments of their broken world.

Eight canal colonies were launched between 1886 and 1916. The first was established in the district of Multan, the second in Montgomery district, and the third in Chunian in Lahore district. The fourth (and the largest), called the Lower Chenab colony, covered parts of four districts (Jhang, Lyallpur, Gujranwala and Lahore). Its creation yielded a new administrative district, Sheikhupura, made up of the 'colony' portions of Gujranwala and Lahore.

The fifth, and almost equally large, canal colony was the Lower Jhelum, located across two districts, Shahpur and Jhang. The Lower Bari doab colony in the districts of Montgomery and Multan was the sixth, followed by the Upper Chenab and Upper Jhelum colonies, the former situated in parts of three districts (Sheikhupura, Gujranwala and Sialkot) and the latter in Gujrat district.

In theory, a canal colony was to be cultivated by 'well-to-do yeomen of the best class of agriculturists with the aid of their families and the usual menials, but as much as possible without tenants'.[16] In practice, while farmers tilling small farms in their home districts indeed comprised a majority of the canal colony grantees, a number of men from other classes were also allotted one or more 'squares' of colony land, each square approximating twenty-five acres.

Thus the man with the biggest grant in the second canal colony, Sohag Para (located in Montgomery district), was Baba Khem Singh Bedi of Rawalpindi district, an eminent Sikh figure from Guru Nanak's Bedi clan. He received several hundred squares in Sohag Para, amounting to no less than 7,798 acres.[17]

Settled between 1892 and 1905, the Lower Chenab colony was populated by grantees described as abadkar (peasants), who received 78 per cent of its land, sufedposh (yeomen), who obtained 8.2 per cent, and rais (capitalists), who were allotted 7 per cent. Retired policemen and soldiers were among those obtaining the remaining 6 per cent. A grantee could not sell his squares, which the Crown owned, but was free to extract profit from them.

The military element became dominant in the Lower Jhelum colony (straddling the districts of Shahpur and Jhang), which was settled between 1902 and 1906. The Raj deciding that horses and mules were needed for its army, 54.4 per cent of this colony's land was allotted for horse-breeding, with each grantee required to maintain five to fifteen brood mares and receiving 1.5 squares per mare.

Eight large stud farms were also allotted in Lower Jhelum, each expected to keep around fifty mares. However, only one stud farm went to a professional horse-breeder, the other seven going to prominent landlord families of northwestern Punjab.[18] Army pensioners not breeding horses obtained another 9.49 per cent of the Lower Jhelum land, while civilians whom the Raj wished to reward got 4.77 per cent. Almost 14 per cent of this colony's land was reserved for 'Janglis'.

Some Punjab officers had questioned Lower Jhelum's horse-breeding emphasis but Calcutta and London overruled them. Punjab's financial commissioner sounded regretful while noting that

> The main object will now be an imperial one, namely to encourage horse breeding and to create a reserve of horses fit for service with the troops.[19]

More openly 'military' than the 'agricultural' colony of Lower Chenab, the Lower Jhelum one was also more 'capitalist'. Punjab's settlement commissioner claimed that Lower Jhelum's 'more wealthy' grantees would also be 'more intelligent' and show 'an advance' over the 'dead level of dull prosperity' achieved in Lower Chenab.[20] Richer farmers engaging sub-tenants and landless labourers elbowed out yeomen in the new colony, and a new town, Sargodha, emerged.

Four out of five grantees in Sidhnai, the first colony, were likely to be Muslim. In the next, Sohag Para, roughly three out of five were Sikh. While the Lower Chenab colony had a large Sikh and Hindu percentage—mostly made up of migrants from eastern Punjab—the Lower Jhelum colony was much more Muslim and also more 'local'.

Punjab's agricultural production and revenue both increased, but the vision of self-reliant farmers creating a model community was not realized. Tenants and landless labourers filled the colonies in unexpected numbers. Many with no interest in farming obtained grants simply because they had served the Raj or were seen as influential. A British colonisation officer noted in 1906:

> One by one they appear, full of forlorn memories of Anarkali or the Chandni Chowk, and beg plaintively for land near a railway station. The best land in the Colony for them is that from which they can get away soonest.[21]

Punjabi bureaucrats involved with the colony schemes became grantees as well. After the Lower Bari doab colony came up in Montgomery district, a senior British officer observed:

> Barring the Colonisation Officer himself, there does not appear to have been a single [government servant] connected with the Montgomery Colony who had not obtained a grant.[22]

The Raj's answer to the scheme's abuse was the Colonisation Bill of 1906, which empowered the provincial government to enforce its conditions of tenure in colony lands by summary or executive process, i.e. without initiating proceedings in civil courts.

An uproar resulted. Throughout 1907, the Bill was assailed in a number of meetings held in the colonies and in Punjab's journals, including the *Tribune* and the *Zamindar* of Lahore. Muslims, Sikhs and Hindus seemed united in their criticism.

Those protesting included Lala Lajpat Rai (1865-1928), born near Moga in eastern Punjab, who had become an all-India figure by this time, and Ajit Singh (1881-1947), raised in Jullundur district, who would have a revolutionary career, including in Europe and Brazil. At a Lyallpur rally, young Ajit Singh's call to the Jat peasant to guard his honour, 'Pagdi Sambhal, Jatta,' evoked a popular response. It was also 'the refrain of a song recited by Banke Dayal' on this occasion.[23] Ajit Singh and Lajpat Rai were both arrested and sent to Burma.

Also protesting was Umar Hayat Khan Tiwana, one of the few Indian members of the Punjab legislative council. In the 1820s, Tiwana's forebears, Rajput Muslims of Shahpur, had forged an alliance with Ranjit Singh. Later, in 1857-58, Umar Hayat's father, Malik Tiwana, provided soldiers to the British for the recapture of Delhi and for combat against the Rani of Jhansi.

Born in 1875, Umar was sent to the new Aitchison Chiefs' College in Lahore, created in the late 1880s for the 'proper' upbringing of the sons of Punjabi nobility. An earlier version, the Wards' School of Ambala, had groomed boys from prominent Sikh families. Named after Charles Aitchison, Punjab's governor at this time, Aitchison College took over and expanded the Ambala school's role. Its first batch of twelve included five Muslims (one was a prince from Pataudi), five Sikhs and a Hindu.

In 1906, apart from serving on the Legislative Council, Umar Hayat was running one of the large stud farms in the Lower Jhelum colony. His loyalty to the Raj was beyond doubt.

Despite Umar Hayat's opposition, Punjab officials dominating the council ensured the passage of the Colonisation Bill. However, the Viceroy vetoed it. Imperial strategy demanded retaining the support of men like Umar Hayat and overruling Punjab's British officers whose sensibility had been injured by Punjabi colonists unwilling to alter their farming practices. Reports of the stir affecting Sikh sepoys who uttered seditious thoughts within their regiments also influenced the Viceroy.[24] Lajpat Rai and Ajit Singh were released and allowed to return home.

Not only was the Bill dropped, the colonists were now able, at remarkably low prices, to buy the lands allotted to them, and also, if they wished, to serve as absentee landlords. Canal colony rules and the Crown's ownership were sacrificed but imperial strategy had prevailed.

Started in 1914 in the districts of Montgomery and Multan, the Lower Bari doab colony was quickly integrated into the Empire's plans for World War I. Aware that the prospect of land grants would stimulate recruitment, the Raj gave military grantees a large share in Lower Bari doab, while also reserving 60,000 acres for Punjab's 'landed gentry', who could help generate new soldiers.

In total, counting all canal colonies, military grantees received almost half a million acres.[25] Though, strictly speaking, pirs and sajjada nashins, custodians of Sufi grounds, were not members of the 'landed gentry', they were encouraged, 'on grounds of real-politik', to apply for colony land under that category.[26]

Imran Ali, scholar of the Raj's canal colonies, informs us that many names prominent in Punjab's twentieth century story, including Noon (or Nun), Tiwana, Daultana and Mamdot, figured on the lists of those who received or were able to buy colony lands.[27]

■

In 1853-54, before the Revolt that is, a judicial commission of the Raj interviewing Muslims, Hindus and Sikhs involved with Punjab's vernacular schools had found signs favourable to harmony. The Sikhs seemed to be losing their inclination for 'fanaticism and political fervour', the Hindus of Punjab appeared to be 'less superstitious and less priest-ridden', and the Muslims were 'less bigoted and less bound by traditional practice' than their co-religionists elsewhere in India.[28]

The Revolt's aftermath changed the picture in some ways. In all communities, the watchword now became purity, not harmony or moderation.

Some Sikhs concluded, looking back, that their deceased kingdom had compromised with purity. Hindu rites had been too readily accommodated in the kingdom's ceremonies. Ranjit Singh's feats notwithstanding, perhaps a king and his court were not what the Gurus had in mind.

Some Muslims in Punjab drew similar conclusions regarding the purity of Islam in the Mughal empire, dead now for half a century. In their view, the 1857 bid to resurrect that empire by (as they thought) a corrupted Muslim like Zafar was doomed from the start. Together with loyalty to the triumphant Raj, a return to a cleaner version of their faith was seen as the way forward.

More willing than Muslims and Sikhs to accept the Raj and embrace its schools, and generally viewing British rule as a blessing that ended Muslim rule in India, Punjab's Hindus utilized the new openings in trade, government service and the professions. But some of them, too, looked for a purer or reformed Hinduism, again joined to loyalty to the British.

Caution continued on all sides in respect of Christianity, which was advocated in Punjab in the 1850s and thereafter by British, American and other missionaries, working from Ludhiana, Lahore, Amritsar and Sialkot. In 1853, the boy-prince, Duleep or Dalip, then eight, had accepted Christianity while under British tutelage. This was followed by the conversion of Harnam Singh

Ahluwalia, a Kapurthala prince with ties that went back to the eighteenth-century Sikh hero, Jassa Singh Ahluwalia.

In Amritsar, a maulvi named Imamuddin and Rallia Ram, a Hindu belonging to one of the city's prominent Khatri families, were among those who became Christians in the 1850s.[29] At about the same time, a man named Ditt of village Marali near Sialkot, a member of the so-called chuhra or scavenging caste, became the first of numerous Christian converts from his local community.[30]

Christian successes sharpened the urge for purity and reform. 'We failed because we did not obey the Guru. People established kingdoms and principalities but neglected their brethren. The result is what you see—the Khalsa has fallen.'[31] This Sikh diagnosis was paralleled by similar Muslim conclusions.

'The Muslims in the Punjab... were caught up in the mire of social evils... Religion... had become a collection of rites and superstitions. At the same time, they faced a grave threat from the increasing proselytizing activities of Christian Missionary societies and the growing economic prosperity of the Hindus.'[32]

Responding to such perceptions, and also because the Badshahi Masjid, recently restored to Muslims, needed repairs and looking after, a few Muslims in Lahore established the Anjuman-i-Islamia in 1869. Four years later, Amritsar saw the emergence of its own Anjuman-i-Islamia. Both bodies attempted to popularize 'religious and modern' education and to 'acquaint the Government with the problems and desires' of Punjabi Muslims.[33] Soon there were similar Anjumans in more than a dozen towns in Punjab.

To directly 'counter, through oral and written word, the opponents of Islam', another association, the Anjuman-i-Himayat-i-Islam, came into being in Lahore in 1884 and was also replicated elsewhere in Punjab. This second set of Anjumans hoped to 'ward off the adverse effects' on Muslims boys and girls of 'the teachings of other religions' and also to 'acquaint the Muslims with the benefits of loyalty to the Government'.[34]

This double aim—guarding their community against perceived threats from other communities while building relations with the British—was nursed by all three communities, Muslim, Sikh and Hindu.

■

One of the first to chastise the Sikhs for supposed compromise was old Baba Dayal, a Malhotra Khatri from Rawalpindi. He spoke—in, it would seem,

1853—of 'the shortcomings of the mighty', criticized 'rites and observances undermining the Sikh faith', targeted 'the worship of images' and insisted on returning to the formless God stressed by Guru Nanak.[35] Hearing of Baba Dayal's impact and teaching, the Christian mission in Ludhiana viewed him and the growing circle of his followers as potential converts, but what followed was a different trajectory, leading eventually, through Baba Dayal's successors, to what mainstream Sikhism would see as the heterodox, if also popular, Nirankari movement.

Although it allowed Christian missionaries to preach, the Raj adhered to its post-Revolt doctrine of divorcing Christianity from its rule and responded positively to separate overtures from Muslim, Sikh and Hindu associations. A joint Muslim–Hindu–Sikh platform in Lahore or elsewhere in Punjab would have presented a challenge to the Raj's guardians, but no such coming together occurred:

> Conditions in the 19th century contributed towards developments on communitarian lines. The British policies too played a role in the birth and progress of communitarian societies and their assumption of communal overtones and politics.[36]

Open foes of the British were now few and far between. Perhaps the most significant among them was Baba Ram Singh (1816-1885), a carpenter's son from Ludhiana district. Baba Ram Singh stressed the value of the Naam (Name) for salvation but he also mobilized Sikhs and Hindus against the withdrawal of the Khalsa-era ban on kine-slaughter, urged a boycott of British-made textiles, and promoted home-made cloth.

Emphasizing Guru Gobind Singh as well as Guru Nanak and also the Hindu goddess Chandi, and playing down the Sikh–Hindu distinction, he was interned by the British in 1863, in his village, Bhaini.

Baba Ram Singh's confinement multiplied the number of his followers, who were called Namdharis and, at times, Kukas. After seven Muslims were killed in a Kuka attack on butchers in Amritsar and in Ludhiana district, eight Kukas were sentenced to death. In January 1872, when the Kukas responded by killing more men while attempting to seize arms—in order, apparently, 'to overawe kine-killers all over the Punjab'—the Ludhiana deputy commissioner, a man called Cowan, reacted—fifteen years after the Revolt—by 'blowing 49 Kukas from guns at the spot'.[37] Backing Cowan's extraordinary action, his superior, Douglas Forsyth, the commissioner of Ambala division, ordered sixteen more Kukas to be blown from guns.

The Raj removed Cowan from service and Forsyth from Punjab. It also sent Baba Ram Singh into exile in Rangoon. Namdhari fervour reached a high pitch in 1885, the year of Baba Ram Singh's death, when it was reported that Prince Dalip Singh, disenchanted with the British after living among them for decades, was returning to Punjab. The enthusiasm seemed to collapse, however, when, in 1890, Dalip Singh 'returned to his loyalty' to Queen Victoria.[38]

The British were more comfortable with the Singh Sabha movement, which seemed to blend better also with general Sikh sentiment. Its start was triggered by an incident in 1873. 'Four Sikh pupils of the Amritsar Mission School proclaimed their intention of renouncing their faith in favour of Christianity. This shocked Sikh feeling.'[39]

Meeting in Amritsar, a group of Sikhs including Thakur Singh Sandhanwalia (a relative of Ranjit Singh's), Baba Khem Singh Bedi (from Guru Nanak's clan), and Bikrama Singh (a Kapurthala prince whose relative, Harnam Singh, had become a Christian) established the Singh Sabha. The Singh Sabha's declared aims included restoring 'Sikhism to its pristine purity', publishing historical and religious books, recovering apostates, and involving 'highly placed Englishmen' in its activities.[40]

The Singh Sabha's decision to propagate its message in the Punjabi language was a factor behind its rapid success in the 1880s and 1890s. Another was its shrewd use of the Sikh soldier.

> The reformist ideology percolated to the Sikh peasantry primarily through soldiers serving in the army or those who retired. One of the regiments had constituted a choir of reciters to go round the villages and sing the sacred hymns at Singh Sabha congregations. The movement picked up momentum and rocked the Punjab from one end to the other.[41]

■

Many among Punjab's Hindus felt that the Gujarat-born Swami Dayanand Saraswati (1824-1883), who visited Punjab in 1877, was the answer to their search. His reputation had preceded the Swami's visit. Opposing idolatry and all rituals except the havan ceremony, the celibate Dayanand was a gifted scholar and energetic debater. Published in Hindi in 1875, his *Satyarth Prakash* (Light on the Meaning of Truth) had urged Hindus to return to 'the pure monotheism' of the Vedas. The book had also criticized Christianity, Islam, idolatrous or corrupted Hinduism, and Sikhism.

The Swami's other views are also of interest. He advocated a woman's right to read scripture and educate herself, opposed untouchability, and held that Europe owed its technological and scientific success not to Christianity but to India's ancient 'Aryas'; in the modern age, however, Indians should learn from European virtues and achievements.

The Swami's Arya Samaj quickly attracted a following among Punjabi Hindus of different castes. Before long, Arya Samaj branches set up 'Anglo-Vedic' schools and colleges in different parts of Punjab to promote education and also an outlook where Vedic beliefs co-existed with openness to the Empire's institutions.

His equivalent, so to speak, in the Muslim community was Mirza Ghulam Ahmad (1835-1908). Born in Qadian in the Bari doab, eleven miles northeast of Batala, Mirza Ghulam Ahmad, the founder, in 1889, of the Ahmadiyya sect, was a talented proselytizer on Islam's behalf. A forebear of his had settled in Qadian in the sixteenth century. In 1834, Mirza Ghulam Ahmad's father apparently submitted to Ranjit Singh, who confirmed the family's title to Qadian and five adjoining villages.

Aimed at proving Islam's superiority over Christianity, Hinduism and Sikhism, Mirza Ghulam Ahmad's writings and utterances won him fame across Punjab during the 1870s and 1880s. He also attracted a wide following in the province, aided no doubt by the fact that he was an authentic Bari doab Punjabi. However, Mirza Ghulam Ahmad invited hostility when he claimed in 1890 that that he was the messiah of whom the Prophet had spoken. An admired champion of Islam was transformed into the leader of a heterodox if not heretical sect.

His interventions on behalf of Islam constituted part of a fierce and often vituperative debate that marked the Punjab of the 1870s and 1880s. Others participating in this religio-political debate included Christian missionaries and representatives of the Arya Samaj and the Singh Sabha. Because many new journals had emerged—in English, Urdu and Punjabi—the debate was re-enacted in homes and arenas across Punjab. While Muslim, Arya Samajist, Sikh or Christian debaters strove to establish that theirs was the soundest faith on offer, the Raj took comfort from the fact that Muslims, Hindus and Sikhs were not thinking of a common platform.

■

In 1881, the launch in Lahore of the *Tribune*, an English-language daily, suggested a wish in some to step out of a small world. The paper was brought out by a trust founded by Dyal Singh Majithia, a prominent Sikh who sympathized with the Brahmo Samaj of Calcutta's Raja Rammohun Roy (1772-1833) and Debendranath Tagore (1817-1905), a tolerant, theistic body believing in the Hindu Upanishads and the Christian ethic. Many Muslims, however, saw the *Tribune* as a Hindu organ, as did some Sikhs.

The *Tribune*'s appearance was part of an all-India trend connected with the end in 1880 of Lord Lytton's viceregal term. Three years earlier, on 1 January 1877, Lytton had held a Grand Durbar in Delhi at which princes from across India marked Victoria's assumption of the title of Empress of India. (One of Lytton's predecessors in Calcutta, we may note here, was John Lawrence, who returned to India to serve as Viceroy. During an uneventful term from 1864 to 1869, Lawrence threw his weight against Indians being allowed into senior levels of government service.)

Assembling the Durbar in the Mughal capital rather than in Calcutta was an expression of post-Revolt imperial confidence. A year later, however, Lytton raised a storm with his Vernacular Press Act, which authorized magistrates to confiscate the printing presses of any Indian-language newspapers preaching disaffection. In response, some vernacular papers in Calcutta became English-language ones, while Madras saw the appearance of a new daily, the *Hindu*, also in English, even as the *Tribune* emerged in Lahore.

The end of Lytton's viceroyalty coincided with a Tory defeat in England. His successor, named by Gladstone, was Lord Ripon, a liberal and recent Catholic. Repealing the hated Vernacular Press Act in January 1882, Ripon enhanced his popularity with Indians by endorsing a bill introduced by the law member on his council, C.P. Ilbert, which empowered an Indian magistrate or sessions judge posted in the districts to try Europeans accused of crime.

Especially in Bengal, Indians had long asked for such a bill. Unlike in Punjab, districts in the Bengal Presidency contained numerous Europeans who worked in non-governmental jobs in plantations of tea and indigo. Until the Ilbert bill appeared, these Europeans stood above the laws that an Indian magistrate could enforce.

Calcutta's British were incensed by these measures. Reporting that a White Mutiny was occurring in India, newspapers in England warned against abandoning a core element of imperial strategy. The *Daily Telegraph* wrote: 'On the day when we surrender the rights and privileges of superior strength and ethnical rank in India we invite our own expulsion.' The *Times* said: 'India can be governed by Englishmen only as a conquered country... [T]he privileges of the English who are resident there... are not anomalies at all...'[42]

Ripon's hands were forced and the Ilbert Bill was modified beyond recognition. But one of Ripon's friends in India, a Scotsman called Allan Octavian Hume (1829-1912), who had resigned in 1879 from the Indian Civil Service, soon responded with initiatives that led to the formation, in 1885, of the Indian National Congress.

Serving from 1849 in India, Hume had in 1857 dealt firmly yet also justly with rebels in Etawah, seventy-five miles east of Agra.[43] Thereafter he told himself and his ICS colleagues that the only way to prevent another revolt was to allow Indians a say in their governance.

Shortly before Hume resigned from the government, Lytton, it seems, offered him the governorship of Punjab. Replying that the entertaining expected from a governor would not suit him or his wife, Hume asked to be made home member on Lytton's council in Calcutta, an idea rejected by Lord Salisbury, HMG's Secretary of State for India.[44]

We can only speculate on the difference a Governor Hume may or may not have made to Punjab's story. Quitting the Raj, he put himself in touch, through letters and quiet travel, with potential Indian allies in different parts of the country. According to a letter he wrote in November 1884, the cities he planned to visit included Lahore and Amritsar.[45] We do not know whether these Punjab cities were in fact visited by him in 1884 or 1885. (During earlier years, Hume had visited almost every part of India, including Punjab, as a student of birds, which he also was.)

In any case, in 1885 (a year after Ripon had ended his viceroyalty) the Indian National Congress held its first session in Bombay, under the presidentship of Calcutta's Womesh Chandra Bonnerjee. Hume served as the INC's active secretary, a role he discharged until his departure for England in 1892.

Hoping to bring India's varied elements—religious, linguistic and provincial—to a single platform, and resolving to convene annually in different parts of India, the INC met in Calcutta in 1886 and in Madras the following year. In 1893, the body gathered in Lahore, under the presidentship of the Parsi luminary from Bombay, Dadabhai Naoroji.

■

At this time, Punjab's Muslims were taking their political cue from Sayyid Ahmed Khan (1817-98), the first Muslim to be nominated to the Imperial Legislative Council and the founder, in 1875, of Aligarh's Mohammedan Anglo-Oriental College (MAO). A scion of Delhi's Mughal nobility and a former judicial officer for the East India Company, Sayyid Ahmed—like Hume—was a graduate of 1857. He had saved British lives in UP's Rohilkhand region and also given the British a candid, if private, assessment of the factors behind the Revolt.

If Hume became Viceroy Ripon's friend, Sayyid Ahmed was quite close to Ripon's predecessor, Lord Lytton, who had visited MAO within days of his January 1877 Durbar. While sharing Hume's wish for Indians to move towards self-rule—the two knew each other and Sayyid Ahmed had supported a proposal by Hume for a native volunteer force—the fear of Hindus lording it over Muslims was a stronger sentiment in the MAO founder.

Suspicious of the INC, Sayyid Ahmed opposed its pleas for adding elected members to the Raj's local or provincial councils and for wider openings for Indians in the civil service. Arguing that the better-educated Hindus would monopolize the service and that any elections would be won by lower ranks among Muslims and Hindus, he asked India's Muslims to stay clear of the INC. It was better for them to ally with the English.[46]

Some Muslims disagreed, including the talented Bombay lawyer Badruddin Tyabji, who chaired, in Madras, the INC's third annual session, but Sayyid Ahmed's reach was wider.

He was knighted in 1888. That year, he formed the United Indian Patriotic Association and invited prominent Muslims and Hindus to join it. In Punjab, the Anjumans that had been established

> supported Sir Syed Ahmed Khan in his attitude towards the Indian National Congress. Most [Anjumans] held meetings in response to his call and passed resolutions opposing Muslim participation in political activities. They also affiliated themselves to the United Indian Patriotic Association.[47]

Sir Sayyid Ahmed Khan was loved and admired among Punjabi Muslims, who 'provided the most liberal and enthusiastic help to the Aligarh movement'. On his death in 1898, the 'Anjumans all over the Punjab held meetings to condole his death,… paid glowing tributes' and raised money for MAO.[48]

■

The religio-political controversies marking Punjab in the last quarter of the nineteenth century did not merely divide Muslims, Hindus and Sikhs from one another. They also produced schisms within each of Punjab's Muslim, Hindu and Sikh worlds.

It is instructive if also ironic to recognize that the Ahmadiyya question faced today by the subcontinent's Muslims owes its origin to the end-nineteenth-century debates, where for years Mirza Ghulam Ahmad appeared to be the stoutest debater for Islam.

Punjab's Arya Samajists, on their part, were stirred into self-confidence and social reform by Swami Dayanand, but they also became part of a more acrimonious Punjab, including a less harmonious Hindu Punjab, for many of the province's Hindus were unwilling to give up traditional Hinduism or the Sanatan Dharam, as they called it.

The Singh Sabhas were as successful as the Muslim Anjumans and the Hindu Arya Samaj branches, and they enthused the Sikh community, yet the present-day separation of Nirankaris and Namdharis from 'Panthic' Sikhism has also descended from the last quarter of the nineteenth century.

Purity was achieved at unity's expense. Muslims, Hindus and Sikhs all pointed to Christian proselytization as the threat. Christianity would not expand as feared, but neither would the unity of Muslims, or Hindus, or Sikhs.

At the end of the nineteenth century, a Sikh intellectual, Bhai Kahn Singh produced a text, *Ham Hindu Nahin* (Not Hindus We), described later as 'a classic exposition of a distinct Sikh identity'.[49] The thesis was an offspring of the Sikh-Arya debate. As a contemporary historian puts it, '[M]ore than the threat of Islam and Christianity, the Singh reformers felt a threat from the Arya Samaj.'[50]

This was not always the case. Until 1888, when Arya polemic crossed a line by seeming to target the Sikh Gurus, several eminent Sikhs were sympathetic to Swami Dayanand's message, notwithstanding *Satyarth Prakash's* criticisms of Sikhism. On the other hand, a few Sikhs with prestigious connections seemed willing, at the start of the twentieth century, to stand with traditional Hinduism. Worshipping idols, they held, was consistent with Sikh tradition,[51] but their position was repudiated by the Singh Sabha.

■

The life of Sir Ganga Ram (1851-1927) showed how individual talent could flower under the Raj. Born to a police sub-inspector of the Bania caste in Mangtanwala, a village about forty miles southwest of Lahore, Ganga Ram became the civil engineer responsible for several of Lahore's landmark buildings as also the city extension called Model Town. In addition, he would be a pioneer in lift irrigation and donate handsomely as a philanthropist.

Lahore's Museum, Post Office, Mayo School of Arts and Aitchison College were only some of the elegant structures he helped raise as an engineer, and the city's Ganga Ram Hospital, later replicated in Delhi, was only one of the institutions he created as a philanthropist. Sir Ganga Ram would die in 1927, in London.

Also part of the Lahore scene in the 1880s was a creator of another kind. Rudyard Kipling (1865-1936) lived there for five years, from 1882 to 1887, as an assistant editor on the *Civil & Military Gazette,* a British-owned daily founded in 1872 and published from Simla as well. The Kipling that Lahore saw was only in his late teens or early twenties and single; he would later recall the *Civil & Military Gazette* as his 'mistress and most true love'.

Brought to Lahore by his father Lockwood Kipling, the curator of the Lahore Museum and also the principal of the School of Arts, Rudyard would be remembered by a colleague on the *Gazette* as someone in white trousers and a thin vest and spotted all over with black ink.[52] Scores of Kipling's short stories, many written in Simla, appeared in the *Gazette.* His *Kim* and *Jungle Book* and the famous poems were written later and outside India, but their themes had been captured in Punjab.

Tho' I've belted you and flayed you,
By the livin' Gawd that made you,
You're a better man than I am, Gunga Din!

Put into the mouth of a British soldier and addressed to an Indian water-carrier, these words were part of Kipling's 1892 poem, *Gunga Din,* written less than four years after he left Lahore; they reveal Kipling's awareness of the Empire's uglier side. His *Recessional,* breathing pride in the Empire yet warning against hubris, was composed in 1897, for Victoria's golden jubilee. *The White Man's Burden,* which kept in mind also a newer empire (the American), came out in 1899; and *If,* the classic reflection on equanimity, in 1906. Portraying a resourceful white boy caught in the Anglo-Russian Great Game, Kipling's novel *Kim* was written in 1900-01.

■

During the period (1859-1919) covered by this chapter, newspapers and journals printed in Punjab—by 1905 the province had 263 of them[53]—promoted the opposite of harmony. Most, including Hindu-owned ones, were published in Urdu, a few in English, and some in Punjabi in the Gurmukhi script. In the eastern districts, a few started to appear in Hindi in Nagari characters.

Verbal hostilities were particularly sharp over language. The questions were real. The language you knew, or failed to learn, influenced your prospects for a government job. If competence in English was deemed essential for entering some levels of government service, what about other levels? In what language, in any case, was the public to communicate with government servants? (After initial retention in western Punjab, Persian had been abandoned.) Again, in what language should the Raj's schools instruct their pupils?

Should it be Punjabi, the language of the people? Or should Urdu come to the fore, the language of Delhi and, until 1900, the sole official language of UP, a language, moreover, that Punjabi had helped create? Or could Hindi in the Nagari script, increasingly competing with Urdu in Delhi and UP, qualify as an alternative to both?

In the north Indian areas ruled by them before Punjab was annexed, the British—along with many of their subjects—had favoured Hindustani, the language spoken in and around Delhi and in parts of UP. By 1835, orders to replace Persian with Hindustani in the Persian script had been passed in parts of UP. However, some speakers of the language steered Hindustani in Sanskrit's direction and called it Hindi. Others led it towards Persian and Arabic and said it was Urdu.

Whether called Urdu, Hindustani or Hindi, it was the language that several of the Raj's officers had picked up before proceeding to serve in Punjab. This became a factor in their decided preference, in Punjab, for Urdu (written in the Persian script) as against Punjabi.

Moreover, British officers running into different Punjabi dialects in different parts of Punjab, and, in the frontier districts, into another language altogether (Pashto), longed for a pan-Indian language. To them Urdu seemed the answer. There was also an inclination, bred by unfamiliarity, to dub Punjabi and Pashto 'barbarous' in comparison with Urdu.[54]

By contrast, in Bengal, including in its Muslim-majority areas, the Raj had ungrudgingly accepted Bengali, the people's language, as the language of administration. Not *written* as widely in Punjab as Bengali was in Bengal, Punjabi certainly carried a handicap. Moreover, in a climate of Muslim-Sikh rivalry it was easy to damage Punjabi's case by linking the Gurmukhi script to the Sikhs' sacred texts.

Punjabi's claims were however underlined by education officers like G.W. Leitner and by a few others. It was pointed out that hundreds of Punjabi-language books existed, most of them in Gurmukhi but many also in the Persian script, including several on the fine arts, and that powerful poetry—romantic and mystical—had been composed in Punjabi.

If, however, script was a problem, why not a Punjabi in Roman letters? The question was asked by the DC of Shahpur district, a man called J. Wilson. With great rationality and equal impracticality, Wilson claimed (in 1894) that primary education and the running of government could both be conducted in Romanized Punjabi.[55]

Pro-Urdu British officers were strongly backed by bodies like the Anjuman-i-Islamia and by preachers in mosques. While the former associated the Gurmukhi script with Sikhism, the latter had little interest in mass literacy, which Punjabi as the medium of school instruction could promote.

The steady advance in UP of Hindi in the Nagari script, a formula advocated for Punjab by the Arya Samaj, did not help Punjabi's cause. When, in 1900, the Raj declared that, along with English and Urdu, Hindi too would be an official language in UP, Urdu's champions in Punjab hardened their stand. The argument that a Hindi wave would also be a Hindu wave found many takers, as also the view that Urdu, not Punjabi, was best suited to withstand it.

As for Punjabi, Miss M. Rose Greenfield, a missionary teacher in Ludhiana, had pointed out in 1882 that many Punjabi girls, Muslim and Hindu, were in fact learning Punjabi in the Gurmukhi script in schools, or in the Persian or Nagari scripts in their homes. Let primary village schools, she proposed, teach Punjabi in Gurmukhi to all children, irrespective of gender or religion. Later they could switch to Urdu or Hindi.[56]

The perspective of people in Lahore, Rawalpindi and Multan differed from that of the Ludhiana teacher. Even so, 'for the most part', Punjabi women who could write at this time, including Muslims, evidently 'wrote Punjabi in the Gurmukhi character'. As a contemporary historian points out, '[W]omen's education in the Punjab owed a great deal to the Gurmukhi script.'[57] Apparently the process had begun in Ranjit Singh's time.[58]

Punjabi lost out, however, and Urdu in the Persian script won, joining English as the language of administration in Punjab, and becoming also the language of instruction in schools. As for Hindi, it was not until 1917 that it was added to the curriculum as an optional subject, which meant that for a long time proponents of Hindi and opponents of Urdu in Punjab presented their case in Urdu newspapers and pamphlets.

In 1909, the vice chancellor of Punjab University, a man from Bengal called P.C. Chatterji, made a fresh bid for Punjabi as the language of instruction. Even though the governor, Louis Dane, supported Chatterji, the attempt failed.

While the *Tribune* and some other papers endorsed the call, it was successfully vilified, in *Paisa Akhbar* and elsewhere, as a Hindu stratagem. Muslims were warned that Punjabi was being used to bludgeon Urdu.

One critic, writing in the *Observer,* said that despite their past association with Urdu—despite 'its pleasing diction and the richness and elegance of its literature'—Hindus had spurned Urdu in UP and now wanted to force Muslims in Punjab to adopt Punjabi as the literate language. After 'cement[ing] Hindu nationality', they were proceeding towards 'injuring the nationality of the Muslim community'.[59]

Some had hoped that a language spoken by all Punjabis might bring them together. Yet, fuelled by the printed word, a language controversy so bitterly divided them that protagonists in Punjab were willing, not just on one side, to speak of two nations, one Muslim and the other Hindu.

Although rural Punjab remained peaceful,[60] Hindu-Muslim clashes occurred in the 1880s and 1890s in the towns of Multan, Isa Khel (Mianwali district), Dera Ghazi Khan, Delhi, Rohtak and Ludhiana. More often than not, a report that a cow was about to be slaughtered, or that a religious procession carrying Hindu idols was interfering with mosque prayers, set off stone-throwing or worse.

An urge to irritate the 'other' abetted the incidents, and behind the urge were underlying reasons. As identified by Ikram Ali Malik, these were a newly-visible assertiveness in some urban Hindus, born of progress under the Raj; resentment of this assertiveness, and at times of Hindu wealth, among urban Muslims; the Muslims' awareness, in part thanks to Sayyid Ahmed Khan, that they too could compete for places in schools and government offices; and Hindu dislike of this Muslim awareness.[61]

In 1881 in Multan, a Hindu demand for a total ban on cow-slaughter coincided with a controversial plan to elevate the spire of Multan's Prahladpuri temple. Though a minority, Multan's Hindus were being assertive. A butcher and two mosques were attacked but retaliation destroyed or damaged twenty-three Hindu temples. In protest, Hindus suspended all trade for a few days.

Religious festivals such as Eid, when Muslims wanted to sacrifice cows, Dussehra, when Hindus took out processions with idols, and Muharram, when Shia Muslims took out their processions and tazias, called for vigilance. Usually, community leaders and local authorities agreed ahead of time as to the place of slaughter or the route of a procession.

Not always clearly spelt out, the Raj's guidelines regarding cow-slaughter in Punjab stipulated, firstly, that slaughter should not occur in the centre of a town and, secondly, that beef brought into populated areas should be covered. On Eid, sacrifice behind walls was at times allowed, but a cow seen in a Muslim locality could generate tension. Rumours of beef found near a temple, of pork near a mosque, of uncovered beef brought to a locality, or of a Muharram tazia 'deliberately' injuring a branch of a sacred pipal tree were always capable of starting a commotion.

However, commotions died down fairly quickly and normal life returned. Also, 'there were instances of mutual help and cooperation'. In September 1883, Hindu and Muslim leaders in Hoshiarpur jointly appealed for cooperation at a large public meeting chaired by a Christian. Three years later, in Ferozepore, 'a number of Muslims contributed subscriptions for a Ram Lila procession' and 'on the whole supported the Hindus' campaign against the opening of beef shops in the city'. Hindus attended Muharram congregations in Lahore, and in the 1893 Isa Khel disturbance 'several Hindu shopkeepers successfully sought help from Muslim friends'.[62]

A study found that local officers were often weak, or slow to react to an imminent clash, but the Raj as a whole, while 'aware of... the utility of communal differences... did not create or deliberately fan or excite religious animosities or prejudices'. Generally taking 'a non-partisan attitude', the administration seemed 'mainly concerned with the maintenance of peace and order'.[63]

After experimenting in the 1880s with elected seats on some municipal boards in Punjab (only the aristocratic, the rich or the educated could vote or contest), the Raj reverted to nominating all members. In many Muslim-majority towns, more Hindus had been elected than Muslims. 'In 96 reported elections [in 1883 and 1884], Hindus won a majority on 72 committees, Muslims on 12, Sikhs on one (Tarn Taran), and there were 11 Hindu-Muslim ties.'[64] It was alleged that Hindu members supported co-religionists during a riot. Nomination gave British officers greater control and enabled them to maintain 'balance'.[65]

Punjab's press apparently contributed to the 'frequency of riots'. While not sparing the *Tribune* or Muslim-owned papers like *Rafiq-i-Hindi, Rahbar-i-Hind, Chaudwin Sadi* and *Paisa Akhbar*, the study of communal riots offers a good word for the Hindu-owned (and Urdu-language) *Akhbar-i-Aam*, which in 1888 admitted the press's role in publishing 'inflammatory material' and asked Hindus to be reasonable in their anti-cow-slaughter campaign. The *Tribune*, too, the study concedes, wrote at times against 'communal bitterness'.[66]

When seen along with the continuing peace of rural Punjab, which seldom made news, the honesty the study found in the urban *Akhbar-i-Aam* suggests that the provocative language of the press in general was not necessarily a true indicator of Hindu-Muslim relations in the period.

By and large, ordinary Muslims, Hindus and Sikhs seemed to experience peaceful encounters with one another—in the village or town bazaar, in school, at work (often in an office of the Raj) or during travel, or at a fair or festival. Hindus continued to visit Sufi shrines. Entering one another's homes was no doubt rare; and it was always possible, especially in a town, to provoke a commotion. Yet ordinary Punjabis of all faiths usually heeded common sense and avoided mutual hostility, just as their down-to-earth ancestors had done.

Punjab's climate was worsened, however, by the death from stabbing, in March 1897, of forty-year-old Pandit Lekh Ram, a prominent Arya Samaj figure. That his murderer was never apprehended added to bitterness among Arya Samajists. Sweeps of premises of Muslim organizations to discover the murderer's identity irritated many Muslims.

Born in Jhelum district, Lekh Ram had taken part in debating contests with Mirza Ghulam Ahmad, among others. Some of his writings (all of them in Urdu) were offensive, which could also be said of the writings and speeches of debaters opposing him. In several towns, the Pandit's assassination was followed by 'a complete trade boycott... instituted by Hindus and Muslims against each other'.[67]

Rivalries between urban Muslims and Hindus were accentuated when word got out of a policy instituted by James Lyall, the province's governor from 1887 to 1892, of favouring suitable Muslim applicants for government posts until the Hindu-Muslim ratio in the native bureaucracy bore 'some relation' to their proportions in the population.[68]

Something significant, ominous even, was happening. Especially in towns, people were being seen and described not as individuals or Punjabis but as slices, identical to one another, of a loaf called 'community', and the latter word was coming increasingly into play. Newly-educated Punjabis were inclined to identify themselves not with the class of educated Punjabis as a whole but with their particular religious community.[69]

We may note here that the Dayanand Anglo-Vedic (or DAV) College in Lahore was started in 1888, with Arya Samaj backing. An Islamia College followed in Lahore in 1892, while the Khalsa College opened in Amritsar, also in 1892.

The marketability of farmland and rise in its value, aided by lower rates of revenue, facilitated borrowings against it. It also led to wasteful expenditure, indebtedness and land alienation. In the 1880s, about half a million acres were lost annually in the province to urban moneylenders.[70] Not surprisingly, destruction of moneylenders' records was an element in some of Punjab's riots.[71] According to one study, the percentage of seriously indebted Muslim farmers reached up to seventy in most western districts and to ninety in Muzaffargarh, Mianwali and Dera Ghazi Khan. Most creditors were Hindu or Sikh moneylenders.[72]

Within the Raj, champions of peasants engaged advocates of market economics in a passionate debate. Taking place in Punjab, Calcutta, Simla (where the Viceroy spent his summers) and London, and before long also in Punjab's press, the debate culminated in the Punjab Land Alienation Act.

Coming into operation in 1901, the Act prevented the sale of agricultural land to persons belonging to tribes and castes not listed as agricultural. The spectre of Hindu moneylenders oppressing Muslim peasants, who in consequence revolt against the Raj, persuaded its guardians, in particular Curzon, the Viceroy at the time, to reject fears shared by many that Punjab's economy would be hit by such a ban.[73]

At meetings across Punjab, 'Khatris, Baniyas and Aroras' led an unsuccessful agitation against the measure.[74] Hindu-owned newspapers criticized it, as did the INC, though at the end of 1900, when for a second time the INC held its annual session in Lahore, discussion of the measure was avoided. Opposition to the proposed law would have lent credence to Sayyid Ahmed's portrayal of the Congress as a Hindu body.

One of the earliest advocates of such a law was S.S. Thorburn, whom we had come across in the last chapter as a DC in Bannu, where he was one of Nicholson's successors. Not content with urging his viewpoint before the Punjab government, Thorburn published a book, *Musalmans and Moneylenders in the Punjab*, which influenced opinion in Calcutta and London.[75]

An equally ardent supporter of such a law was the man we saw in Delhi when Nicholson died: his close Indian aide, Muhammad Hayat of Wah. By now a significant landowner, a member of the Punjab legislative council and member also of a key select committee advising the Raj on the proposed measure, Hayat, a Khattar Jat, asserted that he was a truer representative of the Punjabi farmer than the pro-Congress Harnam Singh, another member of the select committee, who had opposed the measure.[76]

While Harnam Singh was 'an aristocrat', Hayat declared, he himself was a Jat peasant.[77] We may mark here that Harnam Singh was the Kapurthala prince who had become a Christian, an act that cost him the Kapurthala throne. Harnam Singh was opposed also by Charles Rivaz, revenue & agriculture member on the Viceroy's council, who pointed out that Punjab's peasants were 'furnish[ing] the flower of the Native Army'.[78]

In the event, the ban on urban Punjabis buying rural land did not upset Punjab's economy. Nor, however, did it end moneylending, indebtedness, or the alienation of land. Thrifty farmers and those with sufficient land lent money to needy or extravagant farmers and thereby acquired more land. Compared with other agricultural groups, Jats in eastern Punjab and rich Muslim landlords in western Punjab increased their holdings.[79]

■

Lord Curzon (1859-1925), the Viceroy who had pushed through the Land Alienation Act, was a British politician and Central Asia explorer who wanted Russia kept as far as possible from India. His response to fierce clashes between Afridis and the British that had occurred in 1897 (two years prior to Curzon's arrival in India) was to change the governance structure in the Pashtun areas.

In 1901, the year Empress Victoria died, a new unit of British India, the North-West Frontier Province, was created for the Pashto-speaking frontier spaces that Lahore had hitherto supervised, including the districts of Hazara, Peshawar and Kohat and the trans-Indus portions of Bannu and Dera Ismail Khan. Henceforth, the frontier would be managed directly from Calcutta, without an intermediary role by Lahore.

The hard feelings this caused among the Raj's officers in Punjab were nothing compared to the reaction of a larger number against Curzon's next tilt at India's imperial design: the division, in 1905, of the large eastern presidency, Bengal, into two provinces, a western half (inclusive of Bihar and Orissa) with a large Hindu majority, and an eastern half (inclusive of Assam), where Muslims outnumbered Hindus.

Whatever the truth or untruth in Curzon's claim that he was splitting Bengal for administrative convenience, many Hindus in Calcutta and elsewhere saw an intention to weaken a growing nationalist movement. Evidence of Curzon's opposition to the INC, to Bengali intellectuals and to Indians obtaining a say in governance would surface later (it was his wish, he wrote in a private letter in November 1900, to 'assist [the Congress] to a peaceful demise'[80]; but even in 1905, it was clear that Curzon had not only given tangible shape to divide-and-rule, he had also struck at Bengali pride.

By now many Bengali-speakers were also English-speakers, more so than speakers of other Indian languages. Progress in education had brought them leadership roles in the INC and other Indian platforms. Now they were to be diminished in their own Bengal. While the better-educated Hindus would amount to a minority in the eastern half, Bengali-speakers would be reduced to a minority in the western half, which Bihar and Orissa could dominate.

Opposition was expressed through a boycott of British goods and campaigns for swadeshi. The 1905 defeat of Russia by Japan had boosted the sense that Asians could stand up to Europe. While poet Rabindranath Tagore (1861-1941), born in eastern Bengal, came out with *Amar Shonar Bangla* (My Golden Bengal), *Bande Mataram* (I Bow to Thee, Mother), the refrain in Bankim Chandra Chatterji's song in praise of Bengal, became the rallying cry of partition's opponents. In parts of eastern India, bands of Hindus employed the politics of assassination between 1908 and 1910.

The ferment over Bengal was not confined to Bengal. The INC asked for the division to be annulled. Lala Lajpat Rai, who had participated in the Congress's 1900 session in Lahore and helped create Bradlaugh Hall as the INC's space in Lahore, entered the fray, as did the INC leader from Poona, Bal Gangadhar Tilak (1856-1920). With the orator Bipin Chandra Pal (1858-1932) sharing the stir's leadership in Bengal, newspapers spoke of a pan-Indian 'Lal-Bal-Pal' trio.

However, this was hardly the whole story. Not only were most of Bengal's Muslims happy with a Muslim-majority province in the east (there were exceptions), Muslims across India were troubled by the Hindus' opposition to it. Those who remembered that the 1882 novel *Anandamath*, where Bankim's *Bande Mataram* first appeared, had an unmistakable anti-Muslim tinge, became especially pessimistic.

Though in east Bengal men like 'A.K. Fazlul Huq and Nibaran Chandra Das preached non-communal ideas through their weekly *Balaka* and monthly *Bharat Suhrd*',[81] a serious Hindu-Muslim dialogue, was not, as far as one can tell, initiated at this juncture, whether by Muslims or Hindus, Punjabis or Bengalis. What *was* accomplished was a pivotal meeting, in Simla, between a large and influential Muslim deputation and Curzon's successor as India's Viceroy, Lord Minto.

Such a meeting was desired by Muslim leaders in part because of the stir against Bengal's division and also because Lord Morley, the Secretary of State for India—a Liberal in contrast to the Conservative Minto—had hinted in London of a positive response to the INC's long-standing demand for roles by elected Indians in the Raj's councils. Though Curzon's distaste for such a step was widely shared among the Raj's ruling class, withholding it was increasingly hard to justify in India or even in England.

Prepared by now to partially concede the demand for elections to administering or legislating councils, the Raj was aware, too, that elections would involve Indians in mutual squabbles—perhaps, going by the reactions to Bengal's partition, in Hindu-Muslim fights. Blood on India's streets was not what the Raj desired, yet Hindu-Muslim disputes were preferable to India-England ones.

This was the background for the Simla interaction of 1 October 1906. From Aligarh, where Sayyid Ahmed had died in 1898, MAO's honorary secretary, Mohsin-ul-Mulk, painstakingly assembled the deputation, while MAO's British principal, William A.J. Archbold, was in touch with the Viceroy's staff to arrange the meeting.

Led by the wealthy, solidly pro-British and young Sir Sultan Mahomed Shah Aga Khan, the thirty-five-strong deputation consisted of prominent Muslims from every part of India, including at least five from Punjab: Shahpur's Umar Hayat Tiwana, the Punjab legislative council member who was also an army lieutenant and the owner of a large stud farm; two Lahore-based barristers, Mian Muhammad Shah Din and Mian Muhammad Shafi; and Khwaja Yusuf Shah and Shaikh Ghulam Sadiq, prominent figures in Amritsar.

The Ismailis, of whom the twenty-nine-year-old Aga Khan was the head, were counted among India's Shias, who altogether made up only a small minority of India's Muslims, but the deputation had nothing to do with sects or theology and everything to do with politics. It had brought together, for a single important occasion, Muslim leaders from across India, who for the moment formed something like a Muslim national congress.

The address the Aga Khan read on behalf of the deputation had been 'prepared by S[ayyid] H[ussain] Bilgrami* in collaboration with Mohsin-ul-Mulk'.[82] Choosing to focus not on the agitation against a Muslim province in the east but on Muslim representation in any future councils, whether municipal, provincial or national, and in the Raj's services, the address urged the

---

*A senior officer in the administration of the Nizam of Hyderabad.

Empire through its Viceroy to remember 'not merely' the Muslims' 'numerical strength' but also their 'political importance', their service 'in defence of the Empire', and their past position, lasting until 'a little more than a hundred years ago', as India's rulers.

'Representative institutions of the European type', the Aga Khan read on, would be 'new to the Indian people'. The 'greatest caution' was necessary while 'adapting' them. The Muslim community should not be placed 'at the mercy of an unsympathetic majority', which was likely to vote only for 'members of their own community'. India's Muslims were 'a distinct community'. 'In every case', the local authority should 'declare the number of Hindus and Mahomedans entitled to seats on Municipal and District Boards' and each community 'should be allowed to return [its] own representatives as is the practice in many towns in the Punjab'.[83]

The text of the address was in the Viceroy's hands well in advance of the meeting. According to a contemporary Pakistani historian who studied relevant files in London, 'the points raised in this address were discussed at length by the Viceroy, the Secretary of State for India and others'.[84] In his reply, the Viceroy stated, 'Your presence here today is very full of meaning… [A]ll you have said emanates from a representative body'. Underlining Aligarh's importance, Lord Minto referred also—even though the deputation had not brought it up—to the new province of East Bengal and Assam, 'the future of which', he added, 'is now I hope assured.'

Proceeding to what he called 'the pith of your address', the plea that 'in any system of representation whether it affects a Municipality, a District Board or a Legislative council,… the Mahomedan community should be represented as a community', the Viceroy said, 'I am entirely in accord with you'. His concluding assurance was that the Muslims' 'political rights and interests as a community will be safeguarded' in any new political arrangements.[85]

Articulated on 1 October 1906, this historic commitment for separate electorates had evidently been thought through and decided upon by the Viceroy and his advisors a few days before that date.[86] Even as the INC and most politically-conscious Hindus across India were busy demanding Bengal's reunification, the Empire had enabled Sayyid Ahmed's ideological successors to walk off with the prize of a separate Muslim electorate in India as a whole.

Writing right away to the Viceroy, an unnamed British official said: 'I must send Your Excellency a line to say that a very, very big thing has happened today. A work of statesmanship that will affect India and Indian history for many a long year. It is nothing less than the pulling back of 62

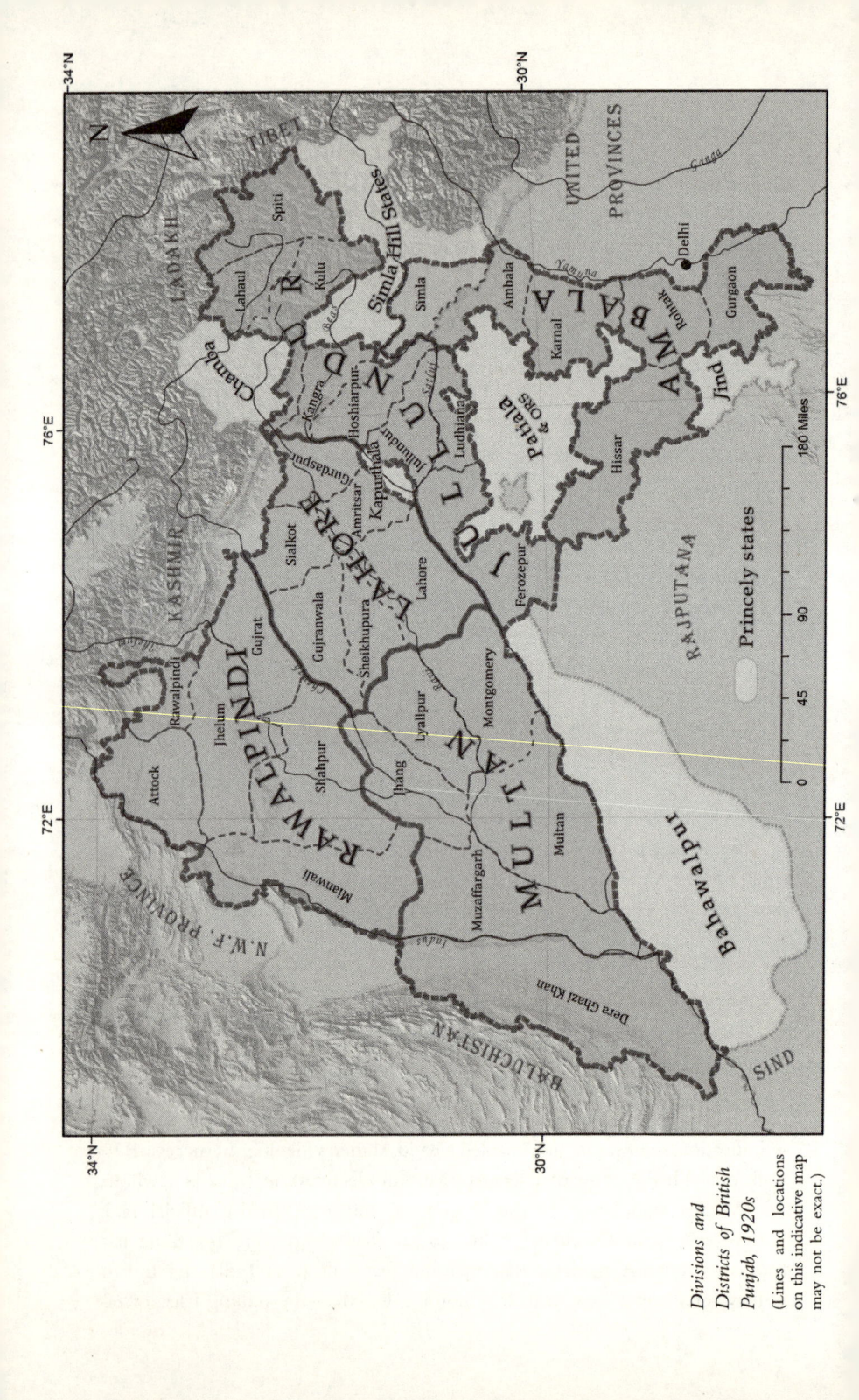

Divisions and Districts of British Punjab, 1920s

(Lines and locations on this indicative map may not be exact.)

millions of people (India's Muslim population at the time) from joining the ranks of the seditious opposition (the Congress).'[87]

Offering his evaluation, Morley told Minto that the Simla meeting 'had completely deranged the plans and tactics' of England's 'Cottonians'—he was referring to a group of Congress sympathizers coalescing around Sir Henry Cotton, MP—who could no longer portray the Indian stage as a 'case of the bureaucracy versus the people'.[88] Morley did not need to add that a picture of Muslims versus Hindus was being presented instead. Later, Minto's biographer, John Buchan, would write that the Viceroy's words were 'accepted as a charter of Islamic rights'.[89]

Learning that the Simla meeting was to take place, the *Bengalee* of Calcutta had, on 13 September, appealed for a united Muslim-Hindu front before the Government. Hindus, the journal promised, would meet Muslim 'brethren half-way', but the belated suggestion evoked no response.[90]

The Simla coup was followed, less than three months later, by the founding of the All-India Muslim League in Dhaka. A Muslim educational conference held on 30 December 1906 and attended by around 3,000 delegates supplied the occasion for the launch. Among the League's founders were Nawab Salimullah of Dhaka, the Aga Khan (who was named the new body's president), Viqar-ul-Mulk (who would succeed Mohsin-ul-Mulk as MAO's honorary secretary in Aligarh), Hakim Ajmal Khan, one of Delhi's best-known medical practitioners, and Barrister Mian Muhammad Shafi of Lahore. Along with the Aga Khan, the last two had been part of the Simla deputation.

In 1909, the so-called Minto-Morley Reforms were unveiled in an Act of Parliament in London. Despite opposition in England from several, including Curzon, the Act permitted the election of a few Indians to provincial councils and to a new all-India Imperial Legislative Council, with the franchise restricted to sections of the propertied and the educated. While Muslims would have reserved seats and a separate electorate, Europeans and loyal Indians nominated by the Raj would comprise the majority in each council. The Empire also agreed with the League that in the councils a minority community would have 'weightage', i.e. a representation larger than what the population ratio warranted.

Since consistent support to Muslim demands violated divide-and-rule, the Empire played an opposite card within two years. Despite what Minto had told the deputation in Simla, the Bengal partition was annulled in 1911. Bengali-speaking areas were reunified—if only for thirty-six years—but Bihar, Orissa and Assam became separate provinces. In another significant policy decision, the Empire moved its Indian headquarters from Calcutta to Delhi, which was detached from Punjab.

The undoing of partition shocked Muslims in Bengal and elsewhere in India. It was alleged that terror had been appeased. Already restive over European attacks on portions of the empire of the world's premier Muslim power, Turkey, Indian Muslims now harboured a powerful new grievance.

The gulf between Hindu and Muslim elites continued in Punjab, where the common 1907 stance over the Colonisation Bill quickly faded in popular memory. Urdu newspapers owned by Hindus (*Hindustan, Punjabi, Jhang Sial* and *Akash*) attacked, and were attacked by, Muslim-owned papers like *Watan* and *Paisa Akhbar*. Hindus as a community were at times targeted, and Muslims likewise.

Occasionally, though, calm was urged. In December 1909, Lahore's Hindu-owned *Akhbar-i-Aam* worried that the abuse exchanged between Arya Samajist and Muslim journals would 'bring about more disastrous results than the throwing of a thousand bombs'.[91] Agreeing on the need for mutual respect, Mahboob Alam, the editor of *Paisa Akhbar*, added in his reply that the sense of an 'Indian nationality' *could* develop among Punjab's different communities, but British rule should remain.[92]

Although the INC again met in Lahore at the end of 1909, its appeal was not expanding in Punjab. Many Arya Samajists 'had developed an attitude of confirmed hostility towards the Congress',[93] and Hindus generally were disappointed by a major INC split in 1907 which placed the two Maharashtra stalwarts, Tilak and Gokhale, in opposite camps, with the Moderates managing to oust Extremists or 'Nationalists' like Tilak and his allies.

The Minto-Morley package, for which the INC could take some credit, was initially disliked by many Hindu Punjabis. They saw the INC as having unwisely pressurized the Raj, equally foolishly sought a joint Hindu-Muslim agenda, and then failed to prevent a separate Muslim electorate. In the opinion of Lahore's *Hindustan*, the separate electorate would 'permanently cripple the notion of a common Indian nationality' and was worse than Bengal's partition. Punjab's Hindus, the journal proposed, should safeguard their 'communal interests', abandon the INC and support the Punjab Hindu Sabha, started in 1907.[94]

Soon, however, many among Punjab's Hindus and Sikhs realized that separate electorates and weightage could work to their advantage. If Muslims could get a separate electorate and weightage in Hindu-majority provinces and in India as a whole, Punjab's Sikhs and Hindus, minorities in their province, were entitled to the same. And if having been rulers in the past qualified for weightage, the Sikh claim in Punjab was at least as strong as the Muslim claim in Delhi, UP and elsewhere.

In another crucial area, education, Punjab's Muslims were registering only meagre progress. Numbering about 53 per cent in the province in 1911-12, they made up only 24 per cent of Punjab's college students and 24 per cent also in the province's schools.[95]

■

One talented Muslim who had joined the INC in 1906 and stuck to it was Muhammad Ali Jinnah (1876-1948), born in Karachi to Gujarati-speaking Ismaili parents and trained in law in London. He was not part of the deputation in Simla. About three months after Minto's announcement there, Jinnah attended the end-1906 INC session in Calcutta where the president-elect, Dadabhai Naoroji, asked for Swaraj, using the Hindi word. Jinnah served as Naoroji's private secretary during the session.

In 1908, Jinnah unsuccessfully defended Tilak in a Bombay court. Deemed guilty of sedition, Tilak was sentenced to six years in prison; he served this term in Burma. But the Congress personality to whom Jinnah was closest was Gokhale, who said of his young Muslim friend:

> He has true stuff in him, and that freedom from all sectarian prejudice which will make him the best ambassador of Hindu-Muslim unity.[96]

Having focused from his law school days on a legal-cum-political career, in 1909 Jinnah—already, at thirty-three, a flourishing Bombay lawyer—took the Minto-Morley opening and entered the Imperial Legislative Council by winning Bombay's Muslim seat. Four years later, after spending eight months in Europe and England in the company of Gokhale, he joined the Muslim League.

This 1913 decision was linked to the turmoil in India's Muslim community over what was happening to Turkey and its possessions. In 1911, when Italy attacked Libya's Tripoli, then part of the Turkish empire, the British had barred Turkey from crossing Egypt to defend its territory. In the Balkan wars of 1912-13, Greeks, Bulgars and Serbs routed the Turks.

Joined to Turkey's humiliation was the possibility of Europe's non-Muslims controlling the sacred sites located in the Turkish empire's territory, including Mecca, Medina, Najaf, Karbala and Jerusalem. India's Sunni Muslims, some of them inclined to think of the distant Turkish Sultan as their religious head, were disquieted, and Muslims who were not Sunnis seemed to share the unease. The Muslim League took up Turkey's cause, and Jinnah, who had not only stayed aloof from it thus far but also questioned separate electorates, joined the League, while not relinquishing his Congress connection.

A year later, when World War I started, and Turkey aligned itself with the Empire's foe, Germany, India's Muslims felt even more conflicted. Yet opportunity, too, seemed close at hand. If only to placate India's Muslims, the Empire might allow political advance in India, especially if the INC and the League jointly asked for it.

Armed with such hopes, Jinnah sought allies and quickly found them. Although Gokhale died in 1915—he was only 49—Tilak, mellower after a long incarceration in Burma and back in the Congress, agreed with Jinnah. Another valuable supporter was an Irishwoman prominent in the INC, Annie Besant, who had made Indian Home Rule her mission.

At the end of 1916, thanks to the efforts of several including Tilak, Besant and Jinnah, who was now forty-one, the Congress and the League, meeting in Lucknow at the same time for their annual sessions, agreed to ask for 'early self-government' based on direct elections, separate electorates for Muslims and Sikhs and weightage for minorities, e.g. for Muslims in UP and for Hindus and Sikhs in Punjab.

For the first time since 1857, Muslims and Hindus had jointly asked for the same thing.

■

In Punjab, Turkey found a champion in the journalist, poet and orator, Maulana Zafar Ali (1873-56), owner and editor of Lahore's *Zamindar,* which his father had started in 1903. Born in Sialkot into a family that evidently saw itself as Janjua Rajput, Zafar Ali went to schools in Wazirabad and Patiala before graduating from MAO in Aligarh. Warm towards the INC and the notion of Muslim-Hindu unity, and a supporter of the successful 1907 stir against the Colonisation Bill, he also sought 'worldwide Muslim unity'. Evidently his 'exhilarating public oratory and lively literary style were immensely popular among Punjabi Muslim youth'.[97]

Under his editorship, the *Zamindar* became Punjab's 'foremost Urdu daily... attaining a circulation of well over 20,000 during the Balkan wars'. Apparently 'some paid two pice to buy a copy and one anna to have it read out to them'.[98] Zafar Ali's uninhibited criticism of the Empire for not supporting Turkey in the Balkan wars annoyed the Raj, which from time to time banned his paper and restricted his movements, but he was unfazed. In 1913, he visited Constantinople and personally handed to the Sultan the donations he had raised in Punjab for the Turkish cause.

Elsewhere in India, Zafar Ali's passion was matched and at times exceeded by Muhammad Ali (1878-1931) in his papers, the English-language *Comrade* and the Urdu *Hamdard* (both published from Delhi, though the *Comrade* had started out in Calcutta), and also by Abul Kalam Azad (1888-1958), whose powerful yet stately prose appeared in *Al Hilal,* printed in Calcutta.

A graduate of Oxford and MAO, Muhammad Ali was born in Rampur, 150 miles east of Delhi; Azad, who was ten years younger than Muhammad Ali and fifteen years younger than Zafar Ali, in Mecca, to an Indian father and an Arab mother. While Muhammad Ali's father, a courtier to the Nawab of Rampur, had joined his chief in supporting the British in 1857, Azad's father had sided with the rebels and therefore ended up in Mecca.

From 1911 onwards, Muslims throughout India were stirred by the words, written and spoken, of Azad, Muhammad Ali, Zafar Ali and many others equally fervent on the question of Turkey and the Empire's attitude to it, even if not always as eloquent.

One man who seemed unwilling to be caught up in the excitement over Turkey, though he helped stimulate it, was Punjab's celebrated poet, Muhammad Iqbal (1876-1938). Born in Sialkot in a tailor's family of Kashmiri Brahmin origin (a forefather had converted to Islam), Iqbal studied in Lahore's prestigious Government College, where he was influenced by Thomas Arnold, a British scholar of Islam who had earlier taught at MAO.

While in his twenties Iqbal wrote powerful Indian nationalist poetry, lauding, in *Saare Jahaan Se Achha,* the country of Hindustan, and rebuking, in *Naya Shiwala,* both the Brahmin and the Mullah for spreading strife. The latter poem called upon Hindus and Muslims to raise a new temple of unity in India. But three years he spent in Europe and England, from 1905 to 1908, changed Iqbal's thinking.

For one thing, the world's Muslim community rather than India now became the object of his devotion. Secondly, identifying dynamism rather than asceticism as the need of his age, and asking India's Muslims to learn that quality from modern Europe, he yet insisted that dynamism's finest example had been offered by early Islam.

He wanted his people, he wrote, to 'glow with the sunbeams of desire' and to learn from the wave, which said of itself,

'When I am rolling, I exist/ When I rest, I am no more.'[99]

But if an action-oriented West had much to teach Muslims, it was nonetheless sick with nationalistic competition, which Muslims should avoid.

They should remember, moreover, that it was the intellectual culture of Islam, disseminated through Spain and Sicily, which had first propelled Europe's advance.[100]

For the rest of his life, Iqbal, using Urdu and also Persian, would be the poet of Islam rather than of India. Composed during a period (1909-13) when Turkey was being humiliated and Bengal's partition was annulled, his *Shikwa* (Complaint) and *Jawab-e-Shikwa* (Reply to the Complaint) spoke of the sufferings of the world's Muslims despite their unalloyed devotion to the One God, and of the luxuries apparently enjoyed by non-Muslims. Lahore's Muslim masses were stirred when, in his magnetic voice, the poet recited these formidable Urdu verses before them. However, Iqbal seemed reluctant to defy the Raj over Turkey.

In his time and later, Iqbal carried a powerful appeal among intellectuals in the Muslim world and beyond, but perhaps he was too urbanized and Persianized to build close bonds with the Punjabi peasant, and he was cautious about inviting the Raj's hostility.

Standing between Iqbal and Zafar Ali as far as Turkey was concerned was the Cambridge-educated Fazl-i-Husain (1877-1936). While his Bhatti Rajput forebears[101] had 'attained... distinction under the Sikhs', Fazl's father, Husain Bakhsh, was forced by the British conquest of Punjab to seek humble jobs. By 'dint of ability and hard work', Husain Bakhsh rose to become a district judge in Peshawar (one of the first Punjabi Muslims to obtain that position); he nursed 'a heart-felt desire' for his son to enter the ICS, and sent him, in 1898, to Cambridge.[102]

A journal that Fazl intermittently kept in Cambridge conveys the inner thoughts of a talented Punjabi Muslim facing the end-nineteenth-century world. On 25 August 1900 he wrote:

> Endowed with more than average intellectual capacities and ennobled with more than average noble blood and descent, not lacking moral upright[ness] and practice, nor standing in want of tolerable symmetry of physique—am I inferior simply because I am not English born? Am I to be a slave because I am an Indian? Little though I find admirable in the Indian life or morals, still I am not ashamed of the land. Inseparably connected with it as I am, I cannot disavow the bonds of over two or three thousand years, which connect me with the land.
>
> During the days of territorial sovereignty, there was no united India, nor ever there will be any unless it is under the sway of... a foreign militant

ruler. But in that independence, that sovereignty of the Rajas there was a social bliss, moral purity and religious candour. What was wanted? Only a political tie to keep these independent Rajas together—a federal union,... but bad luck and corruption could scarcely face the marauding bands which poured into India from the North West Frontier.[103]

This was a very 'Rajput' take on how India lost her sovereignty. Before Cambridge, Fazl had studied at Lahore's Government College, where Iqbal was among his classmates. Though failing to enter the ICS, Fazl passed the London Bar exams, returned to India as a barrister, and for four years practised law in Sialkot before moving to Lahore in 1905.

From later diary entries by him, we get rare pictures of the customs, psychologies and social tensions of turn-of-the-century Punjab. To celebrate Fazl's return from England, his maternal uncle gives a feast for Muslims and Hindus in the home town of Fazl's mother, Batala. In Sialkot, Fazl rents a house vacated by a Hindu barrister called Kaul who had failed to click in the town's courts; but Hindu lawyers in that Muslim-majority town make more money than Muslim lawyers.

Fazl perceives 'enmity' and 'envy' in them when he succeeds. A successful Hindu pleader, Prabhu Dayal, calls at Fazl's home, 'awkwardly' handles the host's 'picture books'—so writes the host—makes 'crude and obnoxious' jokes, and shows no 'power of conversation'.[104] Needing a munshi for his practice, Fazl tries to find a suitable Muslim but has to engage a Hindu called Mangal Sein.

Interestingly enough, Fazl-i-Husain joined the INC in 1905, the year when he moved to Lahore, which was also the year when Bengal was partitioned. But he also went to Dhaka for the 1906 launch of the Muslim League, and started something resembling a Muslim League unit in Punjab. A different, larger and more loyalist provincial unit of the League was put together by Barrister Mian Muhammad Shafi, 1869-1932, an Arain from Lahore who had studied in England nine years before Fazl, and who also went to Dhaka.

Associating with the Anjuman-i-Himayat-i-Islam in Lahore, Fazl-i-Husain also tried to strengthen the still-new Islamia College. However, it was only in 1913, evidently, that Fazl-i-Husain's 'vigorous' interest in political affairs began, linked, we must assume, to the Balkan wars.[105]

In 1915, Fazl-i-Husain—able, ambitious, nationalistic and conscious of a superior social status—was one of two Punjabis seeking to enter the provincial legislative council from the 'general' Punjab University constituency, where Hindu voters comprised a large majority. The other candidate was Kapurthala's

Raja Harnam Singh, whom we have come across more than once before.

Despite his being a Congressman, Fazl was heading to a defeat, above all, it seems, because he was a Muslim. However, Harnam Singh's papers were rejected on the ground that he belonged to a princely state rather than to British Punjab, and Fazl entered the council. The experience convinced him of the usefulness of a separate Muslim electorate.

Thereafter, Fazl-i-Husain went to the end-1916 assemblies of the League and the Congress in Lucknow and joined Jinnah, Tilak, Mrs Besant and a few others as 'the authors of the Congress-League Pact',[106] in which separate electorates were accepted by both bodies. Ten months later, in October 1917, a Punjab Political Conference chaired by Fazl ratified the Lucknow Pact. A Hindu businessman with Brahmo sympathies, Lala Harkishen Lal, served as the head of the reception committee for this conference.

Demanding genuine political reform in Punjab, which Michael O'Dwyer, the province's governor from 1912, was vocally opposing, the conference, it seems, helped 'galvanize' what people elsewhere in India had called a 'politically lethargic' province.[107]

Fazl was now the president of the INC's Punjab unit and also the general secretary of the Muslim League's provincial branch.[108] The cautious Shafi League in Punjab had been disaffiliated by the All-India League and a 'progressive' group led by Fazl-i-Husain accredited in its place.

■

'Out of a total of 683,149 combatant troops recruited in India between August 1914 and November 1918, 349,688—about sixty percent—came from the Punjab.'[109] Also indicating the province's centrality in India's war role was the fact that its governor, Michael O'Dwyer, was the only provincial officer on the committee organizing recruitment in India as a whole. Three members of the Viceroy's executive council, the secretary of the Army Department, and two Indian princes were the others on the committee.

Turkey entering the War at Germany's side in November 1914 added to the vulnerability of the Middle East's oilfields and of the Suez Canal. In consequence, thousands of Indian soldiers were sent not only to France but also to Iraq, Egypt and East Africa. Large early casualties near Baghdad and, earlier, in France, where two brigades of the Lahore division lost half their men within a few weeks of arrival, created challenges for recruitment in India.

The Raj came up with new strategies. New classes and castes were added to the roster of 'martial races'. The limiting procedure whereby army representatives recruited Muslims in Rawalpindi, Sikhs in Amritsar, Dogras in Jullundur and Hindu Jats in Delhi was done away with. Now each district in Punjab did its own recruiting.

Even more importantly, the district's DC, rather than an army officer, was made the chief recruiter. As we have found, in Punjab the DC 'was the government for the vast bulk of the people in his district'.[110] 'The civil and military structures in the province', working separately hitherto, now 'coalesced into a formidable machinery' for generating the soldiers needed.[111]

Virtually every civilian functionary, down to the village level, was given a recruitment target. The zaildar (a big landlord was usually given that post) was expected to find a minimum from the zail of villages he headed, a responsibility he shared with the village lambardars under him.

Also pressed into service during this four-year-long exercise were Punjabis who possessed clout: landlords, pirs and sajjada nashins in the western districts, wealthy Sikhs in central Punjab, and prominent Hindu Jats in the east. Rewards accompanied pressure: 180,000 acres of valuable canal colony lands were set aside for officers and men fighting with distinction, and a further 15,000 choice acres for those who most effectively aided recruitment.[112]

Titles were another inducement. Thus, Shahpur's Umar Hayat Tiwana (who joined battle himself at the European front) became Sir Umar Hayat Tiwana, Khem Singh Bedi became Sir Khem Singh Bedi, and Chhotu Ram, an influential Jat figure in Rohtak district, was made a Rai Sahib. A slew of new nawabs, Khan Sahibs, Khan Bahadurs and Rai Bahadurs emerged. For other helpers, there were swords of honour and grants of money or land. Given 'an opportunity to entrench their positions', many Punjabis 'responded with alacrity and scrambled to furnish men and material'.[113]

There were two difficulties that O'Dwyer and his men had to overcome. One was posed by the Ghadr movement associated with the Delhi-born Kayasth, Lala Har Dayal (1884-1939), and a group of Sikhs residing in North America. A revolutionary, an Arya Samajist and an academic at different points in his life, Har Dayal (who would die in Philadelphia) founded the Ghadr Party in 1913, while in exile in California. Its members made patriotic and revolutionary appeals, including in the journal *Ghadr* (for a time printed in Urdu, Gurmukhi and Gujarati), to Indian immigrants in North America.

When, in the summer of 1914, about 350 Indians on board the *Komagata Maru*, most of them Sikhs, were denied entry into Vancouver and sent back with their ship to India, some amongst them seemed willing to embrace the Ghadrite call. As their ship landed in Calcutta, a riot and firing occurred;

eighteen Sikhs were killed and twenty-five injured.

Between October 1914 and September 1915, Punjab saw bomb attacks and gang robberies at the hands of suspected Ghadrites who included, it would seem, some from the *Komagata Maru*. The militants hoped to hinder recruitment by adding to the anxieties that depressing letters from the front had caused, but their acts were quelled and the danger to the Raj passed.

Whether Muslims in Punjab and elsewhere in India would fight for the Empire against Turkey was an even bigger question. The Raj answered it by declaring that the Empire's primary foe was Germany. In allying with Germany, Turkey had erred. Though fighting Turkey, the Empire was not fighting Islam.

Before Turkey opted to stand with Germany, Muslim leaders in India like Muhammad Ali and his older brother Shaukat Ali had sent cables urging its Sultan to stay neutral. Though their pleas were spurned, the brothers still could not bring themselves to support the Empire against Turkey. Neither could Zafar Ali or Azad. All four were interned and their papers ceased publication, but sympathy for their views was harboured by many of India's Muslims, including in Punjab.

One sign of this was the naming of Muhammad Ali as the Muslim League's president for 1917. In Ali's forced absence, his portrait occupied the chair in Calcutta, where the League, until now a wholly deferential body, gathered for its annual session.

However, Punjab's Muslim chiefs—big landlords, pirs and sajjada nashins—seemed perfectly willing to accept the Raj's assurances and offers. Thanks to the chiefs' wholehearted backing, the districts of Rawalpindi, Jhelum, Gujrat, Shahpur, Gujranwala, Sialkot and Lahore sent tens of thousands of Muslim soldiers to the War. Sikhs from Punjab's central districts and Hindu Jats from eastern districts also joined in large numbers.

A fatwa from Maulana Ahmed Raza Khan Barelvi (1856-1921), the guide of the 'Barelvis', as they were called—who in terms of sect probably constituted the majority grouping among Punjabi Muslims—aided the Raj. Since the Ottomans did not belong to the Prophet's Quraish tribe, they could not claim, the Maulana declared, to be Islam's caliphs. His fatwa cleared the way for many pirs in Punjab to continue supporting recruitment into the army.[114]

Although the Raj successfully met the Empire's war demands, Punjab was altered in the process. First, the civil-military merger that took place had the effect of militarizing the provincial bureaucracy. Secondly, the close involvement of the 'landed gentry' in recruitment created 'an influential rural-military lobby' in Punjab's large countryside.[115]

In July 1918, the Empire responded to the self-government pleas that the Congress and the League had jointly made in late 1916 by announcing the Montford Reforms, named after Montagu, Secretary of State for India, who had made a long India visit in 1917, and Chelmsford, the Viceroy. Enacted at the end of 1919, the Reforms offered only a terminological change at the centre, turning the Imperial Legislative Council into the Central Legislative Assembly, but real, if modest, improvement in the provinces.

Provincial legislatures elected under a restricted franchise—enabling about 10 per cent of India's adult males to vote—would have the power to control a few subjects, the rest remaining under the Raj's governor and his nominated executive council. Each province would thus be governed by a 'dyarchy' or pair of authorities, one an elected 'ministry' and the other an unelected 'council' possessing more vital powers. The Montford Reforms also made it a little less hard for Indians to enter the civil service and the army's officer corps.

Separate electorates for Muslims and Sikhs, endorsed in the Congress-League demand, were put in place by the Reforms, as also weightage for minorities, and a distinction was drawn between urban and rural seats: contests for the latter were restricted to those belonging to designated agricultural tribes. Landowning rural groups and dependable others obtained the bulk of the voting franchise.

In the cities, those paying at least ₹2,000 in income tax or ₹50 in municipal tax could vote. In the villages, loyalty was made as important a qualification as property. All commissioned and non-commissioned officers in the army, all jagirdars, zaildars, lambardars and sufedposhes, and all farmers who paid ₹25 or more in annual revenue were given the right to vote. These rules meant that among Punjab's Sikh voters there would be a 20-to-1 rural-to-urban ratio, among its Muslims 7-to-1, and among Hindus 3-to-1.[116]

For all their limitations, the new provincial councils tempted many in the INC and the League and might have been readily accepted but for new anti-sedition measures the Raj announced two months after the War ended. A wartime committee headed by an English judge, Sir Sidney Rowlatt, and influenced by fears that Germany or Russia (where the Red Revolution had occurred in 1917) might sponsor sedition in India, had recommended the measures. The resulting Rowlatt Bills contradicted any indication Montford might have conveyed of the Empire's willingness to trust Indians.

The Bills authorized arrests without trial and trials without appeal for suspected seditionists, and a two-year sentence for an Indian found with a seditious leaflet in his pocket. The provisions sounded extreme in times of peace. Moreover, the India of early 1919 to which they were introduced was tenser than pre-War India. There was inflation now, with prices doubling in some instances;[117] many felt that recruitment had been coercive; and returning soldiers looking for work experienced difficulty.

For sixty years thus far, the Empire's control over India had seemed completely secure. Now, almost all of a sudden, the scene looked different. Not only did India seem restive; a Gujarati called Mohandas Gandhi, lately emerged from the shadows of South Africa, was winning wide support for novel strategies aimed at loosening the Empire's hold.

Chapter Seven

1919-1922: TOGETHER FOR FREEDOM

Towards the end of February 1919, a post-war Punjab that had been restive even before it learnt of the Rowlatt measure heard Gandhi's call to resist the proposed new law by way of, as he put it, satyagraha, or 'clinging to the truth'.

Employing satyagraha nonviolently in South Africa, thousands of disadvantaged Indians there had evidently achieved fair success in 1913. In 1917, two years after Gandhi's return to India, indigo-growing peasants in Bihar's Champaran district had obtained relief from European planters, also via satyagraha. In the following year, textile workers in Ahmedabad and farmers in Gujarat's Kheda district had similarly realised some of their demands.

While South Africa, Champaran, Ahmedabad, Kheda and satyagraha were strange sounds to most Punjabis in 1919, two intriguing thoughts from Gandhi had come across clearly to them. One was that Indians could openly announce an intention to non-violently defy an unjust law. On 6 February, a pledge drafted by Gandhi and signed by twenty eminent men and women was released to the press from Ahmedabad, along with an invitation to other serious-minded Indians to join:

> We solemnly affirm that in the event of these [Rowlatt] Bills becoming law and until they are withdrawn we shall refuse civilly to obey these laws,... and we further affirm that we will be faithful to truth and refrain from violence to life, person or property.[1]

Newspapers in Punjab published this declaration by the 'Indian covenanters', as Gandhi called them. They included B.G. Horniman, a Briton editing the *Bombay Chronicle,* two women, including the poet, Sarojini Naidu, a Muslim mill-owner from Bombay called Umar Sobhani, and Vallabhbhai Patel, an Ahmedabad-based barrister who had worked with Gandhi in Kheda.

Not for six decades—not since 1857—had prominent Indians announced an intention to defy an imperial law. There was no call, however, to rise against the Empire, from which Gandhi hoped to extract equality. To that end, he had in fact backed the bid for Indian soldiers to fight in World War I.

The other thought passed on by Gandhi was that Muslims and Hindus should together stand up to the Raj. The Lucknow Pact had already brought the INC and the League nearer each other; in Punjab, as we have seen, Fazl-i-Husain was leading the provincial units of both bodies. Yet, Gandhi, who turned fifty in 1919, was aiming for a deeper Hindu-Muslim alliance.

From 1915, the year of his return to India, he had befriended the Delhi-based Ajmal Khan (one of the Simla deputation) and the London-trained doctor, Mukhtar Ahmed Ansari, also of Delhi, who was elected as the Muslim League's all-India president in 1918. Backing the Lucknow Pact, Gandhi had taken care to attend the League's end-1917 session in Calcutta. Befriending, too, Maulana Muhammad Ali (whose portrait occupied the presidential chair in Calcutta) and his older brother Shaukat Ali, both detained over the Turkish question, Gandhi had publicly and privately asked the Viceroy for their release.

Some of this was known to quite a few Muslim and non-Muslim Punjabis as the Rowlatt axe fell, when Gandhi not only proposed satyagraha as India's response; he asked Hindus and Muslims to 'declare with God as their witness that we shall behave towards one another as children of the same parents, that the sorrows of each shall be the sorrows of the other and that each shall help the other in removing them'.[2]

In Lahore, the Rowlatt Bills were first criticized on 4 February, three weeks before the call issued by Gandhi and his fellow-covenanters. At a meeting organized by the city's 'Indian Association' (which Barrister Duni Chand had formed), opposition to Rowlatt was voiced by several, including Fazl-i-Husain, another rising barrister called Gokul Chand Narang, Rambhuj Dutt Chaudhuri (a Brahmin Arya Samajist and leading lawyer), Lala Harkishen Lal, the businessman who had backed the 1917 political conference chaired by Fazl-i-Husain and who controlled *The Tribune,* and Duni Chand.

Despite prominent backing, the meeting drew only a small audience, but the picture was different, following Gandhi's call, at the next gathering announced by the Indian Association. Not only was this 9 March gathering large and inclusive, its unmistakable sentiment compelled Fazl-i-Husain, who was presiding, to sponsor a resolution stipulating that 'the Indian people will be justified in taking resort to some sort of passive resistance' against the Rowlatt measure.[3]

Despite India-wide protests, the Rowlatt measure was enacted on 18 March. Gandhi's response was to ask Indians across the land to observe a hartal on Sunday, 30 March (a date soon altered to Sunday, 6 April), treat the day as one of 'humiliation and prayer' and, if possible, fasting. While a hartal for symbolizing a grievance was not a novel idea for Punjabis, combining it with prayer and fasting was, as was the design of an India-wide protest.

Neither the people of Punjab nor its British rulers were ready, however, for the dramatic and violent events that followed. Taken aback himself, Gandhi would admit in July that launching a satyagraha before training a cadre to keep it non-violent was 'a Himalayan miscalculation' on his part.[4] On the Empire's part, many of its officers had pledged themselves against abandoning Britain's God-given task of protecting an unruly people from their own leaders. No matter what it took, they would enforce the imperial will.

No one seemed clearer about this than Michael O'Dwyer (1864-1940), Punjab's lieutenant-governor from 1913 and throughout World War I. Like several of Punjab's British officers from the 1850s onwards, O'Dwyer was an Irishman. Unlike the Lawrence brothers and John Nicholson, he was a Catholic. (How the Irish functioned as both subjects and agents of the Empire is an interesting question well beyond this study's scope.[5]) The sixth son in a family of fourteen children—Michael's father was a landowner in County Tipperary—O'Dwyer joined the ICS in 1885 and from then on served in Punjab except when briefly posted as revenue commissioner in the newly-created NWFP.

O'Dwyer claimed that 'the interests of the rural masses' required him to resist political reform. Representative government was something which the 'Indian masses... neither desire nor understand'.[6] Urban Punjabis with political aspirations (e.g. men like Fazl-i-Husain, Duni Chand, Harkishen Lal, Narang and Chaudhuri) were untrustworthy, the Montford scheme was a mistake, and any disturbance called for immediate suppression. Quoting the Persian poet Saadi, O'Dwyer warned fellow officers that a spring which a twig could stop would unchecked grow into a river where an elephant would drown.[7]

Particularly objectionable from the viewpoint of men like O'Dwyer was any agitation that brought Muslims and Hindus together. As they saw it, the Hindu-Muslim question was a subject for the Empire, not for Indians.

■

Responding to Gandhi's message, the INC in Lahore and the Indian Association called for a hartal and a rally on 6 April. Two days before the announced protest, Hugh Fyson, the Lahore DC, and the city's leaders (including Duni Chand, Narang and R.D. Chaudhuri) agreed that coercion by protesters or interference from the administration should be avoided.

On the appointed day, as Lahore's businesses and manufactories went quiet, the agreement was kept by both sides. A potentially ugly confrontation between Fyson's police and demonstrators at the Nila Gumbaj Chowk (between Forman Christian College and the University) was averted through the exertions of men like Narang and R.D. Chaudhuri. The huge crowd, which included college students (a majority of them Hindus) and also many of the largely Muslim working and unemployed poor of the city, was persuaded to proceed to the rally venue, Bradlaugh Hall, situated near the northwestern end of the University campus.

Two 'overflow meetings' were held on the grounds next to the packed hall, where Chaudhuri asked Lahorites to realize that satyagraha could 'invite all sorts of suffering'. Several Lahorites fasted, too, and on 8 April *The Tribune* observed that 'patriotic' Lahore had 'faithfully carried out every part' of Gandhi's programme, revealing 'dignity and self-possession'.[8]

O'Dwyer's reply to the success of the Bradlaugh Hall rally and of demonstrations elsewhere in Punjab was to warn the next day in 'most emphatic' terms that the Punjab which did not see disorder during war 'shall not be disturbed in time of peace' and that the ones organizing protests would be held accountable.[9] Two days later, on 9 April, when Hindus marked the Ram Naumi festival, the city answered O'Dwyer with a 20,000-strong procession which a 'substantial' number of Muslims also chose to join.[10] Fazl-i-Husain's son, Azim Husain, would later recall that on this occasion 'members of both communities drank water from the same cups and exchanged head-gears'.[11]

Addressing the procession, Chaudhuri spoke of 'Hindu-Muslim unity as the supreme need of the hour'. Saiyid Mohamed Shah, Lahore's extra assistant commissioner or EAC (the highest post to which an Indian could rise in the Raj's executive branch), observed that for the first time an Indian crowd extended neither respect nor fear towards the city's officers.[12] Just as remarkably (Azim Husain would record), Harkishen Lal and Chaudhuri were permitted to address Muslims 'from the pulpit of the Badshahi Mosque'.[13]

Amritsar, too, saw a joint Muslim-Hindu response, led by ·Dr Saifuddin Kitchlew, a barrister and a philosophy PhD, and Dr Satyapal, a medical practitioner who had served for a year in Aden during the War. In Amritsar, the hartal was observed on 30 March. Some 30,000 persons attended a rally that day, women joined the ranks of the fasting, and many residents signed their acceptance of Gandhi's satyagraha rules.[14]

On 6 April, a second rally was held in Amritsar. Other Punjabi towns—including Rawalpindi, Gujranwala, Hafizabad, Batala, Sialkot, Jullundur,

Ludhiana and Ambala—also witnessed meetings. In some places, women fasted and prayed in their homes. In their secret files, the Punjab police recorded that 'opposition to the Rowlatt Act and admiration of Gandhi are practically universal'.[15]

Never before had Punjab's Muslims, Hindus and Sikhs come together quite like this. In addition to Rowlatt, Gandhi, and the Turkish question, local factors were also at play. In Amritsar, for example, the economic grievances of Hindu traders in cotton piece-goods and Hindu grain merchants converged with the pro-Turkey sentiments of the city's Muslims.[16]

In Lahore, where men like Fazl-i-Husain and Harkishen Lal had long resented O'Dwyer's disdain of urban leaders, the ordinary Hindu had been influenced by the Arya Samaj's sustained preaching for social involvement and the ordinary Muslim by the Turkey-related exhortations of Iqbal and Zafar Ali. The city was therefore ripe for Gandhi's call for a united satyagraha against Rowlatt.[17]

Recognizing that Punjabis needed a better understanding of satyagraha, Satyapal and Kitchlew in Amritsar and Rambhuj Dutt Chaudhuri in Lahore urged Gandhi to visit Punjab. Journeying from western India, Gandhi was about to enter the province when, on the night of 9 April, O'Dwyer had him arrested at Palwal station, just south of Delhi. While Gandhi was sent back on a goods train to Bombay, Kitchlew and Satyapal were arrested in Amritsar on the 10th morning and deported, also on the governor's orders.

Offended by the removal of Gandhi, Kitchlew and Satyapal, the people of Lahore and Amritsar spontaneously declared a hartal that day and took out protest marches. O'Dwyer and his officers were taken aback by the size of the processions and by the fact that Hindus and Muslims were marching jointly.

The 1925 book in which O'Dwyer would defend his actions, *India As I Knew It*, makes plain that in April 1919 it was panic, not facts on the ground, that produced in British eyes the spectre of an imminent revolution in which Afghans, Russians and Germans were also supposedly involved. 1857 was at once recalled, and protecting 'threatened' British women and children became the primary concern of civilian and military officers who had been integrated into the ruling machinery of the state during the War. As O'Dwyer records, cavalries were put in place in Lahore on 10 April, and no doubt artillery too. The governor told the police 'that if they had to fire, there was to be no firing in the air'.[18]

Troubling violence had indeed occurred that day in Amritsar, where demonstrators attacked banks, post offices and the railway station, and were fired upon by police. Those killed in Amritsar included several protesters and also five Englishmen, of whom three were bank managers murdered in their offices and one a railway official. Miss Marcella Sherwood, a British missionary, was assaulted while cycling to shut down her schools. In confused form, word of the Amritsar violence reached Lahore within hours, further agitating its British officers.

But Amritsar's tragic violence was not the opening salvo of a planned or unplanned takeover bid. It was a reckless response to the removal of the city's leaders—Kitchlew and Satyapal—and to Gandhi's arrest. As O'Dwyer would admit, 'The outbreak at Amritsar... was undoubtedly precipitated on 10th April by the deportation that morning of the two arch-seditionists, Kichlu and Satya Pal.'[19]

In Lahore, where no English person was wounded or killed, Chaudhuri led the successful effort to keep protesters peaceful. While O'Dwyer and his men assumed that the marchers were aiming for Lahore's European quarter and used gunfire to disperse them, one of the protesters would claim that their only wish, in case they saw Englishmen, was 'to show their sorrow' at Gandhi's arrest.[20] Taking Amritsar and Lahore together, around three dozen protesters were killed or wounded by gunfire on 10 April. Some in Lahore were holding Gandhi's portrait when gunned down.

Between 10 and 13 April, the Raj's writ did not run in Lahore. A huge rally held in the Badshahi Mosque on 11 April—a Friday—with some 35,000 attending, was addressed by Muslim, Hindu and Sikh leaders. Two-thirds of the crowd was Muslim and largely poor. The gathering's size and its mix of communities and classes were both unprecedented. Speaking to it, Chaudhuri underlined the hartal's success and the unanimous opinion against Rowlatt. He also called upon O'Dwyer to rely not on 'armed force' but on 'honesty, justice and moral force'.[21]

Significantly, Fazl-i-Husain was no longer among Lahore's protesters. Evidently, he doubted that the masses would remain non-violent.[22] Even so O'Dwyer wanted Fazl arrested. However, the arrest orders 'were withdrawn at the intervention of the Government of India'.[23] Fazl's rival in the Punjab Muslim League, Mian Muhammad Shafi, a successful barrister from a well-established Arain family of Baghbanpura, attempted a rapprochement between the Raj's civilian officers and Lahore's popular leaders. The latter seemed open to it, but O'Dwyer, who viewed Shafi as an urban politician unqualified to represent 'the masses', had other ideas.

The military was O'Dwyer's solution. On the 12th, ten unarmed residents were killed by army bullets near the Mosque. Two days later, on 14 April, Chaudhuri, Harkishen Lal and Duni Chand were arrested and Lahore was placed under Martial Law, with Colonel Frank Johnson as the Military Administrator.

By now the worst single episode in the annals of British rule in India had been enacted in Amritsar. Having moved there from Jullundur, where he commanded a brigade, Brigadier-General Reginald Dyer (born to an Irish brewer in Murree) took charge of Amritsar city with O'Dwyer's blessing, if not direction.

In the heart of Amritsar was a ground called Jallianwala Bagh, enclosed on three sides by walls or buildings. On the afternoon of Sunday, 13 April—a day when Hindus and Sikhs were celebrating Baisakhi—around 10,000 people, Hindus, Muslims and Sikhs gathered there. They were responding to a call from city leaders; if some were defying a ban on meetings that Dyer had imposed, others were unaware of it.

The gathering was listening to a speaker when, at about 4.30 p.m., Dyer arrived with (according to his own report written the next day) fifty rifle-carrying troops (Gurkhas, Sikhs and Muslims) and forty additional Gurkhas armed with khukris. The soldiers occupied the entrance to the ground, which was also its sole exit, and Dyer *immediately* ordered fire, without demanding dispersal.

For ten minutes or so, the Empire's Indian soldiers obediently pulled their triggers, stopping only when their ammunition ran out. Almost every bullet found a man. Going by Dyer's report, 1,650 rounds were fired. Curfew was imposed as soon as the firing ended. The city became (in Dyer's words) 'absolutely quiet' with 'not a soul to be seen'.[24] Jallianwala Bagh's dead and dying spent the 13th night with dogs and vultures.

Late on the 13th evening, O'Dwyer (as he would later relate) received in Lahore 'rumours' of what had happened in Amritsar. Some hours later, at 3 a.m., he was roused by 'two British officials' arriving from Amritsar who brought word that Dyer's troops had killed 'about two hundred' and that Dyer *'had used only British troops as the Indian troops had refused to fire'*(emphasis added).[25] The hearsay passed on to O'Dwyer by two half-informed English officers illustrates the panic that misled the province's ruling class in April 1919.

Later, on the 14th, O'Dwyer received (via General Benyon, the Lahore-based army chief for the Punjab region) Dyer's own report on the massacre, whereupon O'Dwyer sent (via Benyon) a message to Dyer: 'Your action correct and Lieutenant-Governor approves.'[26] As continuing punishment for

Amritsar's offence, the city's water and electricity were cut off by Dyer and a 'Crawling Order' was imposed, requiring all using the lane where Miss Sherwood had been assaulted to crawl on their bellies for 200 yards.

For days, stern censorship enforced by O'Dwyer kept India in the dark about the massacre. The numbers involved and the degrading punishments were not known for weeks or longer. Official estimates released much later stated that 379 had been killed and over 1,000 injured in the Bagh, but actual numbers were much higher.

In Punjab, stories of the massacre passed by word of mouth sparked demonstrations, including violent ones, to which O'Dwyer and his officers reacted in a manner that again recalled 1857. In Gujranwala, for instance, where property had been damaged, three RAF aircraft hit residents—Muslims, Sikhs and Hindus—from the air with bombs and machine guns *after* demonstrators had dispersed.

Twelve were killed and twenty-four injured in these air attacks of 14 and 15 April. On the 16th, Martial Law was imposed in Gujranwala district and elsewhere in Punjab. While Martial Law Notice No. 2 of Gujranwala warned shopkeepers of flogging if they refused to serve policemen or soldiers, Notice No. 7 ordered residents to dismount and salute when an officer appeared.[27] In Lahore, Colonel Johnson ordered students of three colleges to report several times a day to military authorities at different venues. Devised to punish presumed sympathy rather than actual offence, the order compelled students to walk up to seventeen miles a day during a hot April.[28] In a spate of summary trials held under Martial Law, scores of Punjabis were sentenced to death or long prison terms.

A non-existent revolutionary plot was crushed by the Raj. Punjab, including Amritsar and Lahore, returned to 'normal'. And Gandhi halted his satyagraha. But the Empire's reputation was in tatters. Soon both O'Dwyer and Dyer were obliged to return to Britain, but they remained unrepentant, and the honours they received from supporters at home—including Rudyard Kipling, a major contributor to a purse presented to Dyer—added to Indian revulsion.

■

At the end of May, O'Dwyer was replaced as governor in Lahore with an ethnographer-administrator, Edward Maclagan, and in October a British judge, Lord Hunter, was asked to head a committee to investigate the Punjab violence.

The Empire was far from being defeated. The rifle was not its sole weapon. While army openings continued to attract peasants in Punjab and elsewhere, the Raj could also dangle jobs before the educated unemployed, councils before the ambitious, and titles before the rich and the vain. Before 1919 ended, Mian Muhammad Shafi, the Baghbanpura barrister, was taken on the Viceroy's council in Delhi.

The Raj could hope, too, for a revival of the Hindu-Muslim divide, which competition for jobs, councils and titles was likely to sharpen. In particular, the new provincial councils (which O'Dwyer had greatly disliked) were capable of trapping politically-minded Indians in personal and communal rivalries.

On his part, Gandhi, released upon his return to Bombay but banned from visiting Punjab, was not finished either. While protester violence in Amritsar, Delhi, Ahmedabad and Bombay had damaged his satyagraha strategy, he tried to recover by instructing a halt to defiance, declaring before a large crowd in Ahmedabad on 13 April that if Swaraj was possible only by slaughtering Englishmen, he 'for one would do without Swaraj',[29] and by connecting personally with Punjab.

At the end of October, soon after the ban on his entry was removed, he arrived in Lahore to learn about what had happened in the province. Dissatisfied with the Hunter Committee's terms of reference, the Congress had named its own inquiry committee of which Gandhi was a member. In Lahore (where he stayed in the home of the imprisoned Rambhuj Dutt Chaudhuri), and also in Amritsar, Gujranwala, Kasur, Lyallpur and a dozen other places, Gandhi used the opportunity to bond with Punjabis.

'One seething mass of humanity' had greeted Gandhi on his arrival at Lahore station. Muslims, Hindus and Sikhs joined in the welcome. In Amritsar, he was honoured at the Golden Temple and taken to a mosque thronged by members of all communities. Many Punjabi women took to the khaddar (hand-woven cloth) and the charkha (spinning wheel) that Gandhi was popularizing. The Punjabis' 'frankness and... plain living' struck him, and he in turn was frank with them. Losing self-control, some in Punjab, he said, had taken to violence; losing self-respect, others had obeyed the Crawling Order.[30]

He also sought funds for a Jallianwala Bagh memorial, not, said Gandhi, to engender 'ill-will or hostility to anyone', but as 'a symbol of the people's grief' and a reminder of 'the sacrifices, through death, of the innocent'.[31] Donations picked up after Gandhi declared that he would, if necessary, sell his ashram in Ahmedabad to finance the memorial. Fear of the Raj, not lack of sympathy, had caused the earlier sluggishness.

Muslim leaders troubled over Turkey invited Gandhi to their deliberations in Delhi in November. Some among them saw the defeated Sultan of Turkey as the khalifa or head of the Khilafat (or caliphate) of all Sunni Muslims, including those living in India. All, including Shias, seemed horrified by the thought that European non-Muslims, victors over Turkey, would control Islam's holy places in Arabia and Iraq, hitherto governed by Turkey.

The Muslims gathered in Delhi saw the Hindu from Gujarat as a friend. Recalling a 1918 promise by Lloyd George, the British Premier, that the Allies were not 'fighting to deprive Turkey of the rich and renowned lands of Asia Minor',[32] they asked Gandhi for his ideas on how to respond to what they saw as betrayal and also, in respect of Islam's holy places, sacrilege.

Gandhi spoke in reply of possible 'non-cooperation'. If the Allies and the British played foul with Turkey, 'which may God forbid', Indians (not Muslims alone) could refuse to cooperate with British rule. They could return the Raj's titles and honours and withhold cooperation even from the councils of the Reforms Act.[33] The suggestion intrigued the Delhi gathering.

■

The climax of Gandhi's Punjab visit was the end-December annual session of the INC held in Amritsar, close to Jallianwala Bagh. More than a year earlier—before Rowlatt—Amritsar's citizens, led by Dr Kitchlew, had invited the Congress to hold its 1919 session in their city. Also meeting in Amritsar at the same time was the All-India Muslim League, chaired by Ajmal Khan, and the Central Khilafat Conference, formed by Muslims dismayed by Turkey's defeat.

Desirous of Indian participation in the new councils created by the Reforms Act, the Raj had released many political prisoners, including the Ali brothers, Zafar Ali, Kitchlew and Satyapal. However, hardened by Punjab events, most INC leaders were inclined to distrust the Empire. Troubled over Turkey and Islam's holy places, the Muslim League and the Khilafatists were even more suspicious.

Gandhi advised giving the councils a trial. His prestige, and support given to him by Jinnah and by the INC chair, Motilal Nehru, carried the day. Despite opposition from influential leaders such as Lokmanya Tilak of Poona and Chitta Ranjan Das of Calcutta, the INC approved in Amritsar a resolution to work the Reforms Act, 'inadequate' and 'disappointing' though it was. Gandhi argued that the release of the Ali brothers signified the possibility that the British would respect Indian sentiments, including over Punjab and the Khilafat.

Also controversial at Amritsar was Gandhi's resolution on the Jallianwala massacre, which while condemning O'Dwyer policy and Dyer's action also deplored the violence occurring at Indian hands. Following strong opposition, the latter reference was at first deleted, but Gandhi successfully insisted on its restoration, saying, 'The Government went mad, but our people also went mad. I say, do not return madness with madness but return madness with sanity, and the situation will be yours.'[34]

It was more than theory. If it came to a fight with the Empire—Gandhi had smelt that possibility—he wanted Indians to hold the moral high ground, yielding which had been part of the folly of 1857.

New things were done or said in Amritsar. Peasants and women attended the Congress meetings. Gandhi was asked to redesign the Congress structure, which henceforth would include village-level committees. At the Muslim League session—where Shaukat Ali, the older brother, wept while speaking of Muslim sepoys fighting Turkey for petty coins from the Empire—and also at the Khilafat rally, Muslims were urged to give up cow sacrifice in appreciation of Hindu support for Muslim sentiments over Turkey.

A significant figure at Amritsar was Swami Shraddhanand (1856-1926), chair of the reception committee for the INC session. Born near Jullundur and a law student in Lahore, Munshi Ram, as the Swami was known before 1917, had headed the Punjab Arya Samaj and founded an innovative yet traditional college called Gurukul at Kangri (near Hardwar), where, in 1915, Gandhi first met him. The two were introduced to each other by a common British friend, Charles Andrews.

One of the earliest to sign the satyagraha pledge against Rowlatt, Swami Shraddhanand became nationally famous after 30 March 1919, when, baring his chest before the Raj's soldiers during a Delhi protest, he dared them to fire. The common stance of men like Swami Shraddhanand and the defenders of Khilafat was part of the fragile newness of Amritsar.

∎

Events conspired to preserve the Hindu-Muslim front. A Muslim deputation led by Muhammad Ali that went to England in March 1920 to urge Prime Minister Lloyd George not to sever Islam's holy areas from Turkish control was told by the premier that there was no reason for Turkey to escape the 'justice, the pretty terrible justice', that Germany and Austria had received.[35]

In the middle of May, Europe's terms for Turkey became known. Not only was Turkey to be deprived of all its colonies and Greek-majority areas,

Mecca and Medina were to be placed under a pro-British chieftain. While France would control Syria, Britain was to 'guard' Iraq, which contained Karbala and Najaf, as also Palestine, which included Jerusalem. Islam's key sites were thus all to fall under the authority of Christian countries.

Following the revelation of these terms, Muslim India's indignation swelled to a peak. A few days later, also in May, India as a whole was offended by the report of the Hunter Committee on the Punjab events. Although Dyer was held guilty of 'a grave error of judgment', the report offered weak recommendations and exonerated O'Dwyer. Worse, the House of Lords gave Dyer a vote of approval and British admirers presented him with a sword of honour and 20,000 pounds.

Not Punjab alone but all of India seemed to feel abused by the Empire. Hindu and Sikh aversion joined Muslim dislike, and Gandhi sensed a 'once-in-a-hundred-years' opportunity (he used the phrase more than once in August 1920[36]) to build a Hindu-Muslim alliance and strike for independence. From May 1920 onwards he presented 'Non-violent Non-cooperation' as a strategy to all willing to fight, including the INC, the Muslim League and the Khilafat Conference.

The last-named body was the first to embrace Non-cooperation, yet before long all were on board. The range of support was quite remarkable. Swami Shraddhanand was in favour. So was Tilak, a hero for many Hindus. So was Lala Lajpat Rai, who had returned to India at the start of 1920. The start of the War had caught him in London, from where he travelled to America, his home for much of the War.

The Ali brothers and Abul Kalam Azad were passionate about Non-cooperation. Jinnah said he agreed with its principle though not with the stage-by-stage programme.

Among Muslim Punjabis, the recently-released Zafar Ali championed Non-cooperation, as did Kitchlew and Ataullah Shah Bukhari, also of Amritsar and a powerful orator. However, Iqbal stayed aloof, and so did Fazl-i-Husain.

For a few days in November 1919, Iqbal and Fazl-i-Husain had together led a city Khilafat committee for Lahore, with the latter as president and Iqbal as secretary.[37] However, Non-cooperation did not attract either of them. Some months later, when, inspired by the Ali brothers, several professors and students left Aligarh's loyalist MAO College and started an independent institution, the Jamia Millia Islamia, Gandhi urged Iqbal to become its first Rector, saying, 'The Muslim National University calls you'.[38] The poet declined the invitation.

In September 1920, Lajpat Rai presided over a special Congress session in Calcutta that endorsed Non-cooperation. Meeting alongside, so did the Muslim League. Later in the year, when the Congress's regular session was held in Nagpur, those who had opposed Non-cooperation in Calcutta also came round. A handful of dissenters in Nagpur included Madan Mohan Malaviya, the conservative Hindu who had chaired the Congress in 1918, and Jinnah.

It was at this session, which confirmed Gandhi's ascendancy, that Jinnah left the Congress. Concerned that mass protests would lead to violence, Jinnah was equally if not more troubled by Nagpur's decision to alter the Congress's goal from 'Swaraj within the Empire' to just 'Swaraj', i.e. whether within or outside the Empire. In 1920, despite Indians' pervasive distaste for the Empire, Jinnah thought that quarrelling Indian groups needed an external authority as an arbiter of last resort.

This, of course, was in line with Sayyid Ahmed Khan's position in the 1880s and 1890s and a view that some Hindus too shared, like Malaviya in Nagpur. Most Indians in 1920, however, no longer accepted the indispensability of the Empire.

In 1920 and 1921, the Non-cooperation train rolled forward with surprising speed. The Congress, the League and the Khilafatists suggested that the agenda could include some or all of the following items:

- Staying clear of the new councils
- Returning the Raj's titles and honorary posts
- Quitting the Raj's colleges
- Quitting the Raj's law courts
- Resigning civilian posts with the government
- Leaving the Raj's police and army
- Non-payment of taxes

There were positive targets as well. For the Congress, these were (*a*) two million charkhas, (*b*) one crore rupees for a Tilak Swaraj Fund (Tilak died in August 1920) and (*c*) one crore Congress members.

Accepted as their guide by the INC, the Muslim League and the Khilafatists, Gandhi claimed that if the positive and negative targets were reached, if Hindus and Muslims stayed together, and if Indians remained non-violent, Swaraj would come in a year. The last five items on the negative list were undoubtedly harder and riskier than the first two, and Gandhi's insistence on non-violence was also a hurdle.

As early as in May 1920, he told his Muslim allies: 'Even if there was a single murder by any of us or at our instance, I would leave.'[39] The point was made to others as well. If they wanted any role from him, participants in Non-cooperation had to accept non-violence as policy even if they did not believe in the principle.

Some Khilafatists advanced proposals of their own. One was hijrat: migration to Afghanistan from an India defiled by the Empire's disrespect for Islam's holy places. Another was inviting Afghanistan to invade India. Acting on the first proposal, thousands of India's Muslims, especially from the NWFP, trudged to Afghanistan, suffered, and returned. Advising against hijrat and announcing opposition to any Afghan invasion, Gandhi claimed that Non-cooperation was an effective alternative to both.

Beginning with 1 August 1920, titles were returned, thousands of students across India left the Raj's colleges, hundreds of lawyers turned their backs on the Raj's courts and, in November, prominent politicians boycotted the elections to the new provincial councils.

Much of India witnessed unusual happenings. High caste Hindus went to 'untouchable' quarters. Muslims celebrated Eid without slaughtering the cow. Town-dwellers streamed into villages. Women stepped out and marched. People wore khaddar and boycotted foreign cloth or burnt it. Hundreds of thousands of new charkhas started to hum, the Tilak fund target was reached, and the Congress enlisted six million new members.

■

As the pitch rose towards the end of 1921, Indians in their thousands non-violently disobeyed laws and entered the Raj's prisons. Remarkably, fear of the Raj had disappeared, as also the fear of discomfort. Eminent figures like Allahabad's Motilal Nehru, Calcutta's Chitta Ranjan Das, Delhi's Hakim Ajmal Khan and M.A. Ansari and Punjab's Lajpat Rai cheerfully invited imprisonment.

Fresh leaders surfaced at all levels, local, provincial and national: UP's Jawaharlal Nehru, Gujarat's Vallabhbhai Patel, Bengal's Subhas Bose, Bihar's Rajendra Prasad and Madras's Rajagopalachari, all of whom courted imprisonment and became nationally known. Central to the campaign and its leading orators, the Ali brothers of UP and Bengal's Abul Kalam Azad also went behind bars. So did Abdul Ghaffar Khan of the Frontier province.

In Punjab, fifty lawyers, including Kitchlew, Lahore's Duni Chand, another Duni Chand (of Ambala), and Agha Safdar of Sialkot, gave up their legal practice, peacefully violated orders of the Raj, and embraced prison. Dr Satyapal, too, would spend the best years of his life in jail.

A remarkable ferment altered the Sikh situation. In 1919, when loyalist Sikhs were willing, even after the Amritsar massacre, to honour Dyer, other Sikhs formed a new pro-independence body, the Sikh League, with the Sialkot-born Baba Kharak Singh (1868-1963), who had been galvanized by the massacre, as its chief.

In the new climate, Sikhs objecting to the control of gurdwaras by lax or corrupt mahants created the Akali Dal to free the gurdwaras. To manage the gurdwaras, the Shiromani Gurdwara Prabandhak Committee (SGPC) was formed by these Sikh reformers. Their efforts meet with fierce resistance. When more than a hundred Sikhs attempted to recover the Nankana Sahib gurdwara, all were brutally murdered.

In the aftermath, Baba Kharak Singh was elected the SGPC president but the Amritsar DC refused to give him the keys to the Golden Temple. The result was a sustained agitation in which 198 persons were arrested, including 'three successive presidents, four successive secretaries and practically the whole of the working committee of the SGPC'.[40] The government had no option but to hand over the keys.

Two years later, when Agha Safdar, serving as the Punjab Congress president, was placed behind bars, Kharak Singh succeeded to the position, only to be arrested later. Sardar Sardul Singh Caveeshar (1886-1963), secretary of the Sikh League and of the Punjab Congress, was also among the numerous Sikhs courting prison terms.

∎

Yet the Raj succeeded—with Indian help—in turning this struggle against the Empire into a Hindu-Muslim or a Muslim-Sikh quarrel. A non-cooperating or prison-going Iqbal could have prevented this from happening, but he stayed out, as did Fazl-i-Husain. Despite energetic efforts, men like Zafar Ali and Kitchlew were unable to enthuse Muslim Punjab for Non-cooperation, which received an early blow in November 1920 when Fazl-i-Husain, who in the previous year had headed the Punjab Congress *and* the Punjab League, announced his intention to enter the new council.

Until then some Punjabis at least had thought of Fazl-i-Husain as one positioned to 'lead the Punjab to the goal of self-government through the path of Hindu-Muslim unity'.[41] His rejection of Non-cooperation was a coup for the Raj.

It also highlighted a major weakness, both within the INC and the Muslim League: the failure to win over the Punjabi farmer, who was central to the imperial project and who in some ways had benefited from British rule. Though Gandhi had tried to involve the Congress with rural India—through khaddar, the charkha and in other ways—and though, as we saw, many Punjabi peasants joined the INC's Amritsar rally at the end of 1919, the Punjab Congress, as also the Punjab League, were essentially urban parties in 1920-21. A strategy for bridging Punjab's urban-rural divide was *not* part of the Non-cooperators' agenda.

Skilfully playing his cards, Fazl-i-Husain, a successful city lawyer rather than a landlord or farmer, became the spokesman for Punjab's landlords and prosperous peasant proprietors (Muslim, Sikh and Hindu), who by imperial design dominated the council. Playing its cards with equal adroitness, and aiming to strengthen opponents of Non-cooperation, the Raj quickly named Fazl-i-Husain and also Lala Harkishen Lal as ministers in Punjab. The men O'Dwyer had scorned—the men who had stood up to Rowlatt—became the Raj's partners. Luring the politicians was shrewder than obstructing them.

Punjab's biggest all-India figure at this time, Lala Lajpat Rai, was fifty-seven when, in December 1921, he was arrested for defying a ban on meetings. Older than Gandhi by five years, respected by Punjabi Hindus of all stripes, an enthusiastic Non-cooperator and desirous of a Hindu-Muslim front, Rai however lacked a Muslim following. Nor did he strive to build it. In June 1920, he had cautioned Punjab's Muslims not to expect unlimited Hindu support, certainly not for anything like an Afghan invasion.[42]

Though Dyer and O'Dwyer had destroyed love for the Empire, desire for its titles and positions survived in Punjab. Also, calls for non-violence and financial contributions did not always find sympathetic listeners. When Gandhi toured Punjab in 1920 and again in 1921 to campaign for Non-cooperation, the Raj's police recorded that his criticisms of violence against Englishmen had not gone down well with everyone, that he was not seen as 'a superman', and that some Punjabis 'sorely resented' the suggestion of renouncing titles and donating money or jewellery.[43]

Zafar Ali's anti-Empire harangues worried the Raj, which responded by mobilizing pro-government Muslims who told fellow-religionists that Khilafat was a political question, not a religious one, and that loyalty to the king—even a king thousands of miles away—was part of India's tradition.[44]

Such arguments were vigorously contested by Maulana Abul Kalam Azad, who also addressed gatherings in Punjab for Non-cooperation. Azad carried great prestige as a scholar and orator, but the fact that he was not a Punjabi reduced his impact.

Non-cooperation faced other blows. The biggest came from Turkey itself. Its emerging leader, Mustafa Kamal, was all set to remove the khalifa—the Turkish Sultan—for whom India's Muslims seemed ready to die. Pleading from India, a Khilafat conference urged the Kamal and the Sultan to join hands, but the two were at war.

A desperate Muhammad Ali now remarked that he would assist an Afghan army that invaded India. Hindus took offence, as did the Viceroy, Lord Reading. At Gandhi's instance the Ali brothers apologized, but the damage had been done.

At ground-level, Hindu-Muslim trust was corroded by suspicion and rivalry. When a fatwa in Punjab asked Muslims to leave the Raj's police and army, it was 'widely hailed by Hindu newspapers', not because the papers were enthusiastic about Non-cooperation, but because 'Muslim preponderance in the police and the army' would be hit. 'But', a Muslim writer would later remark, the fatwa 'had no serious results as very few soldiers and policemen obeyed it'.[45] Old habits were returning: not the Raj but the other community was seen as the problem.

The Empire in any case was not going to tolerate obstacles to its recruitment agenda. When, in July 1921, the Ali brothers declared in Karachi that Muslims should not serve in the Empire's army if it fought Mustafa Kamal, the Raj decided to arrest them. Gandhi and the Congress said they would stand with the Ali brothers, but the Non-cooperation train had run into a storm.

Tempests came from more than one direction. In August 1921, Malayali-speaking 'Moplah' Muslims in Malabar (deep in the south of India) rose first against the government and then against their Hindu landlords. Many Hindus were killed and others forcibly converted. A full-scale military action by the Raj resulted in the deaths of large numbers of Moplahs. Local in origin and aim, the Moplah rebellion had nothing to do with Khilafat or Non-cooperation, and for some time the rest of India knew little about it. Yet, as stories of murder and forcible conversion travelled across the land, Hindu-Muslim trust took a hit.

Non-cooperation's climax, announced by Gandhi, was slated for February 1922, when the farmers of Bardoli in southern Gujarat, where hundreds had been trained in satyagraha, would stop paying land tax. Once Bardoli flew the Swaraj flag, so the thinking went, other places would repeat the example.

As the date neared, however, Gandhi questioned the plan. Reports he received in January had spoken of indiscipline in Non-cooperator ranks in

Calcutta, Allahabad and Punjab.[46] Two months earlier, in Bombay, a crowd of Muslims and Hindus had harassed Eurasian, Jewish and Parsi men and women who were welcoming the visiting Prince of Wales. A statement by Gandhi in December 1921 that 'by our conduct' Indians should 'demonstrate to every Englishman that he is as safe in the remotest corner of India as he professes to feel behind the machine gun' had annoyed some Non-cooperators.[47]

•

Learning (on 8 February) that in Chauri Chaura near Gorakhpur in eastern UP, twenty-two policemen had been hacked to pieces by an angry crowd of about 4,000 Hindus and Muslims, Gandhi made up his mind. In a statement issued from Ahmedabad, he called off the Bardoli defiance. The withdrawal was a shock from which the thousands of jailed Non-cooperators would take long to recover. From his prison, Lajpat Rai, for one, sent Gandhi a seventy-page letter of protest.[48]

Remembering the violent reaction when, in April 1919, Gandhi was stopped from entering Punjab, the Raj thus far had not laid hands on him. Now, after the demoralization, it seemed less of a risk to arrest him. Tried in Ahmedabad for sedition, Gandhi was sentenced to six years in prison.

Eighteen months had passed since the start of Non-cooperation, and the Swaraj that was to come in a year seemed far off, even though the Raj had received a shaking. Before his death in August 1920, Tilak had complained that Gandhi was asking too much of the Indian people. He was proved right. Non-violence, not harming the hated British, embracing jails, Hindu-Muslim unity, giving up titles, contributing money, the abolition of untouchability—each item on the long list was desirable, but also costly. In contrast, collaboration with the Raj brought gains, and there was political profit, too, in the Hindu-Muslim divide.

At least one pillar on which the three-year partnership between the INC and the Muslim League had rested turned out to be hollow. Neither Islam nor India needed a restoration of the Khilafat of Turkey's Sultan. When Mustafa Kamal abolished it, Islam survived, and so did India. However, with no Khilafat to fight for, many Muslims thought they no longer needed Hindu support, while many Hindus and Sikhs felt glad to resume life unburdened by unity with Muslims.

The Ali brothers, among other Muslims, would slowly drift away from Gandhi and the INC. So would Hindu leaders like Swami Shraddhanand, who was deeply affected by the Moplah rebellion. To a lesser degree, so would Lajpat Rai. To many of Punjab's Muslims and Hindus, the Empire once more—even after Jallianwala—seemed a better partner than the 'other' community.

Not, however, to all Muslims or Hindus. Despite Non-cooperation's defeat, a good number from all faiths remained committed to a united struggle for independence. Even those who abandoned a joint struggle acknowledged the worth of the three-year experience. Afzal Iqbal, a future biographer of Muhammad Ali, would write:

> These events formed a psychological watershed in the development of modern India… For the first time India witnessed a mass movement which shook the country and nearly paralysed the British rule. For the first time, India realized a new pride and discovered a sense of unity… For the first time, in a rare manifestation of amity and accord, Hindus and Muslims drank from the same cup…[49]

Thanks to the movement, a middle-class Hindu in Lahore who previously changed his clothes on returning home if a Muslim had touched him in the bazaar, no longer did so.[50] While registering his differences with Gandhi, Lajpat Rai would say:

> It is a fact that from 1919 to the end of 1921 Hindus and Muslims of India were fairly united… For the first time in the history of India, a Kafir preached from the pulpit of the biggest and historically… the most magnificent mosque of Northern India.[51]

Chapter Eight

1922-1942: COLLABORATION AND THE SEPARATION CALL

From an all-India perspective, the three years of Non-cooperation proved useful for the Congress, which was better organized than the League or the Khilafat body. Six million new members had joined the INC, which found footholds in most Indian villages and formed committees at village, town, district and provincial levels. Suspension of defiance did not end its activities. In Punjab, however, the 'composite' INC that remained after 1922, pledged to protect the interests of all Punjabis, was not large.

The future in the province would belong to collaboration, not to Non-cooperation, and in particular to the Unionist party, raised in 1923 'on the foundations of the agriculturalist ideology created by the Punjab Government'.[1] Behind the new party lay the energies of two men: Fazl-i-Husain and Chhotu Ram (1881-1945), a Jat lawyer from Rohtak. An opponent of trader and money-lending interests, a Congressman for four years (1916-20) and an active agent for recruitment during the War, Chhotu Ram became the spokesman in the provincial council for eastern Punjab's Hindu Jat peasantry.

Well-known Muslim and Sikh landowners belonged to the 1920-23 Punjab council, including Firoz Khan Noon (1893-1970), who was educated at Aitchison and Oxford and related to the Rajput Tiwanas of Shahpur/Sargodha; Ahmad Yar Khan Daultana (d. 1940) of the Rajput Johiyas of the Neeli Bar between Lahore and Multan; Makhdoom Raza Shah Gilani of Multan, descendant of a famed Sufi and a prominent sajjada nashin; Sunder Singh Majithia (1872-1941), also Aitchison-schooled and one of the province's biggest landlords; Jogendra Singh (1877-1946); and Baba Kartar Singh, a scion of Guru Nanak's Bedi clan.

Fazl, the city lawyer, was unlike these landowners. Nevertheless, he became their guide. With their help and with the Raj's open encouragement, Minister Fazl-i-Husain and Chaudhri Chhotu Ram created the Unionist party to champion the interests of Punjab's landed peasantry. Fazl won over many of Punjab's urban Muslims, too, by working to increase the Muslim percentage in Punjab's colleges and government departments and in the province's municipalities.

As a minister, he had ensured in November 1921 that seats in Lahore's Government College and Medical College would be divided among Muslims, Hindus and Sikhs in a 2:2:1 ratio. For Muslims, this 40 per cent presence was a great improvement, for, in 1917-18, their Government College share had been only 15.2 per cent. The Muslim presence in the Medical College had been worse.[2]

Then, in early 1923, Fazl secured passage in the council of a measure that increased Muslim representation in municipalities, including that of Lahore. His goal was to bring the Muslim presence in colleges and municipalities closer to the Muslim ratio in Punjab's population, but Hindus were not pleased by the losses they suffered. In protest, Raja Narendra Nath, a wealthy Hindu of Kashmiri Pandit origin, moved for a cut in Fazl's salary. Nath's motion was defeated, but apart from Harkishen Lal and Majithia, both of whom held official posts, all Hindus and Sikhs in the council, including Jat representatives, had voted in its favour.

Charges by Hindu and Sikh politicians that Fazl had become communal only increased his popularity among Muslims. After fresh elections held in late 1923 (under the restricted Montford franchise) had given the Unionists a clear majority in the council, Hindu members tried to prevent Fazl's reappointment as minister. Not only did the Raj stand by Fazl, it named his close ally Chhotu Ram as the 'Hindu' minister' in place of the outgoing Harkishen Lal, rejecting pressure applied on Malcolm Hailey, the governor, to appoint Narendra Nath.

Headed by the poet Iqbal, who was a Muslim League representative in the Punjab council, the province's urban Muslims too were willing to accept Fazl's lead. As the farmers' champion *and* the leader of Punjab's Muslims, Fazl-i-Husain was probably India's most significant Muslim politician in 1924.

Though spurned by the Raj, the Hindu politicians of urban Punjab were no longer inclined to turn to Gandhi, who was released on health grounds in 1924. Unhappy with what they saw as Gandhi's pro-Muslim and anti-Raj positions, they 'stood sternly aloof from his efforts'[3] when, soon after his release, he visited Lahore to improve Hindu-Muslim relations.

On this 1924 visit Gandhi tried to woo Fazl. After a meeting with him, Gandhi wrote: 'I had a very pleasant time with the Mian Saheb. His manners were most charming. He was reasonable and plausible in his conversation.'[4] But in the absence of support from Punjab's Hindu politicians, who disliked the Unionist leader and stayed away from him, Gandhi could not build an accord with Fazl.

In August 1924, Punjab's chief secretary wrote gratifyingly of 'the speed' with which the Montford Scheme's working had 'drive[n] the two main communities into open dissension' and 'urban and rural interests' into 'antagonism'.[5] The chief secretary's appraisal was spectacularly confirmed by Lajpat Rai, by this time a member of the Central Assembly. Writing a series of articles in the *Tribune* (November and December 1924), Rai argued that since Punjabi Muslims were unwilling to grant weightage to Hindus and Sikhs, Punjab should be partitioned into Muslim-majority and Hindu-majority portions. (He proposed a similar solution for Bengal.)

By this time Gandhi had undertaken, while staying in Muhammad Ali's Delhi home, a twenty-one-day fast for Hindu-Muslim unity. Marking the feeling of Punjab's Hindus that 'Gandhi had been much too favourable' to Muslims, Governor Hailey thought in December 1924 that 'our Hindus' were likely hereafter to seek strength 'from Government', not from an alliance with Muslims.[6] A year later, after many of Punjab's Hindu politicians had moved away from the Congress and towards the Hindu Sabha, Hailey rewarded them by kicking Fazl upstairs to the governor's executive council as the member for land revenue.

Though presented as a 'promotion', in reality this was a curb and a sop to pro-Raj Hindus. As Hailey said in a letter to Viceroy Reading (1 December 1925), a minister exercised 'a latitude' which the governor 'need not give' to the higher-paid yet more controllable member.[7] In an additional concession to non-Muslim politicians, Hailey gave the ministership vacated by Fazl not to a Muslim but to a distinguished pro-Raj Sikh, Jogendra Singh, who was close to Lahore's Hindu politicians.

Responding to the advances, these Hindu politicians called off a boycott of municipal elections they had launched following Fazl's legislation for stronger Muslim representation in municipalities. In May 1925, Nath informed the governor, who had been displeased by the boycott, that the Hindus would rather 'delay the attainment of Swaraj than see Muslim supremacy' in Punjab.[8]

In the 1926 elections, an alliance of non-Congress and collaborationist Hindus vindicated Hailey's overtures by defeating 'Swarajist' or Congress candidates in the province's Hindu seats. The INC, which had ended its council boycott, did well in most provinces but not in Punjab, where the success of its Hindu opponents was hailed by the Raj as 'an unmistakably adverse verdict on the policy of non-cooperation'.[9]

In appreciation of their role, one of them, the Cambridge-educated Manohar Lal, was made the education minister. The rural Hindu, Chhotu Ram, was dropped to make room for Lal, who was a Lahorite; but to retain Muslim and Unionist support, Firoz Khan Noon, the Oxford-educated landowner from Shahpur, was made a third minister.

Meanwhile, Fazl and the Unionists were taking care of themselves. In 1924, Unionist pressure forced the Raj to reduce an enhancement of canal water rates. In 1926, the Raj knighted Fazl. Also in that year, a new Punjab law advocated by the Unionists closed loopholes in the pro-farmer 1901 Act. Growing rural indebtedness required the mending: in 1928-29, moneylenders would account for more than a third of the total income tax from industry and business in Punjab.

In 1928, Sir Fazl-i-Husain as revenue member successfully tussled with the Raj and pushed through a Land Revenue Act that reduced the land tax. Nationalist Punjabis, whether Muslim or Hindu, were told by Fazl that he was only implementing the Congress policy of supporting peasants. Though communal disturbances had taken place in Multan (1922-23 and 1927), Amritsar (1923), Panipat (1923 and 1925) and Rawalpindi (1926), these seemed small in scale and did not thwart Fazl's strategy of courting two important sections of Punjabis: landowners of all faiths and urban Muslims.

All sides—the Raj, Unionists, nationalists and communalists—faced a challenge in December 1926, when Swami Shraddhanand was killed in Delhi by a Muslim, and again in June 1927, when the Lahore High Court acquitted an Arya Samaj activist, Rajpal, who had authored a pamphlet that was disparaging of the Prophet. Many of Punjab's Muslims believed a charge—levelled among others by Zafar Ali—that Hindu judges had influenced the acquittal.

In September 1927, a Muslim called Ilm Din stabbed Rajpal to death in his Lahore home. After a trial, Ilm Din was hanged in October 1929. Though, mercifully, violence did not escalate, polarization hardened.

Punjab's temper was being influenced by all-India developments too. These included campaigns among Hindus for sangathan (organization) and shuddhi (recovery of converts)—Swami Shraddhanand had been a leading proponent of shuddhi—and among Muslims for tabligh (religious preaching) and tanzim (organization); and the formation, in 1925, on the initiative of a Brahmin group from Maharashtra, of the Rashtriya Swayamsevak Sangh (RSS), which aimed, through military-style discipline, to protect Hindu interests against perceived Muslim threats.

Affected by polarization but rejecting collaboration, men like Zafar Ali and Kitchlew (the two belonged to the Congress as well as to the Muslim League) turned to tanzim. The Punjab Congress as a whole seemed divided into two groups, one led by Lajpat Rai and sympathetic to the Hindu Sabha, and the other headed by Satyapal, which relied on 'a cross-communal alliance of Hindus, Muslims and Sikhs'.[10]

In 1927 and 1928, Jinnah made a valiant bid for a nationalist accord on the basis of a grand quid pro quo: Muslim acceptance of joint electorates in exchange for three things—acceptance of Muslim majorities in Punjab and Bengal by the INC, the Hindu Mahasabha and the Sikhs; the separation of Sindh from Bombay Presidency to form an additional Muslim-majority province; and a one-third reservation for Muslims in any central legislature.

The bold proposal did not sound unreasonable. Many in the INC responded positively but Punjabi politicians of opposite views knocked it down. Knighted in 1925 on completing a five-year term on the Viceroy's council, Sir Muhammad Shafi, who headed the Punjab Muslim League, called separate electorates non-negotiable and said that Jinnah did not speak for the province's Muslims. Hindu Sabhaites said they would take joint electorates but not give up weightage for Punjab's non-Muslims. Sikh leaders were even firmer in opposing what sounded like mandatory Muslim rule in Punjab.

Sections of the Punjab INC and Fazl were open to the Jinnah plan, although Fazl, more interested in a Unionist-Raj understanding than in a Hindu-Muslim one, wanted to be sure that ministers in Punjab would not be overridden by any elected centre. In any case, at the end of 1928, an All-Party Conference in Calcutta rejected the Jinnah proposal, with the INC adhering to an alternative plan (drafted by an All-Parties Committee headed by Motilal Nehru) which preserved substantial minority weightage for Hindus and Sikhs in Punjab and Bengal and significant weightage for Muslims in UP, Bihar, Bombay and Madras.

The INC had yielded to pressure applied by Punjab's Hindu and Sikh politicians. Fate too played a part, for Lajpat Rai, who in 1928 sounded unexpectedly willing, for the sake of Hindu-Muslim unity, to free Punjab's Muslims from the burden of minority weightage, died in November that year, after being struck by police lathis during a demonstration in Lahore.

Shortly before his death, Lajpat Rai had pointed out that, thanks to their numbers, Muslims had become dominant in Punjab despite minority weightage. If, added Rai, Punjab's Hindus and Sikhs were willing to forego weightage, they would secure joint electorates and de facto Hindu rule in Hindu-majority portions of India and, later, at the centre.[11]

In publicly taking this position, Lajpat Rai had dissented from most Hindu and Sikh leaders in his province. Punjab's story might have taken a different course had the Lion of Punjab, as many of Punjab's Hindus called him, lived longer.

■

By refusing to include a single Indian in the Simon Commission, named after the British jurist heading it and tasked to tour India and propose constitutional reforms, the Empire injected life into a political scene that was stagnating. Across the country, spontaneous protests occurred against the Commission in the latter part of 1927, including the one in Lahore where Lajpat Rai was lathi-charged.

At first Irwin, the new Viceroy, had asked for one or two Indians to be named to the Commission, but Malcolm Hailey, the Punjab governor, and Geoffrey de Montmorency, an officer close to Hailey who had become Irwin's private secretary, persuaded Irwin to accept an all-white body.

A modern scholar of the period has shown that Punjab's white civilians, with whom Fazl had built a rapport, had begun to exert significant influence on Irwin in the late 1920s.[12] In the assessment of this scholar, Irwin was 'introduced to India with the help of a Punjabi guidebook.' On Hailey's recommendation, the Viceroy named Umar Tiwana, the stud-farm owner from Shahpur who had served in African and European wars, to the Secretary of State's council in London.

Between 1927 and 1929, Fazl influenced Delhi 'privately through men like Noon, Sikandar Hayat, Chaudhri Zafrulla and Ahmed Yar Khan Daultana'. After 1930, when Fazl was named to the Viceroy's council, he was able to eexest direct influence.[13]

In 1931, the Punjab officer Herbert Emerson became Home Secretary in Delhi. According to the aforementioned study, Hailey, de Montmorency (Hailey's successor as Punjab's governor from 1928) and Emerson possessed exceptional clarity and shrewdness. However, contempt for India's political class marked these 'Punjabi' civilians who wanted 'continued British control at the centre and the freest possible hand in [their] own province', desires that seemed to coincide with those of Fazl.[14]

Even as the rest of India boycotted the Simon Commission, the Punjab legislative council, influenced by Fazl and his chief Unionist colleagues, Sikander Hayat Khan of Wah and Chhotu Ram of Rohtak, appointed a committee to assist Simon. Headed by Sikander, this committee asked for the retention of separate electorates in Punjab and for eighty-three Muslim and eighty-two non-Muslim seats in a house of 165. Though Narang, Nath and a Sikh legislator on the committee, Ujjal Singh, wrote dissenting notes, Chhotu Ram supported the majority's recommendations.

■

Not even twenty-four when hanged in 1931 for the 1928 murder of J.P. Saunders, assistant superintendent of Punjab's police, Bhagat Singh, a nephew of the Ajit Singh of the 1907 farmers' stir, was born in 1907 in a village in Lyallpur district.

Active from his late teens in the Nau Jawan Bharat Sabha (NJBS), formed by radical young men in Punjab, and in the revolutionary Hindustan Republican Association (HRA), directed from UP (with Chandrashekhar Azad as its driving force), Bhagat Singh, Azad, and a third revolutionist, Rajguru, killed Saunders in Lahore on 17 December 1928 while bidding to avenge the death of Lajpat Rai. (The intended target was James Scott, the deputy police superintendent who had ordered the lathi charge that led to Lajpat Rai's death, but Saunders, newly-wed and newly-arrived in Lahore, was mistaken for Scott and killed.)

Less than four months later, in Delhi, Bhagat Singh—who with the other killers had slipped away—and a fellow radical from the HRA, Batukeshwar Dutt, threw two bombs and leaflets from the visitors' gallery into the chamber of the Central Legislative Assembly. Though a few legislators were injured, no one was killed. Singh and Dutt were seized, tried in Delhi and sentenced to fourteen years in prison. At this time, forensics connected a pistol on Singh's person to the Saunders murder, for which he and others were then tried in Lahore.

Some members of the HRA (renamed, on Bhagat Singh's urging, the Hindustan Socialist Republican Association, or HSRA) confessed their roles and gave evidence against fellow-militants, damaging the organization's reputation. However, large numbers in Lahore and across the country were stirred by the lengthy hunger-strikes undertaken by Singh and Jatindra Nath Das, a fellow-prisoner, for rightful treatment in jail. Bhagat Singh's proud demeanour and fearless utterances in court also made a deep impression.

When the fasting Das and Singh seemed close to death in prison, sentiment in their favour rose to a high pitch. Muslims joined Sikhs and Hindus in processions in Lahore, and the Raj was censured in the Central Legislative Assembly, where Jinnah and Motilal Nehru made forceful statements. Das died after a sixty-three-day hunger-strike on 13 September 1929, but on 5 October, responding to pleas from his father and the Congress, Bhagat Singh ended his fast. Excluding a short break in September, the fast had lasted, according to one account, for 116 days.[15]

Despite pleas for commutation from Gandhi and other Indian leaders, Bhagat Singh and two fellow-militants, Rajguru and Sukhdev, were hanged by the Raj on 23 March 1931.

The 1929 death of Das, which led to the resignation of two Congress members of the Punjab council, Gopichand Bhargava and Dr Mohammad Alam, and the 1931 hangings stirred a great many Indians, and the future would establish Bhagat Singh as an Indian icon. However, the romance of many in twenty-first-century India with the Bhagat Singh legend is not necessarily an accurate indication of the political realities of the Punjab of the hero's own time.

In the late 1920s or early 1930s, the NJBS, the HSRA and a third organization with which young Bhagat Singh was associated, the Kirti-Kisan Party, were not able, separately or together, to unite a sufficient number of Punjabis in an anti-imperialist struggle. Dr Alam's resignation notwithstanding, Punjab's Muslims were generally not drawn to the agenda of the revolutionaries, and Sikh involvement too was minimal. The list of the eighteen men accused in May 1930 in the Lahore Conspiracy Case, as it was called, contains no Muslim name and only one Sikh name, that of Bhagat Singh.[16] Five others who had absconded and five who had turned approver were also, it seems, Hindus. Moreover, many of the twenty-eight charged were from outside Punjab.

While their stoicism won admiration, the violence the revolutionists practised ruled out large-scale participation in their struggle, and their oft-articulated atheism may have baffled the average Muslim or Sikh Punjabi. (In jail Bhagat Singh had produced a thoughtful pamphlet titled 'Why I am an Atheist'.) Others were disappointed at the betrayal by some militants of their comrades.

Bhagat Singh's final position on violence for political aims is not very clear. 'In their last letters', Bhagat Singh and Sukhdev are said to have 'distanced themselves' from bomb attacks that took place in Bengal and Punjab in the latter part of 1930, with Bhagat Singh evidently acknowledging that in the circumstances that existed, throwing a bomb was worse than useless; it was harmful.[17]

At its end-1929 session, held in Lahore and presided over by the forty-year-old Jawaharlal Nehru, the Congress announced complete independence as its goal. The nationwide opposition to the Simon Commission's tour had buoyed its spirits, and Gandhi declared that Civil Disobedience was on the anvil. Soon a march that Gandhi led in western India against the salt tax, which hurt all Indians irrespective of religion or class, triggered great nationwide defiance, including in the NWFP, Bengal and south India, with tens of thousands inviting arrest in the first half of 1930.

Yet, Punjab played only a modest role in this phase of Civil Disobedience, which Churchill described, in the House of Commons, as having inflicted 'such humiliation and defiance as has not been known since the British first trod the soil of India',[18] and which brought the Congress firmly to the fore in most parts of the country. Several factors lay behind Punjab's limited response: the Unionists' understanding with the Raj; appreciation for the Empire entertained by many Sikh and other Punjabi farmers; the INC's failure to regain the support of Muslim Punjabis; and the pro-loyalist tilt of a number of Lahore's Hindu politicians, who did not want Muslim or Sikh Punjabis to pocket all the Raj's favours.

Launched in 1931 against Maharaja Hari Singh, an agitation for democratic rights for Kashmir's Muslim peasants did not receive the Congress's backing in Punjab. As a result, thousands of Punjabi Muslims, including many who had joined the INC during the Khilafat days, deserted the INC and moved to the newly-started Ahrar Party.

In the following year, when, after receiving the Simon Commission's report and holding two Round Table Conferences in London, the Empire announced its Communal Award for Punjab, which gave the Sikhs 18 per cent of seats in the Punjab legislature instead of the 30 per cent they had hoped for, Dr Satyapal did not protest, for Punjabi Muslims had accepted the Award. A consequence was Sikh alienation from the Congress.

Never huge in the first place, the INC's capacity to compete with the Unionists in rural Punjab had diminished. In the early 1930s, the left-wing Kisan Sabha tried to reach out to the rural poor but its impact was largely confined to Sikhs in Punjab's central districts. At this time any rural challenge to the Unionists came not from the INC—or the Muslim League—but from the Akalis, from the anti-colonial and Islamic Ahrars (who had backed the agitation against the Kashmir Maharaja) and, to some extent, from the

Kisan Sabha. In urban Punjab, where the Congress's nationwide defiance of 1930, 1932 and 1933 evoked significant support, conservative Hindus were drawn towards the Hindu Mahasabha, while radical ones gravitated towards the Communists.

•

From the 1920s onwards, Muslim-Hindu mistrust drove some Punjabis to design schemes of separation. We have looked earlier at Lajpat Rai's proposal of 1924. Three years later (on 15 December 1927), Governor Hailey wrote to Sir Arthur Hirtzel, permanent secretary at the India Office in London, of unnamed Punjabi Muslims who 'seriously [thought] of breaking away... and starting a Federation of their own... [which would] embrace the Punjab, parts of the UP, the Northwest Frontier Province, Baluchistan and Sind' and were willing to 'give up... some of our Hindu districts in the Southeast of the province'.[19]

Three years thereafter, in December 1930, Sir Muhammad Iqbal (he had been knighted in 1922) articulated the separation wish while presiding at a Muslim League session in Lucknow. Iqbal said he wanted 'to see the Punjab, North-West Frontier Province, Sind and Baluchistan amalgamated into a... consolidated North-West Indian Muslim State' enjoying 'self-government within the British Empire or without the British Empire', adding that such a state was probably 'the final destiny of the Muslims... of North-West India'.[20]

In this address, Iqbal defined neither the eastern boundary of the Punjab that he saw seceding from India nor the nature of Punjab's link with the latter. While Muslim-majority areas were his primary concern, within these areas he felt a stronger affinity with the cities. In one scholar's words, Iqbal was 'scathing about what he called Punjab Ruralism'.[21]

Three years later, another Punjabi, Choudhry Rahmat Ali, a Gujjar born in 1895 in the town of Balachaur in eastern Punjab's Hoshiarpur district, offered a more precise picture of a Muslim homeland. In a pamphlet he published in 1933 in England (where he studied at Emmanuel College, Cambridge), Rahmat Ali envisaged a sovereign Muslim state which he called Pakistan, comprising **P**(unjab), **A**(fghania—or the Northwest Frontier), **K**(ashmir), **S**(indh) and Baluch(**stan**).

From the Hindu Mahasabha side, Bhai Parmanand had said in December 1932 that he would not mind 'even statutory majority for Muslims' in Punjab provided the province's Hindu-majority areas were separated and joined to Delhi or UP.[22] Prominent personalities like Iqbal, Rahmat Ali and Parmanand were intervening in debates in the early 1930s regarding India's and Punjab's constitutional future.

Pressed by conflicting demands, HMG had invited the Congress, the Muslim League, the Unionists, the Sikhs, the Hindu Mahasabha, the princes, leaders of the 'untouchables' and other political elements to a series of talks in London. While the Congress charged that the Empire was practising divide-and-rule, its Indian and British opponents countered that the INC did not represent all of India. Both claims were valid but the Empire was naturally attracted towards the foes of its chief Indian foe, the Congress.

Churchill in London and men like Hailey in India were troubled by the success of the Salt March of 1930, a Gandhi-Irwin Pact that followed in March 1931, and Gandhi being invited to London later that year. How Hailey and Fazl persuaded Irwin not to let Dr Ansari, the Congress Muslim from Delhi, join the London deliberations has been shown in a recent study by a Western scholar.[23] As a 1970 Pakistani study also puts it, 'Fazl-i-Husain protested, and in spite of Lord Irwin's commitment to Gandhi, it was agreed not to nominate Dr Ansari.'[24] His exclusion made it easier, in Britain, to portray the INC as a body devoid of Muslim support.

The British Parliament's Government of India Act of 1935 replaced dyarchy in provinces with autonomy, while reserving significant powers in the hands of the governor and the Viceroy. The franchise was raised to 14 per cent of the adult population. Separate electorates were retained. In Punjab's 175-strong legislature, Muslims were given 48 per cent of the seats, Hindus 24 per cent and Sikhs 18 per cent.

From the Muslim point of view, this was a distinct improvement for which Fazl, who returned from the Viceroy's council in Delhi to Lahore, could claim at least some credit. Asking Punjab's Sikhs and Hindus to accept a minimal majority for Muslims before the latter demanded their 57 per cent share, he added that Punjab's Muslims—possessing 'brains, physique, virility, and faith in their future' but 'very few moneyed people' and not 'very many large landowners'—were

> a majority only in name, not in voting strength, not in local self-government, not in services. A civilized government should not let a minority be depressed, but what about the government which allows a majority to be depressed?[25]

Elsewhere, however, Fazl revealed excessive respect for the Raj, saying, 'As long as there is a single Britisher in India, the idea of an[y] Indian community dominating ... in a province like the Punjab is moonshine and nonsense.' In his view, it was up to Indian politicians to make the best use of the 1935 Act, a 'constitution [which] the British public through the British Parliament has been graciously pleased to give to India'.[26]

The Unionists intended to use the 1935 Act to extend their influence in Punjab. Despite its dislike of the Act—especially the large role it gave to India's unelected princes in a federal assembly proposed for the future—the Congress, too, chose to contest the provincial elections scheduled for the 1936-37 winter. So did the Muslim League, led by its 'permanent' president from the late 1920s, Jinnah.

Shafi having died in 1932, Jinnah sought an alliance in Punjab with Fazl and the Unionists. 'No one,' he wrote in January 1936 to Fazl, 'can give a better lead to the Mussalmans of India than yourself.' Despite this uncharacteristic overture from the League chief, Fazl declined, in April, an invitation to preside at the League's 1936 session in Bombay.[27] A rebuffed Jinnah went to Punjab to generate independent support there for the Muslim League, whereupon Fazl, who was in poor health from 1934, and Sikander agreed that no one, whether an officer of the Raj or the League president, could be allowed to 'tamper with provincial autonomy'. Jinnah should 'keep his finger out of the Punjab pie'.[28]

After a discouraging visit, Jinnah left Punjab, 'swearing he would never come back'. 'It is such a hopeless place', he wrote.[29] Later in 1936, however, Fazl, the fifty-nine-year-old Bhatti Rajput barrister from Sialkot and Batala who had thwarted fellow-barristers Gandhi and Jinnah, died.

Among other accomplishments, Fazl had brought education to children in numerous Punjab villages. However, his bids to raise Muslim percentages in colleges and the administration had estranged many Hindus and Sikhs. His closeness to the Raj and occasional lapses into obsequious language offended nationalists. Yet, Fazl had created a Muslim-Hindu-Sikh team in Punjab, even if mainly at higher rungs of the social ladder. His long teamwork with Rohtak's Chhotu Ram was particularly noteworthy. His goal, Fazl had declared, was 'a non-communal party run on humanitarian lines in the interests of the masses with due regard to the rights of classes'.[30]

Shortly before his death, he said that the 'Hindu and Sikh press' had accused Punjab ministers like him of being anti-Hindu and anti-Sikh 'without sifting the matter or entering into friendly talk with the Muslims'.[31] Whether or not his complaint was justified, Fazl was certainly one of those Muslim figures in Punjab on whom Hindu and Sikh leaders could have usefully expended more 'friendly talk'.

The Unionists chose Sikander Hayat to succeed Fazl as their leader. A Khattar Jat from Wah, Sikander was a son of the Muhammad Hayat who had served as Nicholson's aide in 1857 before rising in the ranks of Punjab's rural gentry. Sikander's elevation was reluctantly accepted by the influential Tiwana-Noon clans of Shahpur, who were Rajputs like Fazl and also close to the Raj.

Though Jinnah condemned the Unionists as stooges of the Raj, this well-entrenched, Raj-preferred party of landlords and landowners—Muslims in the province's west, Sikhs in the centre, and Hindu Jats in the east—won ninety-five of the Punjab Assembly's 175 seats in the 1937 elections. The Muslim League won only two. Though the INC and its allies performed strongly all across India, including in the NWFP, in Punjab the Congress could only win twenty-eight seats. While Hindu Sabhaite opponents of the Congress secured eleven, different Sikh groups obtained twenty-four and independents nineteen.[32]

Khalsa Nationalists, several Hindu Sabhaites and one of the two League legislators backed the Unionist ministry led by Prime Minister Sir Sikander Hayat Khan, as he was styled (he had been knighted in 1933). Manohar Lal from the Sabha became finance minister. Unionist party ministers included Chhotu Ram (also a knight by now), Khizr Hayat Tiwana, the son of Umar Tiwana, and the Sikh landowner Sunder Singh Majithia.

The opposition comprised the INC, the Akalis, many independents and a sole Leaguer, Barkat Ali. The other Leaguer elected, Raja Ghazanfar Ali, had gone over to the Unionists to become parliamentary secretary.

■

Sharp exchanges between Jinnah and Jawaharlal Nehru, the INC president in 1936 and also in 1937, boosted Jinnah's standing among India's Muslims, including in Punjab. When Jawaharlal stated that only two forces mattered in India, British imperialism and Indian nationalism represented by the Congress, Jinnah countered that there was a third party, the Muslims. Charging that Jinnah was practising 'communalism raised to the nth power', Jawaharlal also said that the Muslim League represented only 'a small group functioning in the higher regions of the upper middle classes and having no contacts with the Muslim masses'.

In his riposte, Jinnah spoke of Jawaharlal as the Peter Pan who refused to grow up, 'the busybody [Congress] President' who 'must poke his nose in everything except his own business'. Rejoining the slanging match, Jawaharlal declared that there were Muslims in the Congress 'who could provide inspiration to a thousand Jinnahs'.[33] An announcement by Nehru that the Congress would promote 'mass contact' with ordinary Muslims was denounced by the League as a bid to influence the ordinary Muslim's beliefs and practices.

In the 1937 elections, the League had fared better in Hindu-majority provinces than in Punjab, Bengal, the NWFP and Sindh. After Congress ministries were formed in seven provinces (Bombay, Madras, UP, Bihar, the Central Provinces, Orissa and the NWFP), Jinnah and the League mounted an unrelenting campaign describing the Congress ministries as anti-Muslim and the League as the Muslims' sole protector.

In letters to Jinnah written in May and June 1937, Iqbal urged Jinnah to bolster the League in Punjab by holding its 1937 convention there and also by linking the League to 'the Law of Islam', which, the poet argued, would attract the masses.[34] Wary, however, of challenging the Unionists inside Punjab, Jinnah chose Lucknow, the UP capital, as the convention's venue, while also inviting Sikander as well as Fazlul Huq, the Bengal Premier, who like Sikander was not a Leaguer, to attend.

Karachi-born but active professionally in Bombay and politically in Delhi and across India, Jinnah was sensitive to Muslim sentiments in Hindu-majority as well as Muslim-majority provinces. The all-India Congress, not Punjab's Unionist Party, was his primary foe. The poet in Lahore, on the other hand, was anxious to strengthen the League in Punjab where, in his view, the Muslims were 'entirely dependent on Hindus'.[35]

The League's Lucknow session of October 1937 was a landmark event where Jawaharlal's strategy of 'mass contact' evoked from Jinnah an element of what Iqbal had urged. Although Jinnah refrained, despite the poet's advice, from identifying the League with 'the Law of Islam', he appeared, for the first time in his political life, in 'Muslim' rather than western attire.

Demanding recognition by the Raj and the Congress of India's Muslims, represented by the League, as a third force, this Lucknow session also produced the so-called Jinnah-Sikander Pact which provided for Unionist autonomy in Punjab in exchange for the affiliation of Muslim Unionists with the all-India League.

Sikander wanted to run his own show in Punjab and was watchful of Jinnah. However, he was aware that in the months following the installation of Congress ministries in UP, Bihar, Bombay, Madras and elsewhere, Jinnah

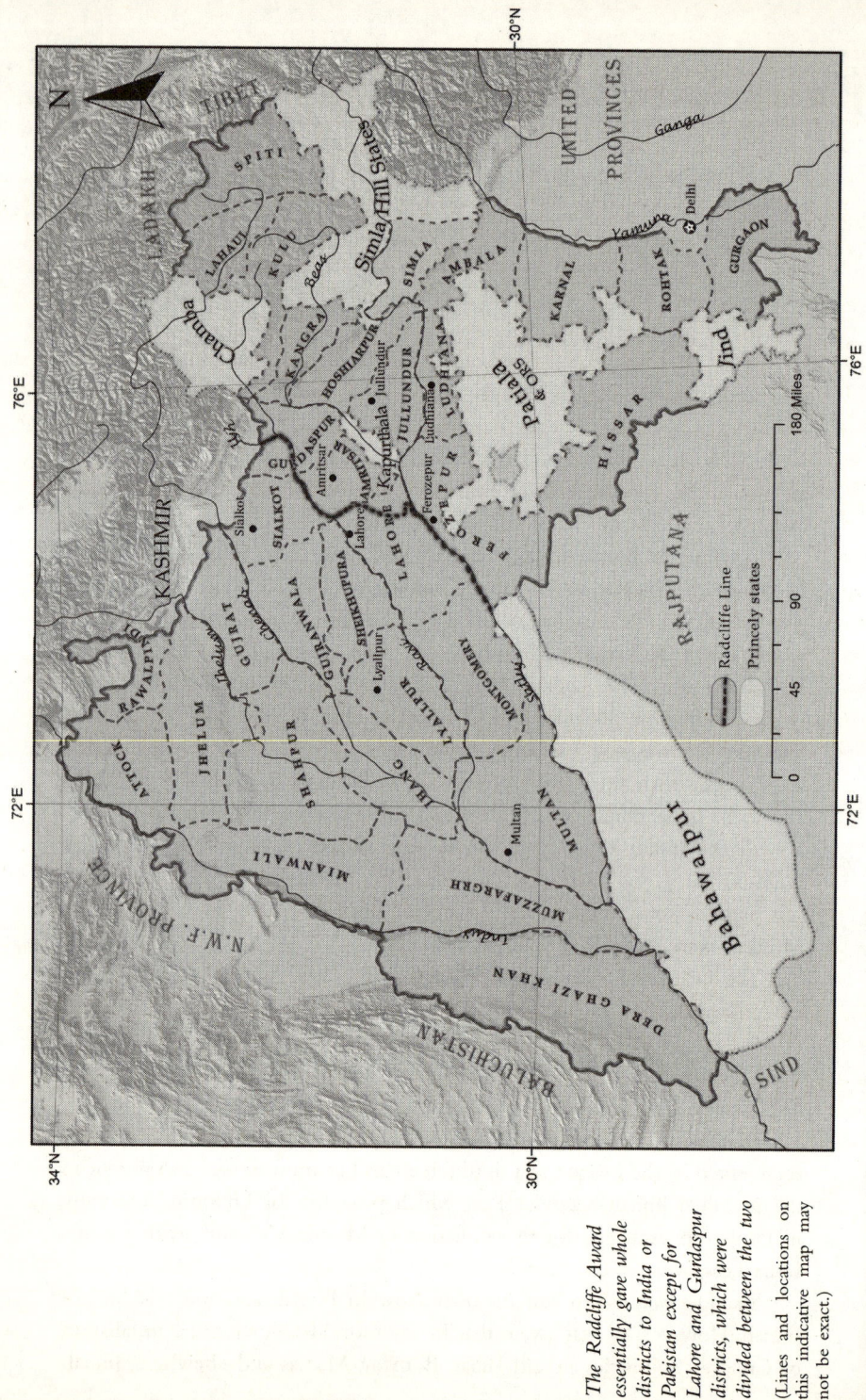

The Radcliffe Award essentially gave whole districts to India or Pakistan except for Lahore and Gurdaspur districts, which were divided between the two

(Lines and locations on this indicative map may not be exact.)

had grown into a force to reckon with. Even in Sikander's province, Jinnah was now being seen as the symbol of resistance to the 'threat to Islam' allegedly posed by the Congress.

As the Unionist Ahmed Yar Khan Daultana, a parliamentary secretary in Sikander's ministry and a prominent landlord from the Neeli Bar, had put it in May 1937, 'All Muslims of the Punjab, whether Unionist or non-Unionist, [are] with Mr. Jinnah in all-India matters.'[36]

Iqbal and other Leaguers in Punjab disliked the autonomy conceded to the Unionists by the Jinnah-Sikander Pact. Non-Muslim Unionists like Chhotu Ram disliked the Muslim Unionists' tie to the League. Sikander's British advisors were unhappy that one outside their circle would now influence the Premier. Sikander was forced into a hard balancing act of assuring Jinnah that he was with the League while persuading the Raj and persons like Chhotu Ram of the opposite.

Iqbal's death in April 1938 removed a major Sikander critic from the Punjab scene. Soon thereafter, when war in Europe seemed likely, the Punjab Premier and Jinnah both realized that they possessed strong cards vis-à-vis the Raj. On August 16, in Simla, when the acting Viceroy, Lord Brabourne, invited first Jinnah and then Sikander for private conversations, each broached a Raj-Muslim deal.

If, said Jinnah, the Raj kept 'the centre as it was now', i.e. if the Raj denied elected politicians, who would mostly be from the Congress, any role in Delhi, and protected Muslims 'in the Congress provinces', 'the Muslims would protect [the British] at the Centre.' Speaking for his province, which provided the bulk of India's Muslim soldiers to the Empire, Sikander assured Brabourne that 'the Muslims, [if] given a fair deal by [the British], would stand by [the British] through thick and thin'. The acting Viceroy passed on the 'offers' from Jinnah and Sikander to the Secretary for India in London, Lord Zetland, whose papers contain Brabourne's report of what Jinnah and Sikander had told him.[37]

Within a month, in September 1938, Premier Sikander 'guaranteed' HMG that in the event of a world war 'the manpower and resources of the Punjab [would] be unhesitatingly and ungrudgingly placed at the disposal of Great Britain and her Allies'.[38] On 25 August the following year, a week before the War would actually start, the Premier repeated the assurance.

Sikander's response to the War differed from that of the Congress and the League. Criticizing the Raj for committing India to the War without consulting the leading political parties, the INC asked to know Britain's plans for India's future before it could announce support for the War, while Jinnah demanded an assurance that no wartime or longer-term constitution for India would be put in place without the League's prior approval.

■

The War strengthened the hands of the Raj's hardliners in India. 'Security' became the watchword with them and 'political progress' in India a dirty phrase. On the Indian side, efforts to develop a united position failed or were hindered by the Raj. Jinnah declined Gandhi's invitation for a discussion on the War. When Gandhi tried to reach out to Sikander, he got nowhere. The Premier was well shielded by officers of the Raj.[39]

The national mood was hardly uniform. Anger towards the Raj had turned Hitler into less of a tyrant in some eyes. Despite a plea from Gandhi (who had called on the Viceroy to express his personal sympathy for England), the Congress working committee withheld even moral backing from the Empire, objecting to the latter's silence on Indian independence. Nehru and the rest of the committee agreed that fascism in Europe needed to be opposed but asked the Empire to first commit itself to Indian freedom.

Striking a sharper note, Subhas Bose, elected the INC president for 1938 and again for 1939, demanded that no 'Indian men, money and resources' should go into the 'imperialist war'.[40] Following differences with Gandhi, Subhas had been forced out of the Congress soon after his re-election in 1939.

At the other extreme stood the Punjab Premier, who at the end of August 1939 said to Sir Henry Craik, the new Punjab governor, that if needed his province could supply half a million recruits within weeks.[41] Hoping (like many Hindus in Punjab) that the Congress would support the war effort, Sikander intended, it appears, to bring Mian Iftikharuddin, the Punjab Congress president, into his ministry if that were to happen.

Indians were told by the Raj that their own divisions blocked political advance, but behind the thick walls of Viceroy's House, Lord Linlithgow seemed pleased. In October he wrote to the King:

> As soon as I realized that I was to be subjected to heavy and sustained pressure designed to force from us major political concessions as the price of Congress's cooperation in the war effort, I summoned representatives of all the more important interests and communities in India, including the Chancellor of the Chamber of Princes and Mr. Jinnah... and interviewed them one by one... a heavy and trying task, but well worth the trouble.

Linlithgow informed the King that it had been decided not to 'give to Congress what they are asking for, which is an understanding... that India will [receive] political independence at the conclusion of the war'.[42]

Like Gandhi, Linlithgow was aware of the importance of Jinnah, who after turning down Gandhi's invitation, accepted, in early October, the Viceroy's. Advised by Churchill as early as in 1937 to build India's Muslims as 'a counter-check on Congress', Linlithgow now strove (as he informed Secretary of State Zetland on 5 September) to 'shepherd all the Muslims into the same fold'.[43] The Viceroy was told by Jinnah that the League would back the war effort provided Muslim interests were protected to its satisfaction in any future Indian constitution.

When, also in October, Vallabhbhai Patel, one of the INC's strongest figures, met the Viceroy, the latter told Patel that if the Congress did not offer support the British would 'have to take the Muslims' help'.[44] After the Empire formally conveyed to the Congress (on 17 October) that Indian independence was *not* part of its war aims, the spectacle of Congress ministers functioning from the offices of an unresponsive Empire became intolerable for the Congress base. The INC asked all its provincial ministries to resign. By 27 November all Congress ministries were out, including the one headed by Dr Khan Sahib in the NWFP.

Declaring that Muslims had reason to celebrate the exit of Congress ministries, Jinnah asked India's Muslims to observe 22 December as Deliverance Day, a call backed by the anti-Congress leader, B.R. Ambedkar, who spoke for Dalits in western India and elsewhere.

At the end of 1939, when the Viceroy suggested to Jinnah that the logical implication of his stand was a separate Muslim state, the League leader, according to Linlithgow, 'blushed'.[45] It would seem that Zafrulla Khan, a member of the Viceroy's executive council, was asked by Linlithgow to draft a note advising the Muslim League to demand a separate nation.[46] By January 1940, Jinnah was saying publicly that Hindus and Muslims were two different nations, and in March, when the Muslim League convened in Lahore, separation was formally called for.

Jinnah was finally ready to challenge the Unionists on Punjab's soil. His new image as the protector of India's Muslims would enable him to avenge the snubs he had received there from Fazl and Sikander, as also his 1937 electoral defeat in Punjab and, indeed, the earlier sidelining—in 1920-22—by the Ali brothers and Azad.

At Lahore, the Bengal Premier, Fazlul Huq of the Krishak Praja Party, who headed a coalition ministry in Calcutta that included the Muslim League, moved the historic resolution asking for 'separate and sovereign Muslim states, comprising geographically contiguous units... in which the Muslims are numerically in a majority, as in the north-western and eastern zones of India.'[47]

Delegates from different parts of India seconded the resolution. Yet, Jinnah was the central figure at Lahore and also a changed one, arousing, unlike the Jinnah of the 1920s, passion more than thought. *The Times* of London reported that prolonged cheering almost drowned Jinnah's remark that he would 'give his life to achieve' a Muslim state.[48]

Gandhi said in response that 'it was worse than anarchy to partition a poor country... whose every corner is populated by Hindus and Muslims living side by side'. 'A Bengali Muslim,' he added, 'speaks the same tongue that a Bengali Hindu does, eats the same food, has the same amusements as his Hindu neighbour. They dress alike.'

> How are the Muslims of the Punjab different [*Gandhi continued*] from the Hindus and the Sikhs? Are they not all Punjabis, drinking the same water, breathing the same air and deriving sustenance from the same soil?[49]

It was indeed the same water, yet Punjabis were usually drawing it from different wells and taps. In the cities, the government had ensured that 'Hindu *pani*' and 'Muslim *pani*' were separately served at railway stations and other public places, an arrangement that did not seem to invite popular protest.

The boundaries of a future Muslim state were not specified in Lahore, and there was also a clear suggestion (later dismissed as a typing error) of more than one Muslim state being demanded. Noting that the resolution, which was passed to sustained applause, did not list the provinces constituting the proposed (and as yet unnamed) new state, a delegate at Lahore wondered whether its imprecise wording would not justify partitioning Punjab and Bengal. In his answer, Liaquat Ali Khan, the League's general secretary, who belonged to Karnal in eastern Punjab, defended vagueness:

> If we say Punjab that would mean that the boundary of our state would be Gurgaon, whereas we want to include in our proposed dominion Delhi and Aligarh, which are centres of our culture... Rest assured that we will [not] give away any part of the Punjab.[50]

Such claims to Hindu-majority parts of Punjab and other Hindu-majority areas 'central to Muslim culture' inevitably invited opposite claims to Muslim-majority areas. Led by Sir Sunder Singh Majithia, the Khalsa National Party, a constituent of the Sikander ministry (Majithia himself was the province's revenue minister), declared on 29 March that the League's resolution 'may mean a parting of the ways' and added:

> It would be the height of audacity... to imagine that the Sikhs would tolerate for a single day the undiluted communal raj of any community in the Punjab which is not only their homeland but also their holy land. As a logical consequence of the Lahore resolution, the Sikhs... would be entitled to claim back the sovereignty of the Punjab...[51]

A 'Khalistan' was accordingly demanded by some Sikhs in 1940.[52] Chhotu Ram and other non-Muslim Unionists as well as Hindu Sabha members supporting Sikander's ministry were also horrified by the Lahore call.

Uneasily present himself at the League rally, Sikander was henceforth forced to speak in two tongues. He was for Pakistan (the name was soon attached to the Lahore resolution) but also against it. 'We do not ask for freedom,' he would say in 1941, 'that there may be a Muslim raj here and a Hindu raj elsewhere. If this is what Pakistan means, I will have nothing to do with it.'[53] He belonged to the League but was not part of it. He was for a sovereign Pakistan but also for a loose confederation. And so forth.

■

The obvious flaw in the way in which the Pakistan demand was spelt out at Lahore was matched by defects in several articulations against that demand. If a Muslim-majority state had no right to Hindu-majority or Sikh-majority districts, did a Hindu-majority state have a natural right to Muslim-majority areas? If not, what was the solution? A division of Punjab and Bengal into Muslim-majority and Muslim-minority halves? If that was too heavy a shake-up, could all of Punjab and Bengal be assigned to a Muslim-majority zone or zones which however remained part of India?

For weighing such questions there was no calm in Punjab, not in 1940, not in the years to follow. Debates became shriller and suspicion became the norm. Feelings were intensified by an HMG declaration in August 1940 which assured minority 'elements in India's national life' that Britain would never allow 'their coercion into submission' to a majority government or permit the emergence of a government 'whose authority is directly denied by large and powerful elements in India's national life'.[54] The Muslim League, India's princes, and other 'powerful elements' had been given a veto over India's political future.

Held in Lahore on 1 December 1940, an Anti-Pakistan Conference chaired by M.S. Aney, a Hindu Mahasabha leader from Maharashtra, and addressed with fire-and-brimstone by Master Tara Singh, the Sikh leader, called the Pakistan plan 'fantastic' and 'vicious' and 'unequivocally' condemned it.[55] 'We will die for Pakistan', was the reply.

Another Anti-Pakistan conference was held in Lahore in March 1941, chaired by the Bengal leader, Shyama Prasad Mookerji of the Hindu Mahasabha, but that was also the month when Jinnah returned to Lahore to preside over a huge rally of the Punjab Muslim Students' Federation (PMSF) where he declared that Pakistan was 'a matter of life and death for Muslims'.[56]

However, Jinnah's argument that the Sikhs would be 'much safer in Pakistan', where 'they would form an important community, whereas in united India they would be a drop in the ocean',[57] found few Sikh takers. In different parts of Punjab, volunteer groups began to be trained for 'defence', and once more the ordinary Punjabi was forced to look around for ways to survive.

■

Wishing to prod an Empire at war without provoking it, Gandhi and the INC came up with the idea of a low-intensity civil disobedience stir. At the end of 1940, about 15,000 carefully chosen individuals, including most of the Congress working committee, courted up to a year's arrest each by pronouncing an unlawful sentence against participation in the War: 'It is wrong to support this War with men or money.' Useful for the Congress's morale in much of India, the campaign evoked little excitement in Punjab, where political passions revolved around the Pakistan demand.

In the summer of 1941—while Nehru, Patel and company were in prison—Sikander was forced by Jinnah to resign from a high-level defence council, sponsored by the Raj, which the Premier had joined without the League leader's permission. Publicly attacked by the PMSF for bypassing Jinnah, a hurt Sikander thought of resigning as Premier and letting Chhotu Ram replace him, but in 1941 there was no question of Muslim Unionists accepting a Hindu from Rohtak as their chief. Sikander quickly abandoned the idea, pocketed his humiliation, and resigned from the defence council instead.

It was a complete capitulation. Though the Raj too had been rebuffed, Viceroy Linlithgow asked Governor Craik to advise Sikander not to publicize his differences with Jinnah. At a time when the Congress was carrying out disobedience, the Viceroy said, 'any fissure in the Muslim ranks' was best avoided.[58] Later in 1941, after Linlithgow learnt that Sikander had sent a private message exploring a Congress-League rapprochement to the Congress leader and recent Madras Premier, Chakravarti Rajagopalachari, then in prison in Trichy in southern India, the Raj's officers in Lahore ensured a termination of the Sikander initiative.[59]

■

Opposed to Pakistan and desirous of an alliance with the INC, Punjab's Sikh leaders did not however share the latter's stance over the War. Places in the Raj's armies had always been important to the Sikhs. By the start of 1941, the Akali Dal modified its stance towards the Raj and committed itself to the war effort. A year later, after a section of the Sikh leadership entered into a pact with Sikander, overlooking the latter's inability to stand up to Jinnah, thirty-nine-year-old Baldev Singh, an affluent industrialist, was taken into the Punjab ministry.

■

The release of Congress leaders towards the end of 1941—their one-year sentence had been completed—was followed by Japan's attack on Pearl Harbor, America's entry into the War, and Japan's sweep across Asia. Alarmed by the possibility of a Japanese attack on southern India, Rajagopalachari sought a three-party agreement between the Raj, the INC and the Muslim League. At about the same time, Winston Churchill (Britain's Prime Minister from May 1940) sent Stafford Cripps, a brilliant cabinet minister from the Labour Party, to India with proposals. Churchill did this not out of enthusiasm for Indian self-rule but to mollify Roosevelt, the American President, who was urging the British to win Indian goodwill.

Cripps was armed with interesting ideas when he arrived in India in March 1942. For one thing, the British were now willing to say, thirty months after the start of the War, that its end *could* see India's independence. Not only that: if India's politicians agreed, a national government could be installed right away, though defence would remain in British hands.

If these ideas were aimed at placating the Congress, the League was told that after the War provinces could secede and become dominions equal in status to the projected dominion of India; the implication was that three or four seceding provinces could form a Pakistan. The Princes, on their part, were encouraged to expect, post-independence, autonomy for their states and possibly more than that.

Briefly tempted by the idea of an immediate national government but appalled by the prospect of India's balkanization, the INC rejected Cripps's proposals. Objecting that Pakistan was merely implied, not spelt out, Jinnah too turned them down. In Punjab, the possibility of a post-War independent Punjab cut off from India alarmed Sikhs and Hindus.

The Sikhs never forgot that the places of Guru Nanak's birth and death as well as the popular Sikh shrine, Panja Sahib, lay in Muslim-majority areas of Punjab, over which Ranjit Singh had ruled in the nineteenth century. Moreover, they were strongly attached to the British-era canal colonies they had helped develop in Lyallpur, Montgomery and other Muslim-majority districts.

Driven by these connections but lacking a majority in *any* district, the Sikhs tried nonetheless to mark out a substantial 'Sikh' Punjab consisting of several eastern Punjab districts where Sikhs and Hindus, taken together, constituted a majority plus a few western districts where, in their view, the Sikhs' earlier role outweighed demographics. If such a 'Sikh' Punjab could not be carved out, the Sikhs would go to any lengths, some of their leaders declared, to prevent a Muslim Punjab.

Punjab's Sikh and Hindu leaders also reacted against proposals that Rajagopalachari and his supporters in the Madras Congress made in April 1942. The southern Congressman had proposed a national government formed by the Congress and the League and an acknowledgment by the INC of the League's claim for the separation of 'certain [Muslim-majority] areas'. It has been suggested without corroboration that a role in Rajagopalachari's new thinking was played by one of his prison-mates in southern India during 1941, the Amritsar-born Cambridge-educated Allama Enayatullah Mashriqui (1888-1963).[60] In the 1920s, Mashriqui had founded the 'Khaksar' movement, which sought a revival of pure Islam and enjoined military-style discipline on its members.

Though in May the INC rejected Rajagopalachari's proposals, causing him to leave the Congress, the fact that a senior Congress leader close to Gandhi had accepted the legitimacy of separation deeply troubled Punjab's Hindus and Sikhs. However, Mian Iftikharuddin (1907-1962), president of the Punjab Congress, defended Rajagopalachari's approach, arguing that acceptance of self-determination by the INC might induce the League to waive the right. In his view, Rajagopalachari had made 'the most effective unity of India move, not a Pakistan move'.[61]

Gandhi now made a sudden and large move of his own. After having advocated for almost three years a policy of not seriously embarrassing a Britain at war, he decided, in the summer of 1942, that the Congress should ask the British to, simply, Quit India.

The call was Gandhi's answer to events threatening everything he had built and hoped for. Hitler and Churchill, and America and Japan, were speaking to the world with bombs and gun-ships. Inside India, while Jinnah demanded Pakistan, Hindu and Sikh voices were asking for anti-Muslim declarations rather than Indian unity. Rival Indian groups, Hindu, Muslim and Sikh, had declared militarization to be their dream.

Leaders long identified with the INC were offering conflicting advice. While Rajagopalachari wanted an agreement with the Empire and the Muslim League, and Nehru wanted a free India to join the global struggle against fascism, Subhas Bose had escaped from British internment in Calcutta and reached Berlin from where, in 1942, he invited German and Japanese help for India's liberation, an appeal that many Indians seemed to welcome.

With Quit India, Gandhi saved his dream of a national nonviolent struggle waged jointly by Indians of all kinds, and prevented a break-up of the organization he had nurtured, the INC. After long and tense discussions (Nehru and Abul Kalam Azad, the Congress president from 1940, were the last to come round), the INC adopted the Quit India call and found the unity that had eluded it since the start of the War.

The response from much of India was extraordinary. Although Gandhi, other INC leaders and thousands of rebels were quickly arrested (on 9 August) and put behind bars, the unrest that followed—in UP, Bihar, Bengal, Bombay and elsewhere—was described by Linlithgow as constituting 'by far the most serious rebellion since that of 1857'.[62]

Not, however, in Punjab, where emotions remained focused on the Muslim-Hindu or Muslim-Sikh divide rather than on India's need for freedom. Moreover, some Muslim, Sikh and Hindu Punjabis advocated participation in the Empire's war to gain expertise and if possible weapons for what to them was the 'real' war that lay ahead: one between Muslims and non-Muslims.

Pulled in opposite directions and unable to stick to one position, Sikander lost support and also physical strength. Muslims attacked him for his pact with Baldev Singh and also for a separation scheme of his own, which attempted to give self-determination rights to Punjab's non-Muslims as well. When Jinnah criticized the scheme, Sikander disowned it.

Visiting Punjab in November 1942, Jinnah argued that while the Hindu-Muslim question was an all-India one, 'the question between the Sikhs and the Muslims' was one for Pakistan: Sikhs, he said, should settle terms with Punjab's Muslims.[63] But after Sikander said in Lyallpur, in Jinnah's presence, that he 'fully subscribed' to the Lahore Resolution, and Jinnah declared that there was 'no question of postponing or shelving the Pakistan issue', adding ominously that Punjab's Muslims 'might stand in need of the sword to prevent any aggression on their right[s]', little possibility of a Muslim-Sikh agreement remained.[64]

Conquered by a man of determination but in the end defeated by his own weakness, Sir Sikander Hayat Khan, Premier of Punjab, a son of one who had been John Nicholson's personal aide in 1857, 'a devout Muslim who rarely missed a namaz or a roza' and took 'far-reaching steps for the renovation of the Badshahi Masjid, involving fresh taxation',[65] was only fifty when he died on 26 December 1942.

Chapter Nine

1942-1947: INDEPENDENCE AND TRAUMA

Sikander was succeeded as Premier by forty-three-year-old Khizr Hayat Khan Tiwana, the Aitchison-educated Unionist son of the old pro-Empire Rajput general, Sir Umar Hayat Tiwana of Kalra in Shahpur district. Punjab's new governor, Bertrand Glancy, had first offered the Premiership to another knighted landowner-politician, the Oxford-educated Firoz Khan Noon, who as member for defence in the Viceroy's executive council was helping recruitment. But Noon, whose Rajput clan, also long-settled in Shahpur, inter-married with the Tiwanas, chose to remain in New Delhi.

At Aitchison, Khizr's friends had included Hindus and Sikhs. After leaving school, Khizr enjoyed riding on the Tiwana grounds in Kalra and managing the estate and the stud. Many of the estate's employees and a majority in the nearest town, Sargodha, were non-Muslims, and a Hindu temple stood on the estate.

Khizr faced an almost impossible task as Premier. As Governor Glancy put it, while the Congress demanded independence and the League Pakistan, Khizr lacked 'any convincing battle-cry with which to rally his followers'. Yet Glancy liked him. In a letter to Linlithgow, he said (July 1943):

[Khizr] has a most attractive personality and he is very pleasant to work with. He is shrewd, even-tempered and blessed with a sense of humour. Though he is at heart an aristocrat and something of a reactionary, he keeps his prejudices in the background and is in my opinion essentially fair-minded. He has shown no signs of communal bias.[1]

But an ascendant Muslim League did not allow Premier Khizr any peace. Even within Unionist ranks, Khizr's position was undermined in July 1943 by Shaukat Hayat, Sikander's son and a member of Khizr's ministry, who said publicly that he would shirk 'no danger or sacrifice' while carrying out the mandates of the Muslim League and that all Muslim legislators belonging to the Unionist Party should do likewise.[2]

Already the League had won over, from Unionist ranks, Nawab Sir Shah Nawaz Mamdot, a veteran landowner (and descendant of Kasur's old Pashtun rulers) whose estates lay in Mamdot, just east of the Sutlej, in Ferozepore district. Lahore's Mamdot Villa became Jinnah's residence on his visits to the Punjab capital. After Shah Nawaz's death in March 1942, his son Iftikhar Hussain Mamdot (1906-1969) headed the League's Punjab unit.

A slogan Khizr did use, 'Rights for the martial races', designed to appeal to Punjabi communities providing soldiers to the British, no longer sounded attractive. When in 1944 Khizr demanded extra voting rights and 'separate and special constituencies for soldiers' in a future Indian constitution, even his British friends, his last line of defence, gave the idea short shrift.[3]

After pro-recruitment currents in 1940 and 1941, Punjab saw a drastic decline in enrolment in 1942 as well as an increase in desertion. Some recruiting officers employed coercion in the countryside, hurting the Unionist image. Inflation and shortages had the same effect: cloth, cement, sugar and kerosene were 'virtually unobtainable in the villages'; and there was also an impression among Punjabi Muslims that 'the Hindu and Sikh business class gained the most' from lucrative government contracts for supplies while 'small Muslim contractors were nearly squeezed out'.[4]

Khizr's situation was made more difficult by directives from New Delhi to requisition, at low prices, Punjab's wheat for distribution in the rest of India, especially Bengal, which saw a great famine in 1943. Khizr and Glancy both objected, but Linlithgow was clear, as he wrote to Glancy, that 'the procurement of the necessary surplus wheat from the Punjab is more important than any political considerations [and] any interests of [Punjab's] ministers'.[5]

In March and April 1944, while his old father Sir Umar lay dying, Khizr was confronted in Punjab by an increasingly assertive Jinnah. When told that the Sikander-Jinnah Pact had bound the League against campaigning inside Punjab, Jinnah replied that 'the League was fighting for the establishment of Pakistan not in Bombay but in the Punjab which was the keystone of the proposed Pakistan state'.[6]

Jinnah's privileging of Muslim-majority provinces displeased Muslims living elsewhere. Heading the Jamiat-Ulema-i-Hind, the association of ulema largely critical of the Pakistan idea, UP's Syed Husain Ahmad Madani (1879-1957) charged that after sacrificing Muslim-majority provinces in 1916 through his formula for minority weightage, Jinnah was now sacrificing Muslim-minority provinces.[7]

In talks with Khizr, Jinnah demanded that Unionist Party legislators and ministers give up their Unionist label and call themselves Muslim League legislators and ministers. This was too much for Khizr, who requested Glancy to 'order' him, in the interest of 'the war effort', to reject Jinnah's demand, but Glancy was unwilling to lend an imperial shield to Aitchison's old boy.[8] Khizr fought back without the shield. Declaring that the electorate which had sent Unionists to office should not be overruled, he warned also against steps that would 'embitter non-Muslims and intensify communal hatred leading to bloodshed and disorder and serious interference with the war effort'.[9]

But he had been isolated. The Muslim League, of which he was a nominal member, expelled him. Inside and outside the legislature, many Unionists crossed over to the League. Jinnah said that the Unionist name should be buried, adding that Khizr was 'a boy leader' and Unionists like him 'traitors' to the Muslim cause.[10]

However, Jinnah had to contend also with non-Muslim critics of Pakistan. Master Tara Singh and other Sikhs 'warned the British Government that the morale of Sikh soldiers would be affected if Pakistan were forced on Sikhs'. Testing whether caste could trump religion, Khizr's cabinet colleague Chhotu Ram tried to highlight, at a Lyallpur gathering in August 1944, the moneylender's grip on Jat peasants of all faiths, but the ploy evoked little interest.[11]

■

Following the Quit India call, Gandhi was kept in detention for two years, the Congress working committee and thousands of others for three years. Yet, Quit India had produced a fresh bonding between the INC and many of the Indian people. Older and thinner than before, Congress leaders leaving their prisons in the summer of 1945 were greeted as heroes across India.

The League too had become stronger, receiving the Raj's goodwill and profiting from the resignation of Congress ministries and the imprisonment of Congress leaders. In 1944, the League claimed two million members across India, a quantum jump from its 1927 membership of 1,400 members.

After being released in the summer of 1944 (the Raj thought he was too ill to be dangerous), Gandhi met Jinnah fourteen times in Bombay in September 1944, with Gandhi walking each time from the Mount Pleasant Road home of his hosts, the Birlas, to Jinnah's large house on the same street. Hopes of a Congress-League accord soared. The new Viceroy, Lord (and General) Archibald Wavell, who had been commander-in-chief alongside Linlithgow during Quit India, thought that the two Indian leaders would at least ask for the release of the still-detained Congress working committee.[12]

If, said Gandhi to Jinnah, the Muslim League joined the INC in asking for a national government, he, Gandhi, would get the Congress to agree to post-independence plebiscites for separation in the subcontinent's Muslim-majority areas. If votes favoured separation, Gandhi added, there should be bonds of alliance between the divided areas.

The talks failed. Objecting that Gandhi's Pakistan was not large enough (it excluded the Muslim-minority areas of Punjab and Bengal) nor, given the 'bonds of alliance,' truly sovereign, Jinnah rejected the offer outright. He also asked Gandhi to agree that Muslims and Hindus were separate 'nations', that voting in any plebiscite would be restricted to Muslims, and that separation should precede, not follow, the end of British rule, propositions unacceptable to Gandhi.

Sikhs and Hindus in Punjab, members of the Congress working committee still in prison, and Glancy, the Punjab governor, all thought that Gandhi's unsuccessful approach to Jinnah had boosted the League chief's prestige and the legitimacy of the Pakistan demand. Yet, Jinnah's stand during his talks with Gandhi had exposed the vulnerability of his position: if he could ask for Hindu-majority areas in a future Pakistan, why couldn't Hindus ask that Muslim-majority areas remain in India?

The War, meanwhile, had progressed well for the Allies. Victory was expected in both Europe and the Pacific. In October 1944—a month after the Gandhi-Jinnah talks—Wavell informed Churchill that Indians wished to end their British connection, adding significantly that he did not think that British soldiers would want to stay on in a post-War India. To 'capture the Indian imagination' and salvage British-Indian ties, the Viceroy sought Churchill's permission to free the Congress working committee.

The Prime Minister sat on the proposal for months and agreed to it only after the Viceroy journeyed to London, stayed there from March to June 1945, and lobbied ministers and MPs. Wavell was exhorted by Churchill to arrange for India's 'partition into Pakistan, Hindustan, Princestan etc.'[13] In Berlin, Hitler committed suicide; and Germany surrendered.

Returning to India, Wavell announced over All India Radio on 14 June 1945 that the Congress's leaders were being released and invited to a conference in Simla, India's (and Punjab's) summer capital, to discuss a possible national government. Also invited were Gandhi, Jinnah, other leaders of the Muslim League, Khizr and other provincial premiers, and a few from outside the two large parties.

At Simla in July, Congress leaders agreed to the Viceroy's proposal of a national government consisting of an equal number of caste Hindus and Muslims, all but one of the former from the INC, all but one of the latter from the ML, one non-League non-Congress Muslim, one Scheduled Caste Hindu, and two or three from other minorities.

Wavell said his intention was to nominate Khizr or another Unionist as the sole non-League Muslim, but Jinnah (who refused to shake hands with Azad, the Congress president) not only flatly opposed the idea of a Unionist member; he also said that the League would stay out unless he, Jinnah, was allowed to choose every Muslim name. The condition was not acceptable to the Viceroy, who abruptly announced the failure of his conference, rejecting the advice of British officials that Wavell should proceed with the INC's nominees and a few others while keeping places vacant for the Muslim League.

After being instructed by London not to blame Jinnah,[14] Wavell declared that the conference's failure was his own responsibility. Irrespective of who caused the failure, its biggest casualty was Punjab's Unionist Premier, Khizr.

There being a bar against cars in the mountain town, all the leaders participating in the talks—Gandhi, Jinnah, Azad, Nehru and everyone else—walked or used rickshaws. All, that is, except Khizr, who as Punjab's Premier was entitled to a car in Simla.

The honour merely underscored his humiliation. Though Aitchison had done much for Khizr, it had failed to teach him two things: empires do not last forever, and departing empires do not reward loyalty.

The Congress was the Empire's chief foe. Faced between displeasing this foe's main Indian adversary, the League (which too had created many difficulties for the Raj), and dropping those who had been faithful to it for a quarter-century, the Unionists, the Empire did not hesitate to jettison the Unionists.

Another consideration weighed with the Empire: the potential of a pro-British Pakistan, were it to emerge, for assisting a strategy to deny the Empire's *new* global enemy, the Soviet Union, access to the Middle East's oil.[15] This factor was also well understood by the Empire's newest custodians, Clement Attlee, Ernest Bevin and others from the Labour Party, which came to power at the end of July, defeating Churchill and his Tory associates.

Even before Simla, the Unionists were declining in Punjab. While Chhotu Ram had died in January 1945, among Punjab's Muslims there was gravitation towards the League, which was being strengthened by men like the left-leaning, Oxford-educated Mumtaz Daultana, a scion of the Daultana clan owning lands northeast of Multan, and Shaukat Hayat, the son of Sikander, who became a League hero when, tiring of Shaukat's criticisms, Khizr dropped him from his ministry.

After Simla, a blow was delivered by Firoz Khan Noon, the Tiwanas' kinsman who sat on the Viceroy's executive council. In September, Noon resigned his Delhi seat in order, he said, 'to go back to the Punjab and help the Muslim League'.[16] Viewing Jinnah as the rising sun, Muslim landlords in Punjab, hitherto the Unionist Party's pillars, started to shift their allegiance towards the League.

With the Raj refusing to dispute Jinnah's claim that the League was the sole representative of Muslim opinion, more Muslim legislators left Unionist ranks in Punjab. By the end of 1945, a third of all Unionist MLAs had crossed over to the League. Iftikhar Husain Mamdot, Mumtaz Daultana and Shaukat Hayat denounced Khizr as a disloyal Muslim. In the Hindu districts, Chhotu Ram's death quickened the Congress's rise at Unionist expense.

Another landowner who saw which way the wind was blowing and went over to the League was Mian Iftikharuddin, whose Arain family owned estates in Baghbanpura near Lahore. Iftikharuddin was a Congressman, in fact the president of the Punjab Congress, not a Unionist, and, despite his background, an avowed leftist. He was a great catch for the League.

∎

New provincial elections held during the winter of 1945-46 accelerated polarization across India around the INC and the League, and in Punjab the movement of Muslims from the Unionists to the League. Formally requested and personally approached to bless the Pakistan demand, Punjab's influential pirs, hitherto allied to the Unionists or detached from politics, obliged the League. Their support of the League, and migration to it of Muslim landowners across the province, transformed an urban party into one dominating the countryside, a process aided by the willingness of some prominent landowners to appear as religious leaders.

As one scholar put it, 'unlikely Sufis' such as 'Pir Mamdot Sharif' (Iftikhar Husain Mamdot), the '*sajjada nashin* of Wah Sharif '(Shaukat Hayat) and the '*sajjada nashin*' of Darbar Sargodha Sharif' (Firoz Khan Noon) were found on platforms in Punjab.[17]

Although their exodus to the League showed the popularity of the demand for Pakistan, Punjab's Muslim leaders did not necessarily believe that Pakistan would bring benefits. Fearing the province's possible division, many 'Punjabi political leaders who finally joined the Muslim League' apparently 'hoped that that the concession of Pakistan in name' would somehow preserve 'a united India in fact'.[18]

Resolved, on their part, to prevent Pakistan, Sikh politicians chose the

Akali party as their instrument, while the Congress, its manifesto highlighting Quit India, attracted the great majority of Punjab's Hindus as also a section of Sikhs.

In some Muslim seats, Congress leaders agreed to back Unionist candidates. However, pro-Congress Muslim voters, many of them supporters of the Ahrars and passionately anti-Empire, refused to vote for Unionists. For the League, three slogans worked beautifully: 'Islam in danger', 'If you are a Muslim, vote for the League', and '*Pakistan ka matlab kya?*' (What's the meaning of Pakistan?) '*La illah illa Allah*' (the Islamic creed).[19]

Gaining also from its success in putting up candidates from the right biradari—a Jat here, a Rajput there, elsewhere an Awan, Arain, Gujjar or someone else possessing a caste base—and from the energies of a Left-inclined section within the party, the Muslim League registered impressive results, winning seventy-five of the eighty-six Muslim seats in a house of 175.

Not enough, however, to form a government by itself. The Congress won fifty-five seats (forty-one 'general', in effect Hindu, seats plus ten reserved for Sikhs), the Unionists and the Akalis twenty-one each. Though clearly outvoted, Khizr and a clutch of Unionist colleagues had put up a plucky fight in the heated climate of early 1946.

A League-Unionist ministry led by Khizr was Mumtaz Daultana's solution but Jinnah vetoed it.[20] A Sikh section led by Giani Kartar Singh briefly held out hopes of Sikh support for a League ministry, while a League section toyed, also fleetingly, with ideas of a League-Congress ministry.[21] Neither plan got anywhere.

Nursing an intense dislike for the Unionists, Nehru seemed in favour of letting the League form a government, but, greatly disturbed by the idea of Pakistan, Azad, the Congress president, blessed a Khizr-led Muslim-Sikh-Hindu ministry and received Gandhi's support.

In the second week of March 1946, after obtaining the backing of the Akalis and the Congress, which swallowed its dislike of a pro-British party, Khizr again became Punjab's Premier, denying that office to the largest single party in the new legislature, the Muslim League. Declaring that the Muslim-majority province would not tolerate a Muslim Premier propped up by Hindus and Sikhs, the League mounted a fierce campaign for Khizr's ouster.

The Premier was reviled as 'Sardar Khizar Singh' and a 'thief'. Unsurprisingly, the ministers did not display great unity, with Bhimsen Sachar, the leader of the Congress group, indicating to the new governor, Evan Jenkins, that he regretted not being able to work with the League, whom he would have preferred to the Unionists.[22]

Again wooing the Sikhs but also probing them, Jinnah said he 'acknowledged that the Sikhs were a separate nation, entitled to their own free state, provided they identified its precise geographical location'.[23] The Sikhs did not take up the challenge, even as Jinnah had refused to demarcate his Pakistan when Gandhi asked him to do so.

■

On 15 March 1946, Premier Attlee told the House of Commons that Britain had decided to leave India. Later in the month, three ministers of the British cabinet—the elderly Secretary of State for India, Pethick-Lawrence, the supposed India expert, Stafford Cripps, who had come in 1942 and was now president of the board of trade, and A.V. Alexander, a trade union leader who had become first lord of the admiralty—arrived in India to try to resolve the Pakistan demand and also to convert the Viceroy's executive council into an interim national government. Viceroy Wavell joined as the fourth member of Britain's negotiating team, which conferred with Indian politicians during all of April and May and most of June in New Delhi and Simla.

Never before had three cabinet ministers from Britain spent three summer months together in India. The main topic of discussion was a promising if complex scheme, thought up by Cripps, of a three-tiered India where provinces, which would remain undivided, would form the bottom tier, two groups of provinces (one in the northwest and another in the east) the middle tier, and a union the top tier. If they agreed to combine, the two groups in the middle, inclusive of all of Punjab, the NWFP, all of Bengal, and Assam, would constitute Large Pakistan, although the so-called Cabinet Mission did not use that phrase.

Jinnah said he could accept the scheme if the union was nominal and the groups could later secede from it. The Congress said it could accept the scheme if the union was meaningful and if provinces like the NWFP, where a Congress ministry had been elected earlier in the year, and Assam, where Muslims constituted a minority, could stay out of the groups.

The Cabinet Mission should have plainly told both the Congress and the League that a meaningful union *and* a large Pakistan space went together. If the Congress wanted League support for an undivided India, it *had to* accommodate a large Pakistan area. If the League wanted Congress backing for a large Pakistan, the latter would have to exist *within* an Indian union.

Instead of speaking clearly (and, if need be, inviting rejection from both sides), the Mission spoke in two voices. On 16 May it produced an ambiguous plan which both the Congress and the League 'accepted' with opposing interpretations, enabling the Mission to claim 'success'.

This 16 May text said in one place (Para 15) that provinces 'should be free to' form groups, and elsewhere (Para 19) that they 'shall' do so. Later, Cripps would candidly say to the House of Commons that the wording was kept 'purposely vague' so as to enable both sides to join the 16 May scheme.[24] The document also said that union and group constitutions could be reconsidered ten years after being framed, a provision welcomed by the League as a door to secession. In short, while the League in effect pronounced the *union* in the 16 May scheme to be optional, the Congress claimed that the *groups* were voluntary.

On 24 May, an aide to the Mission and a future British MP, Woodrow Wyatt, advised Jinnah that though Pakistan had not been conceded, he could accept 16 May 'as the first step on the road to Pakistan'.[25] On 6 June, the League formally 'accepted' the 16 May plan, while adding that 'complete sovereign Pakistan' remained 'its unalterable objective' and claiming that 'the foundation of Pakistan' was 'inherent' in what it described as the plan's 'compulsory grouping' and in the implied 'right of secession'.[26]

Explanations and assurances of the opposite kind were offered to the Congress, enabling it to 'accept' the 16 May scheme even as it held that the phrase 'should be free to' ruled out compulsory grouping in the first place.

'Accepting' these heavily qualified 'acceptances' from the Congress and the League, Wavell installed, in the autumn of 1946, an interim government in New Delhi, formally still called the Viceroy's executive council, composed largely of Congress and League representatives. Nehru, who had succeeded Azad as Congress president, joined as member for external affairs and vice-chairman (de facto Prime Minister, some said), as did Patel (as home member), but Jinnah stayed out, asking Liaqat Ali Khan, who became member for finance, to lead the League group.

This council, the interim government of India, proved above all to be a forum for war between the Congress and the League. It included the Sikh leader, Baldev Singh, as defence member. Another Punjabi on the council, a League representative, was the Jhelum-born Raja Ghazanfar Ali Khan (1895-1963), one of only two Leaguers elected to the Punjab legislature in 1937. Crossing over to the Unionists, Ghazanfar had served in Sikander's ministry, as had Baldev Singh. Later Ghazanfar rejoined the League.

On 5 April, well before the 16 May plan was announced, the Cabinet

Mission asked the Punjab Premier about the impact on Punjab of a possible Pakistan. Khizr replied that if Pakistan 'included the whole of the Province as it now existed, the Muslims would be very pleased'. Otherwise they would react negatively. Sikhs, on the other hand, would forcibly resist inclusion in Pakistan.

Predicting that 'relations between the Muslims in the various parts' in a Pakistan would not 'be free from difficulty', Khizr added that though 'Punjabis, Sindhis, Pathans and Baluchis all had one religion... they spoke different languages and were otherwise very different.'

In Khizr's view, Jinnah should have been 'required at an earlier stage to define Pakistan'. He added, 'Mr. Jinnah himself had not believed seven years ago' in 'the Pakistan idea'. But after being identified at the elections 'with Islam, the Koran and the Holy Prophet', the idea, risky and vague as it was, had taken root. Khizr's plea to the Mission was against dividing Punjab.[27]

Envisaging, in line with Khizr's wishes, a united Punjab, the Mission's grouping scheme was criticized by Muslims in Hindu-majority provinces, who feared reprisals, and also by several Sindhi, Pashtun and Baloch Muslims who feared Punjabi dominance in the proposed northwestern group.[28]

Peace in Punjab now depended on how political leaders, provincial and national, and British and Indian officials conducted themselves, and also on the capacity of the ordinary Punjabi to ignore inflammatory rhetoric. All-India leaders did not improve the provincial climate in 1946.

Accusations by Jinnah that the Congress acceptance of 16 May was dishonest were countered by identical charges about the League's acceptance. An impulsive remark by Nehru in July that, irrespective of what 16 May had laid down, an all-India Constituent Assembly would finally decide the question of groups and provinces led to a call from Jinnah for 'direct action' by Muslims across India in defence of their rights.

In Punjab, the League's provincial chief, Mamdot, declared in June that while the party had accepted the Mission's plan, its 'aim... was still... an autonomous and sovereign Pakistan'.[29]

An ominous pen-dagger nexus threatened life on the streets. Even as the production and sale of knives, daggers, metal-tipped lathis, swords and acids went up, newspapers—Hindu, Muslim and Sikh—printed lurid accounts of the smallest incident. Bands of volunteers, Hindu, Muslim and Sikh, emerged for 'defence'.

In existence in Punjab for several years, the Rashtriya Swayamsevak Sangh (RSS) became active and organized in 1946. So did the Muslim

League National Guards (MLNG). Sikh volunteers were slower to organize provincially but available locally. The RSS had 47,000 members in Punjab in early 1947, the MLNG 23,000.[30]

Demobilized Punjabis from the Empire's armies (an immense pool) and also Muslim, Sikh and Hindu soldiers who had fought alongside the Indian National Army (INA) against the Empire's armies were tapped for training in 'defence'. In early May, 'the most important item on the agenda' at a meeting at Mamdot Villa in Lahore was how to convert demobilized soldiers and ex-INA personnel into 'enthusiastic members of the Muslim League National Guards'. In a speech in Gujrat, Firoz Khan Noon 'urged every Muslim boy to buy a sword and keep it with him'.[31]

Citing danger from the RSS, Mian Khurshid Anwar, provincial organizer of the MLNG, and Mian Amiruddin, leader of the League group in the Lahore Corporation, collected swords and iron-tipped lathis in May 1946. Later that month, a women's unit of the MLNG was started.

In June and July, the Punjab Muslim Students' Federation enrolled all its members into the MLNG, whose guards were given training in Lahore's Islamia College and also in the large Baghbanpura house of Mian Iftikharuddin, the former Congress leader newly in the League.

Also in July, Iftikharuddin's successor as the Punjab Congress chief, Maulana Daud Ghaznavi, who had strong Ahrar connections, left the Congress, making it harder for the party to claim that it spoke also for Punjab's Muslims. Another Muslim once heading the provincial Congress but no longer in the party was Agha Safdar of Sialkot. Men like Zafar Ali and Dr Muhammad Alam had left much earlier.

Growing enlistment into the RSS and the MLNG and the collection of swords and daggers were troubling developments, yet the Raj hesitated to intervene, apart from occasionally enforcing Section 144 to prevent crowds from assembling. 'The colonial state was suffering from a loss of nerve.'[32]

Issued to protest British 'complicity' in Congress 'duplicity', Jinnah's 'direct action' call provoked serious violence in Calcutta in August (where early Hindu deaths were soon outnumbered by Muslim deaths), which was followed by killings in eastern Bengal in September (with hundreds of Hindus killed, raped and forcibly converted), killings in Bihar in October and November (when about 7,000 Muslims perished), and violence in Garhmukteshwar in UP in November, when nearly a thousand Muslims were killed.

In Punjab, 70 per cent of the police force was Muslim. If a major Muslim revolt occurred, would Muslim policemen suppress it? British officials were doubtful. Luckily for Punjab's people and administrators, the 'direct action' call did not incite violence in the province. Even though Shafaat Ahmed Khan, a Congress nominee for the interim government, was stabbed as a 'traitor Muslim' in Simla at the end of August (he survived), the incident did not trigger further violence.

One reason, apparently, was a hope in some Punjabis for a League-Sikh understanding, which Jenkins suspected was also desired by a key Sikh leader, Giani Kartar Singh, who was often in conflict with Tara Singh and also with Baldev Singh. After a long talk with him on 5 December, Jenkins observed that Kartar Singh had been 'intriguing in a desultory way with the Muslim League for some time past'.[33]

Punjab's newspapers were predictably partisan in their reporting of the Calcutta violence in August. Many Muslims and Hindus started collecting 'arms and acids'.[34] In the following month, when Saifuddin Kitchlew, one of the 1919 heroes of Amritsar, called a rally in that city for better Hindu-Muslim relations, only a few hundred showed up, whereas 5,000 or more attended a League meeting.[35]

Cutlery merchants in Wazirabad (most of them Hindus) reported a brisk trade in daggers, though tension seemed to ease partially in October when Jinnah sent his League team (Liaqat, Ghazanfar and three others) into the interim government. But the fact that one of Jinnah's nominees was Jogendra Nath Mandal, a Scheduled Caste Hindu from Bengal, seemed ominous. Jinnah's gambit was followed by the occasional appearance of Scheduled Caste Hindus and Mazhabi Sikhs at League rallies in Punjab.

In November, Madhav Sadashiv Golwalkar (1906-73), all-India head of the RSS, visited Punjab, addressing a few public meetings and several more behind closed doors. According to the Punjab police, Golwalkar asked select groups, in the context of what had happened to Hindus in Noakhali in east Bengal, to 'fight the Muslims without mercy', to train volunteers in the use of lathis, swords and spears, and also to work out their plans in 'utmost secrecy'.[36]

Although a number of 'defence' bands emerged and expanded in Punjab's towns, and press reports about Noakhali and Bihar inflamed tensions, killings did not occur. A 'Bihar Day' called by the League passed without violence. Punjabi sanity seemed intact in the final months of 1946, with Wavell observing in November that that it was 'to [Khizr's] credit and the credit of Jenkins (the Governor) that the Punjab is remarkably steady at this time'.[37]

The League's agitation against Khizr continued, however, as did preparation for 'defence' by Muslim and Hindu bands. Punjab's insecurity was heightened by demands and counter-demands at the all-India level, where the League and the Congress each wanted the other ejected from the interim government.

On 19 November, a worried Jenkins imposed a Public Safety Ordinance with the support of Khizr and his Unionist-Congress-Sikh ministry. Opposition to the Ordinance seemed low-key to begin with but when, in January, Khizr imposed a ban on the RSS and the MLNG, while the former 'succumbed without a whimper', the latter resisted, with the full support of the League's provincial leadership.[38]

Because he stood, refusing to budge, in front of the door of the MLNG office, and did not let the police enter, Iftikharuddin was arrested. Arriving on the scene and also defying the police, Mamdot, Noon, Daultana, Shaukat Hayat and a few others were arrested as well. A wave of anger at Khizr, joined to support for the League, was set off, and 'Muslims were pleased to see their leaders finally willing to rough it out in colonial jails'.[39]

Lacking in natural political instincts, Khizr 'had no idea', Jenkins would write to Pethick-Lawrence, 'that the League would take him on'. He had not intended to arrest its leaders but 'could not yield to a show of force'.[40] In less than ninety-six hours, however, popular Muslim sentiment obliged Khizr to withdraw his bans and release the League's leaders, who resumed their agitation and demanded a withdrawal of the Ordinance.

An annoyed Khizr had the leaders rearrested, and Punjab was thrown into turmoil. Now desperate, Khizr thought aloud before Jenkins about an independent, multi-faith Punjab, separate from India and also from the Pakistan being demanded. The day-dream was late by many a year and Khizr did not pursue it.[41]

While Muslim Punjabis were angry at the fresh arrests, Hindus seemed pleased, for it was clear that the Raj would not allow a League in revolt to replace Khizr's ministry. Recognizing that the League's campaign was pushing Sikhs and Hindus towards demanding the province's partition, Jenkins wired Wavell (8 February):

> It is quite impossible for one community to rule the Punjab with its present boundaries... Muslim League are... wantonly throwing away certainty of Muslim Leadership in a United Punjab for uncertain advantages of a partition which Sikhs will gradually now demand. But nobody has brains to understand this.[42]

A week later, Jenkins wrote to Wavell that the League's objective of 'undiluted Muslim rule all over the Punjab' was unrealizable. While Sikhs and Hindus would not consent to it, the League lacked the ability to conquer all of Punjab.[43] Whether or not they understood this, League leaders intensified their agitation, which Sikhs and Hindus saw as a drive for Muslim rule.

Responding in mid-February, Master Tara Singh called publicly for a Sikh fighting force, an Akal Fauj as he named it. Across Punjab, Sikh bands quickly caught up with the MLNG and the RSS. To obtain the right to carry a spear in addition to the short kirpan allowed to all Sikhs, many Sikhs converted at this juncture to Sikhism's Nihang sect.

A few days later, on 20 February, Punjab was inflamed, not calmed, by HMG's historic declaration in London that the British would leave India not later than June 1948, i.e. in sixteen months or less. Prime Minister Attlee said that a departing Britain would hand over 'to some form of central government or in some areas to the existing provincial governments' or 'in such other way as may seem most reasonable'. Attlee added that Wavell would be replaced as Viceroy by Lord Louis Mountbatten, a forty-six-year-old admiral related to King George VI.

Informed in advance of the coming announcement, Jenkins had advised strongly against it, predicting (on 16 February) that it would cause 'all parties' in Punjab to try to 'seize as much power as they can—if necessary by force'.[44] Apart from being shaken by his dismissal, Wavell too thought that announcing a deadline would drain the Raj's authority and the morale of its officers and soldiers, an opinion shared by General Auchinleck, the commander-in-chief.

But the empire in retreat ignored the advice of its colony-based officers. Built in district after tropical district over a century of toil, British Punjab was abandoned after a few short hours of deliberation in London. Cutting losses was the watchword, as was throwing responsibility onto the shoulders of Indians. 'You asked us to quit. We will oblige. Now it's up to you.' The argument was irrefutable, but it was not as if earlier Indian demands had always been met.

The possibility of 'the existing provincial government'—Khizr and his Hindu and Sikh allies—inheriting all of Punjab was too much for Punjab's Muslims. The League's agitation snowballed. Women took to the streets. Students hoisted the League flag over government buildings and blocked trains. Kinsmen deserted Khizr and relatives criticized him. Apparently the last straw was a remark by a youngster in his family: 'My friends say you are not a Muslim.'[45]

Informed that Khizr was caving in, the League celebrated 2 March, a Sunday, as Victory Day. Khizr resigned that night. On 3 March, after Sikh and Hindu MLAs refused to support an alternative League ministry, which therefore could not be formed, Master Tara Singh unsheathed his sword on the steps of the Punjab legislature building in Lahore and said that Sikhs would not live under Muslim rule nor allow Pakistan to emerge.

In the following few days, Tara Singh's sword-backed exclamation would be invoked in town after town by violent Muslim mobs, and the image would enter almost every future account of the Punjab of 1947.

At another 3 March event in Lahore, held at Kapurthala House near Old Anarkali, Tara Singh was elected to lead Hindus and Sikhs in an anti-Pakistan campaign. Addressing the huge gathering, Tara Singh announced that 11 March would be observed as Anti-Pakistan Day. He also asked Hindus and Sikhs to be ready, like the Japanese and the Nazis, for self-destruction, and declared that having ruled Punjab before, the Sikhs would do so again.[46] Other Sikh and Hindu speakers at Kapurthala House included Giani Kartar Singh.

Killings occurred the next day in Lahore and Amritsar, and quickly also in Rawalpindi and Multan. All four were cities where Muslims and non-Muslims seemed more or less evenly balanced, but a large number of murders also took place in the countryside, where Sikhs and Hindus were in a hopeless minority, around the towns of Rawalpindi, Attock, Jhelum and Mianwali. On 5 March, Jenkins imposed governor's rule and banned all rallies and processions, including those planned for Anti-Pakistan Day.

Accounts of the killings of March 1947 in several towns in Punjab usually state that a Sikh or a Sikh-Hindu crowd raised anti-Pakistan slogans which provoked, or provided a pretext for, the violence that ensued. Except in Amritsar, where more Muslims than non-Muslims perished in a total count of over a hundred dead, Sikh and Hindu deaths greatly exceeded Muslim deaths, and Punjab's policemen were often indifferent or complicit.

A particularly tragic killing was that of Labh Singh, an Akali leader in Jullundur, shot by a Muslim youth even as he was on a tour of Muslim localities to ask for forgiveness for Sikh violence.[47] In almost every place, however, lives were saved because ingenious or brave help came from the other side, while other lives were prolonged by doctors true to their profession.

> As long as we two brothers are alive and our rifles have bullets we will never let you touch the Muslim patients in this hospital.[48]

Addressed to assailants storming (and, soon afterwards, leaving) their Amritsar hospital, these words spoken by Dr Parshottam Dutt on his behalf and that of his brother Dr Narain Das reflected the gallant spirit of many unknown

Punjabis, Sikh, Muslim and Hindu, of March 1947. Yet, the frenzied spirit that was also abroad destroyed around 2,500 lives in Punjab in that month, including that of one of Multan's most-respected men, Kalyan Das, a prosperous Hindu living near the railway station. A man to whom Muslims had often turned for arbitrating disputes with fellow Muslims, Das was killed in his house along with his entire family.

Also nearly killed in Das's home was his house-guest that day, Saifuddin Kitchlew. The killers stripped Kitchlew completely, saw that he was circumcised and spared the Amritsar leader, and that too because an Ahrar group friendly to Kitchlew had arrived on the scene.[49] Reporting to Wavell on 17 March about the Multan deaths, Jenkins thought that 'about 150 people, nearly all Hindus', had been killed.[50]

The area around Rawalpindi saw an even larger number of killings. While flying into the city (on 9 March, in a plane loaned by the Viceroy), Jenkins saw 'six villages burning'. Civil and military officers in the area told him that 'in several villages the Hindus had been massacred'—'Hindus' in this phrase included Sikhs. Raiders had attacked Murree as well, as also the Frontier Mail train; army units had not managed to confront them; and 'the disturbed area [was] full of crowds of villagers armed with lathis, spears, axes, agricultural implements and in some cases firearms'.[51]

The violence seemed to start first in Rawalpindi town, where Sikhs and Hindus, some of them possessing guns, may have shown avoidable bravado. A fairly even fight in the city was quickly overshadowed by countryside massacres. Surviving Sikh and Hindu villagers complained that policemen aided attackers and army units were slow to arrive.

Some lives were saved by daring Muslim helpers (including, it would seem, Khaksars), but two thousand or more Sikhs and Hindus were killed between 5 and 8 March in villages near Rawalpindi and Attock, and tens of thousands fled from their homes. In some villages—in the words of Lt.-Gen. Frank Messervy, the northern command chief and a future head of the Pakistan army—'savagery was carried out to an extreme degree'. Messervy admitted that the army's 'ex-soldiers and pensioners [had] been heavily involved' in the violence.[52]

A good percentage of Rawalpindi district's young men had served in World War II, with 1,420 families in the district apparently sending three or more sons into the army.[53] In the last years of the war, many Punjabi soldiers had deserted, with weapons.

■

Noting two developments that seemed new—(*a*) violence was occurring *simultaneously* in different parts of Punjab, and (*b*) it was occurring in the *countryside*—Governor Jenkins (who rejected the theory that resentment at economic exploitation caused the violence) thought that if the violence 'spread to [other] rural areas in Muslim districts and was not checked, we must expect similar trouble in Sikh districts and later in the Ambala Division where the Hindu Jats are dominant'.[54]

Hindsight recognizes this observation as prescient. Between Jenkins's lines it is also possible to discern a suspicion of a plan being implemented that was more than a response to Tara Singh's gesticulation. This sense was spelt out by Lt.-Gen. Messervy in a note written on or just before 22 March. Expressing shock that 'the normally chivalrous and decent P[unjabi] M[uslim] peasant' had been 'aroused to such frenzied savagery', Messervy added (author's emphasis): 'There has also been *a widespread desire to rid many areas of all Sikhs and Hindus, entirely for ever.*'[55] Messervy was suggesting that ethnic cleansing had entered minds.

Who first thought of ethnic cleansing in northwestern Punjab in March 1947 is as yet an unanswered historical question. Though launched two or three days after Tara Singh's flourish in Lahore, the well-organized drive may have been planned prior to it.

The Raj appeared reluctant to combat the drive. That the Empire was giving up on India and focused on protecting British lives (there were several British families in Rawalpindi) may or may not be a complete explanation. Did some in the Raj welcome a repeat of earlier conflicts between Sikhs on the one hand and northwestern India's Muslim Pashtuns and Muslim Punjabis on the other?

In any case, between March and August there was a steady flow of urban and rural Sikhs and Hindus from Rawalpindi, Multan, Attock, Lahore and other western districts to safe havens in eastern Punjab. In all, about 500,000 may have moved east *before* mid-August.[56]

■

Temporarily chastened, leaders of all communities including Mamdot, Iftikharuddin, Daultana, Shaukat, Tara Singh, Swaran Singh, Sachar and Bhargava formed a Punjab peace committee on 6 March. It would prove toothless and non-serious. On the same day, another politician, Ujjal Singh (who represented one of western Punjab's urban-Sikh constituencies in the now inactive legislature), urged Jenkins to propose a long-term solution.

The constitutional ideas that Jenkins jotted down in response to Ujjal Singh's plea need not occupy us (dismissed by Wavell as impractical, the ideas were never put to the parties), but some of the governor's accompanying observations are of interest. Jenkins wrote that the parties had to choose between 'an agreed partition' and 'a united Punjab with existing boundaries under a constitution and a government that all communities' would accept. However, partition would solve no problem: minorities would remain in both halves and assigning 'middle' areas to one or the other half would be an explosive exercise.

For example, where would Lahore, which, as Jenkins put it, 'ha[d] been created by all Punjabis', go? Producing 'an artificial frontier', partition would split a Punjab which was 'homogeneous in speech and in many other ways'. In Jenkins's view, a settlement was still possible provided 'we think as Punjabis and put our own safety and welfare first'. He added:

> The Muslims must be prepared to negotiate with the non-Muslims as Punjabis.... The non-Muslims on their part must recognize that the Muslims are the majority community and must in certain matters take the lead.[57]

At least Ujjal Singh took an initiative: he went to Jenkins and sparked off interesting reflections in the governor's mind. But did he also say to a fellow Punjabi—Mamdot or Iftikharuddin or even Khizr—'We *have* to sit together and find a way out', that a 'committee' for peace was not enough? We have no evidence that at this stage Ujjal Singh or any other Punjabi politician demanded cogitation from fellow legislators or other Punjabis.

Events were overtaking last-minute baby-steps. On 8 March, pressed by Punjab's Sikh and Hindu leaders and shaken by the violence in Amritsar and Multan (apparently it had not yet learnt about Rawalpindi district), the Congress working committee, meeting in New Delhi, asked for 'a division of the Punjab into two Provinces, so that the predominantly Muslim part may be separated from the predominantly non-Muslim part'.[58]

By this momentous resolution the Congress had conceded Pakistan, while also insisting that east Punjab would stay out of it. (The implied demand that Bengal should be similarly divided was soon made explicit.) When the League asked for a division of India, the Congress had said no. Now, along with Punjab's Sikh and Hindu leaders, the Congress was demanding a division of Punjab.

The League was indignant, and so, for opposite reasons, were the Congress's Muslim supporters inside and outside Punjab: the Ahrars, the Jamiat-Ulema-i-Hind, and others. Was the INC accepting the two-nation theory? Was soon-to-be-free India going to be a Hindu state?

■

No one seemed unhappier than seventy-seven-year-old Mohandas Gandhi, who after 1945 had become, in his own phrase, a 'back-number'. Yes, he retained some influence, as when he successfully pushed for Nehru to become the Congress president in the summer of 1946, preferring him over Patel, the choice of most provincial Congress committees, and also over Azad, who wanted to continue the presidency he had assumed in 1940.

But from the summer of 1945 onwards most INC decisions were made by Nehru and Patel and often independently of Gandhi, who for much of this time was physically far removed from New Delhi, where the working committee and Congress members of the interim government confabulated. From October 1946, Gandhi was engaged in Calcutta, east Bengal and Bihar, trying to bring peace.

When he read in newspapers in Bihar that the Congress had asked for Punjab's division, he sent questioning letters to Nehru and Patel. He could agree, Gandhi wrote, to the province's partition if arrived at by 'willing consent', but to him the resolution seemed pressurized by violence.[59] These were private protests. Gandhi did not oppose Nehru and Patel in public.

Nehru and Patel, and Baldev Singh, who was Wavell's defence 'minister', asked the Viceroy to impose martial law in Punjab, which is what, five months earlier, the League had unsuccessfully demanded in Bihar. But neither Wavell, who was about to go home, nor Auchinleck, the commander-in-chief, nor Messervy, in command in Punjab, was sympathetic to the idea.

While Messervy argued that martial law in Punjab would be interpreted as a step by the Raj against Pakistan,[60] Wavell and Auchinleck were wholly against placing primary responsibility for law and order on the shoulders of British officers and soldiers now focused on their return home and, until that time arrived, on their own security in an unpredictable India.

Making them responsible for the security of Punjabis suddenly sounded completely unreasonable to an Empire that had suppressed not only the 1857 Revolt but also the 1942 rebellion and, more recently, in February 1946, a naval revolt in Bombay and Karachi. Wavell and company were conscious, moreover, that their Indian soldiers had been communalized, at first through imperial policy and more recently by diatribes between Indian politicians. They could not be relied upon, in a crisis, to act impartially.

Seen during decades of strategic thinking as the Empire's agent in his village, nurtured into a relationship with his white officer yet prevented from bonding with mates who spoke his language but belonged to a different religion, the Punjabi soldier—of whom there were hundreds of thousands—suddenly seemed of no use or reliability when the Empire's soon-to-be-free colony faced its greatest crisis in nearly a century.

•

In Punjab, a League-Sikh deal was again explored in mid-March, this time by Firoz Khan Noon, who offered Sikh MLAs five seats in a new eleven-strong ministry. But there was no climate on either side for such an arrangement. While Shaukat Hayat, for one, was asking district League units 'to prepare for the possibility of war', Jenkins heard on 11 March that on the Sikh side Tara Singh was 'still talking in terms of civil war'.[61]

On 20 March, a frank conversation took place in Lahore between Jenkins, who continued to stand for a Punjab-based solution, and Raja Ghazanfar, the League's Punjabi in the interim government in Delhi, who apparently wanted 'the Central picture [to] be complete before any picture of the Punjab could... be sketched'. Rejecting Ghazanfar's sequence as 'topsy-turvy', Jenkins said to him:

> Surely the right course [is] to determine the future of the units in a way acceptable to their inhabitants and *then* to sketch the all-India picture.

In a reference to Jinnah, the exasperated governor added, 'It [is] a ludicrous position in which the so-called League leaders... take orders from Bombay from a person entirely ignorant of Punjab conditions.'[62] Ghazanfar, however, was not prepared to initiate a Punjabi response.

•

Far from Lahore, in Bihar, Gandhi thought up a 'solution' that he felt met Punjabi *and* all-India needs. Conscious of Punjab's armed bands, and chewing on Jinnah's opposition to the division of Punjab and Bengal and on the Congress's dislike of India's division, Gandhi felt that if the Congress accepted a Jinnah-led League or coalition ministry in New Delhi, polarization in Punjab, Bihar and all of India (and in the interim government) could be reversed and the unity of India, Punjab and Bengal preserved.

Since throughout his life Jinnah had been interested in all of India—in Muslim-majority provinces but also in Muslim-minority ones—Gandhi thought that the League leader would be open to the proposal. Travelling to Delhi, Gandhi presented it in the first week of April to Congress leaders and to the newly-arrived Viceroy, Lord Mountbatten.

Let Jinnah (Gandhi told the Viceroy) head an interim government of his choice, comprising League members alone or including others as well. Second, unless an impartial umpire, e.g. the Viceroy, were to rule that a League measure was against the national interest, the Congress, which had a majority in the Central Assembly, would back the League government and its measures.

Three, Punjab's private armies should be disbanded. Finally, if Jinnah and the League were not willing, under these terms, to form a cohesive government, Nehru and the Congress should be given the same opportunity.[63]

However, the young admiral taking over in New Delhi had not only determined that partition *was* the solution—a conclusion that Nehru and Patel too had reached—he had come close to preparing his own plan for accomplishing it. Gandhi's proposal therefore perturbed Mountbatten, who was even more shaken when, on 2 April, Azad told him that Gandhi's plan was 'perfectly feasible of being carried out'. As the Viceroy recorded:

> I told [Azad] straightaway of Gandhi's plan, of which he already knew from Gandhi that morning. He staggered me by saying that in his opinion it was perfectly feasible of being carried out, since Gandhi could unquestionably influence the whole of Congress to accept it and work it loyally. He further thought that there was a chance that I might get Jinnah to accept it, and he thought that such a plan would be the quickest way to stop bloodshed.[64]

Would Jinnah agree to the proposal? Though never putting it to the League leader, Mountbatten indirectly probed him on 9 April by saying (with less than complete honesty) that 'it was a daydream of mine to be able to put the Central Government under the Prime Ministership of Mr Jinnah himself'. Thereafter, according to the Viceroy, Jinnah 'once more appealed' against 'a moth-eaten Pakistan'. Then,

> [s]ome thirty-five minutes later, Mr Jinnah, who had not referred previously to my personal remark about him, suddenly made a reference

out of the blue to the fact that I had wanted him to be the Prime Minister. There is no doubt that it had greatly tickled his vanity, and that he had kept turning over the proposition in his mind. Mr Gandhi's famous scheme may yet go through on the pure vanity of Mr Jinnah![65]

Though promising Gandhi that he would examine the scheme and privately telling his staff that 'it would not be very easy for Mr Jinnah to refuse Mr Gandhi's offer' and that 'basically Mr Gandhi's objective was to retain the unity of India and basically he was right in this',[66] Mountbatten was in fact opposed to the scheme.

Thanks to skilful work put in by his staff, associates and himself, the Viceroy's anxiety was removed. To secure or strengthen the opposition of Nehru and Patel to Gandhi's plan, the Viceroy, supported by Jawaharlal's friend Krishna Menon (who had befriended Mountbatten in London), worked on Nehru, while V. P. Menon (a talented member of the Viceroy's staff who enjoyed a close relationship with Patel) liaised with Patel. V. P. Menon also produced, on 5 April, a detailed note for the Viceroy entitled, 'Tactics to be adopted with Gandhi as regards his scheme'.[67]

The upshot was that Gandhi's Congress colleagues firmly rejected his proposal, which therefore was never put to Jinnah. On 11 April, in a letter to Mountbatten, Gandhi admitted defeat:

> I had several short talks with Pandit Nehru, and an hour's talk with him alone, and then with several members of the Working Committee last night about the formula I had sketched before you, and which I had filled in for them with all the implications. I am sorry to say that I failed to carry any of them with me except Badshah Khan...
> I could not convince them of the correctness of my plan... Nor could they dislodge me from my position although I had not closed my mind... Thus I have to ask you to omit me from your consideration.[68]

A diary entry by Rajagopalachari (a Congress member of the interim government and participant in the deliberations) states that Gandhi's 'ill-conceived plan of solving the present difficulties' was 'objected to by everybody and scotched'.[69] If Azad was among 'the several members of the working committee' with whom Gandhi talked, his rejection of the Gandhi scheme—or silence over it—would have conflicted with his word to Mountbatten that it offered the best hope of stopping bloodshed.

Jinnah scholars in Pakistan have on the whole doubted that he would have agreed to Gandhi's proposal. However, Stanley Wolpert, Jinnah's American biographer, thought that Gandhi's plan 'might just have worked'. 'Surely', Wolpert wrote, 'this was a King Solomon solution'.[70]

On 12 April, just before he left for Bihar, Gandhi signed with Jinnah not the 'solution' he had envisaged but, in the light of the Punjab killings, a joint appeal for peace, which Mountbatten had proposed.

> We deeply deplore the recent acts of lawlessness and violence... We denounce for all time the use of force to achieve political ends, and we call upon all the communities of India, to... refrain from all acts of violence and disorder [and] avoid both in speech and writing any words which might be construed as an incitement to such acts.[71]

■

Although it was not until 3 June (after a visit to London) that Mountbatten made public the British plan for dividing India, Punjab and Bengal, division had become a fait accompli after the Congress, pressed by Punjab's Sikh and Hindu leaders, asked for it on 8 March and then, a month later, rejected Gandhi's 'Jinnah card'.

Until June, Jinnah resisted the application of partition's logic to the provinces. Continuing to ask for all of Punjab and Bengal, and Assam, in May he called the Congress's partition resolution 'sinister' and a 'stunt'[72] and accused 'the Hindu minorities' of Punjab and Bengal of a 'wish to cut up these provinces and cut their own people into two in these provinces'.[73] Yet, he would not admit that Pakistan would similarly split India and its Muslims. Cutting no ice with anyone, and rejected unreservedly by Mountbatten, his stand against dividing Punjab and Bengal was quietly dropped.

Where Jinnah refused to yield, despite pressure from Mountbatten, was over the governor-generalship of an independent Pakistan, which Mountbatten coveted for himself along with the governor-generalship of India, promised to him by the INC. Confident that the League's refusal to defy the Empire during the War had earned him goodwill in the British establishment, confident also of the personal relationship he had built with Churchill,[74] and aware of Pakistan's strategic value to Britain, Jinnah, who had made up his mind to be Governor-General himself, was unmoved when, on 4 July, Mountbatten cautioned him that not having a British Governor-General when India was opting for one could cost him 'the future of Pakistan'.[75]

Jinnah's confidence about the British establishment's attitude had been bolstered by his discovery during a Buckingham Palace luncheon in December 1946 that 'His Majesty (George VI) was pro Pakistan... Her Majesty was even more pro Pakistan and... Queen Mary (the king's mother) was 100% Pakistan!' to quote his account, given on 11 April, to Eric Mieville, Mountbatten's private secretary.[76]

Though they had asked for Punjab's partition, Sikh leaders knew that any probable dividing line would separate their community into two halves. Unhappiness with this likely fate caused them, in May, to listen yet again to Jinnah's offer of Sikh 'autonomy' within Pakistan. The Sikh leaders reckoned, moreover, that talking with Jinnah would improve their bargaining position with the Congress. Patiala's Maharaja, Yadvinder Singh, and other influential Sikhs such as Tara Singh and Kartar Singh took part in talks with Jinnah in Delhi on 15-16 May, when the League leader apparently offered to meet 'all' their demands. With neither side trusting the other, the talks yielded nothing.

On 20 April, Yadvinder Singh pleaded with Mountbatten (the latter would record) to 'reconsider our decision to go'. British departure, the Maharaja said, would make chaos certain and civil war likely. The Viceroy did not budge.[77]

Accepted by the Congress and the League and, more equivocally, by the Sikhs, Britain's 3 June Partition Plan provided for a commission to demarcate a precise boundary for dividing Punjab if MLAs from Punjab's Muslim-minority districts (a majority of them Hindus and Sikhs) voted for separation, which they were certain to do. The Plan did not assume that every Muslim-majority district in Punjab would go *as a whole* to Pakistan, or every Muslim-minority district *as a whole* to India. The commission *might* award to India a Muslim-minority tehsil in a Muslim-majority district, if that tehsil was contiguous to a Muslim-minority district; and the other way round.

The 1941 census had shown that in four west Punjab districts non-Muslims amounted to a percentage close to or more than 30: Lahore, with 35.1, Lyallpur (33.4), Sialkot (31.1), and Montgomery (29.8). In eastern Punjab, Muslims amounted to more than half the population in one district, Gurdaspur, and one princely state, Kapurthala. Other eastern districts with a Muslim percentage of 30 or more were Amritsar (46.5), Jullundur (45.2), Ferozepore (45), Ludhiana (36.9), Gurgaon (33.5) and Ambala (31.6).

In addition to population numbers and contiguity, however, the proposed commission was also authorized to consider unspecified 'other factors'. The Sikhs hoped that history and economic weight would count, but Mountbatten gave them little encouragement. On 4 June he said at a press conference in Delhi:

> It was mainly at the request of the Sikh community that the Congress had put forward the resolution [asking for] the Punjab to be divided into predominantly Muslim and [predominantly] non-Muslim areas.... I have spent a great deal of time... in seeing whether there was any solution... without departing from [this] broad and easily-understood principle... I am not a miracle worker and I have not found that solution.[78]

By May 1947, India's political leaders were expecting partition and the transfer of power to happen in the following year, 'before June 1948', as Attlee had announced. On 2 June, however, they were startled to learn from Mountbatten, by means of a document entitled 'The Administrative Consequences of Partition', that the events would take place 'at the earliest possible date... in any case not later than 15th August 1947'.[79]

This date (hinted at in advance to Jinnah and Nehru) was only a little over ten weeks away. The retreating Empire wanted out as quickly as possible. Claiming during a private discussion among the Raj's British officials that 'an early transfer of power would gain [Britain] tremendous credit', Mountbatten also candidly pointed out that 'such a transfer would involve the termination of present responsibilities'.[80]

On 17 April, when Jivatram Kripalani, who had replaced Nehru as Congress president, said to Mountbatten, 'The only thing we ask of the British is to maintain law and order and be fair and impartial during their last 14 months out here', the Viceroy had replied that governors were no longer powerful and had to do what their ministers told them to do.[81] This, however, was not true for Punjab, where the governor had taken over and ministers were no longer in office. Yet, Jenkins had little resolve or energy left to enforce peace in the province, and the same was true of other Britons in Punjab. As Jenkins told Mountbatten on 16 April:

> Every British official in the I.C.S. and I.P. in the Punjab, including myself, would be very glad to leave [the province] tomorrow.[82]

To his credit, Jinnah on his part 'begged' Mountbatten (on 23 June) 'to be absolutely ruthless in suppressing disorder' in Punjab, adding, 'I don't care whether you shoot Muslims or not, it has got to be stopped'.[83] The plea was addressed to an Empire focused on departure, not on enforcing order.

The months between April and August saw several violent incidents in Punjab's town and villages. By 2 August, according to information reaching the governor, 1,044 had been killed in urban Punjab and 3,588 in rural areas.

(The killings of March were included in this count.) Most districts were affected, including Gurgaon, where 284 had been killed and 125 injured in Jat-Meo violence. Of the roughly 5,000 'probably killed' by 2 August, about 3,800, thought Jenkins, were Sikhs or Hindus, and 1,200 Muslims.[84]

Their economic strength and substantial numbers led many of Lahore's non-Muslims to believe that they could convey the city to India. These hopes in respect of Lahore were matched by Muslim expectations regarding Amritsar town, where Muslims comprised some 47 per cent of the population, compared with the 36 per cent figure for Lahore's Hindus and Sikhs combined.[85]

Shaukat Hayat and other League leaders made frequent visits to Amritsar and told the city's Muslims that they could 'play a historic role in winning Amritsar for Pakistan'.[86] In May, Muslim badmashes in Amritsar mocked their counterparts in Lahore by sending them henna and bangles. The 'gift' was publicized in some Lahore newspapers and seems to have played a role in stoking Lahore's violence.

The RSS was involved in Hindu attacks in Lahore, which however were less frequent than Muslim ones. In July, a bomb was thrown in a cinema in Bhati Gate, a Muslim locality, and the next day at a train compartment. Amritsar too witnessed some RSS attacks at this time.[87]

Lahore's mohallas saw slogan-wars and fireball-wars throughout the summer. The shout of Allah-o-Akbar from a crowd of Muslims was answered by cries of Har Har Mahadev and Sat Sri Akal. Rag-balls lit after being dipped in petrol or kerosene were flung on targeted homes and shops and countered by the enemy's fireballs.

Arson was frequent in Lahore and Amritsar. Between 14 April and 14 July, there were 495 attempts in Lahore to burn non-Muslim property and 116 attempts to set fire to Muslim property.[88] The biggest and most destructive fire was set off in the pre-dawn hours of Sunday, 22 June, when much of the carefully guarded inner-city Shahalmi Market, totally owned by Hindus and Sikhs and seen as something of a fortress, was burnt down.

The Shahalmi fire broke the will of Lahore's Sikhs and Hindus 'to fight and stay on in Lahore'. Evidence that the city magistrate, Muhammad Ghani Cheema, was deeply involved in this arson attack appears to be compelling.[89] Jenkins visited the market after the fire but there is no evidence that Cheema was even questioned.

While about half a million Sikhs and Hindus had crossed over to eastern Punjab by mid-August, there was as yet no comparable movement in the opposite direction. Despite the Congress demand for partitioning the province,

East Punjab's Muslims (a higher percentage than West Punjab's non-Muslims) were not abandoning their homes.

Offered a choice, Punjab-based Muslim officers opted to serve in western Punjab, Hindu and Sikh police officers in the east. Writing on 23 July in Lahore's *Pakistan Times*, a new English-language daily started by Iftikharuddin, Barrister Mahmud Ali said he feared for East Punjab's Muslims if Muslim officers did not remain there. Ali added:

> I know some Muslim officers are nervous about their future... but can they not muster strength to serve millions of brethren who will need their assistance?[90]

The writer's fears were related to a Sikh thirst for avenging what had happened in and around Rawalpindi in March, and to the Sikhs' resistance to a partition which would leave them without Lahore, Nankana Sahib, Lyallpur and Montgomery. Though the Sikhs argued before the boundary commission for control over these places, population figures were likely to assign all of them to Pakistan.

Some influential Sikhs seem to have concluded that the only answer was to reproduce in eastern Punjab the ethnic cleansing that had occurred in areas around Rawalpindi in March. They would push out East Punjab's Muslim population and replace it with Sikhs from the western districts. No documentary evidence may exist of where, when and by whom such a conclusion was arrived at, yet the events of July, August and September point to it.

Even earlier, on 18 April, when he met Mountbatten along with Master Tara Singh and Giani Kartar Singh, Baldev Singh, the Viceroy's defence member, asked for a transfer of populations in Punjab, claiming also that Jinnah would support it. Expressing doubts as to the latter assertion, Mountbatten said that a transfer of populations would be 'appallingly difficult'.[91]

Calling on Jenkins on 19 May, Master Tara Singh (according to a note by the former) ominously 'intimated' the governor 'that in Pakistan the Muslims would massacre all the Sikhs and Hindus and that in the other part of the Punjab the Sikhs and Hindus would massacre all the Muslims'.[92] According to a present-day scholar, Master Tara Singh told him in February 1967, referring to 1947, 'We took the decision to turn the Muslims out.'[93]

On 22 July, when he was in Lahore, Mountbatten directed that the East Punjab Secretariat should move to Simla. This signal that Lahore would remain in Pakistan was a fresh impetus to the movement of Hindus and Sikhs from west to east. As violence against Hindus and Sikhs grew in Lahore and the western districts, attacks by armed Sikh jathas on Muslim villages began in Amritsar district and elsewhere in East Punjab. On 10 August, the *Pakistan Times* reported that several prominent journalists in Lahore, including its own editor, the poet Faiz Ahmed Faiz, had sent an urgent telegram to Mountbatten:

> Organized attacks by highly armed gangs continue in Muslim villages in the districts of Eastern Punjab. The Government Machinery is incapable of giving protection to the Muslim minority. Pray intervene... to stop massacre of innocent people.[94]

∎

By now parties at the all-India level had agreed on a few things. One, India, Punjab and Bengal would all be divided. When the All India Congress Committee met on 14-15 June to vote on Mountbatten's Plan, to which Nehru, Patel and Kripalani had given their consent, Gandhi asked delegates to ratify the consent. He was 'unhappy', he said. But the Congress's 'best workers' had made their decision, and an alternative set of leaders was not around to replace them.[95] Azad also endorsed the Plan.

Those opposing ratification at the AICC meeting included Saifuddin Kitchlew and a few other Muslims who for years had stood against India's division, as well as Choithram Gidwani, a Hindu delegate from Sindh. The Plan was endorsed by 157 votes to 27, with 32 remaining neutral. 'It was the only resolution' a delegate noted, 'other than a condolence resolution, approved in total silence during my forty years in Congress.'[96]

The Raj, the Congress and the League also agreed that the Indian Army and the civil and police services would be divided into two, and that a 7,500-strong Punjab Boundary Force, commanded by a British general but consisting mostly of Indian soldiers, would enforce the peace in critical Punjab districts during the weeks before partition.

Meeting in Lahore in two sections—the eastern and the western—the Punjab legislative assembly voted on 23 June (the day after the Shahalmi fire) to clinch partition. By 50 votes to 22, legislators from the eastern districts defeated a motion by Mamdot that the province should remain united. Though legislators from Muslim-majority districts voted 69 to 27 in favour of a united Punjab, East Punjab had exercised its right to separate. It would remain in India.

As part of the boundary commission, two League-nominated judges,

Justice Din Muhammad and Justice Muhammad Munir, and two Congress-nominated judges, Justice Mehr Chand Mahajan and Justice Teja Singh, sat from 21 to 31 July in Lahore and heard opposing arguments.

The best lawyers were hired: M.C. Setalvad, later India's attorney-general, by the INC; Zafrulla Khan, later Pakistan's foreign minister,* by the League; and Sardar Harnam Singh by the Sikhs. All three sought to justify their sides' maximal claims. The commission's chairman, Sir Cyril Radcliffe, a British jurist, who had arrived in India (for the first and last time) on 8 July, was not present at the Lahore hearings, but all proceedings were flown to him in Delhi.

After the four Indian judges had neutralized one another by their separate and contradictory opinions, Radcliffe gave his own binding decisions: Lyallpur, Montgomery, and Nankana Sahib to Pakistan; most of Lahore district and all of Lahore city to Pakistan; Amritsar district (and city) to India; Ferozepore district, including its Muslim-majority tehsils (Zira and Ferozepore) and a portion of Muslim-majority Kasur tehsil (Lahore district) to India; Gurdaspur district's Shakargarh tehsil, which lay west of the river Ujh, to Pakistan; all the rest of Gurdaspur district to India.

Reached before 14 August, the day of Pakistan's founding, Radcliffe's decisions were however only announced on 17 August, i.e. two days after India's independence.

His verdict on Gurdaspur would remain the most controversial. Muslims (inclusive of Ahmadiyyas, whose founder belonged to the district) constituted a slight majority in the tehsils of Gurdaspur and Batala, which were given to India, and also in the district as a whole. Only Pathankot tehsil, also awarded to India, had a clear non-Muslim majority. In the decades to follow, Pakistanis would charge that Mountbatten influenced Radcliffe to award three-fourths of Gurdaspur district to India, thereby enabling India to gain a route to Kashmir.

The charge was countered by three arguments. One, Pathankot tehsil, which accommodated India's Kashmir route, had a substantial non-Muslim majority anyhow. Two, the river Ujh divided the region naturally. Three, while Muslim majorities in the tehsils of Batala, Gurdaspur and Shakargarh, and in the district as a whole, were narrow, the non-Muslim majority in Pathankot was solid.

Speculative explanations of Radcliffe's verdict (the man himself left no

---

*Sir Muhammad Zafrulla Khan was a leading member of the Ahmadiyya community.

papers) include a wish on his part to compensate for Sikh disappointment with the bulk of his judgment. The fact that two years earlier Wavell had opined, in a private Raj document, that in the event of partition Gurdaspur district *had* to go, for Amritsar's sake, to India is also mentioned as a factor possibly influencing Radcliffe.[97] On the other hand, there is a belief that before allegedly allowing himself to be influenced by Mountbatten, Radcliffe had wanted to give Ferozepore district's Muslim-majority tehsils (Zira and Ferozepore) to Pakistan. In the end these tehsils were awarded to India.[98]

At the time and later, many Punjabis took it for granted that the four Indians on the boundary commission would give separate verdicts. Yet, the four were judges, not lawyers. They would have violated no norm or convention had they sat down together and tried to reach an agreement. That did not happen. In the Punjab of 1947, even persons who sensed the proximity of horror were reluctant—even when they were judges—to step out of their communal cocoons to try to avert it. Prejudices, fears and enmities were reinforced, not questioned, inside these echo-chambers.

■

As violence on persons, homes, villages and trains escalated in the first half of August, and reprisal invited reprisal, Jenkins found it difficult, he informed the Viceroy, even 'to keep track' of all the 'raids and murders'. Pleading for reinforcements he knew he would not get for the Punjab Boundary Force, the governor spoke on 13 August of the 'completely communal regime' that had taken over in Lahore and added:

> The Sikhs probably have two objectives in mind—they wish to take revenge for the Rawalpindi massacre and they wish to assert themselves on the boundary question. It is impossible to defend their conduct in any way, but the Muslims have failed to understand the horror caused by the Rawalpindi affair and seem to think that by reprisals they can bring the Sikhs to a less violent state of mind. I very much doubt this.[99]

On the night of 13 August, the police station chief of Lahore's Mozang quarter evidently masterminded an attack on a historic gurdwara built by Guru Arjan Dev. All the score or so Sikh men and women inside this gurdwara, which stood only fifteen yards from the Mozang police station, were killed and the shrine burnt down. The attack was carried out by about thirty Muslim youths led by 'a devout Khaksar', as Taj Din, the leader, called himself while admitting his involvement in an interview with a contemporary scholar in the year 2000.[100]

On his last day in office, 14 August, Jenkins informed Mountbatten of attacks in Rawalpindi on two eastbound trains and added: 'Situation now will be for new government to deal with.'[101]

■

In scale and degree of horror, the Punjab killings of August-September 1947 stand in a class apart. In terms of numbers of the uprooted, the migrations occurring between June and November, most of them taking place in August and September, also stand out in the subcontinent's history. Probably between half a million and eight hundred thousand in all were killed in Punjab in 1947. About ten to twelve million people were forced to leave their homes and cross the new border.[102]

Scholars broadly agree that Hindus and Sikhs lost more property than Muslims and that more Muslims than non-Muslims were killed and uprooted. Within three years of the 1947 killings, two wide-ranging surveys were provided by Indian writers, G. D. Khosla's *Stern Reckoning* (1949) and Gurcharan Singh Talib's *Muslim League's Attacks on Sikhs and Hindus in the Punjab* (1950). Both offered the argument that violence against Muslims in eastern Punjab was mostly retaliatory. However, Khosla spoke also of 'the many [in India] who boast that the total number of Muslims killed was more than the number of Hindus and Sikhs who perished'.[103]

No comprehensive survey of the 1947 killings seems to have been brought out by Pakistan-based writers, though in 1948 the West Punjab government published three short reports: *Note on the Sikh Plan; RSS in the Punjab;* and *Sikhs in Action*.

Perhaps the fairest and fullest account of the upheaval is to be found in the 2011 study by the Stockholm-based scholar of Pakistani origin, Ishtiaq Ahmed, *The Punjab: Bloodied, Partitioned and Cleansed*, which analyzes available literature and also provides hundreds of eyewitness accounts from every district of undivided Punjab. Ahmed's study is the chief source for many of the passages and recollections that follow in this chapter.

The eyewitness accounts in Ahmed's study and reminiscences obtained by others, including this writer, confirm what several earlier studies had failed to underline: the successful way in which ordinary Punjabis in both halves of their divided province protected endangered 'Others', assisted escape and enabled survival.

The 'poisonous wind'[104] of 1947 swayed thousands in Punjab who killed several times their number, but not the vast majority of Muslim, Sikh and Hindu Punjabis, who did not allow that wind to shake them. In fact, thousands from this majority quietly and courageously saved an immense number of threatened lives.

'How are the Muslims of the Punjab different', Gandhi had asked in 1939, 'from the Hindus and the Sikhs? Are they not all Punjabis, drinking the same water, breathing the same air and deriving sustenance from the same soil?'[105] Aware of their bond with one another, and of the humanness of those threatened, countless Punjabis protected their fellows. That is the under-reported story of Punjab 1947.

Even when it reaches extreme levels, violence gets graded from 'highest' to relatively 'low'. Ishtiaq Ahmed's study suggests that in western Punjab the violence was probably worst in three districts of Lahore division, Sheikhupura (where Guru Nanak was born), Gujranwala (Ranjit Singh's home ground) and Sialkot; in three districts of Rawalpindi division, Gujrat, Mianwali and Shahpur; in Multan division's Montgomery district; and in the city and district of Lahore itself.

Because of a strong DC, Agha Abdul Hameed, violence was checked for weeks in Multan division's Lyallpur town and district, where (as in some other parts of West Punjab) many Hindus and Sikhs stayed on until end-September. Eventually, though, terrible reprisals were meted out to Sikhs in Lyallpur's rural areas. Another strict DC, Raja Sultan Lal Hussain, controlled the situation in Muzaffargarh district (also in Multan division), but after his transfer on 20 August non-Muslims were savagely attacked.

In Baba Farid's Pakpattan, where, as in much of western Punjab, Hindus and Sikhs were a prosperous minority, soldiers and policemen saved lives if not property. Soldiers and policemen were also responsible for preventing large-scale killings in the large princely tract of Bahawalpur. In Dera Ghazi Khan district, where Hindus and Sikhs made up a tiny if affluent minority, there was heavy looting but apparently most of the endangered escaped.[106]

In eastern Punjab, the princely territory of Malerkotla, ruled by a nawab of Pashtun origin, saw the least amount of violence. Three factors may have been at work: Guru Gobind Singh's 240-year-old decree that Malerkotla's Muslims should not be harmed; the nawab's apparent friendship with the Maharaja of Patiala; and arms possessed by Malerkotla's Muslims. In any event, Malerkotla provided temporary space for hundreds of thousands of fleeing Muslims before they crossed over to Pakistan.

Eastern Punjab's worst-hit areas were the districts of Ludhiana, Jullundur,

Ferozepore, Amritsar and Kangra, and the princely states of Patiala, Kapurthala and Faridkot. Some Sikh rajas of eastern Punjab would be accused of organizing and funding the killings.

Ishtiaq Ahmed's study suggests that if 250,000 Sikhs and Hindus were killed in western Punjab, between 250,000 and 500,000 Muslims may have perished in eastern Punjab. The Sikh jathas that attacked Muslims across eastern Punjab after 15 August were usually armed with Bren guns, Tommy guns, grenades, rifles, revolvers, pistols, spears and kirpans. Often, the jathas were motorized: members moved on trucks and jeeps. Among their ranks were Sikhs from northwestern Punjab, wanting revenge.

Because the Muslim percentage was high in several eastern districts and towns—it was, for example, 63 and 59, respectively, in the city-cum-cantonment areas of Ludhiana and Jullundur—most Muslims in eastern Punjab assumed, until Radcliffe's awards were announced, that Pakistan would extend to include their homes, villages and towns. The League leadership in Lahore knew this assumption to be fanciful, but facts and probabilities were never communicated to East Punjab's Muslims. When, suddenly, reality arrived at the latter's door, it wore a terrible face.

In and around Ludhiana and Jullundur, the carnage was of great size. 'I have seen the holocaust of Muslims in this village and around this region. There can be no comparison with the situation in West Punjab', observed Harmail Singh, a Sikh, speaking in 2005 in Gujjarwal in Ludhiana district.[107]

In Hoshiarpur, Jullundur and elsewhere, many Muslims fought back with such weapons as they had and killed a few of the 'enemy'. Likewise, many Sikhs and Hindus fought back in western Punjab and took 'enemy' lives. But the odds were impossible for minorities when district officers and police chiefs often supported and at times directed the attacks, and the Punjab Boundary Force (PBF) proved too small and, at times, unreliable.

Led by Major General T. W. Rees, who was assisted by two Indian officers, a Sikh and a Muslim, the PBF was deployed between 1 and 31 August in twelve central districts of Punjab, six (Sialkot, Gujranwala, Sheikhupura, Lyallpur, Montgomery and Lahore) on the Pakistani side and six (Amritsar, Gurdaspur, Jullundur, Hoshiarpur, Ludhiana and Ferozepore) on the Indian side. With an area of 37,500 square miles, these twelve districts held over twelve million people, but the PBF never mustered more than 9,000 soldiers and policemen.

The PBF successfully escorted several refugee columns and saved a number of lives but its units were often outnumbered by marauders. Given the vast surface the force had to cover, it was hopelessly undermanned. Also, some of its units were accused of joining the violence instead of stopping it.

Thus, in Sheikhupura town, a Baloch regiment with the PBF was widely believed to have gunned down, on 25 and 26 August, thousands of Sikhs and Hindus who, after escaping earlier attacks, had taken refuge in a factory owned by a man named Atma Singh.[108] Providing the other side of the picture in his *Emergence of Pakistan,* Chaudhri Muhammad Ali quoted a British PBF officer's remark, 'There was no case on record of a Sikh or Hindu policeman having shot anyone except a Muslim.'[109] Instances were also reported of PBF soldiers firing upon other PBF soldiers after being inflamed by the suffering of co-religionists.[110]

During the carnage of August and September, many Punjabis cried as they left infirm and elderly relatives and ran for safety. Others escaped while watching loved ones being killed.

> My grandparents could not walk and stayed behind. On the way to the station I saw my father being struck with a spear. My mother went to help but was hit on the head with a hammer. I saw her skull burst open as she fell. I escaped, reached the station and escaped on a train that was not attacked because some Englishmen were on it.[111]

People looked on helplessly as a child or parent was slain, a wife or daughter raped and killed, an infant tossed in the air and caught by a bayonet or spear. Breasts were knifed, vaginas speared. In both halves of Punjab, deeds and sights more horrible than could be imagined were done and seen.

Often the trauma was stretched out. You were seized, raped multiple times and brutally killed. Or, leaving behind dead or living relatives, you fled from an attacked house, joined a column of escapees, slipped into a clump of trees when the column was shot at, found a fresh group of assailants, eluded them—and found yourself trapped by the rising waters of a river. Or you reached a refugee camp—and starved or caught cholera there.[112] Or you were stabbed or clubbed just before reaching the river or the camp.

There was fearsome symmetry. Muslims left Amritsar station, which was littered with Muslim bodies, and arrived at Lahore station where they walked on corpses of Hindus and Sikhs in order to get out. Traumatized Hindus and Sikhs running to Lahore station to flee to the east saw there the traumatized faces of survivors who had fled in the opposite direction, bereft of slain relatives.

The train filled with dead bodies became the enduring symbol of 1947 Punjab. Such trains arrived on both sides of the new border. A tree trunk or a boulder blocked a train loaded with refugees; the engine-driver often fled; armed attackers entered the train, killed as many as they could and flung out others who were dealt with by a waiting mob armed with swords and guns. The attackers, many of them demobilized soldiers, were familiar with railway time-tables as well as with guns.

Those who successfully escaped by train, lorry or bullock-cart, or in foot-columns, saw dead bodies and rivulets of blood first on their side of the border and then again beyond the border. Arriving in Lahore towards the end of August, Haji Mukhtar Ahmed Khan, who fled from his village in Hoshiarpur district, saw that 'the whole of Anarkali and the shopping area on the Mall was burnt down. Hindu and Sikh dead bodies were lying all over'.[113]

One day at the end of August, shortly before his father and about 150 Sikhs and Hindus were slain or burnt to death inside a gurdwara in Gujranwala, twenty-four-year-old Kidar Nath Malhotra reluctantly obeyed his doomed father's injunction and fled. Early in September, an Indian army unit enabled Malhotra and other refugees from Gujranwala to cross the border at Wagah and reach Amritsar. 'The road between Wagah and Amritsar was littered with dead bodies. They must have been Muslims, I suppose,' he would recall in 2004.[114]

Some women jumped into wells or rivers to save their honour, others were slain by their menfolk before the enemy's menfolk could ravish them. A few women were killed in error. In one instance where this happened, a rumour that the Baloch regiment was coming was believed when in fact Hindu soldiers were on the way.

Women who were part of columns trudging towards the border were snatched from helpless husbands, fathers and brothers, and appropriated. Elsewhere, seized women were divided among attackers, with police officers picking first. Murder often followed rape.

•

As the Empire exited on 14-15 August 1947, and Punjab became two Punjabs, Jinnah, Pakistan's Governor-General, asked Francis Mudie, who had been serving as Sindh's governor, to move to Lahore as West Punjab's governor. Though his Ferozepore lands had gone to India, Mamdot became West Punjab's chief minister, with Iftikharuddin as minister for refugees. India's East Punjab province, which included also the districts of today's Haryana and Himachal, had Chandulal Trivedi, a Gujarati member of the ICS, as governor and Gopichand Bhargava as chief minister.

In the first few weeks of independence, these new administrations were as feeble before the carnage as the receding Raj had been; some in the new administrations were complicit. Sensing what was likely to happen, many Muslim officers posted in eastern Punjab, including those in the police, had crossed the border before it was delineated. Many Hindu and Sikh officers had similarly moved east in good time.

Officers who found themselves on the wrong side of the dividing line were quickly disempowered. Policemen were disarmed. A few were killed. The rest, civilians and policemen, made for the border, along with those they might have assisted in better times, the terrified Hindus and Sikhs of the western half or the terrified Muslims of eastern Punjab.

In some cases, officers who crossed the border carried bitter memories and a vengeful spirit that goaded attackers and dehumanized victims. A report prepared on 21 September by the Communist Party of India claimed that 'the Jullundur District Magistrate, one Mr. Midha [told] the people "to do whatever they liked for three days"'.[115] Midha had served until mid-August in Gujranwala, where his son was stabbed.

On 14 October, the governments of India and Pakistan formally agreed that the two Punjabs should exchange their minorities.[116] This was merely an acknowledgment of what had already take place, not an enunciation of new policy. Earlier, on 10 September, when the government of India 'decided' that 'priority should be given to the transfer of refugees rather than the maintenance of law and order',[117] that 'decision' too was only an admission that enforcing law and order had *not* been the primary goal of officials in East Punjab after 15 August, even as it was not the priority of West Punjab's officials.

Seeing the writing on the wall, many businessmen had sold properties in the weeks before mid-August and slipped out of Lahore, or Amritsar, or wherever. Speaking of Lahore, Ishtiaq Ahmed writes,

> In well-to-do localities ugly acts of violence did not occur. Hindu-Sikh bourgeoisie of Lahore could leave more or less safely. It was petty employees, servants, shopkeepers and all who had neither the connections nor the means to arrange for their departure in time that bore the brunt.

A few well-off Hindus in Lahore did not even witness the violence. One of them, living on Egerton Road, would recall in 1999:

Nobody in our family saw the violence with our own eyes because we never went to the old city or other trouble spots. Ours was an upper-class area.[118]

Despite ethnic cleansing, not every single Hindu or Sikh left West Punjab. Those who remained were mostly 'untouchables' who had no resources to make an exit or attract looters. In East Punjab, too, a few very poor Muslims did not, or could not, leave.

Escapees would recall the attackers' common tactics. In both parts, attackers used similar deceptions. For example, if a cluster of minority homes was guarded by defenders, the latter were rushed out by 'a friend' in the majority to fight a non-existent force of attackers a couple of miles off, freeing real attackers to slaughter the undefended.

Frightened groups often sought shelter in a mosque or a gurdwara, only to find that a sacred place merely simplified mass killing. This happened in, among other places of worship, Masjid Rangrezan in Amritsar's inner city, where hundreds of men, women and children were slain on 15 August, and in the Gujranwala gurdwara two weeks later. Similarly, trains and railway stations, destinations of hope, frequently turned into traps of death.

In both halves, escapees retained pleasant memories of life before the carnage. 'Earlier we always had good relations.' 'That teacher, or shop-owner, or postmaster (from the Other group) was such a good, kind person.' 'That woman was like an aunt.' 'We exchanged sweets during Diwali or Eid.' 'Outsiders, not people from our village, did the killing.'[119] And so forth.

The large quantity of such memories would indicate that enmity between non-Muslim and Muslim was *not* the Punjabi norm. However, other recollections mentioned persons close by who did horrible things. 'Men became beasts', was a recurring theme. However, a number of Punjabis would recall that they, or people they were concerned about, were helped by units of the Indian or Pakistani army after mid-August. 'Army people came and removed them (or us) to safety.'

Quite a few also remembered pledges made in their village or locality to protect one another. Men with murderous intent were told, 'Kill us first before you kill the people we have sheltered.' Such declarations usually had an effect but were harder to make once people with tales of outrage arrived from the other half.

Eventually the sheltered had to be told: 'Please leave now and return when normal times are back. Meanwhile we will look after your house and things.' An unspoken cross-border alliance of goodness thus preserved countless lives and also some property.

In some cases, Hindus returned after a year or so to their homes in West Punjab to retrieve gold and silver, though there was no question of resuming life there. There were fewer stories of Muslims returning to East Punjab to recover gold or silver, but then uprooted Muslims contained a larger proportion of the poor as compared with uprooted Hindus and Sikhs.

■

Since Punjab became purely Muslim in the west and purely non-Muslim in the east, a question has at times been asked: could this rearrangement have come about through a peaceful transfer of populations, without the 1947 carnage?

A peaceful transfer of people required prior agreement on a boundary. Such an agreement did not exist in the summer of 1947 and was in fact never sought. Until May of that year, the very idea of parts of Punjab staying out of Pakistan sounded 'sinister' to Jinnah and was dismissed by Punjab's League leaders. The Sikhs similarly dismissed suggestions that Lahore, Lyallpur and Nankana Sahib should or could belong to Pakistan.

As events moved forward in 1947, a peaceful exchange of Punjab's populations was never seriously canvassed by any major party. While Baldev Singh's mention of it to Mountbatten on 18 April is interesting in retrospect, it was not accompanied by an offer to explore a dividing line acceptable to all sides.

On 1 May 1947, in a statement published in *Dawn,* Jinnah too spoke of a transfer of minorities 'at some [future] stage', whenever 'it may be necessary and feasible'. But in the same statement he ruled out any division of Punjab and Bengal.[120] Jinnah seemed to assume that western Pakistan would extend up to the perimeter of Delhi. Given the total disagreement on dividing lines, a peaceful exchange of populations was a fantasy.

Even after 3 June, when the Partition Plan was made public and approximate boundaries were known, no one asked for a population exchange in Punjab. While the average Punjabi prayed that his or her worst fears would not be realized—that partition would not destroy everyday life—others more aware of ugly trends seemed keener on punishing the 'enemy' than on saving lives.

The several League-Sikh talks held before partition were about possible power-sharing in a coalition ministry in Lahore for a united Punjab, not about a dividing line across the province. Had those talks moved forward, and also taken the Congress along, bloodshed might indeed have been greatly reduced, if not averted.

■

'Hordes of gangsters, criminals and drug and alcohol addicts took part in the raids. They were looking for an opportunity to loot and pillage and let loose their evil lust on women.'[121] So says Harmail Singh (in Ahmed's study) about the attacks in Gujjarwal in Ludhiana district. Many other accounts also refer to prominent roles played by local badmashes, armed men with a criminal record and influence in their turf. We saw earlier that Amritsar's Muslim badmashes sent mehndi and bangles to their Lahori counterparts to taunt them into violence.

But the badmash in the Punjab of 1947 was not a character wholly independent of the community he lived amidst. In any case, roles in the Punjab carnage were also played by influential men who were not badmashes in the conventional sense—by police chiefs, officials, politicians and ex-soldiers, by men looking for loot, revenge, control or a killer-image.

Greed for gold and houses played a part. Enraged refugees stoked passions. Former army men, including ex-INA men, provided expertise, leadership and weapons. They deliberately spread false rumours (about hidden guns, for instance), inciting assaults.

For a few weeks, Punjab seemed to face a climate (a 'poisonous wind', a 'fever' that turned some men into beasts, a 'madness', as it was variously called) which enabled the viewing of 'those people' as objects deserving expulsion or death and whose women merited rape. In such a climate, a mob was willing to do anything, especially when deliberately inflamed by stories of horror from the other side.

In those dark days or weeks, the pathologies of some in Punjab found free expression and received applause and imitation. Something in the air valorized the badmashes, who killed, burnt or looted and set off a frenzy that captured others. Even so, individual responses, destructive or life-saving, made a difference. Depending on the officer present, a mob was calmed, dispersed or inflamed. If some Punjabis were receptive to the frenzy, most were not.

As to what precipitated the dark climate, any answer has to include HMG's 20 February announcement that the Empire was leaving. The ensuing scramble for control saw Punjab's politicians making unreasonable and clashing demands. Muslim politicians asked for *all* of Punjab, including large areas where non-Muslims were a clear majority. Sikh leaders asked for *much* of Punjab, including districts where Muslims were a clear majority. From opposite sides Punjabis were pushed onto a collision course.

Unwilling to lower their demands, or agree on a partition scheme, *or* on a coalition government for undivided Punjab, Punjab's Muslim and Sikh politicians, taken together, created an impossible situation which became calamitous when sections in both groups thought of ethnic cleansing as a solution. The province's Hindu politicians, representing a population larger than the Sikhs', contributed nothing constructive as a remedy; and there were no successful interventions at the all-India level either, whether from the INC or the League.

With the Empire impatient to quit India, including Punjab, with no power-sharing agreement in New Delhi between the INC and the League, no Punjabi coalition surfacing to replace the Raj in Lahore, and the provincial press fiercely partisan and unrestrained, it was open season in Punjab—from July 1947 onwards—for looters, badmashes, killers and ethnic cleansers.

Of course, earlier history too was at work, including a ministry opposed by the bulk of Punjab's Muslim majority, and also what had happened before that, including the polarizing campaign for Pakistan. Yet, a historian asked to identify a 'trigger' for the climate that enabled the carnage of August-September 1947 would point the finger at the 20 February announcement.

■

Given their pride in building Punjab, the 1947 killings were profoundly troubling for the British. Given their faith in the remedial powers of liberty, the killings were equally troubling for the Indians. Having surveyed, in the last two chapters, Britain's final quarter century in Punjab, let us identify some longer-term factors in the process that wrecked the imperial vision of British Punjab leading the subcontinent in economic progress and stability, killed, at the same time, the nationalist dream of freedom in unity, and produced the Punjab cataclysm.

With their century-long toil there, involving among other things a sustained focus on agriculture, the British had earned, one might say, a moral right to influence Punjab's future. Though in the end it lost the will to use it, the Empire also possessed the gun to control Punjab.

Until 1946, Punjab's soldiers and land-owning lobby remained loyal to the Empire, but the landowners remained alienated from the people. Worse, soldiers from the start and landowners towards the end were fragmented into Muslims, Hindus and Sikhs. The British policy of divide-and-control undoubtedly prolonged imperial rule, but it did not help Punjab in 1947.

Divide-and-rule was reinforced by annoyance at the Congress-led independence movement. It was to deny gains to the Congress that Khizr was let down at the Simla Conference of 1945. This betrayal of a loyal ally was a fillip to the League's hard line and a signal for sharper polarization in Punjab. Human and understandable as it was, imperial pique contributed to the 1947 carnage and helped destroy a Punjab the British had done much to build.

A year later, a Cabinet Mission eager to return to London with an 'agreement' refrained from candidly asking the Congress, the League and the Sikhs to choose between a Large Pakistan within a firm union and a Small Pakistan firmly outside it.

Given the role that demobilized soldiers played in the Punjab violence, we also have to conclude that two other long-standing British policies, making Punjab the main recruiting ground of the army and making its regiments communal, extracted, in the end, a large price from Punjabi society.[122] That the most Empire-friendly of its Indian provinces should see the greatest violence was a sombre denouement for Britain.

Along with a right to influence Punjab's future, the British had also acquired a moral duty to be responsible while departing, a hard duty no doubt, and one tragically abandoned in post-War fatigue, which was aggravated by annoyance at what was seen as Indian ingratitude and impertinence.

Neither Punjab's political leaders nor the all-India Congress tried seriously to unite Punjabis across the class divide between landed aristocrats and the rest, or across the communal divides. The Unionists tried to unite all large landowners irrespective of religion, but not the bulk of Punjabis. The Gandhi-led, Khilafat-linked movement of 1919-22 cut across all divides and penetrated all parts of Punjab but lasted for only three years.

Gandhi asked Punjabis of different faiths to settle with one another and struggle against the Empire. From 1919 to 1922, the three communities jointly fought the Empire. However, once the Khilafat issue disappeared, each group in Punjab, whether Muslim, Hindu or Sikh, chose to settle with the Empire and struggle against the other groups.

Thereafter, in the enfranchised Punjab that counted, the pro-Raj stance of the Unionists and the communal stance of Punjab's Hindu, Sikh and Muslim leaders proved more appealing than Gandhi's message of non-dependence on the Empire coupled with Hindu-Muslim-Sikh unity.

This was not surprising, for the Empire had much to give. The jobs the Empire could dangle, including with the army, were a strong draw. The Empire could also offer canal-colony lands and ministerships. But Punjab's communities had a great deal to offer one another too: peace in the street and countryside, the benefits of trade, and support in the struggle for independence.

While hard to hold on to in the heat of competitive politics, this truth could have been brought home to all Punjabis by the Congress. However, the Punjab Congress remained too Hindu and too urban to do this. For the failure of the Punjab Congress to grow into a party of all Punjabis, Gandhi and the Congress's central leadership must be assigned some responsibility.

The Congress's failure to retain Fazl-i-Husain was the biggest evidence of its limitations. The anti-feudal sentiment of the Congress Left combined with the anti-Muslim sentiment of the Congress Right to block a possible understanding with Fazl and the others who formed the 'feudal' and 'agricultural' Unionist party.

These anti-feudal sentiments resided in the Punjab Congress and also in the all-India Congress. In the 1920s and 1930s, Gandhi's occasional feelers for an understanding with the Unionists were disliked by progressives in the all-India Congress and even more strongly by the Punjab Congress and other Hindu leaders in the province.

The Unionist Party's prominent Muslims were key to avoiding polarization in the province, but until the 1946 elections the Punjab Congress was opposed to approaching the Unionists. In opting to fight both the League and the Unionists, the Punjab Congress had taken on one foe too many.

In the end, cooperation from the Raj too was necessary for resolving the tension between the Congress's twin goals, freedom and unity. This cooperation was not forthcoming. The Congress's nationwide stirs, including Quit India, had induced in the Empire a wish to hurt rather than assist the Congress.

In his Punjab strategy, Jinnah was in some ways wiser than the Congress. Ignoring the Punjab League, which until 1945 was as primarily urban as the Punjab Congress, he proposed an alliance with Fazl in 1936 and with Sikander in 1937. Failing with Fazl, he succeeded with Sikander.

But wanting India's division and Punjab's unity was a stark inconsistency in Jinnah's and the League's wider goals. To demand self-determination for Muslim-majority areas and deny it to areas where Hindus and Sikhs were a majority was illogical and proved unfeasible. It also contributed to the 1947 tragedy.

Just as an earlier set of local Muslim chiefs had been unprepared, in the late eighteenth century, to resist the Sikh drive, Punjab's Muslim leaders were unwilling, in 1945-46, to resist the League's extreme demands, even though they feared the consequences of Punjab's division. This weakness contributed to the 1947 tragedy and the loss of Muslim lives in East Punjab.

Their unique and centuries-long identification with Punjab and the Punjabi language made the 1947 tragedy extraordinarily tough for the Sikhs. Yet, their leaders cannot escape a due share of responsibility. Their failure lay not in picking more than one foe, or in inconsistency, but in a lack of realism.

To recall Ranjit Singh's Punjab with pride was one thing. But to suggest, a century after the Sikh kingdom's demise, that a fighting spirit could restore Sikh rule over areas where Muslims were a majority was neither reasonable nor prudent. Following on the 20 February announcement from London, this 3 March claim in Lahore accelerated the journey to tragedy.

■

Our survey suggests that the Punjabi individual on the ground—Sikh, Muslim or Hindu—was more tolerant than elites and elected politicians. If some Punjabis were willing to be caught up in the frenzies of 1947, many more were willing to quietly protect the threatened.

At other times, normal life usually prevailed on the ground, and cordial exchanges took place during festivals, though the centuries-old tension between purity of belief and purity of birth was present even in the 1930s and 1940s. If this tension remained part of Punjab's climate, the Punjabis' ability to put it to one side was a stronger part.

But the ordinary Punjabi also bears some responsibility. Punjabi Hindus and Sikhs embraced education, the professions, commerce and industry, but not democracy. While desiring Indian independence, they disliked and also feared popular rule. At several junctures they seemed to want a restoration of the Raj's bureaucracy and an end to elected governments.

This was not anti-Muslim prejudice as much as reluctance to lose a dominance to which they had grown accustomed. In any case, the bid to defy demography and delay democracy proved short-sighted.

Punjabi Muslims, on their part, showed inadequate awareness of the problems that Hindus and Sikhs saw in majority rule. There seems to be little evidence that the average Muslim tried in the 1930s or 1940s to dispel fears about majority rule from the mind of his Hindu or Sikh neighbour.

If the people were not as far-seeing as they might have been, those claiming to represent them did not rise to the occasion. No core or nucleus emerged that spoke for Punjabis as a whole, and those that spoke for their communities refused to discuss possible compromises. As in earlier history, most Punjabis were able, during the 1940s, to adjust, survive, and assist others to survive, but their leaders were unable to lead.

Chapter Ten

1947: *INSANIYAT* AMIDST INSANITY

Carnage was not the whole story of Punjab 1947. In their villages and towns, many ordinary Punjabis protected vulnerable ones and helped them escape. In recent years, attempts have been made to obtain and record these life-saving acts.[1] One such effort was made in Lahore during nine days in July 2005 by this author and Usha Gandhi, the author's wife. The subsequent passages are reports of, and excerpts from, a few of the more than two dozen interviews conducted at the time.

■

Ahmed Hayat Kalyar of Sargodha. Interviewed in Lahore on 23 July 2005, Ahmed Hayat Kalyar (*b*. 1949) told us of what he had heard of 1947 from his father, Mian Mohammed Hayat Kalyar (*b*. 1926). The family had lands about 120 miles northwest of Lahore in district Shahpur (called Sargodha after 1960), mostly in a village called Mir Ahmed Sher Garh.

Kalyar: 'Only one Hindu family owned land in our village—the family of Bhogaram Chugh. Three or four miles from our village stood the big village of Faruka, where Sikhs had established the Khalsa High School in 1906-7. One of the schoolteachers was Master Tara Singh.

'He was well-liked but in 1947 he decided to go to India. The family left for Sillanwali railway station, nine miles from Faruka. The army was protecting a camp in Sillanwali where Hindus and Sikhs... had gathered. Two miles from Faruka, on the way to Sillanwali, the entire family of Tara Singh (six or seven people) was slaughtered on a bridge over a drain. That was the reward given to a great man.

'But my family was able to save the family of Bhogaram Chugh. Soon after the Tara Singh incident, tongas and guards were arranged and the Bhogaram family reached the Sillanwali camp. His son Tilak Raj became a dental surgeon in Chandigarh. He sent us photos of the family. In 1985 or 1986, my daughter Fatima (*b*. 1973) had correspondence with Dr Tilak Raj's family. [We learnt afterwards that] Tilak Raj put Fatima's letter to his eyes and cried.'

Mohammed Saeed Awan, formerly of district Hoshiarpur. Interviewed on 24 July 2005, Mohammed Saeed Awan, originally of village Khanpur in sub-tehsil Mukerian in tehsil Dasooya in East Punjab's Hoshiarpur district, was born in 1925. His father was a headmaster in Khanpur village. The family had lived for generations in Hoshiarpur district.

Mohammed Awan: 'There was a substantial Muslim presence in Khanpur village and in the towns of Mukerian and Dasooya. Many in the Awan clan were in the army. I went to Arya High School in Mukerian. I led a campaign in the school after a Hindu mithai-seller roughly shook off a Muslim boy who had touched his tray of sweets, saying, "Bharasht kardiya"—"You have polluted the sweets." I saw dogs licking his cooking vessels but a Muslim boy could not be allowed to come close. After the agitation led by me, the headmaster, Agya Ram Bhalla, got the mithai-seller to apologize in front of the whole school.

'In 1945, I found a job as a clerk in an office of the public works inspectorate near Baddi Nali railway station between Lahore and Narowal. The inspector, Tikka, and the assistant inspector were both Hindus. The assistant inspector was a Pandit. A day before 15 August I learnt that Tikka had fled, leaving behind everything. There was a plan to kill the Pandit. I asked him to move to my house. He was reluctant, perhaps even suspicious.

'I took out the Qur'an and promised, "Before you die, I will die." He moved in, with two or three families of relatives. I told the others that the Pandit had vanished and got the police to seal his house. Then I arranged for him and the relatives to go to a camp in Lahore, and said to him, "Don't tell me where you are going."'

■

Dawood Perwaiz from no one knows where. Responding to a message from a woman who insisted that she had to meet us, we went to her home in Lahore's 'Township' colony, where we were warmly welcomed by Nayla Perwaiz, her husband Dawood, and other members of the family.

It was her husband's story that Nayla wanted us to hear. Dawood was two-and-half years old, his head and elbow slashed (Nayla said), when in 1947 he was brought to one of Lahore's refugee camps—'the Walton camp, I think.'

Nayla Perwaiz: 'He knows nothing about his family. We do not know if anybody came with him. We don't know of any relatives of his. Can you help find out?'

Dawood showed us the large furrow on his scalp and the scars on the elbow left by the childhood wounds—inflicted by kirpans, so they had heard. The child Dawood had been adopted by Nayla's aunt, and in due course Nayla and Dawood got married. Nayla longed for her husband to find his roots, and though there was nothing we could do to help, she seemed glad to express her wish to people from across the border, where—somewhere—Dawood's origins lay.

That gash on Dawood Pervaiz's head, and his wife's unanswerable plea, underlined the tragic fact that the bulk of 1947's stories will remain unknown and unrecorded, and therefore underlined also the value of gathering what *can* be recorded.

■

Chaudhry Muhammad Hayat of Gujrat tehsil. We met Chaudhry Muhammad Hayat, a retired squadron leader in Pakistan's air force who had played for the joint services cricket team, in his small first-floor office room in a crescent-shaped complex in Lahore's Defence Housing Area. Seventy-six in 2005, Hayat belonged originally to village Sook Khurd, about four miles east of the town of Gujrat on the road from Lahore to Jalalpur Jattan.

Hayat: 'North of Sook Khurd was the village of Nichra where many Nichra Jats lived. There was one dera where five or six Hindu families lived, some of whose members were educated and had found jobs in Rawalpindi. One (Hindu) boy of my age, Chuni Lal, studied with me. I used to visit his home and well remember his father Haveli Ram. His two brothers were working in Rawalpindi. Chuni Lal and I sometimes ate in each other's homes.*

'Two miles south of our village was a big village called Sook Kalaan. In this village, one-fourth were Hindus—hardworking and educated. One of them was Narain Das, an affluent man who helped with donations.'

But Hayat's hero was the Sikh schoolteacher, Bhagat Saab.

Hayat: 'Nobody knew or needed to know the real name of Bhagat Saab. I first met him in 1939 when I was in the fourth class. He was 60–65, had a short beard, a white turban, a pink-and-white complexion. He enjoyed smoking the hookah. We boys kept the angeethi burning for his hookah. He knew all the principals and headmasters of Gujrat tehsil and used to get

---

*This was said with a suggestion that it was unusual. The notion of a Hindu home being polluted if a Muslim ate there came up in more than one interview.

tuition fees excused for poor boys, especially poor Jat boys.

'I was with him once in Sook Kalaan when he said something in Narain Das's ear. Narain Das asked his son to bring some money. He brought thirty rupees. Bhagat Saab gave the money to me.' Here Hayat broke down, but added: 'Bhagat Saab also said to me, "Hisab rakho"'. (Keep an account.)

Hayat's father removed him from school in the sixth class but on Bhagat's persuasion re-enrolled him after four or five months. Hayat went on to matriculate in the first division and start a successful career.

Hayat: 'But for Bhagat Saab, I would still be cutting grass in my village... On 10 August 1947, people said to Bhagat, "Bhag jao". "I will not leave," he said. He was living alone—his wife was dead. Two sons and a daughter lived elsewhere (in West Punjab).'

'He moved to live with our family [on our land], in a shed near our well. One day, he heard that his daughter and son-in-law had been killed... Then news came of a train arriving from the east (from India) with bodies of dead persons—poori gaddi katal ho gayee. After this, Bhagat Saab (now 70 or so) became very shaken and ill.'

Hayat said he carried Bhagat Saab on the back of a bicycle to a hakim in Sialkot town. The forty-kilometre ride to Sialkot and back took two nights and a day. But there was no improvement. Then a train with Hindu refugees heading for India was stopped near Gujrat town. 'All on the train were killed,' said Hayat. 'I saw the scene.' Here Hayat could not hold back his tears.

Hayat: 'After two or three days, Bhagat Saab gayab ho gaye. (He just disappeared.) Inse achha insaan maine nahin dekha.' (I haven't seen a finer human being.)

After Bhagat vanished, there were attacks by outsiders on Hindus and Sikhs still left in the village but the villagers refused to join in the frenzy. 'Leaders of the village sheltered the Hindus and Sikhs and at two in the night took them four miles on foot to safety at a camp for Hindus and Sikhs in Gujrat town. I walked with the party. In the camp I looked everywhere for Bhagat Saab. Lekin Khuda ka banda tha, oopar chala gaya.' (God's good man, he had gone up to heaven.)

Hayat observed that in 1947 a zahreeli hawaa—a poisonous wind—had hit Punjab. Among the things it destroyed was a deep relationship between a Sikh teacher and a family of Muslim peasants. But the wind could not obliterate the memory of that relationship.

■

Abdur Rab Malik of Quetta, Balochistan. The family of Abdur Rab Malik, 84, retired director in the excise department, originally belonged to Batala in Gurdaspur district in what is now Indian Punjab. 'But I was born in Ziarat (hill station near Quetta). Father had settled in Balochistan.'

We interviewed Malik on 22 July 2005 in his house in Lahore's Model Town, where many well-off Hindus and Sikhs resided before partition. A Hindu temple stood near the house but with no sign of worshippers.

Malik was happy to learn that Usha's Sindhi parents had lived in Quetta before leaving for India in 1947. Recalling events in Quetta, he spoke of his Sikh subordinate, sub-inspector Sardar Rajinder Singh, whom he had called to his home to prepare a raid on a cinema house.

'Rajinder Singh came at about 8.30 p.m. By this time riots had begun in the town and we could hear sounds of an uproar outside. The Sardar got frightened. I said, "You are in safe hands, I'll take care of you."'

Malik took out a burqa for the sardar to wear and accompanied him to his house, which was nearby, along with his own wife, also in a burqa, and two constables in uniform. He warned the sardar not to leave his house.

The next morning Malik went to his subordinate's home and personally took Rajinder Singh, his wife and their son, all dressed in burqas, to the railway station. 'We went in a hired car and saw that they sat in the train. From Quetta to Lahore my people travelled with them. They reached their destination (in India), Darwaza Ram Bagh in Amritsar, from where he wrote a letter of thanks.'

Malik spoke too of a Hindu, Seth Hemal Das—'the biggest sweetmeat merchant in town'—who lived three or four houses away. 'The Seth served mithais free of cost to poets in his shop.' (These poets would have been mainly Muslim.)

One night, at the peak of the riots, the Seth's son Lilaram arrived at Malik's house with a bunch of keys in his hand—these were the keys to their shop. 'I went to the Seth's shop, opened his safe, took out Rs. 24,000 and the jewellery inside, brought the stuff home, put a burqa on Lilaram, accompanied him to his house, and delivered the valuables to his father.'

The next day, Malik, along with his sergeants, accompanied the Seth and his family to Machh railway station, fifty miles from Quetta, and put them on a train. 'They reached Karnal (in Indian Punjab) safe and sound.'

But there were those, said Abdur Rab Malik, he could not save.

'Sardar Ram Singh owned a furniture shop. Mr. Scott, the (British) superintendent of police, shot down dozens of rioters. I saw twenty bodies on the road. Going on a bicycle with a friend—I used a cycle those days—I saw Sardar Ram Singh coming in a Morris Minor. He was stopped by a crowd of Hazaras and Pathans, pulled out by his hair, burnt, and placed on the engine of his car...'

'My own eyes, these sinful eyes,' Abdur Rab Malik said, 'have seen that sight.'

∎

Prem Pandhi, tennis star. Samina Akram Sayed, daughter and wife of police officers, told us in Lahore of her father's role in 1947 in protecting Prem Pandhi, one of India's tennis stars in the 1940s and later a leader in industry and education. Samina's account put us on a trail that led to a first-floor office in New Delhi's Connaught Place where, at the end of July 2005, we met Prem Pandhi, 86 at the time, and elicited his story.

A son of Lyallpur lawyer Chamanlal Pandhi, Prem graduated from Lyallpur, excelled in tennis and other sports, did a master's course in history at Lahore's Government College, and later also obtained law and education degrees. A teaching assignment at Aitchison followed, the tennis circuit continued, and then came a job in Lahore with a British firm, Bird & Co.

An older sister, Bimla, was married to Narinder Nath Chopra, who became a police officer in 1947. Narinder lived in Lahore's Fort area, which was overwhelmingly Muslim, along with his brother Kedar Nath, also a police officer, and their mother.

On August 10 ('just before the peak of the carnage'), Prem's parents, his sister Bimla, Bimla's two young sons, and other relatives left for India. Prem stayed on in Lahore, thinking that 'the madness' that had affected Lahore from June or so would soon end.

A week after partition, around August 22, the two police brothers, Narinder Nath and Kedar Nath, came in their uniforms to Prem Pandhi's Bird & Co office on Mall Road, announced that they had been transferred to cities in India (Panipat and Delhi), and asked Prem to take them and their mother, who was waiting in a tonga on the street, to their Fort house in his car.

Pandhi's Ford Prefect was parked on Mall Road. The plan, the brothers said, was to remove their belongings from the Fort house. Three or four tongas had been hired for the purpose, they added.

Pandhi, twenty-eight at the time, tried to dissuade them. The times are dangerous, he said. The brothers insisted, and added that the head of the police station in their area was a friend and had promised assistance. Prem took the brothers in his car to their Fort home.

In three or four hours the tongas were loaded. But a couple of policemen came to the house and said that a big crowd had collected near the car; it was dangerous to go there. 'Don't worry,' said the brothers. 'We are police officers and have revolvers.'

The mother, her two sons, and Prem Pandhi walked to the car and saw that its tyres had been deflated. A crowd of 100 to 200 persons carrying lathis and daggers surrounded them, and several men pounced on the two brothers.

Pandhi: 'One brother was killed on the spot, the other seemed to have still some life left (he soon died), and the mother too was hurt (she was rescued by the police). But nobody touched me. I was dressed in shalwar kameez and Peshawari chappals and taken for a Muslim.'

Policemen took Pandhi to the police station and asked if he wanted to contact anyone. He phoned Anwar Ali, the deputy inspector-general of police (DIG), whom he knew. Anwar Ali (the father of Samina Syed, whom we met in Lahore) said he would come immediately and instructed the station officer to protect Pandhi.

Arriving with two jeeps and policemen with Sten-guns, Anwar Ali took Prem in one of the jeeps, guns pointing outside, to his home. As they were leaving the thana, Anwar Ali said to Pandhi: 'By now the crowd knows you are a Hindu. My men will shoot and kill, but I cannot guarantee that you will remain alive.'

He reached the Ali home alive. After two or three days there (for safety Pandhi was locked up in the bathroom whenever the DIG was not at home), Anwar Ali said to him: 'You had better go away. It is impossible to keep your presence a secret, with servants and all. I have found you a seat on a plane to Delhi. Here is your ticket. You will go confidently to the airport, driving my car. It will be safer that way. No attention will be drawn.'

Pandhi recalled: 'I drove to the airport, left the DIG's car there with the key inside, boarded the plane and reached Delhi.' After a brief pause, he said to us, 'I don't think I have paid Anwar Ali for the ticket.'

■

Sughra Rasheed about Jullundur. On 19 July 2005, in her sister's home in Thokar Niaz Baig in Lahore, we met Sughra Rasheed. In broad terms we had known—from her niece, Aroona Kamal, a friend of ours—that Sughra Rasheed had lost several relatives in the city of Jullundur.

In 1947, she was a young wife and mother in Delhi. Her husband, Abdur Rasheed, was a railway officer from a family hailing from the villages of Singhpura and Uggi near Jullundur. The husband's brother was a young doctor, also Delhi-based. The husband's father (a retired railway officer) lived in the railway colony in Jullundur city.

We asked Sughra Rasheed for the names and ages of those who had been killed in August 1947 in Jullundur. Her answer was given clearly, calmly, and solemnly, and filled with brief pauses as she tried to remember.

Sughra Rasheed: 'Dr Badruddin, the father of my husband. He was sixty. Fatima, his (my husband's) mother. She was fifty-five. Jamila, their newly married daughter, my husband's sister. She was twenty-five. Tahira, their younger daughter, who was twenty-two. Qutubuddin, my husband's nana, who was also my dada. He was eighty. Idu, a mulazim. Idu's wife Fateh. Five children of Idu and Fateh.'

We were moved by this brief re-creation, through naming, of the killed, and perhaps specially by the naming of the servants. Like the vast majority of the killed of 1947, the servants had lacked the means or critical contacts—in the military, or the police, or the railways—that made escape possible for many of the better-off, though not, in this case, for Sughra's relatives.

'The family was living in a Hindu mohalla on the main road with only two Muslim homes. Amne-samne was a Hindu family who had said to my husband's family, 'Don't go away.' I remember two girls from that family, Sheela and Dhannu.

'I don't think the family could have been involved,' Sughra added. 'I think they were helpless before the attackers.'

Sughra had a happier story, too, to tell. Her husband's older brother Sharif was in Solan (also in East Punjab) with his young wife and a two-month-old daughter. Their lives, said Sughra, were protected by Hindu friends who then helped them to move across to West Punjab. But Sughra's nani Ayesha, who was part of a walking caravan trying to reach Pakistan, died on the way, as also the nani's sister Jeena.

After recounting these events, Sughra said: 'Itna Jullundur yaad aata hai. Jab koi Jullundur ki baat karta hai, dil mein kuch ho jaata hai.' (I remember Jullundur so much. Whenever anyone speaks of Jullundur, something happens inside my heart.)

■

Returning to Gurgaon from Lahore, we related portions of our research to close friends of ours for decades, Rajinder Das and Prabha Mathur. We were aware that Prabha Mathur had spent her early years, before partition, in Lahore, but what came out (in Gurgaon, on 26 July 2005) was quite new to us.

Prabha Mathur about Lahore and Simla. 'My father was an officer in the prisons department of Punjab. We lived in Model Town, Lahore. My father had good relations with his Muslim colleagues who told him around 10 August 1947 that Hindus were no longer safe in Lahore and that he should leave at once with his family for India.

'I was thirteen and the eldest of six children. Within hours we packed our belongings and managed to reach the railway station. A Hindu family we knew came to the station with food for our journey. As our train rolled away the father of this family was stabbed on the platform. He must have died. I saw it happening. But my father's Muslim colleagues had saved our lives.

'We moved to Simla. In our home we hid for several days a young Muslim man, a servant. We had known him in Lahore but he happened to be in East Punjab when partition occurred and somehow turned up at our place. It was difficult to keep him without people getting to know. After some days we had to ask him to leave. Fortunately he was able to reach the other side—we heard from him.'

■

A three-part report of our Lahore interviews was published in the *Tribune* on 16, 23 and 30 October 2005. (After partition, the *Tribune* had moved from Lahore to Ambala and then to Chandigarh; it also comes out in New Delhi, in many ways a Punjabi city now.) Letters received in response to our report, some of them published in the *Tribune*, offered accounts of other life-saving acts of 1947 which the senders of the letters had heard of in their families. These accounts confirmed, first, that courageous deeds of protection were widespread in 1947, and, secondly, that those who performed or witnessed such acts recounted them to the next generation. If more such stories are accessed and shared, the under-reporting of the *insaniyat* of 1947 can be corrected.

Chapter Eleven

POSTSCRIPT: DIVIDED PUNJAB AND THE FUTURE OF *PUNJABIYAT*

Before long it will be seventy years after Punjab's 1947 division, the intended terminus for this study, which we reached in Chapter Nine and where we stayed in Chapter Ten. This additional chapter is in the nature of a postscript. It attempts, first, to encapsulate our 1707-1947 survey; secondly, it touches on some post-1947 trends in divided Punjab; and, finally, it tries to capture for our times the legacy of history's undivided Punjab—the strength or weakness of what has been called *Punjabiyat*, which may be translated as Punjabiness.

Following the deaths of Emperor Aurangzeb and Guru Gobind Singh in the opening decade of the eighteenth century, Punjab saw strife for seventy years. Afghan and Sikh forces were the principal antagonists in clashes that culminated in Sikh triumph and, as the century ended, in Ranjit Singh's conquest of Lahore.

The Sikh kingdom established thereupon, lasting for five decades, proved to be Punjab's only indigenous government in 900 years. Earlier, from the eleventh century onwards, varied Delhi-based Turkic dynasties and occasional Afghan rulers had presided over Punjab until, with Aurangzeb's death, Mughal rule began to disintegrate. More distant aliens, the British, ruled Punjab for a hundred years after the Sikh kingdom fell in the late 1840s.

During the period of our study and earlier, Punjabi society witnessed an ongoing clash between purity of belief, stressed by some of the region's Muslims, and purity of race or caste, which many of the region's Hindus sought to preserve. Peaceful relations, generally the norm at ground level, did not prevent a Muslim from looking down at his Hindu friend's faith as polytheistic or idolatrous, or a Hindu from washing with extra energy a utensil used by his Muslim friend, stances that hurt psyches even among people of goodwill and impeded a deeper unity.

In a speech in Chittagong in March 1948, Jinnah provided what from him was a rare non-political explanation for the Pakistan movement. 'I reiterate most emphatically,' he claimed, 'that Pakistan was [fought for] because of the danger of complete annihilation of human soul in a society based on caste.'[1] In this remark Jinnah was giving expression to the injury from caste superiority nursed by many of the subcontinent's Muslims, including in Punjab.

Punjab sustained a plural society where, except for the eighteenth century, periods of peace were longer than phases of violence—a society where Muslims, Hindus and Sikhs usually lived peacefully side by side. It did not, however, become a single nation or entity of all Punjabis.[2]

Still, what on the surface seemed to be a recurring Muslim-Sikh clash for control over Punjab did not necessarily mean enmity in the villages. While influential and often armed Sikh and Muslim groups bitterly fought one another at times, common human values were celebrated by popular poets and peaceful coexistence usually prevailed at the grassroots.

On some crucial planes the Muslim-Sikh relationship was nonetheless marked by memories of bitter wounds, recollections of past periods of glory, desires for revenge, and urges to dominate. Such memories, desires and urges contributed to recurring discord.

British Punjab, where a largely just administration reached down to village level, was an impressive achievement. Yet the imperial urge to prolong European rule produced the policy of divide-and-control which in the end destroyed the Punjab the British had built. A policy of assisting Punjabis to help rule their land and eventually replace the Empire—a policy of requiring Muslim, Hindu and Sikh leaders in the province to turn to one another rather than to the Raj—might have achieved a result different from what 1947 witnessed, but contempt for the colonized and resentment at their agitations came in the way.

The withdrawal of the British just before the middle of the twentieth century did not return Punjab to those whom the British had displaced, the Sikhs. In the democratic age which Punjab too was entering in the 1940s, numbers and votes counted for more than arms. Moreover, in the 1940s the Sikhs did not possess the military superiority over their Punjab rivals which had favoured them in the eighteenth century. Nor did Punjab as a whole go over, when the British left, to the region's Muslim majority. Nearly half of it went to Sikhs and Hindus, who made up a majority in eastern Punjab, and carnage accompanied the division.

Yet, even a magnanimous Empire, one wanting the colonized to replace it, would have failed to create a Punjab solution on its own. In the end it was beyond the capacity of non-Punjabi entities like the Empire or the INC, or individuals like Gandhi, Nehru, or Jinnah, no matter their power, ingenuity, influence or prestige, to solve Punjab's problems. Only Punjabis could devise solutions for Punjab. Tragically, these were not hammered out.

The Punjabi virtues—staying clear of clashes with rulers, recognizing the wind, picking the winner, self-preservation, assisting the endangered—were evident throughout much of the period looked at, but these assets did not suffice against the passions unleashed in Punjab in the 1940s, even as they had not sufficed against earlier eruptions. At more than one critical stage in the region's history, a bold local leadership that stood up to extremist drives was Punjab's unmet need.

■

In a London speech on 27 September 1947, Winston Churchill said that 'the fearful massacres... occurring in India' were of 'no surprise' to him. He went on to predict that the 'butcheries' would continue and indeed lead to 'a vast abridgment' of the subcontinent's population.[3] That did not quite happen. Hindus and Sikhs in East Punjab and Muslims in West Punjab made earnest efforts to put the carnage behind them and rebuild their broken lives.

Gandhi's assassination by extremist Hindus on 30 January 1948 in New Delhi affected both Punjabs. Many homes in Lahore went without a meal, and Mian Iftikharuddin said, 'Each one of us who has raised his hand against innocent men, women and children during the past months, who has publicly or secretly entertained sympathy for such acts, is a collaborator in the murder of Mahatma Gandhi.'[4]

Following the 1947 trauma, poets, writers and artists in both Punjabs searched for meaning and healing. One poem that would be recited again and again was composed in 1948 on a train between Dehra Dun and Delhi by a twenty-nine-year-old Sikh woman born in Gujranwala, Amrita Pritam (1919-2005). Addressed to Waris Shah and written in Punjabi, Pritam's lines asked the poet to rise from his grave and articulate the sorrow of Punjab's women, even as he had given voice to Heer's heartbreak in the eighteenth century. The train being the marker of Punjab's 1947 tragedy, the fact that the words of *Aj Aakhan Waris Shah Nu* (I Ask Waris Shah Today) were jotted down as Pritam's train rolled forward sharpened the poem's poignancy.

As frequently remembered as Amrita Pritam's 1948 cry is the Urdu poem written the previous year, in fact during the night of 14-15 August, by Faiz Ahmad Faiz (1911-84), *Ye Daag Daag Ujaala* (This Stained Dawn), which expressed shock, pain and disappointment at what journey's end had brought. Born in Sialkot into a Jat family, an officer-soldier in World War II before becoming a committed leftist, Faiz is one of the subcontinent's best-loved poets, read and recited in India as much as in Pakistan.

In 1955, shortly before dying in his early forties, the writer Saadat Hasan Manto (1912-55), wrote *Toba Tek Singh,* a searing short story on the irrationality that gave company to the 1947 violence. *Toba Tek Singh* is studied as a classic in many parts of the world. Born in eastern Punjab (in Ludhiana district) in a family of Kashmiri Muslims, Manto was a scriptwriter in Bombay before migrating in 1948 to Lahore, where he died in 1955.

Also viewed as a classic is *Train to Pakistan,* Khushwant Singh's 1955 work. Ninety-seven in 2012 and New Delhi-based for decades, Khushwant Singh, who was born in western Punjab's Shahpur district, lived in Lahore until June 1947. Locating *Train to Pakistan*'s harrowing story in a fictional East Punjab village populated by Muslim and Sikh peasants who live on reasonably good terms with one another until they run into hating mobs, the author fills his creation with believable and doomed characters.

A reason for the force and continuing popularity of the texts cited above, and of similar works by others, is their ability to take us to the bafflements and sorrows of human beings rather than of Hindus, Muslims or Sikhs.

In some cases, Punjabis who had crossed the border in 1947 re-crossed it two or three years later for a brief glimpse of their home, village or town. Others managed to keep in touch with former neighbours. The postal service informed old friends of the loss felt after separation and conveyed remembrances.

When, in 1955, Pakistan announced that East Punjabis were welcome to witness a cricket match in Lahore, thousands of Sikhs and Hindus went across. It was difficult to say who was more moved when they met, the 'Indian' Punjabi or his old friend the 'Pakistani' Punjabi. At a mushaira held to mark the Indians' arrival, when Ustad Daman, the people's poet, said that the red eyes he was witnessing showed that 'you wept, and we wept too',[5] many burst out crying openly.[6]

But state-to-state relations between India and Pakistan rarely showed substantial or lasting improvement. Accusations and tensions mounted, some of them related to Kashmir, and from time to time there was actual fighting. The 1947-48 conflict was limited to the terrain of Jammu and Kashmir, but not the 1965 war, nor that of 1971.

Though, mercifully, neither the 1965 nor the 1971 war was a prolonged affair, around 90,000 Pakistani soldiers, a majority of them Punjabis, were detained in India for more than seven months after the latter conflict ended. Suspicion and hostility became official and national attitudes after these wars, blocking people-to-people contact. Except for rare spells or individual cases, doors were firmly shut to persons longing to visit their old homes and neighbours, or the grave of a parent, spouse, child or sibling.

•

In West Punjab, Mamdot's 1947 ministry had included Iftikharuddin, Daultana and Shaukat Hayat. As for Khizr, unable to accommodate himself in the new Pakistan, he spent many of his remaining years in the UK and in the USA (where his son lived), looking in those far-off places for a world that had gone. Passing away in California in 1975, he was buried in Kalra.

In East Punjab, the first ministry after independence, headed by Gopichand Bhargava and temporarily operating from Simla, included Bhimsen Sachar and Swaran Singh.

After independence, each Punjab grew in size as princely states were merged with it. In the 1960s, however, East Punjab was split into three parts, Punjab, Himachal and Haryana, with the new city of Chandigarh as the common capital for Punjab and Haryana, and Simla (now Shimla) as the Himachal headquarters.

From one angle, this trifurcation was only an application to eastern Punjab of the linguistic principle which determined new provincial boundaries elsewhere in India. More importantly, however, it produced a Punjabi-speaking state that was also a Sikh-majority state. In Haryana and Himachal, the majority were Hindus who spoke Hindi variants.

India's new and smaller Punjab—one-seventh the size of undivided Punjab—was essentially British Punjab's Jullundur division (minus its hill districts) together with the Amritsar and Gurdaspur districts of the old Lahore division, plus Patiala and other Punjabi-speaking tracts previously ruled by rajas. While the hilly principalities adjoining British eastern Punjab along with Jullundur division's hill districts became Himachal, the new state of Haryana was reminiscent of the Ambala division of British days.

Unlike in India, where provinces were renamed 'states', Pakistan continues to have 'provinces', of which Punjab is easily the most populous. However, if the long-sustained movement for a separate Seraiki-speaking province succeeds in obtaining it, presumably with Multan as its capital, Pakistani Punjab too may witness a split. The argument that, similarities notwithstanding, Seraiki is a different language rather than a Punjabi dialect appears to have gained ground, though as of writing the picture seems unclear.

In the 1950s, Mamdot was followed in the chief minister's chair first by

Daultana and then by Noon, who in 1958 became Pakistan's Prime Minister for a few months. From 1955, until his assassination in 1957, Dr Khan Sahib, former Premier of the Frontier province and an old Congressite, functioned from Lahore as the chief minister of a single-unit West Pakistan, which was scrapped in 1969, with the old provinces coming back.

Pakistani Punjab's best-known political figures since the late 1980s have been Nawaz Sharif, an industrialist-politician who served twice as Pakistan's Prime Minister before winning again in the 2013 national elections, and his younger brother Shahbaz Sharif, who as of writing was set to retain the chief ministership of Punjab. By origin the Sharif brothers are linked to Amritsar and Kashmir.

After Pervez Musharraf's 1999 takeover, which ended Nawaz Sharif's second spell as Premier and sent the Sharif brothers into exile, some of Sharif's colleagues in the Pakistan Muslim League (PML) formed a new party, PML-Q, which backed General Musharraf and, later, following the 2008 restoration of democracy, the Pakistan People's Party (PPP) of Zulfiqar Bhutto and his daughter Benazir. But the 2013 elections proved disastrous for PML-Q.

A relatively new and much-discussed face in Punjabi and Pakistani politics is the Lahore-based former cricketer, Imran Khan, whose Pakistan Tehreek-e-Insaf, or PTI, performed very well in the KPK province in 2013 but failed to live up to electoral expectations in Punjab or in Pakistan as a whole.

In Indian Punjab, Gopichand Bhargava and Bhimsen Sachar, both with origins in or long ties to western Punjab, alternated as chief ministers until 1956, when the America-educated Pratap Singh Kairon, who hailed from Amritsar district, assumed the chief minister's post, which he held for eight years. Some months after leaving the post, Kairon, a Congressman like his predecessors, was shot and killed in his car, evidently for reasons of personal enmity.

The smaller Punjab that followed in 1966 has been governed by ministries led by the Congress or the Shiromani Akal Dal (SAD). At intervals it has been under President's rule. Both the SAD and the Congress draw Sikh as well as Hindu support, with the 'Hindu nationalist' Bharatiya Janata Party (BJP) usually allying itself with the SAD. Since November 1966 the chief minister of Punjab has always been a Sikh.

In Haryana, where politics often takes a 'Jats versus non-Jats' shape, elected office has been shared between the Congress, which has supplied Jat as well as non-Jat chief ministers to the state, and the Jat-dominated Lok Dal. In Himachal, which enjoys a lower population density and higher rates of literacy and life expectancy, the principal rivalry has been between Congress and the BJP, with both parties having won elections and formed governments.

Both Punjabs have displayed economic vigour, with the cities of Faisalabad (the former Lyallpur) in Pakistani Punjab and Ludhiana in Indian Punjab showing the highest growth rates in population and production.

■

Between 1947 and the year 2000, Indian Punjab probably saw more violence, in terms of numbers killed, than Pakistani Punjab. Much of this violence was linked to Sikh militancy and to operations against that militancy by the Indian state and governments in Punjab. Waxing and waning over time, this militancy has made cultural, economic and territorial demands, the latter involving Chandigarh city, and at times sought a separate Sikh country called Khalistan.

Sikh militancy reached its peak in 1984, claiming over two hundred lives in the first five months of that year. On the night of 5-6 June, the Indian Army moved into Amritsar's Golden Temple to suppress thousands of militants entrenched inside. In two nights and one day of hard fighting, at least 576 were killed, including 83 army soldiers, but these official figures were probably lower than actual numbers. Among the killed was the militants' thirty-seven-year-old leader, Jarnail Singh Bhindranwale, a Jat Sikh preacher who had become a hero to a section but was seen by others as a sponsor of targeted killings.

Shaken by word or pictures of state armour invading Sikhism's holiest shrine, some Sikh recruits deserted army camps in different parts of India and headed for Amritsar. Hundreds of them were detained and several killed in shoot-outs with loyal units.

About five months later, on 31 October 1984, Sikh members of her bodyguard assassinated Indira Gandhi, the Prime Minister who had ordered the Amritsar action, in her residence in New Delhi. Three days of counter-revenge followed in the Indian capital, where up to three thousand innocent Sikhs were killed in what perhaps was the city's worst carnage after 1857.

Punjab's unrest caused a succession of governors serving under a succession of Prime Ministers to administer presidential, i.e. central, rule from 1983 to 1985 and again from 1987 to 1992. In 1995, Beant Singh, Punjab's Congress chief minister from 1992, was assassinated by militant Sikhs. Since then, elected governments led either by the Akalis or the Congress have run Punjab.

Experiencing three long periods of nation-wide military rule (1958-71,

1977-88 and 1999-2008), Pakistani Punjab has more than competed with the spells of presidential governance that Indian Punjab has gone through, and religious extremism and militancy inside Pakistani Punjab have intensified in the twenty-first century, more than matching their Indian manifestations.

Demands to classify Ahmadiyyas as non-Muslims were raised in Punjab and elsewhere in Pakistan from the early 1950s. Prime Minister Zulfiqar Ali Bhutto yielding to the pressure, a law was passed in 1974 authorizing punishment for Ahmadiyyas who claimed to be Muslims. Demands from a few Sikh groups in Indian Punjab for declaring sects like the Nirankaris to be non-Sikh recalled the focus of Pakistani sections on Ahmadiyyas.

Pakistan's third military ruler, Muhammad Zia-ul-Haq (1924-88), a Punjabi of Arain background, was born in Jullundur (now Jalandhar) in 1924 and educated at St. Stephen's College, Delhi. After deposing his political chief, Zulfiqar Bhutto, in 1977 and presiding over Bhutto's hanging in 1979, General Zia used the Soviet Union's end-1979 invasion of Afghanistan to forge links with the USA and Saudi Arabia and Islamicize the country he had taken over.

Army officers governed Punjab during Zia's years at Pakistan's helm, which saw a proliferation of guns and drugs in the Frontier province (now Khyber-Pakhtunkhwa) and new nationwide regulations in the name of Islam. Laws or ordinances penalized eating and drinking in public during Ramazan, required women TV anchors to cover their heads, raised to death the punishment for blasphemy, and imposed other codes of behaviour.

With the state under Zia championing religious orthodoxy, male government employees exchanged Western-style trousers-and-shirts for shalwar kameezes, new mosques multiplied, and Sunni-Shia controversies as well as attacks on Ahmadiyyas became sharper. Before Zia was killed in 1988 in an air crash near Bahawalpur (along with the American ambassador, the chairman of Pakistan's joint chiefs of staff, and others on his plane), his policies had made Pakistan and its Punjab province more hospitable for extremists. Video and music stores and barber shops were attacked in the name of Islamic purity, and worshippers in mosques were assaulted for the crime of belonging to their sect.

Islamic extremism's numerous Pakistani victims are seldom named. As with the great majority of 1947's victims, their deaths seem anonymous. But they include men like Salman Taseer, a sixty-six-year-old governor of Punjab, gunned down in January 2011 near his Islamabad home by Mumtaz Qadri, a member of the governor's bodyguard. In Qadri's eyes, the offence of Taseer, whose father had been a professor in Amritsar, was to question a death sentence for blasphemy on Asiya Bibi, a Christian woman from a village in Sheikhpura district. In October 2012, Qadri, who admitted to the killing, was sentenced to death by a court in Rawalpindi.

Two months after Taseer's death, Pakistan's minister for minority affairs, Shahbaz Bhatti, a Roman Catholic from a family in Faisalabad district (formerly Lyallpur), was killed when his car was sprayed with bullets not far from his home in Islamabad. An extremist group, Tehrik-i-Taliban Pakistan, claimed credit for the assassination, for which no one appears to have been charged.

Assassinated a few years earlier—on 27 December 2007, in Rawalpindi—former Prime Minister Benazir Bhutto had spoken out against extremism shortly before her death. The Pakistani government headed by the husband of the killed leader had not announced its findings on her killers when its term was completed in March 2013.

Ajmal Kasab, the sole survivor of the Pakistani terrorist group that attacked several sites in Mumbai at the end of November 2008 and killed close to 170 people, was born in a village in Okara district, south of Lahore. The testimony in Indian courts of Kasab, who was hanged in Pune in November 2012, and other evidence satisfied Indian authorities of the involvement in this attack of the Pakistani extremist group, Lashkar-e-Taiba, and of Inter-Services Intelligence (ISI), Pakistan's chief security and intelligence agency. Claiming that it has conveyed the evidence in its possession to Islamabad, India asks for action against the culpable.

■

The blame game in state-to-state relations has from time to time been interrupted by cordial contacts and agreements. In January 1966, soon after the 1965 war, Prime Minister Lal Bahadur Shastri and General Ayub Khan signed an accord in the Uzbek city of Tashkent, then part of the Soviet Union. In July 1972, after the 1971 war, Prime Minister Indira Gandhi and President Zulfiqar Ali Bhutto signed an agreement in Simla.

In February 1999, nine months after India and Pakistan had both tested nuclear bombs, Prime Minister Atal Bihari Vajpayee boarded a bus in New Delhi and arrived in Lahore, where he was warmly greeted by Prime Minister Nawaz Sharif and thousands of others. At a banquet given by Sharif, Vajpayee said:

It is unworthy of two nations the size of India and Pakistan to have wasted so much time in mutual ill will... There is nothing which cannot be solved through goodwill and direct dialogue.... There is nothing in our bilateral relations that can ever be solved through violence.

As we approach a new millennium, the future... demands upon us to think of the welfare of our children and their children and of the generations that are yet to come...[7]

Less than three months after Vajpayee was welcomed in Lahore, Pakistan-backed forces moved into Kargil in Indian-administered Kashmir, causing another subcontinental war, again not a long one, but this time, thanks to improved television coverage, more intimate for millions.

India's Prime Minister from 2004, Dr Manmohan Singh, is a Sikh born in 1932 in Gah village, sixty miles south of Rawalpindi in Chakwal district. When Dr Singh started his premiership, Pakistan's military ruler and president was General Pervez Musharraf, who was born in Delhi in 1943. In 2004-5, the two leaders met three times, twice in New York and once in New Delhi. Encouraging joint statements were issued, including over Kashmir, and India's Premier said he would go to Pakistan, which waits for Dr Singh's visit even as India awaits action against the 2008 culprits. Pakistan's Prime-Minister-in-waiting as of writing, Nawaz Sharif, has spoken of his wish for an early meeting with Dr Manmohan Singh.

■

What from undivided Punjab remains? On the map, four separate pieces, which may grow into five if a Seraiki province is created. In memory, nostalgia in Punjabis born before 1940 and able to recall both the horror and the humanity of 1947.

Then there is language and culture. At times world conferences on Punjabi literature, films or music take place, and a few magazines publish Punjabi pieces in different scripts. Bollywood celebrates Punjabi culture and is conscious of markets in both Punjabs. In Pakistan, filmmakers have made money with Punjabi films like *Maula Jatt* (1979) which highlight the blunt and ingenious Punjabi farmer.[8]

Those raised in the two Punjabs after 1947 spoke the same language but grew up in separate worlds. They were brought up on different and often unconnected stories. On occasion parents and grandparents in both parts talked of the 1947 trauma and also of a period when Muslims, Sikhs and Hindus lived cordially in the same locality or village. Some grandparents spoke of 'the good times' when the British ruled undivided Punjab as well as of proud days when all Punjabis, Hindus, Sikhs and Muslims, jointly demanded freedom.

But the present's demands, and the present's controversies, which are dissimilar in the two Punjabs, have elbowed out recollections of history. Everyday talk in a Lahore or Rawalpindi home in our time has been very different from everyday talk within families in, say, Ludhiana or Amritsar. During times of tension or conflict between India and Pakistan, ugly memories are recalled, and patriotic rhetoric seems to trump *Punjabiyat*. When better times return, poets, musicians and artists from both sides of the border come together, find that *Punjabiyat* is alive, and breathe fresh energy into it.

In the main, however, the two Punjabs have lived separate lives.

■

In the late 1840s, the British contributed to *Punjabiyat* by abolishing the duties on goods or produce travelling in the region, which in the Sikh kingdom's time were apparently imposed up to a dozen times on the same item. To reduce the twenty-first century's barriers to trade, the SAD's Sukhbir Singh Badal, deputy chief minister of Indian Punjab, took a forty-five-strong delegation of businessmen and politicians to Lahore in November 2012.

Badal's move followed Pakistani decisions[9] in the previous year to grant India 'most-favoured-nation' or MFN status (something that fifteen years earlier India had granted to its neighbour) and prune the list of items not allowed in from India. From both sides there was talk of lowering customs duties as well as other 'non-tariff' obstacles such as requiring a licence or clearance from a remote authority for importing some items. It appeared, too, that India and Pakistan would simplify the granting of visas.

For decades, the only permissible land crossing from one Punjab to the other has joined Attari, a village on the Indian side of the border, to Wagah, which lies bang on the Radcliffe Line, with a railway station in its Pakistani half. Although a train, the Lahore-Delhi Samjhauta Express, has for some years covered the two-mile distance between Attari and Wagah, and there is a road as well, moving between the two places has been cumbersome and costly for people and goods both.

Indian passengers taking the Samjhauta Express have to get down in Attari, board the Attari-Wagah special for the two-mile trip, and at Wagah change into the Pakistani Samjhauta Express to reach Lahore. Delhi-bound

Pakistanis must perform a similar exercise.

Despite obstacles, trade between Pakistan and India has multiplied in recent years. In 2010, the official figure for the two-way trade was $2.5 billion. Counting 'illegal' trade and trade re-routed from third countries, the estimated total figure rose to around $10 billion.[10]

India's share in Pakistan's global exports fell from 23.6 per cent in 1948-49 to 1.3 per cent in 1975-76, and its percentage in Pakistan's exports fell from 50.6 in 1948-49 to 0.06 in 1975-76. Pakistan's share in India's exports worldwide fell from 2.2 per cent in 1951-52 to 0.7 per cent in 2005-06; and its percentage in India's imports dropped from 1.1 in 1951-52 to 0.13 in 2005-06. By 2010, however, imports from Pakistan were accounting for 6 per cent of India's total imports.

In 2010, India's exports to Pakistan (sugar and sugar confectionery, cotton, chemicals, coffee and tea, rubber, etc.) amounted to $2.2 billion, compared with imports worth $248 million from Pakistan (fruits and nuts, fuels and oils, salt, cement, lead, hides and skins, etc.)[11] By importing from the neighbour rather than from elsewhere, each country can save hundreds of millions of dollars annually.

In November 2012, Badal called Attari-Wagah 'an important gateway' and expressed the hope that both countries would start trading '6,000 items through this border'.[12] While some Pakistani farmers and industrialists fear that imports from India could wipe them out, more may be attracted by the size of the Indian market and the utility of Indian inputs for what they make or grow.

Following the successful treatment of a number of Pakistani patients, including children, in Indian hospitals beyond Punjab, men like Badal want Pakistanis to know that Amritsar and other places in Indian Punjab too can provide high-quality medical care.

Despite the passage of over sixty years, a journey today between Lahore and Amritsar for reasons of trade or health can also evoke memories of the 1947 trauma. On the other hand, just as in 1947 ordinary Punjabis hid and saved their threatened friends or neighbours even while political leaders spoke against one another, and even as badmashes were initiating rounds of killing, hostility occupies only the top layer of Punjabi memory.

At lower and perhaps deeper levels, the Punjabi psyche contains finer memories as well as longings for a fresh start. Pragmatic more than anything else, this psyche may want Punjabi grandchildren to find a climate of goodwill rather than of hostility.

Nostalgia and enthusiasm mark diaspora gatherings in the US, the UK, Europe, Canada and Australia. Thus the website of the Academy of the Punjab in North America, or APNA, offers access to books and articles in Punjabi (in Gurmukhi and Shahmukhi scripts), Urdu and English, and to albums of Punjabi music (Sufi, folk, film, pop, and Bhangra). APNA describes itself as 'a non-religious, non-political organization of all Punjabis for the promotion of Punjabi language, literature and culture'.

If APNA's rich and diverse website is any indication, *Punjabiyat* is making progress, at least in North America, and has champions on the subcontinent too. Yet South Asia's nation-states have acquired a stake in hostility. Armies, security establishments, politicians and influential chunks of the media have found that enmity generates resources, votes and audiences.

Punjabiyat thus faces gigantic foes. What can brighten its prospects? For one thing, enlarged trade and interdependence. Secondly, unexpected statesmanship from New Delhi or Islamabad, or from Chandigarh or Lahore. Thirdly, an unqualified rejection of extremism and coercion, whether in politics or religion.

Last but not least, individuals can revitalize *Punjabiyat*. In the enmity-filled climate of the 1760s, Waris Shah touched Punjabis of diverse backgrounds with his poem, which continues to speak to us and to which Amrita Pritam added unforgettable lines in 1948. Waris's descendants-in-spirit may, God willing, offer similar works today: a poem, song, play, film or something else, a garden maybe, that helps heal the past and points the way forward.

Healing and renewal may come also from 'ordinary' men and women, Punjabis and others, who, thinking of their children and grandchildren, simply ask one another, 'For tomorrow's sake, can we learn from yesterday?'

NOTES

Introduction
1. http://ireport.cnn.com/docs/DOC-825228
2. Grewal, *Sikhs*, p. 1.

1. Punjab Until Aurangzeb's Death
1. Dani, *History of Pakistan*, p. 178.
2. Sekhon, *A History of Panjabi Literature*, vol. 1, p. 3.
3. Dani, *History of Pakistan*, p. 180.
4. Quoted in Abdulla, *Historical Background*, p. 44.
5. Sekhon, *A History of Panjabi Literature*, vol. 1, pp. 2-3.
6. Chandra, *Medieval India*, pp. 31-32.
7. *Gazetteer of the Multan District, 1923-24*, pp. 32-33.
8. Shireen Moosvi in Grewal and Pall, *Precolonial and Colonial Punjab*, p. 99, citing Sujan Rai Bhandari, *Khulasat ut-Tawarikh*, 1918.
9. From Abdullah Yusuf Ali, *Three Travellers to India*, pp. 40-46.
10. See Dani, *History of Pakistan*, pp. 168-69; Abdulla, *Historical Background*, pp. 172-73; and Wikeley, *Punjabi Musalmans*, pp. 68, 118 & 142.
11. Abdulla, *Historical Background*, p. 130.
12. Abdulla, *Historical Background*, p. 179.
13. Reeti Grewal, 'Natural Vegetation and Wildlife in the Punjab', http://www.global.ucsb.edu/punjab/journal_11_1/4_grewal_r.pdf
14. See, for example, Qureshi, *The Muslim Community*, pp. 51-59.
15. Sekhon, *A History of Panjabi Literature*, vol. 1, p. 5.
16. See, for example, the editor's Introduction in Richard Eaton, *India's Islamic Traditions*, p. 16 & p. 20.
17. See, for example, Ibbetson, *Panjab Castes*, Wikeley, *Panjabi Musalmans* and Dani, *History of Pakistan*. Also J.S. Grewal on Punjab's historical geography, http://www.global.ucsb.edu/punjab/journal_11_1/2_grewal.pdf, p. 6.
18. Mujeeb quoted in Abdulla, *Historical Background*, p. 134.
19. Abdulla, *Historical Background*, pp. 172-9.
20. Contrast Abdulla, above, with Qureshi, *The Muslim Community*, pp. 82-85. See also Harbans Mukhia, 'Conversions to Islam in Punjab' in Saleem, *Punjab Revisited*; and Grewal, *Sikhs of the Punjab*, pp. 12-13.
21. Ansari, *Life, Times and Works of Amir Khusrau Dehlavi*, p. 295.
22. Shireen Moosvi in Grewal and Pall, *Precolonial and Colonial Punjab*, p. 99.
23. See Buddha Prakash, 'People's Struggle against Political Tyranny', in Saleem, *Punjab Revisited*, pp. 220-27, and Sameer, 'A Forgotten Hero Named Jassa', *Chowk*, 6 January

2001. http://www.chowk.com/articles/4960.
24. See Wikeley, *Punjabi Musalmans*, p. 99.
25. Shireen Moosvi in Grewal and Pall, *Precolonial and Colonial Punjab*, p. 99.
26. Shireen Moosvi in Grewal and Pall, *Precolonial and Colonial Punjab*, p. 99.
27. Akbar, *Punjab under the Mughals*, pp. 25-26.
28. Irfan Habib, *An Atlas of the Mughal Empire*. Information found on this Atlas's map 4B: "Punjab (Economic), 1595".
29. S.M. Latif, *History of the Panjab*, p. 147.
30. Akbar, *Punjab under the Mughals*, p. 80.
31. Abdulla, *Historical Background*, p. 137.
32. Shireen Moosvi in Grewal and Pall, *Precolonial and Colonial Punjab*, p. 99.
33. Quoted by William Dalrymple in 'The Empire Strikes Back,' *Daily Telegraph*, London, 3 August 2007.
34. Latif, *Lahore*, p. xi.
35. Latif, *Lahore*, p. xi and p. 41.
36. Lafont, *Maharaja Ranjit Singh*, p. 23.
37. Akbar, *Punjab under the Mughals*, pp. 56-57.
38. Latif, *History*, p. 143.
39. Father Pierre du Jarric quoted in Burke, *Akbar*, p. 231.
40. Grewal, *Sikhs*, p. 6.
41. Uberoi, *Religion, Civil Society and the State*, pp. 90-91.
42. Lafont, *Maharaja Ranjit Singh*, p. 30.
43. Chetan Singh, 'Polity, Economy and Society under the Mughals,' in Banga, *Five Punjabi Centuries*, pp. 74-75.
44. Grewal, 'Historical Geography of the Punjab,' http://www.global.ucsb.edu/punjab/journal_11_1/2_grewal.pdf, p. 6.
45. See, for example, Lafont, *Maharaja Ranjit Singh*, p. 24.
46. Quoted in Latif, *History*, p. 168.
47. H. Blochmann, 'Biographical Notices of Grandees of the Mughal Court,' in James Burgess, *The Indian Antiquary*, Vol. 1.
48. Latif, *Lahore*, pp. 214-16.
49. Latif, *Lahore*, p. 172.
50. Abdulla, *Historical Background*, p. 147
51. Latif, *Lahore*, p. 176.
52. Akbar, *Punjab under the Mughals*, p. 283.
53. Lafont, *Maharaja Ranjit Singh*, p. 27.
54. Quraeshi, *Lahore*, p. 291. Original Farsi verse presented as Poem 98 in Khan, *Diwan of Dara Shikoh*, p. 106.
55. Lafont, *Maharaja Ranjit Singh*, p. 27.
56. Latif, *Lahore*, p. 173.
57. Latif, *Lahore*, p. 174.
58. Uberoi, *Religion, Civil Society and the State*, pp. 89-90.
59. Fenech, *Darbar of the Sikh Gurus*, p. 38.

60. *History of the Sikhs*, vol. 1, p. 31
61. Lafont, *Maharaja Ranjit Singh*, p. 30.
62. Grewal, *Sikhs*, p. 54.
63. Grewal, *Sikhs*, pp. 54-55.
64. Grewal, *Sikhs*, pp. 63-64.
65. Grewal, *Sikhs*, p. 64.
66. Latif, *History*, pp. 255-56.
67. Grewal, *Sikhs*, pp. 65-66.
68. Grewal, *Sikhs*, p. 69.
69. Singh, *Guru Tegh Bahadur*, p. 41.
70. Latif, *History*, p. 259.
71. Latif, *History*, p. 260, and Gupta, *Later Mughal History*, p. 36.
72. Latif, *Lahore*, p. 176.
73. Grewal, *Sikhs*, p. 75.
74. Grewal, *Sikhs*, p. 75.
75. Gopal Singh, *Guru Gobind Singh*, p. 39.
76. Gopal Singh, *Guru Gobind Singh*, p. 38.
77. Gopal Singh, *Guru Gobind Singh*, p. 40.
78. See, for example, McLeod, *The Evolution of the Sikh Community*, p. 11.
79. A.H. Amin in http://www.defencejournal.com/2001/september/analysis.htm
80. See, for example, *www.sikhiwiki.org/index.php/Malerkotla*
81. Latif, *History*, p. 178.
82. Latif, *History*, p. 177.
83. Quoted in Malik, *Modern Nationalism*, p. 86.
84. J. S. Grewal, 'Batala as a Medieval Town', in Grewal and Pall, *Precolonial and Colonial Punjab*, p. 114.
85 Bhandari's text reproduced in Akbar, *Punjab under the Mughals*, pp. 285-311.

2. 1707-1757: Collapse of Authority

1. Latif, *History*, p. 268.
2. Grewal, *Sikhs*, p. 79.
3. Grewal, *Sikhs*, p. 79.
4. Gupta, *Later Mughal History*, p. 44.
5. Grewal, *Sikhs*, p. 82.
6. Gopal Singh, *Guru Gobind Singh*, p. 37.
7. Grewal, *Sikhs*, p. 79.
8. Gopal Singh, *Guru Gobind Singh*, p. 52*fn*.
9. Latif, *History*, p. 180.
10. Quoted in Gupta, *Later Mughal History*, p. 46*fn*.
11. Kazimi, *A Concise History of Pakistan*, p. 47.
12. Gupta, *Later Mughal History*, p. 19.
13. Gupta, *Later Mughal History*, p. 46.
14. Gupta, *Later Mughal History*, p. 46*fn*.

15. Chetan Singh, 'Polity, Economy and Society under the Mughals,' in Banga, *Five Punjabi Centuries*, p. 51.
16. Malcolm quoted in Latif, *History*, p. 275*fn*.
17. Irvine, quoted in Gupta, *Later Mughal History*, p. 47.
18. Khushwant Singh, *History of the Sikhs*, vol. 1, p. 118.
19. Communication to author from Ishtiaq Ahmed, 8 December 2012.
20. Gupta, *Later Mughal History*, p. 48, and Grewal, *Sikhs*, p. 83.
21. Grewal, *Sikhs*, p. 83.
22. Muzaffar Alam, 'Politics Under the Later Mughals,' in Banga, *Five Punjabi Centuries*, p. 77.
23. Gupta, *Later Mughal History*, p. 48.
24. Latif, *History*, p. 180.
25. Latif, *History*, p. 182.
26. Atam Singh, *Songs of Bullah*, p. 7.
27. Khushhal Chand quoted in Gupta, *Later Mughal History*, p. 15.
28. Latif's description. Lepel Griffin suggests that his family was for centuries based in Panipat. See Griffin, *Punjab Chiefs*, pp. 46-47.
29. Muzaffar Alam, 'Politics Under the Later Mughals', in Banga, *Five Punjabi Centuries*, p. 69.
30. Though an explicit statement is lacking, this seems to be the implication in Muzaffar Alam, 'Politics Under the Later Mughals', p. 70.
31. Gupta, *Later Mughal History*, p. 49.
32. Latif, *History*, p. 279.
33. See Uberoi, *Religion, Civil Society, and the State*, p. 97.
34. Gupta, *Later Mughal History*, p. 50, quoting from Forster's *Journey*, vol. 1, pp. 312-13.
35. Latif, *History*, p. 188.
36. Latif, *History*, p. 188.
37. Gupta, *Later Mughal History*, p. 51.
38. Gupta, *Later Mughal History*, p. 51.
39. Muzaffar Alam in Indu Banga, *Five Punjabi Centuries*, p. 71.
40. Khafi Khan cited in Gupta, *Later Mughal History*, p. 52.
41. Gupta, *Later Mughal History*, p. 53,
42. Gupta, *Later Mughal History*, pp. 27-28*fn*.
43. Haroon Khalid in 'The Folklore of Chunian', *Express Tribune*, Lahore, 28 October 2010.
44. Khaled Ahmad's introduction in Rafat, *Bulleh Shah*, p. 7.
45. Grewal, *Sikhs*, p. 89
46. Gupta, *Later Mughal History*, p. 53.
47. Gupta, *Later Mughal History*, p. 54.
48. Gupta, *Later Mughal History*, p. 55.
49. Muzaffar Alam in Banga, *Five Punjabi Centuries*, p. 71.
50. Gupta, *Later Mughal History*, p. 16.
51. Gupta, *Later Mughal History*, p. 17*fn*.

52. Gupta, *Later Mughal History*, pp. 17-18.
53. Quotation from unnamed historian in *Mirat-i-Waridat*, reproduced in Gupta, *Later Mughal History*, p. 20*fn*.
54. Latif, *History*, p. 193.
55. Latif, *History*, p. 193.
56. Latif, *History*, pp. 200-01.
57. Quoted in Gaur, *Society, Religion and Patriarchy*, p. 79.
58. Latif, *History*, p. 212.
59. Khaled Ahmad's introduction in Rafat, *Bulleh Shah*, p. 22.
60. Gaur, *Society, Religion and Patriarchy*, p. 165.
61. Khaled Ahmad's introduction in Rafat, *Bulleh Shah*, p. 1.
62. Rafat, *Bulleh Shah*, p. 191.
63. Rafat, *Bulleh Shah*, p. 177.
64. Atam Singh, *Songs of Bullah*, p. 4.
65. Duggal, *Sain Bulleh Shah*, p. 11.
66. Rafat, *Bulleh Shah*, p. xvi.
67. Khaled Ahmad's introduction in Rafat, *Bulleh Shah*, p. 6.
68. Duggal, *Sain Bulleh Shah*, p. 8.
69. Duggal, *Sain Bulleh Shah*, p. 9.
70. Sethi, *John Lawrence*, p. 15.
71. Gupta, *Later Mughal History*, pp. 62-63.
72. Khushwant Singh, *History of the Sikhs*, vol. 1, p. 127*fn*.
73. Mukhlis, *Tazkira*, p. 139, quoted in Khushwant Singh, *History of the Sikhs*, vol. 1, p. 127*fn*.
74. 'The Palace of Sharaf al-Nisa' in Iqbal's *Javid Nama*, tr. by Arthur J. Arberry, http://www.allamaiqbal.com/works/poetry/persian/javidnama/translation/
75. Latif, *Lahore*, pp. 135-36.
76. In an email for the author, the historian, Ayesha Jalal, wrote (12 January 2011): 'The Afghan raids into Punjab, particularly those of Nadir Shah and Abdali, are supposed to have facilitated Sikh rule in Punjab. Other explanations point to the failure of the Mughal governor to declare independence, thus prompting the emergence of a warrior clan with a unique organization (Sikhs).' Similarly, writing on 'Punjab and the Retardation of Nationalism' in D.A. Low (ed.), *The Political Inheritance of Pakistan* (London: Macmillan, 1991), historian Imran Ali states: 'In ex-Mughal provinces such as Awadh, Bengal and Hyderabad, Mughal viceroys became independent rulers.... Matters were quite different in the Punjab.'
77. Gupta, *Later Mughal History*, p. 68-69*fn*.
78. Gupta, *Later Mughal History*, p. 68.
79. Gupta, *Later Mughal History*, quoting Alexander Dow, p. 225.
80. Latif, *History*, p. 219.
81. J.C. Dua, *British Historiography*, p. 7.
82. Latif, *History*, p. 220.
83. Gupta, *Later Mughal History*, p. 75.

84. Gupta, *Later Mughal History*, p. 76.
85. Gupta, *Later Mughal History*, p. 76.
86. Gupta, *Later Mughal History*, p. 77 and p. 77fn, citing the historians and works recording the conversation.
87. Gupta, *Later Mughal History*, p. 168.
88. Gupta, *Later Mughal History*, p. 78.
89. Gupta, *Later Mughal History*, quoting Malcolm, pp. 78-79.
90. *District and States Gazetteers of the Undivided Punjab*, vol. 2, p. 486.
91. Gupta, *Later Mughal History*, p. 79.
92. Gupta, *Later Mughal History*, p. 80.
93. Gupta, *Later Mughal History*, p. 122.
94. Gupta, *Later Mughal History*, p. 80.
95. Gupta, *Later Mughal History*, p. 82.
96. Muzaffar Alam in Banga, *Five Punjabi Centuries*, p. 80.
97. Gupta, *Later Mughal History*, p. 127fn.
98. Gupta, *Later Mughal History*, pp. 127-30.
99. Gupta, *Later Mughal History*, pp. 130-31.
100. Gupta, *Later Mughal History*, citing sources, p. 132.
101. Gupta, *Later Mughal History*, p. 134.
102. Gupta, *Later Mughal History*, p. 170.
103. Gupta, *Later Mughal History*, p. 170.
104. Latif, *History*, p. 228.
105. Gupta, *Later Mughal History*, p. 173.
106. Latif, *History*, pp. 228-29.
107. Alexander Dow quoted in Gupta, *Later Mughal History*, p. 225.

3. 1757-1799: Adina Beg Khan, Afghans and The Sikhs
1. Gupta, *Later Mughal History*, p. 137.
2. Gupta, *Later Mughal History*, p. 88.
3. Chaudhry, *Punjab*, pp. 185-86.
4. Gupta, *Later Mughal History*, p. 90.
5. Gupta, *Later Mughal History*, p. 91.
6. Gupta, *Later Mughal History*, pp. 90-91, citing several sources, including the anonymous writer, 'probably a Panjabi Hindu', of an 1806 biography (in Persian) of Adina, *Ahwal-i-Adina Beg Khan*.
7. Gupta, *Later Mughal History*, citing sources, p. 94.
8. Gupta, *Later Mughal History*, p. 94.
9. See Gupta, *Later Mughal History*, p. 97fn.
10. Gupta, *Later Mughal History*, p. 103.
11. Latif, *History*, p. 232.
12. Gupta, *Later Mughal History*, p. 99.
13. See Gupta, *Later Mughal History*, p. 99, and Chaudhary, *Punjab*, pp. 185-86.
14. Gupta, *Later Mughal History*, p. 99.

15. See Gupta, *Later Mughal History*, p. 100*fn*.
16. Gupta, *Later Mughal History*, p. 100.
17. Ahmad Shah of Batala quoted in Gupta, *Later Mughal History*, pp. 100-01.
18. Gupta, *Later Mughal History*, p. 101.
19. Gupta, *Later Mughal History*, p. 106.
20. Gupta, *Later Mughal History*, p. 104.
21. Quoted in Gupta, *Later Mughal History*, p. 102.
22. Gupta, *Later Mughal History*, quoting Aliuddin, p. 103.
23. Gupta, *Later Mughal History*, p. 156.
24. Gupta, *Later Mughal History*, p. 177.
25. Gupta, *Later Mughal History*, p. 177.
26. Gupta, *Later Mughal History*, p. 177.
27. Gupta, *Later Mughal History*, p. 185.
28. McLeod, *Evolution of the Sikh Community*, p. 17.
29. See Gupta, *Later Mughal History*, pp. 308-17.
30. Gupta, *Later Mughal History*, p. 191.
31. Gupta, *Later Mughal History*, p. 192.
32. Gupta, *Later Mughal History*, p. 192.
33. Gupta, *Later Mughal History*, p. 192*fn*.
34. Gupta, *Later Mughal History*, p. 194.
35. Gupta, *Later Mughal History*, p. 195.
36. Gupta, *Later Mughal History*, p. 196.
37. Gupta, *Later Mughal History*, p. 197*fn*.
38. Gupta, *Later Mughal History*, p. 214.
39. Gupta, *Later Mughal History*, pp. 210-12.
40. Indu Banga, 'Ala Singh: The Founder of Patiala State,' in Barrier and Singh, *Punjab Past and Present*, p. 152.
41. Salahuddin, *Tarikh-e-Punjab*, p. 358.
42. Lafont, *Maharaja Ranjit Singh*, p. 33.
43. Gupta, *Later Mughal History*, pp. 218-19.
44. Lafont, *Maharaja Ranjit Singh*, p. 28 & p. 32.
45. Allegation on Badshahi Mosque notice-boards seen by the author in the 1990s.
46. *Gujranwala District Gazetteer*, vol. xxiv A of Punjab District Gazetteers series (1935), pp. 15-17.
47. District officers in the later British period would run into the saying in different parts of the Punjab countryside. See, for example, *Montgomery District Gazetteer*, p. 30, and *Gujrat District Gazetteer*, p. 18.
48. A.H. Amin in http://www.defencejournal.com/2001/september/analysis.html
49. *Rawalpindi Gazetteer*, p. 264.
50. Sufi Muhammad-ud-Deen Zaar, *Tazkara-e-Jehlum*, pp. 35-36.
51. Talbot, *Punjab and the Raj*, p. 44
52. Kazimi, *A Concise History of Pakistan*, p. 49.
53. See a discussion of this in Gaur, *Society, Religion and Patriarchy*, pp. 150-82.

54. This observation is borrowed from A.H. Amin, http://www.defencejournal.com/2001/september/analysis.htm
55. Gaur, *Society, Religion and Patriarchy*, p. 91, citing Singh, *Studies in Punjabi History and Culture*, p. 201.
56. Gurcharan Singh, *Warris Shah*, pp. 30-33.
57. Gurcharan Singh, *Warris Shah*, p. 71 & p. 11.
58. Gurcharan Singh, *Warris Shah*, pp. 9-10.
59. Gurcharan Singh, *Warris Shah*, p. 10.
60. Amrita Pritam's phrase, translated, quoted in Gaur, *Society, Religion and Patriarchy*, p. 89.
61. Gaur, *Society, Religion and Patriarchy*, p. 104.
62. Gurcharan Singh, *Warris Shah*, p. 12.
63. Quoted in Gupta, *Later Mughal History*, p. 230.
64. Cunningham quoted in Gupta, *Later Mughal History*, p. 228.
65. Ferrier quoted in Gupta, *Later Mughal History*, p. 227.
66. *Gujranwala District Gazetteer*, vol. xxiv A of Punjab District Gazetteers series (1935), pp. 18-19.
67. *Gujranwala District Gazetteer*, vol. xxiv A of Punjab District Gazetteers series (1935), p. 22.
68. Forster quoted in Khushwant Singh, *History of the Sikhs*, vol. 1, p. 184.
69. Khushwant Singh, *Ranjit Singh*, pp. 35-36.
70. Latif, *History*, p. 305.
71. Khushwant Singh, *Ranjit Singh*, p. 35.
72. Gupta, *Later Mughal History*, p. 280.
73. Latif, *History*, p. 305.
74. Grewal, *Sikhs*, p. 101.

4. 1799-1849: Ranjit Singh and His Successors

1. Khushwant Singh, *Ranjit Singh*, p. 47.
2. Amrik Singh's foreword in Nijhawan, *The First Punjab War*, p. 14.
3. Khushwant Singh, *Ranjit Singh*, p. 31.
4. Khushwant Singh, *Ranjit Singh*, p. 31.
5. Khushwant Singh, *Ranjit Singh*, pp. 30-31.
6. Khushwant Singh, *Ranjit Singh*, p. 48.
7. Lafont, *Maharaja Ranjit Singh*, p. 15.
8. Khushwant Singh, *Ranjit Singh*, p. 51.
9. Khushwant Singh, *Ranjit Singh*, p. 56.
10. Lafont, *Maharaja Ranjit Singh*, p. 15.
11. Khushwant Singh, *Ranjit Singh*, p. 56.
12. Khushwant Singh, *Ranjit Singh*, p. 57.
13. Khushwant Singh, *Ranjit Singh*, p. 58, and Lafont, *Maharaja Ranjit Singh*, p. 52.
14. Khushwant Singh, *Ranjit Singh*, pp. 61-62.
15. Khushwant Singh, *Ranjit Singh*, p. 63.

16. Khushwant Singh, *Ranjit Singh*, p. 67.
17. Khushwant Singh, *Ranjit Singh*, p. 67*fn*
18. Khushwant Singh, *Ranjit Singh*, p. 68.
19. Latif, *History*, p. 366.
20. Khushwant Singh, *Ranjit Singh*, p. 70.
21. Letter of 31 Oct. 1908 (handcopy) from Metcalfe to Edmonsone, Chief Secretary in Calcutta, SN 23, Vol. 1, Book 5, Punjab Secretariat Archives, Lahore.
22. Khushwant Singh to author, New Delhi, 18 June 2011.
23. Metcalfe's letter of 8 November 1808 to Edmonsone, Chief Secretary in Calcutta (handcopy), sent from 'Camp Goongrana', SN 31, Vol. 1, Book 5, Punjab Secretariat Archives, Lahore.
24. Khushwant Singh, *Ranjit Singh*, p. 81.
25. Khushwant Singh, *Ranjit Singh*, p. 91*fn*.
26. Letter of 31 October 1908 (handcopy) from Metcalfe to Edmonsone, Chief Secretary in Calcutta, SN 23, Vol. 1, Book 5, Punjab Secretariat Archives, Lahore.
27. Khushwant Singh, *Ranjit Singh*, pp. 79-80.
28. Khushwant Singh, *Ranjit Singh*, p. 76*fn*.
29. Khushwant Singh, *Ranjit Singh*, p. 77*fn*.
30. See, for example, the remarks of British historians Thompson and Kiernan quoted in Khushwant Singh, *Ranjit Singh*, p. 79*fn* and p. 84*fn*.
31. Khushwant Singh, *Ranjit Singh*, p. 85 & p. 85*fn*.
32. Khushwant Singh, *Ranjit Singh*, p. 92.
33. Khushwant Singh, *Ranjit Singh*, p. 99.
34. Khushwant Singh, *Ranjit Singh*, p. 102.
35. SN 71, *Press Lists* (Lahore 1915), Vol. II, p. 217, Punjab Secretariat Archives, Lahore.
36. Letter of 25 September 1810, SN 54, Book 6, p. 114, Punjab Secretariat Archives, Lahore.
37. Latif, *History*, p. 385.
38. Khushwant Singh, *Ranjit Singh*, p. 105.
39. Khushwant Singh, *Ranjit Singh*, pp. 108-9.
40. Latif, *History*, p. 399.
41. Khushwant Singh, *Ranjit Singh*, pp. 113*fn*.
42. Letter of 13 August 1814, SN 78, *Press Lists* (Lahore 1915), Vol. II, p. 307, Punjab Secretariat Archives, Lahore.
43. Khushwant Singh, *Ranjit Singh*, p. 126.
44. Manuscript about Shaheed Muzaffar Khan written in H 1233 by Fakir Muhammad Issa Qadri, Tarikh Daulat-e-Abbasia (Bahawalpur), MSS 971, Lahore Museum; *Gazetteer of the Multan District, 1923-24* (Lahore: Punjab Govt., 1926; reprint, Sang-a-Meel, Lahore, 1990), p. 46.
45. Latif, *History of the Panjab*. p. 412.
46. Khushwant Singh, *Ranjit Singh*, p. 126.
47. *Gazetteer of the Multan District, 1923-24*, pp. 49-50.
48. Khushwant Singh, *Ranjit Singh*, p. 129.

49. Khushwant Singh, *Ranjit Singh*, p. 130.
50. Khushwant Singh, *Ranjit Singh*, p. 133.
51. Khushwant Singh, *Ranjit Singh*, p. 185*fn*.
52. Khushwant Singh, *Ranjit Singh*, p. 137.
53. Grewal, *Sikhs*, p. 105; and Khushwant Singh, *Ranjit Singh*, pp. 155-56.
54. See, for example, Latif, *History*, p. 408, where some of these Hindu officers are named.
55. See, for example, Griffin, *Punjab Chiefs*, p. 171 (Shahpur).
56. Grewal, *Sikhs*, p. 105.
57. Latif, *History*, p. 432.
58. Latif, *History*, p. 440.
59. Latif, *History*, p. 440.
60. Burnes quoted in Khushwant Singh, *Ranjit Singh*, p. 168*fn*.
61. Burnes quoted in Khushwant Singh, *Ranjit Singh*, p. 171.
62. Grewal, *Sikhs*, p. 113.
63. Lafont, *Maharaja Ranjit Singh*, p. 83.
64. Grewal, *Sikhs*, p. 113.
65. Lafont, *Maharaja Ranjit Singh*, p. 76.
66. Lafont, *Maharaja Ranjit Singh*, p. 83.
67. Latif, *History*, p. 435.
68. A.H. Amin in http://www.defencejournal.com/2001/september/analysis.html
69. A.H. Amin in http://www.defencejournal.com/2001/september/analysis.html
70. Lafont, *Maharaja Ranjit Singh*, pp. 74-75.
71. Lafont, *Maharaja Ranjit Singh*, p. 81.
72. Lafont, *Maharaja Ranjit Singh*, p. 74.
73. Lafont, *Maharaja Ranjit Singh*, p. 70.
74. So the author was told in Lahore in March 2011.
75. Lafont, *Maharaja Ranjit Singh*, pp. 10-11.
76. Khushwant Singh, *Ranjit Singh*, pp. 178-79.
77. A.H. Amin in http://www.defencejournal.com/2001/september/analysis.html
78. Khushwant Singh, *Ranjit Singh*, p. 178*fn*.
79. Khushwant Singh, *Ranjit Singh*, p. 177*fn*.
80. Khushwant Singh, *Ranjit Singh*, p. 177*fn*.
81. Khushwant Singh, *Ranjit Singh*, p. 163.
82. Letter of 25 June 1830 from Wade to Hawkins, *Press Lists of Old Records*, Vol. V, SN 100, p. 148, Punjab Secretariat, Lahore.
83. Caroe, *The Pathans*, pp. 297-98.
84. Nijhawan, *The First Punjab War*, p. 32.
85. Quoted in Khushwant Singh, *Ranjit Singh*, p. 169 & p. 181.
86. Khushwant Singh, *Ranjit Singh*, p. 166.
87. Burnes quoted in Khushwant Singh, *Ranjit Singh*, p. 170.
88. Quoted in Khushwant Singh, *Ranjit Singh*, pp. 170-71.
89. Khushwant Singh, *Ranjit Singh*, p. 174.

90. Quoted in Khushwant Singh, *Ranjit Singh*, p. 183.
91. Khushwant Singh, *Ranjit Singh*, p. 185*fn*.
92. Latif, *History*, p. 464.
93. Fane, quoted in Khushwant Singh, *Ranjit Singh*, p. 202.
94. Lafont, *Maharaja Ranjit Singh*, pp. 41-43.
95. Quoted in Lafont, *Maharaja Ranjit Singh*, p. 43.
96. Grewal, *Sikhs*, p. 107.
97. Grewal, *Sikhs*, p. 107-11.
98. Lafont, *Maharaja Ranjit Singh*, p. 89.
99. Lafont, *Maharaja Ranjit Singh*, p. 11.
100. Quoted in Latif, *Lahore*, p. 98.
101. Quoted in Latif, *Lahore*, pp. 98-99.
102. Quoted in Latif, *Lahore*, p. 99.
103. Lafont, *Maharaja Ranjit Singh*, pp. 71-72.
104. Khushwant Singh, *Ranjit Singh*, p. 189, and Latif, *History*, p. 483.
105. Khushwant Singh, *Ranjit Singh*, p. 190.
106. Khushwant Singh, *Ranjit Singh*, p. 194.
107. Khushwant Singh, *Ranjit Singh*, p. 192.
108. Moon, *British Conquest and Dominion of India*, p. 590.
109. Quoted in Bosworth Smith, *Life of Lord Lawrence*, p. 189.
110. Latif, *History*, p. 476.
111. Quoted in Khushwant Singh, *Ranjit Singh*, p. 207.
112. Quoted in Khushwant Singh, *Ranjit Singh*, p. 212.
113. Latif, *History*, p. 492*fn*.
114. Latif, *History*, pp. 493-95.
115. Grewal, *History*, p. 120*fn*
116. Grewal, *History*, p. 121.
117. Grewal, *History*, p. 121.
118. Moon, *The British Conquest and Dominion of India*, p. 593.
119. Grewal, *History*, p. 122.
120. Khushwant Singh, *How the Sikhs Lost their Kingdom*, p. 66.
121. Moon, *British Conquest*, p. 593
122. Trotter, *Life of John Nicholson* p. 24.
123. Quoted in Bosworth Smith, *Life of Lord Lawrence*, p. 142.
124. Quoted in Bosworth Smith, *Life of Lord Lawrence*, p. 161.
125. Khushwant Singh, *Ranjit Singh*, p. 174, quoting from Baillie Fraser, *Military Memoirs of Lieut.-Col. James Skinner*, 1851, vol.1, entries Oct. 26-31, 1831.
126. Grewal, *History*, p. 123.
127. Grewal, *History*, p. 123.
128. Grewal, *History*, p. 123
129. Moon, *British Conquest*, p. 596.
130. Moon, *British Conquest*, p. 600.
131. Moon, *British Conquest*, p. 599.

132. Moon, *British Conquest*, p. 600.
133. Moon, *British Conquest*, p. 600; and Grewal, *History*, p. 124.
134. Moon, *British Conquest*, p. 600.
135. Grewal, *History*, p. 124.
136. Nijhawan, *First Punjab War*, p. 31.
137. Nijhawan, *First Punjab War*, p. 245.
138. Nijhawan, *First Punjab War*, p. 31.
139. Patwant Singh, *The Sikhs*, p. 162.
140. Grewal, *History*, p. 126.
141. Khushwant Singh, *How the Sikhs Lost their Kingdom*, p. 162.
142. Khushwant Singh, *How the Sikhs Lost their Kingdom*, p. 165; and Moon, *British Conquest*, p. 615.
143. Moon, *British Conquest*, p. 617.
144. Bosworth Smith, *Life of Lord Lawrence*, p. 248.
145. Bosworth Smith, *Life of Lord Lawrence*, p. 251.
146. Major, *Return of Empire* pp. 112-13

5. 1849-1859: British Punjab and the 1857 Rebellion

1. Bosworth Smith, *Life of Lord Lawrence* vol. 1, p. 33.
2. Without providing a direct quotation from Lawrence, this is what McLeod Innes claims in *Lucknow & Oude in the Mutiny*, p. 68.
3. McLeod Innes, *Lucknow & Oude in the Mutiny*, p. 66.
4. R. Bosworth Smith, *Life of Lord Lawrence*, vol. 1, p. 233.
5. R. Bosworth Smith, *Life of Lord Lawrence*, vol. 1, p. 211.
6. R. Bosworth Smith, *Life of Lord Lawrence*, vol. 1, p. 213 & p. 241.
7. R. Bosworth Smith, *Life of Lord Lawrence*, vol. 1, p. 15.
8. R. Bosworth Smith, *Life of Lord Lawrence*, vol. 1, p. 32.
9. R. Bosworth Smith, *Life of Lord Lawrence*, vol. 1, p. 37.
10. R. Bosworth Smith, *Life of Lord Lawrence*, vol. 1, p. 41.
11. Trotter, *Life of John Nicholson*, p. 152.
12. For example, see R. Bosworth Smith, *Life of Lord Lawrence*, vol. 1, p. 2.
13. Charles Raikes, British civilian, quoted in Sethi, *John Lawrence*, p. 3.
14. Quoted in Sethi, *John Lawrence*, pp. 3-4.
15. R. Bosworth Smith, *Life of Lord Lawrence*, vol. 1, p. 59.
16. Charles Aitchison, quoted in Sethi, *John Lawrence*, p. 11.
17. Sethi, *John Lawrence*, p. 11.
18. Charles Aitchison quoted in Sethi, *John Lawrence*, p. 33.
19. Sethi, *John Lawrence*, p. 6 & p. 17.
20. Letter to unnamed friend quoted in Sethi, *John Lawrence*, p. 31.
21. Sethi, *John Lawrence*, p. 31.
22. See Penderel Moon, *British Conquest and Dominion of India*, pp. 609-10.
23. Trotter, *Life of John Nicholson*, p. 153.
24. Bosworth Smith, *Life of Lord Lawrence*, vol. 1, p. 247.

25. Talbot, *Punjab and the Raj*, p. 51.
26. Bosworth Smith, *Life of Lord Lawrence*, vol. 1, pp. 190-91.
27. Bosworth Smith, *Life of Lord Lawrence*, vol. 1, p. 262.
28. Bosworth Smith, *Life of Lord Lawrence*, vol. 1, p. 261.
29. Bosworth Smith, *Life of Lord Lawrence*, vol. 1, p. 261.
30. Bosworth Smith, *Life of Lord Lawrence*, vol. 1, p. 261.
31. Bosworth Smith, *Life of Lord Lawrence*, vol. 1, p. 273.
32. Bosworth Smith, *Life of Lord Lawrence*, vol. 1, p. 282.
33. Bosworth Smith, *Life of Lord Lawrence*, vol. 1, p. 275.
34. R.H. Cust in undated article in *Calcutta Review*, quoted in Bosworth Smith, *Life of Lord Lawrence*, vol. 1, p. 49.
35. See, for example, Bosworth Smith, *Life of Lord Lawrence*, pp. 49-50.
36. Trotter, *Life of John Nicholson*, p. 8.
37. Trotter, *Life of John Nicholson*, p. 11*fn*.
38. Trotter, *Life of John Nicholson*, p. 14.
39. Trotter, *Life of John Nicholson*, p. 19.
40. Trotter, *Life of John Nicholson*, pp. 34-35 & p. 46.
41. Trotter, *Life of John Nicholson*, p. 125.
42. Trotter, *Life of John Nicholson*, p. 125
43. Trotter, *Life of John Nicholson*, p. 143.
44. Trotter, *Life of John Nicholson*, p. 143.
45. Trotter, *Life of John Nicholson*, p. 130.
46. Trotter, *Life of John Nicholson*, p. 147.
47. Trotter, *Life of John Nicholson*, p. 150.
48. Trotter, *Life of John Nicholson*, p. 151.
49. Trotter, *Life of John Nicholson*, p. 162.
50. Trotter, *Life of John Nicholson*, p. 163.
51. Trotter, *Life of John Nicholson*, p. 163.
52. Trotter, *Life of John Nicholson*, p. 180-81.
53. Trotter, *Life of John Nicholson*, p. 169.
54. Trotter, *Life of John Nicholson*, p. 174.
55. Trotter, *Life of John Nicholson*, p. 146.
56. Latif, *History*, pp. 574-76.
57. Bosworth Smith, *Life of Lord Lawrence*, pp. 297-8.
58. Bosworth Smith, *Life of Lord Lawrence*, p. 297.
59. Bosworth Smith, *Life of Lord Lawrence*, p. 298.
60. Trotter, *Life of John Nicholson*, p. 153.
61. Bosworth Smith, *Life of Lord Lawrence*, p. 299.
62. Bosworth Smith, *Life of Lord Lawrence*, p. 350.
63. Trotter, *Life of John Nicholson*, p. 153.
64. Bosworth Smith, *Life of Lord Lawrence*, p. 405.
65. Quoted in Bean, *Yankee India*, p. 255.
66. Bosworth Smith, *Life of Lord Lawrence*, p. 377.

67. Bosworth Smith, *Life of Lord Lawrence*, pp. 387-90.
68. Trotter, *Life of John Nicholson*, p. 168.
69. Trotter, *Life of John Nicholson*, p. 154.
70. Letter of 25 September 1855, R. Bosworth Smith, *Life of Lord Lawrence*, p. 441.
71. Bosworth Smith, *Life of Lord Lawrence*, p. 410.
72. Colonel Urmston quoted in Trotter, *Life of John Nicholson*, p. 195.
73. Bosworth Smith, *Life of Lord Lawrence*, vol. 2, p. 12.
74. Bosworth Smith, *Life of Lord Lawrence*, vol. 2, p. 19.
75. Bosworth Smith, *Life of Lord Lawrence*, vol. 2, p. 7.
76. Kaye & Malleson, *History of the Indian Mutiny*, vol. 2, p. 325.
77. Bosworth Smith, *Life of Lord Lawrence*, vol. 2, p. 10.
78. Trotter, *Life of John Nicholson*, p. 202.
79. Trotter, *Life of John Nicholson*, pp. 203-07.
80. Bosworth Smith, *Life of Lord Lawrence*, vol. 2, p. 32.
81. Trotter, *Life of John Nicholson*, p. 213.
82. Trotter, *Life of John Nicholson*, p. 213.
83. Trotter, *Life of John Nicholson*, pp. 210-13.
84. Trotter, *Life of John Nicholson*, p. 215.
85. Trotter, *Life of John Nicholson*, p. 223.
86. Trotter, *Life of John Nicholson*, p. 223.
87. Trotter, *Life of John Nicholson*, p. 224.
88. http://www.gutenberg.org/files/16528/16528-h/16528-h.htm#XXV5
89. Rudrangshu Mukherjee, 'Satan Let Loose' in *Past & Present*, No. 128 (1990), p. 111, citing Kaye, *History of the Sepoy War*, vol. 2, pp. 269-70.
90. Dodd, *History of the Indian Revolt*, p. 322.
91. Bosworth Smith, *Life of Lord Lawrence*, vol. 2, p. 46.
92. Bosworth Smith, *Life of Lord Lawrence*, vol. 2, p. 3.
93. Bosworth Smith, *Life of Lord Lawrence*, vol. 1, p. 46.
94. Bosworth Smith, *Life of Lord Lawrence*, vol. 2, p. 97.
95. Bosworth Smith, *Life of Lord Lawrence*, vol. 2, p. 97.
96. Bosworth Smith, *Life of Lord Lawrence*, vol. 2, p. 98.
97. Bosworth Smith, *Life of Lord Lawrence*, vol. 2, pp. 85-86.
98. A summary of Bosworth Smith, *Life of Lord Lawrence*, vol. 2, pp. 37-38.
99. A Colonel Ramsay quoted in Bosworth Smith, *Life of Lord Lawrence*, vol. 1, p. 171.
100. Bosworth Smith, *Life of Lord Lawrence*, vol. 2, pp. 72-73.
101. Bosworth Smith, *Life of Lord Lawrence*, vol. 2, p. 92.
102. Bosworth Smith, *Life of Lord Lawrence*, vol. 2, p. 92.
103. Bosworth Smith, *Life of Lord Lawrence*, vol. 2, p. 86.
104. Bosworth Smith, *Life of Lord Lawrence*, vol. 2, p. 153.
105. Cooper, *Crisis in the Punjab* p. 100.
106. Bosworth Smith, *Life of Lord Lawrence*, vol. 2, pp. 62-64.
107. Abdul Ghani Sameen, 'The Role of the Punjab in the Revolt of 1857,' in M. Ikram Chaghatai, *1857 in Muslim Historiography*, p. 655.

108. http://www.apnaorg.com/articles/news-20/
109. Sourced to a letter from Commissioner Thornton to Robert Montgomery. See Tan Tai Yong, *The Garrison State*, p. 48.
110. *Gazetteer of the Sialkot District, 1920* (Lahore: Punjab Govt., 1921. Reprint, Sang-a-Meel, Lahore, 1990), p. 23.
111. *Gazetteer of the Sialkot District*, p. 26.
112. *Gazetteer of the Sialkot District*, p. 26.
113. *Gazetteer of the Sialkot District*, p. 26.
114. Bosworth Smith, *Life of Lord Lawrence*, vol. 2, pp. 107-08.
115. Bosworth Smith, *Life of Lord Lawrence*, vol. 2, p. 155.
116. Abdul Ghani Sameen, 'The Role of the Punjab in the Revolt of 1857,' in M. Ikram Chaghatai, *1857 in Muslim Historiography*, pp. 661-62.
117. *Gazetteer of the Montgomery District, 1883-84* (Lahore: Punjab Govt., 1884. Reprint, Sang-a-Meel, Lahore, 1990), pp. 38-39.
118. http://indopakmilitaryhistory.blogspot.com/2011/08/1857-rebellion-from-january-1857-to.html
119. *Gazetteer of the Montgomery District*, p. 38.
120. *Gazetteer of the Montgomery District*, pp. 38-39.
121. Bosworth Smith, *Life of Lord Lawrence*, vol. 2, 204.
122. http://en.wikipedia.org/wiki/Rae_Ahmed_Nawaz_Khan_Kharal.
123. Bosworth Smith, *Life of Lord Lawrence*, vol. 2, p. 206.
124. *Gazetteer of the Montgomery District*, pp. 38-39.
125. Woodham-Smith, *Queen Victoria*, p. 385.
126. Bosworth Smith, *Life of Lord Lawrence*, vol. 2, pp. 146-47.
127. From Trotter, *Life of John Nicholson*, p. 229, with revised translation of the Hindustani order.
128. Trotter, *Life of John Nicholson*, p. 232.
129. Trotter, *Life of John Nicholson*, pp. 237-38.
130. Trotter, *Life of John Nicholson*, p. 249.
131. Trotter, *Life of John Nicholson*, p. 256.
132. Trotter, *Life of John Nicholson*, p. 272.
133. Trotter, *Life of John Nicholson*, p. 276.
134. Trotter, *Life of John Nicholson*, p. 262.
135. Trotter, *Life of John Nicholson*, pp. 264-67.
136. Trotter, *Life of John Nicholson*, p. 286.
137. Trotter, *Life of John Nicholson*, p. 272.
138. Trotter, *Life of John Nicholson*, p. 278.
139. Trotter, *Life of John Nicholson*, p. 285.
140. See ballad on Nicholson in Trotter, *Life of John Nicholson*, pp. 321-23.
141. Trotter, *Life of John Nicholson*, p. 293.
142. Trotter, *Life of John Nicholson*, p. 300.
143. Hodson's letter quoted in Broehl, *Crisis of the Raj*, p. 113.
144. MacDowell quoted in Hibbert, *The Great Mutiny*, p. 326.

145. Bosworth Smith, *Life of Lord Lawrence,* vol. 2, p. 190.
146. Kaye, *Sepoy War,* vol. iii, quoted opposite the Preface in Trotter, *Life of John Nicholson.*
147. Trotter, *Life of John Nicholson,* p. 323.
148. Trotter, *Life of John Nicholson,* p. 322.
149. Moon, *The British Conquest,* p. 731.
150. Moon, *British Conquest,* p. 731.
151. Woodham-Smith, *Queen Victoria,* p. 384 and p. 467.
152. Hibbert, *Great Mutiny,* p. 212.
153. Dodd, *History of the Indian Revolt,* p. 311.
154. Dodd, *History of the Indian Revolt,* p. 312.
155. Dalrymple, *Last Mughal,* p. 443.
156. Bosworth Smith, *Life of Lord Lawrence,* vol. 2, p. 199.
157. Hibbert, *Great Mutiny,* p. 361.
158. Bosworth Smith, *Life of Lord Lawrence,* vol. 2, p. 236.
159. Bosworth Smith, *Life of Lord Lawrence,* vol. 2, p. 241.
160. Hibbert, *Great Mutiny,* pp. 389-91.

6. 1859-1919: Imperial High Noon

1. *Gazetteer of the Jhelum District, 1904* (Lahore: Reprint, Sang-e-Meel, 1991), p. 73.
2. An account of some of these discussions is provided in Tan Tai Yong, *The Garrison State* pp. 50-53.
3. Grewal, *Sikhs,* p. 129.
4. *Gazetteer of the Rawalpindi District, 1893-94* (Lahore: Punjab Govt., 1895; reprint, Sang-a-Meel, Lahore, 2001), pp. 253-54.
5. Punjab Committee quoted in Tan Tai Yong, *Garrison State,* p. 53.
6. Letter from Wood Papers cited in Mehrotra, *The Emergence of the Indian National Congress,* p. 105.
7. Sir J.P. Grant, quoted in Tan Tai Yong, *Garrison State,* p. 66.
8. See Tan Tai Yong, *Garrison State,* pp. 75-76.
9. Tan Tai Yong, *Garrison State,* p. 75.
10. Tan Tai Yong, *Garrison State,* p. 66.
11. Tan Tai Yong, *Garrison State,* p. 26.
12. Tan Tai Yong, *Garrison State,* p. 96.
13. Grewal, *Sikhs,* p. 139.
14. Denzil Ibbetson, *Panjab Castes,* p. 11.
15. Abdulla, *Historical Background,* p. 187.
16. Quote from *Chenab Colony Gazetteer, 1904,* in Imran Ali, *Punjab under Imperialism,* p. 13.
17. See Table 2.7 in Imran Ali, *Punjab under Imperialism,* p. 47.
18. Imran Ali, *Punjab under Imperialism,* p. 27.
19. Imran Ali, *Punjab under Imperialism,* p. 27.
20. Imran Ali, *Punjab under Imperialism,* pp. 27-28.
21. Unnamed officer quoted in Imran Ali, *Punjab under Imperialism,* p. 88.

22. Imran Ali, *Punjab under Imperialism,* p. 87.
23. Malhotra, *Gandhi and the Punjab,* p. 18.
24. Government of India files of August and October 1907 quoted in Tan Tai Yong, *Garrison State,* p. 95.
25. Imran Ali, *Punjab under Imperialism,* p. 115.
26. Talbot, *Punjab and the Raj,* p. 52.
27. Imran Ali, *Punjab under Imperialism,* pp. 81-84.
28. Minute of the judicial commission quoted in Jalal, *Self and Sovereignty,* p. 112.
29. Harbans Singh, 'Origins of the Sikh Sabha,' in Singh and Barrier, *Punjab Past and Present,* p. 278.
30. Singh and Barrier, *Punjab Past and Present,* p. 279.
31. Singh and Barrier, *Punjab Past and Present,* p. 276.
32. Ikram Ali Malik, 'Muslim Anjumans and Communitarian Consciousness,' in Banga, *Five Punjabi Centuries,* p. 112.
33. Ikram Ali Malik, 'Muslim Anjumans and Communitarian Consciousness,' in Banga, *Five Punjabi Centuries,* pp. 112-13.
34. Ikram Ali Malik, 'Muslim Anjumans and Communitarian Consciousness,' in Banga, *Five Punjabi Centuries,* p. 114.
35. Singh and Barrier, *Punjab Past and Present,* p. 276.
36. Ikram Ali Malik, 'Muslim Anjumans and Communitarian Consciousness,' in Banga, *Five Punjabi Centuries,* p. 121.
37. Grewal, *Sikhs,* p. 143.
38. Grewal, *Sikhs,* p. 144.
39. Singh and Barrier, *Punjab Past and Present,* p. 280.
40. Harbans Singh, p. 280.
41. Harbans Singh, p. 281.
42. S.R. Mehrotra, *The Emergence of the Indian National Congress,* p. 344.
43. Some details are provided in Gandhi, *Tale of Two Revolts.*
44. Wedderburn, *Allan Octavian Hume,* p. 47.
45. Letter of 16 November 1884 to Chiplonkar, secretary, Poona Sarvajanik Sabha, quoted in Mehrotra, *The Emergence of the Indian National Congress,* pp. 381-82.
46. *Sir Syed Ahmed on the Present State of Indian Politics, Consisting of Speeches and Letters Reprinted from the 'Pioneer'* (Allahabad: The Pioneer Press, 1888), pp. 29-53. Modern facsimile version (Lahore: Sang-e-Meel Publications, 1982). Translator unknown.
47. Ikram Ali Malik, 'Muslim Anjumans and Communitarian Consciousness,' in Banga, *Five Punjabi Centuries,* p. 119.
48. Ikram Ali Malik, 'Muslim Anjumans and Communitarian Consciousness,' in Banga, *Five Punjabi Centuries,* p. 119.
49. Grewal, *Sikhs,* p. 146.
50. Grewal, *Sikhs,* p. 145.
51. Grewal, *Sikhs,* p. 146.
52. http://en.wikipedia.org/wiki/Rudyard_Kipling
53. Jalal, *Self and Sovereignty,* pp. 153-54.

54. Circular of Punjab board of administration, quoted in Jalal, *Self and Sovereignty*, p. 107.
55. Jalal, *Self and Sovereignty*, p. 122.
56. Jalal, *Self and Sovereignty*, p. 121.
57. Jalal, *Self and Sovereignty*, p. 121.
58. This was asserted to the author at interviews in Lahore in March 2011.
59. Letter in the *Observer* of Lahore, 8 May 1909, quoted in Jalal, *Self and Sovereignty*, p. 137.
60. Ikram Ali Malik, *Hindu-Muslim Riots*, p. 35.
61. Ikram Ali Malik, *Hindu-Muslim Riots*, pp. 8-16.
62. Ikram Ali Malik, *Hindu-Muslim Riots*, p. 34.
63. Ikram Ali Malik, *Hindu-Muslim Riots*, p. 35.
64. From N.G. Barrier, 'The Punjab Government & Communal Politics, 1870-1908,' *Journal of Asian Studies,* 3 Nov. 1968, quoted in Ikram Ali Malik, *History of the Punjab,* p. 258.
65. Ikram Ali Malik, *Hindu-Muslim Riots*, pp. 25-26. See also S. Qalb-i-Abid, *Muslim Politics in the Punjab*, p. 11.
66. Ikram Ali Malik, *Hindu-Muslim Riots*, pp. 26-29.
67. Jalal, *Self and Sovereignty*, p. 99.
68. Talbot, *Punjab and the Raj*, p. 68.
69. Barrier, 'The Punjab Government & Communal Politics, 1870-1908,' *Journal of Asian Studies,* 3 Nov. 1968, quoted in Ikram Ali Malik, *History of the Punjab,* p. 246.
70. http://ier.sagepub.com/content/2/2/145: Norman G. Barrier, 'The Formulation and Enactment of the Punjab Alienation of Land Bill,' in *Indian Economic and Social History Review,* 1964, 2: 145, p. 147.
71. See Barrier, 'The Formulation and Enactment of the Punjab Alienation of Land Bill,' in *Indian Economic and Social History Review,* 1964, 2: 145, p. 148.
72. Jagtar Singh Rakkar, 'The Punjab Muslims: A Socio-Economic Study, 1901-20,' in Ahmed Saleem, *Punjab Revisited*, pp. 462-70.
73. See Barrier, *Indian Economic and Social History Review,* 1964, 2: 145, p. 148.
74. Barrier, *Indian Economic and Social History Review,* 1964, p. 165.
75. Barrier, *Indian Economic and Social History Review,* 1964, p. 148.
76. Barrier, *Indian Economic and Social History Review,* 1964, pp. 159-60.
77. Barrier, *Indian Economic and Social History Review,* 1964, p. 159.
78. Barrier, *Indian Economic and Social History Review,* 1964, p. 155.
79. Barrier, *Indian Economic and Social History Review,* 1964, p. 161.
80. Curzon to Hamilton, 18 November 1900, taken from Hamilton Papers, vol. xviii, India Office Library, London, in Wasti, *Lord Minto and the Indian Nationalist Movement,* p. 21.
81. 'Partition of Bengal' at http://www.banglapedia.org/httpdocs/HT/P_0100.HTM
82. Wasti, *Lord Minto and the Indian Nationalist Movement,* p. 69.
83. From Appendix XII, containing the text of the deputation's address and Lord

Minto's reply, in B.R. Ambedkar, *Pakistan or the Partition of India*, 2nd edition (Bombay: Thackers, 1945), available online at http://www.columbia.edu/itc/mealac/pritchett/00ambedkar/ambedkar_partition/appendices/12app.html
84. Wasti, *Lord Minto and the Indian Nationalist Movement*, p. 72.
85. www.columbia.edu/itc/mealac/pritchett/00ambedkar/ambedkar_partition/appendices/12app.html
86. See Wasti, *Lord Minto and the Indian Nationalist Movement*, pp. 68-73, and John Buchan, *Lord Minto*, p. 243.
87. Mary Elliot-Murray-Kynynmound, Countess of Minto, *India, Minto and Morley*, p. 47.
88. Wasti, *Lord Minto and the Indian Nationalist Movement*, pp.72-73.
89. Buchan, *Lord Minto*, p. 243.
90. Wasti, *Lord Minto and the Indian Nationalist Movement*, p. 73.
91. Quoted in Jalal, *Self and Sovereignty*, p. 164.
92. *Akhbar-i-Aam*, 1 December 1909, and *Paisa Akhbar*, 16 December 1909, quoted in Ayesha Jalal, *Self and Sovereignty*, p. 164.
93. N.G. Barrier quoted in Ikram Ali Malik, *History of the Punjab*, p. 232.
94. *Hindustan*, 12 & 26 March 1909, quoted in Jalal, *Self and Sovereignty*, pp. 160-62.
95. Page, *Prelude to Partition*, p. 12.
96. Quoted in Bolitho, *Jinnah*, p. 55.
97. Jalal, *Self and Sovereignty*, p. 184.
98. Jalal, *Self and Sovereignty*, p. 184.
99. Quoted in S.M. Ikram, *Modern Muslim India and the Birth of Pakistan*, p. 168.
100. Fazlur Rahman, *Islam*, p. 143.
101. See Khaled Ahmed, 'Word for Word', *Daily Times*, Lahore, 2 May 2004, and Ravinder Kumar, 'Urban Society and Urban Politics,' in Banga, *Five Punjabi Centuries*, p. 193.
102, Ikram Ali Malik, *History of the Punjab*, p. 18.
103. Azim Husain, *Mian Fazli-i-Husain*, p. 65.
104. Azim Husain, *Mian Fazli-i-Husain*, p. 109 & p. 104.
105. Ikram Ali Malik, *History of the Punjab*, p. 426.
106. Ikram Ali Malik, *History of the Punjab*, p. 428.
107. Ikram Ali Malik, *History of the Punjab*, p. 432.
108. Talbot, *Punjab and the Raj*, p. 97.
109. Tan Tai Yong, *Garrison State*, p. 98.
110. Ikram Ali Malik, *History of the Punjab*, p. 226.
111. Tan Tai Yong, *Garrison State*, p. 139.
112. Tan Tai Yong, *Garrison State*, p. 122.
113. Tan Tai Yong, *Garrison State*, p. 132.
114. Naeem A. Qureshi, *Pan-Islam in British Indian Politics*, p. 76.
115. Tan Tai Yong, *Garrison State*, p. 140.
116. Talbot, *Punjab and the Raj*, pp. 77-78.
117. See figures for 1914 and 1918 given to the Hunter Commission by Townshend, director of civil supplies, Punjab, quoted in Ravinder Kumar, 'Urban Society and Urban Politics,' in Banga, *Five Punjabi Centuries*, p. 199.

7. 1919-1922: Together For Freedom

1. Desai, *Day-to-day with Gandhi*, vol. 1, pp. 298-99.
2. Gandhi, *Collected Works*, 15: 203.
3. Ravinder Kumar, 'Urban Society and Urban Politics,' in Banga, *Five Punjabi Centuries*, p. 201.
4. Speech in Nadiad, Gujarat, quoted in Desai, *Day-to-day with Gandhi*, 2: 67.
5. See Kevin Kenny's article, 'The Irish in the Empire,' at http://mason.gmu.edu/~wcarpent/hist635/empire_4.pdf.
6. O'Dwyer, *India As I Knew It*, p. 449.
7. O'Dwyer, *India As I Knew It*, p. 268.
8. Quoted in S.L. Malhotra, *Gandhi and the Punjab*, pp. 37-38.
9. Quoted by Ravinder Kumar, 'Urban Society and Urban Politics,' in Banga, *Five Punjabi Centuries*, p. 205. See also O'Dwyer, *India As I Knew It*, p. 270.
10. Ravinder Kumar, 'Lahore in 1919' in Banga, *Five Punjabi Centuries*, p. 204.
11. Azim Husain, *Fazl-i-Husain*, p. 117, cited in S.L. Malhotra, *Gandhi and the Punjab*, p. 39.
12. Ravinder Kumar, 'Lahore in 1919' in Banga, *Five Punjabi Centuries*, pp. 204-5, quoting Shah's evidence, *Disorders Enquiry Committee Minutes* (1920), Vol. IV
13. Azim Husain, *Fazl-i-Husain*, p. 117, cited in Malhotra, *Gandhi and the Punjab*, p. 39.
14. Malhotra, *Gandhi and the Punjab*, p. 38.
15. *Secret Punjab Police Abstract of Intelligence*, 12 April 1919, vol. xli, no. 15, pp. 152-54, quoted in Jalal, *Self and Sovereignty*, p. 205.
16. Jalal, *Self and Sovereignty*, p. 204.
17. Ravinder Kumar, 'Lahore in 1919' in Banga, *Five Punjabi Centuries*, pp. 218-19.
18. O'Dwyer, *India As I Knew It*, pp. 275-77.
19. O'Dwyer, *India As I Knew It*, p. 273.
20. Student's evidence, *Congress Inquiry Committee Report*, vol. II, cited in Ravinder Kumar, 'Lahore in 1919' in Banga, *Five Punjabi Centuries*, p. 206.
21. Ravinder Kumar, 'Lahore in 1919' in Banga, *Five Punjabi Centuries*, pp. 210-11.
22. Azim Husain, *Fazl-i-Husain*, p. 123, cited in Malhotra, *Gandhi and the Punjab*, p. 114.
23. S.M. Ikram, *Modern Muslim India and the Birth of Pakistan*, p. 215, cited in Ikram Ali Malik, *History of the Punjab*, p. 433.
24. Dyer's report in O'Dwyer, *India As I Knew It*, pp. 284-85.
25. O'Dwyer, *India As I Knew It*, pp. 283-84.
26. O'Dwyer, *India As I Knew It*, p. 286.
27. Details including text of Martial Law Notices in *Report of the commissioners appointed by the Punjab Sub-Committee of the Indian National Congress* (Lahore: Santanam, 1920), pp. 106-11.
28. O'Dwyer, *India As I Knew It*, p. 307, and Malhotra, *Gandhi and the Punjab*, p. 46.
29. In Desai, *Day-to-day with Gandhi*, 2: pp. 323-26.
30. Malhotra, *Gandhi and the Punjab*, pp. 52-53.
31. Gandhi, *Collected Works*; 19: 307.

32. Gandhi, *Collected Works*; 19: 447.
33. Gandhi, *Autobiography*, p. 435.
34. Pyarelal, *In Gandhiji's Mirror*, pp. 5-7.
35. Quoted in Afzal Iqbal, *Mohamed Ali*, p. 199.
36. Gandhi, *Collected Works*; 21: 145 and 21: 183.
37. Jalal, *Self & Sovereignty*, p. 210.
38. Quoted in S.M. Ikram, *Modern Muslim India and the Birth of Pakistan*, p. 160.
39. *Navajivan*, 16 May 1920; Gandhi, *Collected Works* 20: 318.
40. Malhotra, *Gandhi and the Punjab*, p. 169.
41. D.C. Sharma, 'The Truth About Mian Fazl-i-Husain,' *Modern Review*, 1937, p. 641, cited in Malhotra, *Gandhi and the Punjab*, p. 114.
42. Police report cited in Jalal, *Self & Sovereignty*, p. 220.
43. Police reports cited in Jalal, *Self & Sovereignty*, p. 227.
44. Police reports cited in Jalal, *Self & Sovereignty*, p. 226.
45. Ikram, *Modern Muslim India and the Birth of Pakistan*, p. 160.
46. Nanda, *Gandhi: Pan-Islamism, Imperialism and Nationalism*, p. 355.
47. Gandhi, *Collected Works*, 25: 218-19.
48. Remark of Subhas Bose, quoted in Malhotra, *Gandhi and the Punjab*, p. 76.
49. Iqbal, *Mohamed Ali*, p. 285 & p. 394.
50. Som Anand, describing the change in his father, quoted in Ishtiaq Ahmed, 'Forced Migration and Ethnic Cleansing in Lahore in 1947: Some First Person Accounts,' p. 26. Anand adds that Western education, too, had contributed to the change. http://www.sacw.net/partition/june2004IshtiaqAhmed.pdf
51. Lajpat Rai, *Writings & Speeches*, edited by V.C. Joshi (Delhi: University Publishers, 1966), vol. II, p. 170, cited in Malhotra, *Gandhi & the Punjab*, pp. 178-79.

8. 1922-1942: Collaboration and the Separation Call

1. Talbot, *Punjab and the Raj*, p. 80.
2. Page, *Prelude to Partition*, pp. 69-70.
3. Page, *Prelude to Partition*, p. 88.
4. Gandhi, *Collected Works*, 26: 54, quoted in Malhotra, *Gandhi and the Punjab*, p. 115.
5. Chief Secretary to the Reforms Enquiry Committee, in Committee's Report of 1925, quoted in Page, *Prelude to Partition*, p. 90.
6. Hailey's letter of 11 December 1924 to Alexander Muddiman (GI Home Pol 37/1925) quoted in Page, *Prelude to Partition*, pp. 88-89.
7. Quoted in Page, *Prelude to Partition*, p. 91.
8. Letter of 8 May 1925 from Nath to Hailey (Hailey Collection, 7B, IOR) quoted in S. Qalb-i-Abid, *Muslim Politics in the Punjab*, p. 88.
9. Page, *Prelude to Partition*, p. 92.
10. Page, *Prelude to Partition*, p. 129.
11. Jalal, *Self & Sovereignty*, pp. 308-09.
12. Page, *Prelude to Partition*, pp. 151-54.
13. Page, *Prelude to Partition*, p. 151 & p. 144.

14. Page, *Prelude to Partition*, p. 153.
15. The 116-day figure is provided in Nayar, *Without Fear*, pp. 98-99.
16. Nayar, *Without Fear*, p. 116.
17. Nair, *Changing Homelands* p. 125.
18. Churchill's remark in the House of Commons on 12 March 1931 can be seen in Robert Rhodes James, *Winston Churchill*, vol. V (1928-1935), p. 4995.
19. Page, *Prelude to Partition*, p. 162, citing Hailey Papers, File 11B.
20. http://www.columbia.edu/itc/mealac/pritchett/00islamlinks/txt_iqbal_1930.html.
21. C.M. Naim, http://pakteahouse.net/2010/06/15/cm-naim-on-iqbal-and-jinnah/
22. Letter from Parmanand to Malaviya, *Tribune*, 23 December 1932, quoted in Nair, *Changing Homelands*, p. 147.
23. Page, *Prelude to Partition*, pp. 242-43.
24. Ikram Ali Malik, *History of the Punjab*, p. 451.
25. From Fazl's pamphlet, 'Communal Aspirations and their Rational Adjustment', 1935 or 1936, reproduced in Azim Husain, *Mian Fazl-i-Husain*, p. 415.
26. Azim Husain, *Mian Fazl-i-Husain*, p. 416 & p. 435.
27. Jinnah to Fazl, 5 Jan. 1936, quoted in Jalal, *Sole Spokesman*, p. 20.
28. Letter of 1 May 1936 from Sikander to Fazl discussing Jinnah's plans, after being rebuffed by Fazl, to visit Punjab, quoted in Jalal, *Sole Spokesman*, p. 21.
29. Jalal, *Sole Spokesman*, p. 22, citing Azim Husain, *Mian Fazl Husain*, p. 311.
30. Azim Husain, *Mian Fazl-i-Husain*, p. 431.
31. Azim Husain, *Mian Fazl-i-Husain*, pp. 411-12.
32. Figures taken from Jalal, *Sole Spokesman*, p. 23.
33. Sarvepalli Gopal, *Jawaharlal Nehru*, p. 224.
34. Letters of 28 May and 31 June 1937 on http://www.columbia.edu/itc/mealac/pritchett/00islamlinks/txt_iqbal_tojinnah_1937.html
35. Iqbal's letter of 31 June 1937 on http://www.columbia.edu/itc/mealac/pritchett/00islamlinks/txt_iqbal_tojinnah_1937.html
36. Ikram Ali Malik, *History of the Punjab*, p. 485.
37. Brabourne's report in Zetland, *Essayez* (London: John Murray, 1956), p. 247, cited in Stanley Wolpert, *Jinnah of Pakistan*(New York: Oxford University Press,1984)pp. 161-62.
38. Ikram Ali Malik, *History of the Punjab*, p. 542.
39. See letter from Gandhi to Hayat, 1 November 1939, Gandhi, *Collected Works*, 77:72; and telegram from Gandhi to Hayat, 25 May 1940, *Collected Works*, 78: 246.
40. *The Hindu*, 4 September 1939.
41. Tan Tai Yong, *Garrison State*, p. 283.
42. Linlithgow to George VI, 19 October 1939, Linlithgow Papers, India Office Library, London.
43. 1937 letter from Churchill to Linlithgow quoted in Bipan Chandra, *Communalism*, pp. 244-45; letter from Linlithgow to Zetland in Bipan Chandra, *Communalism*, p. 270.
44. Conversation recalling the 1939 talks on 11 August 1950 between Patel and Narhari

Parikh, recorded in the Diary of Maniben Patel, entry dated 11 August 1950, Patel Papers, Ahmedabad.
45. Glendevon, *Viceroy at Bay*, p. 119.
46. Wali Khan, *Facts Are Facts*, pp. 29-30.
47. Merriam, *Gandhi vs. Jinnah*, p. 67.
48. Merriam, *Gandhi vs. Jinnah*, p. 66.
49. In October 1939 and April & May 1940. See Gandhi, *Collected Works*, 77: 27; 78:109; & 79: 231.
50. Quoted in Naim, *Iqbal, Jinnah and Pakistan*, p. 186.
51. Ikram Ali Malik, *History of the Punjab*, p. 513.
52. Grewal, *Sikhs*, p. 172.
53. Talbot, *Khizr Tiwana*, p. 119.
54. Gandhi, *Collected Works*, 79: 466-68.
55. Ikram Ali Malik, *History of the Punjab*, p. 514.
56. S. Qalb-i-Abid, *Muslim Politics in the Punjab*, p. 242.
57. S. Qalb-i-Abid, *Muslim Politics in the Punjab*, p. 242.
58. Linlithgow's letter to Craik quoted in Wali Khan, *Facts are Facts*, pp. 34-45.
59. See Linlithgow to Hope, Governor of Madras, 8 May 1941, Linlithgow Papers, India Office Library, London; and Gandhi, *Rajaji*, pp. 225-26.
60. See Ikram Ali Malik, *History of the Punjab*, p. 563, citing the uncorroborated claim in Safdar Saleem (ed.), *Khaksar-i-Azam Aur Khaksar Tehrik*, Lahore 1967, pp. 15-16.
61. *The Hindu*, Madras, 11 May 1942.
62. Linlithgow to Churchill, 31 August 1942, Linlithgow Papers, F 125/58, India Office Library, London.
63. S. Qalb-i-Abid, *Muslim Politics in the Punjab*, p. 258.
64. S. Qalb-i-Abid, *Muslim Politics in the Punjab*, p. 260; and Ikram Ali Malik, *History of the Punjab*, p. 531.
65. Ikram Ali Malik, *History of the Punjab*, p. 568.

9. 1942-1947: Independence and Trauma

1. Talbot, *Khizr Tiwana*, p. 127.
2. Talbot, *Khizr Tiwana*, p. 151.
3. Talbot, *Khizr Tiwana*, p. 139.
4. Talbot, *Punjab and the Raj*, p. 144, p. 152.
5. Talbot, *Punjab and the Raj*, p. 148.
6. Ikram Ali Malik, *History of the Punjab*, p. 494.
7. Jalal, *Self & Sovereignty*, p. 459, citing Mirza, *Karvan-i-Ahrar*, p. 373.
8. Talbot, *Khizr Tiwana*, p. 167.
9. Talbot, *Khizr Tiwana*, p. 161.
10. Talbot, *Khizr Tiwana*, p. 162.
11. Jalal, *Self & Sovereignty*, pp. 433-36, citing Secret Punjab Police Abstract of Intelligence (SPPAI), August 1944.
12. Moon, *Wavell*, p. 87.

13. Moon, *Wavell*, p. 120.
14. See Singh, *The Origins of the Partition of India*, pp. 121-23.
15. This argument is presented in Sarila, *Shadow of the Great Game*.
16. Talbot, *Khizr Tiwana*, p. 186.
17. Talbot, *Punjab and the Raj*, p. 211.
18. Assessment at the time of the British civil servant, Penderel Moon, quoted in Talbot, *Punjab and the Raj*, p. 191.
19. Jalal, *Self & Sovereignty*, p. 468.
20. Jalal, *Self & Sovereignty*, p. 470.
21. Jalal, *Self & Sovereignty*, pp. 469-71.
22. S. Qalb-i-Abid, *Muslim Politics in the Punjab*, p. 303.
23. Jalal, *Self & Sovereignty*, p. 487.
24. House of Commons Debates, 8 June 1946, quoted by S.R. Mehrotra in Phillips and Wainwright (ed.), *The Partition of India* (London:George Allen and Unwin, 1970), p. 218.
25. Mansergh & Lumby (eds.) *Transfer of Power*, 6: 684-7.
26. Ahmad, *Historic Documents of the Muslim Freedom Movement*, pp. 522-23.
27. 'Note of Meeting between Cabinet Delegation, Viceroy Wavell and Sir Khizr Hyat Khan, Premier of Punjab, on Friday, 5 April 1946,' *Transfer of Power* 7: 147-48.
28. Jalal, *Self & Sovereignty*, p. 488.
29. Mamdot in June 1946, cited in SPPAI, 22 June 1946, and quoted in Jalal, *Self & Sovereignty*, p. 489.
30. Talbot, *Punjab & the Raj*, p. 233.
31. Jalal, *Self & Sovereignty*, p. 482, citing SPPAI, 4 May 1946.
32. Jalal, *Self & Sovereignty*, pp. 482-83. Apart from offering her verdict, Jalal cites police reports.
33. *Transfer of Power*, 9: 287.
34. SPPAI, 31 August 1946, in Jalal, *Self & Sovereignty*, p.492.
35. Jalal, *Self & Sovereignty*, p.492.
36. Jalal, *Self & Sovereignty*, pp. 500-01, citing SPPAI, 16 and 23 November 1946.
37. Talbot, *Khizr Tiwana*, p. 203.
38. Jalal, *Self & Sovereignty*, p. 508.
39. Jalal, *Self & Sovereignty*, p. 508.
40. Jenkins to Pethick-Lawrence, 26 January 1947, *Transfer of Power*, 9: 557.
41. Talbot, *Khizr Tiwana*, p. 204.
42. *Transfer of Power*, 9: 655.
43. *Transfer of Power*, 9: 720.
44. *Transfer of Power*, 9: 729.
45. Kuldip Nayar, Sachar's son-in-law, to author, New Delhi, June 2011.
46. Tara Singh's remarks on the steps of the legislature building and in Kapurthala House are quoted in, among other places, Gopal Das Khosla, *Stern Reckoning*, p. 100; in Jalal, *Self & Sovereignty*, p. 513; and in Ishtiaq Ahmed, *Punjab*, pp. 165-66. Ahmed also quotes several eyewitnesses.

47. Ishtiaq Ahmed, *Punjab*, p. 194.
48. Ishtiaq Ahmed, *Punjab*, p. 185.
49. Ishtiaq Ahmed, *Punjab*, pp. 202-03.
50. Ishtiaq Ahmed, *Punjab*, p. 207, citing letter of 17 March.
51. Jenkins to Wavell, 9 March 1947, *Transfer of Power*, 9: 904.
52. Note by Messervy, *Transfer of Power*, 9: 1006-07.
53. Army figures cited in Swarna Aiyar (1995): 'August anarchy: The partition massacres in Punjab, 1947,' *South Asia: Journal of South Asian Studies*, 18: s1, p. 28.
54. Jenkins to Wavell, 9 March 1947, *Transfer of Power*, 9: 903.
55. Note by Messervy, *Transfer of Power* 9:1006.
56. Ahmed, *Punjab*, pp. 373-74.
57. Letter of 7 March 1947 from Jenkins to Wavell, *Transfer of Power*, 9: 881-82.
58. *Transfer of Power*, 9: 901.
59. Gandhi, *Collected Works*, 94: 153-54.
60. Note by Messervy, *Transfer of Power*, 9: 1006-07.
61. Jalal, *Self & Sovereignty*, p. 515; *Transfer of Power*, 9: 921.
62. 'Note by Sir E. Jenkins' on conversation with Ghazanfar, 20 March 1947, *Transfer of Power*, 9: 997.
63. For the text of his scheme that Gandhi left with the Viceroy on 4 April, see *Collected Works*, 94: 229.
64. *Transfer of Power*, 10: 86.
65. *Transfer of Power*, 10: 104.
66. *Transfer of Power*, 10: 84.
67. *Transfer of Power*, 10: 129.
68. *Collected Works*, 94: 283-84.
69. Entry dated 13 April 1947. Rajagopalachari Papers.
70. Stanley Wolpert, *Jinnah* (New York: Oxford, 1984), p. 317.
71. *Collected Works*, 94: 290.
72. *Transfer of Power*, 12: 778.
73. Ahmed, *Punjab*, p. 258, citing *Transfer of Power* 10: 543.
74. See Jinnah's 26 April 1947 claim, made to Mountbatten, of Churchill's backing, *Transfer of Power*, 10: 453.
75. *Transfer of Power*, 11: 898-900. See also Jinnah's remarks to Mountbatten quoted in Ahmed, *Punjab*, p. 263.
76. Mieville to Mountbatten, 11 April 1947. *Transfer of Power*, 10: 198.
77. *Transfer of Power*, 10: 347.
78. Ahmed, *Punjab*, pp. 277-78. The press conference transcript is in *Transfer of Power*, 11: 115-22.
79. *Transfer of Power*, 11: 53.
80. *Transfer of Power*, 10: 703-04.
81. *Transfer of Power*, 10: 309.
82. *Transfer of Power*, 10: 283.
83. Hodson, *Great Divide*, p. 337.

84. Ahmed, *Punjab*, pp. 361-62.
85. Ishtiaq Ahmed's article of 25 Aug. 2007 in *The News,* quoted in http://www.apnaorg.com/articles/news-25/
86. Sheikh Arshad Habib, Amritsar resident, quoted in Ishtiaq Ahmed, *Punjab*, p. 385.
87. Ahmed, *Punjab*, p. 353.
88. Ahmed, *Punjab*, p. 363.
89. See Ahmed, *Punjab*, pp. 311-12.
90. Ahmed, *Punjab*, p. 354.
91. *Transfer of Power,* 10: 322.
92. *Transfer of Power,* 10: 893.
93. Paul Brass, 'The partition of India and retributive genocide in the Punjab, 1946-47,' *Journal of Genocide Research* (2003), 5(1), 71-101; p. 7 of electronic version, http://faculty.washington.edu/brass/Partition.pdf.
94. Ahmed, *Punjab*, p. 363.
95. Gandhi, *Collected Works,* 95: 286-87.
96. Gadgil, *Government from Inside*, p. 40.
97. Ahmed, *Punjab*, pp. 346-49, citing documents from the *Transfer of Power* volumes.
98. Ahmed, *Punjab*, pp. 346-49.
99. Quoted in Lionel Carter (ed.), *Punjab Politics: 1 June 1947-14 August 1947* (New Delhi: Manohar, 2007), p. 231, and cited in Ahmed, *Punjab*, p. 293.
100. Ahmed, *Punjab*, pp. 366-69.
101. Ahmed, *Punjab*, pp. 372-3, quoting from Lionel Carter (ed.), *Punjab Politics: 1 June 1947-14 August 1947* (New Delhi: Manohar, 2007), p. 234.
102. See a discussion of these numbers in Ishtiaq Ahmed, *Punjab*, pp. xl-xlii.
103. Khosla quoted in Ahmed, *Punjab*, p. xl.
104. See the Appendix in this book.
105. Gandhi, *Collected Works,* 77: 27.
106. Ahmed, *Punjab*, pp. 483-510.
107. Ahmed, *Punjab*, p. 571.
108. Ahmed, *Punjab*, pp. 429-31.
109. Chaudhri Muhammad Ali, *Emergence of Pakistan*, p. 255.
110. Ahmed, *Punjab*, p. 399.
111. Mahinder Nath Khanna, who was 21 in 1947, to Ishtiaq Ahmed in Amritsar, 3 Jan. 2005, in Ahmed, *Punjab*, pp. 460-61.
112. See Muhammad Afzal's account given to Ishtiaq Ahmed and others in December 2004. Ahmed, *Punjab*, p. 549.
113. Ahmed, *Punjab*, p. 574.
114. Ahmed, *Punjab*, p. 442.
115. Quoted in Ahmed, *Punjab*, p. 546.
116. *Hindustan Times,* New Delhi, 15 October 1947.
117. Policy decision cited in Hodson, *Great Divide*, pp. 410-11.
118. Ahmed, *Punjab*, p. 415.
119. Such comments from interviewees (in Ishtiaq Ahmed's *Punjab* as well as in other

studies, including the writer's in 2005) are too frequent to be separately sourced.
120. *Transfer of Power*, 10: 543-45.
121. Harmail Singh to Ishtiaq Ahmed, 29 Nov. 2005, quoted in Ahmed, *Punjab*, p. 571.
122. Swarna Aiyar (1995): 'August anarchy: The partition massacres in Punjab, 1947,' *South Asia: Journal of South Asian Studies*, 18: s1, p. 34.

10. 1947: *Insaniyat* Amidst Insanity

1. Ishtiaq Ahmed's *Punjab* contains numerous interviews, conducted by him and others, where such acts are recalled. Others who have collected similar accounts include Tridivesh Singh Maini.

11. Postscript: Divided Punjab and the Future of *Punjabiyat*

1. Speech of 6 March 1948, http://jinnah.pk/2009/09/27/development-of-chittagong-port/
2. For a further discussion of this point see Ishtiaq Ahmed, *Punjab*, pp. 680-81.
3. Churchill's speech is quoted in *Gandhi, Collected works* 97: 6.
4. Quoted in *Homage* (New Delhi: Publications Division, 1949), p. 27.
5. Daman's Punjabi lines: *Lali ankhian di pai dasdi ay, Roay toosi vi o roay asi vi aan*
6. Ishtiaq Ahmed, *Punjab*, p. 684.
7. *Hindu*, 21 February 1999.
8. See Pritam Singh, 'The Idea of Punjabiyat', http://apnaorg.com/articles/preetam-singh/
9. Not implemented as of writing
10. Mehta, *Trade Relations between Pakistan and India*, p. 17.
11. Mehta, *Trade Relations between Pakistan and India*, pp. 12-17.
12. http://timesofindia.indiatimes.com/chandigarh/17103455.cms

BIBLIOGRAPHY

Abdulla, Ahmed, *Historical Background of Pakistan and Its People* (Karachi: Tanzeem Publishers, 1973).

Ahmad, J. (ed.), *Historic Documents of the Muslim Freedom Movement* (Lahore: Publishers United).

Ahmed, Ishtiaq, *The Punjab: Bloodied, Partitioned and Cleansed* (New Delhi: Rupa, 2011).

Akbar, Muhammad, *Punjab under the Mughals* (Lahore: Ripon Printing Press, 1948).

Ali, Abdullah Yusuf (ed.), *Three Travellers to India: Yuan Chwang, Ibn Batuta and Francois Bernier* (Lahore: Gulab Singh and Sons, 1927; Reprint by Al Biruni, Lahore, 1978)

Ali, Chaudhri Muhammad, *Emergence of Pakistan* (Lahore: Research Society of Pakistan, 1973).

Ali, Imran, *Punjab under Imperialism: 1885-1947* (Karachi: Oxford University Press, 2003)

Anon, *Dabistan-I Mazahib*. Written in Farsi in 1645 by a friend of Guru Hargobind.

Ansari, Zoe (ed.), *Life, Times and Works of Amir Khusrau Dehlavi* (Seventh Centenary Amir Khusrau Society, n.d.)

Aziz, Abdul, *Mansabdari System & the Mughul Army* (Delhi: Idarah-i-Adabiyat, 1972; Reprint of undated publication).

Banga, Indu (ed.), *Five Punjabi Centuries: Polity, Economy, Society & Culture, 1500-1990* (New Delhi: Manohar, 1997).

Barrier, N. Gerald & Harbans Singh (eds.), *Punjab Past and Present: Essays in Honour of Dr Ganda Singh* (Patiala: Punjabi University, 1976).

Bean, Susan, *Yankee India* (Ahmedabad: Mapin, 2001).

Bhandari, Sujan Rai, *Khulasat-ut-Tawarikh*, ed. Zafar Hasan, Delhi, 1918.

Bolitho, Hector, *Jinnah: Creator of Pakistan* (Westport, Conn.: Greenwood Press, undated).

Bosworth Smith, R., *Life of Lord Lawrence*, 2 vols (New York: Charles Scribner's Sons, 1883).

Broehl, Wayne, *Crisis of the Raj: The Revolt of 1857 through British Lieutenants' Eyes* (Hanover: University Press of New England, 1986).

Buchan, John, *Lord Minto: A Memoir* (London: Thomas Nelson & Sons, 1924).

Burke, S.M., *Akbar: The Greatest Mogul* (Delhi: Mushiram Manoharlal, 1989).

Caroe, Sir Olaf, *The Pathans: 550 B.C.-A.D. 1957* (Karachi: Oxford University Press, 1976; first published in 1958 by Macmillan, London).

Chaghatai, M. Ikram, *1857 in Muslim Historiography* (Lahore: Sang-e-Meel, 2007).

Chandra, Bipan, *Communalism in Modern India* (Delhi: Vikas, 1984).

Chandra, Satish, *Medieval India: From Sultanat to the Mughals* (New Delhi: Har-Anand, 1997).

Chaudhry, Aziz Ahmed, *Punjab: Mughlon ke Ahd-e-Zawaal Mein* (Lahore: Punjab Research Foundation, 1980).

Cohen, Stephen P., *Pakistan Army* (Los Angeles: University of California Press, 1984).

Cohen, Stephen P., *Indian Army: Its Contribution to the Development of a Nation* (New Delhi: Oxford University Press, 1990).

Cooper, Frederic, *Crisis in the Punjab from the 10th of May until the Fall of Delhi* (London:

Smith, Elder, 1858, & Lahore: H. Gregory, 1858). Reprint by Sang-e-Meel Publications, Lahore 2005.

Dalrymple, William, *The Last Mughal* (New Delhi: Penguin, 2007).

Dani, Ahmad Hasan, *History of Pakistan: Pakistan Through Ages* (Lahore: Sang-e-Meel, 2007).

Darling, Malcolm, *Rusticus Loquitur: or, the Old Light and the New in the Punjab Village* (London: Oxford University Press, 1930).

Darling, Malcolm, *Wisdom and Waste in the Punjab Village* (London: Oxford University Press, 1934).

Darling, Malcolm, *Punjab Peasant in Prosperity and Debt* (London: Oxford University Press, 1947).

Das, S.T., *Indian Military: History & Development* (New Delhi: Sagar, 1969).

Desai, Mahadev, *Day-to-day with Gandhi*, vol. 1 (Varanasi: Sarva Seva Sangh).

District and States Gazetteers of the Undivided Punjab, vol. 2 (Delhi: Low Price Publications, 1993; reprint of 1914 edition published by Punjab Government and printed at the Civil & Military Gazette Press by Samuel T. Weston, 1914).

Dodd, George, *History of the Indian Revolt* (London: W. and R. Chambers, 1859).

Dua, J.C., *British Historiography on Eighteenth Century Punjab* (New Delhi: Radha Publications, 1992).

Duggal, Kartar Singh, *Sain Bulleh Shah: The Mystic Muse* (New Delhi: Abhinav, 1996).

Dyrud, Lars and Carla Radloff, *Sociolinguistic Survey of Punjab, Pakistan* (Islamabad: National Institute of Pakistan Studies, Quaid-i-Azam University, 2011).

Eaton, Richard (ed.), *India's Islamic Traditions, 711-1750* (New Delhi: Oxford University Press, 2003).

Elliot-Murray-Kynynmound, Mary, Countess of Minto, *India, Minto and Morley, 1905-1910* (London: Macmillan, 1934).

Fenech, Louis E., *Darbar of the Sikh Gurus: The Court of God in the World of Men* (New Delhi: Oxford University Press, 2008).

Gadgil, N.V., *Government from Inside* (Meerut: Meenakshi, 1968).

Gandhi, M.K., *Autobiography* (New York: Dover, 1983).

Gandhi, Mohandas K., *Collected Works* (New Delhi: Publications Division), 100 vols.

Gandhi, Rajmohan, *Tale of Two Revolts: India 1857 & the American Civil War* (New Delhi: Viking, 2009).

Gandhi, Rajmohan, *Rajaji: A Life* (New Delhi: Penguin, 1997).

Gaur, Ishwar Dayal, *Society, Religion and Patriarchy: Exploring Medieval Punjab Through* Hir Waris (New Delhi: Manohar, 2009).

Gazetteer of the Gujrat District, 1921 (Lahore: Punjab Govt., 1921. Reprint, Sang-a-Meel, Lahore, 2007)

Gazetteer of the Montgomery District, 1883-84 (Lahore: Punjab Govt., 1884. Reprint, Sang-a-Meel, Lahore, 1990)

Gazetteer of the Multan District, 1923-24 (Lahore: Punjab Govt., 1926. Reprint, Sang-a-Meel, Lahore, 1990)

Gazetteer of the Sialkot District, 1920 (Lahore: Punjab Govt., 1921. Reprint, Sang-a-Meel, Lahore, 1990)

Glendevon, John, *Viceroy at Bay* (London: Collins, 1971).
Gopal, Sarvepalli, *Jawaharlal Nehru: A Biography*, vol. 1 (New Delhi: Oxford University Press, 1975).
Grewal, J.S., *Sikhs of the Punjab* (Cambridge, UK: University of Cambridge Press, 1998).
Grewal, Reeta and Sheena Pall (eds.), *Precolonial and Colonial Punjab: Society, Economy, Politics and Culture* (New Delhi: Manohar, 2005).
Griffin, Lepel, *Punjab Chiefs* (London, 1900; reprint by Sang-e-Meel, Lahore, 2004).
Gupta, Hari Ram, *Later Mughal History of the Punjab* (Lahore: Sang-e-Meel, 1976, reprint of 1944 edition).
Habib, Irfan, *An Atlas of the Mughal Empire* (New Delhi: Oxford University Press, 1982, in association with Aligarh Muslim University).
Hibbert, Christopher, *The Great Mutiny: India 1857* (London: Penguin, 1980).
Hodson, H.V., *Great Divide* (London: Hutchinson, 1969).
Husain, Azim (ed.), *Mian Fazl-i-Husain: Glimpses of Life and Works, 1898-1936* (Lahore: Sang-e-Meel, 1993).
Ibbetson, Denzil, *Panjab Castes* (Lahore: 1882, reprint by Mubarak Ali, Lahore, 1974).
Ikram, S.M., *Modern Muslim India and the Birth of Pakistan* (Lahore: Institute of Islamic Culture, undated).
Innes, Arthur, *Annexation of Punjab* (Delhi: National Book Shop, 1984, reprint of 1897 edition).
Iqbal, Afzal, *Mohamed Ali* (Delhi: Idarah-i-Adabiyat, 1978).
Jalal, Ayesha, *Self and Sovereignty: Individual and Community in South Asian Islam since 1850* (London: Routledge, 2000).
Jalal, Ayesha, *Sole Spokesman: Jinnah, the Muslim League & the Demand for Pakistan* (Cambridge, UK: Cambridge University Press, 1985).
Khan, Ahmad Nabi (ed.), *Diwan of Dara Shikoh* (Lahore: University of the Punjab, 1969).
Khan, Wali, *Facts Are Facts: The Untold Story of India's Partition* (Delhi: Vikas, 1987).
Kazimi, M.R., *Concise History of Pakistan* (Karachi: OUP, 2009).
Lafont, Jean-Marie, *Maharaja Ranjit Singh: Lord of the Five Rivers* (New Delhi: Oxford University Press, 2002).
Latif, S.M., *History of the Panjab* (Delhi: Eurasia, 1964, reprint of 1889 edition).
Latif, S.M., *Lahore: Its History, Architectural Remains and Antiquities* (Lahore: Sangameel, 2005, reprint of edition printed in 1892 in Lahore at the New Imperial Press).
Major, Andrew, *Return of Empire: Punjab under the Sikhs and British in the Mid-Nineteenth Century* (New Delhi: Sterling, 1996).
Malhotra, S.L., *Gandhi and the Punjab* (Chandigarh: Punjab University, 1970).
Malik, Hafeez, *Modern Nationalism in India and Pakistan* (Washington, DC: Public Affairs Press, 1963).
Malik, Ikram Ali, *Book of Readings on the History of the Punjab: 1799-1947* (Lahore: University of the Punjab, 1970).
Malik, Ikram Ali, *Hindu-Muslim Riots in the British Punjab, 1849-1947: An Analysis* (Lahore: Gosh-i-Adab, 1984).

Mansergh, Nicholas and E.W.R. Lumby or Penderel Moon (eds.), *Transfer of Power, 1942-47* (London: Her Majesty's Stationery Office), 12 vols.

Mansingh, Jasjit (ed.), *Time Out: Stories from Punjab* (New Delhi: Srishti, 2002).

McLeod Innes, J.J., *Lucknow & Oude in the Mutiny* (London: A.D. Innes & Company, 1895, full text by Hathi Digital Library).

McLeod, W.H., *Evolution of the Sikh Community* (New Delhi: Oxford, 1994).

Mehrotra, S. R., *The Emergence of the Indian National Congress* (New Delhi: Vikas, 1971).

Mehta, Pradeep S., *Trade Relations between Pakistan and India*, Pildat, Islamabad, January 2012.

Merriam, A.H., *Gandhi vs. Jinnah* (Calcutta: Minerva, 1980).

Mir Farina, *Social Space of Language: Vernacular Culture in British Colonial Punjab* (Berkeley: University of California Press, 2010)

Mirza, Shafqat Tanvir, *Making of a Nation: A Historical Perspective* (Islamabad: Dost, 2002).

Mirza, Shafqat Tanvir, *Resistance Themes in Punjabi Literature* (Lahore: Sang-e-Meel, 1992).

Moon, Penderel, *Wavell: The Viceroy's Journal* (London: Oxford University Press, 1973).

Moon, Penderel, *British Conquest and Dominion of India* (London: Duckworth, 1989).

Naim, C.M. (ed.), *Iqbal, Jinnah and Pakistan* (Syracuse: Syracuse University, 1979).

Nair, Neeti, *Changing Homelands: Hindu Politics and the Partition of India* (New Delhi: Permanent Black, 2011)

Nanda, B.R., *Gandhi: Pan-Islamism, Imperialism and Nationalism* (New Delhi: Oxford University Press).

Nayar, Kuldip, *Without Fear: The Life & Trial of Bhagat Singh* (New Delhi: HarperCollins, 2007).

Nayar, Kuldip, *Beyond the Lines: An Autobiography* (New Delhi: Roli, 2012).

Nijhawan, P.K., *The First Punjab War: Shah Mohammed's 'Jangnamah'* (Amritsar: Singh Brothers, 2001).

Noorani, A.G., *Trial of Bhagat Singh* (New Delhi: Konark, 1996).

O'Dwyer, Michael, *India As I Knew It: 1885-1925* (London: Constable, 1925).

Page, David, *Prelude to Partition: The Indian Muslims and the Imperial System of Control, 1920-1932* (Delhi: Oxford University Press, 1982).

Punjab District Gazetteers, Gazetteer of the Rawalpindi District, 1893-84 (Lahore: Punjab Govt., 1895. Reprint, Sang-a-Meel, Lahore, 2001)

Punjab District Gazetteers, Vol. XXVII A, Jhelum District, With Maps, 1904 (Lahore: Punjab Govt., 1907. Reprint, Sang-a-Meel, Lahore, 1991)

Pyarelal, *In Gandhiji's Mirror* (New Delhi: Oxford University Press, 1991).

Qalb-i-Abid, S., *Muslim Politics in the Punjab: 1921-47* (Lahore: Vanguard, 1992).

Quraeshi, Samina, *Lahore: The City Within* (Singapore: Concept Media, 1988).

Qureshi, Ishtiaq Husain, *The Muslim Community of the Indo-Pakistan Subcontinent* (Karachi: Ma'aref, 1977).

Qureshi, Naeem A., *Pan-Islam in British Indian Politics: A Study of the Khilafat Movement, 1918–1924* (Leiden: Brill, 1999).

Rafat, Taufiq, *Bulleh Shah: A Selection* (Lahore: Vanguard, 1982).

Rhodes James, Robert (ed.), *Winston Churchill: His Complete Speeches* (New York: Chelsea House, 1974).

Rose, H.A., *A Glossary of the Tribes and Castes of the Punjab and North-West Frontier Province* (first published 1911-19, reprint, Patiala, Languages Dept., 1970).
Salahuddin, Iqbal, *Tarikh-e-Punjab* (Lahore: Aziz Publishers, 1974).
Saleem, Ahmad (ed.), *Punjab Revisited: An Anthology of 70 Research Documents* (Lahore: Gautam, 1995).
Sarila, Narendra Singh, *Shadow of the Great Game: Untold Story of India's Partition* (New Delhi: HarperCollins, 2005).
Sekhon, Sant Singh, *A History of Panjabi Literature*, vols. 1 & 2 (Patiala: Punjabi University, 1993 & 1996).
Sethi, R.R., *John Lawrence as Commissioner of the Jullundur Doab, 1846-1849* (Lahore: National College of Arts, 2003; reprint of undated publication).
Singh, A.I., *The Origins of the Partition of India* (New Delhi: Oxford, 1987).
Singh, Atam (tr.), *Songs of Bullah* (Lahore, 1940, reprint by Punjabi Adaibi Laihr, Lahore, 1982).
Singh, Gopal, *Guru Gobind Singh* (New Delhi: National Book Trust, 1992).
Singh, Gurcharan, *Warris Shah* (New Delhi: Sahitya Akademi, 1988).
Singh, Harbans, *Guru Tegh Bahadur* (New Delhi: Manohar, 1994).
Singh, Khushwant, *A History of the Sikhs*, 2 vols (Princeton, NJ: Princeton University Press, 1963).
Singh, Khushwant, *Ranjit Singh: Maharajah of the Punjab* (London: Allen & Unwin, 1962).
Singh, Khushwant, *How the Sikhs Lost their Kingdom* (New Delhi: UBS Publishers, 1996).
Singh, Patwant, *The Sikhs* (New York: Random House, 2000).
Sufi Muhammad-ud-Deen Zaar, *Tazkara-e-Jehlum* (Lahore: Shoaib Graphics, 1984).
Talbot, Ian, *Punjab and the Raj: 1849-1947* (New Delhi: Manohar, 1988).
Talbot, Ian, *Khizr Tiwana: The Punjab Unionist Party and the Partition of India* (Karachi: Oxford University Press, 2002).
Tan Tai Yong, *Garrison State: Military, Government & Society in Colonial Punjab, 1849-1947* (New Delhi: Sage, 2005)
Tandon, Prakash, *Punjabi Century, 1857-1947* (Berkeley: University of California Press, 1968).
Trotter, Lionel, *Life of John Nicholson* (London: John Murray, 1905; first edition London 1897; reprint by Karimsons, Karachi, 1978).
Uberoi, J. P. S., *Religion, Civil Society and the State: A Study of Sikhism* (New Delhi: Oxford University Press, 1996).
Wasti, Syed Razi, *Lord Minto and the Indian Nationalist Movement, 1905 to 1910* (Lahore: People's Publishing House, 1976; reprint).
Wedderburn, William, *Allan Octavian Hume: Father of the Indian National Congress* (London: T. Fisher Unwin, 1913).
Wikeley, J.M., *Punjabi Musalmans* (Lahore: Pakistan National Publishers, 1948; reprint of earlier edition, 1917).
Wolpert, Stanley, *Jinnah of Pakistan* (New York: Oxford University Press, 1984).
Woodham-Smith, Cecil, *Queen Victoria: From her birth to the death of the Prince Consort* (New York: Knopf, 1972)

INDEX

Abbott, James, 184
Abdali, Ahmad Shah, 86, 88, 90, 94, 107-109, 124-125, 149
Abdali-Sikh confrontation, 110-112
Abdul Hameed, Agha, 354
Adi Granth, 49
Adina Beg Khan, 21, 81-83, 85, 91-92
  against Afghan establishment, 102-103
  death and subsequent events, 106-107
  and Maratha invasion, 103-106
  as nazim, 82-83
  as a revenue collector, 82
Aga Khan, Sir Sultan Mahomed Shah, 264-265, 267
Agar Khan, 150
Agnew, Patrick Vans, 183
Ahluwalia, Fateh Singh, 132, 134, 137, 139, 142, 154-155
Ahluwalia, Harnam Singh, 247, 262, 274, 361
Ahluwalia, Jassa Singh, 88, 100, 110, 115-116, 118, 126, 247
Ahluwalias, 112
Ahmed Khan, 135-136
Ahmed Khan, Sayyid, 160-161, 252-253, 264, 291
Aitchison College, 255
Ajit Singh, 244-245
Ajmal Khan, 280
Ajmal Khan, Hakim, 292
Akbar's marital alliances, 38
Akbar's Punjab, 33-34, 40
  administration, 35-36
  agriculture, 33-34
  coexistence between diverse groups, 37
  Lahore city, 37
  manufacturing and urbanization, 34-35
  tolerance for different faiths, 37-38
Alam, Dr Mohammad, 305
Alamgir II, 91, 93, 100, 107
Ala Singh, 101, 108, 110-114
Alexander, A.V., 330
Ali Ahmed, 168
Alimuddin, Hakim, 44
Allard, Jean Francois, 161
All-India Muslim League, 267
Amar Das, Guru, 47
Anand, Dev, 19
Anderson, W.A., 183
Angad, Guru, 47
Anglo-Afghan treaty, 210
Anglo-Afghan War of 1878-80, 231
Anglo-Sikh treaty, 171-172
Anglo-Sikh wars, 183, 217
Anirodh Chand, 156
Anjuman-i-Himayat-i-Islam, 247
Ansari, Mukhtar Ahmed, 280, 292
Arain biradari, 79
Archbold, William A.J., 264
Arjan Dev, Guru, 41, 47-49, 60-61, 159, 352
Army of the Indus, 170-171
Aroras, 48
Arya Samaj, 250
Asaf Jah, 75, 84, 90
Asaf Khan, 41-42
Atariwala, Raja Chattar Singh, 184
Atariwala, Sham Singh, 180
Attlee, Premier Clement, 327, 330, 336, 347
Auliya, Nizamuddin, 24, 31, 39
Aurangzeb, 17, 43, 50-54, 58-62, 65, 68, 131
  empire of, 55-61

post death of, 17, 21, 71
relation with siblings, 43-46, 116
Avitabile, Paolo Bartolomeo, 161
Awadh, capture of, 233-234
Azad, Maulana Abul Kalam, 290, 292, 294
Azam, 59, 62

Babur, 31-35, 46-47, 65, 131
Badauni, Abdul Qadir, 38
Badshahi Mosque, 53
Bahadur, Banda Singh, 63-69, 116
Bahadur Shah I or Shah Alam, 62-64, 67-68, 71-72
Bahawal Khan, 125
Bairam Khan, 34
Baji Rao, 75
Bakhsh, Husain, 272
Baksh, Data Ganj, 24
Baldev Singh, 341, 349
Bardai, Chand, 25
Barelvi, Maulana Ahmed Raza Khan, 276
battle for Sirhind, 66
battle of Harchoki or Chunian, 73
battle of Manupur, 87
battle of Sabraon, 180
Bayazid Khan, 68
Beant Singh, 382
Bedi, Baba Khem Singh, 243, 249 Bengal army, 178
Bengal partition, 267, 272
Besant, Annie, 270
Bevin, Ernest, 327
Bhagat Singh, 304
Bhandari, Sujan Rai, 26, 61
Bhangi, Gujjar Singh, 115, 117-118
Bhangis, 112
Bharatiya Janata Party (BJP), 381
Bhargava, Gopichand, 305, 380
Bhatti, Rai Ibrahim, 100, 118
Bhattis, 24
Bhawani Das, 149
Bhikari Khan, Nawab, 90-91, 158

Bhim Chand, 56
Bhutto, Benazir, 381
Bhutto, Zulfiqar, 381, 384
Bikrama Singh, 249
Birbal, Raja, 36
Blood, Edwin, 204
Bokhari, Fakir Azizuddin, 132, 142, 153, 157, 167, 169, 171
Bonnerjee, Womesh Chandra, 252
British Punjab (1859-1919)
    agricultural production, 236, 244
    army recruitment strategy, 237-239, 245-246, 274-275
    canal colonies, 241-246
    census, 1881, 240
    Hindu-Muslim relations in, 253-254, 258-260
    1914 incidents, 275-276
    internal migration, 1880s, 241-242
    Lahore, 254-255
    legislative changes, 277
    middle-class, emergence of, 237
    Muslims in, 252-253, 265-278
    during O'Dwyer, 274-275
    Punjabi vs Urdu, 255-261
    Punjab Land Alienation Act, 261-262
    religio-political controversies, 253-254
    religious divide, 247-254, 259-261
    separate electorate, 265-269
    Singh Sabha movement, 248-249, 254
    'tribes and castes', 240-241
Vernacular Press Act, 251
Broun-Ramsay, James. see Dalhousie, Lord
Bukhari, Jalaluddin, 27
Bulleh Shah, 79-80
Burnes, Alexander, 156, 159, 162, 168, 171

Cabinet Mission, 330-331, 363
Campbell, Colin, 232-233
canal colonies, 241-246
Canning, Charles John, 206, 212-213, 231-232, 237
carnage of 1947, 353-357, 360-362

worst-hit areas, 354-355
Caveeshar, Sardar Sardul Singh, 293
Chamberlain, Major Crawford, 210
Chamberlain, Neville, 201, 237
Chand Kaur, Maharani, 174
Chattar Singh, Nazim, 189
Chatterji, Bankim Chandra, 263
Chatterji, P.C., 257
Chaudhuri, Rambhuj Dutt, 280, 284
Chauhan, Prithviraj, 25
Chauri Chaura incident, 296
Chet Singh, 129
Chhotu Ram, 298
Chitta Ranjan Das, 292
Churchill, Winston, 378
Civil Disobedience movement, 306
Civil & Military Gazette, 255
Colonisation Bill of 1906, 244-245, 268, 270
Colvin, John, 218, 232
conversions, 27-30, 37, 159, 247, 295
Cornwallis, Lord, 137
Court, Claude August, 161
Cowan, 248-249
cow slaughter, campaign against, 259-260
Cripps, Stafford, 319, 330
Curzon, Lord, 262

Dalhousie, Lord, 178, 184-185, 189, 193-194, 202
  departure from India, 206
  doctrine of 'lapse', 204
Dalip Singh, Maharaja, 165, 181, 186
Dane, Louis, 258
Dara, Prince, 43-46, 116
Daudpotras, 119
Dayal, Lala Har, 275
Dayanand Anglo-Vedic (or DAV) College, 260
Delhi Sultanate, 24-25
  lifestyle of, 26-27
demography
  British Punjab, 1880s, 240-244
  in Delhi, 1947, 10-11
Dhian Singh, Raja, 152, 156, 163, 166, 173-175
Dhir Mal, 50-51
Dilaram, 99
Din Muhammad, Justice, 351
divide-and-rule policy, 262-263, 267, 362-363
Diwan Chand, 160
Dodd, George, 231
Doloo, Jassa Singh, 134
Dost Muhammad, 153, 169, 184, 186, 205-206, 210, 212
Duleep Singh, 224
Duni Chand, 292
Dyer, Brigadier-General Reginald, 285, 294

East India Company (EIC) rule in Punjab, 15, 187
East Punjab, 50, 155, 340, 349-350, 355, 357-360, 365, 368, 374-375, 378-380
Edmunsone, 141
Edwardes, Herbert, 183, 200, 210, 234, 237
Ellenborough, Lord, 177
Elphinstone, Mountstuart, 142
Emerson, Herbert, 303

Faiz Ahmed Faiz, 19, 350, 378
Fane, General Sir Henry, 171
Farid, Baba, 24, 26-27, 39, 47, 81, 122-123, 223, 354
Fateh Khan, 147, 149, 152-153
Fazil Khan, 95
Fazl-i-Husain, 272-274, 280, 283, 290, 293-294, 298, 301, 309, 364
Friendship, treaty of (1809)/Amritsar Treaty, 145-147, 153
Fyson, Hugh, 281

Gakhar, Jasrat Khan, 32

Gakhars, 24
Gandhi, Indira, 16, 382, 384
Gandhi, Mohandas, 278-279, 287, 299, 320-322
Gandhi-Irwin Pact, 308
Ganga Ram, Sir, 254-255
Ganga Ram Hospital, 255
Ganna Begum, 92
George, Lloyd, 288
George VI, King, 336
Ghadr movement, 275
Ghaffar Khan, Abdul, 292
Ghamand Chand, 106
Ghani Khan, 56
Ghausa, Mian, 150
Ghazanfar Ali Khan, Raja, 331
Ghaznavi, Maulana Daud, 333
Gheb, Tara Singh, 138, 139, 173
Ghulam Ahmad, Mirza, 250
Ghulam Muhammad, 126
Gidwani, Choithram, 350
Gilani, Makhdoom Raza Shah, 298
Gobind Singh, Guru, 54-56, 63-65, 73, 117, 248
Gogera rebellion, 223
Gokhale, Gopal Krishna, 268-270
Golwalkar, Madhav Sadashiv, 334
Gomal Pass, 24
Government of India Act of 1935, 308-309
Granth Sahib, 41, 49
Greenfield, Miss M. Rose, 257
Grewal, Jagtar Singh, 60
Gujral, Inder Kumar, 16
Gulab Singh, 152, 156, 179, 181
Gul Bahar, 165
Gupta kings, 23
Gurmukhi script, 255-257

Haider, Ali, 121
Hailey, Governor, 300, 308
Harappan civilization, 23
Hardinge, Governor-General Lord Henry, 178-181, 183, 188-189, 191, 193
Harimandir, 41
Hari Singh, Maharaja, 306
Harkishen Lal, Lala, 280, 283, 294
Harlan, Josiah, 169
Harsha, King, 23
Havelock, Henry, 214, 232-233
Hayat Khan, Muhammad, 199, 227, 229, 261-262
Heer, 121-124
Hindu-Muslim disputes, 258-260, 262-264, 267-268, 287, 293, 296, 321-322
Hindu-Muslim unity, 281-283, 299-300
Hira Singh, 175
Hirtzel, Sir Arthur, 307
History of the Panjab, 16, 62
Hodson, William, 205
Hogg, James, 197
Holkar, Jaswant Rai, 136
Home Rule movement, 270
Honigberger, Martin, 161
Horniman, B.G., 279
Huddlestone, John, 187
Hujweri, Syed Ali. *see* Data Ganj Baksh
Hume, Allan Octavian, 252

Ibn Battuta, 26-27
Iftikharuddin, Mian, 314, 320, 328, 333, 335, 339-340, 349, 357, 378, 380
Ilbert, C.P., 251
Ilbert Bill, 251-252
Imad-ul-Mulk or Ghaziuddin, 90, 92-95, 107
Imamuddin, Fakir, 162
Imperial strategy, post-1857, 235-236, 262
independence movement (1919-1922)
   Bradlaugh Hall rally, 282
   Chauri Chaura incident, 296
   Dyer's 'Crawling Order', 286
   Gandhi's satyagraha, 279-283, 287-288
   Hindu-Muslim unity, 281-283
   Jallianwala Bagh incident, 285

Martial Law, 286
Non-cooperation movement, 290-296
O'Dwyer policy and, 281-283
outbreak at Amritsar, 283-284
in Punjabi towns, 282-283
against Rowlatt measure, 281
Indian National Army (INA), 333
Indian National Congress (INC), 252, 268-274
India-Pakistan, state-to-state relations, 379
Intizam, 100
Iqbal, Afzal, 297
Iqbal, Muhammad, 271-272, 307
Ishtiaq Ahmed, 358
Islamia College, 260

Jacquemont, 164
Jafar Beg, 168
Jahanara, 44
Jahandar Shah, 90
Jahangir, 41-42, 49
Jahan Khan, 94, 99, 102
Jallianwala Bagh massacre, 285, 289
Jamiat-Ulema-i-Hind, 324
Jamshid Khan, 64
Jaspat Rai, 83
Jat clan, 29, 57
Jat culture, 119-120
Javed Khan, 90
Jawahar Singh, 175
Jenkins, Governor Evan, 330, 334, 336, 339-340
Jhanda Singh, 119
Jindan, Rani, 165, 179-180, 189
Jinnah, Muhammad Ali, 269, 271, 288, 290, 302, 309, 321-322, 325, 328, 331, 345-347, 360, 364
Jinnah-Jawaharlal dialogue, 310-311
Jinnah-Sikander Pact, 313
Jogendra Singh, 298, 300
Johnson, Colonel Frank, 285

Kabuli Mal, 112, 114

Kader Khan, 205
Kahan Singh, 183
Kairon, Pratap Singh, 381
Kam Baksh, 59-60, 62, 64
Kamran, Prince, 152
Kanhiyas, 112
Kanishka, 23
Kapoor, Raj, 19
Kartar Singh, Baba, 298
Kartar Singh, Giani, 329, 349
Kasab, Ajmal, 384
Kashful Mahjub, 24
Kashmir, 19, 21, 32, 35, 42-43, 46, 52-53, 63, 68, 86, 89, 95, 101, 111, 113, 125, 134, 146-147, 149-150, 152-155, 162, 166, 173, 181, 183, 199-200, 351, 379, 381, 385
Kasur revolt, 73
Kauramal, Diwan, 88
Kautilya, 23
Kaye, John, 230
Khafi Khan, 64, 67, 69, 71
Khalsa College, 260
Khanna, Rajesh, 19
Kharak Singh, Baba, 293
Kharak Singh, Prince, 131, 138, 146, 153-154, 167, 171, 173
Kharal, Ahmad Khan, 220, 223
Khatris, 48
Kheshgi, Nawab Hussain Khan, 72
Khilafat movement, 288
Khilji dynasty, 25
Khokhars, 24
Khulasat ut-Tawarikh, 60
Khurshid Anwar, Mian, 333
Khushhal Chand, 139
Khushwant Singh, 19, 165, 379
Khusro/Khusrau, Amir, 31, 41-42
Khwaja Abed Khan, 109
Khwaja Mirza Khan, 90, 93, 101-102, 107, 109
Khwaja Yusuf Shah, 264
Khyber Pass, 24

Kipling, Rudyard, 255, 286
Kitchlew, Saifuddin, 338
Koka, Fidai Khan, 54
Kripalani, Jivatram, 347

Labh Singh, 337
Lahore, 24
  in 1809, 168
  during Akbar's reign, 37-38
  in Bulleh's poetry, 80-81
  Ramayana-linked legend, 72-73
  in 1880s, 254-255
  under Shah Jahan, 42-43
Lahore Conspiracy Case, 305
Lahore Resolution, 322
Lahore treaty, 1806, 137
Lahori, Mirza, 37
Lajpat Rai, Lala, 244, 263, 290-291, 302-303
Lake, Lord, 144
Lakhpat Rai, 76, 85
Lal Singh, 183
Land Revenue Act, 1928, 301
langar (community kitchen), 48
Latif, Syad Muhammad, 202
Lawrence, Henry, 181, 183, 187-193, 195, 202-204, 228-229
Lawrence, John, 187-193, 195-196, 202-204, 237, 251
Lawrence, Richard, 208
Lawrence Schools, 188
League-Sikh talks, 360-361
Lehna Singh, 114, 117
Leitner, G.W., 237
Lekh Ram, Pandit, 261
Linlithgow, Lord, 314-315
Lodhi dynasty, 25
Lucknow Pact, 280
Lucknow siege, 214
Ludhianvi, Abdul Qadir, 221
Lyall, James, 260
Lytton, Lord, 251

Maclagan, Edward, 286
MacNaghten, Sir William, 171
Madho Das, 63
Mahajan, Justice Mehr Chand, 351
Maha Singh, 126, 130
Mahmud of Ghazni, 24-25
Mai Sukhan, 135
Majithia, Dyal Singh, 251
Majithia, Sir Sunder Singh, 298, 316
Majma-al-Bahrain, 45
Malaviya, Madan Mohan, 291
Malcolm, John, 66
Malhar Rao, 101
Malhotra, Kidar Nath, 357
Malik, Ikram Ali, 258
Mamdot, Hussain Iftikhar, 324
Mamdot, Nawab Sir Shah Nawaz, 323
Man Singh, Mansabdar, 36
Mani Singh, Bhai, 73
Manmohan Singh, 16, 385
Mannu, Mir, 87, 89
Manohar Lal, 300
Manto, Saadat Hasan, 19
Maratha Confederacy, 21
Maratha invasion of Punjab, 71, 103-109
Marathas, 17, 22, 53, 59, 63, 71-72, 75, 82, 90, 97-109, 120, 125-137, 140
Mardan Khan, Ali, 43
Marshall, Honoria, 188, 201
martial-race theory, 238
Masson, Charles, 168
Matthews, Captain, 143
Maurya, Chandragupta, 23
Mayo School of Arts, 255
Mehtab Kaur, 130, 138, 144
Mehtab Singh, 225
Menander the Greek (Milinda), 23
Messervy, Lt.-Gen. Frank, 338
Metcalfe, Charles, 140-147, 190
Metcalfe, Theo, 213, 228, 230
Metcalfe, Thomas, 190, 204
Miharban, 50
Minto, Lord, 140, 144-145

Minto-Morley Reforms, 267-268
Mir, Mian, 41, 45, 79
Mir, Mir Taqi, 120
Miskin, Tahmas Beg Khan, 90
Mohammedan Anglo-Oriental College (MAO), 252-253, 264, 271
Mohar Singh, 129
Mohkam Chand, 139-140, 142, 144-145, 147, 150
Mohran, 135
Mohsin-ul-Mulk, 264
Moinuddin Chishti, 24, 39
Mongols, 25-26
Monserrate, Father Antonio, 37
Montford Reforms, 277
Montford Scheme, 300
Montgomery, Robert, 207, 209, 216, 234, 245
Mookerji, Shyama Prasad, 318
Moplah rebellion, 295-296
Mountbatten, Lord Louis, 21, 336, 343-353, 360
Muazzam/Moazzam, 59, 62
Mughal Punjab, 23
 administration, 35-36, 58, 74-76
 Akbar's reign, 33-34
 Aurangzeb's empire, 55-61
 Babur's reign, 32-33
 Bahadur Shah's campaign, 67-68
 Banda Bahadur's campaign, 66-67
 Maratha raids, 71
 Mughal-Abdali confrontation, 87-97
 Muhammad Shah, 72-75
 Nadir Shah's march, 77-78
 Sikhs' rise to power, 84, 87-92, 109-121
 Timur's invasion, 32
 Zakariya Khan and, 73-77, 82
Muhammad Ali, Chaudhri, 357
Muhammad Ali, Maulana, 280
Muhammad Shah, 72
Mujeeb, Muhammad, 30
Mukarrab Khan, 117-118

Mulla Shah, 45
Multan, 23-26, 30-35, 39, 42, 45, 62, 70-79, 86, 88, 91, 112-119, 125, 134-8, 146-147, 150-158, 166, 183-185, 194-196, 208-210, 220-224, 236, 240-242, 257-258, 298, 301, 327, 337-340, 354, 380
Mumtaz, 42
Munim Khan, 62, 65
Munir, Justice Muhammad, 351
Munj, Isa Khan, 72
Murad Khan, 44-45, 100
Musharraf, Pervez, 381
Muslim-Hindu-Sikh platform, 248
Muslim-Hindu-Sikh ratios, 237, 260, 267, 277, 299
Muslim Jats, 69-70, 119
Muslim League, 17, 267, 269, 273-274, 276, 280, 284, 288-291, 293, 296, 299, 302, 306-310, 315-317, 319, 321, 323-329, 333-335
Muslim League National Guards (MLNG), 333
Mustafa Kamal, 295
Muzaffar Khan, Nawab, 119, 134, 151

Nabi Khan, 56
Nadir Shah, 21, 75-78, 82, 85, 91, 115
Nagri, Chaudhri Jodha, 100
Naidu, Sarojini, 279
Najib-ud-Daulah, 93
Nakkais, 112
Nalwa, Hari Singh, 150, 160, 169-170
Nanak, Guru, 38-39, 46-47, 67, 70, 81, 248
Nanda, Gulzari Lal, 16
Naoroji, Dadabhai, 252, 269
Napoleon, 139
Narain Das, Dr, 337
Narang, Gokul Chand, 280
Nargis, 19
Nasir Khan, 76, 113
Nassir Ali, 100

Nathoo Shah, 114
Nau Jawan Bharat Sabha (NJBS), 304
Nau Nihal Singh, Prince, 168, 171, 173-174
Nehru, Jawaharlal, 292, 306
Nehru, Motilal, 288, 292
Nicholson, Charles, 227, 230
Nicholson, John, 184, 197, 224-231, 238, 261, 281, 310, 322
Nicholson, Richardson, 197
Nihal Singh, 217
Nihangs, 135
Nirankari movement, 248
Nishan Sahib, 116
Niwas, Lala Shri, 82
Nizamuddin Khan, 119, 129, 134, 138
non-cooperation movement, 290, 292, 295
Noon, Firoz Khan, 298
Noor Jehan, 19
Nur Jahan, 41-42
Nur Muhammad, 113
Nuruddin, 110
Nusrat Fateh Ali Khan, 19

Oak Creek incident, 2012, 15
Ochterlony, Major David, 145, 147
O'Dwyer, Michael, 274, 281-284, 286, 290, 294
Outram, James, 206

Pakistan, call for, 307, 326, 328-329
  Cabinet Mission, 330-331
  Gandhi's plan, 343-345
  peaceful transfer of people, 360
Pakistan Muslim League (PML), 381
Pakistan People's Party (PPP), 381
Pal, Bipin Chandra, 263
Panini, 23
Panipat battle, 108-109
Paradise Lost, 37
Parmanand, Bhai, 307
Parshottam Dutt, Dr, 337

Partap Singh, 174
Partition Plan, 360, 362
Pandey, Mangal, 207
Patel, Vallabhbhai, 279, 292, 315
Peel Commission, 237
Peshaura Singh, Prince, 175
Peshawar disarming, 212
Pheru Shah, 179-180
Phula Singh, 160
Phulkians, 112
Pritam, Amrita, 19, 378
Prithi Chand, 48
Public Safety Ordinance, 335
Punjab-based regiment, 237-238
Punjab Boundary Force (PBF), 355-356
Punjab Congress, 364
Punjabi/Hindustani 'divide', 231
Punjabi language, 18, 255-261, 365
Punjabi Muslims, 17-18, 58, 116-117, 120, 365
Punjab Irregular Force (PIF), 188
Punjabi tribes, 24
Punjabiyat, 19, 376, 386-388
Punjab Land Alienation Act, 261-262

Qadiri, Shaikh Inayat, 79
Qadir Yar, 168
Qadri, Fakir Muhammad Issa, 151
Qadri, Mumtaz, 383-384
Qalandar, Bu Ali, 27, 108
Qalandar, Lalshahbaz, 27
Qamruddin, Wazir, 86-87
Qamruddin Khan, 73, 75
Quit India movement, 325-326, 364
Qutbuddin, Shaikh, 69
Qutbuddin Kaki, 24, 39

Radcliffe, Sir Cyril, 351-352
Radcliffe Line, 386
Rafat, Taufiq, 80
Rafi, Muhammad, 19
Raghunath Rao, 100-101, 103
Rahmat Khan, Chaudhry, 104

Raikes, Charles, 191
Rajagopalachari, C., 292, 320-321, 344
Rajaram, 71
Raj Kaur, 130, 138
rakhi (protection tax), 112
Ram Das, Guru, 41, 47, 159
Ram Dyal, 150, 154
Ramgarhia, Jassa Singh, 126
Ramgarhia Confederacy, 89
Ramgarhias, 112
Ram Singh, Baba, 248-249
Randhawa, Nihan Singh, 104
Ranjit Dev, 104, 106, 111
Ranjit Singh, 15-16, 21, 127, 129-130
  alliance with the Ahluwalias, 134
  Amritsar, capture of, 134-135
  army, 136, 162, 167
  encounter with East India Company, 133
  governance style, 165-166
  installation in Lahore, 132
  Kabul, entry into, 152
  and Kasur, 138
  and Kohinoor, 149
  negotiation with British, 140-145
  Lahore treaty, 137
  love of horses, 163
  and Marathas, 136-137
  Muslim revolt, 159-161
  new infantry, 135
  and Sikh religious leaders, 131
  Sindh Sagar conquest, 155
  Treaty of Friendship, 146
  triumphs in Multan, Peshawar and Kashmir, 147, 151-153
Rashtriya Swayamsevak Sangh (RSS), 301, 332-333, 348
Rees, T. W., Major General, 355
Reforms Act, 288
riots in Punjab, 259, 261, 276
Ripon, Lord, 251
Roberts, General Frederick, 210, 238
Rohilkhand, capture of, 233-234
Roshanara, 44
Rotton, John, 231
Rowlatt, Sir Sidney, 277
Rowlatt Bills, 277-278, 280
Russell, William Howard, 233

Saadat Khan, 75, 109
Saare Jahaan Se Achha, 271
Sachar, Bhimsen, 330, 380
Sada Kaur, 144-145, 154
Sadashiv Rao, 108
Sadiq, Shaikh Ghulam, 264
Sadiq Beg Khan, 103, 109
Safdar Jung, 90
Saiyid Mohamed Shah, 282
Salimullah of Dhaka, Nawab, 267
Salisbury, Lord, 252
Samad Khan, Abdul, 69-70, 102
Sambhaji, 71
Samjhauta Express, 386
Sandhanwalia, Thakur Singh, 249
Sansar Chand, 137, 146, 156
Saraswati, Swami Dayanand, 249-250
Satyapal, Dr, 292-293
Satyarth Prakash, 249
Sauda, Mirza, 120
Sawan Mal, 151-152
Sawan Yar, 168
Sayyid, Abdullah Khan, 71-72, 92-93
Sayyid, Hussain Ali, 72
sepoy mutiny, 1857, 207-213
  aftermath of, 235-236, 246
Setalvad, M.C., 351
Shafi, Mian Muhammad, 264, 273, 284, 287, 302
Shahabuddin of Ghor, 25
Shah Alam II, 111, 125
Shahanchi Khan, 127
Shah Din, Mian Muhammad, 264
Shah Hussain, 121
Shahir Yar, 42
Shah Jahan, 41-42
  Punjab during, 42-46, 76

Shah Jahan III, 107
Shah Mohammed, 181-182
Shah Muhammad, 79
Shah Nawaz, 85-86
Shah Waliullah, 160
Shaikha, 32
Shaikh Ahmad, 38
Shams Khan, 68
Sharaf al-Nisa, 82
Sharif, Nawaz, 381
Shaukat Ali, 280
Shaukat Hayat, 327
Sher Khan, Jandiala, 123
Sher Singh, 184-185
Sher Singh, Prince, 138, 154, 160, 173
Sherwood, Miss Marcella, 284
Shiromani Akal Dal (SAD), 381
Shiromani Gurdwara Prabandhak Committee (SGPC), 293
Shivaji, 63, 71
Shraddhanand, Swami, 289, 296, 301
Shuja, 44-45, 169
Sialkot rebellion, 225-232
Sikander Hayat Khan, Sir, 310, 322
Sikander-Jinnah Pact, 324
Sikh Gurus, 38-39, 46-52, 121
Sikh-Hindu differences, 157-159
Sikh kingdom, 376
Sikh militancy, 382
Sikh-Muslim relationship, 16, 120, 247-248, 255-261, 293, 337-339, 347-350, 377
Sikh rivalries, 126-129
Sikh rural society, 119
Sikhs' egalitarian outlook, 120
Sikhs in America, 15-16
Sikhs' religious zeal, 118
Sikhs' rise to power, 84, 87-92, 109-121
Simla conference, 264, 267
Simon Commission, 303, 306
Singh Sabha movement, 249
Sirr-i-Akbar, 45
Siyar, Farrukh, 68, 72

Skinner, Colonel James, 178
Slave dynasty, 25
Smith, Bosworth, 195
Sobhani, Umar, 279
Sobha Singh, 117
Sodhi Barbhag Singh, 100
sovereign Muslim state, 307
Suchet Singh, 152
Sufi khanqah, 30
Sufis, 24, 116, 120, 328
Sufi silsila, 30
Sukerchakia, Charhat Singh, 110, 112, 115, 126, 129
Sukerchakias, 112
Sukhjiwan Mal, 111
Sultanate-era Punjab
    castes, 29
    conversion, 27
    Hindu population, 31
    Jatt clan, 29
    Mongol raid, 25-26, 30
    Muslim population, 31
    population, 28-29
    Rajput forces *vs* Ghori, 25
    Sufi activity, 27-28
Sultan Khan, Raja, 153
Sundri, Mata, 57
Sunil Dutt, 19
Sur, Sikandar, 34
Surayya Begum/Mughlani Begum, 90, 95, 99, 106, 158
swadeshi campaigns, 263
Swaran Singh, 380
Syals, 24

Tagore, Debendranath, 251
Tagore, Rabindranath, 263
Taj Mahal, 43
Tarabai, 71
Taranjia, Dharamdas, 100
Tavernier, Francois, 43
Tegh Bahadur, Guru, 51-52, 60, 65, 81
Teja Singh, Justice, 351

Tej Singh, 179
Thapa, Amar Singh, 114, 137
Thoka, Jassa Singh, 83
Thomas, George, 136
Thorburn, S.S., 261
Tilak, Bal Gangadhar, 263, 268-269, 288
Tilak Swaraj Fund, 291
Tilla Gorakhnath (monastery), 23
Tilsit, treaty of (1807), 139
Timur, Amir, 31-33, 46
Timur Shah, 97, 99-102, 107-108, 125-127
Tipperary, County, 281
Tipu Sultan, 121, 187
Tiwana, Khizr Hayat Khan, 310, 323-324, 327
Tiwana, Umar Hayat Khan, 245, 264, 275
Todar Mal, Mansabdar, 36 transfer of populations, 360-362
Tribune, 250-251
Trivedi, Chandulal, 357
Trotter, Lionel, 202
Tughlaq, Muhammad bin, 26
Tughlaq dynasty, 25
Turkey, 268-271, 276, 283
two-nation theory, 330-341
Tyabji, Badruddin, 253

Udham Bai, 74
undivided Punjab
  boundaries, 19-21
  invading forces, 21
  Muslim population, 21
  society and economy, 22
United Indian Patriotic Association, 253
Urdu, 255-261
Usman Khan, 65

Vajpayee, Atal Behari, 384
Ventura, Jean Baptiste, 161
Vernacular Press Act, 1882, 251
Vishwanath, Balaji, 71
Vishwas Rao, 108

Wadda Ghallughara, 110
Wafa Begum, 149
Waraich, Rahmat Khan, 118
Waris Shah, 121-124
Wavell, Lord Archibald, 325-327, 330
Wazir Khan, 57-58, 62, 64, 66
Wazir Khan Mosque, 44
weightage to minorities in electrorates, 267-270, 277, 300, 302, 324
Wilson, Major General Archdale, 224, 227, 230
Wolff, Joseph, 159
Wood, Charles, 357

Yadvinder Singh, 346
Yahya Khan, 85, 87
Yar, Ahmad, 168
Yusuf Ali, Mir, 133

Zafar, Bahadur Shah, 204, 211, 213, 228, 230, 232, 246
Zafar Ali, Maulana, 270-272, 276, 283, 288, 290, 293-294, 301, 333
Zafarnama, 59
Zafrulla Khan, 351
Zail Singh, 16
Zain Khan, 109, 112
Zakaria, Bahauddin, 27
Zakariya Khan, 69, 73-77, 82
Zaman Shah, 127, 129, 133, 147
Zamindar, 270
Zia-ul-Haq, Muhammad, 383
Zohra Begum, 97

PHOTO CREDITS

The author and publisher would like to thank the following for permission to use copyright material:

- Guru Gobind Singh and his Khalsa army from *Sikh Heritage: Ethos and Relics*.
  Courtesy: Roopinder Singh.
- Contemporary portrait of Adina Beg Khan.
  Courtesy: Lahore Museum.
- Portrait of Maharaja Ranjit Singh.
  Courtesy: *www.sikhcd.com*.
- Portrait of Fazl-i-Husain.
  Courtesy: Ishtiaq Ahmed.

While every effort has been made to trace copyright holders and obtain permissions, this has not always been possible in all cases; any omissions brought to our attention will be remedied in future editions.